ERIC VAN LUSTBADER

SHAN

FAWCETT CREST • NEW YORK

Library of Congress Catalog Card Number: 86-10027

ISBN 0-449-20598-3

This edition published by arrangement with Random House, Inc.

Manufactured in the United States of America

First International Edition: April 1987
First Ballantine Books Edition: January 1988

THIS IS FOR MY FATHER
WITH LOVE AND RESPECT.

Special thanks to Kate Bush
for running up that hill.

Kudakutemo
  kudakutemo
    ari mizu-no tsuki

Though it be broken—
  broken again—still it's there:
    the moon on the water.

                    —Choshu

              Fame or one's own self,
                which does one love more?
              Loss of self or the possession of goods
                which is the greater evil?

                              —Laotse

AUTHOR'S NOTE

In the Buddhist religion, the Sanskrit word *kalpa* is used in several ways. It is an almost incalculable period of time. It is also the word used to measure the period between the creation and the recreation of the world. Each great *kalpa* is divided into four parts. So, too, is *Shan*.

Those familiar with my novel, *Jian*, will recall that the Chinese transliteration of *kalpa* is *ka*. The masters of *wei qi*, the ancient board game of warfare and strategy that Jake, Shi Zilin and Daniella Vorkuta play in *Shan*, use the term to mean the point where the contending forces have reached a stalemate.

It is common knowledge among *wei qi* masters, however, that a Jian—a master general of *wei qi*—may find a strategy to break *ka*. It is Shan, the Mountain.

CONTENTS

According to known history there is no highly clandestine espionage organization (originally sanctioned by President John Fitzgerald Kennedy) called the Quarry. Just as, in the summer of 1945, there was no aide to Maj. Gen. Patrick J. Hurley, Ambassador to China, named Ross Davies. But there could be. And there might have been.

"Jake," Rodger Donovan said, without turning around. He seemed quite calm, despite the desperateness of the situation. "You seem to have as many lives as the hero of a novel. I knew we couldn't kill you."

"It didn't stop you from trying."

Donovan winced at the tone. "Of course not. What do you take us for, amateurs?"

"No more talk," Jake said. "Take me to Wunderman."

"Ah, Wunderman. I imagine he'll want to know how you evaded all our security measures."

"Then he'll be disappointed. Come on, let's go."

Jake Maroc, in Hong Kong, dreaming of another time, another place. Of a day nine months before, a rain-swept day. He had flown into Washington's Dulles International Airport after spending hours with Bliss deciphering the papers for which so many people had died, not the least of whom was David Oh, Jake's closest friend. Papers that irrefutably identified Henry Wunderman—now the Director of the clandestine intelligence organization known as the Quarry, for which Jake had worked—as a double agent working for the KGB's Daniella Vorkuta. His code name was Chimera.

General Vorkuta and Chimera, the papers showed, had masterminded the assassination of Antony Beridien just weeks before. Beridien, the Quarry's first Director and its founder.

Now Jake was in Washington, racing by car to Great Falls where, nestled within the rolling emerald hills, Greystoke sat: the nineteenth-century mansion, seat of power for the new Director. And Wunderman, asserting that it had been Jake himself who had murdered Antony Beridien in retaliation for the Director's cutting Jake off from the Quarry, had instituted a number of new security systems at Greystoke.

This is what Jake dreamed of: the day he confronted his father and struck him down forever.

Not that Henry Wunderman was Jake Maroc's real father. But as Jake dreamed of crouching in the high grass just outside the perimeter of Greystoke's eastern boundary, his thoughts were filled up with images from a time when Jake was young, a wild orphan roaming the filthy back alleys of Hong Kong, a great unwieldy anger riding his shoulders like a deformity.

Henry Wunderman had changed all that. He had come to Hong Kong to search Jake out. To recruit him into the Quarry. Henry Wunderman had given Jake's life a purpose, his faith in the young man had redeemed Jake from emptiness and perhaps even self-destruction. He was Jake's spiritual father.

And now Jake was forced to destroy him.

To do it Jake needed *ba-mahk*. *Ba-mahk* meant, literally, "feel the pulse." It was a state of mental preparedness in which one was able to "feel" the energy sources of one's surroundings. Through *ba-mahk* one could therefore discover much that was hidden from the normal five senses. One could even discern the strategies of one's opponent and thus counter them even as they were occurring.

Ba-mahk is what Jake used now at the eastern edge of the treacherous minefield of security traps that Henry Wunderman had devised. He sat and entered *ba-mahk*. For him it was another world entirely; it always had been. Here he was free of corporeal concerns. He was almost entirely spirit or, as the Chinese would say, *qi*. *Qi* was the inner energy that resided in every living thing. It was, in essence, life. Without *qi* a man had no strength, no inner reserves; he was not in harmony with either himself or his surroundings.

In *ba-mahk*, Jake's *qi*, his strength of spirit, expanded. Like the ripples on a lake widening from the spot where a stone had been thrown, so Jake's extraordinary *qi* roved outward, encountering first the infrared units like rogue blades of grass, well camouflaged to the eye, then the ultrasonics, implanted as clumps of speckled mushrooms at the foot of rustling trees.

Ba-mahk revealed to him the outer defenses of Greystoke. He moved around them, above them, so that the electronics were as oblivious to him as they were to the wind that rushed by his side.

Within the double outer ring Jake stopped and returned fully to *ba-mahk*. It was a comforting sensation, as if one were to return to a private world where the very pulse of the

2

cosmos could be felt, examined and absorbed. Jake was aware of how much he delighted in, of how much he depended on *ba-mahk*. It was his ultimate weapon, the manner by which he had gained his victories for the Quarry and, after, for himself and for his father. His real father, Shi Zilin.

It was *ba-mahk*, Jake knew, that made him special. It was *ba-mahk* that guided him through the dangers inherent in the life he had chosen to lead. Without it he would never have been able to make it to Greystoke, sitting like a great old man at the center of the security web.

The dogs were next. Dobermans trained to scent out humans and immobilize them at the point of contact. *Ba-mahk* picked them up, allowing Jake to keep downwind of them, to pass them by without incident.

His dream never revealed to him how many more rings he had to pass through. The number was irrelevant. Infiltration into Greystoke was akin to a game of *wei qi*, the ancient Chinese board game of strategy. It would have been fruitless to take the security rings one at a time, for they had been so set up that often the solution used to penetrate one would have set off the next. *Ba-mahk* allowed Jake to "feel" several of the rings at once.

So it was that Jake had come at last upon Rodger Donovan, the Quarry's wunderkind and number-two man, working on his 1963 Corvette in the driveway beside Greystoke's famous rose garden.

It was Donovan who took Jake into the house itself, into the inner sanctum of the Director. Face to face with Henry Wunderman.

The prodigal son had returned home to face the wrath of his father. The replaying of events of mythic proportion. There should have been portents: thunder crashing, lightning forking. Instead the black skies were almost somnolent, and the only discernible sounds were the droning of the bumblebees greedily gathering attar from the roses two stories below.

The scent of the enormous flowers was in the room. And it was to this aspect that the end of Jake's dream clove. The struggle with Henry Wunderman, while Rodger Donovan looked on, sphinxlike, was inextricably bound to the rich perfume.

Wunderman had pulled the pistol. By all rights he should have shot Jake dead where he stood, not two meters away. But *ba-mahk* had revealed his intent to Jake even before the movement had begun. Enough time—just enough!—for Jake

3

to spill his body forward, the shot passing through the spot where he had been.

Now the die had been cast. The stink of death mingled with the scent of the roses, the strangled sounds of their struggle punctuated the droning of the gluttonous bees.

How many myths in how many different cultures scattered throughout time and place foretold the prodigal son returning to kill his father? Jake, in righteous anger, used *ba-mahk* yet again to penetrate Wunderman's defenses, used the lethal liver kites because of David Oh, because of Jake's wife, Mariana, because of Jake's half-brother, Nichiren. Chimera had had a hand, either directly or indirectly, in all their deaths.

Protected by *ba-mahk* from the terrible implications of what he had to do, death was in Jake's mind, in his hands; death was in his heart. The naked flame of revenge expunging the light of all the pure stars in the vault of the heavens.

And now, in the space of a heartbeat, everything had changed. Instead of the satisfaction of revenge, there was only death, appalling and irreversible. The knowledge and the guilt and the crying inside was too much, too much, mingled always with the scent of roses, powerful as the ocean's tide.

DESTRUCTION
SAMVARTA

WINTER—SPRING
PRESENT

HONG KONG/BEIJING/
WASHINGTON/MOSCOW

Jake and Bliss were down in the Hole. In the night, the sounds of Hong Kong came to them as through a mist. They were so near the harbor they could hear the lap-lap, lap-lap of water against pilings. The high-pitched squeal of rats came to them now and again through walls of packed earth and rotting timbers.

The sounds of gambling took precedence over everything else. That was the essence of the Hole, a warren of underground chambers linked by low tunnels: gambling. The only legal gambling allowed in Hong Kong was the horse races at Happy Valley. But the Chinese were insatiable gamblers.

It was very dark down in the Hole. Jake had no love for it but it was the spot insisted upon for the rendezvous.

"How well do you know this man?" Bliss asked him.

Jake stared at her. "He is one of the half-dozen I have been running for the past six months." He caught her tone. "I trust him."

Bliss shivered a little. "I don't like this place," she said, echoing Jake's own thoughts.

"He must have a reason for meeting us here," Jake said.

Bliss looked around. "Easy to get trapped down here."

"Just as easy to get lost," Jake said. "Don't worry."

She gave him a little smile. "Just nerves." He could see the long sweep of her beautiful neck. "I don't like to be underground."

"You could have stayed home. I told you."

"Not after what your contact hinted at." She moved and the hollow of her throat filled with shadow. "Jake. Do you really think he's that close to the spy who has infiltrated our inner circle?"

Jake was watching the low-ceilinged corridor. There had been some movement there. "Like I said." Click-clack-click

7

of the ivory mah-jongg tiles. "I vetted him himself." Cigarette smoke, blued in the bare bulb light, thick as fog. "As I do all my operatives." Jumble of Cantonese, rising, as the bidding became more heated. "I trust him." Shadow and light, moving. "I wouldn't be down here otherwise."

Bliss turned her head. Jake could feel the tension come into her frame. "Is that him?"

Jake looked at the thin Chinese with slicked-back hair. He was young to be down here. The Hole was generally the province of the older men, who remembered when smugglers used these tunnels. "No," Jake said, watching the thin Chinese stand there, observing the mah-jongg game. When he began to joke with the participants, Jake turned his attention elsewhere.

"He's late," Bliss said, "your contact."

"He'll be here."

"You've had leads before," Bliss said.

"They've all been dead ends," Jake said. He was looking beyond the gamblers. "My operatives get so far, then it's as if a door gets slammed in their faces."

"Time to take another tack."

Jake considered this. He knew how smart Bliss was; that was part of what he loved about her. Maybe she was right. Maybe he should—

He began to move forward. "He's here."

Jake was in the light, and the stocky, mustachioed Chinese saw him. He motioned for Jake to stay where he was. Movement at the mah-jongg game was furious, as the last of the tiles were laid out.

The contact made his way past the gesticulating gamblers. His movements were quick, darting. Then he seemed to stumble, and with a cry, he fell forward, into the midst of the gamblers. The ancient wooden table collapsed beneath his weight, tiles scattered, and the old men shouted, lurched out of their chairs.

Then Jake saw the young Chinese with the slicked-back hair; he was racing back along the tunnel down which the contact had just come.

Jake sprang toward the jumble of the gamblers and their ruined game. Bliss shot past him as he bent over the stocky Chinese, his contact, and turned him over. There was blood everywhere. Jake saw the knife and thought, He got the heart; he's a professional—a good one.

There was nothing in the stocky man's eyes: no recognition,

8

no intelligence; the spark had been extinguished in a second. Life to death, without warning.

Ignoring the shouts of the gamblers, Jake took off after Bliss and the assassin. I should have kept my eye on him, Jake thought. I should have known. Why didn't *ba-mahk* alert me?

Instead he had put Bliss into great danger.

She slammed around a corner and, catching sight of the Chinese with the slicked-back hair, she raced after him. The cloying scent of opium was strong in the air, almost masking the acrid odors. The sweat of feverish gambling was as dense as mist in the subterranean air.

Through a clot of thin old men playing fan-tan. They turned, cursing at her: What was a woman doing down in the Hole anyway? Get back to shelling shrimp where you belong, they shouted. Leave men to their important business.

She ignored them as she had ignored similar poison all her life. She had seen the man with the slicked-back hair dart around to the left and, pushing aside several gamblers adrift on opium currents, she ran into shadows at top speed.

He was waiting for her; a curled arm like steel smashed downward, and Bliss gasped as she felt the pain sweep through her collarbone and neck. Her legs went out from under her and she slid onto the corridor's earthen floor.

Half stunned, she felt herself being dragged into a small, evil-smelling room. The soft stirring of the opium addicts came from all around her. She could barely make out supine shapes in the darkness. Here and there miniature fires were lit; the tears of the poppy was burning in the tiny bowls of long-stemmed pipes.

She felt his presence like a heat above her. She knew he would kill her, just as efficiently as he had killed the contact.

As he stood over her, she knew what she must do. In her mind she could hear the ancient gamblers screaming at her: What's a woman doing down in the Hole anyway? This man was no different from the rest. She would use it against him.

She could hear his panting; it contrasted with the slow, deep exhalations of the addicts among whom she lay.

Bliss lifted a hand, curled it around his neck, brought him down against her face. She could see slivers of yellow light reflecting in his eyes. She could scent his arousal. Killing sometimes did that to people, she had heard.

She needed time: to recover, to fix on a strategy. Bliss

9

opened her legs, thrust her breasts up. All the while the hand she had placed behind his head was moving, ever so slowly. She twisted her breasts beneath his hands. Now the pad of her thumb was just over the right side of his neck. She must give no pressure, no warning.

Bliss knew that she would only get one chance. If she did not get it dead on, he would kill her. She had absolutely no doubt of that.

She concentrated on what she had to do. The carotid. She knew the nerve meridian well. Still she hesitated. So much was riding on the split second of her commitment. Death was waiting for her.

She felt him against her soft flesh and she had had enough. She summoned all her inner strength; she concentrated her *qi* down to this one point on his anatomy. The carotid meridian.

Opened her mouth wide and shouted, as Jake had taught her; simultaneously, she pressed inward at the meridian juncture.

The effect on the assassin was astounding. He jumped, a fish on a line. His eyes flew open; she could see the whites all around. They began to bug out as the color drained from his cheeks.

Realizing what she was doing, he responded instinctually; he hit out. His fists were like blocks of iron. They struck Bliss; tears of pain welled up in her eyes.

Dizzy, grinning, the man hit her again; he laughed. He was enjoying this. Perhaps he was still as hard as he had ever been.

Bliss abandoned the carotid meridian and smote the underside of his rib cage with the heel of her hand. She heard the sickening snap as the two lowest ribs shattered.

Jake, having heard Bliss's cries, slammed around the left turning, racing down the near-deserted corridor of shadows. His peripheral vision brought him the movement of the struggle and he leapt into the opium den.

He grabbed the man with the slicked-back hair and jerked him backward. Bliss, so focused that she was still unaware that he had come into the room, saw her opening and jammed her hand into her assailant's abdomen. As Jake had taught her to do she used her rigid fingers to puncture skin, muscles, organs, all in one blurred motion of such power that it was unstoppable.

"No!" Jake cried, as he saw her begin the lethal blow, but

10

he was too late. She had been fighting for her life, and had become an organism too busy with the business of surviving to be concerned with outside stimuli.

The assassin spit blood and bile as he died. Reaching down, Jake scooped Bliss up off the floor and put the side of his face against hers. He kissed her on the lips. "Bliss. Are you all right?"

"Jake." Her head against his chest.

"Brave one," he said softly, and took her out of there.

Bliss sat in their apartment, a neat Scotch in her hand. Jake Maroc was in her eyes. He was stretched out at her side, his long legs crossed at the ankles.

"I messed it up," she said softly.

"He was going to kill you," Jake said. "You did what you had to do. You had no choice. Not too many people would have been able to survive that, let alone succeed. Concentrate on that."

"But if I'd just disabled him we would have been able to question him." The whiskey was against her opened lips. "Maybe we would've even found out who the spy is."

"He was a professional, Bliss. Chances are we would have gotten nothing from him. I'm just glad we're both okay."

The Repulse Bay crescent was not far away but they were too high up to hear the crying of the gulls. A huge black kite sat in the treetop outside the window, the early morning sunlight turning its feathers iridescent.

"Another dead end," she said, and swallowed half her Scotch. She had taken a long, hot bath, and then she and Jake had made love. That was what she had wanted the most.

"My father," Jake said, staring at the kite. "He must be up for hours already."

Bliss watched from her long almond eyes. After a long time she stirred, as if making up her mind. "Jake, you don't understand. I am part of the *yuhn-hyun*, the inner circle. I am part of you. If I can't be of help . . ."

Jake turned his head and smiled. He reached out, took her hand in his. "What would I do without you, Bliss. *Joss* that my contact was killed; *joss* that his murderer was, too. If I hadn't wanted you with me I'd have made damn sure that you stayed behind."

He frowned. "I need you with me. I don't know what I'd do otherwise, in the middle of the night." He was talking about the long ordeal he had so recently been through. For the entire nine months since he had returned to Hong Kong from Washington, where he had killed Henry Wunderman, Jake had been able to sleep only an hour or two a night. Near midnight he would pass out as if drugged, and Bliss, in the middle of reading, would quickly turn out the lights and slide down next to him.

Between one and two his animal cry of terror would start her awake. He could never remember the nightmare that had gripped him, but Bliss was certain that his guilt at having killed his surrogate father was the source.

Bliss reached out now, her long cocoa-colored fingers twining about his slender waist. They traced the network of long, flat muscles. Out of the corner of her eye she watched the worry lines etch themselves across his face. "The hospital," she said.

Jake smiled absently. "I remember. What a shock to see you again after all that time."

"We were childhood sweethearts, in the streets of Hong Kong."

"Is that what we were?" He pulled himself close to her.

"I always thought so."

"That's because you were precocious." The palm of his hand slid along her cheek. "To me you were my best friend."

Bliss laughed. "You see what I mean? What other boy would think of a girl as his best friend."

"I guess you're right," Jake said. "I must have been in love." Watching as Bliss's eyes closed. To his caress or his words? He was not certain it mattered. "Or crazy!"

Her eyes flew open and now it was his turn to laugh.

"I'm glad you're not angry with me," she said.

"Why should I be angry?" he said, sliding out of bed.

"Because when I came back into your life a year ago, it was as an agent of your father . . . because I was forbidden to tell you about certain things, the inner circle included, before a specific time."

Jake's extraordinary copper-colored eyes were hooded, as dark now in their centers as lead. "You were chosen by my father to lead me back to my family. Because of you, I found my half-brother, Nichiren. I found my real father, Shi Zilin. Because of you I am part of the *yuhn-hyun*, the inner circle of people who will control all of Asia someday."

"You are much more than that, my darling," Bliss said. "You are *Zhuan*. Your father is preparing you to be the new

12

leader. Don't you see, you are becoming the most powerful and influential man in the entire Eastern Hemisphere."

Jake looked away, and Bliss thought, What is wrong? He went barefoot into the bathroom. He did not bother to close the door. Bliss heard him urinating, then the tap water going. She drew her knees up to her chin and watched his shadow blocking the bathroom light. It fell upon the tiles in sharp angles.

When he came out of the shower, he looked into her beautiful face and seemed to see right through to the core of her. "No one else in the world could have done what you did," he said. "You fought at my side against spies and assassins. Like tonight. The extreme danger never fazed you."

"My father trained me well," Bliss said. But her mind was far away. She was thinking of how Jake had changed since Zilin had arrived in Hong Kong. He had become at once more in command and more secretive. She wondered whether the one was part of the other, and found herself fervently hoping that was not true.

Jake was very close to her. She felt the force of him. It was like being bathed by the noonday sun.

"The struggle is just beginning." His voice was very quiet. "It's on a larger scale than any of us could have dreamed. Before it's over, Bliss, we'll all need every ounce of strength we possess."

His words fell like hammer blows. Bliss felt her heart beating fast. "What's happening, Jake? What aren't you telling me?"

He smiled suddenly, and kissed her hard on the lips. "Nothing," he said, and kissed her again. "Speaking of your father," Jake said, "I'll need to see Three Oaths Tsun this afternoon."

"Do you wish to see the inner circle's other *tai pan*, or just my father?"

What was it, she wondered; what was darkening Jake's thoughts? She could feel it. Was it the specters of the dead he had so recently buried? For just an instant, she had a premonition; a remarkable sword of light pierced her consciousness. There was something more. Something that even he might not be aware of. She felt a chill of fear run through her. If Jake was out of phase with his environment or with himself, the consequences could be disastrous. He needed all his concentration in order to formulate his own strategy within the inner circle—and to try to discern the strategies of his enemies. If his *qi* was not in harmony, his decision-making prowess would be in serious jeopardy.

"No. I want to see Three Oaths Tsun alone," Jake said. "Will you set it up for three o'clock?"

Bliss nodded. "Of course." She thought of Three Oaths Tsun as her father because he had brought her up. Bliss had never known her real father, and remembered her mother only as a distant blur, like a badly out-of-focus photograph.

"And don't forget the emergency meeting Andrew Sawyer has called for noon," Bliss said. "That was the soonest all the *tai pan* could be rounded up." Jake nodded.

"Do you know what that's all about?" she asked anxiously. "Andrew sounded quite upset when he called."

Jake said, "Andrew's always upset about one thing or another."

She opened her mouth to tell Jake that she wanted to help him more, but he had turned away; she sensed that he was gone from her just as surely as if he had already walked out the door. His mind, no doubt, was already on this morning's meeting with his father, the great Jian, Shi Zilin.

Before Henry Wunderman, Jake's surrogate father, Jake had had foster parents. Solomon and Ruth Maroc, Jewish refugees in Shanghai, had taken him and his mother in. She had been sick and dying. The Marocs cared for Athena and her frightened child.

By that time, Jake's real father, Shi Zilin, had already gone with Mao, giving up his family, all that he held dear, in order to direct the fate of the new China.

Zilin worked behind the scenes with Mao, consolidating his power, entrenching himself through all the agonizingly bloody years of revolution and struggles for power, through the fall of Mao, the Gang of Four, the abrupt end to the Cultural Revolution. Until he was beyond all the infighting, the internecine warfare that led, inevitably, to the purges. Philosophies eddied and flowed around the seat of power in China. But because he was secreted away from it, Zilin was always spared.

Not that there weren't those who had tried to destroy him. The latest in the long line had been Wu Aiping, who had set himself up at the head of the group known as the *qun*, reactionary ministers who were opposed to Zilin's forward-thinking views on economic and industrial progress.

But Jake's father had outfoxed Wu Aiping, as he had all

14

his other enemies. Now the thinking of those who ruled China had turned his way, and though old and ill he had journeyed south to meet his grown sons, Jake and Nichiren, the child of his mistress.

One son had lived, the other had died in the pitched battle on the veranda of the villa high on the cliffs overlooking Repulse Bay. Nichiren, having found out that his father had also been his Control, had attacked Zilin. Jake had only wanted to protect the old man. His father. And in the process Jake had killed his brother. One could say half-brother, but what in the end was the difference? The same blood—Zilin's blood—flowed through their veins. Neither had known it until the very end. They had spent a good deal of their adult lives hunting one another, hurting one another, as bitter enemies. It had been Nichiren who had been responsible for Jake's daughter's murder at the Sumchun River three-and-a-half years before. As part of the American organization known as the Quarry, Jake had done his best to track Nichiren down. As he had peeled away the layers of deceit, he had gone from seeing Nichiren as a lone-wolf assassin to being controlled by the Russians—by General Daniella Vorkuta. Until recently Vorkuta had been the head of the KGB's most feared extra-territorial wing, the KVR. And then, Jake had discovered that Nichiren was in fact being controlled by Zilin out of Beijing.

It was all part of Zilin's master plan, what the old man called his *ren*, his harvest. Shi had created an inner circle, a *yuhn-hyun* of powerful people. Included in the inner circle were the major *tai pan*—the heads of Hong Kong's most powerful trading houses—and also the dragons, the overlords, of the three largest Triads, the secret societies.

And the man to direct them all? Jake Maroc or Jake Shi, take your pick. The *tai pan* of all *tai pan*, the most special one. Jake was *Zhuan*.

Ever since he had been reunited with Zilin, Jake's obsession had been the old man, his father. His days were spent at Zilin's side, deep in conversation. His zeal taxed even the old man's phenomenal endurance.

They would sit by the shoreline, their trouser legs rolled up, their bare feet in the surf. Even hunger did not stop their dialogue; they ate while they spoke, hardly tasting the food they were brought. Neither of them noticed the Triad members assigned to them, who strolled the beach, looking fondly at babies toddling on still-soft legs, carefully searching the faces of any others who entered the vicinity of father and son. Both Jake and Zilin appeared oblivious to danger.

On this day, there was a mist in the air, as if the night had refused fully to relinquish its hold.

"It is time for you to begin your work as *Zhuan*."

Zilin sat as a child might, his legs straight out in front of him. The brace was off the right leg, but his gnarled hand massaged the atrophied muscles along its upper length.

"Talk is constructive up to a certain point," Zilin said. "After that, only action matters."

Though it was in the low sixties, a winter coat was draped across Zilin's bony shoulders. His baggy cotton trousers were rolled to just below the knee. Still, in spots, the fabric was darkened, splashed by the surf of the South China Sea.

"The *Zhuan* is the *tai pan* of all Hong Kong *tai pan*. He is the head dragon of the inner circle. The *Zhuan* will eventually control all business throughout Asia. He will be the funnel through which Beijing will make its deals, through which the Indonesianized Chinese businessmen will clear their profits. Through him the British will do their trading. As will the Americans, the Japanese, the Thais and Malaysians."

Zilin stared out to where the sunlight was a swath of beaten brass over the waves. "This is the ultimate stage of my *ren*, my harvest. For fifty years this has been my dream—a united China. I have told you how I came upon the beginnings of Communism in China. My first wife, Mai, was Sun Zhong-shan's assistant." He was speaking of Dr. Sun Yat-sen, founder of the Guomindang. "We met in Shanghai at the founding of the Chinese Communist Party.

"I have already told you of my boyhood in Suzhou, of how much time I spent in the garden of my mentor, the Jian. Here it was that I was taught the overriding importance of artifice in life. The Jian's garden looked so perfectly natural that I believed for some time that every tree, bush, shrub, rock and hill in it had been there for hundreds of years—since, even, the beginning of time.

"Imagine then my consternation when the Jian revealed to me his secrets . . . the secrets of the garden. The hillock he had made himself to create a certain calming effect. The stones he had had brought from a brookside; these trees planted from here, those shrubs he had lovingly put in but three weeks ago. Yet all was harmonious, natural. Surely, I had thought, the hand of Buddha had shaped this space—not the mind of one man.

"But it was true. I saw that it was true; I became part of the Jian's plan for his garden.

"All this was never truly out of my mind as I grew up. And by the time my family moved to Shanghai and I went to college I knew that somehow I must employ the Jian's strategy in the game of life. I was already a *wei qi* grand master. On the game board, as well, I was able to use artifice to win matches.

"In those days, Jake, my friends spoke about nothing other than ridding our shores of the foreign devil who had invaded us. The foreign devil systematically pulled the natural resources out of China for their profit and at our expenses.

"But China was divided, at war with itself. How then could it also fend off the foreign devil? This was the subject of many debates. I listened but rarely made a comment, for I saw how clever the foreign devil were. And I thought, if we could only employ artifice—give the foreign devil what they thought they needed—then we could begin to use them as they had been using us. We could begin to harness their talents in the service of China.

"But first China had to be united. I had no clear idea how such a vast country, riddled with poverty and unrest, could be tamed.

"Then I went to the fateful meeting in Shanghai. I came face to face with the concept of Communism. And I knew instinctively that I had found the means of bringing peace to China.

"This, Jake, was the first stage of my *ren*, of my fifty-year harvest. But it required that I leave Shanghai, leave Athena, my second wife and your mother . . . leave you. I had no choice. China came first. China has always come first.

"Now at last we are in the final stages. You will be the conduit through which the power of all Asia will flow. China will at last be whole again. Not by destroying Hong Kong as some in Beijing still fervently wish to do, but by utilizing all the advantages that the foreign devil have given to this Colony: free trade, open markets, an unhindered, unlimited pipeline to the West. Without losing face we can solicit the industrial and electronic aid we so desperately need from the foreign devil.

"Within the spreading arms of the inner circle all China will prosper and grow.

"It is your *joss* to see the fruits of my *ren*, my harvest. Over the years Communism will wane. It was a powerful tool for us in the past. It roused the colossus that is China out of its slumber and moved it to a certain point. But now it is stagnating us. We have been strangling on doctrine while the world around us has moved into another age. If we cannot move also into this great new realm, then China is doomed to backwardness and is in real danger of being subordinated to Moscow. The Soviets have sought for many decades to control the direction of our future."

Zilin moved uncomfortably and for the briefest moment a flicker of pain shadowed his face. "I knew from the beginning, Jake, that I could not go beyond the stage of Jian. I have accomplished enough in my lifetime—now that I have found my son. I am the creator. It was for you to be *Zhuan*, the international conduit through which all Asian and Asian-related business flows. I admit that I could not control all the forces that must now come into play, not only from the Mainland and Hong Kong but in Bangkok, Singapore, Manila, Kuala Lumpur, New Delhi, Tokyo and Osaka. Some of those contacts have been made and have been passed on to you. Others you must make yourself. That is for the *Zhuan* to do—as it is to continue the fight to subdue our enemies."

A junk with a sail the color of pumpkins turned the point, tacking out to sea, its hull canted over as the winter wind took it.

Zilin held out his hand and Jake produced an oval of carved jade depicting two creatures locked in mortal combat. At some time it had been cleaved into four pieces which were now bound together by solid gold clasps. "Now it is not enough to dream and to spin webs of power." He turned the jade over and over in the palm of his hand. "Schemes will fail us in the end, if the *yuhn-hyun*, the inner circle, breaks apart. The bond between those of the ring may be more fragile than you can guess. Yes, the Triad dragons and the *tai pan* of my choosing are bound by this *fu*, the emperor's seal of carved lavender jade that you and Nichiren and Bliss and Andrew Sawyer brought together."

He lifted the oval into the sunlight. Its translucence was aglow with a radiance that almost brought the two carved animals to life. "But consider what the *fu* depicts: the legendary battle between the dragon and the tiger for supremacy of the earth. This is, perhaps, also what we truly speak of when we imagine the enormous task before the *yuhn-hyun*.

First, to protect the new emerging China from its enemies, the Soviets, the British, the Americans, and those in Beijing who are determined that Communism shall not die. Second, to unite Hong Kong and the Mainland, gradually adding Japan, Malaysia, Indonesia, Thailand, the Philippines. To take a strong and homogenous China swiftly into the twenty-first century.

"We must not become divided among ourselves. For now the forces are linked: my brothers, Three Oaths Tsun and T. Y. Chung; Andrew Sawyer, loyal to me and my family through the unimaginable favor I did him so many years ago; the dragons of the three major Triads.

"But these dragons, especially, will be wary, constantly seeking to gain an edge over their rivals within the inner circle. Nor can they be counted upon for substantial amounts of capital. Their support is manifest in other ways. These facts we cannot dispute nor waste energy in trying to change. It cannot be changed. *Joss.*

"We must ever be aware that our enemies—powerful enemies in many countries—seek to smash the *yuhn-hyun*. If they should succeed, then Hong Kong will become a mercantile battleground. Each country, each faction will seek to exploit to his own advantage the riches that flow through Hong Kong. There will be a cessation of profits. There will be war. And China will sink back into the medieval sloth it is only now beginning to outgrow. Divided, we are vulnerable and may be cut down. Seek to avoid this at all costs. You are *Zhuan*. Without your strength and expertise China will never make the transition into a modern world power. Without you and the inner circle there is no hope for us as a people."

Zilin turned his head away from the flat oblate of the sun. Within the shadows, his black eyes sparked with ethereal energy. Any lesser man would have already succumbed to the debilitating pain of his degenerative disease. But though his body had betrayed him, his mind was so disciplined that it could effectively cut itself off from the network of nerves that constantly throbbed with pain.

"Our enemies are known to us, father," Jake said. "In Russia, General Daniella Vorkuta seeks control of the inner circle, and of all Hong Kong. But her agent here, Sir John Bluestone, *tai pan* of Five Star Pacific, is well known to us—though he does not suspect that his cover has been blown."

But already a warning had been sounded. The spies Jake

employed throughout Hong Kong had reported an odd occurrence: a weekend party aboard Sir John Bluestone's 130-foot yacht, *Trireme*. The guest list included at least four powerful *tai pan*. Jake had not been able to find out the names of everyone who was there yet the knowledge that four powerful *tai pan* had been together with Bluestone for a significant amount of time was enough to make him uneasy.

Perhaps the weekend was nothing more than a two-day lark on the South China Sea. After all, Bluestone's entertaining was legendary in the Crown Colony. But there was that warning buzz, that question mark that Jake could not erase no matter how hard he tried. How he would have liked to have a spy among the crew of the *Trireme*. He made a mental note to work on that when he returned to the office.

"You are forgetting the agent, still unknown to us, who informed Chimera that you possessed a piece of the *fu*," Zilin said. "You must find this spy and destroy him. How we have suffered because of his treachery: the death of Mariana; the death of your brother, Nichiren. Retribution must be taken."

"The spy is deeply buried, father." Jake could not get the party on the *Trireme* out of his mind. "I am afraid that many roots will have to be unearthed before we discover who it is."

"Time is a commodity we are short on, Jake."

"Would you have me tear apart the entire inner circle?"

The Jian shook his head. "Absolutely not. The inner circle is all-important. If that is destroyed, then my entire life—all my sacrifices, all the pain, all the deaths I have caused and have been witness to—will have been in vain. Only the *yuhn-hyun* can hold the new China fast against its enemies from without and, just as importantly, from within. But this spy has demonstrated time and time again the ability to hurt us deeply."

He reached out in a rare physical gesture to grip his son's arm. "You are the *Zhuan*. By all means do as you see fit. I know that whatever happens you will not fail me. You must keep the *yuhn-hyun* together at all costs. I must emphasize these words: at all costs. If you cannot be ruthless with your allies as well as with your enemies then you will not succeed as *Zhuan*. And my *ren*, my fifty-year harvest, will have been for naught.

"Consider China's recent history. Our own petty bickering allowed the foreign devil to invade us. Our ignorance of world culture allowed the foreign devil to exploit us all. But it was

20

because China had been turned into a huge nation of poverty-stricken coolies that I knew a concept such as Communism could galvanize even a nation as large as ours.

"But Communism was only a means to an end. Those ministers in Beijing who still cling to its rigid tenets do so only because of the power it gives them. Communism is no longer useful to China. On the contrary, it is impeding our progress. My goal all along has been to use Hong Kong as the sword with which to slowly shed our old, outdated doctrines without losing face. The method was obvious to me. Beijing could not be seen to discard wholesale what it had espoused for so many decades.

"My *ren* has been a constant struggle to save China from itself."

The old man shook his head. "Hong Kong is the key to our—to all of Asia's—future safety and prosperity. Unfortunately, our enemies know this as well."

He bowed his head and Jake said, "Father, what is it?"

Suddenly the Jian seemed old, frail, desperately tired. Like an afternoon sky abruptly devoid of sunlight, Zilin's countenance was bleak, wintry.

Jake felt his stomach tighten in a spasm of anxiety. "Father, are you in pain?"

The old man shook his head. He held himself carefully as if afraid that he would shake apart. "The pain I feel has nothing to do with my illness." He closed his eyes. For a long time not a word passed between them. Gulls cawed shrilly above them, circling in the watery sunlight. Mist lay along the water like dragon's breath. Jake felt the imminence of terror, lurking in the mist.

"Jake, I have hesitated to tell even you," Zilin said at last. "But the time is now such that I no longer have a choice." He held the jade tightly in a fist made white by tension. "The one topic about which we do not often speak is Kam Sang."

"Our trump card," Jake said. "As you have told me, Kam Sang may very well end up being the salvation of China."

Now the Jian shuddered visibly. "Kam Sang was always a two-edged sword. We all knew that going in. In any project of this sort the potential for destruction exists. However, at the time, we felt that the risk was worth taking. We felt that we had built in adequate controls and safeguards." He took a deep breath. "But now everything has changed."

In the deathly silence, Jake could hear the plashing of the waves as if they were rows of crystal smashing. "What has happened at Kam Sang, father?" He could not recognize his own voice; his rapid pulse made his ears ring.

Zilin looked out to sea, beyond the surf and the small junks lifted high on the ocean's crests as they tacked for shore. "A discovery has been made by the scientific cadre there," he said softly. "A frightening, terrible discovery. It was accidental. They came upon it by chance during their experiments." His head swung around and his dark gaze impaled Jake. "It threatens—Jake, it threatens the entire balance of power here; in the entire world. Kam Sang's possibility for destruction is now virtually limitless. The destructive potential is so heinous that you must ensure that it can never be implemented. Sane men—of all nationalities—would shun it. But there are others—" He broke off abruptly, shivered slightly, and turned his face into the wan light. "The Russians would gladly kill for the secret of Kam Sang. So would the Americans and the British. But you, Jake . . . you are its sole guardian now."

He placed the jade *fu* in Jake's hand and said, "Though this jade has been near you and near me, yet is it still cool. Jade is always cool, unlike men, who grow heated with passions and lusts. That is a lesson to be learned."

Zilin placed his hand atop Jake's so that the jade linked them. "There is a saying, Jake," he said, "older than the Tao: 'On the mountain it is dark and cold, but without these discomforts there would be nothing.' "

He moved his legs in the surf. "That is where you are now—on the mountain. You must begin to feel the dark and the cold. Without giving them substance you will be lost; you will feel only fear for the rest of your life."

Jake felt the sand beneath him, felt the salt wind on his cheeks. Somewhere he heard the sound of children's laughter, a dog's yelp of joy. Most of all, he felt the weight, cool and curved, of the jade *fu*. Father, he wanted to say, when I learn your lesson will it make me all-powerful, or just inhuman?

But sitting on the beach at Repulse Bay, next to the Jian, the creator, he made no comment at all. He merely waited for his father to explain to him what had occurred at Kam Sang—and to explain how the world was now a different and infinitely more dangerous place.

Jin Kanzhe was in Qianmen, just south of Beijing's Tienanmen Square, in among a warren of tiny side streets filled with food shops and vendors' stalls. He wore a putty-colored trench coat, belted and epauleted, the hem reaching to the ground. It made him seem even taller and slimmer than he was.

Behind Jin Kanzhe a torrent of bicycles shot along the main streets, the heavy cold damping down almost all sound so that their passing was eerily silent. The smell of coal dust turned the air to molasses.

Jin saw the stocky man outside the carpet shop and approached him. "Good morning, Comrade. And how is our *lizi*, our deadly little plum?"

Colonel Hu sucked on his teeth. "Our *lizi* is as well as can be expected," he said.

As always, Colonel Hu was uncomfortable around Jin. His features, rough-hewn, undistinguished, were a far cry from the narrow elegance of Jin Kanzhe's.

"The mission concerning the girl went well?" he asked. They moved slowly through the throngs of shoppers; Jin Kanzhe liked to be in motion.

"There was no undue difficulty," Colonel Hu said. Jin concentrated on a tonal shading he did not recognize. "The strategy you proposed was the correct one. They are used to being sought out near the rivers. It has been the established way for years. We found Cheng and the girl on the mountainside; we caught them asleep." Colonel Hu shrugged. "Still I lost two men; one more is in a coma. These are resourceful people."

Jin Kanzhe wondered whether it was a note of respect he detected in Colonel Hu's voice. "We used every precaution and still they were able to counterattack."

"It was a pity about her escort," Jin Kanzhe said. "I would have preferred to put him under articulated interrogation."

"Cheng?" Colonel Hu shrugged. "He died a soldier's death. He took a bullet through the heart."

Jin Kanzhe snorted. " 'A soldier's death.' You give it a romantic ring. There is nothing romantic about death."

Colonel Hu said nothing. They turned right as they came to the end of the block. They were in an area adjacent to the railway station. As they walked, they passed a line of traditional apothecaries, their narrow interiors lined with dusty glass cases stocked with deer antlers, ground tiger's teeth, ginseng root and all manner of fungi.

Jin Kanzhe nodded, dismissing the subject. "It is the girl who concerns us, after all. We have Wu Aiping to thank for detecting her presence among the Steel Tiger Triad. His almost pathological interest in the Shis led him to track down, before his death, her identity and whereabouts. This was the legacy left for his friend, Huaishan Han."

"He led us to the girl?"

"Yes," Jin Kanzhe said thoughtfully. "She will soon be the engine of your making."

"There is a good chance," Colonel Hu said slowly, "that what you are asking me to do to her will change her in a very basic manner."

Yes, Jin Kanzhe said to himself; yes. She is like some mythical creature. All men who look upon her face are captivated by her. He stopped, turned to face Colonel Hu. "I must tell you something in no uncertain terms. This is so critical that neither of us can afford to misunderstand the other." He was silent for a moment, allowing his intense gaze to register on the other man.

After a time, Colonel Hu nodded. "Yes, sir." For the first time, he understood the true nature of his discomfort around this man. I am *afraid* of him, Colonel Hu thought, with some surprise. Jin Kanzhe knows how desirable the *lizi* is. Has she so profoundly affected me—her captor? Is Jin Kanzhe making a shrewd guess? What troubled Hu most was that he himself did not know the answer.

"Good, Comrade Colonel. *Zheige lizi hai mei shu ne.* This plum is not yet ripe. But that doesn't mean that she is not dangerous. On the contrary. She is *exceptionally* deadly." Jin Kanzhe abruptly began to walk again and Colonel Hu, taken unawares, was obliged to hurry to catch up.

"You have a point," Colonel Hu said. "However, I must confess that I am unsure whether you are aware of *just* how deadly I have made her."

Jin Kanzhe turned his head. The oblique light flashed off his eyes, as if energy was pouring out of him. "Tell me, Comrade Colonel," he said, "have you ever been to sea?"

Colonel Hu was puzzled. "No, sir. The truth is, the water makes me seasick."

Jin Kanzhe laughed. "Yes. That seems to be the case for many of our countrymen. However, there is a nautical term that you should take to heart when it comes to our *lizi*, our unripe fruit. She is like a beautiful sloop. With her one may come to feel that anything is possible. Therefore, beware of sailing too close to the wind, Comrade Colonel. Otherwise you may find yourself drowned." He glanced at his watch. "I am late."

Colonel Hu knew a dismissal when he heard one. He watched Jin Kanzhe stride off. In a moment the tall man was swallowed up in the swirl of pedestrian and bicycle traffic that ran like an endless river through Qianmen.

Ian McKenna was out with his police unit quelling a disturbance in Stanley when he was handed the briefcase. One moment he was directing three of his men in beating back a phalanx of jabbering Chinese so intent on getting through the doors of the closing Hongkong & Bangkok Trust Bank that they had flung aside the sawhorses McKenna's men had erected, the next a nondescript Chinese had placed something in his free hand. At six-foot-three, McKenna was easy to spot.

For a moment McKenna was not even aware of what had happened. He was intent on parting a Chinese from his teeth, swinging his burnished teak walking stick over his head and bringing it down with a crunch he believed to be one of the most satisfying sounds in the world.

Then, as the blood began to flow and he was about to step over the prone Chinese, he became aware of the added weight. He turned his head, saw the briefcase and the nondescript Chinese at the same moment.

"Inspector Ian McKenna, this is for you."

"Hey!" he called. "Hey, you!" But it was already too late, the figure melted into the riot of color and motion that surged all around him.

McKenna was known as Great Pool of Piddle by all the Chinese who came into contact with him—and this included those who served under him—but never to his face, only when they were among their own, speaking in their native tongue. McKenna was a fire-haired Australian who spoke Cantonese and a smattering of the Hakka dialect with an atrocious accent. He had served his apprenticeship in police work in the Outback down under before emigrating to Hong Kong ten years before. He was made a corporal in the Crown Colony's police force and by a combination of a rough-hewn guile and an often violent force of will, worked himself up to the rank of captain.

He possessed the animal's innate ability to go for the jugular when confronting his enemies. This trait caused him to be feared by almost as many of his superiors as those who toiled in his command.

But there were others who did not fear Ian McKenna. Among them was Formidable Sung, the 489 of Hong Kong's largest Cantonese Triad, the 14K. It was Formidable Sung who, failing to strike a bargain with McKenna, had discovered the Australian's weakness. Photographs had been obtained of McKenna and an eleven-year-old Chinese boy in poses of such extreme intimacy that the public exposure of same would spell not only instant dismissal for McKenna but more than likely criminal prosecution.

Now twice a week McKenna reported the details of his pending workload directly to Formidable Sung; in a break with tradition, it had been the 489 himself who had handed McKenna the sheaf of photographic prints sealed in a glossy crimson envelope.

The symbolic gesture—such a red envelope was tradition-ally given to a defeated business rival along with a token sum of money in order for him to keep some semblance of face—had not been lost on the Australian. He would never forget the moment Formidable Sung placed the thing in his hand. Each sound, each smell, and above all the laughing glitter in the 489's eyes, were indelibly etched into McKenna's brain. He would not forget such an insult, for Formidable Sung—by coming himself to the rendezvous, and by staring openly into his face when he slit open the envelope—had left McKenna with no face at all.

Now, as the men in McKenna's command beat back the last of the would-be rioters, McKenna wondered what new indignity the dragon of the 14K was foisting upon him. His face was red, and not from the exertion of wading through a bunch of hysterical heathens.

McKenna blew his whistle, calling his men back to the wagon that had brought them from the station house. He stared down at the unconscious Chinese and spat heavily into his broken face. What he really wanted to do was spit into Formidable Sung's face.

He turned, stomping back to the police wagon, thinking, One day I'll do just that. Then *I'll* watch *his* face turn red. A pox on him and all his accursed Triad.

McKenna did not open the briefcase until he had returned to the precinct. Even then he did not trust the operation to his office. Instead, he went down the musty-smelling hall to the evil-smelling men's room. One grimy window was painted shut. The black desiccated bodies of flies lay on the rotting sill. Above, one of their brothers, still alive, beat itself feebly against the painted glass. There was just enough sunlight filtering in to give it a false sense of hope.

McKenna paused. The tap-tap-tapping of the fly seemed to echo eerily in the enclosed space, taking on supernormal proportions.

Suddenly, McKenna was back in Australia's Northern Territories outside of Bundooma. The edges of the Simpson Desert where he and his partner had tracked a trio of aborigines accused of stealing six head of steer. McKenna remembered how his partner, Deak Jones, had balked at the sight of the Simpson.

"Not in there, mate," he had said, the eyes in his sunburned face squinting up. "Let the buggers go. They'll fry anyway in there." January in the Simpson was no place for a living thing to be without shade and water in good supply.

"That's their turf," McKenna had replied. "They'll slaughter the animals as they go, drink their blood, eat their flesh. They'll get off scot free if we turn back now."

"They were starving. They stole in order to live."

"They'll see this," McKenna unholstered his .357 Magnum, "they'll know they've done wrong." He licked his lips, cocking back the hammer. "It's our job, Deak m'lad. If we don't have that, we don't have a bloody thing."

"We're going to bring them back, Ian," Deak said, eying the muzzle of the huge pistol. "Let's remember that."

McKenna grinned savagely. "Push off, mate. Push off."

It took them two days to get the scent and overtake the abos. Near to dusk they topped a rise and found the trio and what was left of the cattle. By then they had been in the desert for close to fifty hours and it had taken its toll. They were dehydrated and without sleep and jumpy enough to be spooked by any sound of unknown origin.

"Let's take them," Deak said through crusted lips, and McKenna had headed down the slope, silent as a dog.

The aborigines looked up at the policemen's approach. As McKenna had predicted, they had slaughtered a steer. Its blood was pooled at its open belly.

Nothing was said. The aborigines made no move; there was no animosity on their faces, no remorse, not even, McKenna had thought later, surprise.

"All right," Deak had begun, beginning a speech McKenna knew well. McKenna drew his Magnum and shot them each once through the center of their foreheads. They pitched forward at once, covering the animal they had so recently slit open.

"Christ Jesus!" Deak swung on his partner. "Have you

27

gone mad? We were meant to take them back. Alive, mate. A—bleeding—live!"

McKenna holstered his weapon. "Now you listen to me. We're more than two days into this stinking hellhole. There were three of them and only two of us. How long would we realistically last? D'you think you could stay awake another night? Or get by on four hours sleep? What d'you think would happen if you closed your eyes even for a moment. They'd be all over you and then me, that's what. This was the safest way; the only way."

They camped there for the night, feasting on the carcass of the steer. But the flies had come, scenting the reek of death. It was odd to see them in the desert but they were unstoppable, crawling all over the steer and the abos without a trace of discrimination.

Tap-tap-tap. In the last of the light, McKenna had turned his head. Tap-tap-tap. His gaze followed the sound back to its source. A fly was beating against the open filmed eye of one of the natives as if it was a pane of glass, as if it were trapped.

Tap-tap-tap. Tap-tap-tap, over and over again, without meaning, until the tattoo began to grate on McKenna. He got up and walked over to the corpse. Tap-tap-tap. He looked down, into the opaque orb. Tap-tap-tap.

"God rot you!" His boot lashed out viciously, crashing into the ashen face. "Shuddup!" Wiped what was left of the fly off his sole. The dead abo wouldn't know or mind.

But that night, McKenna had heard the recurring sound again and this time he could do nothing to stop it. He was staked out on the sere desert floor, sunlight blinding him, and he felt them all over his exposed flesh. The flies crawling.

He awoke from the dream, dripping wet, his heart pounding painfully in his chest. Deak Jones was sitting close to him, his knees drawn up. He was staring into McKenna's face. When he saw him awake, he said, "I was wondering if you could tell me how you're able to sleep."

When they had returned to civilization, Jones had asked for a transfer and McKenna had not seen him again. But as for the tap-tap-tapping, that was another matter entirely.

Now, thousands of miles and thirteen years later, that moment in time rushed back on McKenna with the force of a piledriver. In two quick steps he crossed the small room and, reaching out a spatulate thumb and forefinger, squeezed the bloated black fly against the dirt-encrusted pane.

"Like getting rid of a pimple," he said, and went into one of the two adjacent cubicles. He closed the door and locked it, sat down with the briefcase across his lap.

For a time he did nothing. He shook out a cigarette and lit up, taking the tobacco deep into his lungs. The air hissed in exhalation. It was like a sigh. Of resignation, perhaps?

With a sudden flip, McKenna unsnapped the brass latches. He opened the lid. Unconsciously he held his breath. The cigarette dangled loosely from his pursed lips, smoke curling past his eye.

"Christ!" It was a reedy whisper. As if of their own accord, his hands began to flip through the stacks of bills. Three thousand dollars U.S. currency. Part of his mind still numb, he did a recount and came to the same total.

Only then did he see the note. It was taped to the inside of the lid. He opened it. "For services rendered," he read. "Should such a weekly stipend be of interest to you please come to Hair Pin Beach at two thirty this morning. At the second light stanchion three kilometers northeast of Stanley, walk straight down the beach to the edge of the water."

The note, typewritten and obviously untraceable, was unsigned.

McKenna's gaze was drawn back as if by magnetic polarity to the contents of the briefcase. He gave a little shiver as if of anticipation.

There was a small painting by Georges Seurat that Rodger Donovan had brought with him when he had moved into the office that had been Antony Beridien's, until the then-director of the Quarry had been assassinated.

Donovan thought of it as a most extraordinary painting. It had been a gift. Twice daily—at dawn and dusk—when the light from outside was right, the points of seemingly disparate colors swirled through eye and brain to create a unity of tone and, even, quite miraculously, form.

That was, Donovan supposed, why he was drawn so strongly to Seurat's work. It was the miracles the artist could perform. For Donovan was quite certain that no true miracles existed in day-to-day life. Seurat had the ability to take Donovan quite out of himself.

Now, with the heavy gun-metal rain rattling against the windowpanes, he turned away from his contemplation of a miracle. The buzzer sounded again and he said, "Come."

The thick door opened. Between two three-inch mahogany

panels, a sheet of steel-alloy an inch thick protected him from the unlikely event of an attack. Unlikely because of the six-level security system he had had installed after the death of Henry Wunderman.

A tall, lanky figure stood in the doorway. He wore a Donegal-tweed sweater, pleated wool trousers the color of burnt butterscotch and cordovan tasseled loafers. His long frizzy hair and high forehead made him seem no older than nineteen or twenty, rather than his true age of thirty-one. He was pale-eyed and fair-skinned, with cheeks made ruddy in the winter by skiing, in the summer by windsurfing.

Donovan gestured to a bentwood chair. "Take a pew, Tony."

Tony Simbal's long strides ate up the distance between them. Like Cary Grant's, they were fluid, so effortless they attracted the attention of a majority of the female population in his immediate vicinity. He folded himself into the chair. His long-fingered hands neatly folded over his crossed knees.

"How was New York?" Donovan asked.

Simbal grunted. "Grimy. And there's so much traffic these days you're forced underground in order to get anywhere in a reasonable amount of time." He grinned. "Down there you need a .357 Magnum in order to survive."

"Nothing untoward occurred, I take it."

"Not really. I just bared my teeth at the natives. That seemed enough to keep the Zulus at bay."

Zulus. Donovan gave a little laugh, his handsome blond visage breaking its somber façade. That word took him back. Tony Simbal was a relative newcomer to the Quarry. Still, he was one of the closest to Donovan. That was because the new Director had reached out his long arm and snatched Simbal away from the DEA.

Donovan and Simbal had gone through the Stanford mill together. They had been fiercely competitive roommates, fraternity brothers and the best of friends. They had grown up together, their fathers vying for regional chess titles all along the Pacific coast.

In rebuilding the Quarry after the twin debacles of Beridien's and Wunderman's deaths, Donovan's aim was absolute trust. His recruitment of Tony Simbal was the essence of that trust. In high school, the two boys had actually gone after the same girl. She, being open-minded and flattered, had dated each one on alternating Saturday nights until they had asked her to make a choice. She had told them that she could not because each had qualities she loved and did not want to

30

give up, and that comment had sealed their friendship forever. After that, they continued to compete with one another—mostly in the academic world—but neither really kept score of the victories and defeats. They seemed to share the elation and the disappointments equally, remembering what that girl in high school had told them. Now, long after both had forgotten her name, they recalled that moment in time as if it had the magical aura of Arthur pulling Excalibur free of the stone.

"No Zulus in Chinatown," Donovan said now. Zulus had been their word for blacks on the wrong side of the law.

"No," Simbal agreed. "Only one very dead white man."

"How bad was it?"

The tall man grimaced. He got up, restless in high-rises of any kind. He crossed to where the Seurat hung. "Looked like a barbecue gotten all out of hand. His face was basically fleshless. Can you believe this, Alan Thune was roasted by a dragon."

"Pardon?"

Simbal was still studying the Seurat. "It was Chinese New Year. Thune was set to pick up payment for three-quarters of a ton of Number Four opium. The tears of the poppy. Instead he met up with a dragon. It opened its mouth and fried Thune."

Donovan looked at him and Simbal smiled.

"The dragon's traditional at New Year's. A papier-mâché head. People inside. Only this time there was also an anti-personnel flame-thrower."

"There couldn't've been much left of him," Donovan said.

Simbal grunted. "There wasn't. But our boys did a DNT on him. All the molars were in the right place. It was Alan Thune, all right."

"Bastard." Donovan sat back in his leather swivel chair. "I only wish I had been the one to do it."

Behind him, through the dark-blue latticework of the Bali microblinds, Simbal could see the White House, part of the immaculately tended rose garden. Both were partially obscured by the rain. He wondered what it was about Thune that had gotten under Donovan's skin. At Stanford, he remembered, there was nothing that fazed that handsome, placid façade: not the most difficult final, not the breakup with a girlfriend. It wasn't, Simbal had eventually learned, that Donovan did not have emotions, it was that he wasn't fond of putting them on display. As he had now.

"You spent two years in Southeast Asia," Donovan said after a time. "All that time you were monitoring the *diqui*." *Diqui*, the Mandarin word for the planet earth, seemed an altogether accurate name for an organization of such vast power and influence. "Any ideas as to what's going on?"

Simbal was still focused on the Seurat. "This the real thing?"

"No," Donovan said, "a copy. I only wish I had the real thing. I'd have to go back to Paris for that."

Simbal grunted, swung around. The light was fading. "There's no easy explanation as to why a man's fried by a dragon. But one thing's certain: it was a gaudy public way to go, and *that* tells us something."

"A warning?"

Simbal nodded. "No doubt. But of what? Thune was the *diqui*'s top American courier. Was he skimming from the *diqui*? Is someone making a move against them? Was it a personal vendetta? Did the *diqui* itself have some gripe against Thune?" He shrugged. "Right now it's impossible to say."

Donovan's gray eyes regarded his friend for a time. A French antique carriage clock tick-tocked on a chrome and rosewood sideboard across the room. Outside the window umbrellas were being shredded as the wind picked up. It sounded as if disgruntled demonstrators were throwing pebbles against the steel-mesh glass.

"I don't care for the word *impossible*. What's your best guess?"

Simbal went back to the chair, folded himself into it again. For a time, he said nothing. The carriage clock marked the interstices of silence. "I've run as much as I have through the computer." Simbal's voice carried a tone of absolute authority. "But you know what I think of computers, Rodger. They only spew out what other people have programmed into them. Federal agents are, by and large, nitwits. They are trained to think in terms of budgets and of what has happened before. They lack imagination and therefore their informational data banks possess the same drawback."

Donovan laced his fingers, began to tap their tips together. "Don't tell me that brain of yours hasn't narrowed the possibilities."

Simbal smiled thinly. "My nose says that it wasn't the *diqui*'s doing. I've traveled after Thune for a long time. Unless he's done something very bad while I've blinked, his standing inside the *diqui* was solid. In fact, I suspect that he was being readied to move up. Someone was grooming him for bigger things than the Fun City run."

"Like who?"

Simbal shook his head. "Sorry. I haven't been able to get that far yet."

"Then take another tack." Simbal watched Donovan's head. It seemed he was holding it still with some great inner force and once again he asked himself, What's gotten under Rodger's skin? "Whatever it takes."

Simbal's eyes opened wide. "Schiffer won't like it." He was speaking of his dry section case officer. Field operatives were wet section. "He didn't even like it that I went off to New York without letting him know. He chewed my ear off about it first thing this morning."

"That's all in the past," Donovan said.

"Meaning?"

"From now on you report to me and me alone. Clear?"

Simbal's eyes seemed as pale as winter sunlight on inimical ice. "When I was in Burma, I met a woman. A girl, really. She was a Shan. She had that almost Polynesian beauty the Burmese possess.

"She was uneducated from a Western point of view, but she could outshoot three-quarters of the DEA's marksmen including me and her father possessed undreamed-of wealth, mainly in uncut gemstones, though I seem to recall that he dealt in the tears of the poppy as well.

"In the Shan States, Rodger, there is no such thing as civilization. There is only life and death. Only love and hate. That realization shook me apart. It was why, I realized, I had come there, why I turned down that plum job at Cray Computers that the rest of the top ten percent of our class probably would have killed for.

"I am not, I suspect, a civilized man." Simbal hunched forward now and Donovan could see the power in his hands. "I do not like civilization's dictates and its rules. Cray was not for me. Neither was DEA, which has rules up the yin-yang. You couldn't pee without writing up forms. I don't like writing forms."

"And you didn't like reporting to Schiffer," Donovan said. "I know that." He looked at Simbal. "In my predecessor's time, the Quarry was mainly concerned with the machinations emanating out of Moscow. That was, perhaps, inevitable. Antony Beridien founded this organization during the reign of John Fitzgerald Kennedy."

Simbal snorted. " 'Reign'? Isn't that a little grandiose to describe an American president's term of office?"

"Not when we're talking about JFK. Beridien spent many hours talking about those times. Camelot. Remember that's how the press spoke of Kennedy's reign. The shining hundred days." Donovan grunted. "Everything in America's reduced to the parameters of an advertising slogan. Advertising's what catches the American public's attention, Tony. Otherwise, they're too busy buying new Toyotas and Subarus to be aware of anything. But we both know advertising for what it is: bullshit."

Simbal contemplated this all-American, fair-haired prodigy that his long-time friend had evolved into. Who'd have thunk it? he thought wonderingly. Back in the Stanford days we were just two sex-charged boy geniuses. Look at the misfits we've turned into. "So the both of us need to get out."

"Out?"

"It's civilization, Rodger. It stinks. I've said it. Now you have, too. In your own way."

Donovan thought about that for a moment. "I was speaking about Antony Beridien."

"And Kennedy."

"Kennedy gave the Quarry its original charter. It was Beridien's brainchild but it was JFK who breathed the breath of life into it. The Quarry, Tony, was born out of paranoia. The world was shrinking at a terrifying, overwhelming rate in the sixties. It seemed as if the Russians were right next door. The Cuban missile crisis proved that dramatically.

"Anyway, Beridien and Kennedy were asshole buddies. The President knew strength when he saw it and he gave Beridien his head. But there was a caveat. Each incoming president had the option to cancel the Quarry's charter within the first month of his term of office. That was for a specific reason.

"The Quarry is the President's responsibility, period. We don't have nosy senators ferreting around; we're not dependent on Capitol Hill for funds. No one knows us or what we really do. We're a lone-wolf quantity . . . undoubtedly the last in American governmental history. I want you to remember that."

Donovan put his hands flat on the table. "It was Beridien's obsession to go after the Soviets, not mine. These days, there are other, more pressing matters that require our attention.

Which is why I appropriated you from the DEA. The *diqui* was your bailiwick there and we need that experience here in the Quarry."

"International dope smuggling's not exactly the Quarry's thing," Simbal said. "DEA's got that tied up pretty tightly and I don't have to tell you how my old boss, Max Threnody, guards his territory. He gets bent out of shape if someone extra-agency even requests DEA data."

"That's just fine by me," Donovan said. "Threnody can have all the cocaine and opium his operatives can lay their hands on. You're right, dope's not our thing. But Kam Sang is. I've been trying to get a line on that top-secret Chinese project for a year-and-a-half. That's the main reason I tried to reenlist Jake Maroc some months ago. I got a hunch he knows what Kam Sang's all about. I have reports that his father has some link to Kam Sang. What the old man knows, I figure Jake knows too."

"Why don't you ask him, then."

"Very funny. Jake was loyal to the old Quarry regime. Then they threw him out. He wouldn't tell me the time of day if it didn't suit his purpose."

Simbal came over to the desk. "What has Kam Sang got to do with Alan Thune's incineration?"

"I don't know," Donovan admitted. "Maybe nothing at all. But all of a sudden our Far East signals eavesdropping is detecting *diqui* interest in Kam Sang. Why? That's not their bailiwick either."

"Anyone been on this?" Simbal wanted to know.

"Powers and Choi."

"Shouldn't I speak to them in person?"

"You'd better have a line on a good medium," Donovan said. "They're six feet under."

"Dead?"

"Shot through the eyes, both of them."

"*Diqui* trademark." Simbal wondered whether this was why Donovan was pissed off.

Donovan stood. "I've got a feeling, Tony, that something's been started and now it's out of control. Alan Thune's death may be the start of an international bloodbath."

Simbal watched Donovan's face. "About Threnody," he said. "What do I tell him?"

"Oh, Christ, use your imagination," Donovan said. "But whatever you tell him, make sure it isn't the truth."

Just east of a section of Connaught Road Central was Sawyer Place, the only street in Hong Kong named after an American. The centerpiece of the two-block narrow thoroughfare was the Sawyer Building, a white-stone and blue-granite affair that had been built in the mid-1930s when such grandiose workmanship was still affordable. Now even the Bank of China had to have its stone cut in Canada to help defray the impossible cost of labor.

Many companies were housed within this structure that stood between Connaught Tower and the equally ornate building that had until some months before been the home of Mattias, King & Company, once the oldest and most renowned of all the major trading houses in Asia.

Mattias, King & Company's new London-born *tai pan* had seen fit, perhaps at the urging of the Queen herself, to move the venerable house's headquarters to Bermuda. Ostensibly that had been to ensure a tax-free haven for the company but, privately, the other *tai pan* in the Crown Colony knew that it was a panic move away from what the British obviously saw as Communist Chinese intervention on the free-market running of Hong Kong.

While it awaited the building of its gargantuan new office tower designed by I. M. Pei, the Bank of China had temporarily moved into the Mattias, King building. It was, Andrew Sawyer said, a sign of the changing times.

The old *tai pan*, his snowy hair much receded on his freckled scalp, turned away from the ten-foot-high windows that looked out at all of Kowloon, Victoria Harbor and the hazy recesses of the Asian continent from his office aerie atop the Sawyer Building.

Sawyer & Sons was one of the handful of most successful Western trading houses in Hong Kong and it had been so for many years. In Shanghai, where the firm had been started by Andrew Sawyer's father, Zilin had begun a clandestine partnership with Barton Sawyer. The Shis were not only a secret part owner of Sawyer & Sons, but Andrew Sawyer owed Zilin a personal debt he could never fully repay. Without Zilin's intervention when he had been young and foolish, Andrew Sawyer would never have become *tai pan* of the trading house. That exalted position would have gone to Chen Ju, Barton Sawyer's trusted comprador.

"Peter Ng's being revealed as a Soviet spy," Andrew Sawyer said now, referring to his former comprador, "was the beginning of our woes. It left security in a goddamned mess, and the first thing I want to do is to hang Sir John Bluestone up by his thumbs."

"I don't think that would be the most prudent thing to do." Jake, sitting in a leather sofa at the side of the enormous office, said this slowly and calmly.

There was enormous tension in the room; it had generated even before this extraordinary meeting of the *yuhn-hyun*'s principles—Jake, Sawyer, Three Oaths Tsun and T. Y. Chung—had gotten under way. It was Sawyer, the ring's day-to-day caretaker, who had called the emergency session. Since the business feud between Three Oaths and T. Y. Chung—a ruse dreamed up by Zilin to allow both his brothers to amass fortunes and allies who would never have joined the two together—was still very much a public issue, it was most dangerous for the two to be seen together. Nothing less than a full-fledged emergency would have caused Andrew Sawyer to bring the men together in broad daylight. He felt that he had had no choice.

"It was fornicating Bluestone who turned my comprador; it's Bluestone who is the Soviets' most high-ranking agent in all of Asia," Sawyer said angrily. He tapped a manila envelope. "We've got more than enough hard proof to convict him. I told you before that we should have shut him down. Give me one good reason now why we shouldn't have Special Branch come and haul him away."

"The primary one is that we now know who our enemy is," Jake said reasonably. "You are asking me to give up an enormous advantage and that I will not do. We are in a position to monitor Sir John Bluestone, the Soviets' most important agent on this continent. If he is removed, who will Daniella Vorkuta replace him with? We won't know the man until, perhaps, it is too late. Also, Bluestone's networks, which we are finally beginning to infiltrate, will be blown along with him. His control at Moscow Center, Daniella Vorkuta, is sure to see to that. She'll close everything down and start over. We'll be in the dark again. Is that what you want?"

Sawyer came and sat down in a chair at Jake's left. He ran a thin hand through the wispy strands of hair combed down over his mottled skull. "Of course not, no." His cool blue eyes flashed. "But I want my justice against Bluestone."

"And so you shall have it," Jake said evenly. "In time. The season has not yet come for reaping, Andrew."

"Meanwhile, our empire is falling down around us. Bluestone is fighting us by proxy for control of our company—which includes Pak, the subsidiary invested in the Kam Sang project. It is vital that we maintain a majority interest in that warren of companies, isn't that so, Honorable Tsun?"

"I created the companies," Three Oaths said. "I would say, yes. Without that subsidiary we would lose close to two hundred million dollars American."

"And the *yuhn-hyun*'s control of Kam Sang is absolutely vital," Jake said. "There can be no debate about this."

"But our fight for control of Pak combined with our own increased investment in Kam Sang, has seriously depleted our liquidity," Sawyer said.

"Do you know what that means?" T. Y. Chung jumped in. "Never in my life have I seen so much capital expended so quickly as we have poured into InterAsia Trading. We are three of the most wealthy *tai pan* in all of Asia. Yet because of the extraordinary guidelines laid down to us by Shi Zilin, we have assigned all our assets over to the *Zhuan*. I do not even know where my capital has gone to."

"Overextension," Three Oaths said. "I dislike saying it but perhaps the Jian has erred." He turned to Jake. "I still do not understand why we needed to start up this new entity, InterAsia Trading. At a time when, as the Honorable Chung has pointed out, we are all expending our ready cash to keep Kam Sang on line, it seems to me a grave miscalculation to have generated an entire new corporation. Especially one in which all our accumulated wealth has been sunk. Gods, all our money is in InterAsia Trading. This can no longer be a secret from our enemies. You know that, *Zhuan*. I fear that InterAsia will become a lodestone, attracting the business sharks. What that dung-gatherer Bluestone wouldn't pay to take control of InterAsia Trading."

"There is the other side to consider," Jake said quietly. "Because of my father's maneuvering, we now have a new business entity without a history or a modus operandi. We can, in short, utilize InterAsia Trading for *any and all purposes* we desire, without causing even one eyebrow in the business or governmental sectors to be raised. Such freedom is impossible with our existing companies, including Southasia Bancorp, our banking subsidiary. It is impossible with any of our other sector companies engaged in shipping, warehousing, real eatate and so on. InterAsia Trading is an entity for the future; a company to mold as we see fit. Eventually, it will become an umbrella of new sector companies."

"But precisely what businesses will InterAsia be used for, *Zhuan*?" T. Y. Chung asked. "We are still in the dark as to why we have all put our entire financial empires on the line."

"InterAsia is not the subject of this session," Andrew Sawyer interjected. "Pardon me, *Zhuan*, but I have withheld this news too long as it is." Using a linen handkerchief to wipe his sweating pate, he continued. "It is my sad duty to inform you that as of midnight this morning our auditors have found that the comptroller of our Southasia Bancorp arm has systematically funneled over twenty-five million dollars into private holdings outside the Colony."

Jake sat very still and he thought, When this hits the press, we'll be ruined.

"All gods strike down worm-ridden bankers!" Three Oaths exploded. "Nothing good ever came of those institutions. I put my gold bars underneath my bed and don't have to worry about such defectors!"

Jake waited patiently until the tirade ended. Then he said, "You're certain it was Teck Yau."

"Absolutely," Sawyer said. "We've traced him to an Air India flight to New Delhi. He is no doubt already in Switzerland or Liechtenstein, laughing his head off about how much he stole from us."

"Leaving us to deal with the mess he made." Jake tapped his finger against the arm of the chair. "The first thing we must do is make sure there is no scandal. One whiff of this in the local press, and the Southasia Bancorp could suffer an irreversible loss of confidence among its depositors." He did not have to add that the majority of them were Chinese who, like Three Oaths, did not have much confidence in such Western concepts as banks to begin with. A scandal of this magnitude could cause a run that would shut down the Southasia Bancorp within a week. Since a majority of the *yuhn-hyun*'s free-market cash flowed through the institution, such an occurrence would be an utter financial disaster. One from which, Jake very much suspected, they could not recover.

Surely, he thought, my father could not have anticipated this. Perhaps my uncle is right. Perhaps I have overgambled our position. He thought again of Bluestone's weekend boat party; what did it portend?

It would be unthinkable for him to go to his father in this

situation. That would undermine his authority permanently. No. He was *Zhuan*. He must take control, and immediately.

"Andrew, I want everything you've gotten so far on the loss." Jake turned to Three Oaths. "Uncle, I want you to contact the Triad dragons who are part of the *yuhn-hyun*. All their power is to be exerted in clamping down on the incident. If it reaches the press, we're dead in the water."

"Even they won't be able to keep tongues from wagging forever, *Zhuan*," Three Oaths said. "You know how rumors spread in this city."

"True," Jake said, rising. "But all we need is a week or so. By that time, I'll have found a way to siphon money back into Southasia."

Three Oaths nodded. "I'll do what you ask. And so will they. I'll see to it personally."

"Good," Jake said. And he thought, We are already on the brink. One tiny gust of wind will send us tumbling over the edge.

He thought of what he had once learned many years ago. *One must seek to injure the corners when one comes up against a strong enemy*, Fo Saan, his teacher, his guide, the extraordinary man Zilin had sent to train him, had counseled Jake. *If you attack a foe who is obviously stronger than you in a direct fashion, his spirit will overcome you and he will smite you down. Seek then to strike swiftly at the corners of his force. In that way, the main body's spirit will be weakened and you may find a path to your enemy's heart.*

In a moment Jake had made his decision. It was obvious to him that the person who would benefit the most from the dissolution of Southasia was Bluestone—and Daniella Vorkuta. Could Bluestone have infiltrated the inner circle yet again? He had done it once, as Andrew had been quick to point out. Why not a second time?

Jake rose and looked at the other men. "I'll leave you to get down to work, then."

He hardly remembered going down in the elevator and getting into his car. The moment he left Sawyer's office, he had pushed the Southasia fiasco to the back of his mind. Nothing to be done about that until Sawyer delivered more detailed information.

Jake turned his mind to the news reports coming out of Tokyo and Osaka. Bliss had called him in from the shower and, dripping, he had watched the television cameras recording the shattering aftermath of what the announcer called

40

"the bloodiest clash yet in the recent territorial wars between the rival Yakuza clans, Kisan and Komoto." Jake's closest friend, Mikio Komoto, was *oyabun*, boss of the Komoto clan. Jake was most concerned about Mikio.

"These scenes of death and destruction"—three twisted bodies, headless and bloated; a burned-out building in Osaka; flames engulfing yet another structure in downtown Tokyo, following a thunderous detonation that many apparently took to be an earthquake—"follow hard on the heels of a tactical battle that until earlier this month had remained very much in the shadows as an ongoing series of skirmishes."

More shots, panning, terrified faces, more blood, black and smeared by the imperfections of the broadcast medium. "Now the wholesale slaughter that some officials of Tokyo's special anti-Yakuza task force had been predicting is here at last.

"The only question remaining is: where will it end?"

Jake had made a grab for the phone and called his friend. But Mikio Komoto was not at home, he was told. Yes, his message would be passed on. Any way Jake could be of help, he would.

This morning, after reading the newspaper dispatches, Jake tried to phone his friend. No answer. On his way into Sawyer's office, he had asked Sei An, Sawyer's secretary, to try Mikio Komoto's home number again with the same negative result.

Where is Mikio? Jake asked himself. What has happened to him?

When Tony Simbal arrived at Max Threnody's townhouse in Georgetown, the party was already in full swing. Threnody, a tall, slight Bostonian, had about him a rather donnish air, as if he had come straight across the quad at Oxford and was brushing the ivy leaves off his academic robes.

Because of this image, nobody in his right mind would believe that he was one of the ranking members of the Drug Enforcement Agency. He had also been Simbal's immediate superior in the DEA; it had been Threnody's devious mind that had put Simbal in the Shan States to begin with. The Shan States, in the middle of the Golden Triangle, was where the majority of the world's opium was harvested and refined into heroin. Of course it was a major DEA target.

The Shan States, a mountainous region of northern Burma, shoved up against the China border, were ruled by any number of tribal warlords whose armies were at constant war with

41

the Burmese and Chinese governments. Both governments wished to wipe out the opium trade.

Threnody's cream-colored townhouse was on R Street in the hinterlands of Georgetown. From his kitchen windows could be seen a generous corner of Dumbarton Oaks. From his upstairs bedroom, one could see patches of Lovers' Lane through the brushstrokes of the trees.

The party was mainly DEA, but as Simbal strolled through the downstairs he saw a sprinkling of representatives from State, Congress, even the CIA. There was nothing official about this party, so whoever was here was strictly on "amorous" status with DEA. In other words, it was a friendly affair.

The place was cozy, filled with French Provincial furniture more comfortable than might be expected. The color tones tended toward the earth range, built, it seemed, around the paintings displayed with such loving care. Whatever investments Threnody had made were in the form of art which, besides his work, was his lone passion. He loved the Impressionists such as Degas, Monet and Manet, and the related but less subtle Pissarro and Cezanne, whose almost hallucinatory work he could absorb for hours on end. Like them, he shared that tangential resonance with later luminaries, so that it was not surprising to find a small Picasso drawing here, a minor Braque there, among the work of their artistic forebears. The house had always had a calming effect on Simbal.

He picked up a beer and went to say hello to his host. Threnody was in the kitchen, his hands deep in some concoction he had just pulled from the Cuisinart.

Simbal had to squeeze out of the way as a couple of young, modish DEA types came laughing through, looking for the ice. Threnody directed them in good-natured fashion.

Simbal felt a pressure against his back and turned around, to find himself staring straight into those violet eyes. "Hello, Monica," he said.

He heard Threnody say from behind him, "See you later, Tony." Then with a little laugh, "Maybe."

"It's been a while." Monica Starr's voice was just this side of husky. Her midnight hair was long, cascading back from her face, down her shoulders. The effect was breathtaking. When Simbal had known her, she had had short hair and there had been a pixieish quality about her that was now gone. But she had been younger then, he told himself. The hunter-green sweater over the sienna-colored gored tweed skirt showed how she had filled out.

After a while, Simbal became aware that she had begun to lead him out of the jammed kitchen, weaving a path for them through the boisterous crowd.

The lights were off in one of the downstairs back rooms. The bed was piled high with coats, hats, scarves and handbags. A streetlight filtering in through the window provided ghostly illumination.

Monica was wreathed in shadows. She wore little makeup, diamond studs in her ears, like a prima ballerina, he thought, a small gold watch with a green lizard band on one wrist, no other jewelry.

"Monica," he said.

She smiled and slapped him hard across the face. "That's for walking out on me."

Simbal stood very still. "It was a mission, Monica. Jesus Christ. What did you expect?"

"To hear from you when you got back. I had to go to Max and ask him if you had gotten back at all." There was a quiver there, and a thickness to her voice as her emotions swelled, threatening to break through her iron resolve. "Do you have any conception of what that cost me? It is Max Threnody's considered opinion that running is too dangerous for women. We're too unpredictable—I think that was his word—for field work; too emotional.

"Up until the moment when I burst into his office in tears— *in tears over you, you sonofabitch*—I think I was doing okay with him; wearing him down to the point where he'd give me the go-ahead to do some running on my own.

"Then he saw what you'd done to me and that was the end for me. Do you understand what that means? I put my guts into this job; if I have anywhere else to go, I sure don't know about it."

Simbal thought he saw a glitter in her eyes, the cusp of tears she had, perhaps, promised herself he would never see.

"Even a dog gets treated better than you treated me."

"Monica, I'm sorry." He reached out but she shook him off.

"That won't make it right. You know it won't." He could sense how much it took for her to keep herself together. "Max told me I was mad to feel anything for you. He was right, wasn't he?"

The silence brought a bubble of laughter bursting in on

43

them, an ironic intruder. Someone came in—neither of them saw who—said, "Oops!" and hastily departed.

"Answer me." She had not raised her voice, only lowered the pitch. The result was akin to an animal's warning growl.

Simbal recalled his discussion with Rodger Donovan. How could he explain his feelings about civilization to this woman? She had been born in Philadelphia, had been educated in the best Eastern private schools before going to Smith. What kind of experience could she have had with the primitive side of life; how could she possibly understand the lure of the absolutes that civilization sought so hard to dissipate: life and death, love and hate. No trappings, no psychological baggage, no modern jargon. High up in the mountains of the Shan States if someone crossed you, you didn't say, "Fuck you!" you killed him. *Finis*. Because it was wild up there. The poppy fields brought danger, secrecy, double-crosses. In the Shan States, the strong survived, feeding off the weak.

He wanted very much to lie to her but just as he was about to do so he paused, biting his lip. Why should he lie? That was the civilized thing to do and he was tired of civilization.

"I saw something in you," he said, "that I thought I'd never see again."

"Why?" She tossed her head. "What do you mean?"

"The last time we made love, the night before I left. I had my eyes open. I saw the look on your face. I wanted it to last. But I knew that good Smith girl that you are, I'd most likely look for that emotion again and never find it."

Monica moved and the streetlight, oblique and opaque, struck her. She was shadow-striped and Simbal recalled another woman, striped in just the same way by the jungle foliage, high up on a mountainside. He could scent again her peculiar muskiness, the animal smell of the jungle itself and, behind them, in her father's house, the heady perfume of the crates of uncut gems.

"You're too civilized for me, Monica." It was out before he had a chance to bite his tongue. Oh shit, he thought, now I've gone and done it.

Monica threw her head back and laughed, a harsh, bitter sound. He watched her long neck, the argon streetlight turning her dusky flesh pale. The arch of her throat made him feel heavy in his chest.

"Is that it?" She was virtually weeping with brittle laughter. "What a schmuck you are, Tony. Really. I went to Smith, sure. For two-and-a-half years. Then I dropped out. It wasn't

44

the pressure that got to me. I never felt any. It was something else entirely. Something I couldn't define for a long time, not to my college adviser, not to my parents, not even to myself.

"I worked for a year at a Baskin-Robbins on the Upper West Side of Manhattan. While I was there, we were held up maybe a dozen times, a girl standing right beside me got shot to death. We had bums coming in and throwing up all over the shiny counter; we had guys come in and make a grab for us—serious grabs. They were interested in doing a lot more to our asses than pinching them.

"But don't feel sorry for me. I put in my time. I made my own money because I didn't want to touch my old man's, I was fed up with that, as well. That was part of it, the feeling I couldn't quite define.

"So after my year in hell, I got out. Of New York, of the U.S. of A., of the world as I knew it. I went to Tahiti and saw a McDonald's sign. I nearly vomited on the spot. I went further, past Bora Bora, until I got to a beach that had no one on it, where the nearest town was made of bamboo and dried plantain leaves, where nobody would bother me.

"For eighteen months I was alone with the blue-green sea and the golden sky. I watched the birds and they, I suppose, watched me. They didn't care what I looked like or how I felt, which was just fine with me."

"Why did you come back?" Simbal said softly. He could see just a hint of the amethyst in her eyes. He thought her face had never looked more feline or full of energy. "Because I found that you can't—or *I* can't, at any rate—live my life without human contact—intelligent human contact. Learned people."

"But being away from it all," Simbal began.

"Is what makes coming back all the more fascinating."

"I'm sorry," he said again.

Monica's eyes went opaque the way they did when she was confused. "Now I think you mean it."

"I suppose I didn't before," he conceded. "Not really."

"You're arrogant, Tony." Her soft tone went right through him. "You were so sure you knew me through and through."

"The perfect rich girl. Breeding and schooling, what more could a family ask of its child. You must have broken your mother's heart."

"My father's, too." Her full lips were back. The tight compression, another outward sign of her rage, was gone. "I never came out, I never finished college, they don't even know what I really do. 'Government work,' my father tells his colleagues, as if he's describing rat poison. To him, I am something incomprehensible: a bureaucrat."

Tony laughed. "Maybe you should take Max home one day. That would seal your fate."

"On the contrary," she said, "I should really take *you* home to meet my parents."

He thought she was joking until he saw in her eyes that she was quite serious.

"You would shake daddy's tree something fierce," she said.

Simbal was abruptly aware of how close Monica was to him. Her perfume hinted of jonquils and jasmine. He reached out and this time she did not brush him away. She made no move at all. Simbal felt his heart beating heavily. This was not why he had come to the party. There were some things he needed to find out and this was the place to begin; the only place.

He had ferreted around for several days, casually dropping in on known DEA hangouts in Georgetown and Washington's Northwest sector at lunchtime. Nothing heavy, just a casual beer and a subtle bump, "Oh, hi, long time no see," that sort of thing.

That's how he had found out about the party. He knew that Peter Curran would be there if he was in town. If not, someone there would certainly have a line on Curran's whereabouts. Curran was the man Simbal knew he had to see; Curran had taken over Simbal's role as chief *diqui* hunter at the DEA. That meant he had been in Southeast Asia or at least running—DEA-speak for field work—while Simbal had been in the necessary but frustrating transition period in Washington learning the Quarry system and training at the Movie House, the sprawling farm the Quarry maintained in rural Virginia.

For this reason alone, he had told himself, he had come to the party. Now he knew that he had been at least partially fooling himself. He did not understand how badly until this electric moment.

"Smith wasn't a complete waste," she was saying now. Her eyes were half mocking. "Here's something interesting I learned there."

Simbal felt his belt loosening, then his trousers. In an instant her hand had encompassed him.

Monica made a husky sound. "You never wore these tiny

46

briefs when I knew you. Who's been buying your underpants lately?"

"Are you crazy?" Simbal was regaining his equilibrium. "What if someone comes in?" But he was already hard and Monica had peeled down his briefs. Now she moved so that she had her back to the doorway. Shadows danced in the room like ghosts spilled over from the party. It could have been in another universe for all the meaning it had for the two of them.

"If someone comes in," Monica said softly, "I'll give her a reason to leave."

She put one foot on the low window sill and, with her free hand, lifted up her skirt. Drew Simbal against her. He gasped and she smiled. She wore only a garter belt beneath her skirt and he felt the tangle of jungly hair caressing the end of him.

"Let's get you wet," she said, moving him against her lips. "Monica . . ."

"What? Tell me what?" But his eyes were already closed. She took a fierce, greedy delight in watching the emotions play across his face. His desire had made him a tabula rasa. She no longer recognized him; it was as if the burden of civilization had already been dispelled from him.

The hard streetlight fell across her breasts, rising and falling now with greater energy. The area of her flat stomach was shadowed. And, below, the bunched tweed hid their hot liquid connection from sight.

Just the head of him was inside her. Monica circled her hips, swaying. Her full lips were half-parted and her breath was getting away from her.

Simbal felt intoxicated. He felt the exquisite sensations of her on him, just a brief silken swirl across the most sensitive part of him. He had hold of her shoulders, was urging her on. Max's house was overheated and the window was open from the bottom. A couple of guests were apparently outside in Max's garden. They were speaking in soft, whispery tones, the sounds floaty, rising like steam in the night.

In Simbal's mind these half-heard words mingled with Monica's caresses to create a kind of erotic intoxication, a web of sound and feeling. He shuddered heavily. He wanted to penetrate her more fully but when he thrust he felt her fist encircling him, preventing any forward movement.

"Monica," he whispered.

"Kiss me," she breathed.

His lips came down over hers and as their tongues touched

47

she let go of her grip and he slipped all the way in. A great groan escaped him, filling her mouth with vibration. Monica's hips began to move, then buck against him as he moved out, then all the way in.

His hands slid over the soft wool of her sweater, lifted it, then felt her bare breasts. They were warm, the nipples hard and so sensitive that she gave a little cry, ground her hips in a circle hard against him when his thumbs touched them.

"Make me come, Tony," she panted in his ear. "I'm dying for you."

I'm dying for you. The words reverberated in his head. Is that what he heard wafting in through the window from the sere garden downstairs? *I'm dying for you.*

He felt her heat suffusing him. There was a great weight in his loins so that he remained on his feet with the greatest difficulty. He felt the muscles in his calves, behind his knees, begin to tremble. He felt as if her weight was on him. He felt, he felt, he felt . . .

In a moment he was aware of her fingertips sliding between his thighs, lifting his testicles, squeezing in gentle rhythm.

I'm dying for you.

"Oh," he groaned. "Oh, Monica!"

"Yes!" Her whisper? The whisper of the couple in the garden?

Simbal raced upward into her as far as he could go. His heartbeat was in his throat and he lost all ability to breathe. He gasped and began to shoot heavily into her.

"Ohh!" Monica's eyes flew open and she groaned into the side of his neck. The liquid heat at her core began her own spasming. Her face flushed and she felt the ripples spreading outward from the juncture of her thighs. She ground herself into him, feeling the harsh scrape of his pubic hair against her intimate flesh. Strangely, this made her orgasm blossom to such a point that she lost all control.

Climbing atop him she tumbled them from their precarious stance and they fell backward onto the pile of coats on the bed. One of them began to laugh.

Simbal, covered by the folds of her skirt, looked up into her amethyst eyes. "How could I have been so wrong about you?"

"Like I said, you're a schmuck." She explored beneath her pooled skirt, found him, wet and still hard. "And what a schmuck."

In the garden below them, the couple had ceased their whispering.

The gleaming black Chaika stood waiting at the side of the runway at Domodedovo Airport. The snow lay pale and gleaming in the moonlight, piled in the aisles between the runways. The winter chill, still deep at this time of the year, turned the exhaust as thick and white as clouds.

Fifteen kilometers to the northwest, the lights of Moscow put the moon to shame, reaching up into the night, banishing the darkness.

Inside the limousine, General Daniella Vorkuta lay back against the leather seat. Her thick sable coat was opened around her like a bedspread. Its opulence contrasted with the severe line and color of her army uniform. It was the dress uniform she had worn to Yuri Lantin's funeral, the creases pressed to an almost knife-sharp edge. The triple line of medals above her left breast shone dully in the cold blue airport lights.

For the moment her thoughts were far away from Moscow and the man she was here to meet. As usual her brilliant mind was reviewing the latest intelligence Mitre, her main asset in Hong Kong, had transmitted to her. Hong Kong! That great teeming port was all Daniella thought about lately. The money that flowed through the Crown Colony drew her as unerringly as a magnet to true north.

It was not that Daniella Vorkuta was venal. Far from it. She was one of a select few who could see beyond capital's gleaming immediate value. To her, money was power. Especially in Hong Kong. And she knew that Hong Kong was the key to China, possibly even to all of Asia.

She knew that this was also Shi Zilin's belief. Shi Zilin! The master strategist whose plan for China she had been attempting to infiltrate for three years now. Even though her best source to Shi Zilin, his assistant, Zhang Hua, was dead of a heart attack, she had something better: lines of intelligence gathering into his most secret organization, the *yuhn-hyun*.

And, Daniella thought now, even though she had been thwarted in every effort to infiltrate Shi Zilin's other secret, the Kam Sang project, she now suspected that Mitre had provided her with another mode of access.

To control Hong Kong, that was Daniella Vorkuta's most devout wish. For she knew that if she controlled Hong Kong, she would control all of China. Hong Kong was, and always would be, China's gateway to the West. Without Hong Kong as a middle ground with which to deal with the West, she knew that China would be doomed to return to its backward past. Without Hong Kong, China had no future at all; it could never begin to compete in the modern world. Therefore, Hong Kong was a priceless—and irreplaceable—commodity to China.

And now she knew the best way of gaining control of Hong Kong: wresting the power that now resided in the *yuhn-hyun*, and making it her own.

This was essentially why she had had to destroy Anatoly Karpov, her predecessor as head of the First Chief Directorate, and his even more powerful ally, Yuri Lantin. The two had concocted a scheme, code-named Moonstone, that involved the military encirclement of China and a puppet war against it using North Vietnamese regiments in Malipo County in Yunnan province.

Her predecessors had wanted the destruction of China. Stupid men! Their scheming had brought Russia dangerously close to a world war that could have devastated the entire planet.

Daniella had a better fate in store for China: subjugation, with its profits funneled into Soviet coffers. That was Hong Kong's role in her strategy. Hong Kong would bring her enormous wealth—and with that wealth, great power, an awesome victory. Only she, a master player of *wei qi*, was an equal match for Shi Zilin. He was the Jian, the supreme champion of the ancient board game. If one was not weaned on *wei qi* strategy, one had no chance at all of finding Shi Zilin's weak spot and exploiting it. She understood the strategy of *wei qi*.

At last she felt herself in position for taking the breath from Shi Zilin's *wei qi* pieces. She would have total victory. Millions of rubles would flow into the Kremlin. And into her pockets. Power undreamed of in Asia would be hers. Soviet supremacy, a dream Russian patriots had nurtured since the emergence of that false Communist, Mao Zedong. And when that was accomplished, what further elevations in rank lay in store for her?

With an effort, she pulled herself away from the seductive multifaceted jewel of her vision. "He's late," she said.

The driver, a KGB officer permanently assigned to her staff, said, "The storm. They would have hit it on their way over.

In any case, the delay can't be major or I would have been informed."

Daniella turned her beautiful head in his direction. Her thick blond hair fell across her throat and she pushed it back with curled fingers. She disliked his tone, the use of the "I" in his statement. Alexei was not as selfless as she would perhaps like him to be.

"Lyosha," she said now, using the diminutive, "please be smart enough to keep your mouth shut when he gets here."

"Don't worry," he said, his dark eyes on her in the rearview mirror.

Daniella leaned forward, breathing in his ear, "Don't give me cause to worry." Her tone was as hard as flint. He merely nodded, his gaze now straight ahead.

"*Jahwohl*, *Herr* Comrade General," he said in his best clipped German.

Daniella laughed, ruffled his thick black hair. From her position she could not see his sharply delineated widow's peak or the precise Serbian features of his face. But she could easily bring to mind his lean, sinewy athlete's body, the long flat planes of his abdomen and belly that she often painted with sweat.

She looked out the Chaika's smoked-glass window. There were more than a dozen men in coarse blue overcoats and fur hats. Police, she thought. Not *sluzhba*. The colloquial term for the *Komitet Gosudarstvennoi Bezopasnosti*, the KGB. Daniella was the head of its First Chief Directorate, the largest and most powerful subdivision of Russia's most feared *apparat*.

"The plane is down, Comrade General," Alexei said.

Daniella steeled herself. There was already movement among the policemen. She could see more of them now, the blue flashing lights, the glint off the Kulspruta machine pistols, and she thought, Who is the maniac who ordered drawn weapons?

He appeared out of the darkness, his visage made indistinct by runway and airplane lights. Daniella could not as yet see his face but she recognized that walk. It was the walk of a dangerous man, quick and lithe, full of power and hinting at lightning speed. There was nothing of the hulking deliberation one associated with most of the high-echelon Kremlin officials.

He was surrounded by six plainclothes KGB operatives. Daniella's men. Despite the cold she had insisted they not wear their greatcoats. "Your concealed armament will be no good to you beneath all that padding, if an emergency should arise," she had told them at the briefing this afternoon.

The blue-coated policemen parted like the Red Sea as he approached. "You have the route down," Daniella said, and Alexei, hands on the steering wheel, noted the tension in her voice.

"Yes, Comrade General," he said formally.

The group had stopped. One of Daniella's men reached forward to pull open the door beside her. Then Oleg Maluta was climbing into the warmth of the limousine's interior.

"Greetings, Comrade General." His voice was like sandpaper over cement.

"Comrade." Daniella was aware of the heavy smells of tobacco and sweat. It was work sweat, the smell of a mover and shaker after a long day of complex negotiations.

Alexei put the Chaika into gear.

"A drink," Maluta said.

He is not even civil, Daniella thought as she reached out a bottle of Azerbaijani brandy. As she poured, she remembered that Yuri Lantin's favorite liquor had been Starka, aged vodka. That was how she had killed him: overdosed his nightcap with his own sleeping pills, then put his head in the oven to make it look like suicide. In so doing, she had taken the late unlamented Anatoly Karpov's place as head of the First Chief Directorate and, consolidating her power, had taken Yuri Lantin's spot in the Politburo. She was the first woman to rise so high in the Soviet hierarchy.

Oleg Maluta could destroy all that with one wave of his hand.

He had an oval face. It was not the visage of a Muskovite. Rather he had the odd, almost almond eyes, the flat planular cheeks of a Mongol. His salt-and-pepper hair was shaved close to his scalp on the sides. The bald patch on the back of his head gave him a benign aspect, to those who had had no real contact with him. To such an ignorant eye he might be an honored chess master, his scheming mind turned to essentially harmless pursuits.

Nothing could be further from the truth.

Maluta accepted the glass from Daniella, downed three fingers of the fiery stuff at once. His uptilted head revealed his prominent adam's apple, bobbing as he swallowed. He handed her the empty glass, wiped his lips with the edge of a yellowed forefinger. He turned his head to watch the nighttime parade by him, as if it were there for his benefit alone.

Following Daniella's instructions, Alexei veered off the Kashira Highway in order to take the streets that banded the Moskva River. Maluta loved the river almost as much, Daniella suspected, as he loved the ballet. His apartment overlooked the river; his offices were within one of the stuffy encrusted Kremlin towers from whose windows he could keep the Moskva in sight.

"The moonlight looks fine on the water," he said now as he shook out an unfiltered Camel. He did not offer her one, which was just as well. Lantin had made her smoke and she had detested it. Now the stench nauseated her, associated in her mind with the cloying odor of cooking gas.

"It is because of the ice," she said.

They were running along the embankment. The gnarled and twisted shadows of the bare tree branches were like an old man's fingers stretched across the Moskva's silver expanse.

The Chaika's interior was filled with smoke. Daniella opened the window on her side a sliver.

"How was Leningrad?" she said now, swallowing hard to rid her throat of the acrid smoke.

"Stultifying," Maluta said. He continued to stare at his beloved Moskva. As they streaked toward the city he sat turned partially away from her, staring intently out the tinted window.

"Comrade, may I ask—"

But his nicotine-stained hand was waving her words aside. "I am hungry." It was a rebuff, pure and simple. Because I am a woman, Daniella wondered, or is it something else, something I'm unaware of? "As I digest my supper," he continued, "you will digest my words."

Sitting next to Oleg Maluta, Daniella decided, was akin to coming into contact with a dark star. The sensation of negative energy was enormous. After ten minutes in his presence she felt chilled and drained. She began to fight that feeling, knowing that she would need all her mental acuity this night.

Daniella had instructed Alexei to make reservations at Rossia on the Moskvoretskaya Embankment. The hotel had nine restaurants. Daniella often went to the one in the basement because it boasted the best dance orchestra. The restaurant they went to now was on the twenty-first floor. It had a most spectacular view of the Kremlin and the green, terra-cotta and yellow onion domes of St. Basil's. She thought this sight would please Maluta, and she was not disappointed.

53

"How splendid Moscow looks," he said as they were seated at the best window table. "Clean and sparkling." He ordered vodka and *zakuski*: two kinds of Caspian caviar, cold sturgeon in aspic, pâté. He did not bother to ask what she would like.

Daniella closed her eyes; she thought of her *wei qi* board. Whenever she could, she played the ancient Chinese board game that the Japanese knew as *go*. It was said that a player's strategy in *wei qi* was a mirror of his or her personal philosophy.

She wondered why Maluta bothered to play these games with her. Plainly, he detested her, as he seemed to hate all women. Certainly, he resented her promotion into the sanctum sanctorum of male power: the Politburo.

The liquor came almost immediately, yet another demonstration of Oleg Maluta's power. He had chosen a *pertsovka*, one of Daniella's winter favorites. The hot peppers gave the vodka a delicious, soul-warming kick.

Maluta waited until the appetizer tray had been set before them. He made no move to eat though he had told her he was hungry.

"We must know what Kam Sang is all about."

Said without preamble, what he said was a shock. Kam Sang was the project in China's Guangdong province that she had been trying to penetrate for almost a year without success. Two men knew its secret: Shi Zilin and his son, Jake Maroc. Why was Oleg Maluta suddenly interested in Kam Sang? Daniella did not trust him. If he needed Kam Sang's secret, that meant that he would make certain that she was out of it when it came time to hand out the medals. Kam Sang's secret could provide undreamed of power to Daniella or Maluta. But not to both.

"That will be most difficult to do," Daniella said carefully.

"It must be done, Comrade General." Maluta's eyes were blazing. "I mean to become the successor to Fyodor Leninin." He was referring to Fyodor Leninin Genachev, Soviet leader, head of the Communist Party. "Without the power Kam Sang's secret will bring me, it will be next to impossible. With friends like Reztsov and Carelin inside the Politburo one cannot fart in bed without Genachev knowing."

Carelin. Had Maluta another reason from bringing up that name?

She tried slow breathing. She had been right. What mad scheme was he hatching? Whatever it was, he meant to enmesh her in it. Her mind was reeling. She fought to remain calm.

"You should have been there, Comrade General. In Leningrad. You should have seen Genachev. He walked through the crowds, smiling and calling out to them. 'I am close to you now,' he said. 'I am here to aid you, to listen to your problems, and to solve them. I am here to begin a new Russia!' " Maluta took a deep breath. His face was that of one who had just smelled rotting flesh.

"When I was a young man, I saw Nikita Khrushchev. He appeared in public all over Russia. He lapped up the adulation of the crowds, visibility affected him like a drug. He even went to America, to Disneyland. I thought of him as a kind of hero. Do you understand? A man of vision, who had set his sights on affairs outside the Soviet Union.

"Until one day I heard my father speaking. He was vilifying Khrushchev. 'This personality cult that Khrushchev spends so much time building is a clear and present danger,' he said. 'Khrushchev spends too much time on Khrushchev. He apes the power and prestige of the American President, Kennedy. Theirs is a war not of ideology, not of nations. But of egos.' "

Maluta began to put food into his mouth, because in Russia one did not drink vodka without eating; it was taken as a sign of drunkenness. "For two days after that I locked myself in my room. I did not eat, I did not see anyone. All I thought about was Khrushchev and what my father said about him. In time, I came to understand that he was right. Khrushchev was driven by his ego—a dangerous attitude for the leader of all the Russias."

She took a deep breath. "Do you really think that this talk is wise, Comrade?"

Maluta's head snapped around. He was like a falcon who had found its prey flying calmly a half mile below. Daniella felt transfixed by his terrible Medusa's gaze. A thin line of sweat trickled down the indentation of her spine, and she thought, I am terrified of this man. She fought it, knowing with an absolute certainty that that very fear could kill her.

"Are you questioning my judgment, *Comrade General*?" His heavy emphasis on her title made it clear that he had no respect for it. And again she thought, Is it because I am a woman?

"No, Comrade." It was a trial to keep her voice firm and sure. "I am merely questioning the circumstances. Out here—"

"Here there is noise, so much of it that no microphone could possibly pick up our conversation." He continued to stare her down. "Are you certain that this is the reason you are uneasy?"

She kept her head still. "What do you mean?"

Maluta popped another appetizer into his mouth, and shrugged. "The people love him. Genachev is fifty-five, young by the standards of the Kremlin. He shows them energy and they respond. He announces that he will institute sweeping changes in the agricultural system. The economy—the economy. It is all he speechifies about. A four percent growth rate, without any military cutbacks, is what he promises the people. The people, Comrade General. Then he brings his wife and daughter to parades, to official functions. At the Moscow Art Theater, the three of them arrive and are seated in the stalls along with everybody else, instead of the balcony, the traditional spot."

He reached inside his suit and pulled out several glossy pages. "Have you seen this?"

Daniella took the cover and article from the current edition of *Time*. She saw the Genachevs on the cover, a rich color photo of the three of them smiling happily at some official function, ecstatic crowds in the background. "First Family, Soviet Style," the caption read. She handed it back to Maluta without opening it.

"There's very little space in which to maneuver," he said, putting the magazine away. He handled it as if he suspected it of being contaminated. "Each day this new-style leader of ours usurps more and more power. Each day his personality cult grows in stature. Genachev turns to the internal side of Soviet politics without an understanding of what it will take to get this country moving again. Words to the people will not make a four percent net increase in the economy.

"But it has taken him away from the international arena. Genachev ignores the China threat, the Afghan war. We have suffered severe and I am afraid almost irreparable loss of prestige in Africa after a decade of solid and consistent gains. We have lost control of South America and all efforts to bring Southeast Asia into line have failed.

"Yet what is Genachev spending his time on? Getting close to the people, talking to the farmers, reassuring them that their time of trial is at an end." He snorted. "Soon we will have farm subsidies, just like in America."

Maluta's hand curled into a fist, white with tension. "It is enough! When you deliver to me Kam Sang's secrets, I will prove to the entire Politburo the truth of what I have been saying. It is time to regain control over Africa, over South and Central America. It is time for the Soviet Union to push forward across the globe. It is time for us to be more aggressive abroad, rather than attempting to get our out-of-date farm collectives to deliver more produce.

"But as long as Genachev holds sway, no other voice in the Politburo amounts to anything."

Wanting to defuse him, at least temporarily, she gestured. "Shall we eat, Comrade? I'm starving."

They ate in silence for a time but she could see that Maluta's attention was not on his food.

"Of course," she said, after the remains of the *zakuski* had been cleared away, "you always have another option. You could strike an alliance with Genachev, use a little give and take. Even perhaps persuade him to use you as his adviser on international affairs."

Maluta said nothing but she could tell by his expression that his mind was turning over what she had said. He spread his hands, shrugged. "I cannot see how Comrade Genachev could afford to take any kind of advice from me. Mikhail Carelin is his guru. Carelin: the man with no face. Isn't that how he's known?"

"In some circles," she said. Thinking about *wei qi*, strategy. Trapping Oleg Maluta. She thought about being able to implicate him in a plot to assassinate Genachev, amassing evidence; irrefutable evidence that would sentence him to immediate execution.

"Carelin. He's egoless, they say. Content to remain in the background, whispering in Genachev's ear. Perhaps Genachev's idiocies are in reality Carelin's. You see? It's hard to determine what's what between them."

Slowly, slowly, she thought, her heart hammering. "Suppose Carelin himself recommended that Genachev elevate you to adviser status."

Maluta tapped the center of his liver-colored lips with a forefinger. He took out a Camel and lit it. Daniella concealed her disgust.

"Now this is interesting, Comrade General." There was a certain expression on his face, and with dawning understanding she felt appalled. It was a smile but the kind of smile that was more a rictus, as if he did not have full control over his facial muscles. "But of course you are joking. Why should Carelin cede any of his power to me?"

"Because I'll ask him to."

"Oho, and I suppose just like that he will comply."

Daniella put down her teacup. "Perhaps six weeks ago Mikhail Carelin phoned me. He invited me to dinner. I assumed it had to do with some Politburo lobbying. As the most recent member, I am perhaps perceived to be more vulnerable to persuasion on certain issues.

"He took me to Russkaya Izba, a surprise since it is somewhat out of the way—forty minutes from the center of town. Very romantic. Also to my surprise there was no talk of business. Instead, we spoke of small things: our backgrounds, childhood memories and the like. We were getting to know one another."

"Carelin asked you out on a date?"

"A date," Daniella confirmed. "That was it exactly. He wants to see me again."

Maluta thought of Carelin's wife, squat and dumpy, their two daughters, built in their mother's image. He grunted. "What is the American phrase? 'Quiet waters run deep'?"

"Close enough."

"And what did you answer our *gospadin* Carelin?"

"I gave him neither a yes nor a no."

"Women," Maluta said, as if that one word explained everything. He was silent while they served. He did not look at his plate or at his still-lighted cigarette. When the waiter left, he said, "Well, perhaps in this case your female, er, indecisiveness, has served us in good stead."

He did not immediately elucidate but, rather, lit into his *pelmeni* with gusto. Somewhere during the recent conversation he had regained his appetite. It was not until he finished, pushing up the last of the meat dumplings onto a thick slab of black bread, that he spoke again.

"I want you to be my sparrow with Carelin," he said, around a mouthful of food.

"And get him to use his influence with Genachev." Thinking, I have him now.

Maluta nodded, rinsed his mouth with a large gulp of the spiced vodka before swallowing. "That would do me very well." He smiled his odd, bone-chilling smile; she suppressed a shudder.

Daniella felt the triumph like a dove fluttering against her heart. She did not downplay the danger of such a double

58

game, but the risk was acceptable considering the circumstances. She had also found out something quite vital about Maluta: he did not have surveillance on her. Otherwise, he would have known that she had already been to bed with Mikhail Carelin.

Feeling more relaxed than she had all evening, she said, "All right. I think I can manage it."

"A direct line into Genachev's mind." He was deep in thought.

She nodded. "It is possible, yes."

"Good. Initiate it."

As they retrieved their coats, Daniella thought, I will be his sparrow; I will spy for him, yes. If it means that I can bring him down, it is worth doing this. Even for such a monster.

In the aftermath of the party Simbal and Monica ate overstuffed sandwiches he had slapped together from odds and ends lying around Max Threnody's refrigerator. Shoulder to shoulder, they tore into them voraciously, like little animals, bent over the outsized double sink in the kitchen. From the living room emanated the sounds of Max seeing off the last of his guests. DEA types were tightly wound. They tended to blow off a lot of steam in relaxed circumstances. That was only to be expected; it was in fact the major reason for Max's infamous parties. Steam was far better blown off in a private place than in public.

In the heat of all the emotion being thrown around, Simbal hadn't forgotten why he had come here. Around a swig of Dos Equis Amber he said, "I didn't notice Peter Curran around tonight. Did I miss him?" And suddenly the blood drained from Monica's face.

She put down her half-eaten sandwich. In a small voice she said, "What made you say that?"

"Say what?"

"Mention Peter."

He shrugged, on his guard now. He watched her carefully. He wanted very much for her to face him so that he could see the full run of emotion in her. "Peter and I knew each other fairly well when I was here, that's all." He waited a second. "Monica, what is it?" A worried friend, nothing more. Above all, he must convince her that he had no special interest in Peter Curran.

"I didn't know that you and Peter were friends," she said, still not looking at him.

"We weren't really. It wasn't easy to get close to Peter as I remember. But we were in Burma together for about six weeks before he was pulled out." Watch it!

"Yeah. I remember that." She picked up her sandwich again, licked Russian dressing off her fingers. She seemed abruptly tired, as if even this much talk about him exhausted her. "I didn't know you were there at the time."

"I don't think we'd met yet," he said easily. "It seems to me I ran into you after I got back that first time. It was here, I think."

She gave him a wan smile. "You remember, then." Her mind was clearly on something else. Peter Curran.

"He wasn't here, I take it."

Monica jerked as if he had pricked her with the tip of a knife, and he thought, What the hell is going on?

"No," she said, so quietly he had to bend closer to hear her, "he wasn't."

Simbal looked down, saw her thumbs had gone all the way through the thick sandwich, from the pressure she had been exerting. Best to ignore that, he decided.

"So he's on assignment then."

"Can we talk about something else?" Her head swung toward him; he was surprised at how pale she had become.

"Sure. I'm sorry." He touched her. "Monica, I wish you'd tell me—"

"Take me home, Tony." There was no expression on her face. She wiped her hands on a paper towel. "Just take me home. And don't say another word, okay? *Okay?*"

It wasn't okay but he was determined that she should not know that.

The Chaika still stank of smoke even though Alexei, at Daniella's unspoken command, had done his best to air out the interior while she and Maluta had been at dinner.

"It's cold in here," Maluta said. "Get some heat up."

They pulled away from the curb and he sat back in the seat. His old-fashioned suit smelled of ashes.

"I have regards for you from Uncle Vadim." He was referring to Vadim Dubas, the current head of the Communist Party in Leningrad and her late father's brother.

"How is he?"

"Old and stubborn—as always," Maluta said shortly. "He

60

seems never to change." He shook out another Camel. Abruptly, Maluta leaned forward. He tapped Alexei on the shoulder. "I want to go to the monument. Do you know the one, Lieutenant?"

"Yes, Comrade Minister."

It was in the outskirts of Moscow, the angular steel crisscrossed almost like a modern sculpture atop its cut-stone plinth. Except that the steel was real, a portion of the four hundred miles of antitank traps and trenches erected by the remaining citizens of what Stalin dubbed "the Hero City," in the flush of their victory over the seventy-five Nazi divisions that had been massed over the hills leading to Moscow.

Alexei slowed the Chaika, pulling to the side of the highway. It was late, past eleven, and the roads were deserted. There was little or no nightlife here, or anywhere in Russia.

Maluta made no move until Alexei opened the back door. Alexei handed him a flashlight but Maluta made no comment, merely flicked it on. His shoes cracked the icy snow as he went across the verge to stand beside the monument.

Daniella, right beside him, was astonished to see tears sparkling in his eyes.

"So much blood spilled here," Maluta said, his voice thick with emotion. "So much heroism. The revolutionary spirit shone like a beacon in those dark days."

He was silent for a time. The beam of light sparked like fireworks against the precise edges of the steel bars.

"The snow," Maluta said into the dark. "I love the snow, Comrade General. The snow is pure and white like the spirit of Lenin, which guides us always." He put his foot out, the toe of his shoe scraping away at the snow until the black earth was eventually revealed. "But the snow also covers a multitude of sins." The beam of light stayed steady on the war monument but Maluta's gaze was fixed on Daniella, making her skin crawl. "These are still dark days, Comrade General, no less dire than they were forty-odd years ago. We are still fighting for our very existence. This is war, plain and simple."

Daniella stood very still. A pulse throbbed in the side of her head. She knew she was in the presence of a very dangerous man indeed—dangerous not only for herself but for the country as a whole.

"Let me tell you something, Comrade General," he said. His voice was like acid. "In this war, you are either with me or against me. Do you understand?"

Daniella nodded, not trusting herself to speak.

"Words," Maluta said. "I deal with words twenty hours a day. The more I deal with words the more I am convinced that lies are commonplace and the truth is lost to sight." He lit up a Camel, took his gaze from her. He stared meditatively at the memorial. The steel bars seemed to waver in the hand-held beam of light.

The moon had gone and it had grown more chill. The air was heavy, incipient with snow. The storm that had delayed Maluta's flight was catching up with them. Daniella pulled her sable coat closer around her. A sudden gust of wind caught her thick hair, whipping it across her face. She made no move to pull it back.

"The trouble with you, Comrade General," Maluta said after a long silence, "is that you are beautiful." He exhaled, took a bit of tobacco off his lower lip. "Because of this, you believe that you can extract anything from the men around you. You open your thighs for Anatoly Karpov and you become head of the KVR." Maluta was referring to the clandestine section of the First Chief Directorate, more commonly known as Department K, when it was referred to at all. The KVR was responsible for extraterritorial assassination and wet—field—counterintelligence. "You did the same for my late lamented colleague, Yuri Lantin. And, following his untimely death, you succeeded him."

Still he would not look at her. He smoked at leisure, as if they were two close friends discussing nothing more momentous than vacation plans. "On the one hand, I admire your guile. I believe you to be an ingenious woman."

He threw away the butt. It sparked in the night, the only brief flash of color in the landscape before it died in the snow. "On the other hand, I am aware of your ambition. Acutely aware. I want you to understand that you cannot do with me what you have done with Karpov and Lantin and, I am sure, several others before them. I am immune to your beauty. I do not dream at night of your cunt."

His use of the derogatory term was deliberate. It shocked her, as it was meant to.

"Now," Maluta continued, "I want you to make your choice. Either you are with me or you are against me. You have no other options, I will tell you that much. Do you think for a moment I believed your little fantasy scenario back there? Mikhail Carelin whispering in Genachev's ear that he should elevate me to adviser status alongside Reztsov and Carelin himself?" There it was, that unsettling rictus of a smile was back. "Oh, no, no, no, Comrade General. Even if your lovely cunt would have persuaded me to believe such nonsense, I know that you would never propose such a thing to Carelin. He would laugh in your face, Comrade General—and your file reports that you do not care for such treatment."

Daniella was shaking. She suspected that she had seriously underestimated Maluta, and that, in fact, in taking Yuri Lantin's place so quickly she had undone herself. She wondered whether she was prepared for the rarefied atmosphere of the Kremlin upper echelon or whether she was now truly in too deep.

She knew that she had to answer now, suspected that he would only allow her one option. "I am with you." She had had to open her mouth twice; the first time, her throat was so dry she knew only a croak would come out.

Maluta nodded. *"Horosho."* Good. "Now Alexei will not have to shoot you in the back of the head."

"What?" Again, he had meant to disconcert her, and he had.

His malevolent head turned toward her and she saw that awful rictus that passed for a smile. "Yes, didn't you know that your Alexei reports to me? All your movements, Comrade General. *All* of them are known to me."

Now Daniella knew that he was lying. If this was so Maluta would know that she had already begun her affair with Mikhail Carelin. She steeled herself to play his game at his own level.

Maluta was watching her face carefully. His black almond eyes glittered fiercely. "I see that you doubt my word. That is understandable." He reached inside his greatcoat, producing a small wrapped packet. He handed it over with yellowed fingers.

Daniella stared down at the packet as if it were a poisonous thing. Her pulse rate rose and she felt the tremor again in the side of her face.

Slowly, she unwrapped the thing. Holy Mother of God, she thought, staring down at the contents.

It was odd, Daniella thought, with a kind of hysterical calmness, how ungainly and almost comical two people looked when they were making love; especially when one of those people was oneself.

Shot after grainy shot of Daniella and Carelin in naked embrace, writhing, in obvious ecstasy, flushed in orgasm.

Maluta took the photos from her nerveless fingers. He shuffled them like a deck of playing cards before extracting one. "This one, I think, is the best." He went through the pile. "Or perhaps this one."

"Stop it!"

He wanted that reaction and, having gotten it, obediently put the damning photos away. "Now," he said, "I want you to do something for me. It is a symbol that will bind us together much more securely than you and Comrade Carelin are bound in that little tête-à-tête." His voice was soft now, almost tender. "I ask this of you, Comrade General, because you have lied to me. I assume that you have done so only once, in the instance of Mikhail Carelin, but"—he shrugged—"who knows, there may have been other instances in the past.

"But you see I do not care about the past. Only the future." He had produced it from somewhere beyond the limits of her sight. "I want this to be an object lesson for you, Comrade General. Take off your gloves, please."

Daniella did as he bade, her mind partially numb. How, she thought, could I have misjudged him so completely? I was so certain that I had him.

He laid it into her bare chilled hand: the pistol. It had a silencer screwed onto the end of the muzzle. Daniella noticed that it was German-made, not regulation Russian army. A personal handgun, a strictly forbidden item.

"Now I want you to shoot Alexei." She heard Maluta's voice as if in a dream. "Do it as you have been trained to carry out an execution, through the back of the head. That was, you recall, how he was to kill you."

This is a nightmare, Daniella thought. Panic and fear raced through her like a brushfire. She could not think. It was as if the reasoning part of her brain had gone to sleep. Wake up! she thought desperately. What am I to do?

"It shouldn't be too much of a task," Maluta was saying. He was smoking again, the wind bringing the vile smoke back into her face. "After all, there is a revenge motive. He had gained your trust and, in return, was spying on you. It is only just, don't you think, to punish such a heinous crime?"

I am in bed with a true monster, Daniella thought. Her stomach was a cold, twisted knot. She felt vertigo overcome her. She was frozen to the spot. I cannot do what he asks, she thought. I cannot.

"Why do you hesitate, Comrade General?" Maluta's voice had returned to rasping hardness. "This indecision is a poor trait for a member of the Politburo. I shall have to report this. A serious offense. A man would never show such weakness." He pulled on his cigarette. "Perhaps I should call Alexei out here and have him kill you after all."

His eyes blazing, Oleg Maluta crunched through the brittle snow. He put his lips against her ear. The tobacco smell was a nauseating miasma undaunted even by the chill and the wind. "Do it, Comrade General. Do it now or your life is ended here, at this moment."

Daniella could not believe it herself, but her body was moving toward the car. She had no idea who was directing it; surely not she.

Inside, she saw Alexei's eyes on her in the rearview mirror. "What's happened?" he whispered. "You look as white as a ghost."

Daniella saw herself lean forward, her arm lift up. She opened her lips to answer Alexei. Just before the muzzle touched the back of his head she pulled the trigger.

She was gagging when she emerged from the back of the Chaika. Her nostrils were clogged with the stench of death.

Maluta moved very quickly. He produced a clean white handkerchief and, using it, took the gun from Daniella's hand.

"Your prints," he said, wrapping the thing with the utmost care and slipping it into his greatcoat pocket. "I want you to understand that I can have you brought up on murder charges at any time. I have no patience with liars. I would have had you killed but I need your acute mind."

Daniella turned away from him and vomited. Maluta made no move but played the flashlight beam over the rippling surface of her sable coat. The exquisite fur shone like platinum. For a time he hummed tunelessly to himself.

"You need me for what?" There was a bitter taste in her mouth that she was certain even mouthwash would not be able to take away.

"Why, to get into Shi Zilin's mind, of course. You see, when I do my research I am quite thorough. I know that the secret to Kam Sang resides in that old man's head. You're going to extract it for me."

Daniella felt as if she had suddenly been struck a blow from a hammer. "That is impossible," she managed to stammer.

Maluta's heavy eyebrows lifted. "So? In that case, Comrade General, you are ordered to terminate Shi Zilin."

Mouth dry, Daniella said, "Shi Zilin and Jake Maroc are inextricably linked."

"All right," Maluta said, "I am a reasonable man." The

65

dry rustle of the snow, like a living thing, moving. "Kill them both."

Daniella felt an icy ball of fear turn her insides to water. "I don't think you understand what you are asking."

His teeth came together with a clack. "Kam Sang, Shi Zilin, Jake Maroc. One, two, three. What could be simpler?"

Daniella said nothing. She could hear the rushing of her blood in her inner ears as if it were part of a spring thaw. She knew now what he was up to, knew that she could not have been subjected to a more thorough investigation had she been within the dank caverns of the Lubyanka.

"I run the China section," she said. "There are long-range operations in progress. You can't ask me to just—"

"Oh, but I can, Comrade General." Maluta took a long drag on his cigarette. He was very sure of himself. "The problem is that when one has free reign over such a powerful lever one's mind turns to thoughts of personal use." He leaned toward her, hissing smoke into her face. "*Personal* ends, Comrade General, as opposed to those that will best serve the State."

That awful clacking of teeth again. "Chimera is your power, Comrade General," Maluta said, "but I know that China is your overriding obsession. I am not asking so much, am I?" His voice had turned syrupy. "After all, I could demand you reveal to me Chimera's identity. I could even take this asset away from you." He grinned. "Then where would you be? You see? Seen in this light, it is not so much what I ask of you. To find out about Kam Sang. And to get rid of Shi Zilin and Jake Maroc."

Daniella was trembling. For years her complete control of Chimera had been the key to her rapid advancement. Without the fantastic flood of classified information Chimera provided for her, she would never have climbed so far, so fast, in what was, quite literally, a man's world.

In that, Maluta had been right on target. Chimera sat at the very center of the Quarry. Though Jake Maroc believed that he had killed Chimera during a confrontation at Greystoke nine months before, in fact the mole was not Henry Wunderman, Maroc's long-time mentor. Daniella's maneuvering had camouflaged Chimera perfectly, and had fooled everyone, even Shi Zilin.

Now her situation was desperate. She was not fooled by Maluta's words. Unless she could find some way to deflect or forestall him, Maluta would take full control of her China operations. This is what his orders were leading to. With Shi Zilin and Jake Maroc out of the way, and with the secrets of Kam Sang in his hip pocket, Maluta would be invincible. Even Carelin's and Reztsov's aid would not stop him from bringing Genachev down. Russia run by this madman was unthinkable. Maluta already had so much power that if he was able to use Kam Sang to add to it, he would be able to persuade the other members of the Politburo that what he had done— destroy Genachev—was in fact in the Soviet Union's best interests. And where will that leave me? Daniella thought. Permanently under his thumb. Because once Maluta believes that he no longer can control me, he will destroy me as well.

By "the State," Daniella knew Maluta meant himself. "Are you saying that I am not fit to run the China operations?"

"Possibly." Maluta nodded, threw the glowing butt of the cigarette far out into the night.

The rage building in her sought an outlet; she was mad with it, and so she spoke without thinking. "You talk of the State. But there is nothing of the State in you, Comrade. This is personal, pure and simple. You are generating a power play and I'm to run interference for you." She felt tears burning behind her eyelids and closed them tightly so that he wouldn't see them. She began to pray for strength. "I'm to provide you with your silver bullet to lay Genachev low. And if, for some reason, security is breached, I will be the one they put to the stake."

"Ah, Comrade General." Maluta smiled down on her benignly. "You have pleased me in so many ways tonight. Yes, you're quite right in your assessment." He shrugged. "But you will do as I ask, just the same, won't you?"

Daniella nodded numbly. What choice did she have? At least he would no longer spy on her.

Companionably, he took her arm as they went back to the Chaika. "Besides," he said, more easily now, "getting rid of the Shis will be best in the long run. I do not care for the power base they are forming in Hong Kong." It had begun to snow. Together they maneuvered Alexei's corpse into the trunk.

He handed her a chamois cloth, took one himself, and together they wiped away what little blood had seeped onto the front seat. They threw the bloody rags back into the trunk.

Maluta, looking down at the white frozen face, said, "He looks so surprised." He slammed down the trunk. "Well, I'm not surprised, really. He was quite loyal to you, Comrade General."

Daniella felt the ground give way beneath her. She made a grab for the fender of the Chaika, missed and went to her knees.

Maluta made no move to assist her. He stood over her, watching her behavior with the kind of total curiosity a scientist exhibits toward a laboratory specimen.

"Do you really think that I would be foolish enough to allow you to kill my surveillance of you? Had Alexei actually been doing what I told you he was, he'd have been far too valuable for me to waste this way.

"No, my dear Daniella. I lied to you about Alexei. In that regard he was as pure as the driven snow. You see now how it feels to be lied to." He watched with a kind of trembling intensity the tears dropping from Daniella's eyes. They made dark indentations where they hit the snow.

"Soon," he said thickly, "I will have photos of you weeping. My surveillance of you will see to that." With his breath clouding in the cold night, he seemed to be panting.

"The day after tomorrow is your birthday," Three Oaths Tsun said. "Where would you like to go for dinner?"

"To Gaddi's at the Peninsula," Neon Chow said immediately.

Three Oaths Tsun, standing on the just-washed deck of his junk lying to at the floating Hakka city in Aberdeen Harbor, eyed his mistress. *Oh ko*, he thought, of course Gaddi's. For her twenty-fourth birthday why shouldn't she be taken to Hong Kong's finest and most expensive restaurant.

"Gaddi's!" he exploded. "By the Celestial Blue Dragon, if I know you at all, you'll try to bankrupt me there!" That was not to say that one should not show reluctance, Three Oaths Tsun thought. In his seventy-one years he had learned all the tricks—or so he believed—of the female mind.

"I'll do nothing of the kind," Neon Chow said, pouting deliciously. She came across the deck to him. "I'll only be twenty-four once. Should I not be happy?" She fondled the emerald necklace he had recently given her. "Aren't I worth Gaddi's?" Her pout deepened. "I know, you think I'll embarrass you in such a fine place."

In fact, Three Oaths thought, nothing could be further from the truth. Whenever he took this exquisite woman out, all heads turned in their direction—female as well as male. Neon

Chow, who worked part time for the governor, could easily have been a recording or film star. The only thing that would have stopped her, he supposed, was that she was essentially a lazy creature. Neon Chow had never done an hour of hard work in her life and that was, he was quite certain, just how she liked it.

"It's true, a *tai pan* of your stature cannot afford to be publicly embarrassed," she went on sulkily, "so I shall rescind my request. Take me to that dirty old fishmonger's you like so much in Causeway Bay. I suppose I deserve nothing more anyway."

Three Oaths tried not to smile. In reality, she could ask anything of him and he would gladly grant it if it was within his power. But it would do neither of them any good for him to make that manifest to her. Her powerful effect on him was similarly best kept to himself, he believed. No woman he had ever known—and in his lifetime he had known many—could move him as Neon Chow did. And when they made love he was thirty years old again, the clouds and the rain more dizzying even than when he had been in his rampant youth. Just watching her sent tremors of arousal through his sacred member.

"As it happens you are in luck," he said now. His voice betrayed none of the emotion he felt energizing him. "I phoned the place in Causeway Bay but it's not available because of a private party." That was a blatant lie; he'd had no intention of taking her anywhere but the restaurant of her choice. "So I suppose Gaddi's it must be after all."

"Eeeee!" Neon Chow screamed, throwing her arms around him. She ground her liquid hips against his loins, crushed her breasts against his chest. "How wonderful!"

Yes, Three Oaths thought, it certainly is.

"Honorable father, they are here!"

Three Oaths turned from her embrace to acknowledge his number one son's voice. He went, limping, across the deck as Jake and Bliss came aboard. My daughter looks more beautiful now, Three Oaths thought, than she ever has. Bliss's skin is as translucent and glowing as alabaster. It is as if she has waited all her life for Jake Maroc Shi to return to her—to return to her love.

"Greetings, *Zhuan*," he said and, turning to Bliss, "Daughter." His face was serene; none of his inner emotion showed.

"May Bliss go below?" Jake asked. "My father has asked for the services of her healing hands."

"Certainly," Three Oaths said, leading the way. Ever since he had made the journey from Beijing to be reunited with his family, Shi Zilin had chosen to live on his brother's junk, because, he said, "It reminds me of the old days when we ran the tears of the poppy for the foreign devil *tai pan* in Shanghai."

Jake and Three Oaths watched Bliss descend the companionway. Jake was aware of Neon Chow staring at him. He did not look at her or acknowledge her presence. He preferred to treat her as an object, much like the bales and crates littering the freshly swabbed deck.

He did not think about Neon Chow. In his mind she was his uncle's responsibility. Certainly he did not consider her family. He suspected privately that she was more interested in Three Oaths's money than she was in him. He had come across many beauties like her who had nothing more to barter with in life than their bodies. A part of life in Asia. *Joss*.

Below, Bliss smiled into Shi Zilin's face and picked up his hand. She squeezed it, stroking its back with loving affection in her eyes. She kissed both his cheeks.

"Where is your pain the worst today, *a-yeh*?" she asked softly, and when Zilin told her, she nodded. "We'll begin then with the Liver Meridian." She moved down, took off his shoes. "The sedating point is here"—picking up one bare foot—"on the sole just below the base of the middle toe. Now as I press here, imagine the energy flow moving from the opposite end of the meridian, the inner end of the collarbone, down through the ribs into the pubic region, down the inside of the leg to the knee, then down farther along the inside of the ankle bone, circling there until it reaches the point where I am pressing. Close your eyes now, *a-yeh*."

Up on deck, Three Oaths Tsun watched Neon Chow's slim back as she went forward. When she had disappeared, he shifted his gaze to the silver sky and then spat heavily over the side. "No sun; no rain. This is no weather at all. Bad for fishing, bad for fornicating anything, *heya*?"

Jake's hooded copper eyes were watching far out at sea. Tankers, black and low, filled with oil from the rich emirates, steamed in two-dimensional silhouette. They had come, no doubt, through the Strait of Malacca, one of the smallest and most strategic bits of territory in this modern petrofueled world.

It was at the Strait of Malacca as well as at the Mainland,

Zilin had informed his son, that the Soviets meant to strike.

As he stood there, Jake blotted out his uncle and Neon Chow, recalling the conversation he had had with Zilin earlier in the day. The old man seemed obsessed with their old enemy, the KGB. And in particular two high-ranking officials.

"Over the last three-and-a-half years," the Jian had said, "the Russian army, with the vital political backing of Anatoly Karpov and Yuri Lantin, has begun a massive upgrading of their fifty-eight border divisions. Nine of them are now fully armored. All are arrayed along China's northern frontier.

"In Eastern Siberia, where we are historically the most vulnerable, our latest intelligence tells us that approximately one hundred TU-22 bombers and one hundred fifty SS-20 mobile missiles armed with nuclear warheads have been deployed."

"Are those the Backfire bombers?" Jake had asked. And when his father had nodded his assent he had thought, They are currently the most modern the Russians have: five-thousand-mile range, nuclear capability with either bombs or air-to-surface missiles.

"They are all around us, Jake," Zilin had said. "But these are only machines. Machines need guidance. The human mind. Here is the crux of the issue. We have a new nemesis in the Kremlin: Oleg Maluta. He is far worse than Karpov and Lantin ever were because his power base is virtually unshakable. And if the time comes that he is ever elevated further, Buddha protect us. His militancy is well documented. Afghanistan and Pakistan were two of his pet projects.

"The question we must now ask ourselves is in which direction is Maluta turning his adder's head. Will he make those Backfire bombers take to the sky?"

Zilin's glossy black eyes were depthless, ageless. The degenerative disease that continued to wrack him with pain had nevertheless failed to dim the inner energy or the acuity of his extraordinary mind.

"How did Maluta come to your attention, Father?" Jake had asked.

"Through Daniella Vorkuta," the old man said. "Always and forever it is Daniella Vorkuta. It is her eye that is constantly on China, Jake. Never for a moment forget that fact. It is she, of the Russians now in power, who understands the importance of controlling Hong Kong. If the Russians can gain enough hold over the trading companies here, they can cut all revenue off from the Mainland; they can suck Mainland

71

companies establishing themselves in Hong Kong into bad ventures. Daniella Vorkuta's hold in Hong Kong must be broken forever or China can never gain her destiny as a future world power.

"Though Maluta is dangerous because of his avowed militancy against us, it is Daniella Vorkuta who can truly destroy us: financially, economically, for all time.

"General Vorkuta plays *wei qi*; she knows the strategies. Through Sir John Bluestone, she has a substantial foothold here and though we have him in view we should not underestimate her mind. Only she, of all the Russians, understands our potential here."

"How much does Daniella Vorkuta know about Kam Sang?" Jake had asked.

Zilin had let out a long sigh. "She has already tried twice to infiltrate the project. So far we have managed to, ah, appropriate her agents before too much information was leaked back to her. But she will keep trying."

"But this in itself seems to me to create a problem of its own," Jake had said. "The very fact of the intense security surrounding Kam Sang should be cause for alarm on her part. She is smart enough to read the military implications in such massive security."

Zilin had looked at his son. "Indeed. And if she becomes sufficiently alarmed, so will Oleg Maluta. And Maluta will order the Backfires up."

"Are you sufficiently relaxed, Jian?" Bliss asked.

Zilin opened his eyes. His mind, freed of the network of pain within which it had been gripped, was floating. He was in the center of *dai-hei*, the great darkness where, he had found, all incorporeal essence resides, when Bliss's voice called him back.

"Yes," he said thickly. "You have done wonders for me, *bou-sehk*. Precious gem, that is what my Younger Brother calls you." He moved slightly. "I thank you ten thousand times over."

"I have only taken away your pain," she said, overwhelmed that he would call her by the loving term her father did. "I have given you nothing at all."

"On the contrary," his luminous eyes sought hers, "you have given me part of yourself. *Bou-sehk*, listen to me. Your body is only part of what you have to offer others; it is, perhaps, the most insignificant part. Yes, your body can give and receive enormous pleasure. But that pleasure is at best fleeting. The mind, on the other hand, is nourished by your aura, your essence, your *qi*; that which makes you unique. This is in the end what the mind remembers. What the soul cherishes."

Bliss knelt beside the reed pallet, her head bowed. Her hands were clasped in her lap.

"Tell me," he continued, "do you know of *da-hei*?"

"No, godfather."

"Touch the tips of my fingers with yours." His voice was but a whisper, coming to her in waves like the tide that lapped gently at the hull of the junk. "Look into my eyes now. Look into my eyes."

"What am I supposed to see?"

"Nothing," he said. But it seemed to her as if his mouth had not opened at all. "Nothing."

There was a darkness in the room that was not gloom, not shadow. To Bliss it was a source of illumination, although she had no idea how darkness could be a source of light.

In the depths of Zilin's eyes was a spark of color unknown to her. She stared long at the hue, in an attempt to decipher its mystery. And all about her the darkness crept, stealing the light. Then the cabin disappeared.

And Bliss heard the world calling.

Up on deck, Jake was saying, "I have ten thousand threads, all of which I must weave into one tight skein."

"That is the *Zhuan*'s job," Three Oaths said, watching carefully the famed intensity of Jake's formidable gaze.

Though his uncle's tone was carefully neutral Jake still picked up a subtle undercurrent, and a warning siren went off in his head. "You do not approve of my father's choice of successor, do you, Elder Uncle?"

"Oh, no, no. Nothing could be further from the truth. I just do not see how the *yuhn-hyun* will survive without the Jian. I mean no disrespect, Younger Nephew; I could not love you more were you my own son. But the Jian has had eighty-odd years of experience. The *yuhn-hyun* is his creation—it has been evolving in his mind for fully fifty years. The thought of losing him now, at this most critical time, fills me with dread."

The day was waning but the air was completely still. Forward, Jake watched Neon Chow chatting with Three Oaths' number two daughter.

"Will you stay for dinner, *Zhuan*?"

"Unfortunately, I cannot," Jake said. "Too much work to do." He tried to smile but his face felt wooden. There was too much happening, too quickly. Jake wished desperately that he could talk to someone about his strategy—to Three Oaths or to Bliss. But he knew that in this he was alone. He must be. It was part of being the *Zhuan*. He could afford to trust no one. But he felt a burning in his heart; he wondered how much it was costing him to push Bliss away. Part of him wanted to take her into his confidence. Because he loved her so. But another part of him—the *Zhuan*—knew that the information he possessed was far too explosive for any other person to have. The enemy was too close, too well hidden within the inner circle to take the risk. Still, he was chilled by what he was being forced to do. Bliss was an integral part of his life. He could not imagine living without her.

A junk, its high triangular sail a glowing red in the dusk, gradually swung into the harbor mouth from the east.

Jake put his elbows on the top rail. His sleeves were rolled up; Three Oaths could see the sinewy power in those wrists and fingers. The lines of callus along the edges of Jake's hands were as yellow as ancient ivory.

"Uncle," he said, "do you believe that Bluestone is behind the embezzlement at Southasia Bancorp?"

"Without doubt," Three Oaths said decisively. "It's clear the motherless dog who actually took the money did not have the brains to put such a scheme together. He would have soiled himself first. No, the scheme required a brain such as Bluestone's."

As the crimson-sailed junk made for the typhoon shelter, Jake saw that the black smudge along the horizon had broadened. A wind had sprung up. "But perhaps," Three Oaths said heavily, "Bluestone is inside the *yuhn-hyun* deeper than any of us imagine."

Jake said nothing, watching the horizon with a blank look.

"Chimera—the Soviet mole inside the Quarry, your former mentor, Henry Wunderman—knew about the emperor's jade seal of power, the *fu*, pieces of which my brother left with you, your half-brother Nichiren, Bliss and Andrew Sawyer. How did he know about the jade?"

Jake took a deep breath. "Bluestone is nothing, Elder Uncle. He is nothing more than a conduit. Daniella Vorkuta is behind the scheme to bankrupt Southasia. Daniella Vorkuta is inside the *yuhn-hyun*; it is her brain at work here. Daniella Vorkuta runs Bluestone. As she runs Chimera."

"Runs Chimera?" Three Oaths said incredulously. "What do you mean? Chimera is dead. You killed him with your own hands."

"I killed Henry Wunderman, Elder Uncle," Jake said, the pain in his voice now evident. "He was—in fact—not Chimera."

"What?"

Jake still did not move. Three Oaths realized he stood as still as stone—as death. "A week ago an agent of the Quarry contacted me. Never mind who, it was a deep cover asset, code-named Apollo. Beridien and Donovan, perhaps a few others at Quarry Central knew about Apollo. But no one except Henry Wunderman knew Apollo's identity. When Apollo heard through high diplomatic circles of Wunderman's death, and why he was killed, it set him thinking. He knew—he *knew*, Elder Uncle—that Wunderman could not possibly be a double agent. Apollo confirmed this. He also confirmed that Chimera is still operating. Over the months since, Apollo has been doing some thinking. He has deduced the identity of General Vorkuta's mole inside the Quarry: Rodger Donovan."

Jake watched a *walla-walla* carrying three Mandarin businessmen, somber as reptiles, as it negotiated the narrow lanes between boats, on its way to one of the floating restaurants moored in the harbor. Oily water lapped at the side of the junk.

Jake turned to face his uncle. "Donovan's name is the only one that makes sense. The ploy Vorkuta used on all of us to persuade us that Wunderman was Chimera was as audacious as it was meticulous. She used false intelligence to convince me that Henry was Chimera; while she used other intelligence—just as false—to convince Henry that I was behind the assassination of Beridien.

"The whole plot was dangerous to Chimera. At any time, Henry or I could have stumbled onto the truth about Chimera. So the reward must have been very high indeed."

"I'd say that Vorkuta's mole taking control of the Quarry is high reward indeed," Three Oaths said.

"Oh, yes," Jake said morosely.

Three Oaths watched the oily patches of water lap against the junk. Out in the harbor, Jumbo, the giant floating restaurant, was abruptly lit up, sending gaudy red, green and blue lights dancing over the waves.

"Are you certain of this? Perhaps this is another of accursed Vorkuta's diabolical ploys."

Jake shook his head. "No, I don't think so, for two reasons. One, she would have no earthly reason to stir up my suspicions now—the whole idea was for me to believe that Chimera was dead. Two, Apollo told me what his last directive from Wunderman was: to terminate Daniella Vorkuta. I have reaffirmed that directive."

"May she die a hundred deaths for what she has done to you, Younger Nephew!" Three Oaths said, spitting over the junk's side.

"One will do, Elder Uncle," Jake said bleakly. "General Vorkuta caused me to kill one of my oldest friends." He was watching something from very far away. Perhaps it was not anything in the real world. "She set us one against the other and neither Henry nor I saw what was happening. She destroyed everything we had between us: friendship, love, trust. Like a master magician she paraded before us our own supposed deceit, betrayal, fear. She separated us and, thus, defeated us. Worse, she caused us to defeat one another. She suspected, rightly, that our mutual love could be twisted into hate, and that that hate would blind us to her illusion.

"Buddha, how she must have gloated when I killed Henry. And became her assassin."

"Ahhhh." It was a long drawn-out sigh of recognition. "General Vorkuta is a devil, *Zhuan*. She is intent on our destruction. How to believe such a diabolical mind resides in the head of a female."

The wind sang an eerie tune through the shrouds; a tern called, wheeling above them. The light that surrounded them seemed abruptly leaden, a deadening weight. It was a long time before Jake's gaze shifted, and even when it happened Three Oaths knew enough to say nothing.

"Look, Elder Uncle." Jake pointed at last to the thickened black smudge out to sea. "Here comes your rain."

Ian McKenna pulled at the collar of his shirt. It was still and muggy after the brief evening rain. The dark beach was stippled as if by a painter's brush. The tide washed detritus ashore. McKenna shone his flash this way and that. It was the middle of the night, and so quiet he could hear the hoot of a ship far off across the water.

"Put it out, if you don't mind."

McKenna stood very still. Chinese voice. Instinctively, McKenna's hand went to his service revolver. Calm down, he told himself. You'll give yourself a heart attack if you go on this way. He shut off the flash and was cloaked in darkness. A light phosphorescence—the conglomerate of lights from nearby Stanley—rode the water, reflecting nothing but abstract patterns.

He felt a presence approaching over his right shoulder. It came around until it was standing by his side. "Good evening, Mr. McKenna."

Turned his head and saw one wide-open white eye glaring at him. Round moon face, wide button nose. A typical southern Chinese face, disfigured by a livid scar that pulled the bottom of the left eye downward, creating a perpetual glare. Inwardly, McKenna shuddered at the bad *joss* of this man.

"I am White-Eye Kao."

McKenna grunted. "You're all alike to me. Shanghainese, Cantonese, whatever. You're all bloody bandits."

For a moment, White-Eye Kao said nothing, then his lips curled upward in a smile. "That did not stop you from accepting my money," he said evenly.

"Money has no loyalty," McKenna said. "I don't care where it comes from."

"Does the amount seem sufficient?" White-Eye Kao asked.

Thinking, Jesus, I may have found the goose that lays the golden egg, McKenna said in his most self-important voice, "For the time being, I believe it to be adequate. But final judgment depends on what you want in return."

"Ah, Mr. McKenna, it is really nothing at all." White-Eye Kao put his hands behind his back. Though he stared out to sea, his ruined orb continued to glare at McKenna. The pale phosphorescence of the water lent it a ghostly hue, as if it were the clouded eye of a dead man—a dead man with a fly tap-tap-tapping in its glutinous surface. Stop it! McKenna screamed silently to himself. He fought to calm his stomach but he could not suppress the image of the great fires along the outback, sparks cracking upward, threading across the dead black sky. The chanting . . .

". . . all right?"

"What?" Dragged himself back from the terrifying memory. "I didn't hear you."

"I asked if you were all right, Mr. McKenna. Your face is pale."

McKenna wiped his face with a shaking hand; it felt clammy. "I'm—no, I'm quite all right. I'm fighting a bit of a stomach flu, that's all."

"You must take care of yourself, Mr. McKenna." White-Eye Kao had taken out a cigarette. He lighted it and inhaled deeply. "Much depends on you now."

Back to business. "What is it you want me to do?"

White-Eye Kao had had about enough of the foreign devil's bad manners. "I wonder what your superiors would do to you if they got wind of the young man who lives with you?"

Color suffused MeKenna's face. "What the hell does that mean?"

White-Eye Kao clucked his tongue. "Formidable Sung, head of the largest Triad in Hong Kong, knows this secret, does he not, Mr. McKenna? He uses it against you from time to time, to get you to deliver advance information on police raids."

"That's utter nonsense!"

"Is it, Mr. McKenna?" White-Eye Kao smiled. "How old is he, Mr. McKenna, your house mate? Eighteen? No, too old. Sixteen, maybe? Does fifteen sound more accurate?" The Chinese laughed.

He knows, McKenna thought. The little bastard knows it all! Suddenly the rage was there, glowing red at his core. The idea of dancing on a string held by these little slant-eyed whoresons was too much to bear. With a low growl, he reached for his gun.

But White-Eye Kao had anticipated him and he was so close his body was up against the larger's man. The gleaming blade of a knife was shoved against McKenna's throat.

"That was not an intelligent move, Mr. McKenna." Those last two words were squeezed out of White-Eye Kao's mouth. Only the fact that he was under strict discipline stopped him from slitting this foreign devil's throat. "You may be powerful inside your precinct house but out here in the night you are nothing but a piece of stinking meat I can hang out to dry for the rats to find. You'll give them a festival feast, Mr. McKenna. I don't want you to forget that."

McKenna's rage bubbled to the surface. His head trembled with the force of it. But he could feel the biting edge of the steel blade across his adam's apple. You're the one who's dead meat, he thought, that's bloody well the truth, mate. His lips were drawn back in an animal snarl. No one treats me like this. No one.

78

In a moment, the steel blade had disappeared. All appeared normal again. "The first service you may provide me," White-Eye Kao said just as if no threat had been uttered, "is confirmation of a rumor. I have heard that there has been some trouble—some very recent trouble—at the Southasia Bancorp.

"I bank at the institution and am understandably concerned as to the continued welfare of my money. You understand."

McKenna laughed. "This is all on your own. Yes. I understand." Thinking, this wog may have given me a leg up on Formidable Sung. That bastard has been blackmailing me long enough. Sung owns a part of Southasia Bancorp. If there is a problem at the bank it will give me great pleasure to see the look on his face when I report it. "All right," he said, making an effort to throttle back his burning rage. Visions of Formidable Sung's thunderstruck face helped. "I'll see what I can find out."

"Quickly," White-Eye Kao said. "Do it quickly, Mr. McKenna. Now go home. Throw your arms around your little boy and drift off to sleep. In time, perhaps—if you run your errands faithfully and well—I will give you that which you need in order to destroy Formidable Sung's hold on you."

Darkness. And within it, whirling, was the light. How was that possible? It was. Because the light was not illumination.

It was pain.

Pain so delicate, so exquisite, so palpable that it took on an actual presence. It hung—that was as close as one could get using a conventional verb—in the center of her universe spinning blurrily like a scythe. Cutting her nerve ends, leaving them raw and open and bleeding—a pain she was certain would never end.

Eventually, however, it did.

That was because Colonel Hu Xujing ordered it.

Qi lin heard his voice quite clearly over the discordant din that was but one component of her pain. Over the course of her internment, she had lost her bearings. She had no real words to describe the amount of time this pain, this light had enveloped her: a day, a week, a month, or a century, it was all the same to her. Before—before the pain, that is—she recalled that her sense of time had been acute. She had never needed an alarm to wake her up, never needed to glance at a watch in order to make a rendezvous; she was always on time.

Time. The pain ate time, consumed it greedily in its maw of light, then regurgitated what was left: not time, not emptiness either, for that would have meant the absence of pain. The pain was always there, a light in the stygian blackness. Her only light. And because it was made so for her, it became, in time, her oasis, her one friend.

Until Colonel Hu.

Colonel Hu made the pain stop. At first, Qi lin hated him for that—for taking away her one and only light. Now there was only the darkness. Sheer emptiness encircled her, a rage of silence, of aloneness. Once, she remembered dimly, she could hold her pain closer to her. It assured her that she was still breathing, her heart was still pumping: that she was still alive.

After the pain went away she was not sure. For a time, she suspected that she was dead. She could feel nothing, see nothing, smell nothing, hear nothing, taste nothing. What *karma* was this that had brought her to this unknown and horrific place? Was this the beginning of the Wheel of Life? What arcane sins had she committed to find herself here?

Then Colonel Hu brought her out from the nothingness. Qi lin believed later that it was like being born again. Literally. There were no words to encompass the enormity of her gratitude.

He showed her light—real light, with color and gradation— and so delighted was she that she reached out in order to bring it closer to her.

He brought to her ears the whisper of the wind through the trees, the brief fluttery calling of the birds; when he ordered it, it began to rain and the soft comforting sound caused her to weep with joy.

Colonel Hu told her that they were the tears of a pure heart and a pure mind. Those were the first words she could recall his having spoken to her. She took his hand, shivering with the feel of his callused palm across her fingertips.

The first gulps of water he fed her went down her chin. She was ashamed until she felt him wiping her off with a soft cloth. He gave her a gentle kiss on her cheek and she was warm inside. She slept.

When she woke she was ravenous. Colonel Hu was there to feed her. She tried to do it herself but it was as if she had forgotten what chopsticks were for. She began to eat with her hands but he stopped her.

Instead, he fed her with the chopsticks, slowly and carefully, in a most instructional manner so that soon she was able to feed herself under his watchful gaze.

In all this time she had not said one word. She found that she had no difficulty in understanding the simple things Colonel Hu said to her. As with the chopsticks, she seemed to have lost the ability to speak.

This, too, Colonel Hu taught her in the most patient manner possible. Qi lin could not imagine anyone being as patient as he was with her and she loved him all the more for it.

There were flashes of course. Times when she would remember with breathtaking clarity her "other" life—before she had been born again through the bright light of pain. At those times she would speak up, tell Colonel Hu that he was wrong, that she knew the meaning of this or that, the true meaning, and why was he lying to her?

Then the darkness would come down like a suffocating blanket and she would not even have the pain—the very personal oasis—to clutch to her breast. Instead, she would be returned to the nothingness from which she had been born.

The first time this occurred, Qi lin said, "This cannot be happening, I have already been reborn." But no sound whatsoever came out and, besides, she almost drowned on the rush of fluid that filled her open mouth.

Pain had long ago ceased to frighten her. She knew instinctively that she could withstand any amount of agony because she knew the secret of turning it around. Like an alchemist she could transform agony into light, a light that would keep her safe, sound, whole.

During the ensuing episodes she kept her mouth tightly shut. That saved her, perhaps, from drowning but it did little to allay her terror. There was nothing, she concluded, more horrifying than being thrust back into an endless void. It was like dying for all eternity. Or worse, not dying . . . yet not living either.

Eventually, she learned to hide these bursts of what she termed "color memory" from those around her, especially Colonel Hu, who seemed to be watching her particularly for these so-called "regression episodes." In any case, they began to occur less and less.

By the time Colonel Hu presented her with her target, Qi

lin hardly remembered another life, other than the one she had been leading here in the outskirts of Beijing.

He floated on a lacquered ocean. Free of pain, he was able to expand his *qi*, his intrinsic energy, so that he stretched out across the whole of the South China Sea. Sunlight, warm and life-giving, radiated down, infusing him. He watched the dolphins at play, clowning through the foamy troughs made by the oil-stained tankers. In another quadrant, he saw a herd of blue whales sounding. They worked their flukes, diving deep, through layers of blue increasing to midnight. In the blackness they sped, the cows guiding their young with gentle nudges while silvery streams of bubbles trailed behind them and lazily rose into daylight.

"Are you relaxed, *a-yeh*?" Bliss asked. It was just before sunset and she had been working on his body for more than two hours.

"Very relaxed. Yesterday's pain is gone, and today, I have very little. Your hands work wonders on this ancient body."

Warmth suffused him, keeping, for the moment, the disease at bay. She is the only one, Zilin thought, who calls me Grandfather. To the others, I am Jian. Even to my son. Though Bliss was more a goddaughter to him, he loved that she called him *a-yeh*. Grandfather was something Lan, Jake's daughter, would have called him. Lan. He turned his mind to thoughts of her.

He no longer felt Bliss's hands kneading his ancient flesh. His *qi* was expanded: he saw and felt other, more momentous things; the petty concerns of the flesh were shut away for some time.

But, in the end, he returned to more human concerns. I am Jian, he thought, half dreaming. I spent my entire life seeking to attain that exalted state. Now I can have no regrets about what it has brought me.

But oh, I do, I do! It has cut me off from the life of a normal human being. I come home to no wife, no family gathered around the fireside. I have sacrificed the traditions of the ages—traditions that have made us the most unique and civilized people on earth—in order to secure a safe pathway to the future.

We must learn new traditions if we are to survive and prosper, but I do not know what they are. I have nothing of that sort to pass on to Jake. I am truly suspended between two worlds. I am of the old Middle Kingdom, antiquated with superstition, so I deliberately cut myself off from that level of thought. The first Jian, the master of the fantastic garden in Suzhou where I was born, taught me the meaning of artifice in building a new world. In school, in Shanghai, my peers thought me odd, a rebel whose views they could not fathom. I can never forget my debt to the Jian. And I thank Buddha every day that his living legacy, Bliss, his great-granddaughter, is here with me now in Hong Kong.

Zilin could still remember that day when Bliss's mother came to him. He was still a rebel, with Mao, hiding out in the hills of Hunan while Chiang Kai-shek sought a way to destroy the Communist army. He had done all he could for her in those dark days: he had fed her and, when she was sufficiently rested, had used his influence with the leaders of the Shan tribes in Burma to get her through to Hong Kong and his brother Three Oaths Tsun.

Only microns thick, his *qi* spread itself across the vastness of the lacquered ocean. Zilin was surprised by the continuance of its strength. The disease that had been ravaging him for years now could only affect his body. Still, because of the intense pain that would otherwise incapacitate him, he had been obliged to draw more and more heavily on the power of his *qi* to keep himself sane and functioning. It was good to know that he could not deplete that mystical reservoir. In that sense he was as potent now as he had been when he was in his twenties. No, he thought now, even more so because he developed the wisdom to know how to use his *qi* in ways he could not have imagined at that younger age.

But he also realized that his flaccid body required a trigger now to release his *qi* so completely. It was no easy accomplishment these days. With his nerve points so blocked with disease and pain, it was difficult to maintain the free flow of energy throughout his system that allowed the release of his *qi*. Bliss worked his body like a magician, using one set of unblocked points to aid her in freeing the next set, and so on all along the nerve paths under siege by the ravages of time.

"Bliss," he said now.

"I am here, Grandfather."

"You are good for an old man. You make me feel young again."

"Thank you, Grandfather," she said, her head down. "But as to the other, you are like granite. You will never die."

"Ah, my precious gem, all who live must die. It is Buddha's

will. To defy that is to be greedy." He sighed at something she could not discern, some inward vision perhaps. "Do you know what happened to the greedy man?"

"I don't, no."

"He at last came over the rise of a hill—the last of many in his travels—and saw before him a valley so vast that he could not determine its dimensions. And this entire valley was encrusted with everything he had sought to possess during his lifetime. Everything. He spent days running from piece to piece, examing and sifting, happy beyond all imagining.

"At first his intense excitement and joy pushed the thought of food and drink from his mind. But eventually the sight of his endless possessions began to pale beside his gnawing hunger and thirst.

"Now he stumbled through the encrusted valley but no longer did he care which bauble he passed. Hunger consumed him; thirst dizzied him."

Zilin was silent then, and Bliss was forced to prompt him. "Then what happened?"

"The man found that he could bear his thirst and his hunger no longer. He had no choice. For the valley was indeed endless, and nowhere within it was there food or drink. All his life he had coveted riches and at last they were his. But because his desire for them was so omnivorous, there was no room even in that endless valley for food to grow or water to surface, or for another soul to inhabit his universe."

Bliss shuddered. "It seems a cruel fate."

"Cruelty breeds cruelty," he said softly. Adrift on the lacquered ocean, he became aware of a disturbance. It was as if a storm was brewing on the far horizon. Stretching his *qi* to its limits, he sought its source.

"We are through for the day," Bliss said. "How do you feel?"

"Wonderful," Zilin said, feeling his *qi* rushing back to his core as if with the onset of night. "Because of you, wonderful." Still, he thought of that far-off storm and because of that he said, "Are you ready again to journey to *da-hei*?" He spoke of the great darkness within which all human spiritual energy dwelled.

Bliss nodded. "But I do not understand."

"A cat does not understand why it is able to fall from a great height and land on its feet. A bird does not understand how it is that it can fly. It merely seeks the air and becomes one with it." Zilin held out his hand. "It is the same with

84

you. Do you imagine that anyone may enter the sphere of *da-hei*?" He grunted. "Now give me your hand, your eyes. Here. And here. Are you afraid?"

"No."

"Not of *da-hei*. That I can feel. I mean are you afraid of that which has no explanation?"

"I have been trained not to be."

"Yet you are afraid."

She bowed her head and whispered, "Yes."

"Then you must know why it is you are afraid." Zilin waited until her head came up and their eyes met again. "It is because that which has no explanation is also without limit."

"The responsibility." The small cabin echoed her words, her feelings. And when she passed through with him into *da-hei*, her exhilaration and her dread.

Jake was dreaming of his daughter, Lan. He often did that and it was never pleasant. Always he was on the banks of the Sumchun River. The muddy water flowed over his feet so that he could neither see them nor feel them.

His daughter was running toward him. She had her mother's body. She was very beautiful. She was clothed in gossamer instead of the ragged Triad uniform she had actually had on that day.

She ran in the water. She did not sink but rather ran on as if she were on solid land. Jake, fearful for her, opened his mouth.

"Lan!" he called. "Lan!"

But no sound came out. He strained to call to her but there was no response from inside him. At that moment, Mariana, his second wife, appeared beside him. She was laughing so hard the tears were streaming down her face. "What are you doing?" She could barely get the words out. "Don't you know you were born without vocal cords?" Just as she was about to cry for real, she vanished, leaving him alone with Lan.

Coming across the Sumchun River at full speed. She saw him now and she smiled. Her arms opened wide. Then the blood started to flow from neat round holes in an oblique line down her body. A fountain of blood. Her face filled with terror and she slipped, sinking into the river.

Jake, shouting, tried to get up. But the river had his feet. His legs ended in ankle stubs, callused and worn. He could not even hobble.

With a herculean effort he flung himself into the river.

Down and down into its sluggish depths he sank. Without feet to propel him he was like a stone. His arms and hands were useless.

Near the muddy bottom he found her, twined in weed and fern. She swung, blue-white, through the aimless current. An errant eddy swirled her black hair across her face so that he was obliged to pull it away as he came up on her. It was as tenacious as if it were alive. It seemed vital to clear her face, so he devoted himself to the task. It took all his energy.

And when at last he had succeeded, he let out a scream of sheer horror.

It was his face he saw swinging slackly before him. *His* face. *His face . . .*

Woke up in a rush. His chest was heaving like a bellows gone mad, his skin slick with cold sweat. Sound filled the room.

"Jake."

There it was again, chilling him.

"Jake, stop it!"

Sound upon sound. He began to shiver, then to shake, to sweat.

Bliss tried to get her arms around him but he fought her, hurting her, not meaning to, not yet seeing her or even knowing she was with him.

The sound echoed eerily through the core of him. It had substance, as much shape as a shadow. He associated a color with it, a deep nut brown, rich and glossy, filled with hidden tones. Skin tones . . . skin running with crimson blood, exploding mahogany trees piercing the sky like javelins thrown by giants.

"Jake. Jake."

Together they struggled while the demons of sound howled and cried out.

His daughter calling out to him, across the gulf of the Sumchun River, "*Bah-ba. Bah-ba. Bah-ba!*" While the bullets tore into her and she stumbled, falling to her knees in the sluggish eddies, regaining her feet, turning and falling almost immediately, the mahogany trees exploding upward in a great fiery burst as the mortars hit, fountains of blood and rock chips.

Three-and-a-half years ago when Jake was still an active member of the Quarry, on a mission at the border of the New Territories and Mainland China. Working with a secretive splinter Triad, misfits and daredevil maniacs, outcasts of the major Triads who patrolled the northern border of the New Territories, pulling fleeing Communists across into the Colony.

Jake and his group—his *dantai*—had been assigned to safeguard a crossing of three high-level Chinese scientists. For that, he had had to enlist the aid of the Triad.

But something had gone very wrong. Someone had been pulled in at the last minute, perhaps, and been made to talk. Their operation had come unraveled beneath a withering counterattack. The strategy had been flawless and Jake had recognized the hand of a *wei qi* master at the head of the enemy: Nichiren, the assassin he had been chasing, the man who had shot Jake's daughter, Lan.

. . . Lan falling into his already bloody arms, her skin a deep nut brown so much like her mother's, but already cool. Her eyes were distant and dark. Her long hair, undone, cascaded into the swirling river.

Lan dying in his arms and her murderer, Jake's half-brother, Nichiren, on the far shore, directing the counterattack. The *wei qi* master. Jake had gone after him, after him across the river, into the jungle. And then, unsuccessful, he had returned, to find only the bodies of his massacred group. The Triad had gathered up their own casualties and faded back into the burning trees.

From that moment on the Triad had severed all contact with Jake, believing that they were betrayed by someone inside the Quarry. A disaster on many levels for which Jake had paid dearly for years afterward.

"Lan!" he screamed now, beating Bliss back against the wall. "Lan!"

"Jake," she called to him breathlessly, "Jake! It's only a dream. A dream!" She fought aside his fists. "You are awake now!" Beating aside his frightened blows. "Listen to me! You are awake! Lan is dead! Do you hear me! Dead!"

Jake's eyes were wide open, he knew where he was, but all he saw was the Sumchun River, the exploding trees, the stumbling body of his long-lost daughter.

Ba-mahk, he thought desperately. *Ba-mahk* was the way to energy, calmness, order inside oneself. It was the way to see others' strategies, to win battles, even wars. *Ba-mahk*: feel the pulse. It was the first lesson that Fo Saan had taught him.

He tried to concentrate.

Feel the pulse.

And for the first time since it had been introduced to him Jake felt nothing. *Ba-mahk*. It was gone; its power was closed to him.

Only a great roiling at the core of him. Lan. Lan. Lan.

Before he knew it, he was crying into the hollow of Bliss's shoulder.

"It's all right," she whispered. "It's all right."

Stroking him over and over, wiping off the sweat, brushing back the hair that had fallen over his forehead. Her palms against his chest, kneading the tension out of the muscles, the tips of her bare breasts crushed against him, doing everything she could think of to bring the heat back into a frame that had gone cold as ice.

It was as if he died—or at least a good part of him died—during these episodes. His flesh turned cold, his color paled, his pulse became rapid and erratic, his breathing was dangerously shallow as he exhaled in rapid pants.

Rubbing her breasts against him, breathing warmth into him through parted lips, drawing him out because he was withdrawing and she feared that one time he would do so with such severity that he would no longer be able to return to her. It was her opinion—but one that he had made her keep to herself—that his episodes were becoming more and more severe. Once he dreamed of Lan perhaps once a month. Now, it was several times a week, and the violence of the visions had increased at an alarming rate.

Moved one hand down his body, stroking his lower belly and inner thighs, caressing his sacred sac, squeezing ever so slightly, grazing the sensitive skin with the edges of her nails until she felt the heat of him beginning to emerge as she placed the engorged tip of him against the flanges of her jade gate.

Allowing their natural movements to move him against her slowly, achingly so that without any other help, her sex flowered open to him, arousing him even more.

She gasped as he plunged into the core of her, her head thrown back, her breasts thrust into his chest. His lips came down onto her exposed neck, sucking there until she moaned with pleasure.

Never once did her talented hands cease their work across his flesh, never once did she allow him to slow; circling her hips, she thrust herself to the limit onto his hot pulsing sword.

Long strokes, then short, quick strokes, up and up until

88

each moment hung suspended in ecstasy, precious and sublime, tender.

They entered each other in an entirely other way, then, and her *qi* sought to cleanse him of the remnants of his nightmare.

Each scorching instant brought them closer together, merged into time and space, until Jake could draw it out no longer and, throbbing, he shot and shot into her liquid depths, groaning deeply, exhaling the long-held air out of him all the way down to his loins.

Bliss, trembling like a leaf in a gale, felt his orgasm reach out and surround her in heat. In that moment, she felt the onset of the clouds and the rain and abandoned herself to his inner core.

Vulnerable and open to her widest extent she unwittingly entered *da-hei* for the first time on her own, and instead of confronting the coruscating colors of Jake's exceptional *qi* she encountered something else entirely.

Da-hei, the great darkness, where all incorporeal essence resides, revealed to her all that she needed to know. Her black eyes flew open and she looked upon the face of her beloved, now relaxed, drifting off to sleep, his arms tenderly around her.

I will not weep, Bliss told herself. But in this she was not successful.

McKenna went looking for Big Oysters Pok. He had been electrified by the thought that Southasia Bancorp might be in financial trouble. If the rumor's true, he thought, Formidable Sung's in a real mess. Half his life must be tied up in Southasia's vaults. If there really is a case of fiduciary malfeasance at Southasia I sodding well better find out about it.

McKenna prowled the nightside clubs of Wan chai. He went from one sleazy joint to another. A world of revolving red and green lights, watered-down drinks, and pathetic whores, addicted to the tears of the poppy at twelve, old at fifteen, masters of sleight of hand and deceit.

He had only ever seen Big Oysters in one of these places. McKenna supposed the Chinese lived in that world in a kind of permanent way. Big Oysters, the Chinese said, knew everything that went on within the Crown Colony. The fact was that he made McKenna nervous. He fell into none of the preconceived stereotypes that filled McKenna's head, and therefore he was a threat. Usually, McKenna did not sit still for threats, but Big Oysters was different. McKenna needed him so he left him alone.

McKenna found him inside the White Teacup, an utterly ridiculous name for an establishment that dispensed swill and gonorrhea with equal indifference.

Big Oysters was sitting near the rear where, McKenna was quick to notice, the red and blue strobe lights were more subdued, the music not as deafening and the drinks were full strength.

McKenna made his way through the sailors on shore leave with the kind of exaggerated swagger that had helped earn him his nickname—Great Pool of Piddle—from the Chinese.

Big Oysters was with a woman, and not one of the local B-girls. This one had class. She was dressed to kill. McKenna, getting an eyeful, fairly drooled over the cleavage and thigh the woman's theatrical and expensive dress revealed.

Seeing McKenna, Big Oysters squeezed the woman on the elbow and she rose, disappearing into the smoky pall of the nightclub.

There was nothing on Big Oysters' face to indicate how he felt about this grossly oversized man sitting down across from him. The fact was that McKenna's very size made the Chinese's sacred sac pull up inside itself. There was something intimidating about all that height and girth. Big Oysters hated himself for feeling as he did but there was nothing he could do about it. *Joss*.

"You've disturbed my evening," he said, sipping at his Courvoisier.

"Mind if I have a drink?"

"Help yourself," Big Oysters said.

"Don't tell me you eat at joints like this?" McKenna sneered.

"I have business here," Big Oysters said. "I eat at Star House in Causeway Bay."

"Sure, I know it," McKenna said, nodding. He looked at Big Oysters through the glass. "I need some information about Southasia Bancorp."

Big Oysters winced inwardly at the foreign devil's total lack of manners. The civilized man would have sat and drunk at least one full round with his host; he would have asked after the host's family, the state of the host's business enterprises; he would have, perhaps, made a small wager on when rain would again fall. When one sat down with a toad, Big Oysters thought resignedly, one must expect to be spattered with slime.

"What about Southasia?"

"I was hoping you would tell me."

Big Oysters watched those terrible pale blue eyes that looked as if they had witnessed something they should not have. "What do I get in return?" he asked.

"Twenty-four-hour advance warning on the next Special Branch raid in your territory."

"I want those raids to stop altogether."

Christ, McKenna thought. "Even I don't have that much authority. Besides, even if I did, it would cause too much talk at the commissioner's level. They'd no doubt hear about it in London and then there'd be a real flap, a full-scale investigation, and it all would be gone—your protection, our arrangement, everything."

Big Oysters turned his head and spat. "So much for the foreign-devil British. Their time here is done."

"When and if they go it won't be the best scenario for the likes of you, I can tell you," McKenna said gracelessly. "The Communists'll come in here and pull all the hairs from your sacred sac."

Big Oysters laughed to cover the enormity of his disgust for this barbarian. "I wouldn't worry about the Communists," he said. "We've got a surprise or two for them."

"The Southasia Bancorp," McKenna said. He had no desire to debate politics with an ignorant Chinese.

"Why did you come to me?"

McKenna finished his brandy. "I have it on good authority that someone may have embezzled a lot of money out of there."

Big Oysters considered what Great Pool of Piddle had told him. "I have heard nothing of this," he said. "Nothing. And that is the most interesting aspect. Either your information is incorrect or—"

"Or what?" McKenna prompted.

"Or," Big Oysters said, "the embezzlement is so big they've put a total security net over the whole thing."

"Then I'm wasting my time with you."

"On the contrary." How I detest this foreign devil, Big Oysters thought. But I need his information to keep my profits high. I use him the way his kind have used us over the years. "Be here this time tomorrow. You'll have your answer one way or the other."

"Bloody good," McKenna said, getting up.

"Oh, one thing."

"Yes."

"Those raid warnings," Big Oysters said, shuddering inwardly at the man's abominable height. "You'll provide them free of charge for six months."

"Impossible!" McKenna exploded.

"Nothing's impossible to a man of your rank," Big Oysters said evenly. "Tomorrow. At this time."

Choking on his fury, McKenna nodded. Then he spun around and stalked out. There was too much noise for him to hear Big Oysters's laughter.

Every day of the working week, Jake went into Sawyer & Sons, laboring at the *Zhuan*'s business out of an office Andrew Sawyer had set up for him, next to his own, on the top floor of the tower. On weekends, Jake worked either from home or from Three Oaths' junk.

There was much to be done. Lines of communication into Communist China, into Singapore, Bangkok, Manila, Jakarta, Toyko and Osaka had to be maintained. Every day, new contacts were being established, increasing the depth and scope of the *yuhn-hyun*'s sphere of influence. Companies hewing cedar trees in Indonesia, building light machinery in Singapore, inventing new kinds of computer chips in Tokyo were all linked together in a far-flung skein of interrelated commerce.

And all had to be coordinated by the *Zhuan*. Mornings and evenings were devoted to telephone and Telex link-ups with various company presidents and key division personnel. In between, Jake was busy reviewing those companies' computer readouts relaying updates on inventories, production schedules, leveraged buy-outs, long- and short-term debt, market share and, in the case of the public corporations, how they were faring on their national stock markets.

The days were long, and inevitably filled with problems. But finding solutions was very much akin to planning moves across a *wei qi* board. Problem-solving became second nature to him—as the Jian knew it would—precisely because of his *wei qi* training. Jake was fascinated by the manipulations, and the strategies he conjured up and implemented.

Near evening, he wrapped up his last call and, slinging his jacket over his shoulder, went down in the private elevator only he and Andrew Sawyer used. Out on the sidewalk, the air was thick with humidity. Overhead the sky was clear, streaked with a russet and amethyst sunset. Refracted off the spires of Central, it seemed to fill the air to the bursting point. But to the west, clouds were already pushing in, and he scented rain on its way.

Jake knew there was someone there as soon as he got into his Jaguar. The car was parked just outside the Sawyer Building.

A tick in tall grass, he thought, beginning to work out the vectors open to him. All the while thinking two thoughts: Why is there someone following me? and Who is running the operation?

Several other things occurred to him as he made his way along Queen's Road.

Why choose this moment to begin a tail on him? Was it coincidence, or something more sinister? In Jake's experience it was dangerous to take an occurrence at face value.

His gaze flicked into the image in his rearview mirror: silver-gray Alfa-Romeo Spider Veloce, low and sleek. The driver allowed a cordovan-colored Mercedes 500 SEL, then a Mitsubishi truck to get in-between. The Spider moving up and back in the traffic flow: sign of a very canny driver. Yet Jake might not have been aware of him for some time, had he not misjudged the timing: Jake heard his engine start up, and then the Alfa's a millisecond later. If his window hadn't been down he doubted that he'd have heard the double sound at all. *Joss*. Bad for the tick, good for him.

It was not until Jake had parked his Jaguar in the Western District that he got a clear look. The tick was a woman. She did not have a typical Cantonese or Shanghainese face. That did not mean that she did not fit in with her surroundings. On the contrary, she was chicly dressed, in one of those oversize Japanese sweater-blouses, a gray-brown-taupe striped thing with bat sleeves and an enormous cowl neck that hung around her throat like jewelry. She wore mahogany-colored leather pants and ankle-high suede boots.

She could move, too, Jake observed. He had not once looked at her directly but, instead, was using what the territory naturally provided him: shop windows, glass doors.

It was imperative that he get the measure of her skill before he tried to lose her. Because it would give him an impression of how good the opposition was—and that, by extension, would give him a clue to the identity of the control. Also, it would give him a better idea of which escape maneuvers would work best against her.

Jake was due at Three Oaths' junk in fifteen minutes for

a meeting alone with his father, a date he was now unlikely to make on time. That was all right. The first order of business after spotting the tag was to change his destination. Ticks were as often interested in where their subjects were going as they were in their subjects themselves.

That was why Jake had gone in the opposite direction. He needed to cut out the tick and, in isolation, go to work. That was of course impossible while they were both mobile. On foot, there were innumerable methods of cut out and contact. Losing the tick in the Jag had occurred to Jake, but was dismissed. First, know your enemy, Jake had been taught. He hurried back toward the populated Central District.

He was already working within an emergency situation. Bluestone had apparently seen to that. In a red sector, he knew, evasion tactics were a waste of time. *Evasion*, Fo Saan had told him, *is a delaying strategy at best. Therefore it is a weak strategy in all but the most specialized circumstances. Evasion has no part in the killing ground.*

On the other hand, time was against him. Cut outs required time. There were complex, often elegant affairs. Jake's meeting with his father, in fifteen minutes, was of the utmost importance. Zilin was ready to tell Jake of the "shadow enemies," as he had put it.

So Jake did the only thing he could: he went off the street.

Taking the steps three at a time, he bolted up a staircase leading to the network of raised and covered walkways that joined the huge office towers of the Crown Colony's Central District.

Jake pushed people out of the way, up against the billboards. Crossing to the Island side of Connaught Road Central. Turned a corner and, using the glossy façade of an advertisement, saw the woman right behind him, her face in ghostly passage.

Boutiques were no good because they were too small, no place to get lost in and, anyway, no back entrances. Restaurants were another matter and he ducked into one, brushing past the line snaked up for tables. But it was no go, she was too close behind him and he got out of there.

The skywalks were a trap, he saw now, and he went down to the street at the first chance. She was good, this unknown tick. As good on foot as she had been in the Alfa; and now he was doubly glad that he had used a number of feints to get the feel of her, because he knew this wasn't going to be easy; knew too that he would have to lose her before he could head toward his meeting. There was no way he could lead her to his objective.

He hurried down Ice House Street until he came to Des Voeux Road Central. Hung around the curb as if undecided as to what move to make next. Swung aboard the westbound tram at the very last instant and watched as the woman ran, lunging for the open back doorway. She wouldn't have made it either but some eager-beaver tourist reached out and pulled her aboard, lifting her off the pavement with his powerful, suntanned arms.

He was still talking to her, laughing and bobbing his head, as Jake edged away through the crowd toward the front of the tram.

Where they turned onto Tung Street, Jake leapt off, not caring now to hide his movements. They were in the all-Chinese Western District, full of warehouses, shipping firms, snake shops, fish markets and apothecaries.

She came down off the tram and began to follow him as he turned onto Jervois Street. That was all right. During the time on the tram Jake had thought of how he would handle her and he did not want to lose her. At least not yet.

He went two blocks, then abruptly cut to his right up a narrow alley rank with the scents of gutted fish and drying skate. The light was coming down, the pale winter sun already dropped below the bosom of the sea. The last watery fingers of its light played across the very tops of the Mid-level residential skyscrapers that rose like groves of bamboo from the steep slopes of Victoria Peak.

Shadows were everywhere. Their spread across the cracked cobblestones running dark with fish blood reminded Jake of Mikio Komoto. He had tried to reach him twice again today, but even Kachikachi, Mikio's faithful adviser, could offer no hope of finding Komoto. That was an unpropitious sign. Mikio had been forced out of his Tokyo compound by the escalating Yakuza war. Had he been injured? Was he now in a secluded hospital surrounded by members of his clan armed to repel an assassination attempt? Was his power in the Japanese underworld gone? There were no answers to these questions. In desperation, Jake had phoned his information source in Tokyo. He was not home at noon, which was unusual. That was the time he and Jake had set upon for their electronic rendezvous. If Jake had not had the Southasia Bancorp crisis on his hands he would have taken the next plane out of Kai Tak bound for Tokyo. As it was . . .

On Ladder Street, he began to ascend. The way was steep and narrow, hence it name. It was lined with doorless shops, small spaces, dim even at noontime, within which were stacked square cages. Jake ducked into one of these and quickly made his purchase. The price was exorbitant because of the time of year but he had no time to enter into an extended round of bargaining. With his back to the street he tucked his purchase away and continued up Ladder Street. His movement had been so quick and the light was now so bad that his tick had not been certain what he had done. So much the better.

At the head of Ladder Street was an alley without a name. He headed into it, engulfing himself in shadow. He went perhaps fifty yards down the fetid tunnel, his back against the walls. He stopped and listened. Now would come the test. Either she would follow him into the alley or she would stay where she was and wait for him to come out. Either way he would be ready for her.

He waited. It was late for the Western District, which closed up shop between five and six. A dog barked and then, snuffling, moved on. Somewhere above his head a baby began crying. He heard the lilt of a female voice singing in Cantonese. Soon the baby grew still.

Now there was nothing and Jake found himself thinking of Mikio Komoto again. Was he, too, crouching in the darkness somewhere waiting for an assassin to strike? Was he carrying a modern weapon or an ancient one? Gun or bow and arrow? Blood spilled in rivers in Tokyo and Osaka. How many men had he lost? And Kisan's clan as well. The battle for territory. And honor. One must never forget the Yakuza's fierce honor.

Giri. Jake felt it now. His obligation to his friend. With all the weight on his shoulders that being the *Zhuan* brought, it was ridiculous that he should add to it. But *giri* was hardly a matter of choice. One either felt it or one did not, it was as simple as that. He felt duty bound to help his friend.

All the while his ears were open for any sound that might disturb the fragile integrity of the environment. He checked his watch with a flick of his gaze. It had been fifteen minutes. She was not going to venture in. Well, that said a great deal about her.

Smiling to himself, Jake crept away from the head of the alley. He had picked this one deliberately because it had the appearance—like many of its neighbors—of being a cul-de-sac. What he had discovered quite by accident some time ago was that at its far end was a space between two warehouses just wide enough for a man to slip through.

Tak Ching Road beckoned to him beyond the gray interstice. Jake took one last look behind him at the head of the alley. Shadows crept along the wall like cringing dogs. But there was no sound at all, no sign of pursuit. Let her guard her entrance well, he thought as he slipped through the narrow fissure. She'll find nothing there.

He was through the narrow space, struck by the lights of Tak Ching Road, and the muzzle of a .22 pistol pressed against his face.

The cowl neck of her sweater framed her face with shadow.

When Jake was leaving his office, three Japanese couples were deplaning from their flight in from Tokyo.

At Hong Kong's Kai Tak airport they passed through Immigration and Customs without incident. They were young and of approximately the same age, perhaps in their early twenties. They might have been affluent newlyweds off on an expensive shopping spree in Hong Kong. A typical custom for many of the Japanese rich. And so they engendered the minimum of attention at the crowded airport, as they collected their matched Louis Vuitton luggage and were met by a uniformed chauffeur. They piled into a gleaming white Rolls, the men first, the ladies standing about wide-eyed and giggling in their Albert Nipon and Gianni Versace outfits.

They stayed at the ultramodern Regent Hotel because it was closest to the water and the harbor views were breathtaking. But they went across the street to the most luxurious bastion of the British Colonial occupation of Asia, the Peninsula Hotel, because its spectacular lobby was the place to see and be seen while having tea or drinks.

They spent perhaps an hour there, time enough for the haughty Japanese to come to the attention of almost all the staff, who in any case resented the Japanese and saw them as uncivilized louts.

During that time, it might have been noted—had anyone cared to pay attention—that the women jabbered on much as all women would who were embarking on an exciting sojourn in a foreign land. But the men spoke not at all, rather they smoked furiously, downing Suntory Scotch with almost mechanical regularity.

One moment there were six of them, sitting comfortably; the next moment only the women remained. The three men were already down the marble steps and through the semi-circular courtyards filled with Rollses and Mercedeses.

They did not go back to the Regent but rather hailed a taxi to Kai Tak. Once at the airport they split up. One of the men went through the main terminal to a bank of metal rental lockers. Using a key, he opened one and withdrew three vinyl flight bags, dark-blue overprinted with a white airline logo. He took these into the men's room.

Inside, he kept one, distributing the others to his two companions who were waiting for him. All three used the cubicles.

Ten minutes later, the first man emerged. Over the course of the next five minutes the other two came out. All carried their dark-blue-and-white flight bags, but save for that element they were unrecognizable as the young affluent Japanese who had arrived at the airport thirty minutes before. At some point before leaving the terminal, all three disposed of their bags in separate trash cans.

Two took different buses, the third climbed into a taxi. Despite the fact that they were using differing means of transportation, they were all headed for the same destination: the harbor at Aberdeen.

In an unusual display of public affection Three Oaths took Neon Chow's hand. He could not help himself. She was so dazzling, he felt intoxicated by her presence.

It was the evening of her birthday, and—as she had requested—they were at the elegant Gaddi's, one of Asia's finest restaurants. This was where Neon Chow had wanted to go and she had shown her appreciation by wearing his favorite dress that showed off the emerald necklace he had given her. Also out of deference to him she wore no other jewelry. There was nothing to compete with the necklace.

Three Oaths felt better than he had in thirty years. There was not a man present who was not looking or had not looked at Neon Chow. Men far younger than himself. He thought, There are some fires that age cannot diminish. He was so happy that even the prospect of eating *loh faan* style did not bother him. One night ingesting food that had been chopped, minced, puréed and whipped into consistencies that bore no relation to their natural state would not kill him. He might have indigestion later on, but Neon Chow knew how to cure that. He smiled at the thought and his sacred member began to thicken underneath the table.

"*Eeeeya!*" Neon Chow cried as the sommelier brought over

a bottle of Dom Perignon. "My favorite!" She had developed a taste for fine champagne, from the governmental functions she attended with the governor. Personally, Three Oaths thought all champagne tasted like cat piss. But, he thought, this is her night and she will get what she wants.

He watched her stuff herself with foie gras and caviar, and later, venison flown in from Buddha only knew where, dripping in a reduction of juices and cream so rich that it made him bilious just to inhale the aroma. But what did any of that matter as long as she was happy?

Neon Chow's pleasure was at this moment very precious to him. When she was happy she made him happy, and considering the monumental business problems confronting him he needed her radiant energy like a fragile plant needed a fiery sun.

The final accountings at Southasia had come in while he was again at Andrew Sawyer's office. As was their habit, he and Sawyer had been going over the monthly revenue returns on the tanker fleet owned by the inner circle and run by Three Oaths. When the shock had worn off enough for them to regain their senses they had tried to locate Jake. But it was late in the day and Jake had already left the office.

Three Oaths had called his daughter. Bliss had been on her way to Aberdeen, to give the Jian another acupressure treatment aboard Three Oaths's junk. She had no idea where Jake might have gone but she knew that he was due at the junk that evening, to see his father.

Normally a couple of hours would not have made a difference, but the news the full audit had given them was chilling. Not twenty-five million but closer to fifty-five million dollars American had been embezzled. It was a staggering sum, and a certain death blow to Southasia, as far as Three Oaths and Andrew Sawyer could determine.

It was difficult to conceive how such a vast sum of money could be filtered out of an organization without anyone suspecting, Three Oaths had said. But Sawyer had explained the subtly veined network of international companies that surrounded Southasia. The bank sat at the very heart of them, their nerve center. An accountant and a comprador of sufficient guile and daring could manage to steal that much money over a specific period of time. The trouble was, Sawyer had said, that neither man had seemed to him capable of taking the enormous risk such a deception would entail.

Three Oaths had said, "The fact remains that the *yuhn-*

hyun has lost fifty-five million dollars. We are without sufficient funds to make up what has been embezzled. In effect, we have lost our depositors' money. If even a hint of that leaks into the Colony, Southasia will be shuttered almost immediately."

Dessert was a dense chocolate cake layered with praline buttercream. Three Oaths's stomach screamed for surcease but he ate his piece anyway, hoping that the fragrant oolong tea would calm him.

Of course, they could abandon their fight to retain control of Pak. That would certainly free up enough cash but at what price? It was unthinkable. Pak Han Min was the inner circle's key into Kam Sang. Three Oaths did not know why Kam Sang was so vital to the *yuhn-hyun*, though it had been he himself who had created the labyrinth of interlocking companies known as Pak Han Min. He had been under discipline to his elder brother, Zilin, to do so. Why?

All the companies that comprised Pak made an excellent profit due in large part to Three Oaths's acute business acumen. But that profit was funneled through a complicated and wholly clandestine method directly into Kam Sang. Why?

To his knowledge only the Jian was privy to that secret information. Three Oaths only knew that they must not lose Pak Han Min. Did that mean, then, that they would have to let Southasia Bancorp shrivel and die? What would be left of the *yuhn-hyun* if that should happen?

"What is the matter, *si ji*?" Since there was no definite word in Cantonese for "dear" or "darling," Neon Chow used other nicknames. *Si ji* meant lion.

"What?" She had broken in on his musings.

"I saw you shudder. Do you have a chill? Is that why you have only been half listening to me all evening? Are you ill?"

"I am not ill, " Three Oaths said gruffly. He did not like it when she treated him like a child; it reminded him of his age. "And if I have not been as attentive as I should be, I've not been aware of it."

"But that shudder," Neon Chow persisted, seeming concerned.

"Only the air conditioning," he lied. "I should have asked them to change the table."

Seemingly mollified, she said, "I know you've had a lot on your mind lately. Since you've been spending so much time at the Sawyer Building I see new creases on that beautiful lion's face. I don't like that."

"I am *tai pan*," he said, "with a *tai pan*'s responsibilities. You know that."

"Somehow things were simpler . . . I think you were happier before Jake Maroc became *Zhuan*."

"You two do not get along."

"What is he to you?" Neon Chow said. "Just your nephew."

"He is the Jian's son," Three Oaths said.

"And *he* is *Zhuan*. Why not one of *your* sons? Your number one son is more than qualified. Isn't he deserving of such a signal honor?"

"Perhaps," Three Oaths said. "But this was not my decision to make."

"Are you not a great *tai pan*?" Neon Chow insisted.

Three Oaths said, "Why do you harbor these thoughts?"

"Because Jake Shi says nothing. If he were mute he would say as much to me. I do not trust him."

"You are being foolish. It is part of being *Zhuan*," Three Oaths said. "It is not an easy thing to do to cut yourself off from all outside disturbances. He must concentrate all his energies on leading the *yuhn-hyun*."

"Toward what end?" Neon Chow asked. "Don't you think all of us deserve to know that?"

"One China," Three Oaths said, his eyes shining. "That has been the Jian's dream for many decades. Mine, as well. A united China, strong, in the forefront of twenty-first-century world trade. A modern China: the remaking of the face of Asia."

"To do that," Neon Chow said shrewdly, "Beijing would have to divest itself almost entirely of Communism; it would have to become firm allies with the capitalist West."

"Yes, that's quite true."

When sufficient time had passed, Neon Chow excused herself. She went into the ladies' room. In a tiny wallpapered antechamber was a pay phone.

She dialed a number and waited while it rang.

"Waaaaay?"

"Peony," she said, identifying herself. "I need a rendezvous with Mitre as soon as possible."

"I'll see what I can do," the voice said, tonelessly. "Please hold."

Neon Chow began to sweat in the tiny airless cubicle. Come on, she thought. What could take so long?

"Seventy-two hours."

And that's the best these dung-eating bureaucrats can do,

she thought. What do they know of the emergencies that arise in the field?

"*Dew neh loh moh* on that!" she shouted down the line. "This is Peony."

"All right, all right," the voice said. "Forty-eight hours. But that's the limit."

By all the evil gods in hell, she fumed silently. If I were a man Mitre wouldn't treat me this way. Damn all men!

She went into the ladies' room. She tried to calm herself while she urinated. At the mirror she stared at her face as if she had never seen it before. Flaws and the marks of time were becoming more and more manifest. With a sudden wave of disgust she found that she hated her face.

Great Buddha! she thought. Communist China allied with the West! What a monstrous idea!

She knew that she could not return to the table in this agitated state. Three Oaths would pick up her inharmoniousness immediately. Above all, she knew, she must give him no cause for alarm. If she made him even the least bit suspicious, all would be lost.

She called upon her training, breathing deeply and slowly. Thus, she purged herself of all negative emotion. When she was ready she returned to the dinner table. Three Oaths had called for another pot of tea.

"Sit down, please," he said, filling her cup. "I have something to ask you."

Fear rushed like a stream through her and for a moment she was so dizzy that she thought her knees would not hold her. Calm yourself, she thought fiercely. Do you want to die so young?

She sat opposite him and because she knew that this was what was called for, she sipped at her tea. All the time she was thinking, I must get us back to the junk as quickly as possible. But how?

"What can it be," she said when she could trust herself to speak, "that gives you such a serious face? This is my birthday, after all. All serious topics are traditionally banished for the night."

"I've waited as long as I was able," he said by way of apology. "But certain business, er, problems dictate that the traditions be turned aside this one time."

"All right, *si ji*," she said, in her little girl's voice. "It will be as you wish." Gods, what has been going on between the *tai pan* up at Sawyer's office?

"Not as *I* wish. Not at all. *Joss* dictates this."

"Then I accept my *joss*." She smiled a smile as false as her words.

He nodded. "As I knew you would. I want you to contrive to meet Sir John Bluestone in the course of your job at the governor's office."

Neon Chow had ceased to breathe. She was certain that all the color had drained from her face and she thought frenziedly, All gods bear witness! He knows!

"I want you to be as friendly as you can, even flirt with him. I want, in short, for you to present yourself to him."

Then she thought, He only suspects and is playing with me.

"I want, ultimately, for you to become his confidante. Convince him that you are growing tired of me. I am an old man, after all. Perhaps my sexual prowess isn't what it once was."

"But, *si ji*—"

"It is a logical tack to take; it is, I think, what Mr. Bluestone would like to believe. I think, further, that it will tickle him to cuckold me. Especially when you tell him that you will spy on me for him."

"*Si ji!*"

"Now, now, that is only what I wish him to believe. In reality, you will be spying on *him* for *me*."

"Oh," she cried, clapping her hands, "you have the most deliciously clever mind!"

"The *yuhn-hyun* is desperate for inside information on Bluestone's next moves. Will you do it?"

She was laughing to herself. He doesn't know after all, he doesn't even suspect! She wanted to burst into tears of relief. "Of course I'll do it," she said, leaning toward him across the table. One hand had disappeared.

In a moment, Three Oaths felt her nimble fingers at the apex of his thighs. Even through his trousers she could do things that aroused him to a fever pitch.

"Come," she whispered huskily. She encircled his sacred member as it unfurled. "Let us go home as quickly as possible. I want to consummate my birthday . . . and our new business arrangement!"

The snake, when it came out of Jake's shirt, was already hissing. He had bought it in the shop on Ladder Street. This was the time the hibernating snakes were divested of a fluid said by the Chinese to promote health and sexual prowess.

The warmth of being next to Jake's skin had revived it from its winter torpor and now it was inquisitive about its immediate environment. Jake threw it at the tick.

She threw her arms up as the snake got tangled in the huge cowl neck of her sweater. The gun went clattering down the alley. Jake watched, fascinated, as she struggled with it. In this, he made a mistake.

She struck him two lightning kites, partially missing with the first but connecting fully with the second. All the breath rushed from Jake's lungs and he began to double over.

The snake was on the ground, coiled, its scales gleaming dully. It hissed. The woman's left knee came up, catching Jake's cheek. His vision blurred and he fell to the pavement.

Then she was bending, ripping off one high-heel. He turned his head and saw her gripping the top of the boot. The heel was turned toward him and he could see the streetlight catch along the tip. It was steel-sheathed.

The weapon swung downward and Jake rolled at the last possible instant. Heard the sharp report of the steel striking stone, sparks shooting up, and the arm already pulling back for the next strike.

Jake in *sumi otoshi*, his fingers sliding around the woman's forearm and immediately he twisted to the left, pulling her with him, sucking her into the circular path of his own momentum.

She stumbled, went down on one knee, scraping it hard against the rough pavement. Jake used a kite at her wrist and the boot went skittering away into the permanent shadows of the alleyway.

He could hear the panting of her breath and he knew that he had a chance now, regaining his feet as she did, facing each other as she threw her other shoe into the darkness, equal terms reestablished; it was as if the last frantic few moments had never existed.

Until she came at him in a circular pattern and used the double palm change, and disrupted his strategy, he not fully prepared and cursing himself as he went down in great pain, having failed to follow Fo Saan and, ultimately, Lao Tzu, who counseled: in combat listen not with your ears which hear only ordinary things, listen not with your heart, which records only information of the rational world. Rather, listen with the breath so that one may await extraordinary events in a noncommittal fashion.

He had heard with his heart, had reacted to the woman,

the rational, despite what his new-found experience told him: that she could not be as deadly as a male opponent. Had not been noncommittal but had anticipated and in so doing had sealed his defeat.

Went down in a blinding welter of pain that made his ears ring, leached strength from his arms and shoulders. She had used a strike from *Pa-kua*, one of China's oldest martial arts, one of the original war arts or *wu-shu* that stressed circular movements in attack and defense much like *aikido*, which was Jake's mainstay.

Caught thus off-guard, he was defenseless. Her eyes followed the path her palms were taking. She moved first through her waist, low center of gravity, then, summoning the energy from that reserve, transferred it into her arms. Moved with blurring speed, got in four or five serious blows before Jake could recover enough to block the next two.

That surprised her and gave him a bit of breathing room. But again he anticipated, sure that she would continue the attack with *Pa-kua*. Instead, she ripped the gold chain from around her throat, flicked it outward in a *kasumi* throw just as if the gold links were the steel *manrikigusari*, the Japanese weighted chain.

Struck him in the eye and immediately she had wrapped the chain around his neck. Pulling from both ends, her knee pressed into his chest.

Threw up both his hands, slamming the wrists against the inside of her arm, making her twist to her right, grasping her right wrist as she did so with his right hand, pulling it sharply down to his right while jamming his heel of his left hand against her right elbow.

Heard a crack, then a brief cry of surprise and pain from her as he pulled her hard forward, throwing her completely off-balance.

She was against him and his intention was to use an *atemi*, a hard percussion blow, wanting only to stun her. But saw the point of the knife just in time, divining her intent and knowing there was no time at all because of how close they were.

Had no choice then but to use the *jut-hara*, one of the lethal *atemi*, the one that broke the tips of the fifth and sixth ribs, using them as internal weapons, the concussion of the blow jamming them up into the heart.

Within six minutes he had boarded a red double-decker bus heading east. He went immediately to the upper level so that he had a better vantage point of the environment. The bus pulled out and he watched the street behind them until he was absolutely certain he was not being followed.

At the next stop, he got off, walked four blocks, using natural cover as an added precaution. Took another bus back west into Central.

The busy nightlife engulfed him. It turned the red bus phosphorescent. Faces of the passengers were blue with reflected neon. The tick had possessed no I.D. Jake would have been surprised if there had been any. Pockets contained some money, no keys. Nothing at all save a tiny, hastily wrapped parcel wedged into the seam of the lining. Felt the shape of it in the palm of his hand. He unwrapped it and took a look. An uncut opal with exceptional fire.

At the stop he needed, Jake descended at the last possible instant. He was about to make his final run to his rendezvous and he was understandably cautious. If there was one tick, there might be others.

At last he felt safe enough to return to his parked Jaguar. With a squeal of burnt rubber, he took off, heading up, over the Peak, toward Aberdeen and the Jian.

Bliss was reading the Jian a story. It was one of his favorites, the one about the hare and the sister stars who return to the Middle Kingdom in the form of human beings.

The stories the Jian liked the best, she had found, were the ones involving transmogrification. She suspected that was because he believed this is what had happened to him.

It gave Bliss immense pleasure to read to him, though in point of fact much of their quiet time together was spent with him telling her stories about her great-grandfather, the first Jian, and the legendary garden where Zilin's own philosophical nature had been formed.

Bliss, for all the love and training Three Oaths and his family had given her, felt essentially rootless. She barely remembered her mother and the time they had spent with the mountain tribes in the Shan States—though many years later Three Oaths had insisted that she go back to the Burmese highlands as if she would discover a sense of place there. As for her father, she did not even know his name. He had died while Bliss's mother was six months pregnant with her.

In the Jian she had come home again, full circle. Within the special glow of his loving presence she had found the place she had come from. It was as if she had been conceived in the fabulous garden of her great-grandfather, which Zilin drew for her in his evocative word-pictures.

She discovered quite without warning that she loved him with a fierceness and dedication that she had previously thought impossible. It was not the kind of love she felt for Jake or even for Three Oaths. This was a transcendent emotion that made her feel as if she were truly a part of the earth, the sea, the sky. She had never been a practicing Buddhist but the love she experienced for the Jian made her wish that she was.

She revered him above all other men but she was fully aware that he was a man for all that. The Jian believed that he was one of the celestial guardians of China. Thus his *ren*, his harvest that took the form of the *yuhn-hyun* in Hong Kong, had been born and was given shape by him over the course of fifty years.

It was a monumental enough undertaking for an entire country. For one man it seemed impossible. Yet, she knew, the Jian was not one man. He commanded a vast network throughout all of Asia—perhaps even farther; who really knew the extent of the *ren*? She suspected not even Jake was as yet fully aware of the scope of the network Zilin had created. It was in the nature of the Jian to keep his secrets. He had needed to do so for so many years that it was now quite impossible for him to do otherwise.

Slowly, now, he was teaching Jake the meaning of the term Jian. Jake was not Jian but rather *Zhuan*—Jian meant creator; *Zhuan* meant manager—and the difference was vast. Privately, in the most secret recesses of her own heart, Bliss wondered whether Jake would one day earn the title of Jian.

She had finished the story. The hare had heroically served his role, aiding the sister stars who, now, had returned to their place in the heavens. All was right with the world.

Bliss looked down at the reclining figure. His ancient face was partly in shadow; she was not sure whether he was awake or asleep. She heard all about her the soft creaking of the junk's fittings. It was very quiet. The guards made no sound. No one else was aboard. Bliss suspected that if her father had decided to remarry instead of taking a mistress such as Neon Chow, the children would have been made to stay aboard evenings. She did not know whether or not that would be a good thing. As Three Oaths was always quick to point out, today's children were not like those of the past. They had less sense of their forebears, of tradition. He fought that loss, she knew, with every fiber of his being. But keeping the children locked on the junk was no answer and he knew that. Besides, he was just as often ashore with Neon Chow until late in the night.

She rose, certain that the Jian had fallen asleep.

"Are you going, Bliss?"

"No, *a-yeh*." She sat down again. "I thought you had drifted off."

"I almost did." His voice was as brittle as rice paper. "The pain woke me. It kept me suspended between."

Bliss glanced at him and he said, "What is it, *bou-sehk*?"

"Nothing. I just . . . I don't know why you must shoulder so much pain," she said.

Zilin peered into her shadowed face. "If I did not feel the pain, I would no longer be certain that I was alive. I am alive now, *heya*? You must think of that."

He struggled to sit up and she reached to help him. When their flesh touched, she jumped.

"What did you feel?" he wanted to know.

"A current . . . an electric shock. But that is impossible."

Thinking of Senlin he said, "Nothing is impossible. You know that very well."

"Yes. But some things . . ."

Out of the ensuing silence, Zilin said, "There are no limits. Whatever may happen in the future it is imperative that you keep this thought close beside you."

In a moment, he had twisted her around. Their faces were very close. He saw the soft light falling like a mantle across her golden skin and he thought of her mother and how he had aided her in her time of need.

"You have served me well and faithfully in the past, *bou-sehk*. You kept my son safe under the most trying circumstances. Do not think that for a moment I have forgotten this service." He shook her a little. "Now I know that you have something to tell me and you must do so."

"You have so many other—"

"Do as I say, child!"

Her eyes locked on his and she thought that the entire universe must reside there. "I want to, *a-yeh*. I so much want to."

"But you are afraid," he said, intuiting as was his wont.

She nodded wordlessly.

"You are not easily frightened, *bou-sehk*. This I already know. *Da-hei* has frightened you. What else?"

She shook her head again. "Only *da-hei*," she whispered. "Only that."

"What has happened, *bou-sehk*?"

"I used—" She took a deep shuddering breath. "I used it. Or, more accurately, it came to me. Jake and I were in bed. We were . . ."

Zilin nodded. "I understand. Go on."

"At the end, just before the . . . the clouds and the rain I was opened up; I was, I don't know, an empty vessel waiting to be filled up. Filled up with Jake's love. I reached out with my *qi*, seeking to embrace his. And I found—"

She broke off. She was pale, her eyes were averted.

"You found what?" he prompted.

Another shuddering sigh and he could feel the emotion tremoring all through her frame. "Nothing." Breath like a mist at dawn. "I found nothing at all. It was as if I had fallen down a well and instead of hitting bottom just continued to fall."

Now that it was out, the hideous secret was shared, Bliss searched the Jian's face. "What has happened to Jake, *a-yeh*? What is it that I found?"

For a long time there was no sound in the room but the creaking of the fittings as the junk rode at anchor. Every now and again a quiet plash of water against the hull.

At last, Zilin said, "Do you remember the story of the mouse who asked, 'What is it?' "

"I don't think I ever heard it."

"No?" The Jian seemed surprised. "Well, then, it is high time that you did." He settled down into a more comfortable position. "It was his friend, the rat's, birthday and there was a present waiting at the edge of the rat's burrow. It had a delicious smell, the mouse thought. What is it? he wondered. Carefully, he undid the wrapping. It is not my present, he thought, but after all the rat is my best friend. How could he possibly mind if I take a little peek at his present?

"It was a piece of cheese, one that the mouse was not familiar with. It had the most delicious smell, wafting even stronger now that the wrapping was undone. Well, he thought, the rat is my best friend and I love him like a brother. Would he not invite me to share in his present were he here? Of course he would, the mouse decided, answering his own question.

"He began to nibble on the cheese whose flavor, though unknown to him, proved to be quite delectable. So that without quite knowing how it came about, the mouse ate up all his friend's present.

"When, sometime later that night, the rat returned from his nocturnal foraging, he found his friend, the mouse, stiff and cold in front of their burrow. The rat grew cautious and sniffed the area. When he crept close to the dead mouse his keen nose scented the rat poison, familiar to him but totally unknown to the mouse."

Zilin was quiet for some time. From abovedecks, Bliss could hear the low growl of a *walla-walla* passing close by.

"Are you saying that I should not ask what it is I found?" she said then.

The Jian's eyes were already closed. She heard his stentorian breathing. She had asked a question and he had told her this story. Why? There was danger in the story . . . and death. Was that true here? Was Jake in danger or was she?

Then an even more important thought came to her: Zilin had not been surprised when she had told him of the well without a bottom. Why?

Suddenly that question overshadowed all the others.

The three Japanese rendezvoused near the docks at Aberdeen Harbor. They checked and rechecked to make absolutely certain that their security was intact, though none of them believed that they had been followed.

Now they were dressed as Tanka sailors and in the softly glowing night it would have been difficult save at very close range to determine their true ethnic origin.

They were exceptionally well disciplined. They knew the way to the proper quay as if they had been born here rather than in the Japanese highlands. They worked as a team rather than as individuals. In Japan they were known as a *dantai*, by far the most deadly of raiding groups. This was because the *dantai* developed a group identity. *We think, therefore I am.* In effect, the individuals did not exist separately. They thought as one, moved as one. This was coordination of the highest order.

A *walla-walla* was waiting for them at the foot of a narrow concrete stair cut out of the side of the quay. It was unattended and ready to go, which was unusual in Aberdeen Harbor.

One man climbed in to check the outboard engine while a second began to untie the small boat. The third stood at the foot of the tiny pier casually smoking a cigarette. All the while his highly trained eyes were taking in the immediate environment in calculated sectors.

When all was ready a low whistle brought him around. He threw his butt into the water and jumped in. The *walla-walla* took off.

The man at the outboard carried no map save the one that he had memorized. Though he had never before been to Hong Kong he knew the maze of Hakka and Tanka waterways and junks that composed this floating city almost as well as did its oldest residents.

While he steered, the two others huddled amidships. They withdrew Gion 30-09s from oilskin bags tucked into their waistbands. These were miniaturized machine pistols with the stopping power of a .357 Magnum handgun. While they were maneuvered through the shadow-shrouded waterways between the high hulking junks, they pulled the Gions completely apart, checking all parts for alignment and oil. When they were through with theirs the steersman gave them his and they performed the same painstaking checks.

By the time they were finished, they were almost to their destination.

"I feel the storm, *bou-sehk*." His voice, or rather what he said, made Bliss start.

"What storm, *a-yeh*? I don't understand. It has been clear all evening." Heart hammering against her rib cage with such force that she could feel herself trembling.

"I speak now of another kind of storm," he said in a reedy voice. "A storm far more violent than any that nature can create." He stirred. "Can you feel it, now, *bou-sehk*? Do you feel the evil?"

She could say nothing, she only knew that the Jian, his *qi* stretched out wide upon the velvet night, was in touch with some element of which she was not yet aware.

"My *qi* tells me that it is time for my life to end, *bou-sehk*."

"No!" she cried, flinging herself upon him as if in this manner she could protect him from all evil. "*A-yeh, a-yeh,*" she chanted. "Do not say such a terrible thing."

"It is the truth, *bou-sehk*."

"But how? How?"

"My *qi* is still strong, my child. My second sight has been my shield and my sword for seventy years. Do you think that it would fail me now."

"But I love you. I will take you away."

"It is too late," Zilin whispered. "Listen."

The small hairs on the back of Bliss's neck lifted. The soft *put-put-put-put* of a *walla-walla* very close and dying away at the same time, penetrated the bulkhead of the cabin. She grew very still until she felt as if she had ceased to breathe. Felt the gentlest of bumps.

"Who?" Her whisper echoed his. "Oh, *a-yeh!*" She clutched him as tightly as a mother does her child.

"*Bou-sehk*, listen to me." His voice was the only sound in the cabin, permeating even the darkest shadowed corners. "That my death comes is meaningless. *Joss.* One lives, one must die. It cannot be otherwise." She could hear the rustle of clothing as he moved beneath her. "It is the manner of my death that concerns me. I do not wish to die by an unknown assassin's bullet." He was lying face up now and his thin bony fingers gripped her arms. "Do you understand me, *bou-sehk?*"

At first she did not. Her mind was gripped by a cold dread. It was as if his physical paralysis had seeped into her brain, numbing it.

"I don't—"

"Bliss!" His eyes were black, burning with a kind of green fire she had never before seen. It was as if he were some incarnation of an ancient god: Vishnu or Buddha. And she swore to herself later that she had actually seen the soft aura engulfing him, pushing back the darkness of the cabin. "There is no time left. You must do as I tell you. Take the pillow upon which my head rests."

"Ah, dear Buddha!" A rising terror gripped her. Now she could not breathe. Her mind was on fire. Nevertheless a moment later she found her hands gripping the pillow and she never knew whether it was the ethereal green fire in his eyes or the sounds of the timbers creaking above their heads that caused her to do as he said.

She felt the presence of others aboard the junk—the guards Three Oaths had left? Intruders?—and she wondered whether this was because she was now linked so intimately with the Jian. She had never really understood the expansion of his *qi* as he had described it to her, before this moment. Now she experienced it intimately. With a gasp she felt the three men as they crept across the junk abovedecks; she felt the chill of their intent, the searing cold of their determination. For the first time in her life she experienced the true meaning of evil. It was a stench that caught in her throat and made her gag.

"Now, sweet child. It must be now. They are too close to hesitate." She heard his voice as if from the mists of some unknown void, and she knew that he was right. She could feel them silently descending the companionway.

She was weeping uncontrollably. *"Jou-tau, a-yeh."* Good night. She could not bring herself to utter the words goodbye.

In a moment, the cabin exploded in deafening fury as the three Japanese assassins emptied their Gion 30-09s into every corner.

"It's a matter of economics, plain and simple." Jin Kanzhe was far too agitated to sit still.

He paced the study of the villa. Beyond the glass doors, he could see the vast tiled veranda. But then every room in this splendid house was vast. It did not seem like China here—at least China as it had been since 1949. This villa was the dwelling place of an emperor. The furnishings were precious antiques, painstakingly selected from the finest works of the most skilled of the dynastic artisans. But the antiques not only encompassed the history of China but of other Southeast Asian cultures as well. There were Tibetan prayer wheels, patinaed wooden reclining Buddhas from Thailand, black-rubbed bronze sitting Buddhas from Japan. There were a series of exquisitely carved stone Apsarases, sacred dancers, from Cambodia's richest archaeological treasure trove, Angkor Wat; miniature Mandalay temples, carved of gold and precious gems so intricately that it made Jin Kanzhe dizzy to look at them. What small portion he had seen of the contents of the villa were worth many times more than the totality of the Beijing Historical Museum.

"I don't see how we're going to be able to finance this." His breath steamed the air. What he thought but would not say is: Your obsession is going to undo us in the end.

"I trust you are quite finished," said a voice from out of the shadows. "Or are you merely out of breath for the moment?"

Jin Kanzhe swung around. His expression said more forcefully than any words how serious he was on this subject.

A withered hand lifted, fell like a dying butterfly. "Come and sit down, Jin *tong zhi*. Have some chrysanthemum tea. It will restore your calm."

"It won't take care of the money that is needed." But all the same, he came over and sat beside the shadowed chair on the end of a rattan settee. He accepted the tiny porcelain cup, drank the tea without tasting it.

"I think," the voice out of the shadows said, "that you must beware of your own obsession, Jin *tong zhi*."

"Meaning what?"

"Your tirades are becoming more frequent as well as more vitriolic."

"Finances are my concern."

"And they are mine as well, Jin *tong zhi*. Please do not do me the discourtesy of thinking me ill prepared."

"Huaishan *tong zhi*, the future is unknowable. One cannot prepare for all eventualities. Even you."

"Of course not. But the prudent warrior is able to translate the terrain about him into the variables he must consider."

There was silence for a time. The great dog which slept by the shadowed figure's side stirred, growling in its sleep, perhaps dreaming of a kill. Jin Kanzhe stirred as well. He did not like dogs, especially ones that had been trained to rend flesh on command.

"You leave the money-gathering to me," Huaishan Han said. "I have many friends, many political connections still."

"But even they, Comrade, must someday come to the bottom of their pockets. I fear that day has come."

"Do you see the extent of your obsession, Jin *tong zhi*? I told you that money is no problem. It flows through my hands like an endless river. I no longer concern myself with money." The old man's eyes were blazing, his breath filling the room with his expanding *qi*. "I think, instead, of our *lizi*. Our plum who is our trigger. How very ironic . . . and fitting . . . that it should be she who will seek out Jake Maroc. And at the proper time, the time *I* shall choose"—here the old man began to laugh—"he will rush to meet her. We will dislodge him from his own territory. And he will run headlong to meet his own doom!"

Huaishan Han's head was trembling with emotion. "I do not have to remind you of our great good *joss* in discovering her. Colonel Hu will work his magic on her mind. He can turn night into day. I myself have seen him do it.

"Ah, my vengeance will be sweet indeed. So long in coming, now all the sweeter." What spoke to him in horrendous incendiary glyphs? Jin Kanzhe wondered. What was the source of the eerie light that glowed behind his eyes? "How much

114

suffering should my revenge engender, Jin *tong zhi*? You cannot see it but, oh, how I can! Suffering enough! More than any human should have to bear."

The atmosphere in the villa seemed charged with the force of Huaishan Han's hatred and rage. "Jake Maroc—or should I say Shi Jake—he is my ultimate target. And aren't we training the perfect assassin for him!" His voice, once so fragile, seemed to echo through the rooms filled with treasures. "Think of it, Jin *tong zhi*. His own daughter will hunt him down and kill him!"

Jake saw Neon Chow and Three Oaths strolling down the quay several hundred feet in front of him, and he was about to call out to them when the screaming sound of the machine guns began. And, even as he began to run, he thought, Gion 30-09s!

His heart froze and his soul withered as he flung people from his path. The night had exploded into ten thousand incandescent fragments. He could not catch his breath. Fires were lit inside him as well, and he thought of the woman who had followed him, of how much sooner he would have been here had she not delayed him. Delayed him.

And from out of the past, Lan, covered in blood, sprawled half in the river, calling, *Bah-ba, bah-ba*; dream and reality converging with the sudden impact of a granite slab hitting him in the chest.

"Jake . . . Jake . . . *Dew neh loh moh*, Jake!"

Neon Chow running alongside him. Her fear in the air as he jumped aboard the *walla-walla*. "Call the police!" he cried, pushing her away as he shoved off.

Gunning the engine, slipping through the narrow harbor lanes between the high junks and the small craft. Gemlike lights winked merrily in the background while the night was filled with cruel explosions, the stink of cordite, while death groaned out its horrific litany, a runic chant as old as time.

What's happened? he thought. What's happened?

Intent on the navigation of the craft, he wound his tortuous path through the floating city, and came up on Three Oaths's junk.

Saw the *walla-walla* tied up by the side of the junk and he cut the engine, drifting in without a sound; copper eyes searching the shadows, every square inch of the upcoming environment, all senses alert.

The *walla-wallas* touched, bumped, and Jake was already

over the side. Climbing the rope twisting over the side, hand over hand, his breath sounding in his ears, the pounding of his heart overwhelming.

Shadows enshrouded the deck. The lights of Jumbo were far away, their brilliant sparkle too weak to pierce the chill.

The stink of cordite floating like a miasma, bitter and choking. Soft noises from below, as if rats had invaded the kitchen.

There were two exits from belowdecks and Jake picked up a crate, setting it atop the closed forward hatch. Then he crept along the deck, heading aft.

The night was very dark. It had begun to drizzle and he shivered as he made his way aft. Stopped suddenly, went as still as stone. Then, crouching, he reached out a hand, felt the warm, sticky wet, and knew before his eyes deciphered the black mounded forms in front of him. Three Oaths's guards: one, two, three, their necks had been sawed almost through, with wire.

Jake crept around them, stared down into the blackness of the open hatchway. Dark as the entrance to hell, he thought, and something caught in his throat, Oh, Buddha, keep my father safe! But it was so still now, and he shivered again. The tiny rhythmic lapping of the wavelets against the hull of the junk seemed magnified, a crashing of the elements against the creation of man.

The stench of cordite was even stronger here. Haze rose in spectral languor from belowdecks. It was not a time to think clearly, to consider options. He knew that his father was down there and that invaders armed with Gion machine pistols had let loose their fire.

We have many enemies in many countries.

Who was down there with his father? What evil wind had brought them here? If Zilin was dead, then the Chinese would say *joss* and go on with their lives. But Jake could not. Though he was half-Chinese himself, his Western half cried out against a world this hideous. His wife, his daughter, his friends . . . and now his father? All dead? What evil *joss* was this? Far from being the *Zhuan*, he was the unluckiest man in the world.

If you cannot be ruthless, Jake, then my ren *will have been for naught.*

Jake felt as he did when he woke up screaming, the dream of Lan still clogging his brain. And had Bliss been beside him at that moment she would not have recognized him, seeing instead the terrible mask, monstrous with hate, rage and fear, like the disfigurement of some mythic creature.

Anguish and agony were his companions as he dropped through the hatchway, taking the steep companionway in the manner of a nocturnal animal, gliding and spidery, clinging only here and there as it aided his headlong descent.

Within the bowels of the junk, the whiff of death blew straight at him, a night wind off the mountains, animals stirring after the kill.

And the shadows erupted into whirlwind motion.

Jake feinted left, hurled himself bodily to the right. Bright lightning and the eruption of thunder. Wood chips whirring and spinning and he was forced to shield his eyes; it was easy to be blinded by a near miss in these close quarters.

Kicking out, hearing the grunt and gagging within the hollowness of the awful silence.

Moved back to the left, striking out with his fist, saw a head snap back, brief flash of wide eyes, then the jaw coming up and with another smash, the cracking as the bone shattered.

Blood upon him, hot and sticky, turning his hands black in the dimness, a grim surgeon doing his work, cutting and slashing with frightening precision.

The Gion, or its twin, erupted close, very close, and Jake took the breaths needed and, opening his mouth to its fullest, gave out with *kiai*, the warrior's bloodcurdling cry, meant to confuse and terrify the enemy.

The effect achieved, he plowed on, able to pick out the living shadows from the inanimate ones. Heard gagging and almost slipped on a slick of blood creeping across the deck beneath his feet.

They had said not a word and this worried him. He did not know how many were there, only that his enemy numbered more than one. He felt the silence of the professional and something more, an element with which he was all too familiar.

Dantai?

Could it be? No time, as they attacked in concert—the wounded one as well? Impossible!

On his back after a succession of vicious kites to his rib cage robbed him of all breath. He inhaled their breath, their sweat, the stench of animals on kill: A pack. *Dantai*?

The butt of a machine pistol crashed into the side of his skull, setting off flashing lights behind his eyes. He was effectively blind for the space of several heartbeats and they took swift advantage of their gain, working on the same spot on his rib cage, forcing the breath back out of him yet again.

A kick and he groaned inwardly. Another one of those and his ribs would crack and splinter, like his enemy's jaw, and the internal bleeding would begin. The end.

He lashed out from his prone position and missed. And knew. Discovered what it was that Bliss had already discerned. He was without *ba-mahk*. In a flash he knew it was not going to come back. The ability to sink into his surroundings, to find the pulse of *qi* energy surrounding him was gone, forever! He felt like a man who, upon waking, finds that he has mysteriously lost his sight.

Ba-mahk was what Fo Saan had taught him. It was how he won at *wei qi*, how he planned his strategies in life. It was how he saw in the dark, divined the intent of those around him. How he prevailed in combat.

Now there was nothing inside him but an open wound, a pit blacker than the darkness enveloping him. He was like everyone else. He felt helpless.

The butt of the Gion found him again and he grunted, reaching blindly out with questioning fingers. By accident and proximity, he found the machine pistol and used the grip in an *aikido* throw, employing the other's momentum, his own immobile position as the strong fulcrum, to bring his enemy close to him, inward in an arc.

At its apex, when the enemy's panting breath was full in his face, brought the edge of his free hand down at the angle that would offset his own lack of leverage.

But from his prone position he was not able to exert the proper amount of force. The vertebrae of his assailant's neck did not crack. Felt the enemy gathering his strength and rolled because otherwise he would be dead in the next instant, the butt of the Gion descending again and this time smashing his skull.

One arm was pinned beneath him. He struggled to free it but he was right up against the bulkhead and there was no room. Felt movement above him, the intent to kill, and he shot his free hand forward, extending his fingers together, stiff as a blade of steel. Without conscious thought, rammed the weapon of his hand beneath the lower edge of his adversary's sternum; through skin and muscle, tendon and sinew. Felt the curve of the heart and squeezed.

Rush of blood and feces as the sphincter let go in death.

But he had spent too long on his one enemy and the others—
were there two or three?—were on him. They had scented
their compatriot's death even, if this truly was a *dantai*, feeling
the ending of his life.

A Gion went off and Jake felt the onrush of another figure.
Kicked out, thinking, they were too dependent on those things.
Missed and he was punished brutally for his error. He thought
he felt a rib give way this time and he knew that this was
where he was going to die—in this narrow black corridor,
with the stink of cordite and blood and excrement thick as
fog. He felt the fear rising in him. Because he was without
ba-mahk and his enemies' strategy was opaque to him, the
moments incremental and separate, not part of a growing
organic whole that he could use to defeat them.

Two came at him and he had no chance, chose one and
attacked there while he was vulnerable from the opposite
side. Consciousness was going, the flashing behind his eyes
becoming irregular, interspersed for longer and longer periods of absolute blackness from which he awoke startled and
dismayed at his disorientation.

And like a man going down in icy water for the last time,
he grasped out in desperation. He ceded control. Conscious
thought was forgotten; he had even perhaps the wish to die
here with his father because there seemed no reason to continue this cursed life. Instead, the unconscious or, more accurately, that part of the mind which exists between the two
and which governs so much intuitive thought, rose to save
him.

In this cramped environment the normal *atemi* or percus-
sions were useless, so the primitive mind sought to use the
lack of space to the organism's advantage.

Jake lashed out, staggering another one of his enemies. But
there was the third—Jake had worked out their number by
now—who was already attacking. This close, Jake knew instinctively that this was the one with the broken jaw. Used
that, the heel of his hand slamming crosswise, had enough
momentum for that at least and was rewarded with the sound
of a heavy grunt. Not even crying out then, part of him storing
the fact.

Went immediately for the cricoid cartilage buried behind
protecting lines of cartilage in the center of his enemy's throat.
Used both thumbs in concert to break through, and the body
above him was done, a soft sigh like air escaping a balloon
at a children's party.

119

Shaking his groggy head, Jake rose, his senses already questing in the gloom for his last enemy. Saw the glint of the Gion and rushed toward it, red rage suffusing him and now the stars exploding behind his eyes, his brain dull and working it out slowly as he pitched toward the Gion, clutched in the stiffening grasp of a dead man.

Bliss heard the chatter of the Gion once, twice, the silence then so long and unnatural that she was tempted to emerge from her hiding place within the cavern of the great horizontal clothes locker. But that would have been a mistake, she knew; and she had discipline.

Patience, she thought. Patience. She jumped when she heard the third outburst from the machine pistol. She heard nothing after that save the lapping of the water. Slowly, carefully, she crawled out. And froze.

Her eyes, staring hard into the darkness belowdecks, began to discern movement.

She could see from the formation that it was one figure, but she could not discern much more. The angle was acute enough so that even the ability to discern height was lost to her.

Jake, she said to herself. Where are you?

The figure was creeping along the corridor, a dark shadow coalescing out of the eerie twilight belowdecks. Somewhere a lamp shone, swinging crazily, alternately throwing shadow and light.

The figure disappeared, then abruptly reappeared disconcertingly near her, the head raised. And her eyes locked on its own and she screamed.

He was upon her in a blur of motion. The Gion came up, a block of metal, and struck her across the chest, knocking her backward. Her foot caught on a rope slickened by the drizzle and she fell heavily on her hip. She felt his weight on her and she tried to twist away, striking with an *atemi*, but the angle was all wrong and he brushed her weak blow aside without difficulty. She was vulnerable to a body strike and he came in at an oblique angle, confusing her.

Pain filled her side and he increased the pressure of his pin because in that position she could get no momentum behind her percussives.

Her eyes opened wide in fear. They were nearer the crazily swinging light and she could see her target. She whipped her head toward him, biting down at the last instant with all her strength. Her teeth broke through the skin of his neck. She ground down, severing muscle and tendon, and saw his head snap back in reflexive motion.

His hand let go of the Gion to scrabble at her, trying to pull her away. But this was her only hope and she was not to be deterred. He shook and she shook with him, a dog with a sizable bone, refusing to let go of her bloody grip. She tasted his blood, salty and sweet at the same time, and fought not to choke on the hot flow.

His thumb found her throat and he began to press. It was quick, an improvisation, and he wasn't able to find the right grip. She growled deep in her throat and twisted, his thumb slipping away. But not before she had to stop herself from gagging.

His thumb was back and now he had thought it out, the grip beginning, and once he had it she would be done for, because he would cut off her air supply unless she let go of him.

She felt the depression of his thumb, the pressure beginning to build and she was struggling for air.

Working her legs into the right position and bringing her leg up in a quick powerful motion, she jammed her kneecap into the juncture of his thighs. Heard him grunt; their eyes were very close, entwined in as intimate an embrace as was possible without making love. His hand had come away from her throat, the strength going out of him.

He coughed, and Bliss bit down again. And she thought, I have a chance now.

He struck her just beneath her left breast and she felt her heart lurch. A wave of dizziness swept over her and she thought, I underestimated him. Nausea overcame her so that she was obliged to open her jaws.

He hit her again in the same spot. Bliss's mouth went slack, she groaned. Her gorge rose into her throat and she was gagging.

He staggered to his knees, one hand grabbing at the gaping wound her teeth had made in his neck. His shirt was hanging away from his shoulder. His lips were pulled back in a snarl. He hit her again. Bliss vomited.

He stood up and kicked her, grunting with the effort and the pain in his arm. He kicked her again and again, in a frenzy now, raging at himself for having been stopped so surely by a woman.

He slipped in the wetness and in one last desperate effort

Bliss reached out, grabbing hold of his wounded arm. He cut off a strangled scream and, using his good arm, chopped down at her. Bliss grunted but held blindly on. She was covered in blood and slime.

He chopped down again, this time more viciously, and her grip slipped, her fist ripping down the sleeve of his shirt, exposing his bare flesh from shoulder to wrist.

For a moment her eyes opened wide at what she saw there, then he had regained his feet and, rocking there for a moment, he kicked her again with all his remaining strength. There was nothing left for her to hold on to in the utter darkness that suddenly engulfed her.

Her unconscious mind thought, I am the world.

Bliss, connected with the Jian in the act of committing merciful murder—if such a thing truly existed and was recognized by Buddha—had become a part of the Jian's expanding *qi*.

There was a time when their hot breaths were linked on either side of the pillow, when their essences had mingled through the eiderdown.

Terrified, Bliss had become aware of a stirring below her. She had opened her eyes, only to see his frail form still as a statue beneath her. Perhaps he was already dead. She had surmised that it would not take much to take life from him now.

But when she closed her eyes again, she felt the stirring and could not tell whether it was coming from around her or within her.

The theater of her mind was filled with images, as if she were dreaming, or her lungs were filled with the tears of the poppy.

She was stretched across the bosom of the South China Sea. It was night, the sky full of rain and wind. But still she could see the dolphins streaking through the inky blackness of the ocean, following the bubbly, luminous wake of the great whale herd. They dove and leaped about, calling to each other in bursts of odd high piping which contrasted with the whales' low ululating dialogues, drawn out like taffy, an underwater symphony that brought tears to her eyes.

She was weeping for all the life around her. It was as if she had been deaf and blind all her life until this revelatory moment.

Her *qi* was everywhere at once, and all that it touched it

122

embraced with the fierceness that only true love can engender. Where did such pure feelings stem from, she wondered. She had never before experienced such emotions.

Then she became aware that it was not her *qi* at all but another's *qi* upon which she rode. And knowing that, she understood whose *qi* it was. It was unmistakable, and she was stunned that she had ever assumed it was her own.

But you are dead, she thought. You bade me kill you in this humane fashion, so that your *qi* would not be defiled by an assassin's bullets. Does this mean that I have not succeeded?

But she knew the answer deep down in her soul. The Jian was dead.

Then what was happening to *her*?

She turned, distracted by the ineffable beauty of the musical recital below the waves of the South China Sea.

Into the depths she dived, on the wings of this powerful *qi*, until she was surrounded again by the sleek creatures, creations too, of almighty Buddha.

Jake awoke spitting blood. He choked briefly, even as full conscious cerebration rose to the fore. He gained a kneeling position and leaned against the bulkhead. Pain lanced through him, firing into his nerve endings, making coordination and concrete thought difficult.

The third man. Jake remembered his mistake, lunging at the dead man because he had seen the Gion. The third man had come at him from behind. How helpless I am without *ba-mahk*, he thought.

He reached out and the motion almost made him scream. My ribs, he thought, and he felt around the area, wincing with the pain. But it did not seem that there was anything broken.

Picked up the Gion. He had to unwrap the corpse's fingers one by one. Using the bulkhead as a brace, he rose to his feet. Stepping gingerly over the corpse, he moved down the corridor toward his father's cabin.

Felt the night wind blowing even before he reached the open doorway. Stuck his head in and thought, Oh, Buddha, no! The bulkheads, ceiling, deck were riddled with holes, cracks, loose shards swinging in the wind. The place was still thick with cordite.

He went in, feeling nothing at all, as if his legs were not his own. Pulled the trigger of the Gion, and the third man

123

pitched forward revealing the fragments of sheets, pillows, table legs. And what lay beyond. The feet were crossed at the ankles, one arm flung up across the face, either by the momentum of the fall or the force of the fusillade of bullets.

Jake threw the Gion aside and ran to take his father into his arms.

The Jian was so light, so light that he might have been composed of air. The stained pillow by his side might have weighed more.

To find him after so many years, only to have him taken away now . . . like this. How cruel and uncaring was life! *Joss.* What was *joss* after all, but a concept. How could one accept such a monstrous fate? It would be inhuman to do so.

How I hate this life! His mind echoed with his cry. There might have been danger all around him, but he no longer cared. All that existed at this moment was loss. A love that had sprung up inside him greater than any he had ever known, and like the desecration of some precious flower it had been cut down even as it had begun to bloom.

He was overcome by grief, and a terror he found insupportable. For all his life he had been without the trust, protection and solace only a father can bring. The advent of his real father into his life then had been a psychic relief of enormous proportions. The presence of Zilin had reached down, stirring Jake's very essence.

And now . . .

Bliss!

His head jerked up and his heart beat faster. Hadn't she been here too? Had she been here during the attack? Jake remembered that Bliss had been easing his father's pain.

Tenderly he set aside the shell of his father and, limping a little in pain, went down the corridor. At the foot of the forward companionway he paused, lifting his head. He listened, but could hear nothing but the creaking of the junk.

He began to retrace his steps, then, looking over his shoulder, he saw the crumpled shapes. Went back down. Realized that he should have been aware of them long before. *Bamahk* would have revealed their presence to him.

He saw her and knelt down. "Bliss," he said. Lying on her side, something running along the deck, black in the darkness. Blood. "Bliss!"

He turned her to him, cradling her in his arms. Brushing dark hair, plastered by blood, away from her pale face, he

124

said, "Bliss." He kissed her dry lips and as if he were in the middle of a children's story, her eyes fluttered open.

"Jake." Her voice was barely recognizable.

And he thought, Thank Buddha she's alive. "Don't talk, Bliss. You're all right." Fingertips probing over her in expert fashion, how bad was it? "Keep still now." As she struggled to speak again, her lips moving spasmodically, her tongue flicking out. "Hush," he said.

"Jake." Something in her eyes now that he knew he could not deny and he nodded. "Jake." He saw that her eyes were filled with tears. "He was Yakuza."

At first, he thought he had misunderstood her. "What? He was what?"

"Yakuza, Jake. Yakuza."

"Impossible, Bliss. You must have been mistaken. We'll talk about this—"

"The tattoos." He went very still at her words. "Tattoos of a phoenix and a spider." *Irezumi*—the traditional Japanese tattoos. Worn only by the clans of the Japanese underworld. "He was Yakuza," she whispered.

"Bliss, what did he . . ." But her eyes were closing, her breathing was deepening, lengthening, and Jake thought, I must get her to a hospital.

He took her up the companionway and, cradling her in his lap, reached up, throwing the crate off the closed hatch cover. Gained the deck, poking his head up cautiously. It was raining harder now and he could smell the sea, fresh and clear, sharp with phosphorus and salt tang.

He lifted his head. Father, I need you. Why have you gone when I need you so? But there was no answer.

Everything had been set in motion, and now the die had been cast. Truly, there was no turning back. And what if he had been wrong? If he had misjudged his enemies' strategies? What then? Who would save him? Who could possibly protect the *yuhn-hyun*? Jake, the *Zhuan*? At this moment, he felt as if he could not safeguard the life of an insect let alone the fifty-year creation that would eventually remake the face of Asia.

The sea lapped at the hull of the junk as it always had; the stars, hidden behind the rain clouds, continued to wink down, cold enigmatic signals. The universe continued, uncaring, used to human suffering.

Jake shivered. He was cold, sitting in the darkness. The rain beat against him, drumming along the deck, and though

125

he was aboard his uncle's junk in Aberdeen Harbor he knew that he was on that legendary mountainside that Zilin had spoken of.

Father! Oh, Father! There had been so little time!

He was weeping now, his tears mingling with the chill rain. He bent over Bliss's insensate form, rocking her, but also rocking himself.

Shan, he thought. It rose black and forbidding in the symbolic geography of his mind.

The mountain.

There was a time when all things were possible.

Like a fable come to life—an eerily twisted Far East Arthurian mythos—there was an era in China when great dragons roamed the mountainsides, when thunder cracked the sky, when rivers ran red with blood. It was a time for heroes and villains.

And it was the time when Zilin returned to life—and also where the seeds of his death were sown. And all because of a girl.

On the face of it, it seems impossible. And yet, though it occurred in modern times, this was a period in which not only heroes but an ancient form of magic manifested itself—perhaps at the behest of the celestial guardians of China.

Nowadays Chongqing, sitting at the confluence of the Yangtze and Jialing rivers, is a modern, bustling town of wide streets, indifferent architecture, the rocky promontory on which it was built angling steeply into the waters filled with sampans and produce-bearing junks.

In those days of dragons and lightning, when the town was still known as Chungking, it was built on stilts, and composed of tiny, cream-colored houses with slate-gray tiled roofs. Bowed-backed women in straw hats carried faggots of wood or open baskets filled with raw tea up narrow lanes.

Then as now the summers in Chungking were stifling, and people not used to such weather sought the sanctuary of the lower reaches of the shade-shrouded Jinyun Shan—the Red Silk Mountain.

On a day late in August 1945, Mao Zedong and his circle were settled at Number 50 Zengjiayan. They had made the journey—Mao's first by plane—to meet with Generalissimo Chiang Kai-shek and the ambassador from President Roosevelt, Major General Patrick J. Hurley. They were meeting to hammer out a compromise between the two Chinese factions.

Roosevelt had been outspoken against a resumption of the civil war that had been put on hold only by the larger global struggle. But privately, Roosevelt feared Mao and the ideology he espoused.

Mao, too, was inclined toward a compromise with Chiang. He was well aware of how war had depleted China of its natural resources. His own fear was for the future of his country. He knew that China desperately needed to industrialize if it was to compete in the postwar international arena. To do this, he knew, China would require foreign capital.

But the wily Chiang was already ahead of Mao on this score. Only days before, he had signed the Sino-Soviet Treaty of Friendship and Alliance. In addition, playing upon the well-diagnosed American phobia against Communism, Chiang had made alliances with the United States as well.

In Zilin's mind, at least, Chiang had made a grave error. "His feet straddle two divergent paths," Zilin had told Mao on the flight south, "and this could prove disastrous for China, should he continue to represent the country."

"In a coalition such as the one I have in mind," Mao said, "he could at least be controlled."

"I seriously doubt that, Mao *tong zhi*. He who controls the army, Chiang has often said, rules the nation. As long as he believes that, he will be intractable.

"American military advisers have been at Chiang's elbow, whispering their expertise into his ear. At the other elbow stand Stalin and Molotov. The Russians are already sweeping through Manchuria. They destroy our common foe, the Japanese, yes, but do they not also have another, more sinister reason for invading Manchuria? They covet that territory, Mao *tong zhi*."

Mao had been silent for a long time. Ever since the incident in the mountains of Yunnan two years ago, when Zilin's military strategy had defeated the arm of the Nationalist army Chiang had sent to destroy the then rebel leader and his upstart peasant army, Mao had kept his eye on Zilin, a most remarkable man.

It was Mao who gave the orders; thus, it became Mao's strategy, the victory his, and because of it, Mao's renown had spread through the southern provinces like wildfire. Even Mao could not say how many men had been recruited into the army because of that one victory. He only knew that in

1936, his forces were hovering around the eighty-thousand mark. Now the regular army numbered almost one million, and the militia was over double that figure.

Zilin had never asked to be known as the decision-maker; he had never even asked for recompense of any sort. In fact, when Mao wanted to elevate him in ministerial rank Zilin had refused.

"I thank you, Mao *tong zhi*," Zilin had said, "but the humility of a lowly station is useful. It serves to remind me of our place in the world." He bowed his head. "If, on occasion, you and I speak and the product of our thoughts is constructive then that is sufficient." He smiled and Mao was to get one of his few glimpses into the workings of the inner man. "Besides, I think you will agree that you have enough public advisers as it is. I believe that I can be more useful to you and to the cause if I remain hidden in the shadows, unknown and unnamed."

Mao sighed now, gazing down at the landscape of his beloved China.

"We are in an untenable position," he said to Zilin. "We need outside help. The Soviets fear us. As you know, both Stalin and Molotov have called us 'margarine' Communists because I have not strictly followed Moscow's directives. Besides, they argue, a true Communist revolution comes about through the proletariat, not the peasants."

He grunted. "Our only hope is America. They are already here; they love to stick their noses into the internal affairs of other countries. I believe that our postwar industrialization should come about through free enterprise. They'll like that. They have money, far more than the Soviets . . . if we maneuver them properly I think we can get our capital from them. Toward that end I want you to spend time with this ambassador's aide of theirs, Ross Davies. He was a major once and, from what I hear, a good one. Speak to him of Sun Tzu. Maybe, though he is a foreign devil, he will recognize a kindred spirit through the Art of War.

"I understand Ambassador Hurley tells him everything. I want to know what President Roosevelt is thinking. I want to know whether he will back us."

Zilin held out no such hope for American aid. He knew that the Americans were very cleverly using Chiang as their cat's-paw in China simply because they could control him. They had no such illusions about Mao. "And what," Zilin said with this in mind, "will he do if a fire starts in China?"

"Let us set our minds," Mao said, "that there will be no fire."

But even if Mao had not had a specific mission for Zilin to accomplish he would not have wanted him at the bargaining table when he met with Chiang. Zilin's first wife, Mai, had been assistant to Sun Zhongshan—Dr. Sun Yat-sen. When, in 1925, Generalissimo Chiang broke with Sun's Guomindang, his strongarm men had returned to Shanghai, then the Guomindang's main base, and had destroyed them all.

Chiang's men had come for Mai in the night and had taken her away. Fearing for her safety, Zilin and Hu Hanmin had run after her and, confronting her abductors, Zilin had shot them down. But not before Mai herself had been killed.

Perhaps after all this time Chiang had forgotten the incident and the manhunt that had ensued. Mao did not know. But he was certain that he could not take the chance of the two coming face to face. He had, in fact, debated whether to take Zilin along with him at all. But in the end his need for the younger man outweighed the possible danger.

Zilin's first encounter with Ross Davies occurred early one morning. Zilin was in the midst of *tai chi chuan*. The air was very still. Although the sun had not yet crept above the rooftops, the air was already heavy with the day's moisture. Below, the river shone blue-white. Already sampans plied its currents. Somewhere down the narrow lane a cock crowed.

Davies had awoken in a cold sweat. Sitting up in bed he had tried to get oxygen into his lungs. He looked around. It was dawn but it was not cool. He had been in China for some time but he had been unable to grow accustomed to the climate. Summer was the worst for him; he sweated through his clothes even at night.

He rose and, dressing hurriedly, went outdoors. His tiny room seemed to be closing in on him. Wiping the sweat from his face, he heard the cock crowing and, in a moment, he became aware of Zilin at his exercises.

Davies had taken the book on Roman war tactics with him, intending to calm himself by reading beneath the shade of a tree. Now he stood in the dappled sunlight watching Zilin at his morning rituals.

It could not have been the first time that Davies had seen *tai chi* demonstrated but it was certainly the first time that he had seen it performed with such liquid, weightless grace.

This man was the only one of Mao's retinue on whom Hurley had not been able to get a military dossier. In fact, almost nothing was known about the man. Even his function within the Communist hierarchy and his relationship to Mao were unclear.

In the relative cool of the shade, Davies was sweating. He was a large man with an athlete's body that had not run to middle-age fat as many of his contemporaries' had, simply because Davies worked at it. He did forty-five minutes of strenuous calisthenics twice daily. Except during the summer in China when he found it too hot to do much of anything.

As he watched Zilin, he marveled. It was as if he had never seen the slow ritualized movements before. The man had no trouble breathing though he was in direct sunlight; Davies could discern not a bead of sweat anywhere on his exposed flesh.

At length, Zilin was done. He held the last position for what seemed to Davies an eternity. In the courtyard a breeze caught an eddy of dust, lifting it in a tiny devil at Zilin's feet. It was the only movement in the vicinity.

A dog barked and Zilin came out of what might have been a trance. He saw Davies standing on the doorstep, book in hand, and smiled.

"Good morning," Zilin said.

Davies nodded, somewhat embarrassed. He wondered whether he had transgressed. Two-and-a-half years in China and he was still unsure about customs. "I was struck by your early morning exercises. I hope you don't mind."

"Not at all." Zilin came across the courtyard to where Davies stood. "I don't mind company." He smiled as he had learned the foreign devil did. It put them at ease somehow, like animal signals. Zilin had read an account of the habits of the mountain gorillas of Africa. One approached them with eyes downcast and a neutral expression, to show that no aggressive intent was meant. Baring one's teeth on the other hand would surely bring instant attack.

Faan gwai loh, Zilin thought, foreign devil—they were much like gorillas: powerful and dangerous and primitive, and in dealing with them one had to make certain of their motivation if one were to make use of them.

"You speak English very well," Davies said, unaware of the condescension in his tone.

It is he who thinks of me as the monkey, Zilin thought. Ah, well, the civilized man must put up with all manner of boorishness in order to gain his ends with barbarian devils.

"I learned many years ago in Shanghai," Zilin said, as if

131

nothing were amiss. "A friend from Virginia was good enough to be my patient teacher." A white lie but an excusable one under the circumstances.

Davies's eyes lit up. "I'm from Virginia," he said. Which Zilin knew very well. "My family has a farm outside Roanoke. My father raises horses. Race horses. What is your friend's name?"

"Sawyer," Zilin said. "Barton Sawyer. His family, too, were farmers, though I don't believe they had anything to do with horses."

"I don't know the name," Davies said, obviously disappointed. "But Virginia's a big state and I haven't been home in some time. Since I was a young boy, actually."

Zilin, watching the expression softening Davies's features, thought, Well, at least some things remain universal. "You must miss Virginia as much as I miss Suzhou."

Davies gave a rueful smile and his face turned boyish. He had a wide, mobile mouth, clear blue eyes and the kind of straight patrician nose unheard of in Asia. His shock of curly reddish-blond hair covered the back of his neck in thoroughly unmilitary style. "I suppose I do." He took out a chased silver case, plucked out a cigarette. He offered one to Zilin, who politely refused. Davies struck a match. "I was once quite a fine equestrian—horseback rider."

Zilin suppressed the urge to grunt and hoot like an ape. Since he believes that I have a limited English vocabulary, he thought, I will not disabuse him of the notion. I may be able to make use of his ignorance in the future.

"Horses are something of an oddity in China," Zilin said. "I don't suppose there's been much chance to ride."

Davies laughed, blew out smoke. "Not a one."

"Well, perhaps there's a farm near here where we can find you"—he bit back the word *equis*—"a noble steed to ride."

"Really!" Davies came down off the steps, relinquishing his added height advantage. "That would be most welcome. Quite fantastic, really." He thought a moment, tapping ash off his cigarette. "Look here, Shi *tong zhi*, how would you like to learn how to ride?"

Not on your life, Zilin thought. With an inward shudder he imagined himself atop the gigantic creature. "That would be most interesting, Mr. Davies. I would like that."

Davies's blue eyes got shrewd—or, Zilin thought, in his case, as close as they could come to shrewd. "Look here, would you consider teaching me *tai chi chuan* in exchange for equestrian lessons?"

A decade of plagues on your horses, Zilin thought. "A most splendid idea, Mr. Davies. I would be most pleased to assist you on such a worthy journey. Shall we say tomorrow at five thirty?"

Davies swallowed. "In the morning?"

Zilin gave a little bow. "You learn quickly, sir."

Davies thrust out his huge hand. "You've got a deal." Grinning just like a gorilla.

In fact, Ross Davies proved an exceptionally quick study. While there was nothing fast about *tai chi*, the American was swift to pick up on the mental aspects of the discipline. This surprised Zilin somewhat since it had been his experience that most foreign devils failed completely to understand the philosophic nature of *tai chi*, relegating it to the province of old men and those too infirm to apply themselves to a "real" discipline involving speed, strength and stamina.

The fact was that *tai chi* required great strength and stamina, since to perform exercises slowly took far more control and agility than to run through positions by rote. As for speed, one had to have it in order to keep it in check, as one did in *tai chi*. Besides, the mind was at work here, which made it a far cry from army calisthenics.

Davies brought up this point to Zilin at the beginning of their second week of morning meetings. "I start to do my jumping jacks," he said, "and in this weather I'm overheated within a minute or two. With *tai chi*, we can work at it for over an hour and I'm still comfortable. Yet my body feels as if it has gotten as complete a workout as if I'd done my full complement of calisthenics."

"I don't know much about what you call calisthenics," Zilin said. "But I do know that the body and the mind must be made one. Exercising the one without the other makes little sense."

They were sitting on a bench in the courtyard, sipping tea.

"I sleep better since I've started *tai chi*. I smoke less," Davies said. "And here, look"—he drank back his tea—"I can put away hot tea in the summertime and not break out in a sweat. What do you make of that, Shi *tong zhi*?"

Zilin laughed. "That you're becoming Chinese."

He had made inquiries and had found them a farm. It was up near the slopes of Jinyun Shan, the Red Silk Mountain, where they harvested the area's fine Jinyun tea. Zilin supposed that was why the horse hadn't been killed and eaten. Here, because of the tonnage of the harvest, he was more valuable to the peasant family alive. Indeed, he was an excellent specimen, Davies assured Zilin on their first visit. He ate as well, if not better, than the family itself.

All the young men—there were five brothers—were off at war, leaving the father, who was close to Zilin's age, the mother and three daughters. Yes, indeed, that horse was important, their lone means of survival through the bleak years of the war. Up here on the fertile slopes of the *shan*, where multitudinous subtropical plants grew in riotous profusion, there were no mean seasons. The carefully cultivated tea grew strong and full, and in China there were always empty teacups to fill.

On their first visit, Zilin brought presents of fish and egg noodles, staples to a *faan gwai loh* such as Davies, but manna from heaven for the Pu family.

"Why don't you just give them some money?" Davies said. Prompting Zilin to think that, no matter how tempting, it is unproductive to believe that apes will ever be able to think.

To Davies's way of thinking there was an awful lot of bowing and palaver, considering these people were just a bunch of peasants. But he did what Zilin bade of him. These people may be peasants, he rationalized while on his knees, bowing, but they have a horse.

"This is some animal," he said sometime later, in the ramshackle structure that served as barn. He ran the flat of his hand across the animal's fetlock, feeling the long ropy muscles ripple beneath his palm. "I'm amazed they take such good care of him."

"Did you ever try to take a half ton of tea leaves down a mountainside on your back, Mr. Davies?"

Davies, continuing his assessment of the stallion, said, "I see what you mean."

"Accordingly, we must be extremely careful with this animal." Zilin made sure that he stood well away from the monster. He had no desire to be kicked in the head by this unthinking creature. "Without him, the Pus would most assuredly starve or work themselves to death first."

"No problem," Davies said, and with a startlingly swift motion, he vaulted onto the stallion's back. There was a soft whinnying and a certain amount of nervous stamping which, had Davies been more observant, he would have seen panicked the other man. Zilin clung to a beam as if it were a spar off a broken ship, clutched in a storm.

Davies was bent over the stallion's arched neck. His hands gentled the creature while he spoke directly into its ear in a soft, singsong whisper.

In a moment, the horse was still, save for the odd reflexive shiver running down one leg or another. Davies urged it forward by a method unclear to Zilin.

He followed Davies and the horse cautiously out. It was near midday, the time when the family traditionally rested from its labors and the intense heat. It was no accident that Zilin had picked this time to take Davies here. He never would have thought to interrupt the family's daily routine with such an idiotic request as to borrow their precious animal, for sport.

The girls had come out of the house to watch the hideously tall *faan gwai loh*. They giggled and stared and one of them asked Zilin why if the barbarian's hair was on fire he didn't burn up.

Zilin watched in fascination as Davies bent forward and the horse leapt ahead, galloping along the steepening slopes, racing in and out of the singing trees. Birds called, scattering away from the pair's progress. Zilin saw the white tail of a rabbit bounding out of their way in a terrified zigzag.

He heard an odd sound. The Pu girls heard it, too, for they had fallen silent. And then Zilin knew. Buddha protect me, he thought, the barbarian is laughing. For a long time after that, Ross Davies's cries of sheer delight echoed down the slopes of Jinyun Shan where no such sound had ever been heard before.

In time, Davies returned. He came back at a slower pace which, he informed Zilin later, was important, since the animal needed to walk off the sweat of his galloping pace.

Davies, red-cheeked and grinning from ear to ear, swung off the stallion and said, "Now it's your turn."

Zilin's bowels turned to water. "What?"

Davies cocked his head. "You don't think I've forgotten, do you, Shi *tong zhi*? If you taught me *tai chi*, I promised to teach you how to ride."

Is this my reward for living an honorable life? Zilin thought. "It is getting rather late," he said. "Perhaps another day."

"Nonsense!" Davies patted the horse's back. "It's easy. Here, you're not as tall as I am so I'll give you a hand up."

He laced his fingers tightly together and bent over. "Step right into there," he said. "Come on. You won't believe how much fun it can be."

"I don't know, Mr. Davies. The prospect seemed somehow more appealing back at Chungking."

"I understand," Davies said, his emotions so transparent Zilin could almost see the light bulb going on over his head. He swung back up on the stallion's back and leaned over. Before Zilin knew what was happening, he felt himself being pulled up behind the American.

"Just put your arms around my waist, Shi *tong zhi*," Davies said and dug his boot heels into the horse's flanks.

Oh, Buddha, this will never work! Zilin thought. Such physical contact in public was for him—as it was for all Chinese—something one did not even contemplate.

But as they lurched forward, he was almost thrown off, sliding backward along the creature's sweat-slick back, and he reached desperately out, seeing how far below him the ground was. Terrified of falling, he wrapped his arms tightly around the barbarian, closing his eyes and praying that none of his ancestors were awake and watching this humiliation.

He felt the rushing of the wind in his face and hair. He heard the thrumming of the horse's hooves, felt the complex coordination of muscle, bone and tendon as the great creature carried him along on its back.

He opened his eyes, and almost passed out, as the first wave of vertigo swept over him. The world rushed by in a blur of brown and green and blue.

The sense of rapid movement without a vehicle's intervening walls and floorboards turned Zilin's stomach upside down. As a child suffering with a high fever and uncontrollable shakes, he had vomited up the warm fish soup his mother had fed him. He had been old enough and aware enough through the gauzy layers of his illness to feel the shame at wasting the food that other members of the family had foregone for him.

Now, as he felt the nauseating contractions in his lower belly, he became terrified that he would do again as an adult what he had promised himself as a child he would never do a second time. His loss of face would be incalculable . . . and to a barbarian. It was unthinkable!

So he closed his eyes and prayed to Buddha to calm his tumbling innards enough to keep his gorge down. Toward this end as well he began to exert the power of his inner discipline. He concentrated on his inner core, seeking the place where his *qi* resided.

Zilin was not yet as well acquainted with the extraordinary power of his *qi* as he would be in the coming decades. It was still an essentially raw and primitive source over which he exerted only sporadic and limited control.

Now he made his connection to a place known as *shuijing ban de xiao-lu*, the crystal path. It was a place midway between the conscious and the unconscious mind, a place where contemplation could—with experience and practice—be transformed into action, deed, positive strategy. It was a shining field with a vantage point on the world akin to no other. From its heart one could discern the strategy of one's foes, formulate one's own strategy by assessing the whole rather than a series of disassociated pieces. Within the aura of *shuijing ban de xiao-lu* everything was seen to fit into everything else, the connections like glimmering skeins, illuminated by an inner-directed light. It was *qi*, intrinsic energy, but it was something more as well.

Without quite knowing how, Zilin reached out and gained the crystal path. Now he was no longer afraid. Rather, he was connected with the powerful beast beneath him; he could see it for what it was: a mighty engine.

He felt with all of his senses the superb coordination of this animal and its power became his. Zilin's eyes opened and his heart expanded to the elation such a swift passage through the world could bring.

High atop the galloping stallion Zilin embraced the streaming foliage all about him. He flew with the plovers and skylarks as they raced just above the treetops, below fleecy scudding clouds. He bounded through forest pathways, an animal on the move. He was one with the universe.

Much later, they rested in a glade beside a sparkling stream where water spiders skidded and frogs watched from the indolent shade of overhanging ferns. The buzzing of the insects was thick, the sound somehow applying itself to the honeyed sunlight, lending it a heavy, aqueous quality.

At their backs, giant Jinyun Shan, the Red Silk Mountain, rose on long, steeply sloping ridges, hairy with growth. The peculiar scent of the tea plants, young green shoots not yet ready for the harvest, laced the air.

The horse was gone, back at its mundane but crucial labor for the Pu family. Still, they smelled its essence on them, a rich musk that wafted like perfume from a row of jasmine.

Ross Davies pulled out his silver case, lit a cigarette. He squinted as he stared out into the deep golden light that lay along the slopes like a carpet. "One of these days," he said, "I must really give these up." He smoked leisurely, truly enjoying it; Zilin knew that he never would quit.

"How is it," Davies said, "that you never ask questions? I ask questions all the time; that's what I was taught to do. This cigarette case was a present from my father, a kind of graduation present. He was the first person who taught me to ask questions. How do you learn anything if you don't ask questions?"

"Perhaps," Zilin said gently, "there are other ways to learn." He watched an ant make its laborious way toward them. "I do so by observation."

"That's what I don't understand. In China, I've done my share of looking but I'm none the wiser for it. There are still so many things I can't fathom."

"That may be because you look but you do not observe. The two are hardly the same."

Davies sat up. "How d'you mean?"

Zilin pointed. "Take this ant, for example. What do you see?"

Davies shrugged, watching as the ant approached the line of his outstretched legs. It began to climb his trouser and he brushed it off. "All I see is an annoying insect."

"Now you must observe him, Mr. Davies. Watch him with your heart instead of with your eyes."

"I haven't the vaguest idea what you mean by that."

"If we were back in our courtyard at Number Fifty Zeng-jiayan, beginning our *tai chi*, you would not say that."

"Mental discipline is one thing—"

"Excuse me for interrupting, Mr. Davies," Zilin said, "but mental discipline is not merely for certain times in one's life. One does not turn it on and off like running water. Mental discipline must be employed at every moment if one is to take advantage of life."

"But what does that have to do with an ant?"

"You see how it comes back from the tremendous blow you have dealt it?" Davies nodded and Zilin continued. "Now it approaches the spot where it was defeated before. What does it do?"

"It climbs."

"Yes, Mr. Davies. And without hesitation. To the ant, you

are *shan*, the mountain. Imagine yourself climbing Jinyun Shan, Mr. Davies. Imagine further that you get to a certain spot and a storm of furious proportions throws you back down the mountainside. What will you do? Will you retreat? Or advance?"

"I'm a man, not an insect, Shi *tong zhi*," Davies said. "I possess the ability to reason. This creature merely knows that it must go forward, even if that means being killed by some unknown force." Here he reached out and, taking the ant between his thumb and forefinger, crushed it into dust.

"Ah, Mr. Davies," Zilin shook his head, "tell me how you can have so much love and compassion for the stallion you just rode, and yet have none for the ant you have destroyed."

"How can an ant be useful to me?" Davies said.

"I see. That is your criterion for life and death." Zilin stared at the American. "Tell me, then, Mr. Davies. Would you kill me if you found that I was not going to be useful to you?"

"Don't be ridiculous!"

Zilin rose. "It is not I who has been ridiculous, Mr. Davies." He began to walk off.

Davies jumped up, came after him. "I have offended you, Shi *tong zhi*," he said. "Please excuse me, though I confess I have no idea what I have done."

"That, I believe, is the heart of the matter." Zilin stopped and contemplated the other. "What is of concern to me is whether or not you can be made to learn."

Davies bridled visibly. "Like an animal."

"Or, to be blunt, a barbarian. Quite correct, Mr. Davies."

Davies blinked his large blue eyes. "I suppose I should be offended."

"Don't be. Most of my brethren believe that the *faan gwai loh* are without the ability to learn . . . that they can never become civilized."

"I see."

"No, Mr. Davies, I regret to say that you do not." Zilin sighed. "You speak without sufficient thought; you see without observing. In short, you go through life as if the world were your own private playground, taking this and that at will, at your own pleasure, as if there were no other consequences involved.

"You are here but this is not your land. You are an alien and you are unwanted. You are feared, hated, at times barely tolerated. I should not have to remind you of this. It is humiliating for both of us."

Davies's boyish cheeks were flaming red and there was a look of pain and hurt in his eyes. "Damn you," he said. He was shaking with rage. "You certainly are a bastard."

Zilin said nothing. His ears took in the sounds of the birds twittering, insects humming, the wind ruffling the treetops. These were sweet sounds; they were the sounds of life.

In time he said, "I meant what I said before. I think you can learn. I think, Mr. Davies, that you possess the ability to make your time in China constructive. This is, I believe, exceptionally rare in a Westerner, and I would give it the maximum amount of thought were I you."

"But you're not me, Shi." Davies's voice was strained with anger. He took out a sidearm from a hidden pocket. It was not particularly large but Zilin judged that its discharge would be lethal just the same. "You could never know what it's like to be me; to be Caucasian. You've got yellow skin and slanted eyes and you talk a bunch of nonsense—dangerous nonsense, if you go by what's said by some mighty powerful people back home."

He cocked the hammer of the gun. "I could kill you now just as easily as I killed that ant. How do you like that for power?"

Zilin shook his head. "What you present to me here is not power, Mr. Davies. It is force. The two are often confused and that is most often when lives are lost."

"Stupid talk!"

"Is that so? If you kill me, Mr. Davies, you are defeated. Why? Because you have lost me."

"On the contrary, Shi. I will have killed you, taken your life. I will have exerted my power over you in the ultimate fashion."

"No, you will have done nothing more than you accomplished with the ant. A useless—and far worse, a careless act. You will exert a tangible power over me if you protect me, keep me alive and become my friend. Then you will have recruited me to your cause or, at the very least, obtained an ally in times of trial. Then you will have acted with forethought and courage. So your strategy will be created."

For a long time the two stood facing one another. Between them the gleaming barrel of the pistol, the hammer cocked, as ready as an adder to strike. An ethereal stillness had come between them. For years afterward, Ross Davies would swear that he felt a tangible presence spring up in that glade on the lush slope of Jinyun Shan. He had, he would tell his drinking mates, been choked by rage and humiliation. He could admit to himself only much later that Zilin's words had struck him to the very core of his being. At the time, however, he only knew that he had been made to feel small and insignificant. All the anger he had been bottling up at his inability to puncture the tensile fabric of this strange and fascinating country had welled up, exploding in the face of Zilin's admonition.

It was most odd, Davies would think in years to come, just how close he had been to pulling the trigger. An army man, he knew well the draw of the killing urge and he felt it now as strongly as if a fire had been lit along the mountainside. The smoke he scented was the smell of his own ego being singed.

It was at this precise instant that the peculiar stillness crept over him. It was as if he felt the heartbeat of the earth upon which he stood rising up through him, entering his body by what means he knew not, suffusing his bloodstream.

He thought of *tai chi*, of the rivers of silver thought that, like strings from a master puppeteer's fingers, lifted leg and arm, turned torso and neck, locking him into the rhythms of the rising day.

In a moment, he blinked. He stared down at the weapon in his hand and, abruptly aghast at its portent, dropped it into the thick grass.

"What happened?"

It was night. Darkness crept along the slopes of Jinyun Shan as, hours before, sunlight had slid away before the blue of the lengthening shadows.

One of the Pu girls, the one who had asked about the fire in the *faan gwai loh*'s hair, had brought them food: a sharing of the gifts Zilin had given the family, and which they could not now refuse.

They had eaten in silence, concentrating on the workings of their mouths and the tastes of the food. It was only after they had put aside their bowls and chopsticks that Davies had spoken.

"There are some questions," Zilin said quietly, "that require no answers."

"But—"

"You must learn to accept mysteries, Mr. Davies. Often enough life does not enjoy giving up answers to its enigmas." He looked up. Through the inky blackness of the leaves the stars glittered in blue-white splendor. It had been some time, he realized, since he had seen such a sight. For far too long the starshine had been blurred and dimmed by the vapors of war.

"I will tell you a secret, Mr. Davies. It is a mystery how I enjoyed myself so much this afternoon."

"Did you really like riding?"

"I did, indeed."

The cicadas' clatter was magnified by the vast wall of the mountainside.

"They think you're the Devil incarnate, you know." Davies's voice seemed very close in the night, as if he were whispering in Zilin's ear. "In the Bible's Book of Revelations, it speaks of the Beast. According to Allan Dulles you are the Beast. You and Mao and all the rest of the Communists."

"Is Mr. Dulles the only one who thinks so?"

"Good God, no. A great many wealthy and influential people agree with him. Henry Luce, Bill Donovan, Henry Ford, the lot of them." Davies turned his head. "Do those names mean anything to you?"

"I believe they do, yes." Zilin pondered whether to ask the question. He felt the thunder of the horse still beneath him, his connection to it. His closeness to Ross Davies. And, of course, he thought of the stillness that had overcome both of them in the afternoon.

"And does President Roosevelt agree with these wealthy and influential people?"

"To be honest, I don't think it matters a good goddamn what Mr. Roosevelt thinks."

Zilin thought about this. It had been his opinion that the American president hated and feared Mao. "The President runs the country, does he not?"

"Ye-es," Davies said, "but only in some senses. Besides there being checks and balances built into our constitutional system of government, the President in a very real sense is subject to the pressures brought to bear on him."

Davies could not see Zilin nod in the darkness. "And of course the universal law is that the wealthier one is, the more pressure one is able to exert."

Ross Davies stirred beside Zilin. "I think, yes. You've caught the nature of the situation."

At their next meeting on the slope of Jinyun Shan, Davies was not alone. Zilin recognized an officer from Chiang's hierarchy. He said nothing, waiting to see what was on the American's mind.

"Shi *tong zhi*," Davies finally said, beginning the introductions, "this is Huaishan Han. A lieutenant colonel in the Nationalist army."

"And a confidant of Generalissimo Chiang," Zilin said. "I have heard of you." He gave a stiff little bow which was returned in much the same manner.

"Well," Davies said, rubbing his hands together, "shall we have lunch? I had our cook prepare something." His clear blue eyes darted from one man to the other as if waiting for the first bright spark to ignite. He set down a large wicker basket beneath the shade of a tree. The day was unusually stifling, the afternoon air somnolent and without breeze, weighing them all down.

Davies busied himself pulling out sandwiches, salads, condiments from God alone knew where, and a bottle of white wine.

"Are either of you hungry?" he asked hopefully. "I don't want all this food to go to waste."

Huaishan Han eyed the alien food. He was whip thin, with the kind of lower jaw one found among the Manchus and the peoples high up near the northern frontier. His ears were small, fitting close to his head. Through the bristle of his coarse hair could be seen the beginnings of the inkblot outline of a purple birthmark crawling along his scalp. Perhaps because of the dominance of his jawline, his nose and eyes seemed crowded into the upper portion of his face.

Davies, looking around after spreading out the repast, said, "Doesn't any of this appeal to you?"

"Sandwiches," Zilin said.

"There is no tea?" Huaishan Han said.

Clouds obscured the sun for a time; the glade seemed to lose dimension, some of its quietude rolling away down the slope. In the near distance, the men could see Mr. Pu with his stallion, loading him up as his daughters handed over bushel after bushel of harvested tea plants.

"Won't the wine do?" Davies popped the cork, extracted crystal goblets from the recesses of the wicker basket.

"I don't mind," Huaishan Han said, settling himself next to the American, "but I doubt whether our *comrade* here will be similarly inclined." He turned his head as Davies handed him the glass and, taking a sip, lifted the sparkling crystal in a mock toast. "You needn't bother with this wine, Comrade, you'll only choke on such elitist liquor." He nodded his head and the sprawling birthmark appeared in full. "There's a small brook we passed on the way up. The liquid of the earth is more fitting for a Communist to drink."

Zilin sat down on the other side of Davies. He wondered why the American had brought a member of Chiang's staff along. Very quickly he determined that there was nothing for him to do but observe. Attitude was all. The men's attitudes would reveal the answers to the puzzle.

Davies set a glass of wine before Zilin, having the good grace not to attempt to hand it to him.

Huaishan Han leaned forward. Liquor was glistening on his thin lips. "The wine is quite fine, Comrade," he said to Zilin, his voice slightly mocking. "Why not try it, after all? It, too, has its origins in the earth." He smiled, small even teeth showing like bits of patinaed ivory. "No matter that it is the drink of choice for capitalist captains of industry." He grunted. "But pardon me. I forgot that *industry* is a word you Communists know precious little about. I shudder to think what this country would come to if Mao gained power."

Zilin said, without a trace of rancor, "Without Communism, China is doomed to perpetual piecemeal warfare. Communism's cause is the only effective rallying point for the millions of peasants who comprise the bulk of our populace. Without the unity that Communism provides, China will remain weak, broken into shards through which the *faan gwai loh* will continue to pick like so many carrion-eaters."

Huaishan Han grunted in disgust.

"They are omnivores," Zilin went on, "the *faan gwai loh*. They have no sense of culture, propriety; no sense of the universality of nature. Without the bulwark of Communism to protect us, they will surely pick our bones clean. They will take out of China all that is prized and useful. Only then will they go, leaving a wasted hulk."

Huaishan Han said, "You are as good with words as is your god, Mao."

"My god is Buddha," Zilin said. "I would have thought that self-evident." He had picked up several slender shoots of bamboo. Now he pulled a folding knife from his pocket and commenced to make cuts here and there, bending the supple shoots in a complex pattern.

Davies, eating a triangle of sandwich, said, "What are you doing?"

"I am hungry," Zilin said. "I am doing something about

144

it." He rose and, reaching up, brought down a handful of hemplike vines. His hands moved in a blur, then he went off, disappearing into the underbrush.

Several minutes later he reappeared and came back to where he had been seated before. "I think," he said, "that I will have a bit of this wine now." He sipped it with slow deliberation, savoring it on his tongue and in his throat. "One does not often find such excellent wine in China these days."

"Listen to him," Huaishan Han said. "Does he sound the Communist now?"

"Politics follows the force of conviction," Zilin said. "It is those who are dogmatically righteous in life who are most often struck down."

"Conviction by its very nature is unbending," Huaishan Han pointed out.

"I speak of the conviction of purpose," Zilin said. "In maintaining the good of the people one discerns the elasticity of means. If we are dogmatic only, then we shall surely fail in our goal of protecting the people from poverty, ill health, foreign intervention."

Huaishan Han downed the last of his wine, asked for a refill. "My belly grows empty," he growled.

"There at least," Zilin said, "a Nationalist and a Communist may agree." He rose again and disappeared. When he returned from the underbrush, he was carrying a hare which had been caught in his homemade snare. "Lunch," he proclaimed, and, as he set about killing and skinning the creature, he said, "You see, Mr. Davies, the land must support its people. It is a universal law."

Davies brushed crumbs off his lap. "Didn't Buddha preach that killing—any killing—is wrong?" He opened his silver case, took out a cigarette. Huaishan Han took one as well. Davies put a match to both. "I have heard that priests will not even put a spade into the earth for fear of killing an insect or a worm," he said, drawing smoke into his lungs. "Is this true, Shi *tong zhi*?"

"It is," Zilin said, gutting the hare, "but I am not a priest. We all have our various functions on earth, Mr. Davies. Perhaps I am more like the fox than I would prefer to be. But the world, you will find, is an imperfect place at best. One must learn to accept what one is. Don't you agree?"

Without being asked to do so, Huaishan Han made a fire, first clearing a bare spot in the ground. In time, the two Chinese were roasting the beast on a rough-cut spit made of green branches. The fat crackled and hissed as it dropped into the fire and the aroma of roasting meat perfumed the air.

Davies could not find it in himself to indulge—he saw only the head with the dull glazed eyes staring blankly at him. He much preferred his tobacco.

Zilin and Huaishan Han shared the fragrant flesh, seeming totally absorbed in eating. Nothing more was said until they were done. Davies was astounded to see that nothing whatsoever was left over. Even the innards, wrapped and slow cooked in the embers while the flesh was consumed, were devoured at meal's end.

"Perhaps you've been wondering why I invited Huaishan Han along this afternoon," Ross Davies said.

Zilin said nothing. He had found that gratuitous responses were the province of the foolish.

"What we—that is he and I—would like to enquire is whether you would consider"—Davies cleared his throat; he seemed to be staring at the shiny tips of his boots—"coming over to, ah, our side."

Another man might have leapt up in indignation. An ideologue, a righteous man. Zilin contemplated these two men and wondered what about this situation was wrong. There was an inconsistency, a sense that whatever strategy was on display here was subtly out of kilter.

"By 'our side,' " Zilin said carefully, "I take it you mean the Nationalist cause."

"It is the American cause as well," Davies said.

Zilin nodded. "Yes, Mr. Davies, we have already been made abundantly aware of your patriotism."

Davies looked sheepish. "It shows that much, huh?"

"Like a shining beacon in the darkest night," Zilin said with more than a trace of humor. "But there is something refreshing in your transparency. I hope that, at least, will not be ravaged by war and time."

"All this banter may be very amusing," Huaishan Han said, "but you have not answered our question, Comrade."

Zilin looked directly into Huaishan Han's dark eyes. "That is because I did not take it seriously. Besides, I do not for a moment believe that it was 'our' question at all. Mr. Davies would know better than to ask something so fatuous of me." But already Zilin was aware of the tension that had come into Huaishan Han's frame, the intensity building, and he thought, What is it that I am missing here?

146

"This is not a joke, Comrade," the other Chinese said, switching to Mandarin. "It is a matter of some urgency for us to elicit a true response from you."

"But my dear sir," Zilin said in the same dialect, "you have already gotten it. I would no more contemplate joining the Nationalist forces than I would think about taking my own life. All of China hangs in the balance. Her future and her well-being is of the utmost importance to me. You are not asking me to betray Mao *tong zhi* but rather China itself."

Huaishan Han, who had been studying Zilin during all of this, gave a quick decisive nod. But, oddly, it was directed at Ross Davies.

"Well," Davies said, beginning to gather up the leavings of their lunch, "I believe it is time we returned to Chungking."

Deep in the night, Zilin was caught in a dream. The spirits of those Chinese who had died at the hands of the *faan gwai loh* wailed, speaking to him in tongues long lost. A rhythmic tattoo.

Rain beating against the window of his room. The same sound as the gossamer sheets of his dream, shredding. The bamboo shutters rattled. A shadow beside them. Long, angular, rising along the edge of the closed door. A shadow that should not have been there.

Zilin set his breathing, deepening it, returning to the crystal path, *shuijing ban de xiao-lu*, in order to determine the identity of the anomaly in the room.

Now he could hear the breathing, his and another's, through the other sound of nature: the storm. Another brief flicker and then the thunder crashing heavily, rolling across the heavens.

He had been looking at the right place at the right time. The crystal path had shown him the way. Huaishan Han was in his room!

Zilin remembered the Nationalist's tension, the intensity in his eyes. *This is not a joke, Comrade. It is a matter of some urgency for us to elicit a true response from you.* He remembered, too, the pistol that Davies, this man's ally, had leveled at him.

Slipped out of bed, his mind prepared for battle. He had no intention of attacking; but he knew that he would defend himself to the death.

"Shi *tong zhi*."

Rain like a mailed fist.

147

"Shi *tong zhi*!"

Rattling the shutters angrily.

"I am here." After he spoke, he moved to another place in the room, but the Nationalist made no aggressive move.

"I must speak with you."

"You choose an odd and mannerless method."

"No more mannerless than the war within which we find ourselves."

"True," Zilin acknowledged. "Speak your piece. I will turn on the lamp."

"No!"

Zilin was stopped by the urgency of the voice.

"I beg you make no light here. There must be no hint at all that I have made this visit."

"Huaishan Han," Zilin said carefully, "you will pardon my skepticism, but you are a rabid Nationalist; you made that absolutely clear yesterday afternoon. Further, you have sought to recruit me, to turn me into a traitor to the cause for which I have sacrificed everything in life. In short, you are my enemy. Tell me, then, if you can, why I should not report your actions at once, to my superiors and yours."

"Because," Huaishan Han said in his reedy whisper, "my superiors have you marked for death."

In the eerie silence that followed, thunder rumbled, at some distance to them.

"Explain yourself."

"As best I can," Huaishan Han said. "But you must promise to keep the lights off."

"All right."

"Somehow Chiang caught a glimpse of you."

Zilin's heart picked up, his pulse thrumming.

"He still remembers the murders of his men by a man who was married to Sun Zhongshan's assistant. He still remembers the manhunt he directed; he still remembers its fruitless end. Now he has marked you. He will kill you here."

"Nonsense," Zilin said with a good deal more confidence than he felt. "This is politics. The whole of China is at stake. If Chiang and Mao can come to terms, the coalition—"

"There will be no coalition," Huaishan Han hissed. "That I can guarantee you."

"Then what is the reason for this summit meeting?"

"From the Generalissimo's point of view, it is merely to placate the Americans and the Russians who have been pressuring him to negotiate. The Chinese people as well, if it comes to that. They are weary of war. But I can guarantee you, Shi *tong zhi*, that Chiang's mind was made up before you and your contingent ever set foot in Chungking. It is a victory for him to have the 'great Mao' come humbly into his domain to sue for peace." Huaishan Han shook his head. "But a coalition is out of the question. Chiang plans to procrastinate here, then blame the breakdown of talks on the intractability of the Communist position. Then he will take his army and smash you."

Zilin was stunned, because this was what he had believed Chiang would do all along. Mao knew this but still he refused to believe it. Zilin did not believe in this mythical coalition and now, it seemed, neither did Chiang. If Huaishan Han was telling the truth.

"There is no reason why I should believe any of this," Zilin said. "You are my enemy. After what happened yesterday."

"That's just it," the Nationalist said. "You are not yet aware of what really transpired at lunch. I had no intention of recruiting you, Shi *tong zhi*, merely of getting to the heart of you—of your conviction. I wanted to know beyond all doubt whom I was dealing with.

"Davies had told me that I could trust you but I didn't fully believe him. He is a *faan gwai loh*, after all, no? And what do barbarians know of Chinese?"

"So you decided to see for yourself." The pieces were beginning to fit together.

"That's right," Huaishan Han said. "That is why I baited you, why I tried to recruit you. Now I know that your heart is pure. Now I am certain that I can trust you."

"Trust me? What for?"

"It is I who wishes to be recruited, Shi *tong zhi*. I cannot stand Chiang or his militaristic ideas. His mind is filled with the glories of war—the supposed glories. He believes only in the army. For him it is the end and the beginning. About the people he cares scarcely at all."

"So you wish to be a Communist."

"I wish the best future for my country. I know that Chiang will not be able to deliver it."

"Of course you told Ross Davies all this when you approached him to be the go-between."

"Absolutely not," Huaishan Han said indignantly. "Do you take me for a fool? What I told him was that I wished by informal means to advance the prospects of the coalition. 'Perhaps,' I told him, 'if I approach one of Mao's advisers

149

and we begin negotiations on a sub-rosa level, we can speed up the process.' "

"And he believed that?"

"Why not? You know Davies as well as I do. That notion is one that has great appeal to him. He had to comply, you see. It was the patriotic thing to do."

Zilin laughed. "Yes, yes. The patriotic thing."

"The best quality of the noble savage," Huaishan Han said.

"He's not a bad sort, Davies," Zilin said. "For a *faan gwai loh*."

Huaishan Han moved into the room. "I shall help you pack," he said. "Together we shall flee northward, out of the stronghold of the Generalissimo."

"No," Zilin said. "That will solve nothing. And your defection will create a major problem for Mao. We must think of a better solution."

"Solution?" Huaishan Han echoed. "How can you think of such a thing when you may be killed at any moment!"

"Calm yourself, Comrade," Zilin said. "Chiang will not have someone creep into my room at night and slit my throat. He could ill afford such a scandal. If what you have just told me is true he desperately needs to emerge from this stalemate with clean hands. The Americans, at least, will insist on it as a stipulation for their continued support. And without the Americans, Chiang is lost. So, Chiang will take his time. He knows that as long as Mao is here I'm not going anywhere. It must be made to look like an accident. No culpability must be able to be traced back to the Nationalist camp."

"Yes, yes, I see that," Huaishan Han said. "But still . . ."

"Patience, my new comrade. Patience. We will find a way."

In the morning Zilin did not feel quite so confident. For one thing, Ross Davies did not show up for his *tai chi* lesson. This was the first time that had happened since he and Zilin had made their pact and it was a potentially ominous sign. Though Zilin did not relish jumping to conclusions it was no secret that he did his exercises every morning at this spot at this time. Further, if Chiang wished to assassinate Zilin he certainly would not want an American as a witness. Some reason could easily be found to keep Davies away from the killing ground.

To add to his anxiety, Zilin had found upon arising that Mao and his negotiating contingent had already left for their daily session, though it was barely six o'clock. Zilin could not even report the information he had received from Huaishan Han. On Zilin's suggestion, Han would remain in place until he received an appropriate signal. Zilin had assured Han that he would be of more use to Mao for the moment right where he was inside Chiang's camp.

The dawning day was still. The ground of the courtyard was wet from the night's drenching. No cock crowed, no dog barked. The heavens were obscured by a thick and unremitting layer of zinc clouds.

Zilin began his exercises with only half his mind attuned to the moves. His senses were questing outward, beyond the walls of the courtyard, for any alien sound. He kept one eye on the arched doorway to the street.

As he worked, he felt the short hairs at the back of his neck rise. His skin felt charged with electricity. He could almost feel the barrel of a long gun swinging in his direction, the sniperscope zeroing in on the back of his head. The steel-jacketed bullet whirring toward him, the tiny sound increasing to a buzz just before the point buried itself in his skull.

Movement!

With an effort, Zilin restrained himself from turning his head. He continued with his exercises, trying to calm his tautened nerves.

Used his eyes to discern if the movement he had picked up at the periphery of his vision was real or imagined, an actual threat or a bird flitting off a branch.

A small movement, yes.

The door!

It began, after a moment's hesitation, to swing inward. Zilin ran silently on the balls of his feet from his position in the center of the courtyard to a spot just behind the door.

All was still, as if whoever was on the other side of the door was taking a long look into the courtyard to determine his whereabouts. His breathing was controlled but he found himself sweating, and he recalled Davies's remark to him, *With tai chi we can work at it for over an hour and I'm still comfortable.*

The sweat scrolled off Zilin; he realized that he was afraid. He did not want to die. The urge to live rose up inside him like a kite, and he found the anger that would keep him alive—the anger at someone who would seek to destroy him. Without that anger, Zilin knew that he could not take another human being's life.

The gate, only an inch or two in front of him, began to

tremble, then open very slowly. Zilin's skin crawled at the thought of Chiang's discovery, at what the Generalissimo would do to him.

Now he could detect the presence of someone on the other side of the door. There was motion and, beyond that, intent. Whoever it was was entering the courtyard and Zilin knew that his time had come. It was kill or be killed, he knew that very well. He had killed before, Chiang's men to be exact, in order to save his wife Mai. He had had no choice.

No choice now either, but he thought of Buddha and his teachings. In that, at least, Davies had not been wrong. Or naïve.

Movement began in a headlong rush; he was given no more time. Thought ceased and action took over, the organism seeking to protect itself at all costs.

The blur of a figure on the run. Zilin lunged out from his hiding place, arms wrapped, his strength combining with his momentum to bring them both down. His arm was raised to deliver the killing *atemi* when the image filling his eyes registered on his brain.

His arm came down and the heavy shudder of the excess adrenaline moving about with no release went through him. The anger was gone.

"What are you doing here?"

She thought he was angry with her and she began to cry. It was Pu's daughter, the one who had seen the fire in Ross Davies's hair.

It was not good and Zilin knew that it was not going to get any better.

The horse had stumbled. Perhaps its load had been too heavy or his hoof had caught in a root or a rock fissure. It didn't really matter, that part.

What mattered was that a thousand pounds of dead weight had come crashing down on Mr. Pu. The horse's leg had fractured on impact, of course. Zilin determined that Mr. Pu's lower intestines and spleen had been ruptured. He had drowned in his own blood.

In the meantime, the horse went on suffering. With his broken leg, he would be of no use to the Pus now except as table meat. But Zilin had to do something about the animal's pain.

He thought of Ross Davies and his wild, exultant cries as his hands slid over the horse's sweat-soaked hide. He thought of his own wild rush at freedom astride this animal's strong back. He found the nerve juncture and pressed inward with a short sharp jab, so that the light went out of those wildly rolling eyes.

The girls were weeping openly but their mother remained stone-faced. Her stoicism reminded Zilin of the countless faces of war victims he had observed, empty-eyed and empty-hearted. He wondered whether in these pragmatic times the old woman mourned the loss of her husband or her horse the most. Without Mr. Pu they would go on, at the very least survive. But the death of the horse was another matter entirely.

"We have not even the money to pay for a proper funeral," Mrs. Pu said later. Her voice was as thin as the wind outside.

Zilin and the girls had stayed behind to butcher the animal since its flesh needed to be eaten fresh. The old man lay where he had fallen, covered in black, clotted blood and a shower of tea leaves.

"What will become of his spirit if it is not properly ushered into the next life?"

She spoke not to any one person, though Zilin and her daughters sat beside her, but to the house as a whole. It was as if she felt the spirit of her dead husband still inhabiting the rude rafters and floorboards, and she expected the answers to emanate from there.

Zilin had gotten the idea while he was working shoulder to shoulder with the Pu girls on the horse. He had said nothing, but rather had begun to turn it over in his mind like a rare and fascinating jewel that needed to be observed from every angle.

It was a daring idea—more than that, in fact, it was crazy. But, then, he told himself, these were crazy times. And, of course, there was a kind of Buddhist symmetry to it, a balancing of loss and gain that was appealing to that part of him that demanded a final accounting between what was right and what was wrong.

As he watched the pale light flow across Mrs. Pu's face, as he absorbed a portion of the anguish that racked her, he thought of what he was about to ask. Did he dare? But he knew that the question was, rather, dare he not?

Strictly speaking, what he would ask of her was morally wrong according to the tenets of Buddhism. But China was at war; survival was the goal, at least for the short range until

153

conditions improved. And survival was precisely what Zilin would be offering the Pus. Survival in exchange for . . .

"Madam," he said, leaning forward so that he would not have to raise his voice. There was no point in getting the girls involved at this point. "I know a way that you may ensure that your husband's spirit will be properly escorted to the next life."

Her head came up. She brushed strands of prematurely gray hair out of her eyes. She had been weeping silent tears, her head bowed so that her daughters would not see. There was nothing, Zilin saw, tired about her eyes. They held his with a feverish intensity. Hers was a hard life. This fact had long ago ceased to disturb her. She had accepted her *joss* with the absolute faith of her forebears. It was the way; the only way.

"Our loss is great, Shi *tong zhi*," she said. "But you have already done more for us than I could have asked or even have imagined. It is wrong to ask more of you."

"On the contrary, madam," he said carefully, "it is I who now must ask of you a terrible favor. I have it in my power to grant your wishes. I can provide the proper funeral for your late husband. I can, further, provide your family with another horse."

Mrs. Pu said nothing, though she had ceased to weep. Her wise eyes searched his face. At last she said, "The war is universal in the pain it inflicts, *neh*?"

Zilin bowed his head in acquiescence.

"We must survive, Shi *tong zhi*," she said with a voice grown stronger. "No matter the cost. If you can ensure that, then I and my daughters will be in your debt for all time, this I pledge to you."

Zilin knew that it was he who was in her debt but he was intelligent enough not to argue. "I wish to tell you what it is I require before you give your consent."

Her eyes narrowed momentarily. "You will not take my daughters from me?"

"Never, madam."

"I thought not." She settled herself like a bird upon its perch. "I know you, Shi *tong zhi*. I have observed your heart. That is not your way." She nodded gravely. "Do as you will, then. We shall survive. Tragedy will not break us, though we bend like the supple bamboo."

"I wish you to know."

She shrugged. *"Joss."*
Zilin nodded. *"Joss."*

"You are insane," Huaishan Han said. "Absolutely insane."

"Why?" Zilin said. "Because I want to die?"

Huaishan Han snorted. "You'll never get away with it."

"With your help, I will."

"Impossible!"

Zilin had sent one of the girls into Chungking with a message for Huaishan Han. He did not arrive until well after dark. His face was pale and drawn. "Buddha," he said a bit breathlessly, "when you disappeared from town, I feared the worst. What has happened?"

Zilin told him. Then he began to explain about his plan. "Now," he said, leading Huaishan Han out of the farmhouse, "I will demonstrate why it is not impossible."

He had built several small fires around the periphery of the area where Mr. Pu still lay. He had not wanted to move the body but something had to be done to keep the animals at bay.

"Look," Zilin said, taking Han inside the circle of fire. "We are of approximately the same age. Our height and weight vary only slightly, certainly not enough for anyone to notice."

Huaishan Han grunted. "You don't look much alike."

"True enough," Zilin said. "But when we get through with him, that won't matter."

Huaishan Han turned to stare at Zilin. "You're mad."

"On the contrary, I have found the path out of the dilemma Chiang has put me in. It is quite simple, really. My death will put an end to everything. Chiang's vendetta will be nothing more than a whiff of smoke."

"How did you think of such a thing?"

"This man is dead," Zilin said. "I did not wish it but it is so. His family has nothing. Without a horse who knows what will happen to them. For the loan of this husk from which the spirit has already departed, I will give them that which they need in order to carry on."

"Tell me something, Comrade with the pure heart," Huaishan Han said with an edge to his voice, "what would you have done if Mrs. Pu had said no? Would you have allowed them to starve?"

"I would have done precisely what I am doing now. I would

155

have assured Mr. Pu of a fine burial; I would have found them another horse. There really is no other way."

Huaishan Han regarded him for some time. The crackling of the fires lit up the night, the smell of woodsmoke almost drowned out the sickly sweet smell of death.

"I think Mrs. Pu was aware of all this," Zilin said. "But her indebtedness to me precluded her turning me down. As long as she knew I wasn't planning to take away her daughters, she was willing to comply. The exchange satisfied her sense of debt as well."

Huaishan Han looked away, down toward the corpse. He leaned down, picked up a stiffened arm. He turned the hand over so that it faced him palm up. "The face we can disfigure," he said. "But what about these." He brandished the hand, thick and yellowed with peasant's callus.

Zilin laughed and held out his own hands for inspection. Their heavy layer of callus shone with the translucence of ivory. "You forget, Comrade, that I am a true revolutionary. I worked long years in the fields with the peasants. I am one of them, as all Communists should be.

"When we exchange clothes, when we set my ring upon his finger, when we've set the accident and it is you who finds the body, I will be pronounced dead, all right. Of that I am certain."

And it was as Zilin had said. No major inquiry was held, at Mao's request. The body of Zilin, found along the slopes of Jinyun Shan, at the foot of a long drop off the roadside, provided no ominous overtones. It was obvious to everyone that he had been walking at night and had been struck either by a vehicle or a large animal and had been pitched over the side of the cliff. Regrettable, certainly, but hardly suspicious. *Joss*.

At Mao's express wishes, Huaishan Han remained in place within Generalissimo Chiang's inner circle. And the wealth of information he provided Mao was to a large part—at least in Zilin's opinion—the tide that turned fortune toward the Communists.

Mao stayed on in Chungking until almost the middle of October of 1945. Even though he knew from Zilin that Chiang had no intention of entering into a binding coalition agreement, still his sense of duty and, Zilin supposed, propriety, dictated that he remain.

In the fall, Mao left Chu Enlai to continue the fruitless

negotiations, though this was little more than a sop to the insistent but increasingly frustrated Ambassador Hurley.

Returning to Yunnan, Mao set up his council of war. The Russians had at last entered the war against Japan, Stalin's keen nose scenting the kill. Divisions of the Soviet army penetrated south into Manchuria, wiping out the Japanese units as they went.

This was of paramount concern to Mao, whose greatest fear at the moment was that Chiang's Nationalist army would be allowed by the Americans to take over the so-called liberated zones as the Japanese divisions were defeated. There was, Mao knew well, a wealth of war ordnance and matériel that could be of incalculable assistance to his ill-equipped army. He shuddered to think of what would happen if the Nationalists gained the strength of that hardware and put it to use against his forces.

This fear he made manifest to Zilin who, alone of all his advisers, he was candid with. "Chiang has the superiority of number," Mao said, one bleak, rain-filled day near the end of the year. "He has the backing of both the Americans and the Russians. His is the government recognized by the world. He has the power now, I fear, to destroy us utterly."

Zilin, standing against the stone wall of the cave they had made their headquarters, said, "That Chiang's troops outnumber ours will not figure in the outcome of this conflict."

Mao, sitting cross-legged on a rug that had been spread along the floor, regarded his most trusted adviser. "Please continue, Comrade."

Zilin closed his eyes, put his head back against the cool stone. Outside, the rain was a gray-green sheet, obscuring the countryside.

"Sun Tzu has said, Mao *tong zhi*, that though the enemy may be as multitudinous as stars, if he does not know your military situation he will not know how to prepare for your coming.

"We must change our strategy. Chiang will become confused, for by now he feels that he has divined our purpose. That much Han has assured me.

"If you further disturb his regular military patterns with unannounced forays into his territory, it will increase his confusion. If you then follow a secret strategy—a strategy known only to ourselves, and not even to the generals of our armies— then truly you can say that you are the creator of this most important Communist victory."

For a long time, Mao said nothing. He rose and began to pace the cave. "Manchuria is the key," he said finally. "I can feel it. Manchuria is the key to Chiang's victory. That is why he has been so insistent about it in the negotiations. If we can trap him there, then we will have a victory."

Zilin's eyes were still closed. "To that end, then, Mao *tong zhi*, let us commit ourselves heavily to Manchuria."

"Yes."

"Let us draw Chiang northward into Manchuria. Let us create for ourselves a memorable defeat in Manchuria."

"What?" Mao stood stock still.

"Yes," Zilin said. "Yes. Let us show our strategy to Chiang. We will mass an army at a city crucial to the taking of Manchuria. Which one?"

Mao, fascinated despite himself, said, "Ssuping would do nicely."

"Let it be Ssuping," Zilin said, nodding. He opened his eyes. "It will mean great loss of life, I am afraid. But from this defeat, Chiang will surely believe that he has gotten a feel for us. His superior strength will work against him." Zilin outlined his plan.

In May of 1946, the Communist army suffered heavy losses in its defeat at Ssuping. Two months later, Mao declared that his forces were henceforth to be known as the People's Liberation Army.

Now, Mao gave orders that his army abandon all cities in Manchuria that could not be guarded by a minimum force. The majority of the People's Liberation Army began their new life as a guerrilla force, highly mobile attack units.

Chiang, puffed up by what he thought was a decisive victory at Ssuping, viewed the PLA change in strategy as another victory for his Nationalist cause. Accordingly, he directed massive numbers of divisions to move into the Manchurian towns left behind by—in his opinion—the fleeing Communist forces.

Added to this, in the spring of 1947, Chiang, buoyed by his successes in Manchuria, began a furious offensive strike against the Communist forces. As Mao's armies split apart, as Mao and his advisers took to the hills of Yunnan, Chiang's mind was filled more and more with the glittering prize of ultimate victory.

To this end, he ordered more and more cities taken and

garrisoned in the enormous spaces of Manchuria. Until, as Zilin had predicted, his forces were badly overextended.

Cued by Han, Mao's People's Liberation Army now began their first serious counterattack. Months long and unremitting, it began to have its effect. Within nine months, Peng Tehuai, the Communist field commander, had defeated the Nationalist army at Sian. This effectively cut off Chiang's potential line of retreat from Yunnan. Now, the Communist forces drove inward from two sides for the killing blow.

The Americans poured advisers and money in ever increasing numbers on the Nationalist side. The worse the situation became, the more terrified they were, the more money they spent.

Months before, Major General David Barr had pleaded with Chiang to abandon his positions in Manchuria. Mao had left only skeleton divisions in Manchuria but, acting on his directives, they recruited the remnants—three hundred thousand strong—of the Manchurian "puppet" army of Manchurian Chinese used by the Japanese and left behind after their defeat in the war, and the Russians' subsequent withdrawal. Now the PLA was strong in the north without having had to sacrifice divisions in the south.

But Chiang, abetted by some of his advisers—among them Han—refused to abandon so vital an area. General Barr was, after all, a *faan gwai loh*. He could not be expected to understand the historical imperative of gaining control of Manchuria.

In November of 1948, the Communist army, under the overall leadership of Chen Yi, commenced an offensive of immense proportions in the central eastern provinces. Fully half a million Nationalist soldiers were annihilated in just three short months.

Now Chiang was ready to sue for peace. But the march to liberation had begun and not the Generalissimo or the monied Americans or the truculent Soviets could stand in the way of the massive dreadnought created out of intervention, bitter hatred and despair.

In April, Mao's forces had captured Nanking. By the autumn, complete victory was theirs. On October 1, 1949, in Peking, the People's Republic of China was born.

Mao—Chairman Mao—how he was hailed on that day! As for the man who walked at the end of the line, cast in shadow, few knew his face and none knew his name.

II

EMPTINESS
SAMVARTASIDDHA

When he had heard the machine-gun fire and had seen Neon Chow running back from where Jake had pushed off in the *walla-walla*, Three Oaths had run back down the wharf to call the police. He had already determined that the gunfire had emanated from his junk, and he steeled himself for the worst.

His third cousin worked the night shift as desk sergeant at Aberdeen and so the response to Three Oaths's call was quick. Three Oaths accompanied the four officers on the police launch as they threaded their way through the floating city.

Three Oaths stood, fidgeting, near the bow of the launch while just behind him the officers checked and rechecked their weaponry in much the same professional manner as had the three Japanese members of the *dantai* some time before.

The rain stippled the dark water, drummed against the hulls of the junks and launches. Three Oaths wiped it from his eyes. He saw Jake sitting hunched over a long shape shrouded in shadow as they boarded.

"Stay here," one of the officers hissed as Three Oaths identified Jake; he had already given them descriptions of the three family members he knew to be on board: Jake, Bliss and Zilin.

"Bliss!" Three Oaths fell to his knees as he recognized the supine shadow Jake clutched to him. "Oh! My *bou-sehk*." His trembling hands reached out to brush the slickened hair away from her face. His fingers came away bloody.

"Jake," he whispered. "Jake!"

"She needs a hospital, Elder Uncle." Jake's face was pale. His hooded copper eyes, normally so filled with inner fire, were colorless.

"Are you all right, Younger Nephew?"

"Yes." It was a whisper.

163

"And the Jian?"

Jake blinked. "My father," he began. His eyes stared at Three Oaths. "My father's life is ended."

"Ah, evil gods that foresaw this day!" Three Oaths' hands reached out again for his adopted daughter. It was an instinctive gesture, but no less important for that. The family had been diminished; now each member was that much more precious to him. "Did you see them, Jake? The assassins?"

Jake nodded. "I found them belowdecks. There were three of them. The damage they did was with Gion 30-09 machine pistols." He shook his head. "They were very good. Very professional. A *dantai*, I think."

How could he tell his uncle about his loss of *ba-mahk*? How could he explain the unexplainable? How could he express the burden of guilt weighing him down? He believed *ba-mahk* would have alerted him to the assassination attempt. It would have, at the very least, allowed him to dispatch the three assassins before they had a chance to hurt Bliss. He held her tighter.

"A hospital, Elder Uncle," he said. "We must get her to hospital."

"The police launch is here. They'll take her as quickly as can be managed." He raised his head as the police officers reappeared from out of the hatchways fore and aft.

"Three men dead," one of the officers said. Another was busy scribbling in a notebook. "Lots of blood. Place is pretty well broken up. Looks like machine guns were used all over belowdecks. Like a hurricane."

"Three men?" Three Oaths repeated. "Who?" The officers stared at him blankly and he returned his gaze to Jake. "Who were they?"

"We'll have to wait for that," the officer said. "We found nothing on their bodies that would be useful for identification purposes."

All gods great and small, Three Oaths thought. What am I doing standing here talking to these corrupt sons of idiot sea slugs? They know nothing and, even if they did, would tell me nothing. He stood, trying desperately to bring his emotions under control. "My daughter is in desperate need of medical attention, officer," he said in a brisk, businesslike tone. "If you will be good enough to take her to a hospital."

"What do you know about this incident, sir?" the officer with the pad said.

"Nothing," Three Oaths said. "What could I know? Nothing at all. Why do you ask me such an inane question?"

"Purely form, sir," one of the officers said. "We'll have to talk to your nephew. And to your daughter."

"Please," Three Oaths said. "That can all be done in the morning. Right now my daughter is unconscious. I have no idea how badly she is injured. My nephew is in shock. You have my word that everyone involved will give full and complete statements. But right now . . ."

The officer in charge looked from Jake to Bliss, and nodded. "All right." He gestured. "Take her up, boys. That's right. Easy now, easy. Watch her head there." He watched as they took Bliss down to the launch. He stepped up close to Three Oaths. "I should caution you not to disturb or touch anything on board until the forensic men from Special Branch arrive. Also, the coroner's people are on their way. You'll give them free access."

"Yes, of course."

The officer looked away. The searchlight on the launch silvered his wide Cantonese face. "My condolences. This is bad. Very bad indeed." He took a breath. Fumes from the launch's engines plumed upward hanging in the heavy night air. "Does your nephew require medical attention as well?"

"I'll take care of him," Three Oaths said. "Please see to my daughter."

The officer touched his cap; he was waiting for Three Oaths and Jake to move. Then he swung down onto the launch, the engine pitched downward as they cast off, and in a moment they were slicing the night.

"This really takes me back. There was a time when I couldn't afford any of these."

Tony Simbal looked at the paintings, displayed in their ornate gilt frames.

"This is the one."

It was a particularly aggressive Cezanne, the artist's palette knife slathering thick streams of pigment that took on a demented, almost physical aspect. Simbal did not understand it at all, nor did he like it.

"The thing that attracts me most to Cezanne," Max Threnody said, "is his treading on the brink of anarchy. To create an entire universe that is so chaotic, yet so well ordered, is extraordinary, don't you think?"

Threnody made some notes in the booklet he had been

given when he had registered at the auction house on Wisconsin Avenue. "Didn't see much of you at the party the other night."

"Monica and I got to dredging up old times."

Threnody snapped the booklet shut and grinned. "Is that why my coat room was off limits for an hour or so?"

"I guess so."

"Let's get a seat, shall we?" They moved off to the bidding hall, where rows of gray metal folding chairs had been set up. The place was perhaps a quarter full.

"It didn't end well, I take it."

"It didn't end at all." The place was filling up fast. Threnody had been right to want to take seats.

"I suppose Monica told you that I was asking about Peter Curran," Simbal said.

Threnody opened his booklet, made some more notes. "Why would you think that Monica would tell me anything?" Threnody asked. "But now that you've brought it up, in your own clumsy way—I think we've got a problem."

Later, after he had missed buying the Cezanne when the bidding went unexpectedly high, they began to walk west, down toward the water. The afternoon was overcast, heavy for a late winter day. The wind off the Potomac was as cutting as it had been when snow had blanketed the city and people had been skidding on the ice.

Threnody, who wore an old loden coat more suitable for a student at nearby George Washington University, tucked his head down, like a turtle. "Now what's this sudden interest in Peter Curran?" he asked.

"You said before that you thought we had a problem. What kind of problem? Is it with Curran?"

"I wish," Max Threnody said, "that we could stop fencing."

"I don't work for you anymore, Max. The DEA no longer controls me."

"Yet here we are, together again. How do you explain that?"

Simbal relented. "I need information."

They had reached Virginia Avenue. They began to follow it northwest.

"If you don't come clean with me," Threnody said, "I don't see how I can help you. You know you can't con information out of me. And without access to the DEA computer you wouldn't be able to—" He broke off abruptly. "Monica. The party." He nodded his narrow head. "I gave you the perfect opening, didn't I. I must be getting old."

"The thought had occurred to me," Simbal said, "to have Monica lead me back to the DEA computer. It didn't work out."

"I've got to give the girl credit. She's far from stupid. But her heart aches for you, Tony. God knows why, you're such a bastard. Given time, she'd relent all right. But then I suppose she doesn't know you quite as well as I do."

"You don't have to sleep with me."

Threnody's eyes opened wide. "My goodness, does that mean she's more in tune with the *real* Tony Simbal?" His voice was heavy with sarcasm.

They had reached the southern edge of Rock Creek Park. From their vantage point they could see the dam at the point. Behind them the Watergate Hotel reared its plush and now infamous bulk.

Simbal was silent for a time. He watched the sluggish water, gray as a whale's back, and wondered why he couldn't think of a retort. "Will you help me or won't you, Max?"

"As you said, you don't work for me anymore."

There was something that Simbal had to work out, something going on here that he wasn't quite reading. It had been happening at the periphery of his awareness ever since they sat down at the auction. What?

"Maybe," Simbal said, "it's time we tried to be friends."

"I trusted you and then, when you came home from Burma you left the DEA because your college roommate called. Who said the British had the monopoly on old-boy networks."

They stopped then in the silence, staring at each other, absorbing what the other one had said.

A barge, invisible around the bend in the river, hooted and Simbal shivered. "Jesus," he said, "this sounds like a marriage gone bad."

"Maybe it is."

Simbal took a deep breath. "Can we end this animosity, Max? I'd really like to."

Threnody looked out along the river as if he expected to see the barge. At last he nodded. "That suits me." He put his hands together. Their backs were raw and red-looking. "I always admired you, Tony. You were my best operative. It hurt to lose you."

"I was restless, Max." Simbal took another deep breath. "That's all."

"Sure." Threnody nodded with a kind of positive force. "We all have to move on. It's part of life."

They walked on in silence for a time. A pair of business types in sweats came jogging by. "Christ, but they make me feel old," Threnody said.

"Peter Curran is your resident *diqui* expert, right?" Simbal said. "Alan Thune was murdered in New York last week while on his way to a routine rdv with his regular contact. I figure Curran knows more than I do about the *diqui*'s current activities."

"I can't figure your interest." His pop eyes were always weepy in the wind. He wiped at them now with the handkerchief. "Correct me if I'm wrong but shouldn't you be leaving the *diqui* to us and the SNITs." He was speaking of the CIA's Strategic Narcotics Team.

"The *diqui*'s just part of the beat Donovan's assigned me. Southeast Asia. He wants to know everything and, if it's moving, why, how and where to. So how about you setting up a meet between me and Curran?"

"That's hardly possible now," Threnody said, staring hard at Simbal. "Peter Curran has been terminated."

In this warm light her skin was as tawny as a cat's. With her thick sheaf of blond hair and her cool gray eyes she could have been an enchantress. Lorelei, or, perhaps more accurately, Circe, for to Mikhail Carelin there was a quality about Daniella's beauty that seemed descended from ancient Greek legend.

Carelin, an ardent student of history, saw in her aspects he associated with the peoples of Asia Minor—the Mesopotamians, Assyrians, Babylonians. She did not, in any case, possess a modern face. Her chiseled features were straight out of antiquity; he often joked with her that she was the reincarnation of some ancient queen.

"I am Russian," she would say. "I don't know anything about Babylonia or Assyria."

One time when she said this, he thrust a book into her hands. "What's this?" she said. "I don't have time to read."

"It's a history on the military career of Alexander the Great," he said. "I think you should make the time to read it."

"Why?"

"Because he tried to conquer the entire civilized world," he said. "And damn near succeeded."

Carelin believed that Daniella wanted to conquer the entire

civilized world. "These days," he said, "one needs more help than Alexander had in his time." He believed that she was overly ambitious and that this trait—which, in Daniella's opinion, was what made her strong and resilient in a man's world—was also her hubris. "From the Greek, *hybris*," Carelin said to her, "meaning arrogance. The dictionary defines hubris as exaggerated pride or self-confidence—"

"What's wrong with that?" she had countered.

"—often resulting in retribution."

She had shut up then, thinking of Oleg Maluta. It had been because of Uncle Vadim that she had first met Oleg Maluta socially. Uncle Vadim liked her to come to Leningrad at the end of December. The other members of the family assumed that was because it was the best time of the year for Daniella.

Only she and Uncle Vadim knew the true reason. Daniella's mother had been a member of the Russian Orthodox Church. This she had to keep a secret from Daniella's father. Uncle Vadim was a member as well and he liked Daniella to be with him at Christmastime.

It was in Leningrad that Daniella had first met Oleg Maluta. She had just been named to the Politburo where Maluta was already a senior member. Uncle Vadim had arranged the dinner at the Del'Fin, one of the floating restaurants in front of the Admiralty. Of course at that time of the year the Neva River was frozen solid. Though, at fifty miles, the Neva was one of the world's shortest rivers, its current was so strong that there was little salt content in the gulf near the city. Therefore, it was usually frozen all winter long, from the beginning of December through May.

"This man can help you, Danushka," she remembered Uncle Vadim saying on the way to the Del'Fin. "If he takes a liking to you, many doors will open up for you and your most difficult time—the next six months—will be made infinitely easier. Oleg Sergeevich knows where all the brooms are in the closet."

Not brooms, Daniella thought now. Bones. Your Oleg Sergeevich Maluta knows where all of them are buried, Uncle, and to whom they belong.

It was ironic that she had been elevated to one of the most powerful jobs in all of Russia yet, because of the evil cunning of one man, she was trapped like a fox in its lair. She dared not move against Maluta in any overt manner because she had not yet begun her own consolidation of power. She was

169

new to the Politburo and it would take time for her to learn her way in what had been strictly male territory.

She could not even use her own networks to defeat him from a clandestine position since he had made it clear to her that she was under constant surveillance. That was not so easy a thing to do to the head of the *sluzhba*'s First Chief Directorate; she was not like an ordinary citizen, after all.

The First Chief Directorate was a vast bureau and she was far from coming to know personally all its department heads. Many were from Anatoly Karpov's regime. She was certain that Maluta had suborned one of them. It was the only way to keep her in view without eliciting a whiff of smoke: use Daniella's own people.

Now as they stirred together in the big bed, beneath the thick eiderdown comforter, she wondered whether to tell Carelin of Maluta's treachery. What would he do if he knew that Maluta had secreted away photographs of him and Daniella in the act of making passionate love?

A murderous rage overtook Daniella; she jerked herself into a sitting position.

"What is it, *koshka*?" Carelin liked to call her that: cat.

"Just chill," she said. Tears in the snowy night; Maluta drinking in her sadness and remorse like some dark vampire while someone in the night snapped photographs, obscene closeups of the weakness, the tears leaking out of her eyes. "Nothing at all."

Carelin sat up, put his arms around her.

His face was in all respects nondescript. He could be said to be neither handsome nor ugly. His was a face that would never be noticed in a crowd. The Kremlin watchers in England and America, poring over their surveillance, passed him by time and again in favor of the Genachevs and the Reztsovs and the Kulagins, men with charisma who reached out and grabbed for power. What then could a man such as Mikhail Carelin offer them?

Yet, for Daniella, who had schooled herself to the catechisms of power, Carelin was a man who held infinitely more allure than the more notorious powermongers inside the Kremlin. He possessed something far more valuable, principally because he did not seek the international limelight: an exceptional inner strength.

That was why Genachev came to him for advice. Carelin was not a man who sought continually to expand his power base. He possessed a confidence of self that Daniella greatly admired. He moved in the shadows, along the corridors of power, whispering in the right ears and creating policy while avoiding the lethal purges that were part of any highly ideologized political system. Maluta had called him egoless; the truth was that Carelin had subordinated ego to strategy, and that was rare indeed in the world.

It seemed to Daniella that Mikhail Carelin was filled with a wonderful, ineffable peace. And sharing that peacefulness brought her a great deal of joy.

Joy as opposed to pleasure. Daniella had sought and gained pleasure from a great many men. The male of the species, she had found, could be trained to give enormous pleasure. Not so with joy. Joy was an innate characteristic. It could not be taught. On the contrary, it was so elemental a quality that it simply was. But its existence was rare—very rare indeed, according to Daniella's experience. Mikhail Carelin gave her joy and thus he was precious to her as no man before him had ever been.

This, of course, was a continual source of surprise to Daniella. She was used—had become used perforce by circumstance—to manipulating men as a defensive counter to their manipulation of her. It was when she moved from defensive to offensive strategy—as with Karpov and Lantin, in whose bed they now sat—that her career took off like a rocket.

Carelin was different. Perhaps it had begun in the same way. Had she seduced him? Memory—and emotion, of course—tended to obscure certain facts and now their romantic origins were misted over, as if they were the stuff of Carelin's legends instead of, simply, her life. The mythos of Daniella and Mikhail. The thought of that sometimes made her laugh. At other times, it caused her to hug his lean strong body to hers.

It was at those times that Daniella understood that she was afraid of his leaving her. It was an irrational fear, to be sure. She had no doubts about Carelin. He loved her fiercely and completely, but with none of the slavish devotion that had disgusted her in many of her lovers.

She knew the difference. In them, she had manufactured their love, and so, in the end, it had turned rancid in its artificiality. She had had to do nothing in Carelin's case. He loved her. Period.

"Come, *koshka*," he whispered. "Lie down again."

And Daniella listened to him, as Genachev listened to him

during the day. Her body relaxed, surrounded by his warmth. She melted, her eyes closed, She sighed deeply.

In her sleep, she spoke Oleg Maluta's name and Carelin, wrapped up in her, staring at the play of pale lights across the bedroom ceiling, heard her.

Maluta, he thought.

And when she awoke near dawn, he said, "Tell me about Oleg Maluta."

On her guard, Daniella said, "I don't understand."

"Tell me, *koshka*," he said, "why you are frightened of him."

"Why do you say that?"

"Because he stalks your dreams." Carelin turned to her. "Even in your sleep you speak his name with hate and fear."

She reached out and touched his cheek with the flat of her hand. "Why weren't you asleep, *lyubimi*?"

Carelin smiled. "I was listening to the night. I was thinking. And I heard you call out his name. 'Maluta,' you said."

"What else?"

"Only 'Maluta.' "

Now Daniella was on the cusp. It had been an eternity since she confided anything in a man. She wished to with Carelin, which was precisely why she hesitated to do it. There was danger. In matters of the heart one was always betrayed. This she had learned by hard experience. Still, a heart in love longs to share, for that sharing brings with it another kind of intimacy. The kind that transforms pleasure into joy.

"I want to tell you—" bit off her words in midsentence. Remembering: *In this war, you are either with me or against me*, Maluta had said. The snow, the stillness of the night, the rasp of Oleg Maluta's voice across her heart. The taste of ashes in her mouth as she saw the light go out of Alexei's eyes, her finger trembling on the trigger, her ears echoing with white sound in the aftermath, choking on the cordite fumes.

And Maluta taking the pistol from her hand so that only her prints would be on it. A weapon hidden away, never to be fired again but ready to be used against her. *I want you to understand that I can have you brought up on murder charges at any time*.

"*Koshka*—" Carelin said.

"Make love to me."

"*Koshka*, the pain I see behind your eyes—"

172

"Do as I ask, *lyubimi*." Her hands moving along the planes of his torso. "Please."

Carelin enwrapped her, his palms cupping her hard high breasts. The pads of his thumbs rubbed her nipples and she gasped, burying her head in his shoulder. A thick wing of hair passed across his face, smelling of lavender and citrus.

His hand wove patterns down to her belly and beneath. Found that she was already wet and open. He turned, lifting her over and up, on top of him. Her thighs opened like the petals of a flower.

He entered her and at the same time bit into her cinnamon flesh. Daniella thought that she would faint. Her back rested against his muscular chest. She could feel his heartbeat, his pulse accelerating as he slid further and further up into her. Her head went back and her eyelids fluttered.

She felt him inside her like a second heartbeat. The pleasure as he bucked up against her was a solid cylinder that reached all the way up to the top of her head. She was on fire.

His hands kneaded her breasts gently, pulling at her nipples, making her shiver and pant with wanting. "*Lyubimi*," she said. "*Lyubimi*."

She began to rotate her hips, giving an added motion when he was in all the way so that her inner muscles caressed the very end of him. She could hear his little cries, feel his hot breath in her ear. He seemed to be talking but it was in a language that registered only on her soul. It was as if they were joined from the inside out instead of the other way around.

Her fingertips urged him onward; at the same time she was urging herself on.

"*Koshka!*"

She felt that part of him not inside her drawn up, as hard as rocks. He expanded inside her. He was so deep.

Daniella's eyes, glazed and unseeing, opened wide. She could not catch her breath. Her thighs were trembling and they closed inward, trapping him, pushing him even further as he began to convulse beneath her.

In so doing he pushed hard against the roof of her and she cried out. Grinding her hips down hard against him, she was flooded with intense heat. Her insides had turned molten and she brought her own hands up over his, squeezing in on her sensitive breasts.

She did not stop moving until he popped out of her. Then

she turned and whispered, "Hold me tight, darling. Hold me very tight," for the first time feeling fully the importance of this, too.

With the dawn's cool blue light, she said, "I want to tell you about Maluta." *In this war, you are either with me or against me.* Her fear of him blew like a cold wind against her heart. "I want to tell you everything." Because Maluta had made her cry, bitter tears stinging her cheeks and the snow all around her. The isolating snow, the tears he had forced out of her which had bared her heart to his avid gaze. He had accomplished what no man since Daniella's father had been able to do. He had made her feel like a little girl. He had forced her to shed her adult façade. He had stripped her naked before him and in a terrible way that would be indelibly etched in her mind he had raped her. Nakedness of the body was nothing compared to nakedness of the soul.

"Like a good Catholic, I want to confess."

Carelin, lying with one leg thrown across her thighs, said nothing. He felt the thick sheaf of her hair against his cheek, the sweetness of her breath. He stared into those cool gray eyes and thought of the storm-tossed Black Sea.

Outside, the wind had picked up. Handfuls of dry snow came rattling against the windowpanes and, now and again, the sounds of a vehicle passing could be heard, chains clinking.

"How has he hurt you, *koshka*?"

"I work for him now." Her voice was low. If they had not been so close, Carelin did not believe that he would have heard her.

"Bastard," he said quietly, evenly.

And by the tone of that single word he caused Daniella to relax. I am safe with him, she thought.

"He forced me to murder Alexei," she said in a choked voice. "He told me that he was using Alexei to spy on me. Then after I had put the gun—*his* gun, Maluta's weapon—to Alexei's head and shot him, Maluta told me the truth. That a man was out there in the night, taking pictures of me.

"He's there now, I've no doubt."

"Have you ever seen him? Do you know what he looks like?"

"No."

Carelin thought for a moment. "What happened to the murder weapon?"

Daniella sat very still. Her eyes were dry; she seemed to

174

have ceased to breathe. "Maluta took it. It has my fingerprints all over it. It is untraceable to Maluta. He has photos, as well."

"Of the murder."

Now came the crunch. "Of other things," she whispered. From unnatural stillness to unnatural movement. She had begun to shake all over again. What if, because of this, Mikhail left her? Her nerve ends were on fire at the thought. She did not think that she could face Maluta again, knowing that she was utterly alone.

"What other things?"

Daniella, burning up as with a fever, remained mute. Her tongue clove to the dry roof of her mouth. She felt a pressure on her vocal chords.

"*Koshka,*" he said gently, "now you must finish what you have begun." He took her hand in his and just as if they were teenaged lovers beginning the intimidating ritual of physical intimacy, twining his fingers between hers, pressed hard in order to transfer his courage into her. "What could be so terrible?"

Daniella closed her eyes. She felt as if she were about to jump off a boat into ten fathoms of water. "What would your wife do, Mikhail, if she found out about us?"

He laughed, startling her. "Why worry about that, *koshka*? The only one she could hear it from is you and you won't tell her, will you?" Then he saw the expression of agony on her face.

"Maluta?" His voice was like the tolling of a bell in the room. "Maluta has photographs of us?"

Daniella nodded. She did not trust herself to speak.

Carelin put his head back against the wall. "Oh, *koshka*," he said, after a long time, "I think you've done us in."

"So you see," Threnody said, "it is most unlikely that either you or I will be afforded the opportunity to speak with Peter Curran again."

Simbal now understood Monica's reaction when he had brought up Curran's name. He and Max began to walk again, cued by some unspoken signal.

"What happened?"

"His car was turned into a ball of fire by a pound of plastique."

"Ouch." Simbal stopped. They had been walking for quite some time and the cold was getting to him. "I.D.?"

"We had only the skeleton to work with," Threnody said. "It's a physical match. DNT was impossible since Curran hadn't any dental work done. But he always wore a peculiar signet ring." Threnody took it out of his pocket. "He belonged to something called the Hellfire Club at college. Yale, I think it was. Anyway, we found the ring inside the car. Had to peel lots of blackened skin off it to make the I.D."

"That's it then."

Threnody blew on his hands. "It doesn't have to be."

Now Simbal had it. The something that had been going on at the periphery of Max's responses ever since they had met this afternoon clicked home.

"You want me to take Peter Curran's place infiltrating the *diqui*," Simbal said with some awe in his voice. "That's what you've wanted from the beginning."

"Yes and no." Threnody raised his hands. "Before you get your Irish up give me the benefit of the doubt. Hear me out. Then if you want to say no, just walk away and that will be the end of it.

"The truth is I need someone from outside the Department to continue this investigation. But, no, I do not want you to take Peter's place. He was up to some very unusual stuff. Which is precisely why I need you.

"After Peter left on this last mission it was discovered that certain, ah, documents of a sensitive nature were missing from our files."

"Curran filched company goodies?"

The wind had shifted, gusting in from the water. Threnody pulled the collar of his loden coat up around his ears. "It would seem that way, yes."

"Can you tell me what he took?"

"Names, dates, places, operation networks."

"Jesus."

"Well put, Tony. Our friends on Capitol Hill would love to pull us apart on something like this. Congressional subcommittees live off mistakes like this."

Simbal turned to him. "Is that what you call it, a mistake?"

"Whatever name you care to put on it," Threnody said, "it needs to be fixed. And fixed with the utmost discretion. It would be most embarrassing if this got around, even interdepartmentally." Simbal knew that he meant Donovan.

From behind them a siren sounded. When the ambulance had passed and the normal traffic flow on the street had started up again, Simbal said, "I'll need full access to the DEA computer."

Threnody nodded. "You'll get whatever you need, Tony." He held out his hand and, when Simbal took it, gripped it hard.

The last of the rain slid down the glass. Inside the room it was very still so that the rhythmic sound of the respirator seemed harsh and alien.

Three Oaths played with the cord of the blinds, turning gray light darker, then lighter in minute increments. He stared through the bars the blinds made as if he were in prison.

"All gods destroy our enemies!" Three Oaths said. The sound of Bliss's deep breathing, the most tangible sign of her sedation, was like a knife twisting in his heart. Each tidal sigh brought another wave of anguish.

"The fornicating doctors know nothing," he despaired. "They are helpless, they say nothing. They will not even admit to ignorance. Bliss could die this very instant and they would not be able to do anything about it or even tell us what happened."

"Calm yourself, Elder Uncle," Jake said. "The doctor told us that the x-rays were negative. The EEG showed no internal trauma."

"Then why do they want to make more tests? Probe my daughter with their *gwai loh* machines?"

" 'Certain anomalies in her brainwaves' is how the doctor put it."

"I don't understand," Three Oaths said.

"Neither, I think, do the doctors."

"There, you see!" he cried. "It is just as I said."

"Routine, Elder Uncle. The anomalies are not life-threatening. Just puzzling."

"Ah, Buddha!" Three Oaths collapsed on a chair beside the high bed. "What evil *joss* has overtaken us, Jake? What onerous deeds did we perform in a previous life to have generated such violent and powerful enemies?"

"First," Jake said, "we must discover who our enemies are."

Three Oaths looked at his nephew. "You said Bliss saw their tattoos."

"*Irezumi*," Jake said. "She said they were Yakuza."

"I don't understand," Three Oaths said. "We have no enemies in Japan."

"If she's right, we do now." Jake rose and went to the window. A flood of neon disfigured the ceiling in much the same way the special tattoos marked the Yakuza warriors. "There is a war going on in Japan," he said into the void of the neon-lighted night. "A Yakuza war. My friend Mikio Komoto is under siege."

"And you think that"—Three Oaths gestured—"this had something to do with that friendship?"

Jake shrugged. "Why not? Perhaps they were looking for me. Perhaps they killed my father out of frustration in not finding me."

Three Oaths was not persuaded. "They were professionals. They were very good. I am using your words now, Younger Nephew. You called them a *dantai*. You yourself created two such *dantai* when you were working for the Quarry. I am not mistaken in thinking that a *dantai*'s qualities include extraordinary courage and discipline. I ask you two questions. One: would a *dantai* not be able to pinpoint your whereabouts? Two: would a *dantai* resort to wanton and, to them quite useless, destruction out of frustration?"

Jake said nothing but continued to stare out at the vibrating darkness. He was thinking about the operative who had tailed him, who had kept him busy, away from the junk just long enough . . .

If he had been able to use *ba-mahk*, he would almost assuredly become aware of the larger strategy. It could have turned events on their side. *Ba-mahk* could have saved his father's life—

Fool! he thought savagely. That is your Western half thinking. Use your Chinese mind. What has happened has happened. *Joss*. Get on with what must be done now.

"In any case I will go to Japan," he said after a long silence.

"And leave Bliss and this fornicating mess with Southasia Bancorp?"

"Bliss," Jake said, "will not recover any the quicker with me here. As to Southasia Bancorp, I have the entire *yuhn-hyun* to think of."

"There is the matter of your father's funeral." Three Oaths's tone had turned hard. He remembered what Neon Chow had said at Gaddi's about how qualified his own number one son was to be *Zhuan*. "It is a son's duty—"

"Do not presume to tell me," Jake said, swinging around to face his uncle, "what is or is not my duty. I am *Zhuan*. I understand my obligations. The body will be cremated tonight. You and I and T. Y. Chung will attend a service at dawn tomorrow. My father's ashes will be scattered into the South China Sea, as were his wishes.

"But as to business, something must be done here while I am away." He handed a small packet over to his uncle. "Choose one of your sons—I leave that decision to you. See that he finds out all he can about that."

Three Oaths unwrapped the packet. Inside smudged bits of newspaper he discovered an unset opal. Its predominantly red flame winked and shone at him as he turned it this way and that.

"Where did you get this?"

"From the pocket of someone who was foolish enough to follow me," Jake said.

"When was this?"

"Just see that it is done," Jake said curtly. To bring up the tick was to remind himself of his loss. *Ba-mahk* . . . the Way of strategy. Jake concentrated, tried to feel the pulse. Nothing. And he could not say a word to Three Oaths. "By the time I return I want to know where it was bought, when and, most importantly, by whom."

Three Oaths rewrapped the parcel, pocketed it. "It will be done," he said. His eyes dropped to his daughter's pale face. "She is a part of me just as much as the children of my loins. And she is more. She is a piece of Shi Zilin. My *bou-sehk*."

His tone was entirely different when he raised his head. "Now I want you to go downstairs and let a doctor take a look at you. If you must persist in your course of action I want to be assured of your continued physical soundness. For the sake of the *yuhn-hyun*, you understand."

"Yes, course." The tension between them would not dissipate. This was surely not how my father planned it, Jake thought. Oh, Buddha, I cannot believe that he is gone. Give me the strength to carry out the strategy. "I am counting on you to keep the lid on the Southasia situation."

"You are indeed a hard one, Younger Nephew." Three Oaths sat very still. Though he said nothing for a moment, his tone precluded any further comment from Jake. "Perhaps my Elder Brother was correct after all in believing you *Zhuan*. One must be cold and uncaring indeed to carry the weight of such a superstructure as the *yuhn-hyun* on one's back. I know that it would break mine."

His uncle's words stung him, pricked his heart, decided his next action. He took out an envelope. "Elder Uncle," he said thickly. "I do not know where I will be in the next days. Or what will happen. *Joss*, eh? But I have made some provisions." He held out the envelope. "Inside you will find the name of Apollo, our mole in Russia. While I am gone you must maintain radio contact with him. He must be made to feel that his lifeline out of Russia is absolutely secure. I cannot risk his abandoning his directive. Do you understand?"

Three Oaths looked at his nephew. His heart swelled with pride. "Perfectly, *Zhuan*." So Neon Chow was wrong, after all, he thought. Deep down he had known it to be so. Still, it was gratifying to get this tangible proof of the esteem in which he was still held.

"Forty-eight hours after I am gone," Jake said, "you will open the envelope and follow the instructions for contacting Apollo. Thereafter you will maintain a forty-eight-hour schedule until my return."

"Which will be when, Younger Nephew?"

"When Buddha wills it."

Jake handed over the envelope.

McKenna returned to the smoky labyrinth of the White Teacup at the appointed time. The police report on the incident in Aberdeen—since it had been remanded to Special Branch—had crossed his desk and he had read the account by the dispatched officers with more than passing interest. Three Oaths Tsun was part owner of the Southasia Bancorp and he wondered if this attack on his junk had something to do with the rumor that White-Eye Kao had passed on to him.

He threaded his way through the packs of sailors and B-girls, seeing Big Oysters Pok at his usual table. He thought, I will have my answers soon.

Big Oysters Pok was sitting alone and he waved a hand as McKenna came up. "Sit down," he said. "Have a drink." And laughed. "Or are you on duty, Lieutenant?"

McKenna contrived to ignore the joke and poured himself three fingers of Johnnie Walker Black. He downed the whole in one great swig as if he thought that this gesture would give him face with the Chinese—a commodity he felt was in short supply at the moment. He did not care for Big Oysters Pok's attitude but he was hardly in a position to remark upon it. No, at least, until he got what he wanted from the bastard. McKenna bared his teeth. Soon, he thought, I will teach him a lesson. I will teach him to respect an officer of the law.

"What d'you have for me?" McKenna asked.

"Lieutenant," Big Oysters Pok said, "you remind me of the hare who could not wait to get across the highway." Languidly he reached out, poured himself some whiskey. He took up the glass and, swirling the amber liquid around the curved side, stared into its clear depths. "It bolted across. Just in time to be struck by an oncoming truck. The offside tires flattened it into the baking tarmac." He took a careful sip of the whiskey. "One must learn the art of patience."

"Patience, my ass," McKenna said. He felt in a vise—a double vise really. Between Formidable Sung and White-Eye Kao, he felt as if he was being squeezed dry, as if he had lost all initiative. He was back again in the Outback, the fires burning, sparking in great long sweeps like spectral writing across the ink-black skies. As if from close at hand, he heard again the chanting, echoing through the scrub-dusted wilderness.

"I want answers!" He was shouting, his great ham fist banging down on the table, making the bottles and glassware rattle, like the bone teeth the abos wore. McKenna was shuddering. "Answers!" He wiped sweat off his face.

Big Oysters Pok sat back, regarding the big *gwai loh* as one peers at a strange and not altogether pleasant creature in a zoo. This man is not to be trusted, he thought. I must take care.

"I have your answer," he said.

"Good," McKenna said. "Bloody good." He poured himself another drink and threw that one back as quickly as he had done the first. "Let's have it. I haven't got all night."

Feeling as if he were crouching in an evil-smelling cave with a dangerous bear, Big Oysters Pok said, "There is a problem at Southasia Bancorp."

"What kind of problem?"

"Their comptroller is no longer with them."

"Fired?"

"Fled is how I'm told it went."

McKenna's eyes were alight. "Then there must be money involved."

Big Oysters Pok nodded. "Undoubtedly. The only mystery is how much."

McKenna was rolling his glass around and around. "It matters a great deal how much the comptroller embezzled, don't you think?"

"Are you asking my opinion?" Big Oysters Pok inquired. McKenna looked up. "What? Oh, yes, of course."

"The only way it would matter was if this man somehow managed to take out of the company sufficient funds to make it impossible for the bank to cover a serious run."

"That's right," McKenna assented. "Any hint of fiduciary malfeasance to the depositors of Southasia would create havoc."

"Only under the condition I just outlined."

"The lid is on very tight," McKenna mused. "That could be significant. If they've in fact got a shortage of cash the last thing they could afford would be to risk a run."

"Why does it matter to you what financial state Southasia Bancorp is in?" Big Oysters Pok said, thinking, I know how much was embezzled but why should I tell him?

"None of your bleeding business, mate," McKenna snapped. "But I'll tell you what you can do. Get a line on how much's missing. And fast."

"I am your errand boy now?" Big Oysters Pok's face was bland.

McKenna leaned forward across the table. His face was flushed and his eyes were filled with the sparking fires that showered the Outback. "Listen to me, mate. The minute we began our little arrangement, you put yourself in my pocket. I can break you and haul you in any time I want to, on any one of half a dozen complaints including conspiracy to bribe an officer of Her Majesty's peace force."

"You would only be implicating yourself," Big Oysters Pok pointed out.

McKenna barked out a laugh. "And who d'you think would believe you over me, eh? No judge in Hong Kong, that's for sure. Use your head, mate. Play along like a nice little doggie and do what you're told. That way all's well that ends well, okay?"

"I've done what you asked me to do," Big Oysters Pok said evenly. "We have our bargain. That is as far as I care to go. I am at risk already."

"You little bastard, you're already at risk with me, don't you know that? I'm the one to fear and no mistake." Fly buzzing against the film opaquing that staring eye. Rising and falling, rising and falling. "I'm white, mate. *I* have the power."

For a moment, Big Oysters Pok said nothing. Then he gave

a curt nod and rose. "Good night, Lieutenant." He threw some money on the table. "And good-bye."

Daniella and Oleg Maluta at the ballet. Watching *Sleeping Beauty*, the splendor of crescendos of music, of pas de deux, of the principals' swirling, elegiac movements.

Daniella's senses took in the overrich colors of costume, the thickly textured rococo sets, the melodramatic music. She felt like a reveler at the end of a long night of banqueting.

Idly she wondered why Maluta had insisted that she go with him to the ballet. For years he and his wife had been an almost permanent fixture in this gilt-edged box at the Bolshoi. Then his wife's sudden, enigmatic death had put an end to his attending his beloved ballet.

That was many years ago. Nowadays, there were many people Maluta could take to the Bolshoi, and gain political advantage. Sitting so close to him, Daniella thought about the current of his temper.

Sometimes Maluta seemed to be a dog in the early stages of rabies: he shouted, he screamed unreasoningly; he was physically abusive. At other times, he was perfectly calm. However, he was at his most malicious when he was calm.

Daniella, of course, had no desire to accompany Maluta anywhere. She would have much preferred to be with Mikhail Carelin. His late meeting with Genachev should have been over by now.

But she could not deny Maluta anything. She thought of the room where he kept securely locked the pictures of her and Carelin making love, the gun with which she had shot Alexei. The photos, no doubt grainy because of the high-speed film that was used, of her weeping by the side of the car in which Alexei's still warm corpse lay slumped across the steering wheel. More than anything she wanted those photos. Until she destroyed them, their negatives and the man who had taken them, she would feel utterly defiled. Maluta had in his possession not only the means of her political destruction but also a glimpse into her secret heart. That he had the power to make her cry made her hate him with an intensity that was almost palpable.

And the absolute worst part was that she was utterly helpless against him. Though her desk at work was piled with reports and feasibility studies from several key departments, she had spent the better part of the day digging deeper and deeper into her Directorate's computer's heart in an attempt to find even the smallest chink in Maluta's armor. In vain. His school record indicated that he was at near-genius level by the age of fifteen. He was a zealous Marxist, as were his parents. Maluta's father had been an engineer working all his life in the service of Mother Russia.

Maluta's own rise within the Soviet hierarchy had been swift and unerring. If he had made any enemies they were no longer in power. The only piece of tragedy in his life was the death of his wife twelve years ago in a raging fire that had consumed their *dacha* in Zvenigorod, in the thickly wooded hill country favored by many artists.

According to his dossier, Maluta had asked for and received a leave of absence and had almost single-handedly rebuilt the *dacha* on the ashen foundation of the first one. His form of mourning. He must have loved her a great deal since he had never remarried. In fact, his file was devoid of reference to any liaison.

Had he been celibate all that time? Daniella had wondered, or was he too clever for the watchers who oversaw every person of power within Russia?

Now, as the Tchaikovsky music built to yet another crescendo, Daniella forced herself to relax. That was the most difficult part about being in Maluta's company. She never seemed to be able to relax. She remembered Uncle Vadim saying to her once, "The male is the superior sex because he believes himself to be." Daniella thought that defined Oleg Maluta very well.

Sverdlov Square was alight when they emerged from the glitter of the Bolshoi. There seemed to be a sea of sables swirling like great, dark tutus. It was still snowing and the sound of the chains on car and truck tires was a clear rhythmic pulse, echoed back by the walls of the edifices fronting the square.

In Maluta's thrumming Chaika, they took off into the night made pale by the snow and low clouds off which Moscow's lights reflected.

The privacy screen was up between the back seat and the driver in front. Maluta, leaning forward, rapped his knuckle against the steel-reinforced glass. The driver was completely unaware of the sound.

"No one but us," Maluta said, sinking back into the seat. He was turned partway toward her. Daniella glanced out the window. It appeared that they were headed for the Moskva. They were not going directly to her apartment. She felt a slight queasiness in the pit of her stomach. Now she would find out why he had issued the command for her to come tonight.

"How is the great love affair coming, my sparrow?"

She did not like his tone of voice. "If you had left me alone tonight I would have found out the substance of Carelin's crash meeting with Genachev."

"Oh, you'll be home in plenty of time to ply him with the fur between your thighs." Maluta gave a quick laugh. "Besides, I enjoy the looks of envy and concern I receive when I am out with you at such an affair. At the Bolshoi, my colleagues come not only to enjoy the arts, but also to see who is in attendance with whom."

Though they were both members of the elite Politburo, Maluta had used the phrase "my colleagues."

"You've got a pessimist's heart, Comrade General." Maluta sucked on his cigarette. "Possibly that is because you are female. Will you faint at the sight of a mouse running across your ankles, I wonder?" He laughed again and curled his hand into a fist. "I think not. I have already seen you wield a gun. You are an excellent shot. But what will happen to you when you are tempered in the ultimate fire? Will you harden into crystal? Or will you break apart into ten thousand shards? That is what I wish to know."

The Chaika turned off the highway and slid to a stop. Ducking his head, Maluta got out. He stood holding the door for her until she stood by his side.

Together they went down a stone path. At its foot, it petered out with a series of broken pieces of slate. The bank was fairly steep here and with the snow it was difficult to feel one's footing.

The lights of modern high-rises glittered off the ice that, before this last snow, had begun to break up. The Moskva looked as dull and inert as lead. Nothing was moving along its length or its banks.

"This is a favorite place of mine," Maluta said. And then, in case she might mistake this for a bit of confidence, he added, "It is where I come for private conversations. Here I can be assured I will not be overheard or recorded." He lifted his arms wide. "There is nowhere to hide. I would see even a crouching figure."

The snow seemed pink in the haloed illumination coming off the city. It drifted straight down in a night devoid of wind.

Maluta brought them to a halt just a scant pace from the

waterline. "It was just here that I almost died." The end of his cigarette glowed, an evil all-knowing third eye. "I was fifteen and still foolhardy, absolutely unmindful of rules." He flicked ash into the darkness. "It was spring. Just about this time of the year, I suppose. The ice was thin, treacherous, my mother warned me. I never listened."

Maluta took a deep draft of the smoke, let it out slowly. He stood with his head slightly cocked, as if he were listening for the soft grinding of the splitting ice. His pose was arrogant, his tone of voice angered her further.

But this was Oleg Maluta: somber, opinionated, sharp to the point of cutting, supremely arrogant, and utterly brilliant.

Again, Uncle Vadim's dictum rang in her inner ear: *The male is the superior sex because he believes himself to be.*

Daniella wanted desperately not to be intimidated by this particular male. But she suspected that part of her inability to break free of her fear of him was the intensity of that desire.

"I went skating that day," Maluta was saying. "I believe there was a wager and I was either too brave or too pigheaded to back down. I went out on the ice. I had enough experience to know that there was a problem right away. It didn't feel right. In patches it was dark, which is a bad sign. Good, thick ice is pale. Very pale.

"I went down." His arm lifted and the glowing end of his cigarette described a brief arc. "Just there. I heard the crack and thought someone had shot off a pistol along the river. Then I plunged into the river. It was very cold and very dark." He finished the cigarette and flipped the butt away. "Now I take people here when their usefulness is at an end. Another form of termination."

Typically he had not completed the story and Daniella knew that he never would. It was enough, in his opinion, for the listener to know that the lesson of long ago had been learned. It was self-evident that he had not drowned in the Moskva.

Maluta laughed now. "But take heart, my dear Daniella Alexandrova, I have not marked you for termination of any kind. You are much too special a creature. You are, rather, to be treasured."

"And shown off in public." She watched him. "That *was* what you did with me tonight."

"At the Bolshoi? Why, of course. It's all part of the game."

"What game?"

Shadows broke along Maluta's thin face as if its angularity

had the power to slice up light. "You were intelligent enough to work your way into the Politburo. Up until this moment, you've had it all your own way. You have trapped men—bright men, even brilliant men, in my opinion—because you were able to exploit a common weakness in them.

"Because they wanted to possess you—because you were clever enough to feed that desire in them—they provided you with all you needed to rise up the *sluzhba's* structure. Imagine! They would have gone to the ends of the earth for you. They sold their souls to you, bowed their heads before you, conferred to you all that made them powerful. For this—" His hands pressed roughly against her breasts. "And this." Found the swelling mount at the apex of her thighs.

Listening to this outpouring of the collective masculine ego, this litany of distortion, made Daniella ill. It was as if he believed that she merely had to open her legs to Karpov and Lantin and they had become children.

A red rage began to suffuse her and she could feel her rational mind closing down in just the same way that one feels cold at the extremities when one is severely depressed.

She stopped that and began to think. Do not, she thought, become what he has accused you of being: a purely emotional creature devoid of intelligence or rational planning. He has said that you think, that you decide with your cunt. Will you now prove him right?

Maluta's eyes gleaming, city lights on the Moskva behind him, a nocturnal animal's glimmering. The river seemed to breathe along with them, its current a sigh or moan, silent punctuation.

"These were not men," he continued relentlessly, "at least not by my standards. You feel that you have arrived, that you deserve a measure of respect, even of equality. Nothing could be further from the truth. Now you must be shown your proper place. You must, in fact, learn the humility of your station . . . and of your sex.

"You dared much when you insinuated yourself into this cynosure. Perhaps some comment on your audacity, and foolishly admire it.

"Audacity is to be admired only in great men and in the noblest of animals."

"And women fit into neither category." She knew he was baiting her but she seemed incapable of ignoring him.

"Indeed not." He lit another cigarette. By the flare of the lighter Daniella could see the hatred in his eyes and wondered

187

at it. "By my lights you never should have been elevated into the Politburo. I fought against the nomination. But too much was already being made of the intelligence you have gathered for the *sluzhba*. So much for my minority opinion. I pride myself on my pragmatism. Now that you are here I shall endeavor to make the most efficacious use of your talents."

"I'm glad you think I have some."

"When you open your legs, men listen." He spit out tobacco and, perhaps, something more, something intangible. "That you are a slut is a given. It is because you are that I can use you."

Daniella had to restrain herself from leaping at his throat. The flush of anger was so intense she felt her body break out into sweat.

Maluta gave her a thin smile. "You'd love to kill me, wouldn't you, Daniella Alexandrova? You're good at that, too, I'll give you that. Sex and death, your metier, eh?" He laughed again.

"But I will have you by my side, even when I become Party President. You are far too valuable an asset for me to squander away. In any event, I need you and, as I have indicated, I am a supremely pragmatic man. Which is why I am slightly disappointed in you tonight. True, you found a clever way to destroy Shi Zilin. But your attempt on Jake Maroc's life was a disaster. This does not please me. And are we any closer to penetrating Kam Sang? Perhaps I should punish you. I have contemplated that all through *Sleeping Beauty*. Tchaikovsky's music lends itself to such thoughts."

When Daniella said nothing, Maluta took a step toward her. She smelled his cologne, the residue of tobacco, the accumulation of the day's sweat, a miasma threatening to choke her. "You surprise me, Daniella Alexandrova. I expected you to raise your voice in your defense." His head cocked to one side. "No? Well, no matter. No defense would really suffice." He shrugged. "Who knows? Perhaps you have already figured that out."

Recovering herself somewhat, she said, "What about Carelin and Reztsov? Do you think they will stand around and watch you gather power? Either of them would be next in line, should Genachev die."

"Is that so?" Maluta said. It was just what he had wanted her to say. She is so predictable, he thought. "Termination is not the only way to remove obstacles from one's path."

"What do you mean?"

Waiting for the fear to appear on her face and finding it, he reached out and grabbed her by the front of her coat. He swung her around with astonishing power. Slammed her back against a tree trunk.

"Look at yourself. I have paralyzed you, Comrade General. You, the head of the First Chief Directorate of the *sluzhba*. You know I can do the same with Mikhail Carelin. Do you think that Reztsov is beyond my power?" Abruptly his face darkened. "You are with me now, remember that. If you are stupid enough to disobey me, you will be immediately picked up and charged with premeditated murder. It will be Lubyanka for you, or a gulag for the rest of your life."

With a sound of disgust, he let her go. "You've still to deliver to me Jake Maroc's head. As for the secrets to Kam Sang, if you do not deliver them within ten days I will be forced to take other measures."

"You are asking too much," Daniella said desperately. "These things—"

"Will get done, Comrade General. Otherwise, I shall be forced to order the immediate destruction of Kam Sang."

"What?" Her heart beat fast. The destruction of a military installation inside China's border? Was he insane?

"Oh, come," Maluta said, "these matters are easily arranged. Pilot error, an unfortunate mistake, et cetera, et cetera. It is nothing we have not used successfully before." He grinned at her. "And it *will* be done, Comrade General, believe me. One way or another, Kam Sang will be rendered useless to the Chinese."

In a moment, she could hear the sound of his boots crunching through the crisp layer of snow as he climbed the bank of the Moskva, which lay thick and glowering, heavy undercurrents sweeping reflected light downward into its murky depths.

From where he sat at the restaurant's table, Huaishan Han could see the Hill of Longevity rising up on one side. He was at the best table at the Ting Le Guan, on the north shore of the lake beside which the Summer Palace was built.

The restaurant, which specialized in fresh fish brought out of the lake each day, was in fact within the precincts of the Summer Palace, some forty-five minutes from the heart of Beijing.

Huaishan Han's ancient eyes traced the contours of the Hill of Longevity within whose shadow he now sat. It is both ironic and fitting, he thought, that this hill should be manmade. Nothing goes on forever, but still man in his egotistic way must strive to bring into his life the possibility that part of his essence at least will survive the decay of his corporeal body. Did the engineers who designed the Hill of Longevity, Huaishan Han thought, have this in mind when they began their project?

The pavilions within which Ting Le Guan was housed had recently been restored, their glazed tile roofs, handsomely decorated columns and interior walls bringing back a semblance of the former splendor of the capital—at least that was how it appeared to Huaishan Han. That was why he dined here often in the Pavilion for Listening to the Birds Sing. That and because here he could be near the Hill of Longevity and contemplate its meanings for him. Though his villa was not far distant, it had no view of the Hill.

Though Ting Le Guan was well known for its food, Huaishan Han certainly did not frequent it for that reason. He had not been able to taste anything for so many years that he ate by color. What appealed to his eyes he ordered and, in some way unfathomable to his intimates, enjoyed.

It was a bit early in the year still for the birds to be flitting through the trees lakeside, but Huaishan Han did not mind a bit. The quiet of the lake, the security of being surrounded by the complex structure of the Summer Palace and all the memories it conjured up for him made his time here exceptional. And there was always the Hill.

It was his impression that Shi Zilin—when he had been alive—had liked manmade hills. But then Shi Zilin had been partial to *yuan*, the carefully sculpted gardens of Suzhou. Huaishan Han supposed that was because Shi Zilin had been born in Suzhou and therefore had harbored a particular affection for the gardens. He himself found them confining, overrefined.

Abruptly, he understood that it no longer mattered. This inner debate about *yuan* was as dead as Shi Zilin. That pleased Han a great deal.

"Huaishan *tong zhi*?"

"Yes."

"Shall we order?"

Huaishan Han broke his gaze from the magnetic force of the Hill. He looked into the long, thin face of Jin Kanzhe. "Your stomach growls, does it?" He grunted. "I no longer feel hungry just as I no longer require sleep. I am long past the age where three meals or eight hours of sleep are a daily necessity. When I close my eyes now, I do not sleep. I dream of battlefields and blood, of the politics of change, of the requisites of Communism. I hear the people of China calling me from the border of sleep. In the blink of an eye I rest now, out of age or of habit I do not know. I am not sure that it matters." He waved a thin hand, as bony as a fish. "But go on, then. Do not allow my speaking to interfere with the gratification of your stomach." He grunted again. "No prawns for me tonight, no. Just a couple of *jiao zi*, that's all."

Jin Kanzhe did as he was bade, ordering the deep-fried dumplings for the old man, a whole fish for himself, and *mao tai*—a white liquor—for them both to drink. The spirits came almost immediately and was poured for them. Then they were left alone. Jin Kanzhe would have preferred to order more courses but he was careful not to do so in the old man's presence. Considering Han's disability, it would have been disrespectful.

"Tell me, Jin *tong zhi*," Huaishan Han said, "did you dream last night?"

Jin Kanzhe, who by this time was used to the old man's seemingly bizarre questions, said, "Yes, I did. I dreamt of carp swimming in a clear brook. They were golden and when the light struck their scales they shone like miniature suns."

"Hmmm," Huaishan Han said contemplatively. "This is an auspicious omen." The skin of his face seemed to be folded over again and again upon itself, so that tissue-thin layers lay in translucent creases that appeared to have no beginning and no end. His hands and jowls were heavily marked by liver spots, dark whorls upon his rice-paper-like skin.

"The carp represents China," Huaishan Han said. "Or, more accurately, the people of China. The golden people." He nodded now, his head bobbing on its stalklike neck. It was a simple gesture made odd because of how the old man was forced to sit, one misshapen shoulder higher than the other. Jin Kanzhe had heard that Huaishan Han had broken his back many years ago. "It is good." Huaishan Han mused for a bit, his eyes opaquing as they often did when he was deep in thought. "Tell me," he said in his odd floating voice, "do you have children?"

Jin Kanzhe sighed inwardly. The old man not only knew that he did indeed have children but also how many, their names and ages. Han had met them many times. Nevertheless, Jin Kanzhe repeated like a *sutra* the list of his six children, their names and ages.

Huaishan Han nodded as if hearing all this information for the first time. Then he said, as he always did, "It is a blessing, Jin Kanzhe, to have children." This was the only time the old man used Jin Kanzhe's full name. "Children are the most important aspect of life. I myself tried for many years after my first wife died to procreate. I took three other wives and, once, a mistress with translucent skin. I have outlived them all but I have nothing to show for it. None of them were able to conceive.

"Doctors. A pox on all doctors!" he cried with more animation than he had shown all evening. "None of them were able to tell me a thing. My women were fertile. I was potent. Potent, they told me, until I was almost eighty. Yet I have no children.

"You do not know what that is like, Jin Kanzhe. You cannot. You are not cursed as I am."

Were those incipient tears sparkling in the corners of his eyes, Jin Kanzhe wondered. It was entirely possible. Huaishan Han was obsessed with the subject of children. Any other man would have rested now, knowing that his enemy was dead.

But not Huaishan Han. He wanted more. He wanted to destroy Shi Zilin's son as well. His enemy's child.

"I do not think of children," Jin Kanzhe said carefully. "My expertise lies in other areas. Like Hong Kong."

Huaishan Han grunted. "Hong Kong. Another curse! That disgusting den of capitalist greed will be the downfall of China yet. Damn Shi Zilin to ten thousand flaming purgatories for his incursion into that place! What evil gods possessed him to believe in such a quarter for the salvation of our country." He shook his head sadly. "How misguided are people . . . important people. People whom other people listen to and rely upon for accurate information.

"Shi Zilin believed himself a celestial guardian of China." He laughed sourly. "What an idiotic notion! What rubbish all this mystical claptrap is. Celestial guardian, indeed! He sent his family into Hong Kong and he wished to give them power—to transfer his vast power to them. To an area outside of China. Whatever we do or *say* we will do in the future, one thing is very clear. Hong Kong will always be Hong Kong. Now and forever it is what the foreign devil made of it. The corruption of it goes too deep. We will waste our time in trying to change it. Better by far to cut ourselves off from it, to forget that it exists."

The food had come some minutes ago but Huaishan Han appeared oblivious to it. Jin Kanzhe longed to dig in but he could not begin without his elder and it would have been unforgivable of him to remind the older man of what was so obvious. Therefore, Jin Kanzhe did nothing but listen. That was all right. He was in the presence of a power so strong that it was tangible. Jin would—and indeed had—put up with much more than hunger for that.

"Why is Jake Shi still alive?" Huaishan Han demanded. "Why isn't the shape of my revenge taking place?"

"Colonel Hu requires more time," Jin Kanzhe said. "It is, he says, difficult to induce our plum to ripeness." He watched Han carefully. "In any case, he told you quite clearly at the beginning that in dealing with the human mind, rigid time-tables were impossible to keep. You said—"

"I've waited long enough!" Huaishan Han shouted. "You tell Colonel Hu that!"

Increasingly Huaishan Han was losing track of time and place. He seemed to Jin Kanzhe to be living in another world altogether. The old man's mind dwelt increasingly in his own inner landscape. But if that were the case, whence did his incalculable power stem? He possessed riches beyond the imagination of any Chinese Jin Kanzhe knew. Where did they come from? This was the man's essential enigma that Jin Kanzhe wanted to solve. "Our *lizi* is most precious. I trust we are agreed on that."

At this, Huaishan Han smiled. "Our dangerous little plum, yes. Our precious one." He gave Jin Kanzhe a sharp look. "Why should there be a question at this late date as to her disposition? It has all been arranged."

Jin Kanzhe hid his exasperation. There was something seriously wrong with Huaishan Han. Perhaps it was merely old age. Alzheimer's disease was not uncommon, or any one of a number of similar brain dysfunctions. What would become of the old man's plans, he wondered, if he were not around to see to their implementation. And what was his reward for keeping everything running smoothly? Huaishan Han treated him as if he were an accountant. He wanted—he *deserved*—his share of the old man's wealth.

"Yes. It is all arranged, Huaishan *tong zhi*," he said easily. "But, fortuitously, Shi Zilin is dead. Do we really need to go on now?"

"What do you mean?" Huaishan Han said. "Doesn't Shi Zilin live on?" And Jin Kanzhe thought, It has finally happened; he has lost his mind entirely. "Doesn't Shi Zilin live on through his son, Shi Jake?" Huaishan Han's wizened head was trembling. His hand grasped at the tabletop, seeking perhaps something tangible to crush.

Jin Kanzhe made no comment; there was none appropriate.

Huaishan Han glowered at his companion. "I have waited in the shadows for so long, Jin *tong zhi*. So long. Shi Zilin's power was such that I could not return to Beijing for a very long time. But he could not stop me from making inroads for myself with those ministers in power whom I singled out. Sometimes I used my own name, at other times, I employed a false one. It did not matter other than it kept Shi Zilin from finding out about me.

"Now, though you and others call me minister, I am nothing of the sort. I am more like a natural resource of China. My power is still outside the government. Because of Shi Zilin. His wretchedly long life has given me precious little time in which to work.

"But now my time has come, Jin *tong zhi*. Now my star is in the ascendant. All my preparations were for a purpose and that purpose is at hand. With Shi Zilin's departure from Beijing ten months ago, I was welcomed here by the friends I cultivated for years on end. My private army is assembled; it but awaits my final commands.

"And now that I possess the means to wipe out Shi Zilin's entire line, now that he will be truly dead, I will be able to give those commands."

Slowly, as if recovering from a dream, Huaishan Han became aware that there was food before them. He seemed surprised, as if he had forgotten that they were in a restaurant or what such an establishment was for.

"I am hungry," he said. And with that pronouncement he commenced to devour the dumplings after first having splashed them with a generous amount of soy and chili sauces.

Nothing more was said until the food was gone. This did not take Huaishan Han long. When he was finished, he put aside his chopsticks and set his gaze on the middle distance. It was as if his companion had ceased to exist or had never been there at all.

The moment Jin Kanzhe was finished and tea had been brought, however, Huaishan Han said, "Where did you serve your tour of duty while you were in the army, Jin *tong zhi*?"

"In Cambodia, mainly," Jin Kanzhe said. "Just like Colonel Hu."

"Ah, Hu," Huaishan Han said. "He learned some dark tricks among the Khmer Rouge, did he not?" His laugh was eerie. "There is a blackness about his spirit, as if somewhere inside of him he has been singed."

"I suppose it is so," Jin said, thoughtfully. "Colonel Hu was wounded twice. The first was not bad. But the second time, he was not so lucky. A tracer bullet caught him in the gut. The wound required extensive surgery. They took a yard of his intestines out. The pain will never really go away." Jin shrugged. "I suppose that is why he is so bitter about our offensive in Cambodia. His pain made him lose sight of China's political imperative.

"The Russians were backing the North Vietnamese. The Americans had taken up the French position of luring Prince Sihanouk with their siren songs.

"China's was an elementary decision, from my point of view: back the insurgents, the Khmer Rouge. Their barbarism was wholly justified, don't you think, given the circumstances? They were given the task of burning an entire nation's politically and morally corrupt past. And, in its place, creating a new regime, a new politic, a new society."

Huaishan Han's eyes contemplated his companion. "Tell me, Jin *tong zhi*, what was Cambodia like?"

Jin Kanzhe pushed his plate away. There was nothing whatsoever left of the fish, not even the bones. "Have you ever been to hell?" he said.

For the first time since he knew him, Huaishan Han's expression showed something other than his inner pain and the overriding thirst for revenge which, despite his disclaimers to the contrary concerning the future of China, appeared now to be his sole reason for living.

"Hell," the old man said, "is where I have been residing for the past thirty-eight years."

"Gone? Gone where?" Bliss asked.

"To Japan."

"Where? Where in Japan?"

"That is his business, *bou-sehk*," Three Oaths said. "It is not for us to question the goings and comings of the great *Zhuan*."

Bliss heard something in his voice but she was too distracted to dwell on it. "Why isn't he here?" She had just returned from the hospital where every test imaginable had been run through her brain. The doctors, having found nothing of a conclusive nature, wanted her to remain several days longer to be subjected to further tests. She had refused.

"What is wrong with me?" she had asked them.

"We don't know," they had said. "Nothing." Grasping sheets of computer printouts delineating the wave patterns of her brain. "We suggest that you stay here longer."

"Why?"

"So that we can find out."

"Find out what?"

"Why all our tests show us nothing."

"Then there is something," she had said.

"There is nothing," they had replied, "that we can find. So far."

"The EEG?" It always came back to the EEG, the center of their concern.

"Certain spiky responses," they said. "One or two giving the pattern a skew out of the norm."

"Then in your opinion there is a problem."

"Not that we know of. So far. If you would submit to several more—"

She got out of there, fed up with their enigmatic replies. They were like ancient Greek oracles: they opined and said nothing; left you to manufacture your own fears in private.

Three separate crews were hard at work repairing her father's junk. Three Oaths had borrowed a junk from his vast fleet and, mooring it near the first one in Aberdeen Harbor, had installed himself and his family on the unfamiliar vessel. This was where he had brought Bliss when he had taken her home from the hospital.

He had said nothing to her about Jake or his whereabouts until they were aboard. Though she had queried him several times in the hospital, Three Oaths had managed to avoid any answer. She had enough worries without adding to them.

"Where in Japan?" she repeated.

"That I do not know, *bou-sehk*." He shrugged. "Tokyo, most likely. That is where his Yakuza friend is, *neh*?

"Mikio Komoto? Yes."

"Yakuza murdered the Jian. He has gone to find out why."

For the first time Bliss became aware of the extraordinary tension emanating from her father. That is normal, she thought. Shi Zilin was everything to him.

She had fought not to think about the Jian during those

moments in the hospital when she had been lucid. Most of
the time she had slept, drugged and insensate. At other times
it seemed as if she was drifting through clouds of dreamstuff
so tangible she wanted to reach out and feel them. She dreamt
of light and sensation; she dreamt of floating, of flying. And
of spheres more vast than her imagining. Spheres which spun
in stately time within the bosom of a spangled blackness deep
and wide.

Often she would awake certain that one of the spheres—
the closest to her—had about its terrain a disturbingly familiar
cast. Then, with a start so palpable it made her shudder, the
familiarity was brought into focus: the face of Shi Zilin just
before she placed the pillow over it.

Compulsively, then, she would race away from the image,
engaging the doctors or, if he was available, her father, in
conversation. Speaking about anything at all so long as it kept
her away from the image.

But once, she dreamt of the image. And in that moment
became aware of the expression on the Jian's face as it was
occluded by the white cloud of the pillow. His eyes were
closed, of that she was certain. Yet she was just as sure that
he was watching her. How was that possible?

She thought of *da-hei*, the great darkness where all that
was incorporeal about man resided.

She wondered if Buddha would ever forgive her for what
she had done. But Shi Zilin had asked it of her as a favor.
She was saving him from assassins' bullets.

Now, for the first time since the incident, Bliss wondered
how the Jian knew that they were coming; knew even before
the *walla-walla* bumped against the junk's hull. If he knew,
she thought now, why didn't he act to save himself? Surely
he had time to get us both off the junk.

"Bou-sehk!"

Heard Three Oaths's voice as if from a great distance.

"You did not answer my question."

I did not hear your question, Father, she thought.

"Are you all right?"

She opened her mouth to answer him, though, indeed, she
did not know the answer. Instead she was overcome. The
strange emotion inside her that had been stirring like a snake
in spring, emerging from slothful hibernation, gyred upward.
And in its ascendancy it transported her.

Once again she was stretched over the skin of the heaving

South China Sea as she had been when she had been bent over the dying form of Shi Zilin.

She saw the black bulk of the tankers, newly from the Strait of Malacca, full of flaming dark oil. She heard the sea erns calling, saw their great flecked bodies dipping and gliding on the air currents above her. Below she heard the deep drawn-out symphony reverberating through the ocean current. Carried for miles on end, the whale schools communicated in an ancient arcane song. Elemental and powerful, their speech filled her up as if she had been an empty vessel, waiting upon the bosom of the sea.

And in their cries was recognition, just a flash, a white-hot instant of revelation that shook her to her core. It froze her consciousness even while it galvanized the inner heart of her mind. She saw and felt at once the source of this strange emotion. She felt her *qi* linked and she thought, All gods bear witness this cannot be happening. I must be losing my mind!

"—look like?"

A mi tuo fo!

"—seen a ghost."

Felt herself being shaken and at last her eyes focused on her father's concerned face. "By the Celestial Blue Dragon," he said, "you've gone as white as milk. Are you ill?"

Buddha, she thought. Buddha protect me from this madness. "I'm not—" She put her hand to her forehead. "I'm not feeling at all well in fact." She stood on wobbly legs. "Will you excuse me?"

She clutched at the railing, her body bent over. She tried to vomit and could not.

"Bou-sehk!"

She wanted to stop this feeling of being in two places at once. The South China Sea beckoned with all its thrumming animal sounds.

What is happening to me? she thought wildly. She clutched at her head as her *qi* plunged downward into the depths of the water, listening to the atonal symphony. Listening . . .

"Art is truth," Fo Saan had said to Jake. "Art takes nothing—a blank page, a white canvas—and makes of it something affecting. Art can only be defined by the emotion it engenders in the viewer. It does not presuppose; it does not contend. Like the great seas and rivers of the world, art is one of the Lords of the Ravines. Its power comes from keeping low."

It was Fo Saan who trained Jake in the ways of the mind and of the body. It was Fo Saan who, unbeknownst to Jake, had been sent by Shi Zilin to do just that when Jake was just a boy of seven. Fo Saan in his own way had been a part of the *yuhn-hyun*, the inner circle. He had also been responsible for training Jake's childhood playmate, Bliss.

It had been Fo Saan who had taught Jake about *cham hai*, sinking in, and its ultimate phase, *ba-mahk*.

"There will come a time," Fo Saan had said to his young pupil, "when you will find yourself contending against shadows. Perhaps you will know your enemy, perhaps not. In any event, his intention will be hidden from you. You will strike out here! There! But you will strike nothing. Only shadows.

"Then you must heed my words and seek to become one with the Lords of the Ravines. You, too, must keep low."

This was what was in Jake's mind when he told Three Oaths Tsun that he was going to Japan. Of course his anxiety for the safety of Mikio Komoto was a major factor. But Jake was acutely aware that the *yuhn-hyun* was under attack. He did not know who his enemies were or what their ultimate goal was. The time that Fo Saan had foreseen for him had at last come and by taking himself away from Hong Kong, from the center of the arena of contention, he was keeping low. Hopefully then, he would gather to him the power of the Lords of the Ravines.

Fo Saan's bright button eyes dominated Jake's dream as he slept on the flight out of Kai Tak airport. He had slept fitfully for weeks, and not at all since his father's death. And his fight with the *dantai*, though effecting no permanent damage, had taken a lot out of him both physically and emotionally. The thought that a Yakuza clan was involved in his father's assassination made no sense. It chilled him to the bone, for his connection with the Japanese underworld was directly through Mikio. Had the raid signaled a sinister turn of events in the Yakuza war? Was Mikio already dead, the victim of a rival's *katana*?

Fo Saan:

"You are no longer a child; no longer safe." He takes Jake by the hand and leads him into the night. The skies are pellucid so that the stars seem a shower of sparks raining down upon the earth. The bowl of the heavens is alight and afoot.

"Where are we?" Jake asks.

"Upon the mountain."

"Where are we going?"

"Up."

They walk for a very long time. Above their heads the blazing stars wheel in their predetermined arc. An owl hoots and, flapping its powerful wings, takes flight. Its predatory head, filled with enormous orange eyes, scans the darkness before the bird plunges downward to the earth.

The man and the boy both hear the sharp crunch of tiny bones breaking with an almost suprareal clarity.

"*Shan*," says Fo Saan, "from *shan* do the *dieh loong*, the earth dragons, greatest of all the species, get their power."

"From this mountain?" Jake asks. "From any mountain?"

"Ask the winds and the water," Fo Saan says.

"*Feng shui.*"

"*Feng shui*, yes. The art of geomancy; of reading the magical portents from earth, air, fire, water and metal: the five cardinal elements." Fo Saan, back bent against the incline, seems tireless though the way is long and, at times, arduous. "There is *qi* in the earth," he says, "just as there is *qi* in all of us. *Qi* is a great spiral. Sometimes it is inhaled toward the center of the earth, at other times it is exhaled upward into the valleys, rivers, streams . . . and *shan*, the mountains. It is in these places that man seeks to live."

It is near to dawn by the time they reach the summit. The stars are visibly closer but already beginning to dim in the east. Above, the bowl of night is still dominant.

"Lie down," Fo Saan says. Jake does as he is told. "Close your eyes." He does so.

"In order for you to fend off death," Fo Saan continues, "you must generate sufficient power to carry out the maneuvers you have been learning. Practice is one thing, the killing ground quite another. Speed, dexterity, flexibility in body and thought is vital if you are to survive your first real encounter in the killing ground.

"Force, energy, power. *Qi*." Jake feels rather then hears the movement but he does not open his eyes. "You are no longer a child; no longer a baby." Is there hidden significance in Fo Saan's repeated words? Jake does not know. "You must begin all over again. You must learn the bare essentials of life if you are to live it henceforth in this manner."

Now Jake gasps but does not cry out. There is a weight on his chest of such proportions that he is certain it will crush him. His eyelids flutter and Fo Saan says, "Do not open your eyes." Jake obeys.

"I cannot breathe," Jake says in a strained voice. "I will die."

"There is a stone on your chest," Fo Saan says. "A great heavy stone. Perhaps it is a scale from *dieh loong* that has been shed at the end of winter."

"I cannot breathe."

"Then you must learn to breathe all over again," Fo Saan says and Jake understands the meaning of his mentor's re-iterated words. *You are no longer a child; you are no longer a baby.* There is no oxygen left within him. Weight presses down upon him as if it were the *shan* itself atop his chest. *You must begin all over again.*

"You will ask," Fo Saan says, "why do you not teach me to breathe all over again in tranquil surroundings, with a pleasant breeze ruffling my cheek and an infinite amount of time in which to perfect my learning?" The voice was closer to Jake's ear, an insect buzzing near the gently curved shell.

"My answer is that this is another form of learning. We speak here of instinct. When you are attacked, instinct dictates that you hold your breath, your muscles tighten. *Qi* ceases its flow. Then you will die.

"Instead, you must learn to breathe under attack, to keep your muscles supple, the *qi* flowing. You are under attack now. You must breathe."

The voice subsides in the night. There is a red rim around Jake's eyelids. He sees this aurora and wonders what is causing it. His heart hammers in his chest, his rib cage strains beneath the enormous weight. His pulse thunders in his ears. I will die, he thinks.

Then, his body or his mind—he does not know which—moves. It comes to a clear space, an otherworldly space. Here he feels no pain but rather the rippling of some gleaming constant flow. Is it *qi*, as Fo Saan has suggested?

Jake concentrates on this one spot, a patch of silver moonlight pouring into the midst of a dense and stifling forest. He moves within this glade. He moves upward.

And as he does so he gathers power. His muscles ripple and contract in unison as if galvanized by one momentous surge of inner energy.

Upward he thrusts. Off comes the weight. He hears the thunk of the stone. He breathes.

And in his ear, Fo Saan whispers, "*Jeuih-jahp lihk-leung.* You have gathered together the power. You have learned to breathe all over again."

Jake opens his eyes. Dawnlight shimmers the horizon, illuminating at last the mountain upon whose back he has labored.

Tony Simbal at the DEA computer getting the lowdown on Encarnacion. A town in southeast Paraguay. It was where, Threnody had told him, Peter Curran had bought it. Simbal wasn't getting the usual stuff—population, typography, agriculture, climate and the like. He could have used the *Encyclopaedia Britannica* for that.

The DEA files were gravid with information on that quadrant of the world from 1947 on. With good reason. That was when the futures of certain South American countries began to change—including Paraguay's. Certain leaders abruptly became stronger, their private armies larger and better equipped. Enormous sums of money had been infused into these countries in an astonishingly short period of time. And, further, within the space of five years new industries had sprung up and others were burgeoning. All these industries were clandestine and, at least in the majority of the world, illegal.

The smartest and most powerful of the Nazis who had made it out of Germany and Europe, evading both the burning of Berlin and the subsequent Nuremburg war crimes tribunals, had set themselves up for life deep within the emerald jungles of South America.

Paraguay was high on the DEA computer file list of countries whose regimes had aided and abetted the fleeing criminals. For a price, of course. A price exacted that would ensure their own security among a populace stricken with intense poverty, disease and educational ignorance.

Encarnacion, Simbal learned, had been nothing more than a backward town before the Nazis had come. They had terraformed nearly a continent. Now the *diqui* had begun to take over there. Why? No one knew. It was what, apparently, Curran had been tracking down.

"Who was in Encarnacion when Peter Curran was?" Simbal said out loud.

"I don't know," Monica said softly from a point just behind him. She was peering over his shoulder. The terminal screen was brightly lighted, pulsing with information.

"Anyone from DEA?"

"Not that I know of."

"Let's bring that up and check. What's the file name?"

"Travel Folder."

Simbal found it, coordinating the dates during which Curran had been in Paraguay. Drew blank.

"Okay," she said. "What next?"

He smelled the lemony tang of her soap, mixed with the hint of perfume she used. A stray strand of her hair brushed his cheek. He felt her warmth.

"Vacations," Simbal said and she gave him the file name. He called it up and went down the list. There were six names. None of their itineraries precisely coincided with the dates and, in any case, all were required to file destinations and local phone numbers with Threnody's office.

Monica pulled these. There had been occasion to call three of them during the course of their vacations and they had indeed been where they had logged in. Three others were still out and had not been contacted. None were anywhere near South America, let alone Paraguay, but then Simbal did not expect anyone to broadcast that fact.

"Do you know what you're looking for?" Monica asked him.

"Just following my nose," Simbal said, dialing the first number. He put Monica on and she made up a story about why she had to call. It was late. Everyone was in bed just where they said they would be.

"So much for vacationers," Monica said. "Satisfied?"

"How powerful is this baby?" Simbal patted the side of the monitor.

"Plenty, why?"

"Are you networked?"

"Sure. But it depends on the agency and, within that agency, on how the material is classified."

"How about FBI, CIA, SNITs."

Monica put the flat of her hand over the keyboard. "Whoa," she said. "Before I possibly incriminate myself and this agency I think you'd better tell me what you have in mind."

"I can't."

"Then this is as far as we go together." She reached to shut down the terminal and Simbal took her hand.

"Monica."

"No soft soap, Tony. This is getting creepy. I agreed to let you in here. It's strictly against the rules of the house."

"Max knows all about it."

"Really? Well, he's said nothing to me about it."

"Do you want to find out who had Peter Curran killed?"

Monica gave a little shudder. "I already know that. The *diqui*."

"Possibly."

"Meaning?"

"Meaning I want to know what the hell the *diqui* is doing in Encarnacion . . . a place where they have no right to be."

"Because of the Nazis?"

"Because of the Nazis."

There was silence for a time. The twilit offices were still around them. The air was off and it was stuffy.

"What do you think happened to Peter?" Monica said after a time.

"He ran afoul of someone," Simbal said. "But I'm not convinced that it was the *diqui*."

"Who then?"

"Would you let me find out?"

Monica hesitated for just a moment. Then she said, "Which agency?"

Drew blank with the FBI and the CIA both. But the CIA's Strategic Narcotics Team—the people Simbal called SNITs—had their own computer network.

"I think I'd better take over," Monica said, displacing him in the console chair. "The SNIT files are like minefields. They're so paranoid over there the calling up of certain files triggers an internal alert."

"Any way to get around it?"

"What are we looking for?"

"Same thing," Simbal said. "Assignments, vacations."

Monica's fingers flew over the keyboard, calling up and putting back files. "Nothing that fits," she said, "in either category."

"So I see," Simbal said morosely.

She was just about to pull out of the SNIT files entirely when she caught an electronic asterisk.

"What's that?"

"I don't know," she said. "Let's follow it." A moment later the answer swam up onto the screen.

"A leave of absence," Simbal said. "Jesus Christ."

"The dates are right," Monica said. "The leave began two days after Peter left for Paraguay."

"And he's not back yet. You know this guy Edward Martin Bennett?"

"Zip."

"Personnel."

Monica complied, switching files. "Ooops," she said. "This one's mined, all right. I'll have to find a way around it." And did, in twelve minutes. "Okay," she announced, "here's their scoop on Bennett." The screen began the scroll of data.

BENNETT, EDWARD MARTIN, BORN 3/13/36, DULUTH, MINNESOTA. PARENTS—

"Skip that," Simbal said.

EDUCATED SINDON GRAMMAR SCHOOL, FITZSIMMONS HIGH SCHOOL. TRANSFERRED TO VARLEY PREP IN VALLEY FORGE, PENNSYLVANIA 1/4/50. B.A., M.S., FROM YALE UNIVERSITY, CLASS OF 1956. MEMBER OF SWIM, LA-CROSSE, SOCCER TEAMS. PHI BETA KAPPA. VARSITY SOCCER CAPTAIN, 1956. MEMBER HELLFIRE CLUB—

"Stop it right there," Simbal said, feeling excitement growing in him. "This guy and Peter were at Yale together."

"Coincidence?"

"Also the Hellfire Club."

"Is that significant?"

"Yeah," Simbal said, remembering the signet ring Threnody said had been found. "It just may be."

Monica withdrew from the SNIT files and they switched over to the airline schedules.

"Pick it up two days after Peter left." Monica reviewed the carriers.

"This could take some time."

"Nope," Simbal said, his forefinger stabbing at the screen. "Here it is!"

PAN AM FLIGHT 107, DEPARTING 11 A.M., JFK, ARRIVING 7 P.M. BENNETT, EDWARD MARTIN.

"Mexico City," Simbal said.

Monica's fingers continued to work the keyboard. "There's no connecting flight to Paraguay but there *is* a flight to Buenos Aires." She hummed a little. "His name's not on the passenger manifest."

"I'm not surprised. I wouldn't advertise if I was going that way, either."

"Found his name again," Monica said. Simbal's excitement was becoming contagious. "Here's the flight plan: Mexico

205

City—he left there a week after we were notified of Peter's death. He flew to San Francisco. After a day's layover, he flew out to Miami."

"He still there?"

Monica hit the keyboard. "Well," she said, "he hasn't flown out."

After they had shut down and left the offices, she said, "I wish you could come back with me tonight." He helped her on with her coat.

"Your family comes first," he said. In truth, he was thinking about other things: like Edward Martin Bennett in Miami. "You haven't seen your cousin in, what? a year?"

"Just about." Monica hesitated at the doorway. Her eyes when they looked into his shadowed face were luminous. "You're going to Miami, aren't you?"

He said nothing and she followed him out, locking up behind them. The night was unseasonably warm. From where they stood, they could see the Washington Monument lit up, cool, white, majestic.

"Don't lie to me, Tony. Not again."

He nodded. "I'm going."

"Is Bennett the one?"

"I won't know until I get there."

"Why don't you let someone else do it this time?" Simbal was quiet and Monica nodded. Then she quickly turned away and went down the marble steps and got into her Mazda. She took off.

Simbal watched her go, a little sadly; he would have liked to spend his last night in Washington wrapped in her warmth. Then he remembered that she had forgotten to supply him with the new entry code for the DEA computer. He'd need that to run deep background on Edward Martin Bennett on his own.

He ran down the steps, shouting for her, but she was too far away. He ran to his Saab, turned the ignition and set off after her.

Through nighttime Washington they went, a glittery world filled with public monuments, parks, pools, ponds, fountains.

Into Georgetown, and suddenly Simbal felt a chill seeping into him. Monica lived in Alexandria, which lay in the opposite direction. She had made a point of telling him that her cousin, Jill, was flying in from San Diego that evening and would be spending a couple of nights at Monica's. Yet she turned into R Street. And Simbal, continuing after her with his headlights doused, thought, What the hell?

He stopped the Saab down the block and across the street. Watched with mounting dread as she went up the steps and rang the bell. Watched his old friend Max Threnody come to the door and usher her in.

Tony Simbal, sitting in darkness, listening to the Saab's cooling fan quiet the powerful turbocharged engine, felt an odd queasy sensation, a knowledge of being betrayed. A sense that home was no longer secure.

Bluestone was a tall, angular man with ruddy cheeks, a decidedly Roman nose, a wide straight brow beneath which blue eyes peered out at the world with a great deal of inquisitiveness. He wore Savile Row suits, spurning the efforts of even the best of the Hong Kong tailors. His shirts were handmade by Turnbull and Asser, his shoes handlasted by Church of England. It was Sir John's opinion that one could not pay too much to be dressed smartly and, above all, correctly.

"And how is my little flower?" Bluestone said.

"I have something for you."

"I know," he said and smiled. "It is why I derive so much pleasure from having lunch with you."

"Lunch was my idea," she said, correcting him.

He frowned. "And an odd one, too, I might add." He spread his hands. "This is a very public place." They were sitting in the Central District branch of Princess Garden, high up overlooking the pedestrian walkway above Chater Road.

"Oh, yes," she agreed, "very, *very* public."

"There is, I expect, a good reason for this." She looked smashing, every inch a model or television star. All heads turned—male and female—when she came into the restaurant. She wore a black shantung silk skirt and jacket beneath which peeped out an oyster white camisole edged with delicate open embroidery. Her only jewelry was a massive emerald ring. He knew where that came from. She had the ability to use Western makeup to bring out the exoticism of her Eastern face. How many women he knew would kill to possess that talent?

"*Prosit*," he said, lifting his glass.

"*Das vidanya*," she said in a ludicrous Russian accent.

He scowled. "Don't be idiotic."

"Idiotic?" Neon Chow said. "I am not idiotic. Three Oaths

Tsun knows who you are. They all know: Jake, Sawyer, all of them."

Bluestone put his glass down very carefully. "What, precisely, do you mean, they know who I am?"

"They know that you are the KGB's top Asian operative," Neon Chow said. She was openly enjoying his consternation. "Don't look so sour," she said, sipping at her drink. "They want me to spy on you for them. That's why I asked you to lunch when you came by the governor's office yesterday."

Bluestone watched her face, his mind working furiously, and in a moment he had worked it out. Perhaps this wasn't the disaster it had at first seemed to be.

"Christ," he said, "Three Oaths Tsun wants you to keep tabs on me?"

"That's right," Neon Chow said.

The waiter arrived and they ordered. When he had departed, Bluestone said, "This may be better than ever. Obviously they want to keep me in place. A known enemy is far better than an unknown one. And I have already deceived them concerning the Southasia scheme."

"Oh, yes," Neon Chow agreed. "As I reported to you, they suspect that you are behind Teck Yau's embezzlement."

"That's all right," he said, still working out the refinements of his plan. And because of that suspicion, he thought gleefully, they also believe that the scheme to embezzle funds from Southasia is the full extent of my plan to defeat them. He thought a moment. "Listen to me. I have a way to overcome their discovery of my identity. If I can deceive them by running you back at them, I may have everything I need to destroy InterAsia Trading and all who back her."

"But there's more," Neon Chow said.

"Have you found out who's behind Shi Zilin's murder?"

"Forget about that," she said quickly. "The old man was killed by a bunch of Yakuza. Rivals of Jake's Yakuza friend, I forget his name." She put her empty glass aside. "What I have for you is far more important. When Three Oaths took me out for my birthday, I got him talking about the *yuhn-hyun*. Their purpose is somehow to link certain *tai pan* here with interests in Mainland China."

Bluestone seemed stunned. "What are you saying? Hong Kong and Beijing would be in some kind of collusion?"

"Yes."

"Impossible! Even when China takes full control of Hong

Kong in 2047 the business interests here will fight the change-over to Communism with every breath."

"According to my information," Neon Chow said, "there won't be a changeover to Communism. There will, instead, be *one* China. One political system. One economic system. And that system will most assuredly not be Communism."

Bluestone already knew that. But one was always safest confirming one source with another, totally independent one. This was a lesson Daniella Vorkuta had taught him and it had proved invaluable more than once.

Espionage, Bluestone thought, staring hard at Neon Chow, was not a game for amateurs. Only the seasoned professionals survived.

Taken completely out of time, Qi lin floated. Colonel Hu had learned his trade well.

He had been warned by Jin Kanzhe how tough this subject's mind would be. Her mind and her will. There was no doubt that she had exceptional *qi*. One needed—to be successful at this peculiar and twisted trade of mind sculpting—to be fully aware of the subject's *qi* before one employed any technique. *Qi* could change everything.

Colonel Hu had observed this during his time in Cambodia. The Khmer Rouge, whom he had aided, had been rather crude in their mind-sculpting techniques. One had difficulty dealing with them, and early on Colonel Hu had ceased to give them advice. One could not have a dialogue with fanatics; one merely spoke *at* them. Either they listened or they didn't.

During his time in Cambodia, Colonel Hu had learned to despise the Khmer Rouge. Learn from them he did, for sometimes their techniques were wholly effective. But he hated every minute in that blood-filled land.

If the truth be known (and Colonel Hu only dwelt on this loathsome fact deep in the night while in solitary separation he drank) he had been terrified of the Khmer Rouge. They were as unthinking as robots. They had been programmed as effectively as their pitiable subjects. Colonel Hu had, of course, confronted many fanatics in his time—China itself was well known for its ideological fanaticism. But none was on a level with those he found in Cambodia.

In his mind, their animalistic barbarism was forever linked with the stench of burning flesh and scorched hair. There was not an hour he spent in Cambodia when his nostrils were not clogged with the smell. After a time, he learned to live with it as he had learned to live among the vicious primitives.

It was also true that Colonel Hu drank to blot out the emotions that these dread people had engendered in him. When he at last returned from his tour of duty in Cambodia, he had knelt down when no one was watching and pressed his lips lovingly into the soil of his native China.

He drank to forget, but he could not forget. The terror crept through even the most serious drunk. Only when he passed out near to dawn was his mind washed clean for a few hours. But when he awoke, the memories rushed back at him again like howling demons until he wished only to rip his own brain apart.

Instead, he steeled himself and got on with his job. And now his job was brainwashing Qi lin.

This was no easy task. In fact, she presented a number of unique and at first baffling problems. That was quite all right with Colonel Hu. The more difficult the subject, the better he liked it because the deeper his mind was occupied. Work at least kept the hounds inside his head at bay.

The nights were what Colonel Hu dreaded most.

Now his men were asleep, and Huaishan Han had departed, having spent all day with Hu and his special subject; Hu was alone, face to face with the chill solitary night filled as it always was with the scrabbling of nocturnal creatures, the wind rustling down the trees like faraway voices . . . voices of the dying, of the damned. It was then that Colonel Hu reached for the bottle.

At times, he would not even bother with a glass; it made the river of surcease flow too slowly.

On this night, consumed by gusty winds that rattled sand from the Gobi against the windows, Colonel Hu lay in a semitorpor. He had not dared to touch liquor while old, crooked-backed Huaishan Han was here. But Huaishan Han had left hours ago and the night grew long. Colonel Hu drank. One hand now grapsed the neck of a nearly empty bottle of liquor with the kind of desperation only a drowning man summons up.

Tiny droplets of sweat glistened like sad diamonds in his brush-cut hair. His eyes were filmy with the tread of ghosts marching in an endless parade through the interstices of his skull. His uniform shirt was open at the neck and deep crescents of sweat showed beneath each arm and down the front where the starched fabric clung to his fluttering chest, losing all shape.

His feet were bare; he seemed to feel the squelch of that mixture of mud, blood and offal peculiar to ravaged Cambodia. It had seemed to him that there was no soil left in the country. This putrid compound slid across the valleys, fields, and lakesides like the effluvia of some monstrous volcano.

Colonel Hu started and shuddered, hiccuping. He said something, indecipherable even to himself.

Then he looked up. Qi lin was framed in the doorway.

There was nothing but utter blackness behind her and this stygian color seemed to dwarf her completely, lending her the appearance of a street waif, thin and ill-fed, living from moment to moment.

"Is Huaishan Han gone? Already?"

"What are you doing here?" Colonel Hu asked with slightly slurred diction.

"My sleep was filled with . . ." Qi lin's quavery voice trailed off. She seemed so young, so . . .

"With what?"

"With life. Teeming life."

Colonel Hu thought of his own sleep and what it was like without the utter oblivion alcohol provided. He shuddered again and swallowed.

He raised his hand, discovered the bottle still in it and waved the thing at her. "Come in." There were guards all around the perimeter of the encampment but none at her doorstep. That was not considered sound psychological practice. "Sit down."

Qi lin did as she was told, perching herself on a bamboo-and-canvas ottoman. She looked like a bird, thin and frail seeming, peering at him with those huge dark enigmatic eyes. They were odd eyes; they had held Colonel Hu's attention from the moment he first saw her. They were bright with intelligence, glossy with a more elemental quality he could not name. They were Chinese eyes, to be sure. But they were also something else. There was a Western aspect to them, as if the epicanthic folds were not complete or had been subtly altered in the formless genetic state. Colonel Hu knew where that came from.

Her eyes held him now, their intensity burning through the deadening liquor like hot sunlight through a morning haze.

"Tell me about your dreams," Colonel Hu said.

"I was in a city," Qi lin said obediently. "It was big, big

as a hive. It was built on a hill . . . on many hills so that the streets were never flat. Never ever. They rose and fell like the ocean tides. It was strange."

"In what way was it strange?"

"I felt perfectly at home there," Qi lin said with a bit of wonder in her voice. "I don't see how that's possible. I know the jungle. I know that is where I have been, where I feel at home. You have told me that time and again."

"It is true."

"Then the city—"

"The city is a dream."

"But it felt so real. I dreamt in such detail . . . the streets, the houses, shops. Even the people."

"What people?" Colonel Hu was sitting up straighter. He ran a hand through his hair, wiped the wetness away on his trouser leg.

"I don't know."

"But you said you dreamt in such detail."

"I did."

"Then describe the people."

"I can't."

"You are lying to me."

Qi lin gasped and her eyes were filled with fear. Such a pity, Colonel Hu thought, because all the gloss went out of them. They were dulled to opacity and then they became merely eyes as everyone had eyes, nothing special at all.

"No!"

"Then tell me!"

"I can't!"

"Tell me! *Tell me!*" Colonel Hu became aware that he was shouting. He had hold of her and was shaking her violently. He felt a constriction in his throat, a rage suffusing him as the choir of the damned sang its funereal dirge in his inner ear.

Qi lin was sobbing, a tender shoot trembling before the force of a gale. "Oh, Buddha!" she gasped. "Buddha protect me!"

Colonel Hu's rage doubled and he shook her maniacally. "Why do you invoke the name of Buddha here? That is forbidden! Strictly forbidden!"

His rage fell upon her like cruel sleet, blinding her, making her choke and pant for breath. She felt gripped by forces beyond her control, forces which threatened to rip aside the fabric of this life to which she had become acclimated. That would mean a return to the pain—the awful, ringing, echoing, reverberating pain, behind which lurked the nothingness that froze her marrow.

Thus she struggled, hurling herself against him so that her tears streaked his cheeks, running into his eyes, salt droplets clinging to his lips, trembling just before he swallowed them.

Colonel Hu felt her against him and he felt warmth. Her tremors went through him. It was as if he was feeling her soul shaking itself apart. And without even thinking, he gathered her into him.

Just as two animals in the wild—enemies even—will seek one another out and share in bodily warmth in order to survive the bitter cold of nature's cruelest months, so Colonel Hu acted out of instinct. It was as much for his own survival as it was for hers, though he might not yet understand that.

All he was aware of was the suffering.

"Little one," he murmured. "Little one," hearing her tiny whimpers and within them the anguished cries of the multitudes who had been mutilated in the name of a blasted, nihilistic ideology without heart or soul. Those same multitudes through whom he had tramped, their muck seeping into his boots, squelching between his toes.

He felt her curling up against him, her sobs slackening, her tears drying, and with them, the terror in her soul.

Warmth began to suffuse him and he wondered at it because it was a warmth from an outside source. Colonel Hu was not a celibate. He took his pleasure from a variety of women. But all of them had thighs like alabaster, cool and ungiving. Their jade gates were like marble, smooth, drawing from him his hot seed during the clouds and the rain but nothing more.

Now it seemed to him as if he had the sun in his lap instead of this small frail woman who had appeared to him tonight as a girl. And gradually it dawned on him that the heat had worked a specific source in him. His loins were burning up. He was as stiff as stone.

Qi lin moved on him and he groaned.

Unplanned and unwanted. Worse, unthinkable. Nevertheless, Colonel Hu's sacred member arched upward and where it encountered the heat between Qi lin's thighs, the sensation was exquisite.

Colonel Hu did not wish to be aroused but he did not want an end to this life-giving warmth. Thus he hugged Qi lin to him as she hugged him, surrounding her with his arms and being thus surrounded himself.

He told himself that he did not desire her, that he could not, in fact, desire her. Her jade gate was as forbidden to him as invoking the name of Buddha was for her. He had been warned in no uncertain terms. In Qianmen, Jin Kanzhe had said, *"Zheige lizi hai mei shu ne."* *The plum is not yet ripe. But that doesn't mean that she isn't dangerous. On the contrary. She is exceptionally deadly.*

Such warmth could never emanate from death, Colonel Hu decided. In his mind, along with the singing chorus of the dead, all he wanted was to hold her. Other parts of him felt differently. He was warring with himself and had not Qi lin herself become an active factor he did not know what the outcome would have been.

That was all made academic, however, because she reached inward and gently grasped the head of his sacred member. The touch was so electric that for a moment Colonel Hu felt robbed of all breath. Volition went as well, and he surrendered to her touch.

In that moment he heard the rain begin to lash itself against the tiny windowpanes like an angry dragon's tail.

Colonel Hu felt the buttons at his fly being opened one after another. Each one brought him closer to the heat. He reached up and began to open the buttons on Qi lin's blouse. It was rough cotton, as were her drawstring trousers. Not prison garb—that, too, would have been unsound psychological practice.

He bared her firm ripe breasts at the same time that she wrapped her hand around his naked member. He shuddered and drew her breasts against his mouth. His lips opened to encompass the point of first one then the other.

Qi lin, licking her palm with her tongue, used the moisture to aid her ministrations. A storm tossed Colonel Hu as the storm outside bowed the tall trees, lashed at the groundcover and the buildings of the encampment.

Colonel Hu wanted with such desperation to touch her bare thighs that his fingers shook as they attempted to unknot the drawstrings. In the end, Qi lin was obliged to help him.

She slipped the trousers off without putting her feet to the floor. She was partly nude, since her blouse, though open, was still on, and this inflamed Colonel Hu even more. His sacred member was trembling as much as his hands.

He caressed her thighs and found them warm, not cool as alabaster. The flesh was smooth and soft beneath his callused fingers. The backs of his hands brushed against the thick thatch of hair and he inhaled quickly.

Qi lin, turning her palm in a circular motion across the head of his sacred member, guided him to the portals of her jade gate. She left him there, the bloated tip throbbing against her.

Colonel Hu groaned in anticipation. He felt the unutterable softness of her brushing against his sensitive flesh and he felt the almost painful drawing up of his sacred sac.

He felt her slim arms come up over his shoulders, caressing his hairless skin. Her moist lips came forward, burying themselves in the side of his neck so that he felt little electric thrills race downward into his crotch. All sensation was gathered there. He felt comfortably bottom heavy as blood flowed into his engorged penis.

Fingers in his ears and he could stand it no longer. With a deep, drawn-out groan he heaved his hips upward, slicing through the fluttering portals.

At that instant, Qi lin's grip became sharply painful. One hand was on either side of his head, her left elbow braced against his face. Using the heel of her right hand as pressure and her left elbow as fulcrum, Qi lin jerked his head violently to the left.

The motion should have been enough to break his neck. She performed the maneuver quite correctly, just as she had been taught in the *Gong lou-fu*. It was Colonel Hu's amorous thrust that had changed all the vectors.

She heard a sharp crack, to be sure, but this was followed by his explosive string of expletives and her insides turned to water.

Colonel Hu felt a singing in his ears. His vision was blurred and there was pain somewhere along his nervous system. He was in a state of semishock and his physical reactions at least were sluggish because of the pooling of blood in his lower belly and thighs.

Yet his mind knew instantly what had occurred, and Jin Kanzhe's words bubbled up to him again. *She is exceptionally deadly.*

His hands were pinioned by her lithe thighs and he tried to free them. Pain lanced at him, canting his head at an angle. The chorus of the damned bleated shrilly in his head like lambs to the slaughter. His mind was filled with the yellow bilious skies of Cambodia, stained by napalm, rent by bombs and artillery fire.

215

She had hurt him badly. Twice he might have been killed during his tour of duty but was spared. His *joss* was good. He was not going to die now. Bunching his muscles mightily, he freed one hand and slashed it across her chest. She cried out but his extremity felt as heavy and unresponding as a sack of cement. His vision had cleared somewhat but there were still inconstant patches of blurriness that made him sick and dizzy with vertigo.

Oddly, insanely, he was still inside her, poking and prodding as he fought at her. The pain had not withered him and he could not understand that. He punched her in the stomach but he lacked any real momentum because they were at such close quarters.

He freed his other hand and hit cruelly at her breast. Then he felt her arms come around his head and he knew that she was going to try it again. He fought her with all the strength he had left in him. The trouble was that he was seated and thus much of his superior strength was negated. Too, she had damaged a number of nerve networks in her first attack.

Colonel Hu used his spatulate thumb, digging into the soft flesh at her collarbone. He had gone for her carotid but she had twisted, deflecting him. Now she had hold of his head and was applying pressure.

He gasped and swallowed, almost bit his tongue in two. He choked and coughed, tasting the salty sweet taste of his own blood.

He dug inward farther and felt a bone snap. She cried out and jammed her elbow into his eye, blinding him. Dizzied, Colonel Hu nevertheless raised his hand upward, feeling the slack place she had left open when she had retaliated. Felt her neck and elation soared within him. The carotid! Jammed his thumb inward in a vicious strike and felt the pressure come off his head for an instant.

Then blinding pain hit him between his thighs, pain that shot upward, turning his stomach inside out, clamping his heart between iron fists.

His thumb came away and Qi lin got the placement right and jammed the heel of her right hand against the side of his head.

Snap like thunder and Colonel Hu arched up as if struck by lightning. Qi lin let go and crawled off him. She kept her eyes on him as she picked up her trousers, backing away across the room. She put them on, buttoned her blouse, wincing with the pain of the small bone he had broken.

Outside, the night was alive with rain, silvery and flickering in the lights. She knew where he kept his gun and, taking it, checked it for ammunition. It was fully loaded. She jammed it into the waistband of her trousers and, grabbing up his military jacket, slung it around her shoulders. Then she went out into the unquiet night.

Colonel Hu, alone again, fell from his ungainly position in the chair. The fall revived him somewhat. His head was at an unnatural angle. He could hear a sound akin to a gushing water faucet and wondered at it.

He could not stand nor could he sit. Instead, he crawled. It took him a long time to reach the open door. He saw only intermittently. In between, like a landscape quickly revealed in lightning bursts, he saw the Khmer Rouge camp that had been his home for nearly two years. He heard voices shouting, harsh, guttural, the growling of hungry wolves. He heard the flowering of the bombs, bringing with them the pink flecks of flesh and slimy organs that stuck to one's face and clothes like glue.

Saw, also, the bowed backs and exposed napes of necks so obscenely vulnerable of those found wanting by Angka, the mysterious Khmer Rouge hierarchical organization that seemed forever shrouded in shadowy rumor. The pistol shots, rhythmic and rapid, as those deemed antithetical to Angka were coldly executed. A merciful death, he had been informed by a grinning monkey of a lieutenant. "In the old days," he said laughing, "when we were still struggling for power and did not yet have your benevolent backing, we could not afford to waste a bullet. We used clubs to beat them to death." He had spat. "That was the better way, I think. It developed fortitude among our own soldiers."

Out in the storm, Colonel Hu was dying. He was only dimly aware of his surroundings. Consciousness was turned on and off in bright, pain-filled bursts. Within one of these machine-gun-fire episodes of lucidity, Colonel Hu realized that the sound of the gushing faucet that was following him was emanating from inside himself. His lungs felt heavy and full. It was a labor merely to take a breath.

He curled up on the ground. The rain beat down on him and the mud crept through his toes. That was his last memory, the squelching of the muck, the ground-up paste of humanity feeding upon itself, combining with the earth.

In time the wailing of the damned disappeared altogether, memory in a mist, an end to their hideous strength.

It took Jake almost three hours to get into the heart of Tokyo from Narita Airport. It was nothing special, just modern-day Japan. The superhighways were clogged with bumper-to-bumper traffic from start to finish and, when he was at last dropped off at the Okura, he was as exhausted as if he had taken yet another plane ride to a different time zone.

While the porter was opening his bags for him, Jake threw all the papers he had picked up at Narita onto the bed. There wasn't one whose front page wasn't filled with news of the Yakuza wars.

The police were working around the clock but as was usual in a country where violent crime was, by and large, not a way of life, they were having minimal success.

The special anti-Yakuza task force had been beefed up at the direct urging of Prime Minister Nakasone. Some arrests had been made—the latest one as recently as early this morning—but the raid had netted only underlings. The Yakuza *oyabun* remained at large and, in *Asahi Shimbun*, at least, there was a blistering editorial aimed at the incompetence of the police.

Of Mikio Komoto there was no mention whatsoever, though his clan was often cited in the detailing of the war. Was that good news or bad? Jake was unable to read the portents.

Alone in the room, he thought of Bliss. Her voice was only a phone call away yet he made no move for the receiver. He did not want to speak with her now, did not want any soft emotion to creep around inside him. Softness or any lack of concentration could get him killed here.

He stared into space. His father's voice swam in his head. His father's presence. There was a senescent aroma when he was near Jake that was peculiar to him: warm, rich, comforting. It reminded Jake of the beach at Shek-O where they would sit for hours in the sunshine, the wavelets of the South China Sea lapping around their ankles. Speaking of many things . . . and sometimes of nothing at all. Merely being together. Basking in the closeness that the intervening decades had made new, unique, more powerful.

Gone. All gone.

We have many enemies in many countries. They will seek to smash the yuhn-hyun.

An enemy in Japan among the Yakuza? What was the connection with the *yuhn-hyun*?

He put his elbows on his knees, rested his weary head in his hands. His body felt as if he had just gone fifteen rounds with the heavyweight boxing champ. His mind was whirling with possibilities.

With a slight groan he rose and padded across the Japanese-style room. His shoes had been left at the doorstep. Took a long, scalding shower. He lifted his head up to the water flow, trying to wash the fatigue, pain and fear from his body and his mind. He knew that he was in a lethal area. The *yuhn-hyun* was under attack and unless he found the source at once, the delicate ring of people his father had spent more than fifty years drawing together would blow apart. *The Triad dragons, especially, will be wary,* Shi Zilin had told him, *constantly seeking to gain advantage over their rivals. Divided, we are vulnerable and may be cut down.*

Fear flooded through Jake once again. The fear of failure. He was on the mountainside in the dark and the cold. His father had designated him *Zhuan,* the special one. Perhaps he had been wrong, perhaps his love for his one remaining son had blinded his visionary instincts. Perhaps he only *wanted* Jake to be *Zhuan.* Had Shi Zilin chosen the wrong person?

Jake toweled himself off and dressed in a cobalt-blue linen suit, dove-gray shirt, blue-on-blue polka-dot tie. As he brushed his hair, he stared at himself in the mirror. He saw the intense, hooded copper eyes, deeply set beneath a wide straight brow. His curly black hair—a genetic gift from his maternal grandfather—seemed unruly no matter how much he worked at it. He threw the brush down and, gathering up a couple of small items, went out of the room.

It was early afternoon, local time, just after lunch, so that the streets were merely crowded, not jammed. He had eaten on the plane but had tasted nothing. His stomach was full, nothing more.

Traffic, as usual, was at a standstill. In any case, he felt like walking. The day was sunny and exceptionally clear. There was still a bit of a chill in the air but the first cherry blossoms were in bud and the air smelled fresher and cleaner than it had any right to.

Jake strolled up to Sotobori-dori, turning left down the wide avenue, heading into the Akasaka area. Near the Mikado Theater, he went down off the street, taking the Choyoda subway line three stops to Meiji-Jingumae. He emerged in Harajuku. In the old, post–World War II days, this had been the site of Washington Heights, where the majority of the United States occupation forces were housed within the precincts of Tokyo.

Nowadays, Harajuku was more the province of the wealthy younger classes. Trendy boutiques vied for the visitor's attention with restaurants serving Western food. If one was in the mood for a hamburger and French fries rather than sushi or *soba*, this was the place to go.

Along the wide, beautifully tree-lined boulevard known as Omotesando-dori, young people danced on bright Sunday afternoons. Dressed in fifties-style leather jackets and winklepicker boots, they wended their way into Yoyogi Park, site of the towering Meiji Shrine. To the insistent beat of blaring portable boom boxes, they swirled and gyrated in an almost lunatic frenzy.

Harajuku was also where Mikio Komoto had his corporate offices. The skyscrapers of Shinjuku were where one might have first thought to look for them since that was the real hub of Tokyo's corporate life. But for many reasons, Mikio had decided to headquarter farther south.

It had proved a canny decision. With Harajuku's blossoming popularity, more and more small businesses were descending on the area in an effort to free themselves from Shinjuku's stifling atmosphere.

Mikio's offices were within Seicho No Ie just across from the Togo Shrine, within sight of the park's South Pond and noted iris garden. It was next to a high-tech *kissaten*, a stylish coffee shop where for two dollars one received a tiny cup of the liquid. The sum was also a form of rent for the table where one sat and watched the world go by. A relatively new Japanese custom borrowed without shame or excuses from a much older European one.

This place, with the odd name of the Barking Fish, was done in glossy green walls, highlighted by deep blue neon strips hidden behind polished-wood valences hanging from the glittery ceiling. Tiny marble tables were surrounded by midnight-blue lacquer chairs.

Jake pushed through the smoked-glass doors beside the *kissaten* and ascended in an elevator to the top floor of the building. At the end of a polished-granite and brushed-bronze hallway he went through the seeing-eye glass doors on which was printed KOMOTO SHOMU KOGYO in English and *kanji*. This translated roughly as "Komoto Commercial Industry," a rather nondescript name which could encompass virtually anything and everything.

Jake had no clear idea how the company actually made its money. Mikio was into just about everything: electronics, fiber optics, robotics, you name it. If it was an up-and-coming industry on the MITI—the Ministry of International Trade and Industry—priority list, Mikio was certain to be in it. MITI was the vastly powerful bureaucratic agency which, since the end of the war, set industrial trade policy for all of the private sector. One effective method was to offer businesses certain incentives to start up *kobun*—firms—in the areas that MITI had targeted as important for the country's economic expansion.

Just after the war heavy industry such as petrochemicals and steel had been at the highest priority. Now the emphasis had shifted to light industry—electronics and robotics, computer generation and the like.

Mikio's outer offices were paneled in *kyoki*—Japanese cypress. The built-in desks, consoles and cabinets were all in gleaming black lacquer. The floor was covered with an industrial Berber carpet, rich in tones of gray and brown. Seating in this area—at least for those waiting admittance—was composed of a line of attached wood squares, covered on top with *tatami*.

Jake went over to the Plexiglas screen. There was a male receptionist, young and nattily attired. Jake gave his name and when the young man asked the nature of his business, Jake told him that it was personal.

As he leaned in, a woman—the Office Lady, Jake assumed—turned and looked at him. She was wearing a severely cut suit of dark cotton. Her gleaming black hair was square-cut in a style Jake had not seen here since the mid-sixties. Her wide eyes regarded him for a time. Then, as if a trapdoor were slamming shut, she blinked and, swiveling around, returned to her work.

"Please be seated," the young man said, after taking Jake's business card. "I will contact Mr. Komoto's secretary." He spoke English clearly and overdistinctly as if he were being careful about going too fast.

"Thank you," Jake said and went back across the room. He sat. He was by no means alone. Dark-suited businessmen congregated like birds on a wire. From time to time one or sometimes several were summoned by a bowing functionary

221

who emerged from behind the internal barrier to greet them in polite fashion and usher them inside.

As appointments departed others arrived and the process was repeated. Jake had been waiting for just under an hour when he got up and stuck his head through the opening of the Plexiglas screen.

"I beg your pardon," he said to the young man, "but I have heard nothing as yet."

"I handed your card personally to Mr. Komoto's secretary," the young man said, as if that were in itself an explanation.

"That was fifty minutes ago."

"It's a busy day," the young man said. His hair glistened. It was brush cut and, with the assistance of some modern-day pomade, stood straight up. The intercom gave a muted buzz and he said, "Excuse me." He stabbed at a button, spoke softly into the wire headset he had on. In a moment he had rung off.

"I'm a good friend of Mr. Komoto's," Jake said. Out of the corner of his eye, he saw the Office Lady turn her head. Was she watching him again? "When can I get in to see him?"

"When I know," the young man said, "so will you."

"May I speak with Mr. Komoto's secretary then?"

The young man glanced down at his glossy PBX. "I'm sorry but she's on the phone right now. Please have a seat."

Another twenty minutes of that and Jake was back at the Plexiglas window. The young man looked up. He seemed disappointed when he saw who it was.

"Yes?"

"The bathroom?"

"Out the door, down the corridor to your left. Last door."

Jake nodded and went out. The men's room was as shiny and modern as the rest of the building. But not large. There were two urinals and when the door opened and a man came in, he and Jake were wedged tightly together.

The only sounds in the small room were of the men passing water. Jake saw that the other man was a Japanese in his mid-forties. He was wide-shouldered with salt-and-pepper hair. Like every other businessman in Tokyo he was dressed in a dark suit. The only difference was that he looked ill at ease in his. Muscles bulged beneath the sleek fabric. Old scars shone in his cheeks. He looked neither to the right nor the left but seemed fascinated by the blank wall in front of him.

Jake was finished, zipping up when the man said, "A cup of coffee might be in order."

He said it softly but quite distinctly. He had not turned his head and when Jake looked at him he made no sign that he was aware that anyone else was in the room with him. He zipped, washed up and was gone.

For a moment, Jake stood in the washroom wondering if he had actually heard the man speak. He thought for a time. He was getting nowhere at the offices of Komoto Shomu Kogyo.

Out in the corridor he looked both ways. No one was about. Jake took the elevator down to the lobby. Out in the street he went left. He passed a chic Kenzo boutique, decorated in the latest Japanese minimalist style: flat gray walls, black rubberized wire racks, gray carpet flowing up from the floor to cover low counters on which piles of clothes were set.

He gave it a glance and went by. Then he stopped and went back. In the window was a highly stylized mannequin. She had orange and green hair and nails the color of topaz. She was wearing the suit the Office Lady at Mikio's had on.

An Office Lady wearing a Kenzo outfit? That would have cost her a year's salary. Unless she wasn't an Office Lady at all. Then who was she?

A cup of coffee might be in order.

Jake back-tracked farther to the entrance of the coffee shop in Mikio's building, the Barking Fish. The *kissaten.* He went in slowly, taking some time for his eyes to adjust to the change in light. The neons were softened cast against the deep lacquer paint of the walls. He took a look around.

And saw the Kenzo suit sitting at a marble table. The Office Lady sat in Western style with her legs crossed. She was smoking a cigarette. A minuscule cup of coffee had been set before her. She smiled at him.

He went over and, as naturally as if they had made this date to meet, sat down across from her. He ordered a coffee and when they were alone said, "Who are you?"

Her full lips moved into a mock pout. "You are very rude, Mr. Maroc."

"Pardon my barbarian manners," he said in Japanese.

"That's better," she said, switching from English. "I'm glad you got the message." Her eyes twinkled. "It was amusing to guess at how long your bladder was going to hold out."

Jake was not amused. "Where is Mikio?" he said. "Is he all right? I need to speak with him."

223

The woman watched him with her glittering eyes. Her flat face was all cheekbone and brow. She was not Jake's idea of beautiful but she would certainly be someone's.

"Do you know Tsukiji?" she asked.

"Yes."

"Be there tomorrow morning just after four-thirty."

"Will Mikio be there?" The Kenzo suit was already standing. She looked down at him for a moment before walking briskly from the restaurant. She did not look back.

Bluestone in his study, watching the play of indirect light redefine itself as it passed through the exquisite translucent skin of the priceless Qing vase. It stood on a black lacquered pedestal, alone along one wall. Its pale, opalescent green was the only slash of a color other than black and Chinese red in the entire room.

The ceiling was painted a rich glossy black, the walls were papered in a pattern made expressly for Bluestone: black-on-black, a gloss-and-matte pattern, with a scattering of tiny red chrysanthemums.

The couch along the wall opposite the Qing masterpiece was of black leather; the matching chairs black. The wall-to-wall carpeting was black overlaid with red pindots. The antique Roman-style desk was carved ebony. Massive and intimidating, it was the only other objet d'art in the room besides the vase.

Bluestone sat behind the desk now and watched the Qing's inner power redefine light as he listened to White-Eye Kao's report.

"I have tracked Great Pool of Piddle to the dens of his usual newspaper sources. My sources have confirmed that he has already shot off his mouth—for a suitable amount of *h'yeung yau*." He was speaking of the fragrant grease—the bribes one needed to pay.

"Naturally," Bluestone concurred. "God forbid that our unwitting foil should surprise us."

The Chinese sitting on one oversized chair seemed dwarfed by its proportions. Bluestone liked that. The Chinese turned his head and the light turned his one milky eye opaque.

White-Eye Kao laughed. "No chance of that."

"Good," Bluestone said. "You have made certain that the Honorable Pok has no inkling that the information about Southasia Bancorp's regrettable fiscal plight was deliberately leaked to him?"

"Absolutely," White-Eye Kao said with great certainty. "His sources had to struggle to get every bit of it."

"Better and better," Bluestone said, staring intently at the Qing vase. "I was particularly impressed with the manner in which you disposed of Teck Yau, Sawyer and Sons' comptroller."

"That was a pleasure," White-Eye Kao said. "That pox-infested sea slug was more foreign devil than Chinese." He laughed. "My third cousin—you know, the one who works in the butcher shop on Po Yan Street—was all too happy to play along. He has no love for the *loh faan*, either." White-Eye Kao laughed. "The shop, as you know, sells to all the big hotels catering to the foreign devils. Ha, ha! What a tender meal the stupid *gwai-loh* must have eaten that night, *neh*?"

"Watch your tongue," Bluestone said sharply. "I am also a foreign devil."

"No," White-Eye Kao said with some fervor, "you are a Communist. You have a plan for all of Asia, for all of the world. I know how you aid those unfortunate peoples oppressed by the *loh faan* in every country. It is different with you."

"Yes," Bluestone said. The light passing through the Qing had changed subtly, he couldn't say how. "It is."

The buzzer sounded on his desk and he picked up the receiver, listened for a moment. "Send him in," he said and replaced the phone on its cradle.

Bluestone, who employed a full-time secretary at home as well as at his office—since he was fond of working out the most complex business problems away from the hubbub of the Five Star Pacific offices—turned at last from his contemplation of man's mastery over nature.

White-Eye Kao, alerted, turned his head as the door opened and Sir Byron Nolin-Kelly came in. He was a portly Scotsman with wide white muttonchop sideburns and an immaculately groomed mustache, waxed and curling upward at its ends. His shock of thick white hair was combed straight back off his wide forehead. His ruddy complexion and his bulbous clown's nose conspired to make him appear to be everyone's kindly uncle.

In fact he was *tai pan* of Pacific Overland Trading, an influential firm almost as venerable as Mattias, King & Company, the Colony's oldest Western trading company.

Sir Byron was something of a tyrant, controlling Pacific Overland for the past fifty-five years despite attempts by other members of his family to wrest power from him. He was nasty and powerful and Bluestone had spent much time romancing him.

The thing that Sir Byron liked most was a winner. Conversely, he hated to lose . . . at anything. But especially in matters concerning his company's business. It had been Bluestone's contention that the consortium of *tai pan* who founded InterAsia Trading were doomed to failure. The problems of capital shortfall at Southasia Bancorp—which had been revealed to Sir Byron as well as the other *tai pan* aboard the *Trireme* that weekend—had persuaded him.

"Good afternoon, *tai pan*," Sir Byron said.

Bluestone returned the greeting, turned to White-Eye Kao. "This is Ping Po," he said casually. "One of my compradors."

As Bluestone had intended, Sir Byron gave the Chinese a perfunctory nod and forgot about his presence.

"I have just now come from Macao," he said, waving away Bluestone's invitation to a drink. "Dark Leong Lau and Six-Toe Ping have arranged their financing."

"And the buying?" Bluestone said, leaning forward in excitement.

Sir Byron nodded. "It has begun. Bobby Chan has seen to it. It is being distributed through enough unrelated brokers so that only a specific check would unearth the chain of buying."

"Then you and I will commence our purchases tomorrow."

Sir Byron nodded. "As we agreed."

Bluestone watched the other *tai pan* carefully, waiting for a hint as to why he had actually come. This information could have been just as easily communicated via phone.

"Are you sure you won't have a seat?" Bluestone asked, gesturing to the empty chair vacated by White-Eye Kao, who was now discreetly across the room, staring into the lovely depths of the Qing.

"All right," Sir Byron said, relenting. He sat as stiffly as he stood. A retired colonel whose training would never leave him.

"Before you and I embarked upon our end of this venture, I wished to ask a number of questions."

Bluestone shrugged. "You had ample time over the weekend on the yacht."

Sir Byron's ice-blue eyes studied Bluestone. "Not in front of the natives, old man. This is just between you and me."

And White-Eye Kao, Bluestone thought, who you think of as part of the furnishings.

"I want a true assessment of the danger factor."

"The risk," Bluestone said without hesitation, "is great. I cannot deny that." He also knew that if he did, Sir Byron would get up, walk out the door and that would be the end of his involvement. "We are up against clever *tai pan*. But I believe that their power is on the wane. Shi Zilin is dead. And his son, well, his son has disappeared."

"Disappeared?"

"Wherever he is," Bluestone said, "he's not in Hong Kong. Who is going to run InterAsia now? Sawyer? The old man's headed for senility. Three Oaths Tsun? His business is the sea, that's where he excels. On land, he relies on others.

"Now they have run out of money. And we have a chance at the Kam Sang project. If we control that, with its revolutionary desalinization plant, we will control all of Hong Kong. I don't have to reiterate that water is Hong Kong's constant, overwhelming need. Kam Sang will allow us to control its flow. We will be able to, in effect, set our own price for water."

There was silence while Sir Byron digested this. At length, he nodded. "I'm satisfied," he said. "I'll relay my recommendation to the others."

"Excellent," Bluestone said, standing. Clearly the interview was at an end. The two *tai pan* shook hands. When Nolin-Kelly had left, Bluestone turned to White-Eye Kao, said, "Do you think he believed me?"

"Buddha, yes, of course. It's what he wants to believe. The others as well. It's in their own best interests to believe you. How could they know that we desire control of Kam Sang for more than its desalinization plant?" White-Eye Kao grunted. "You had only to watch his eyes to see that he's already blinded by the fantasy of money and power you've served up to him."

Bluestone sat back down, swiveled in his chair. He stared again into the extraordinary translucence of the Qing vase. "I wonder," he thought aloud, "what our friend Mr. Nolin-Kelly would say if he knew he was making an enormous financial contribution to the furtherance of the Soviet Union in Hong Kong?"

In the blackness of the tunnel all public conversation was drawn to a muted hush. The smell of charcoal dust was strong until, with a rush that was almost euphoric, the trolly burst out onto Mayakovsky Square and, rumbling past the Hotel Peking, braked to a halt in front of the Moscow Planetarium. Mikhail Carelin liked this place especially, he said, because it was just across the street from a little place that seemed squeezed in between its neighbors, the home of Anton Chekhov, now turned into a memorial museum.

Inside, comets spun into the twinkling darkness, their lighted vapor trails sparkling like diamond dust in Daniella's thick hair. They passed up a slide-show lecture on the Sayut that they knew to be overblown, almost stridently patriotic for the benefit of the many tourists who crowded through the doors.

Outside it was gray, raining instead of snowing, which was at least a change of a sort. Here, it was almost possible to believe that one was part of the weightless, airless, extraterrestrial nonatmosphere of space. One had the sense of spinning in orbit so high up, so detached that one saw the entire world revolve serenely at a distance vast enough to reduce all tension, all worry. In the cosmos there was no anxiety.

Daniella was worrying what to do about Maluta. Time was running out on her. She had done all she could behind his back. She was terrified that he would somehow get wind of her operation with Sir John Bluestone and take that over. Now that she finally knew the vast extent of Shi Zilin's *yuhn-hyun*, she understood why he had gone to such lengths to hide its true nature from her.

Mitre—Bluestone—had finally come through. And Daniella now knew that elements in Hong Kong and Beijing were in collusion. She was stunned at the thought of the resulting economic and political colossus that was being created. She knew that it was not enough now to have burrowed her way inside the *yuhn-hyun*; she must either control it outright—or destroy it completely.

She was certain that should Maluta ever get his hands on this intelligence he would take the Chinese operation away from her. This she could not allow. But how to defeat a man who terrified her so? His dossier was as clean as virgin snow.

"What is it?" Carelin said, tracing the furrows in the flesh above her nose. "Maluta?"

She nodded. "I fear that I have destroyed us, Mikhail. Maluta has us both in a vise. You cannot go to Genachev. That would destroy you utterly, given how he feels about personal morals. And if Maluta threatens to expose us?"

Carelin stirred uneasily. "He hasn't yet, has he?"

"No," Daniella admitted. "But only because he has a use for me. And, who knows, for you as well."

The comet, its tail green-and-red fire, came arcing down the sky overhead, passing behind Daniella's left ear. For a moment, her cheek was blushed by the simulated starlight, then it fell back into shadow. Carelin felt his heart lurch. His eyes were filled up with her, his body expanded. When he was with her, there was a heaviness between his legs that never went away.

"Is there something you're not telling me, Danushka?"

The blackness of space abruptly seemed lonely and desolate, more than any place on earth could possibly be. "He has made me his stalking horse," she whispered hoarsely. "I am carrying out his directives but everything is in my name. If anything goes wrong, I will be pilloried and he will remain blameless."

"What is it precisely that he wants you to do?"

It had been a dangerous line that she had been walking all afternoon and now she did not know which way to go. Certainly it would be easiest just to put her head back and tell him everything, continue his role as her priest-confessor. She was tired of the web of lies within which she was enmeshed. Each new lie she was compelled to utter seemingly enervated her more. She was like a patient with a degenerative illness, sinking further and further away from the world of normalcy and light. She was ill and without a cure.

She took several steps away from him, into the pale lavender light of Jupiter. Its ethereal aura flooded her features with the kind of illumination one only finds on a clear summer's night, deep within a densely foliaged forest. In a clearing. Moonlight filtered by treetops, the engirding atmospheric layers, 485 kilometers of space.

Carelin thought again of Circe and felt himself ensorcelled by this extraordinary woman. He knew from the first that his affair with her was stupid and, worse, dangerous. But nevertheless he persisted. It was as if he was split in two. One side of him protested this liaison, the other did not care, and ignored all dangers.

Then, six months ago, the high-speed scrambled transmission had come in and he had been undone. SELENE. The activation code. Selene. Goddess of the moon. Is that why he had thought of the moonlit glade?

"It's—an operation centering on Hong Kong," Daniella

lied, and something inside her gave off a long sigh. The patient dying another death. "Maluta has usurped Mitre, my asset in Asia." The best lies, she thought, always contained a core of truth—or a version of it. "Maluta's taking over my operation there." Almost told him the truth. Almost mentioned Kam Sang. What a disaster that would have been! He would have gone straight to Genachev with word of what Jake Maroc could tell them about Kam Sang and both of them would have been dead from that moment.

Maluta would have known the origin of the leak and the evidence of the murder and their adulterous affair would have surfaced. *Finis* for both of them.

She knew Carelin well enough. His sense of fairness was acute; as was his sense of loyalty. He was a fanatic about both, in fact. His first—his only reaction would be to run to Genachev. Never considering the consequences for both of them.

Time. That was what Daniella needed most. Time to find a way to defuse Maluta. But Maluta wanted Jake Maroc dead now.

Aware of the ethereal light on her face, she began to move away from him, into the shadows, but Carelin took her arm and held her fast.

"Don't do that," he said. "I want to see you."

Mary, Mother of God, she thought, don't let him find out the truth. Her mind raced. It was up to her to save them both.

He pulled her close against him so that her scent came to him and a wave of her thick honey hair brushed his cheek.

Because he wouldn't let her out of the light and the light revealed what was behind her eyes, she let her head go forward so that her forehead was pressed against his chest. "Oh, Mikhail, he's going to take all my power away from me. I can't allow him to do this to me, Mikhail. It will destroy me."

"You've still got Chimera," he pointed out.

Daniella nodded. "I never suspected that he would rise to the level he has," she acknowledged. "But even an asset of Chimera's caliber will not save me now, Mikhail. Perhaps I'll just shoot Maluta and be done with it."

"Bang! Bang! Just the way Mickey Spillane writes 'em, eh?"

"Stop making fun of me!" she cried.

"Then stop acting like a child. Problems are not solved with a gun. You, of all people, should know that."

Daniella raised her head. "But Maluta's got a spotless file. There's nothing in his past to make him vulnerable." A wave of despair washed over her. What was the point, she thought, leaning against him, of describing how debilitating it was to be under Maluta's thumb; of being the subject of his scrutiny?

He put his arms around her, his face was lost in the fragrant mane of her hair. Never, he thought, had he loved a human being as he loved her. "Perhaps I can find a way to take you with me when I go to Geneva with Genachev next month," he said.

"What made you think of Geneva?"

Carelin shrugged. "I don't know." He looked around. "Perhaps it was this place. One does not feel that one is even in Moscow here. It made me think of the Geneva trip, a foreign place, away from Maluta's prying eyes, his veiled threats; away from all the intrigues."

It made Daniella want to weep, this small kindness in the midst of Maluta's monstrously labyrinthine intrigue. Hers, as well, she realized dully. She had done nothing but lie to Carelin.

"Standing here at the edge of Jupiter's orbit," Carelin went on, unawares, "made me think that to us even Geneva might seem like the ends of the earth."

For an instant, Daniella drew a blank. Like a sleeper awaking from a tomb of dreams, remembering dreaming but nothing more, she heard a reverberation inside her head. What was it?

. . . *the ends of the earth.*

Then she had it: Maluta saying in his sardonic, superior tones, *Imagine! They would have gone to the ends of the earth for you. They sold their souls to you, bowed their heads before you, conferring to you on bended knee all that made them powerful. For this—* His cold hands upon her breasts, squeezing joylessly. *And this.* And inward against her mons.

But now, oddly, in this atmosphere that detached her from the earth, his words held another meaning. *Bowed their heads before you . . . on bended knee.* Why had he used such terms? Did he pull them out of a hat? The hat of his subconscious?

Daniella wondered now what it was in life for which Maluta would travel to the ends of the earth. *Bowed their heads before you . . . on bended knee.* Like a goddess, or a sorceress like Carelin's Circe. In that case, hadn't Maluta already conferred upon her some kind of power? Did he in fact fear her? Is that where his contempt and hate stemmed from?

231

What, really, did Maluta see in her? What powers, imaginary or real, did he suspect that she possessed? And, finally, how could that power be used against him?

Turning their conversation around again in her mind, Daniella vowed to find out, even if it meant that she must do what she most feared: plunge into that fearful dark star that sucked in all power, that negated all life, Oleg Alexeevitch Maluta.

The fish stared at him with an eye the color of gold leaf. It was a great red tuna, lying on its side. Just below its head, a square paper sticker denoting size and weight was pasted over the scales.

The tuna was one of many at Tsukiji, Tokyo's vast fish market on the banks of the Sumida River.

It was a quarter to five in the morning. A light wind was gusting across an oyster-colored sky. Much of the city lay shadowed, sleeping. In the distance the great steel-and-glass towers of Shinjuku thrust upward into the low sky, their silvery tips partially obscured by cloud.

In Tsukiji, the tuna were just being brought in off the boats and trucks for, oddly enough, some of them had been flown in over the pole from Montauk, Long Island. Jake could remember a week during one summer when he had stood on the pier at the most eastern tip of the Island watching the Japanese trading representatives frantically bidding for the tuna as the deep-sea fishing boats docked in the late afternoon.

Young men with short gaffs went among the tuna, lifting them this way and that across the wet concrete by hooking them in the gills. Other men walked slowly among the deepening rows of fish, spraying them with water.

All the while a pearlescent mist rose about their feet, the spray from their hoses bouncing off scales and concrete to form miniature rainbows in the air.

At five minutes to five, the men began stacking the most enormous mounds of pink and white sashimi, sparkling, dewy fresh, ready—along with the great fish—for auction.

The market was filling up with people: buyers, sleepy sightseers, revved-up revelers who were making this their last stop among many during the long night.

"Maroc-san."

Jake turned, saw a diminutive Japanese come around from behind a stack of squid.

"Kachikachi-san!"

They bowed to each other, performing the greeting ritual of the Yakuza.

"When I saw you last you were tied up."

"By your own hand, Maroc-san."

"A thousand apologies. The circumstances . . ."

Kachikachi nodded. "Komoto-san explained everything afterward."

"It is about Komoto-san that I have come," Jake said. "Is he here?"

"Let us have breakfast," Kachikachi said. He led the way across the concrete running with sea water and fish blood to a small restaurant that was no more than a counter beneath a striped awning.

Over sashimi and Kirin beer, Kachikachi said, "Komoto-san sends you his greetings."

Jake said nothing.

"He apologizes for the manner in which you have been led around. As you said, circumstances . . ."

"The war."

"You come at the worst time imaginable," Kachikachi said, crunching into a thick slice of abalone cunningly shaped to resemble a butterfly.

"I know."

"There is talk of an escalation of the war."

Buddha, Jake thought. It is already a bloodbath.

"Times are most difficult, Maroc-san. I spent fifteen minutes here making sure that you had not been followed before I made contact."

"Followed by whom?"

"These days," Kachikachi said, dipping squid into soy sauce, "there are many enemies."

Jake thought of his own situation. "I feared that Komoto-san was already dead," he said. "I have been calling for days."

"Security, Maroc-san." Kachikachi ordered more sashimi for them both. "And Komoto-san has no wish to involve you in this extreme danger."

"It's too late for that," Jake said. "I'm already here."

Kachikachi's face darkened. "I am afraid that it would be best if you left."

"Left?"

Kachikachi handed him a slim packet. "Immediately."

Jake opened it, found a one-way ticket to Hong Kong. "What is this?"

233

Kachikachi's eyes were sad. "It is my *oyabun*'s wish."

Jake put the packet on the counter between them. "This did not come from Komoto-san."

"I regret to say that there is no choice, Maroc-san." Kachikachi's eyes were downcast. "One should not have to speak to a friend in such a manner, but I, too, have been given no choice." He reached into his pocket, threw some bills on the counter. "Please be on that flight." He stood.

"I want to see Komoto-san."

"Goodbye, Maroc-san."

"I *will* see him, Kachikachi-san. I must."

But Kachikachi had already disappeared into the mist. Pocketing the ticket, Jake left the restaurant and went carefully through the market. It was just past five thirty and the first auction had begun. The crowds had increased and he had plenty of cover.

He spotted Kachikachi and worked his way through the throng, careful to change vectors frequently since Kachikachi was already sensitive to security.

At the land end of Tsukiji, the small man paused, looking around. They were in the east end of Tokyo. Kachikachi turned right, hurrying up the street. Jake followed, crossing and recrossing the street several times, using shop windows and, where he could, mirrors to keep the small man in sight. At the same time, he kept an eye out for ticks who might have picked either him or Kachikachi up at the market. He saw no one.

Kachikachi went into Asashicho. He was heading directly for Jisaku, a well-known restaurant where one could still see *geisha* performing with lunch or dinner, though the woman was more likely to be sixty than twenty. Nowadays all the young ones were selling their bodies along the Ginza. This tradition, at least, was dying out.

The place looked like a temple structure with its long sloping tiled roofs and ancient appearance. Kachikachi passed into shadow under the eaves.

Jake paused on the street and took a hard look around. There were a number of cars parked along the curb. One of them he recognized as Mikio's company Mercedes. It was impossible to tell if anyone was inside because of the tinted glass. But in the cool morning air Jake could see the soft swirl of exhaust emanating from the car's tailpipe. The engine was on, the Mercedes ready to roll.

Keeping one eye on Jisaku, into which Kachikachi had

disappeared, Jake went out into the street and hailed a cab. At this time of the day, with people streaming in from nearby Tsujiki, it was not difficult to find one. The automatic door opened and Jake ducked his head inside. He spoke to the driver in rapid idiomatic Japanese, unfurling several bills of high-yen denomination as he did so.

The man nodded, pocketing the bills, and Jake stood up. He was about to return to the restaurant when he saw the front door open. Kachikachi came out along with a large Yakuza. They stood in the mist, watching the street. Jake turned away, leaning on the open door of the taxi.

Reflected in the window of the car he could see another man emerge from the shadowed doorway of the restaurant. Now the three were on the move. They were definitely on their way to the Mercedes.

Jake climbed into the taxi and the door sighed shut. There was a miniature TV that the last passenger had left on. Jake switched it off and watched the three hurry down the walk. Jake studied the third man. It was difficult to get even a partial view of his face because of the intervening bulk of the big Yakuza, but Jake recognized the wide shoulders and narrow waist, the close stubble of his shorn hair.

Mikio!

So he had been here after all.

Something about his walk—had he been hurt? Jake was about to climb out of the taxi when he heard an engine cough to life across the street. He turned his head, saw smoke coming from the tailpipe of a blue Nissan.

"The Mercedes," Jake told the driver, and the man nodded.

Mikio and his crew were already in the car and now the Mercedes was pulling away from the curb.

"Wait," Jake told the driver, "for the blue Nissan to pass." He saw the quick flick of the driver's eyes in the rearview mirror.

Then they were all in motion, wending their way through Tokyo's thickening traffic: Mikio, Jake, and the unknown enemy who had somehow known about this meeting.

In Jake's mind, Kachikachi's words echoing, *There is talk of an escalation of the war.*

When Tony Simbal drove his Saab up the long snaking drive leading to Greystoke he did so at slow speed. He had the windows and the sunroof open. Golden light poured into the velour interior with unaccustomed warmth. Though a breeze whispered through the tall sycamore and pine it contained not a trace of winter's biting chill.

All around him it seemed birds twittered and sprang from twig to branch as if delighted to be home again. Fleecy clouds hung in the sky, given a glow by the sunlight striking them, and every so often he spotted a rabbit or a pheasant scurrying away from his passage along the verge of the graveled driveway. Once he was certain he caught a quick glimpse of the rear end of a deer, bolting from his line of sight.

Simbal inhaled deeply, abruptly aware that, perhaps strictly out of defense, he had been breathing shallowly all winter long. In a sense, he thought, one barely lived in winter at all. Bundled and packed in layer upon layer of overclothes, one plodded through bleak days short on light and warmth and even color while one's nose slowly turned red and one's extremities became numb.

Simbal was thinking of Burma, of the Shan States, and the mysterious murders of Peter Curran and Alan Thune when he pulled up to the great nineteenth-century mansion owned by the Quarry and occupied by its Director. The gabled, turreted house sat within fifty acres or so that encompassed rolling emerald hills and a spacious valley in Great Falls, Virginia.

The place still bore the stamp of Antony Beridien, the Quarry's former Director, so lately assassinated in the end phase of a plot, or so it had been rumored, devised by General Daniella Vorkuta and her mole inside the Quarry, Chimera, a.k.a. Henry Wunderman.

Beridien had been an inveterate collector of antiques, and the rooms and hallways of Greystoke were still filled with a rainbow of period pieces ranging from Federal to Chippendale to Louis XV to God only knew what.

As he cut the Saab's engine and the deep throb of the turbo died, Simbal saw Donovan hunched over his '63 Corvette. The car was Donovan's rather manic hobby. Every week it seemed that he was working to improve this or that aspect of the engine.

Donovan picked his head out of the automobile's maw and smiled, waved a hand holding a wrench. It was Sunday and Donovan was dressed casually in a pair of old, faded chinos, a similarly hued Ralph Lauren Polo shirt and worn Topsiders without socks. A green metal toolbox was at his side, along with a tray filled with a pitcher of lemonade, an ice bucket into which had been poked several bottles of Lite beer, and a variety of glasses.

"Help yourself, Tony," Donovan said, ducking his head back beneath the raised hood of the 'Vette.

Simbal went across the gravel and popped the cap off a beer. He took a swig, watching the Director's work without much interest. He knew almost all there was to know about automotive engines of all sorts. So much time in the jungle made that a necessity. But it was hardly a love. He had other things to occupy his thoughts.

He looked around. Someone was working in the rose garden, carefully pruning on bended knee. Soon the bushes would be in bloom and that side of the mansion would be suffused with a scent as delicious as ardor.

"So," Donovan said, his head and shoulders out of sight, "what have you been up to?"

Simbal put the empty bottle aside and leaned against the warm fender of the car. "You remember a woman named Monica Starr."

"Mmm, sounds familiar. Girlfriend or business?"

"Both, actually." Simbal crossed his arms over his chest. "We had an affair while I was at the DEA. I ran into her the other evening."

"Oh, really? Where?"

"A party."

"That wouldn't've been Max Threnody's bash?"

"As a matter of fact it was," Simbal said. "Why?"

"No particular reason. I just like to know which hole my operatives are poking their noses into."

"You don't like Max, do you, Rodger?"

"*Like* him? Hmm, I never considered *that* alternative. Let's just say that I don't approve of the DEA, period. It's too much of a bureaucratic boondoggle for my taste, tied to Congress's apron strings. I don't think having to suck up to those idiots on Capitol Hill ever did anyone any good. Especially people in our profession. We need to be left alone by politicians. Autonomy is the only effective means of doing business. That way, instead of having to cut through red tape, one avoids it entirely."

There was a clanking from inside the Corvette and Donovan grunted. "Don't really understand how you managed to stay there so long. Compared to us, it's a very bourgeois operation."

"Maybe so, but their computer is the key we've been looking for against the *diqui*."

Donovan at last reemerged from his place of refuge. "Is that so?" He wiped his greasy hands on a rag and poured himself some lemonade. "Tell all."

Simbal told Donovan about his talk with Monica, about her unease regarding Peter Curran. When it came to Curran's death, Simbal did not leave out anything but, strangely—or so it seemed to him—he made it seem as if the DEA computer and not Max Threnody had divulged the classified information.

"How'd you get access to the computer?" Donovan asked shrewdly. "The girl?"

Simbal nodded.

"Chasing after skirts," Donovan said ruminatively. "We did an awful lot of that together in college."

Simbal smiled. "We were terrors."

"No responsibilities then."

"No power, either."

Donovan looked at him. His clear blue eyes and handsome features made it appear as if he had just stepped out of a Calvin Klein ad. "But we *did* have power, Tony. A very real kind of power over women. They all wanted to be with us, remember?"

"Yeah." Simbal shrugged. "But to tell you the truth, now I'm not sure how much of that was real and how much we made up."

"What do you mean?" Donovan asked sharply. "We had them all . . . anyone we wanted, we bedded."

"Except Leslie."

Donovan put down his glass and pointed. "Get behind the wheel and start her up when I give you the signal." He did some tinkering and then said, "Okay."

Simbal turned the ignition and the thing began to purr like a great cat.

"Superb!" Donovan made one last-minute adjustment and closed the hood. "Let's take a spin."

Simbal got out and Donovan took his place behind the wheel. As soon as Simbal was in the passenger's seat, Donovan took off, sending a great spray of gravel upward in a graceful arc as he slewed them around.

"Do they know about this?" Simbal said, hanging on for dear life as the Corvette thrummed along.

"Who?"

"The government firm that pays our insurance," Simbal said over the mounting noise. He stole a glance at the dashboard, saw that they were closing in on 110 mph.

Donovan laughed and Simbal shouted, "How fast does this mother go?"

"We're going to find out right now," Donovan said, pushing the accelerator to the floorboards. He whipped around a curve with such force that Simbal felt his neck crack uncomfortably. The road straightened out; the needle trembled at the 150 mph mark.

"How's that?" Donovan shouted, grinning.

Simbal, who was more at home in a jury-rigged World War II Jeep or on a donkey's back, heading down an Asian mountainside, said nothing; he was concentrating on keeping his stomach in place.

After what seemed an eternity, Donovan slowed to a more reasonable pace. Sunlight spun off the hood, refracting colors. The hills on either side of them were already lush, as if they were eager for summer to begin. They seemed haloed with the first misty buddings of springtime, ethereal, almost divine.

"Why did you bring up Leslie?" Donovan said after a time.

Simbal shrugged. "I don't know, really. Except that it seemed appropriate. We were waxing nostalgic weren't we? I don't know about you but I can't think about college without Leslie coming to mind. Unobtainable Leslie."

Donovan slowed even more; now they were merely cruising like any other sightseers out for an afternoon's spin. "She was probably gay."

"Gay? Jesus!" Simbal laughed. "What in God's name makes you say that?"

"She wasn't interested in us, right? She was the only one, buddy."

"I didn't say she wasn't interested in us," Simbal said a bit more soberly. "I said that she was unobtainable."

"Same thing," Donovan observed, "when you come down to it."

Simbal gave the Director a quick look. "I guess I'd forgotten what an ego you have when it comes to women. Face it, Rodger, they didn't all fall for the lousy lines we were handing out in those days. Anyway, all we wanted then was to fuck. Two studs out to rut. Our intellectual pursuits we reserved for the classroom, if memory serves." He shrugged. "Maybe that's why Leslie wasn't interested."

"Christ, but I've never forgotten her," Donovan said all

of a sudden. It came out with such intensity that Simbal felt compelled to remain silent. "She seems like a dream now, almost."

Donovan had slowed, pulling over to the shoulder. Now he stopped the car and turned off the ignition. The sudden cessation of noise was quite shocking.

"I remember her long blond hair streaming out behind her as she walked across the campus. It was as thick as honey. And her gray eyes could see right through you, it often seemed to me." Donovan put his head back against the leather seat. "Jesus, I wanted her."

"Sure you wanted her. Because you knew you couldn't have her," Simbal said. "Because without her pussy in your belt you weren't batting one thousand."

"No, you're wrong," Donovan said thoughtfully. "I wanted her because of *her*. I wanted Leslie." His eyes stared unseeing up at the underside of the roof. Outside, the calling of the birds continued to wash the entire valley in soft, arhythmic melody.

"I never told you this, Tony," Donovan said. "I never told anyone this, but one night just after we'd graduated, I went to Leslie's house. You remember her folks lived quite near the campus.

"I didn't call or anything. I don't think I had the nerve. I remember the look of the place, so warm and inviting in the dusk. I could imagine her with her folks and her younger sister sitting down to dinner and I felt this, I don't know what—a compulsion?—to join them.

"I remember climbing those stucco stairs, going past the huge yucca, all blue and a green so deep at that time of the evening it was near to black. It brushed my cheek.

"I rang the doorbell. I did it the instant I reached the top step. I knew I had to or I wouldn't do it at all.

"I suspected that her father or her mother would come to the door and I had rehearsed a kind of speech for either eventuality. I wasn't prepared for what happened.

"Leslie opened the door. Leslie herself, with that warm light burnishing her honey hair, outlining her body. It was a magical moment . . . something straight out of every fantasy I'd conjured up about her.

"Then I heard someone say, 'Who's this?' It was a male voice, a young voice; certainly not her father's. Then I saw that he had come up behind her. His arm slipped around her waist, his body pressed against hers from behind. 'Who's this, honey?'

"I had no answer to that, no explanation. So I turned and ran. A block away I stopped long enough to vomit into the bushes." Donovan closed his eyes and let enough air out so that Simbal knew he had been holding it in for the space of several breaths.

"I'm sorry I brought her up, Rodger."

"Don't be," Donovan said. "I think about her all the time." He shook his head as if clearing mental cobwebs. "Now Leslie's taken on the aspect of the unicorn or the Holy Grail. Perhaps she's not out there at all. Perhaps we both made her up."

In a moment, Donovan started the engine. "The afternoon's growing old and we haven't finished our business." He made a broken U-turn and headed back to Greystoke.

"What about this woman, Monica whatever?"

"Starr," Simbal said. "Monica Starr. What about her?"

"She still got a thing for you?"

"She was having an affair with Peter Curran."

"Curran is dead, so you have informed me," Donovan said. "Was she also in love with him?"

"I don't know."

"Is she in love with you?"

"I don't think that matters."

For the first time this afternoon Donovan laughed. "Good old Tony. You're still loving them and leaving them. Well, in this case it's no doubt for the best. Who knows what Uncle Max has up his sleeve? I don't care that you once worked for him, you don't now. I don't believe he'd care for you doing your spook number in his territory."

"What does Monica have to do with that?"

Donovan did not like that question and he showed it. "Everybody's got a blind spot, Tony. Yours is Max. Didn't it ever occur to you that he put this Monica woman onto you deliberately?"

The little chill that had begun to coagulate in his lower belly when he saw Monica walk into Max Threnody's house the night before blossomed into all-out nausea.

"What's the matter, Tony?" Donovan said. "You don't look so well."

Simbal thought he'd better get it over with. "I never thought I'd say this, but Max is playing games with me. First he plays footsie, getting as close again as the Dutch uncle I thought he had been. Then he sics Monica Starr onto me and we reignite flames. Then he says, Go use her, buddy, she'll be your guide in the purgatory of the linked governmental computer files."

"So far, so good," Donovan said. "You've got your lead. Edward Martin Bennett. What more do you want?"

Simbal told him of the accident by which he ended up following Monica to Max's house.

Donovan grunted. "Now you see that Threnody's no better than the rest of the spook community," he said, overhauling an elderly couple in a Datsun. "He's got you covered six ways from Sunday, Tony. I wouldn't make the mistake of letting down your guard with him again."

"What I can't figure is what he wants out of all this."

"Don't be dense, it annoys me," Donovan said shortly. "He wants you to go after Edward Martin Bennett. If Bennett's involved with Peter Curran, it's a sure bet he knows who snuffed him. In any case, this one's a bitch, all right. Too many DEA pieces have gone belly up. Which is precisely why your friend Max has gone to such lengths to rope you in.

"You're perfect for the purpose, Tony, don't you see? Ex-DEA operative who's smart and seasoned. You know the ropes yet you're not tied to the DEA now. You're clean as a whistle. You can slide down the hole into this hellpit someone's created and it won't cost Uncle Max the skin off his nose."

"But this is our ops. The Quarry's."

Donovan gave Simbal a quick look. "Use your head, Tony. You're going to be monitored every step of the way. Who do you think will show up just as you get to the kill? Uncle Max. To mop up and get the glory. And in the process gain a measure of revenge for his fallen pieces." Donovan had the disconcerting habit of calling other organization's operatives pieces.

Simbal nodded unhappily, thinking, This has turned into one helluva afternoon.

"Okay," Donovan went on. "Now that I've prepared you for the joust go out and get Bennett and whoever else may be mixed up in this. If you need help, ask."

"I work alone," Simbal said. "In the field I'd rather be responsible for my own life."

"Yes, I know." Donovan accelerated again, the last of the

sun spinning off the windscreen in a semblance of a rainbow. They were almost back at Greystoke.

"What do I do about Max?" Simbal said.

Donovan turned into the gates, handed his and Simbal's laser-coded I.D. cards to the guard at the gates. In a moment, the way was clear and he took them down the winding drive. "Nothing." The wind whispered in the maples and poplars. Somewhere a power mower was droning. "Let Threnody hang by his own rope. Now that you know what a liar he is, you'll know the proper time to set him to swinging, Tony.

"After all, you've got plenty of experience with him."

Toshima-ku. Mikio was heading back to his house. Leading his enemies—surely his assassins—right to the killing ground. Kaname-cho: a subdistrict within the *ku*.

Jake was familiar with this area of Tokyo—as familiar as he was with Mikio Komoto's house. Jake had once cased it thoroughly in order to break in and gain secret information concerning the whereabouts of his half-brother, Nichiren.

The mists of early morning had dissipated, leaving the skies clear and bright. Hurtling just under the speed of sound, lowering into Narita airport fifteen thousand feet aloft, one would no doubt be aware of the haze that almost perpetually enwreathed Tokyo. But here on the ground, the air seemed clear. Sunlight showered the ancient boxwood and thin, soldierly cryptomeria which stood silent guard around Mikio's compound.

Jake saw the familiar iron gate in the twelve-foot bamboo fence. He could see the sloping rooftops of Mikio's house and beyond, the barren sprawl of Rikkyo University's baseball grounds. Practice was beginning and every once in a while Jake could discern the solid sound of ash bats connecting with horsehide baseballs.

He had the taxi stop just at the top of a rise that overlooked Mikio's house. The Mercedes slid through the open iron gates and disappeared. Jake paid his fare and got out. The taxi made a U-turn and departed.

Jake was studying the blue Nissan. It had drawn to a halt at a point directly outside the spot along the wall where Jake knew Mikio's study was secreted. The enemy was well informed.

From out of his pocket he produced a pair of Zeiss binoculars. They were tiny and foldable. He put them to his eyes and took a good look at the Nissan. Sunlight shattered into ten thousand shards against the Nissan's windows. He could not see inside.

He took the binoculars away as he had been trained to do. One was never to peer through magnifying lenses for too long a period during surveillance because one was all too apt to miss some crucial occurrence across the larger field of play. This—as it was with many things—Jake had learned through *wei qi*. One could not concentrate on one section of the board alone.

Now he saw a shadowed figure hurrying out from a side gate. It clung to the long dark spaces along the bamboo wall before running full tilt toward the blue Nissan. The figure bent down and the side window scrolled down. Jake peered through the Zeiss lenses and sucked in his breath.

Kachikachi!

Mikio's right-hand man was selling him out, pointing to the spot most vulnerable in the compound's defenses. Now the diminutive Yakuza was sprinting back toward the house, leaving the gate unlatched. Deliberately.

Kachikachi a traitor! Jake found it difficult to believe. But the twists of war—especially an internecine war such as this—were hard to fathom. Perhaps Mikio was losing; perhaps Kachikachi wished to be on the winning side. In any event, Jake knew what he was witness to.

Using the binoculars at intervals, he made his way around so that he was at once closer to the house and had a better angle through the still open side window of the blue Nissan.

He caught movement inside and adjusted the lenses to maximum power. There was one man plus the driver. He saw the man on the passenger's side working on a piece of hardware. *Dew neh loh moh* on all enemies! he thought. In a moment he recognized it: a Riverton Bison, a miniaturized handheld launcher that fired a specially made fragmentation grenade at approximately three hundred feet per second. That was how they were going to do it. Everything would go up in a big bang and Mikio would be plastered all over the walls.

Jake was about to make a move for the car when he saw the driver pull out a Gion 30-09 and take off the safety. He began to check quadrants radiating out from their immediate vicinity. He was very good; he missed nothing.

Jake shrank back behind a boxwood and took a look at the environment. They had parked the Nissan well. There was no immediate cover and that left Jake out in the cold. There was no way to approach the vehicle clandestinely.

That left the house. Jake knew that he had little time. He pocketed the Zeiss lenses and, making his way carefully away from the lines of sight afforded those inside the Nissan, he approached the bamboo fence. He pulled a nylon cord out of his pocket. It was anchored with a clawed iron weight. This he threw over the top of the bamboo and pulled down hard immediately. There was no give.

Then he went up.

He went over very fast, leaping down onto the grass with knees deeply bent to cushion the landing. He heard birds calling and somewhere a squirrel or other small animal scurrying. Otherwise, it was still. The muted sounds of traffic were a background wash. Once he even heard the crack of the bat from the nearby diamond.

Where in Buddha's name was everyone? What had happened to Mikio's vaunted security?

He went quickly along the side of the house, skirting the long narrow *kyujutsu* practice lane where he and Mikio had engaged in a monumental battle of wits and prowess in the ancient *samurai*'s art of archery.

Jake checked his watch. He had been too long in getting here. He went up on the *engawa*, tried the *fusuma* to the room adjacent to Mikio's study. It was locked. No time to pick the lock; used the calloused edges of his hands, the flat of his right heel to crash through.

Now he was fully committed and could not turn back. The danger of the Bison was ever present in his mind but it was no deterrent. He had to pull Mikio out of harm's way.

The house was eerily, unnaturally quiet. There should have been the pounding of running feet, shouts raised by the noise of his abrupt entry. There was nothing.

Jake went hurriedly through the dark, closed-up room. Pushed aside the inner *fusuma* out into the hallway.

Saw Kachikachi coming from the opposite direction. Someone at least had been alerted by his break-in.

"*Amida!* Maroc-san!"

"*Muhon-nin!*" Jake cried. Traitor. They grappled for a moment in the narrow hall before Jake threw the other aside. Turned, pulling the *fusuma* to Mikio's study open.

"Get away from there!"

He heard Kachikachi's frenzied cry but he had spotted his friend deep in meditation, kneeling on the *tatami*.

"How did you get here! You fool! Do not go in there! Do not disturb—!"

Mikio in his kimono with the clan *kamon*, the crest, printed in a great three-lobed wheel across the back. The *oyabun* began to turn his head.

"Mikio!" Jake shouted. Grabbed a handful of kimono and began to pull his friend upward when the window shattered with explosive force.

The Bison, Jake thought. And then, Oh, Buddha, I'm too late.

White-and-yellow light screaming in nova, all sound, sight, smell coalescing into one elemental bellow that echoed on and on as the room collapsed in upon itself with a thunderous howl.

Then the fire began, running like a river of death.

It had been Generalissimo Chiang who had taught Mao that whoever commanded the army would, in the end, be victorious. War, Chiang believed, decided conflicts of all nature.

Extrapolating from this, Mao had said, "Political power grows out of the barrel of a gun."

This, of course, had been of much concern to the Americans. But what they feared most about Mao was that his strategies were hidden from them as they were from the multitudes, and outsiders found this opacity both dangerous and unpredictable. Certainly, the Americans harbored no illusions that they could use Mao as they had used Chiang to further their own political ends in China.

Only Mao, sitting atop the ungainly pyramid of power that he and his inner core had created, knew that this was due principally to two men. Sun Tzu had shown him the Way to keep his strategy secret. Zilin had told him, "In politics, it is the threat of violence that is an end in itself."

The truth is that Mao and, to a good degree, Zilin were ready and willing to listen to American ideas concerning a coalition government in post–World War II China. Mao, above all others, believed that American intervention could be important—indeed, even crucial—to his country's future. That was, Zilin believed, principally because Mao had been stung to the quick by Stalin's and Molotov's unkind insult, calling him a "margarine Communist."

Zilin had been the first to understand Moscow's unease regarding the direction of Chinese Communism. Stalin especially, the iron-fisted commander, was able to discern strength in a leader. It was Zilin's firm belief that Moscow was terrified of Mao. It was not only what Mao stood for—that is, a form of Communism divergent from that of Moscow's—but also Mao himself.

Stalin was a genius, of that Zilin was certain. His understated manipulation of Roosevelt at war's end was proof enough of that even if one had not already been convinced by how Stalin had handled his troops during the war.

It was Zilin's theory that Stalin had taken the measure of Mao himself and had seen in him, perhaps, many of the qualities that made himself so powerful.

Stalin and Molotov had called Mao and his followers "margarine Communists" because their revolution had come via the peasants and not the proletariat as was strict Karl Marx scripture.

Mao had taken this jibe to heart. Though Zilin saw the insult as ridiculous, he could not convince Mao.

"China is unique," Zilin would say. "It is an agrarian country, a land whose interior Marx could not have imagined let alone conceived of how to tame. Yet we have done just that, Mao *tong zhi*. Is that not proof enough of Stalin's lies?"

Mao would shake his head. "No, you are wrong, Shi *tong zhi*. Much as it pains me to admit it, Stalin and Molotov are right. Our revolution—the true Communist revolution—must come about through the proletariat."

"Moscow is baiting us," Zilin would say. "That is all."

"No. We *are* an agrarian nation, it is true. Now. But in order to survive the coming decades we cannot afford to remain so. For our decimated economy to revive and prosper after the war we must industrialize. When that happens we will be creating our own proletariat. Do you not think, Shi *tong zhi*, that we will be forced to move our economy through a capitalist phase in order to reach a profitable standard of industrial productivity? Well, then, we must be certain that we reach this new emerging class. It is they—not the dwindling peasant population—who must carry our cause forward into the nineteen fifties.

"Toward this end, the Americans can be of enormous assistance. Only they have the capital and the industrial knowhow to set us on course. After the war, do you think that Moscow will be in any financial shape to send us the amount of aid we will require? Not likely!

"No, Shi *tong zhi*, the Americans are our only hope."

In this, Mao was quite correct. It was at that time—during the height of the war—when a fairly balanced American foreign policy in China would have opened many doors as well as creating a firm power base for the country in one of Asia's most important nations.

But the great capitalists of the time would not brook any form of what they referred to as "Communist handholding." On the contrary, they saw a bit of themselves in Generalissimo Chiang and they were to a man dead certain that Chiang would be America's strongman bulwark against the spread of Communism. They were blind to the political and, worse for them, the sociological upheavals wracking China. They could not see—as Zilin had early on—that Communism was the only logical method of unifying a country as vast and—generally speaking—as poor as China.

Thus during the war America poured aid only into the coffers of Generalissimo Chiang. During the outbreak of the Chinese civil war when American policy makers still had a chance to deal with the situation objectively, they provided aid only to the Nationalist forces by airlift and sea transport alike. Even while the American embargo of military matériel to China was still in effect from August 1946 to May 1947, thousands of tons of ammunition held by U.S. forces stationed in China were clandestinely transferred to the Generalissimo's garrisons.

The Americans then left Mao no choice. In December of 1949, Mao embarked on a trip to Moscow where he and Stalin hammered out the Sino-Soviet treaty of alliance. Thus was the fate of modern China sealed. From that time on, America was shut out of the formation of Chinese policy, obliged to watch the progress of Asian politics molded and remolded by Russia and China without chance to inflict its own predilections on the dynamics of change. Thus had America lost the one precious possibility of real Western involvement—rather than coercive intervention—in Far Eastern affairs.

Because of his role in Chungking and afterward, it was perhaps not surprising that Zilin should have taken Huaishan Han to see Lo Jui-ch'ing. Lo was the head of the Ministry of Public Security. His responsibilities were many and extended throughout the country.

Huaishan Han's expertise in security—in spying, to put a fine point on it—was already manifest to Zilin and certain other members of Mao's inner circle. Now was the time to put it to good use from inside the country.

This interview occurred near the time when Mao was returning from his sojourn to Moscow and the timing was to prove quite important.

Even though Huaishan Han was quartered next door to

Zilin, the two friends saw little of each other during the next several months.

Mao had returned with mixed results—at least as far as Zilin was concerned.

"And that," Mao said, "is precisely why I declined to take you along to Russia. If you have a blind spot, my friend, it is with the Soviets. I had mine with the Americans but that is all over with now. You were correct on that score. But as for the Russians, now that America has abandoned us utterly, we must take our infusion of capital from whatever source makes itself available."

However, Mao's "infusion of capital" was not quite what he had been hoping for. Stalin agreed to supply China with the equivalent of three hundred million dollars. The catch was that it was in the form of credits rather than by the grant of a simple loan. This meant that China was now quite literally tied to the Soviet Union. It was not free to form the source of its new industry and rebuilding but rather must depend wholly on Soviet technology, technicians and material.

This, a depressed Mao told Zilin privately, was the best he could come up with. "Stalin still distrusts us. How many times he invoked the name of Tito and his 'mockery'—I use Stalin's own words—'of a Communist state' I cannot begin to count. He was like a broken record on that score.

"I had no power base from which to bargain," the dispirited Mao said. "After all, it was the Russians as well as the Americans who were agitating for the coalition government. We went directly against Moscow's wishes when we plunged into civil war. 'How do you expect me to trust you after that?' Stalin said, like an aggrieved elder uncle."

Zilin was not surprised as Mao had been but he said nothing. His anti-Soviet bias would get him nowhere with Mao on this matter. He knew full well that even if Mao had been able to produce hard evidence that it was Chiang who had begun the civil war Stalin would have found another excuse to offer only credits. This was Moscow's way of gaining a semblance of control over what it viewed as its wayward—and potentially lethal—stepchild.

After a long leisurely dinner at Mao's residence during which nothing at all was said, Mao took Zilin out into the house's inner garden. It was cold. Snow was falling lightly, dusting straight down all around them, muting all sound. There seemed no wind.

Mao pulled his coat closer around him. "When I was in

Moscow, there was a blizzard to the north of the city. Fifteen feet of snow. Can you imagine, Shi *tong zhi*!"

Zilin said nothing. There was no reason for them to be out here in the frigid night but security. His heart beat fast. What was it Mao wanted no one else to know?

"There is another problem," Mao said now. He was facing out into the night. The back wall of the garden was overgrown with ivy. The zeal of the revolution precluded at least for the moment the tending of such items of luxury. "Stalin spoke to me of another issue. That of Korea." Mao waited a moment before continuing. "With Moscow's backing, the North Korean Communists will invade the South."

"How soon?"

"Next June."

Zilin knew what was coming. "That means war, surely."

Mao nodded mutely. His face was very sad. "Our poor people. They have just finished with a war that went on far too long."

"Then Stalin gave you no choice."

Mao turned to Zilin. "None at all." Then he went inside.

"I have found her!"

Zilin looked up from the paperwork he had been poring through. He saw Huaishan Han dressed in a uniform rush into the offices.

"I have found her, my friend!" His lean face was alive and animated.

Zilin peered around him to see another figure enter hesitantly through the doorway.

Huaishan Han gestured impatiently. "Come in, Senlin! *Hao jia huo!* Come in!"

She was a woman who—so it seemed to Zilin—must always have been slim. Now she was thin to the point of emaciation. Her face, which still held a certain pellucid beauty, was gaunt and haggard. Her color was poor and judging by her skin alone she appeared to be in poor health. Her eyes—large, luminous and wide apart—were filled with fright. She blinked constantly, perhaps a physical manifestation of her intense anxiety.

Huaishan Han put his hands on her back, propelling her forward. Zilin saw the wince she tried to hide.

"Shi *tong zhi*," Huaishan Han said with an odd kind of pride, "this is my wife, Soong Senlin."

"Your wife." Zilin was so astonished that for an instant he

251

forgot his composure and allowed his shock to show. He covered by giving a little bow. This gesture, at once familiar and polite, brought a flicker of a wan smile to the young woman's stricken face.

"Are you all right, Senlin?" he asked.

"Of course she's all right," Huaishan Han said a trifle too loudly. "Or at least she will be as soon as I take her to hospital. Just routine, you understand."

Zilin offered the young woman—she must have been twenty years Huaishan Han's junior, she was not yet thirty—his chair. She sat gratefully. Some of the hard lines of tension etching her face eased immediately.

Taking up his teapot, he served her. She gripped the small handleless cup with both hands as if determined to absorb all of its warmth into herself. Her head bobbed, she murmured her thanks and drank greedily, as if she had not tasted proper tea in some months.

Zilin looked up at his friend. Huaishan Han shrugged. "She was captured by the Communists."

"Captured, you say?"

"Their commander knew of me. A well-known Nationalist, *neh*? That is what I was to everyone but you and Mao *tong zhi*." Huaishan Han gestured. "In the end she was their enemy. Because she was my wife; the wife of Huaishan Han, the Nationalist. So they captured her, tortured her too, I think, though I cannot get her to talk about it. In fact, I cannot get her to talk much at all."

"I did not know that you were married." Zilin was appalled at the barbarism of his own people. But then he should not have been surprised. He had been witness to plenty of the aftermath of the bloody and bitter civil war. Somehow, though, this one pathetic creature, caught between two warring sides through none of her own doing, affected him more deeply than the rest.

Perhaps it was because the gross injustice of his situation served as a powerful metaphor for the madness that drove countrymen against their brothers. Of a sudden, he was aware of just how monstrous was this game in which he had chosen to play. "If you had only told me," he said weakly, "I would have dispatched men to see to her safety."

Huaishan Han turned away. "It was not a time when I could think of her, Shi *tong zhi*. I had my job to do. It was dangerous, this double game, and I found all my mind concentrated on placing one foot in front of the other in the dark, making my way in the tunnel down which you and Mao *tong zhi* sent me."

He turned back to Zilin. "Considering your own personal circumstances, I think you of all people can understand that."

It had not been meant as anything other than a compliment, a show of the degree of intimacy of their friendship, but this statement cut Zilin to the core. It was true. He had abandoned Athena and the baby Jake as well as his mistress, Sheng Li, and their child who would, in adult life, take the name Nichiren. All for the sake of protecting China, of carving out for it the proper future. He had sacrificed everything for his devotion to his country.

Zilin looked at his friend and said, "I do not recognize that uniform."

"It is of the Public Security Forces," Huaishan Han said, the pride returning to his voice. "Lo Juiqing has put me in charge of the Peking district bureau."

"The secret police," Zilin said.

"That is how I came to find Senlin, my friend. Our internal forces are powerful now. Our strength is growing every day. I sent my people out to find her and find her they did." He turned and his voice changed. "Senlin! We must go now."

Zilin watched her as she rose. She handed him the empty cup, then bowed to him quite formally.

After they had gone, Zilin sat at his desk. The lines of calligraphy swam in front of his eyes. He tried to concentrate on them but could not. Instead, he saw Senlin's hands as they gripped the white porcelain cup: her long palm, the slender fingers, so delicate and white as powder. Only their nails, cracked and bitten to the quick, marred their transcendent beauty.

When he next saw her, her nails had grown out. And they had been worked on by an expert. They were glossy with lacquer and as gently curved as a swan's neck.

"I don't know what to do with her," Huaishan Han said. They had come to Zilin's for dinner. Leaving the women— Zilin had invited a female acquaintance over as well as another couple in order to get away from four, an evil number in Chinese numerology— the two men had made themselves comfortable in Zilin's study. The third couple, who had a newborn infant at home, made an early departure.

"What is the problem?"

Huaishan Han smoked a thin black cigarette of Russian

manufacture. He had a habit of flicking it even when there was no excess ash. But then Huaishan Han, in Zilin's opinion, was a rather high-strung individual who rid himself of excess energy through his work. When he was between assignments and merely doing the drudgery of paperwork he was difficult to be around for long. As now.

He rose and began to pace back and forth across the deep wine-colored carpet. "The problem is Senlin. Frankly, she's not the woman whom I left when I went to war."

"She has been through a lot," Zilin advised. "Why don't you give her some time."

"Time!" Huaishan Han snorted. "I don't have time. There is far too much to do already. My head is filled with my work. Important work, mind you! I cannot have these constant interruptions at home."

"Mmmm. What kind of problems?"

"The doctors. Tests. Reports. Interviews. Buddha alone knows what else." Huaishan Han delivered this last in quick staccato bursts, as if his anger and frustration was making him tongue-tied. Through all of this he continued to prowl the room like a caged tiger.

"What, precisely, is Senlin's problem?" Zilin asked.

"I don't know."

"Well, is it medical or emotional? What?"

Huaishan Han blew out a long cloud of smoke. His breath hissed like that of a great dragon's. "No one knows. Buddha, the doctors can tell me nothing. They've tried acupuncture, acupressure, herbs. It would take all night to list them."

"And Senlin?"

"You saw it yourself tonight at the table. She ate nothing at all. Didn't you think that odd?"

"She wasn't hungry."

Huaishan Han threw up his arms. "Buddha, she's *never* hungry! She drinks tea. But that is all she consumes."

"She is losing weight."

"What?" Huaishan Han puffed away like an engine. "Yes. Of course she is. What creature wouldn't?"

"She was already dangerously thin when you found her."

"Way below normal."

"Then, from what you've been telling me," Zilin said, "she should be dead by now." His friend stopped his pacing long enough to stare at him. "And yet she is not. Perhaps that is what the doctors seek an answer to."

"Whatever the question," Huaishan Han said, resuming

his prowling, "they have found no answers. And time is running out."

"Why?"

"I have been given an assignment of the utmost political importance by Lo *tong zhi*. It entails my leaving Peking." Huaishan Han ceased his pacing at last, perching on the arm of a carved wood chair. "I am going south, my friend. To Hong Kong and thence, perhaps, even to Taiwan. Guomindang agents emanating from the Nationalist regime in exile in Taiwan have been found to be infiltrating our military units. Perhaps—and this is Lo *tong zhi*'s theory—even our political bureaus." Huaishan Han's face was dark. "There may come a time when a purge will become a political necessity. When we will have to weed out the traitors from within our midst. And when that time comes, it will be our people who will find these vile traitors."

This was the second time that Zilin could recall his friend using the phrase *our people*. Huaishan Han was referring to the Public Security Forces. There was, Zilin thought, no more fervid ideologue than the converted one. Huaishan Han, once having made the jump from Nationalism to Communism, was now its most ardent—and rigid—enthusiast.

"I cannot leave Senlin at home alone."

"A nurse, perhaps. Or a female companion."

Huaishan Han shook his head. "Neither will do. I have no intention of making my wife into an invalid. I want no nurses around. As for a female companion, there is none that I know or trust sufficiently for the task."

"But surely she must have family."

"Naturally she does. But Senlin is a Soong . . . descended from *the* Soongs, so she tells me. There is not a Soong or a Kung of note left even on the island of Taiwan. They have all fled to America with their lives and their wealth." He shook his head. "There is no one." He stubbed out his butt in an iron ashtray. "That is why I must ask you, my friend, if you will look after Senlin. I know that you are wise. If anyone can find out what is wrong with her I trust it is you."

Zilin said nothing. He had dreaded this moment from the time he became aware that Huaishan Han might ask this of him. The thought of having Senlin around the house . . . but there was no question of his answer. He could not refuse his friend. It would be impolite and worse, a slap in the face of their friendship.

Zilin at last nodded. "All right," he said.

Huaishan Han stood. He possessed a military bearing now that was unmistakable. To a politician such as Zilin, this was a disturbing sign. Politicians learned to use the soldier but never to trust him.

"What a great pleasure it is to look at this lake," Mao said.

He and Zilin strolled side by side along the bank of Kunming Lake. They were within the impressive precincts of Yiheyuan, the Summer Palace. This series of buildings, temples, pavilions, gardens, walkways and mounded islets eleven kilometers northwest of Peking had been built for the successive generations of Chinese emperors who felt the need to abandon the heat and high humidity of the imperial city during the high summer.

"Even you, Shi *tong zhi*, cannot know how many times Kunming has changed shape and size. Each dynasty had its complement of architect-landscapers who saw fit to redesign this lake over and over." Mao put his hands behind his thick back. "Yet here it still stands, its waters unchanged. There is, I think, a lesson to be learned from this spot on earth." He breathed deeply. "I often come here and gaze out upon the water. I let my mind wander, as if that way I may be able to discern all its previous shapes, all its previous lives." He shook his head. "Yet I find myself reluctant to absorb its message.

"China must change, Shi *tong zhi*. And I have no illusions about that change. It will be painful and it will be bloody."

"It has already been bloody enough for me."

Mao gave one of his tiny enigmatic smiles. "Hush! That is not in the spirit of the true revolutionary, Shi *tong zhi*. You have a heart that I find impenetrable. Death is part of change. In all upheavals—in all true revolutions, Shi *tong zhi*—blood must be shed. The old must give way to the new; it is the blood of the old regime that enriches the earth that the revolutionary tills."

"Our revolutionaries wield guns, not plowshares."

Mao nodded. "For the time being that is so. And perhaps it will always be thus. Our enemies—not ourselves—will determine that. China has been insulted enough by the unwanted presence of the imperialist barbarians. We will never again allow ourselves to become weak, a target for invasion. The Americans themselves have seen to it that I have an iron fist. They pour aid into Taiwan. They train Guomindang agents to infiltrate our Mainland society in an attempt to destroy us. I tell you they will not succeed!"

This interested Zilin since it paralleled his conversation with Huaishan Han. "You have been talking with Lo Jui-qing."

"With Lo *tong zhi*, yes," Mao acknowledged. "And with Huaishan Han."

They paused at the apex of Mirror Bridge. Across the shimmering water they could see South Lake Isle with its pagodalike Dragon King's Temple. The islet was connected with the shore by the stunning seventeen-arch bridge. The buildings, vermilion, turquoise, orange and verdigris green, rose up from the still blue waters across which white herons and egrets swooped in long, arcing dives. The birds skimmed the translucent surface of the lake, plucking thrashing fish, shining silver and gold in the sunlight, from just beneath.

"There," Mao said, "you see how the birds feed there. That is how the imperialists have treated China. They have plucked from us our natural resources. For decades they have grown rich off our land, caring nothing for the suffering and poverty of our people."

Zilin thought of the succession of Chinese dynastic rulers who had done the same thing. But it was not his place to say such a thing. Besides, his mind was filled with what Mao had said just before.

"It is my belief that Huaishan Han received his orders from Lo *tong zhi*."

"Not for some months," Mao said. "What a find that man is! I really must congratulate you, Zilin. I have kept my eye on him ever since you brought him to the Ministry of Public Security. The man is fearless—he proved as much to me during several missions."

"I knew nothing of these."

"Of course you didn't." Mao commenced to walk again and Zilin was at his side. "Internal security is not your province. Besides, I know that the firm hand I am forced to keep at home displeases you. Why then should I burden you with the details of such, er, unpleasant operations."

"What has Huaishan Han been doing for you?"

"Oh, he is part of the state machine," Mao said easily, "and you have heard me say more than once that the state machine is often an instrument for oppression."

"That is what concerns me."

"Why?" Mao asked. "Are you not also part of the state machine?"

Zilin made no reply. He was thinking of Huaishan Han's repeated references to "our people." Since Lo Juiqing had created the Public Security Forces within his ministry, they had grown in size and power far beyond Zilin's expectations. He said so now.

"Nonsense," Mao replied. "Our revolution—as all revolutions—has spawned radical changes in our society. Of course there must be pockets of those who believe in the old ways. Of course there must be pockets of those who do not believe in the sweeping changes we have made and are continuing to make. And the tasks of regaining control of an economy destroyed by war and of establishing a nationwide administrative hierarchy sensitive to Peking's desires only add to our burden. And then there is the external threat of the Nationalist-American alliance.

"Authoritarian methods are sometimes the only alternatives. Without them a country would collapse during periods of rapid social and economic change. Tell me, Shi *tong zhi*, how else am I able to stabilize a country this vast under these circumstances?"

Zilin walked in silence, his head down. Lost to view were the magnificent pagodas and temples, shaded walks and whispering trees. He saw with his mind's eye that a cord linking modern China with her past had now been severed. He saw, too, what no one else did: that this separation was irreversible. China could never go back. There might be gain—would have to be—in order to justify all that would be irrevocably lost. The old skills will wither and die away beneath the banner of the revolution, he thought.

When at length he looked up again he saw that these magnificent structures had been built by a people already alien to him. His heart broke in unutterable sadness.

"There is unhappiness in your eyes," she said. "And pain in your heart."

Senlin. Her name meant great forest, and in a very strange and compelling way it was apt, for Zilin felt lost when he was near her.

He was a man who had spent almost all his life developing a strategy adapted from that used by his childhood mentor, the Jian. The Jian had lived in Suzhou, a town of the most renowned and spectacular gardens. These *yuan lin*, which were in fact villas surrounded by gardens, were carefully tended, painstakingly built. The Jian lived in one such and slowly he revealed to the young Zilin the secrets of the *yuan*: how hills, ponds and the like could be fashioned by the hand of man to seem as confluent to the environment as if created by nature. This art of remarkable artifice, Zilin eventually discovered, could be translated to the world outside the *yuan*. One could become whatever one chose to be so long as one knew how to create the artifice appropriate to the circumstance.

Thus Zilin had eventually joined the Chinese Communist Party in order to fulfill his destiny as celestial guardian of China. His commitment to Communism was purely a pragmatic one. He had seen very early on that it was the concept behind which all of his countrymen—so long wrapped up in petty internecine warfare—could unite in order to return control of China to the hands of its native sons.

To this end—even to have developed this strategy in the first place—his *qi* was extremely powerful and well developed. It was his *qi* which allowed him to see into the very hearts of those around him in order to don his many disguises and thus get that which he wished.

Senlin—the great forest—was the one person with whom he had contact whose internal riddle he could not solve. This was at once a subject of concern and attraction to him. Compounding the enigma was the fact that he knew her own *qi* to be strong. He could in fact feel that hers was almost as powerful as his. Yet he was at a loss as to how it manifested itself. Few indeed would be the people who would see her as "strong." Certainly it was clear that her husband did not.

Then there were the incidents—increasing in frequency—when she was able to see through this meticulously constructed artifice. No one, not Athena or Mai, had been able to do that.

Now as they sat within his villa on a dark, still evening, she had done it again. Zilin had given up denying her insights. The first time he had done so, she had looked at him with her wide-apart ebon eyes and had said, "Is there a reason why you are lying to me?"

He had been astounded. But there was nothing but the simplest honesty in her voice and on her face. Like a child yet to be sophisticated by the adolescent and adult worlds, she had opened her mouth and said what was in her heart.

Zilin was to recall that imagery with great clarity in the weeks to come.

For now, he said, "It saddens me to see what has become of us."

"I do not understand." She had the most endearing habit of canting her head to one side. Her thick black hair, gleaming richly in the lamplight, slid across her shoulder.

"Repression appears to be the only way in which to keep China functioning at the moment. The internal and external pressures are far too great for us to long tolerate. We have already gone through immense and painful political and social upheavals. My sense is that the agony for us is far from over. Many lives are yet to be lost. There is not yet enough blood spilled. How can the future dictate such cruelty when the present is so brutal."

Senlin, watching him in the pool of soft light, said, "Ask Buddha. In him we must seek our refuge."

"Unfortunately," Zilin said, "Buddha has no place in modern-day society."

"Is that what Mao *tong zhi* writes? If so you would be well rid of him. My husband as well." Abruptly she turned her head away. Shadows fell across her cheek, spilling downward like a river at night.

Zilin wondered what had made her break off so precipitously. Was it the realization of her antirevolutionary words or something else? He wondered what else Huaishan Han had not told him. His friend had lied to him about the source of his assignment. He had mentioned Lo Juiqing by name when he had not had to. Why? Perhaps it was only for security reasons. That would be acceptable. And in all probability the notion would have successfully pacified Zilin had Huaishan Han's recent behavior remained the same. But the fact was that he was rapidly becoming unrecognizable as the man with whom Zilin had formed a bond on the slopes of Jinyun Shan.

Like the new China itself, Huaishan Han was hardening his heart. Donning the colors of the revolution he was striking out with Mao's gun in his curled fist, Mao's philosophy filling his head, to perform Buddha only knew what unspeakable tasks.

He is part of the state machine. Mao's answer to his question, offhand and evasive, stuck in Zilin's mind like a warning flag. Huaishan Han believed that what he was doing was making China a safer place in which to live. He might even be right . . . which was even more frightening. Because Zilin suspected that when Mao sent his friend abroad in the land, people died. Silently, swiftly, without even a ripple of comment, the instrument of oppression carried out his appointed commissions.

Does Senlin know what he does? Zilin wondered. Does she suspect what he has become?

He rose and went to the window. Outside he could hear a nightingale's iterative call. He inhaled deeply, scenting rain. It was still some distance away but it was coming. As he watched, the darkness came alive with the forked flicker of lightning. When the second outburst licked downward, he judged the distance.

"The rain will not last long," he said even as the first rumble of thunder echoed in the hills. "Tomorrow will be a fine day. Perhaps you will venture out." Except to see one doctor or another, Senlin never went outside the villa.

When she made no reply he turned from the window to contemplate her. You cannot remain in here forever, was what he should have said, but he could not bring himself to do so. It was something, perhaps, with which Huaishan Han would have scolded her. That Zilin would not do.

She was so frail looking. It seemed to him, watching her now in the soft lamplight, that her skin was as fragile as eggshell. Her luminous eyes regarded him without apparent emotion and, not for the first time, he found himself wondering by what magical art she was able to conceal the nature of her spirit from his probing powers.

"Huaishan Han told me several times before he left that you would not speak," Zilin said. "He feared there might be something wrong with you."

Senlin held out her hands palms up. Her crimson nails glittered. "There is a world here," she said softly, raising her right hand slightly. "And here"—now the left—"another."

"The doctors—"

"The doctors enjoy enigmas," she said. "When they can find none to occupy their minds, they create them."

Zilin came away from the window and sat down next to her. "Do you mean, then, that there is nothing wrong with you?"

Senlin stared at him wordlessly.

"Would you go outside tomorrow if I went with you?"

"I do not care for the world outside." Emotion, electric and fleeting, transformed her face. "It is harsh and ugly. It is evil. I long only for the days before the war."

261

"We will never return to that."

"You can be most cruel." There were tears trembling at the corners of her eyes.

"I speak only the truth."

Those enormous eyes dropped from his and when she spoke next it was in a tiny whisper. "You asked before why I spoke with you and not with my husband. Now you have answered your own question."

Zilin thought about that for a moment. "He has lied to you."

Her head came up. "Only because he lies to himself."

The confirmation of his own suspicions came like an electric shock. He saw the tiny tremor in her temple and decided to change the subject. "You cannot stay inside the villa for the rest of your life. That is a kind of death."

"What does it matter? I am already dead!" Her eyes held in their depths the green burning flames of a land wholly alien to Zilin. He did not know what to do for her. He only knew that he must try to end her strange inner-directed torment.

Outside a crack of thunder reverberated nearby. Senlin started, her head jerking around on her neck. Her eyes were open wide as the first burst of rain slapped against the windowpanes.

"It is nothing," Zilin said. "Only the rain."

"It is everything." But she seemed not to be talking to him. "Senlin."

She gave a great shudder and her eyes fluttered closed. He reached out and she slid against him. His arms went around her to hold her up. Then just to hold her.

Her face was but a breath from his. He felt her warmth and more, the pulse of her. He felt as if he had downed a bottle of whiskey in one thirsty gulp.

Light-headed, unable to catch his breath fully, he drew her closer to him.

"Senlin."

Her lips were half-open and her sweet breath fell upon his cheek like spring rain. The heavy cascade of her hair fanned out. It seemed to caress him as if, with a life of its own, it was part of some mythical creature—a Qilin, perhaps. Then he realized that she was swaying, her long pent-up emotions breaking through the barriers of icy iron she had erected so that now the two of them, linked by the warmth of their bodies, were tossed as if on a tide.

Closer and closer so that Zilin felt the softness of her cheek, a peony's petal, against him.

"No!" With an inarticulate cry, Senlin broke away from him and, staggering to her feet, ran across the length of the study.

"Senlin!"

"Please . . ." Thunder booming, rain beating its rapid tattoo. "Please!"

He took a quick step toward her, not knowing what she would do or even what she meant by that single strangled word.

The reflection of the rain ran obliquely across her pained face as she wrenched open the glass door out to the garden and the weather came rushing in with the fierce whip of a tiger's tail.

The shades rattled, an eerie unsettling sound, and Senlin rushed out into the rain. Zilin followed her, calling her name. The deluge had turned night into the pitch blackness of a well. Branches like a spirit's withered arms juddered and shook in the wind which, caught between the side of the villa and the high garden wall, swirled around upon itself, picking up strength. The sound of its passage through the trees moaned in their ears.

Zilin caught up with her just as a violent streak of lightning forked downward overhead. By the flutter of its acid illumination, he saw her abruptly reverse herself, flying into his arms, burying her head in his shoulders, molding her body to his.

He moved to bring her inside but she refused to be budged. She brought her face up to his, her lips opened. Rain danced off her face, flew through her hair as if they were both part of the wind. Zilin felt as he had atop the horse, riding bareback with Ross Davies up the slopes of the Red Silk Mountain. Together, they dropped to the sopping ground.

He pulled aside her clothes as she frantically opened his. Never had he felt such urgency, not with either of his wives, not with his mistress or all the women who had followed him into his bed. The physical, the emotional were both supplanted at this moment. But by what he could not say.

His flesh tingled at her touch, her lips, when he enclosed them in his, tasted of the most exquisite nectar. The rain drumming on them, all around them, pressing leaves and twigs to their bare flesh, felt to them like an extension of their own molten passion. The rumbling of the thunder sounded in their ears like the growling of some great primitive cat, rampant and eager.

When Zilin bared her breasts he nearly wept with longing. His fingertips traced her skin, drinking in its superb smoothness, free of blemishes or wrinkles. His lips soon followed as he moved down her.

In the shadowed dell between her thighs, he discovered the heat and he made her cry out, her lithe body undulating upward, her head back, mouth open, drinking in the downpour while her neck arched.

In a moment she had taken him in her two hands, guiding him through portals flowering open like an anemone. Instantly he felt in the midst of a dream. In China, it was this way: as one slept, one's *hun*—spirit—emerged through the top of one's head at the spot where the bone was the last to harden at the beginning of one's life. What one dreamed, one experienced. It was as simple as that. Dreams, therefore, were no less real than waking life.

Now as Zilin penetrated to Senlin's soft, clinging core, his spirit rose out of his body. In the midst of the kinetic storm it mingled with that of his partner's.

Upward they flew in an endless helix of motion, sound, color, scent. The sweet smell of wet grass, the cant of a curious pair of plovers huddled within the shivering branches of a pine, the color of the wind, turned mauve and electric blue by the raging tempest. Motion.

Force.

Qi.

As their cries of pleasure mingled with the long moaning cries of the wind, Zilin was at last made witness to Senlin's unleashed *qi*.

And understood everything.

"War."

As Zilin had predicted, the following day had turned out fine. But Mao was in a foul mood; even the exceptionally clear weather had failed to soften his attitude.

"War," he fumed, "is all around us. Our economy can ill afford another war—especially one in the foreign land of Korea. Our people cry out for peace. They look to us for leadership and support not for a further effort which will leave Chinese blood soaking into the ground of another country."

"Perhaps," Zilin said, "we should be looking for a way to turn war to our advantage."

"You do not understand," Mao said impatiently. "The Americans, the Nationalists are like hungry sharks lurking in the waters just offshore. If we go to war they will wait until the military expenditures have further weakened us. Then they will strike. As of now the counterrevolutionists are relatively few and weak. A renewal of war will give them fuel. Like pouring kerosene on a fire, their cause abetted by the Nationalist agents will begin to pose a serious threat. Do you suppose I can allow that to occur?"

"Not at all," Zilin said.

Mao stood quite still. They were still in quarters that had been turned into a suite of offices from hotel rooms. Out the window was Tienanmen Square. The whirring of the clouds of bicycles through the wide avenues was a constant sound through the open windows. "I want you to understand this clearly so that, at a later time when, perhaps, you have a different taste in your mouth, you will not come to me with your conscience bleeding and petition me for surcease."

"What are you asking me?" From another office, Zilin could hear the clack-clack of a barrage of antiquated typewriters upon which propaganda leaflets were being banged out by a squadron of efficient clerks.

"Just this," Mao said. "War with Korea will bring disaster here, no matter what advantage you may cook up for us internationally. The economy will collapse yet again and, worse, there is the distinct possibility that our actions will create our own political nemesis.

"In order to forestall such a catastrophe, we will be forced to depend more and more on the Ministry of Public Security."

"The secret police."

"If you would call them that, yes."

"I cannot condone a reign of terror."

For an instant, Zilin feared that he had gone too far. There was some color to Mao's cheeks, unnatural as women's rouge. There was silence between them so taut that Zilin could imagine biting through it with one snap of his jaws.

Mao sat down. He closed his eyes, massaging the lids with his thumbs. When he was sufficiently calm, he said, "I do not believe that either of us have a choice. You believe that war with Korea is inevitable."

"Inevitable," Zilin said, "and desirable."

Intermittently, there were bells ringing, tiny sounds as the typewriters came to the end of their lines. Some minister stopped in to ask Mao a question and was quickly dismissed.

After a time, Mao said, "You had better make yourself clear, Shi *tong zhi*. I am in no mood for jests."

"You know me better than that, Mao *zhu xi*."

Hearing the formal address, Mao turned. "Let us be rid of this tension between us, my friend. It serves both of us ill. I have no wish to be at odds with my most trusted minister."

Zilin bowed, pressed the palms of his hands together in front of him, moving them up and down in the honorific.

As a physical manifestation of his words, Mao set about making tea and nothing more of a business nature was said until it had been brewed, served in the traditional manner and savored by both men. By that time, they had talked about many other topics of a personal and, sometimes, trivial nature.

Following the natural pause at the end of the easy dialogue, Mao said, "Please be good enough to explain to me your theory concerning war with Korea."

Zilin nodded, poured himself more tea. "You have already told me that Stalin is adamant about acting should the Americans cross the Yalu and invade North Korea."

"I have said that he is of two minds about this," Mao corrected. "He is committed to seeing that all of Korea is eventually ruled by the Communists. To this end he sees no alternative but to dispatch Russian troops to the site of the conflict."

"If the Americans come to the aid of the South Koreans, such a decision would spell disaster for both sides, perhaps the entire world." Zilin shook his head. "No, Mao *tong zhi*, it is China which holds the key to Stalin's dilemma, and with it we may open the door to our own salvation."

"How?"

"We inform Stalin that should MacArthur advance across the Yalu we will send troops into Korea. We are in a much better position than he to do this since we can say to the world at large that we have merely sent volunteers to aid a neighboring fraternal Communist regime. Will any Westerner not believe that the Koreans are our brothers? In that way we may join the battle even if the United States intervenes. They will be on as tentative ground as will we. They could not afford a direct attack on us. World opinion would be against them."

"Yes, I see," Mao said. "And Stalin would be put into our debt. I could get out of him more aid—perhaps even unencumbered aid this time. But there is the matter of troops to be sent."

"Transport the remnants of the Guomindang armies stranded here. Let them shed their blood for our cause; let them be the first Chinese to join the Koreans in expelling the Americans from the North." Zilin put his teacup down. "And we both know that will happen, Mao *tong zhi*. We have made it our business to study General MacArthur. He *will* cross the Yalu."

"So this is to be our fate," Mao said. "We must serve as Moscow's cat's-paw in order to earn their trust and their capital aid."

"It is always thus with the weak," Zilin said. "But history is mutable. We must endeavor to make our own so that one day we will be strong enough that Moscow will fear us, not the other way around."

The first thing they saw was Fazhan's spirit screen. In its center was the symbol of the creation of the world which, as every Chinese knew, came about as the result of the union of a tortoise and a serpent.

Surrounding the central symbol were arrayed the Eight Trigrams. These consisted of a series of combinations of continuous and broken lines, symbolizing male and female, respectively. The possibly mythical emperor Fu Hsi claimed that the Trigrams were the basis for mathematics. Every possible combination and juxtaposition were to be found within the Trigrams from power to submission, to representations of all the important animals in the Chinese mythology to the points of the compass.

The spirit screen was a sign. In accordance with the precepts of *feng shui*, the ancient art of geomancy, screens such as this were set at a site filled with evil spirits. In order to get past this screen, evil demons were obliged to make a right turn, which every Chinese knew that they could not do.

In Fazhan's foyer was an enormous mirror. It was painted in the same manner as the spirit screen outside had been carved. This was a further sign of the virulence of the evil influences that must be deflected in order to make this place safe.

Senlin balked when she saw the mirror. The spirit screen and its obvious significance had disturbed her enough. The mirror seemed to unnerve her completely.

She turned away from it and Zilin felt her trembling like a doe against him.

"It is all right," he said, staring at their reflection in the interstices of unpainted mirror. "There is nothing here to fear."

"Why have you brought me to this place?" Her voice was small, wavery as water.

"Because you must be helped," Zilin said gently. "Your husband was correct on one count. No physical doctor can cure your malady. That is why we have come here."

"But it is an evil place."

"No," he said, "it is merely a place where evil dwells. Fazhan, the *feng shui* man, picked this spot specifically in order to draw the evil spirits inward, to confine them, chain them down and thus render them powerless."

"But the spirit screen, this mirror. Both will repel them."

Zilin nodded. "The evil is not within this house. Within Fazhan's garden is a well. A spirit well. It is, he says, a well without bottom. It is within the spirit well's depths that he imprisons the evil spirits."

Something in his voice caused her to look up into his face. "You do not believe any of this, do you?"

"I believe there is a *xin jing* in Fazhan's garden," Zilin said slowly. "But as to what dwells within its depths I am not at all certain."

Senlin gave a great shudder and, drawing in her breath, said, "Well, I am. I'm very sure."

Fazhan had a fierce Mongol's face. His skin where it appeared from out of the voluminous folds of his black robes was as parched and leathery as an elephant's skin. His head was long and narrow; his body followed suit. He was also tall, which added immeasurably to the sense of power he exuded.

Fazhan was a Black Hat *feng shui* man. There were many forms of geomancy; this was the most ancient and the most mystical.

The origins of Black Hat *feng shui* were said to have been in India, the birthplace of Buddha. From there, it traveled northward into Tibet. When at last it migrated from out of the land of great mountains, it drifted south into China. By then it had gained power and influence from each country and culture where it had been practiced over the centuries.

268

Zilin bowed in front of the *feng shui* man and Senlin did the same. She was plainly terrified of him.

"Greetings, Great Lion," Fazhan said, using a play on Zilin's name. "It is good to see you again." His voice was a vast rumbling, seeming to fill the room like faraway thunder.

"The good fortune is mine, Silver Buttons," Zilin said, "to be here." With that he handed over a slim red envelope. For just the space of a heartbeat it appeared. Then it had disappeared within the folds of the *feng shui* man's robes.

Senlin observed these exchanges silently but with a great deal of interest. Neither of these men used the modern honorific, *tong zhi*, comrade. Further, they used nicknames that connoted a deep and abiding personal friendship.

Zilin turned and, speaking softly, presented Senlin and a capsule summation of her recent history. Even before he was done, Fazhan had begun to move. Zilin stood off to one side of the room, leaving Senlin on her own in the center.

The *feng shui* man's gaze, so much like black fire, was intolerable for her so she kept her mind occupied by staring at her surroundings. They were in a room nine meters by nine meters. The ceiling was painted a stark white but the walls were overhung by a series of calligraphic scrolls. While Senlin could not read them since the style of writing was ornate and the language archaic, she was certain that these were *sutras*, or perhaps extracts, since one complete *sutra*, she knew, could fill an entire book. Oddly, she did not question how she knew such an arcane thing.

By the time Zilin had finished recounting Senlin's history, the *feng shui* man had made three complete circuits around her. At length, he stopped in front of her. He said, "She has the aspect of the phoenix. That is good. The phoenix has its roots in royalty. With the dragon, it rules the capital of China." He turned and lit three *joss* sticks. He placed them one at a time before a small apple-green figurine that crouched by the side of a gilt Buddha.

"Please speak to me," Fazhan said and Senlin trembled at his voice. It was dark as woodsmoke and seemed to her to be as aromatic. Surely it was the *joss* sticks she was smelling. Had voices a scent? "You were tortured." It was not a question.

"Yes," she whispered.

"How were you tortured?"

"Silver Buttons—"

But the *feng shui* man's upheld hand cut Zilin off.

Senlin stared into that long Mongol face and thought she saw someone else. A countenance she knew yet did not know.

"If it is painful," Fazhan said, "think of how a wound aches even as it is healing. Consider that it must do so in order to heal."

"There were shadows," she began. "I remember there were shadows all around. Perhaps they came from the men moving beyond the fires. There were fires burning all around, did I mention that?" Her voice held an odd echoey quality, as if she were speaking to them from some distance away. "The men came at me with the fires at their backs. I could never see them . . . see their faces. The absence of light and heat gave me clues as to their movement but always firelight was in my eyes. There was an overpowering stench that made me want to gag. There were piles of broken bones. Those were all black and scorched as if they had been roasted in the fires.

"They were the bones of the Japanese, the shadows told me. And bones of the Nationalists. A shadow bent down and I felt the passage of something. It must have been a weapon because I saw the shadow hold up the severed arm of a Chinese soldier.

" 'See,' he said. 'See what we do to Nationalist scum!' And he thrust the hand into the flames. There was a great crackling and hissing as the dripping blood sizzled. And the fingers . . . the fingers began to move. I began to scream and the shadows began to laugh. I screamed and screamed as I watched the fingers moving even as the fire ate through the skin, even after I realized that the movement came from the fire itself, the heat, the inner combustion. I saw that hand blackening, writhing still as if in the most intense agony.

"When the hand was gone and nothing remained of even the bones, the shadow threw the stump into the night. I heard dogs barking, panting and padding just outside the circle of the firelight.

"Then the shadow grabbed me and untied me. It took me toward the flames. Now I knew the origin of the cloying stench. It was the burning of human flesh. I saw how the soldiers were defiling the Ming corpses . . . cutting off their manhood and pressing the sides of their jaws so their mouths gaped open . . . it was hideous, unspeakable."

Senlin's breast was heaving uncontrollably and her words were gasped out almost as if she was being choked by them. She was shivering as if with the ague, but by a commanding gesture the *feng shui* man held Zilin back from her.

"You said 'Ming corpses' just now," Fazhan said.

Senlin started as if he had put a branding iron to her flesh. "I did?" She blinked heavily. "I don't remember. Of course I meant the Japanese corpses. It *was* the Japanese corpses." There was a hollow look in her eyes. "Why would I say Ming? The Ming Dynasty was overthrown three hundred years ago."

Fazhan turned and lit three more *joss* sticks. He placed them beside the first three, already half-burned.

"In sixteen forty-four, to be precise," he said. "By the end of the fifteenth century, the end the Ming Dynasty was in sight. Remorseless Mongols from the north, barbarous Japanese pirates along the east coast were constant threats. Chronic poverty caused by the ever increasing popularity of large servant-tended estates. Lower and lower bowed the back of the pitiful peasant until, at length, these inhuman injustices brought on a groundswell of protests and then strikes by the workers in the major mercantile sectors.

"Despite the intervention of a newly formed secret police, the people cried out for justice, banding together. And all the while, the power of the Ming emperors was waning until, by the time of Wanli at the close of the century, much of the dynasty's power had devolved into the hands of the court eunuchs.

"In sixteen twenty-one, shortly after the time of Wanli's death, those who opposed the Mings' rule overran Peking. This internal war was the signal the Manchus had been waiting for. Down from the north they swept. When they reached the capital there was tremendous bloodshed. Eventually, the victorious Manchus proclaimed the Qing Dynasty."

The room was filled up with the curling scent of the *joss* sticks. There was heat as if somewhere out of sight a fire had been lit.

"What do the Ming and the Manchus have to do with Senlin?" Zilin asked.

"In *feng shui* one deals with many aspects of the world," Fazhan said. "Some are obvious, others are hidden in dark corners. Ordinarily, however, one deals in *ru-shr*, that which is within the scope of our experience. In these cases, cures are often simply effected since humans have within them the five elements: earth, fire, water, metal, wood. All people possess these five to one degree or another measured upon a scale of one to seventy-two. Imbalances in one or more of these elements are most often the cause of an individual's *feng shui* problem."

Fazhan took up three more *joss* sticks and lit them. Now there were nine grouped around the jade figurine and the gold Buddha. Nine, the full figure in numerology. The most fortuitous of numbers.

"Occasionally," Fazhan went on, "very infrequently, one comes upon a subject for which *ru-shr* is inadequate. When one has exhausted all the known quantities at one's disposal, one is obliged to seek answers elsewhere. In *chu-shr*, areas outside one's experience."

Zilin could see through the smoke that Senlin was trembling. She turned to him and said, "Please take me back to the villa. Zilin, I implore you!"

Zilin looked from her pained face to the *feng shui* man, who stood silent as a statue, the tips of his long fingers touching. For the first time in his life, he did not know which course was the correct one. His mind told him to stay but his heart, torn by what his eyes saw, urged him to take Senlin and flee.

"Zilin, please! There is evil here." Her eyes were wide and staring. She was clearly terrified. "I fear the evil will consume me."

"And so it shall," Fazhan said, "if you leave here now."

"No!" The one word was torn out of her throat.

Fazhan spread his hands. "I cannot stop you from leaving. Neither can Zilin. No one has that right, Senlin. You must understand that. If you do not stay of your own free will there is nothing I can do to save you."

"Save her?" Zilin said. "Save her from what?"

"From whatever is consuming her from the inside."

"What is it?" Zilin asked.

"*Chu-shr,*" the *feng shui* man said.

Senlin gave a little cry so strangled and full of despair that Zilin took her by the wrist and led her out of there.

Down the long dark corridor he heard sobbing, an eerie echoing sound as if, like the voice Senlin had used to recount the horror that had befallen her, it came from far away.

At the entryway, they passed by the spirit mirror. Senlin turned to glance at it and stopped so abruptly that for an instant Zilin was thrown off balance.

"No," Senlin said in another voice entirely. "I cannot leave. Not yet. Not yet. The evil—"

They both started as Fazhan appeared. From out of which shadow he had stepped Zilin could not say nor would he wish to try.

"It is time," the *feng shui* man said. "Earth, fire, water, metal, wood. None of the five will avail us an answer. *Chushr*." He began to lead them in another direction.

"Where are we going?" Zilin said.

"To the edge," Fazhan replied, "of the *xin jing*."

The garden at night. It was filled with white mulberry trees. The same species cultivated by the weavers and off which the precious silkworm fed.

There was an odd spicy scent about them that was unfamiliar to Zilin. There was a cold silver sliver of moon, the horns of the dragon, so it was said. The height of the feeding cycle for nocturnal predators.

They made nine circuits around the small garden. Nine, in Mandarin, meant long life. Much of Chinese numerology stemmed from the fact that Chinese, in all its varied dialects, was a homonymous language. Often numbers sounded like other words and, therefore, took on the significance associated with those words.

"The nine is important tonight," the *feng shui* man said. "Perhaps even crucial. This is the twenty-fourth day of the fourth month. Four twenty-four, the most inauspicious day of the calendar."

Zilin, who knew Cantonese as well as Fazhan did, understood why. The number four in Cantonese sounded like the word die. Thus four twenty-four was die and die again, a number to be shunned at all costs. Why, Zilin wondered, had he decided to bring Senlin here this night?

"Still you are here," Fazhan said, echoing Zilin's thought, "and that is significant in and of itself. If the four twenty-four is the proper time, then so be it. The Tao of perpetual change tells us that only at the apex of the darkness can the first light appear."

Fazhan then led them to the center of the garden. Here there were vines all around, and the luscious scent of roses though, surely, it was too early in the year for such blossoms.

When they were completely enclosed within the bower formed by the overarching white mulberries, the *feng shui* man placed them as he saw fit. "Senlin," he said, "face this way, toward the slopes of the black tortoise mountain. Zilin, here, this is where you must stand, near the rock formation of the crimson phoenix. And I, here, at the mouth of the green dragon." He nodded his long head. "Now the *qi* will rise, bubbling like lava, from where it swirls endlessly at the core of the planet."

Senlin was aware of a great darkness before her. "What is this?" she said, pointing.

"The spirit well," Fazhan said.

There was no wind at all, and no clouds to speak of. The dragon's horn moon rode in the firmament as the final enigmatic punctuation on an otherwise blank page.

Now Fazhan began to speak in a kind of rhythmic litany. His words were of no Chinese dialect Zilin had ever heard. Perhaps they were not Chinese at all, he thought, but rather some ancient Tibetan or Indic tongue.

It seemed that the heat that had suffused the room of *sutras* had followed them out into what had once been a cool spring evening. Now it was as hot as high summer. The budding mulberry leaves seemed to droop, and sweat sprang out on all of them.

Zilin looked at Senlin. Her eyes were fixed and staring into what invisible space he could not guess. As if in some trance she took a step forward, then another until she was at the lip of the spirit well. Her hands came up and by the cold light of the horned moon, he saw her grasp the stones at the well's top. She began to lean over until her face was hanging suspended over the great maw whose inky blackness was beyond color.

Senlin could not breathe. She tried to inhale but it was as if she had entered an airless space where her lungs refused to work. She no longer heard Fazhan's arcane incantations. Rather, she felt it. His words cloaked her and at the same time began to pull her out of herself. She felt again the sensation she had experienced with Zilin when they had joined their flesh in the storm of the previous night.

The top of her skull seemed to dissolve and something—a part of her—began to emerge. Then she felt the pain and knew—*knew*—that there was someone else inside her.

This was the source of the evil, not Fazhan's house or garden or *xin jing*. It had been this malevolent presence inside her who had sensed a danger here—for itself, not for Senlin.

Senlin's jaws were clenched, her eyes were tearing and there was an agony inside her beyond all understanding. Curved talons raked against her insides, weals of pain sprouted, and she tried to cry out. She could do nothing.

Inside the airless space over the spirit well's mouth, she swayed and would have collapsed into those infinite depths had not Fazhan woven his invisible web around her.

Now a blinding light shone inside her head and for an

274

instant Senlin was transported back in time to the sacking of Peking by the enemies of the Ming. She relived the atrocities inflicted by the conquerors upon the vanquished. She was witness to the death of the dynasty, the bloody, terror-filled ending. She was the Emperor's consort and she recognized the face of Li Zi cheng, the general who had once been her lover and was now her mortal enemy.

Li Zi cheng ended her Emperor's life with one appalling blow. Then he took her up and threw her across the room. She withdrew a dagger from its sheath against her breast and tried to kill him. But he only laughed and struck her so hard across the face that she let go the weapon. Then he was upon her. He raped her, taking his time about it, his member hard as jade all over again, thrusting viciously into her a second time. When he was through, he ordered all the soldiers in the room to take her. By ones, twos, even threes, they eagerly complied.

She was a long time in dying. At least her physical body had perished. But not her spirit. It had survived and even now it craved revenge. It sought only to destroy. Was there any intelligence within it beyond that one elemental desire?

Zilin knew none of this, of course, until later. But he did see Senlin bent over the well's mouth. He saw her convulsed by awful spasms. He saw her mouth come open far wider than he thought possible in human anatomy.

And he saw the flash of light, blue-white, corrosive enough so that it seemed to sear his eyes. His vision blurred painfully and after that he was never certain whether he saw or merely imagined he saw . . .

. . . the smoke of centuries curling like that of the nine *joss* sticks in the room of the *sutras* from out of Senlin's gaping mouth. It seemed to him that it streamed and floated at the same time and that, simultaneously, his nostrils caught a heavy whiff of that same sickly sweet stench that Senlin had described and which Zilin had himself smelled so often during the war. Flesh was burning.

And now the smoke began to curl, forming itself into a shape. The apparition of a young woman made itself manifest. Its eyes were large around, its nose a skeleton's fleshless socket.

There were arms as well, ending in fingers—or perhaps, knowing the predilection of the Mings, nails—nearly half a meter long. But the torso was as thin and undefined as a serpent's body.

As an astounded Zilin continued to watch, that reptilian form commenced to entwine itself first around Senlin's shoulders and then around her neck and head.

He cried out but in that instant Fazhan stepped aside so that the *feng shui* man no longer stood in front of the mouth of the rock known as the green dragon.

Zilin was aware of a rising wind and looked around for its source, for the tops of the high mulberry trees were as still and droopy as ever they had been since the trio emerged into the garden.

It was then that he saw that the unnatural wind, as cold as an icy stream in winter, seemed to have its origin within one of the horizontal crevices that indented the green dragon.

The horrific apparition that was part of Senlin and was also trying to kill her turned its head as it felt the first gust of wind.

Then the water came. Another rainstorm one might have said, except that the water was running horizontally!

Into the face of the apparition the icy water flew. Smoke spinning, water spitting, the rush of a heavy wind and the burning in the trembling, shimmering air.

A howling, a gusting and, in a silence wholly unnatural in its completeness, the apparition was gone, the heat was gone. The garden, still and utterly serene, shone peacefully in the moonlight.

Fazhan picked Zilin up off the ground. Zilin looked the *feng shui* man in the eye. "What happened?"

Fazhan smiled. Opening his cloak slightly he said, "You see, Great Lion, I still have the row of silver buttons sewn inside my clothes. Nothing has changed."

"Did I see—"

"Nothing has changed," Fazhan reiterated.

"And Senlin?"

"The garden is yours. Do with it what you will. The spirit well sleeps now."

Alone within the bower of the mulberry trees, Zilin went to where Senlin stood, trembling. She was still gripping the lip of the stone well but as she sensed his presence, she turned and he saw that her eyes were clear.

"She is gone."

Zilin said nothing. He wondered if this had all been a dream.

"The consort of the last Ming emperor. Hu chao."

Zilin knew it was nonsense. Of course it was a dream. She

276

was swaying like a drunkard at the end of a long evening. Perhaps she did not even know what she was saying. He took her up into his arms.

"Her lover became her enemy," she whispered reedily. "He was a general named Li Zi cheng." Her head rested against his chest and he felt her words like the rumbling of faraway thunder. He carried her along the circuitous path out of the garden. Her eyelids were heavy.

It was not until they had returned to the villa and he had put her to bed that Zilin went into his study. Searching along the rows of books, he plucked a history down and leafed through until he came to the period of the decline of the Ming Dynasty.

In 1621, during the sacking of Peking that brought the Manchus to power in China, a rebel army was indeed led by a general named Li Zi cheng. There was likewise a reference to the last emperor's consort, but since a good deal of his power had already been usurped by the imperial eunuchs and he was thus considered by many Chinese scholars to be unimportant, her name was not mentioned.

Zilin went from history to history but no matter how detailed they otherwise were, he could find no trace of the consort's name. But all of Peking was at his disposal and at length an obscure library tome delivered up to him her name.

Hu chao.

III

FORMATION
VIVARTA

Amid the storm, with the pain that enwrapped her, this is what Qi lin thought: I am an animal. I have been an animal for months without end. If I am to survive now, I must become civilized.

Easier said than done. Qi lin raised one filthy hand to the wide purple bruise, the enflamed vampire's kiss where Colonel Hu's spatulate thumb had dug in and, in desperation, had snapped her collarbone. Pain throbbed through her but that was something she was used to.

Pain was her friend, her only constant companion, while Colonel Hu convinced her that black was white, love was hate, pain was feeling and comfort nonfeeling; that death was life.

Using *prana*—deep breathing—she assigned the pain to a specific compartment of her mind while she tested the use of her arm. It was all right as long as she kept it below shoulder height. Beyond that point, she could feel the broken ends abrading, and from shoulder to fingertip, her arm went numb, which meant there was a nerve involved. She knew enough to understand that she needed to get to a doctor.

That, she suspected, would not be the problem. It was silencing the questions she would have to worry about.

But first the forest. She needed to rest but she was all too aware that she was a fugitive. On foot, in this weather, there was a finite distance she could travel before she passed out.

Her pursuers would know that and certainly they would already have calculated a circle using the compound from which she had come as its central point. No matter where she went, they would eventually find her. So the trick was not to fall into the trap of trying to outrun them. Better by far to outthink them.

She looked up and the rain beat against her fluttering eyelids. She grasped what she had to do. It meant using both her hands, her arms, lifting them up over her head. The alternative was death.

Gritted her teeth and, reaching up, grasped at a jutting branch. Went off the forest floor, high up into the arboreal foliage. On a limb, perhaps one hundred fifty meters off the ground, she stretched out and, holding her aching arm, fell into a deep and dreamless sleep.

When she awoke, it was almost dawn. Scenting the air, she came down from the tree, swinging and half-sliding. She heard voices and froze, clinging to the bole until they faded away. Then she put her feet on the forest floor and got out of there as quickly as she could.

Just over two kilometers away, she broke into a farmhouse and stole clothing and some food staples. She knew that it was as good as leaving her spoor for the dogs but she had no choice.

Insinuating herself into a group of women working an enormous stretch of paddy fields, Qi lin worked all day pulling up the tender shoots of rice and, at day's end, received a ride on a belching, rusted truck. She made friends with a woman and, on learning her name, moved off to another part of the field after lunch, introducing herself around as the woman's fourth cousin. No one seemed curious and she was required to answer few questions.

It was after dark when she reached town, where bleak unadorned housing reminiscent of barracks stood brooding in militarylike rows. On the way they passed a series of mills, sprawling factories, sparking ironworks and the like. She found the physician's residence and knocked on the door. Because of the lateness of the hour, she was obliged to wait several minutes. At last, a small window on the second story opened and a head peered out. Streetlight flashed on round, steel-rimmed spectacles. In a moment, a hand beckoned her around the corner.

Qi lin followed the directions and was admitted through a small doorway hidden in the shadows of an alley.

"Younger Sister?"

He was a homely man, bandy-legged and pot-bellied. He wore an old-style coat and pajamalike trousers. His long mustache quivered when he spoke; his mouth was small as if echoing his soft voice. His spectacles shone in the lamplight, sending reflections batting off the walls like frightened moths.

She kowtowed in the old manner, intuiting that would impress him. "Elder Uncle, a thousand pardons for my appearance. Early this morning I slipped on a root in entering the paddy fields." Her fingertip gingerly touched the bruise just below the hollow of her neck. "I think I broke a bone."

The stoop-shouldered doctor clucked his tongue. "You should have come right here then."

Qi lin made her eyes go big and round. "Oh, I could not, Elder Uncle. I could not afford to miss even an hour's wages. You see, my boy—he's only three—is quite ill. In hospital. I must travel constantly to see him. He cries for his mother. Isn't it right that I should be by his side?" Bringing tears to her eyes. "But I have other children I must feed, Elder Uncle, and no man to provide for the family."

"But surely the State—"

"The State, the State!" she cried, working herself up. "I would not be an orphan of the State nor suffer my children that fate either."

"Ah, Little One," the doctor said, "you know what Confucius said about pride." But he was obviously moved. He shuffled forward. "Now let me see how badly you have injured yourself."

Qi lin watched as he parted her blouse and began his work. "Tell me, if you will, exactly where I am, Elder Uncle."

"You are just past the *shen dao*, the way of the spirit, the Sacred Way down which the Ming emperors rode during their funerals. On their way to the tombs." His touch was light and deft. Nevertheless she made herself gasp when he was probing and he clucked his tongue again. "This village is known as Jiao zhuang hu. Perhaps you have heard of it. It has an important place in our modern history.

"During the war, the peasants here built a network of underground passages in order to hide from and spy on the invading Japanese. They stand to this day, a monument to the ingenuity and courage of the Chinese mind."

He paused a moment, then turned and, swabbing the area with chill alcohol, inserting two long needles into her flesh. The pain was instantly gone. Qi lin looked at him as he said, "I must now set the break, Little One. Perhaps you will want to look away."

Qi lin laughed so hard to herself that she almost began to cry again. Oh, old man, she thought, if you only knew the blood I had seen. More in my short time on earth than even you. She averted her gaze because it was his wish.

"There," he said, after some time. "It is done." He began

283

to apply an herb poultice, wrapping it with adhesive bandage, a true blending of the old and new. Then he went over to a small gas stove and began to heat water.

She watched as he unscrewed bottles, jars, flagons, flasks, pouring first this liquid, then that powder into the pot on the stove. Out of one container, he produced a solid object from which he cut a piece and, using a mortar and pestle, ground it up. That, too, went into the pot. He hummed a little as he worked.

It wasn't until after he had obliged her to down the foul-tasting concoction that he went across to his small, shabby desk. He took up a quill pen and produced an official-looking sheet of paper. "Now, Little Sister, I must have your name, address and work number."

The first two would not be an immediate problem, Qi lin knew, but the third would be impossible. He would require that she present her documents. This, of course, she could not do. Other than the setting of her collarbone, this was the reason she had come here. Now that she was on the verge of civilization again, she needed the proper documents to move about at will. That was not easy for a fugitive in Communist China.

"The tunnels," she said, slipping down off the examining table.

"I beg your pardon?"

"This famous underground labyrinth you spoke of." She approached him carefully. "So ingenious. I would like to see it. Will you take me?"

"When? Now?"

"But of course now." Pumping enthusiasm into her voice. "What better time? Isn't this when our ancestors took to the tunnels in order to spy on the Japanese?"

"Well, yes, but—"

"Then what good would it be to see them in the light of day?" She smiled. "Besides, right now I need something to take my mind off my shoulder."

After a slight hesitation, he nodded. "All right." She had hit all the right buttons. Colonel Hu would be gratified to know that a significant part of him lived on within her.

The doctor led the way. He lit a magnesium torch as basement stairs turned a corner into a blank wall. He pressed something—an irregularity in the rock formation—and they went through.

In the flickering semidarkness, she said, "I want you to show me the way to Beijing."

He paused. His old rheumy eyes looked into hers. "You will need papers in the capital," he said.

"Then you will provide me with them."

He shrugged. "I am no forger, Little Sister."

She smiled. "I saw the photograph of her on your desk. I saw her dress shoes in a corner of the room." Her eyes were steely. "Your daughter."

He held the torch higher so that the shadows danced like madmen along the seeping walls. "Who are you?"

"I am Chinese," she said. "I am not Chinese."

He heard the defiance in her voice. "You are not from anywhere around here."

"No."

"Not from the Mainland."

She watched him.

"Taiwan."

She laughed. "I am not the enemy. Not the Guomindang."

"But you would not hesitate to kill me."

"Elder Uncle," she said, "you would not want to have lived my life."

" 'The heaven cannot help being high, the earth cannot help being wide. The sun and the moon cannot help going around, and all things of the creation cannot help but live and grow,' " he said, quoting from Laotse.

"Then you will give me your daughter's papers."

"It is futile to contend." The doctor squinted into her face. "I see that you have yet to learn that lesson," and he nodded. "You are older than I, Little Sister, yes, I see that. I yield to your desires."

Thus he took her back up to his office and conferred upon her all the identification she required to move about in the world outside. Back down in the labyrinth, he took her to the western edge of the warren of tunnels.

"Here," he said, pointing up at a rickety wooden staircase. "Through the copse of firs you will come upon a road. It is well traveled by vehicular traffic. No doubt you will get a ride to your destination."

Qi lin said, "I might still kill you."

"Yes."

"You have seen my face. You know in which direction I travel."

"I have seen also the face of the fox outside my window,"

he said. "I know in which direction the wind blows. Others actively seek what I already know but they are defeated."

"Why?"

His gaze was penetrating and with a little shiver of recognition Qi lin saw that there was more to him than she had imagined. "They do not follow the Tao," he said. "They contend, therefore others contend against them."

"Like me."

"You have killed before, Little Sister. I see death in your eyes."

"I have killed to survive."

"And in so doing, you have killed yourself," he said softly.

She snorted, despite a growing pain gripping her heart. "You wish me to believe that you want to help me."

"I have no such power, Little Sister."

"But you do not believe me," she insisted. "I killed out of necessity."

"Is that so."

The pain was strong within her, the blackness seeking to overwhelm her. It was the blackness—or more precisely the fear of it—that drove her to kill Colonel Hu. "He was my creator." Her voice had dropped to a whisper, reedy and ghostly. "And I destroyed him."

The old man watched her with black beady eyes. His face betrayed no emotion. Her inner agony was evident.

"He built me over, took the essential clay and— He transformed me."

"Now he is gone."

"Now I am free."

"You yourself can see the folly of those words," he said.

Qi lin said nothing. She knew that she should strike him down where he stood and be done with it. Leaving him alive was risking a clear trail behind her in the moonlight.

"Perhaps this is what your creator did," the old man said. "Turned you into this soldier I see before me. Must I tell you that soldiers are the instruments of evil? The Tao knows the Way. One who controls others possesses muscular resources. The strength that endures comes from controlling one's own nature."

She put a hand to her aching head. "I do not even remember what it was he was training me for. Something comes and goes. A shadow on the wall—"

Something passed across his face. "What has been done to you perhaps even the Tao cannot change."

Shadows chasing after shadows. The pain in her head! And coming after the shadows, the blackness. Qi lin gave a soft cry, hit the side of her head with her balled fist. "You are dangerous," she gasped. "Through you they can catch me."

"Then you must see that never happens."

He said it with such openness that Qi lin was taken aback. "Your death means nothing to you?"

"Oh, yes," he said, "it means something to me. But it is insignificant compared to the rivers that flow in the sea."

"Meaning?"

He was so calm. "Those who are able to cease action as well as initiate it will long endure. All others are doomed to die young."

Qi lin looked at him for the longest time. She was aware of her heart beating, the blood coursing through her veins. The flick and pop of the magnesium torch, close to guttering. Shadows extending themselves along all sides, sliding up the dank, curving walls, meeting at the arch of the ceiling. *All others are doomed to die young.*

Took one last look, drinking him in as she shoved the papers into her waistband. Up the rickety stairs, ascending out of the inconstant light. She would not kill him. Was that a victory or a defeat? From out of the darkness, she said, "Good-bye, Elder Uncle."

"Remember the rivers," he said into the space she had just vacated, "that flow to the sea."

When Bliss closed her eyes she saw the gem. Its fire shone out across the bosom of the ocean, red, gold, a flash of bronze. And she thought, why is this opal so important?

On board her father's junk, she arose from sleep and, hearing voices, pulled clothes around her body and went out of her cabin. On bare feet, she moved down the corridor. It seemed to her that she had heard these voices in her sleep, that they, in fact, had been the reason that she had woken. But they were so soft that she could scarcely believe such a thing.

Still, was it any odder than the episodes she had been having ever since Zilin had died. Putting the soft down over his sunken face, pressing down while some other voice—his voice!—in her mind commanded her to do what she herself could never have faced doing.

Buddha will forgive you, bou-sehk, he said. *As I forgive*

287

you. But could she ever forgive herself? That was still a question with which she grappled.

Voices in her head like time elapsing, a week, a month, a year. The eons spoke to her while her conscious mind slept. She felt, sometimes, as if an entire host resided within the recesses of her mind. She was not alone. And she was not afraid.

Zilin—the Jian—was with her. He had died, yes, and she had been his executioner. What had transpired between them at the moment his mortal self had ceased to function, she could not say. Perhaps, she thought now, they had both somehow passed through the resonant membrane into *da-hei*, the great darkness. In that magic, arcane space, who knew what transformation had been worked.

Of one thing Bliss was certain: this—whatever *this* was— was part of Zilin's plan. He knew of his death, had wanted her with him at that moment. Hadn't he trained her for it? Hadn't he brought her to *da-hei* times before? In preparation. She was sure of that now. In preparation.

For what?

"—is, as you can see, of exceptional quality." Heard her father, close now, speaking in hushed tones. "Great red fire, a superb example."

"Australian, isn't it?" Danny, number three son.

It was very late, four in the morning, almost.

"I want you to find out where this was bought."

Bliss at the cabin door, fingertips pressed against the wood, picking up the vibrations of conversation. Still half immersed in *da-hei*, aware that her place was inside the cabin rather than in the corridor.

"Father?"

Three Oaths looking up, Danny's round face, so similar to that of his father's, swinging around.

"Bou-sehk. Are you all right?" A constant query these days, the look of concern on his face an agony inside her. But how to explain to him what was taking place inside her when she herself was unsure?

"Yes," she said. "I'm fine. I was dreaming of a great jewel, a fire opal filled with crimson flame." Glancing down and seeing in the center of the table the object of her dream, the opal, the very one. And before either of the men could say or do a thing, she reached between them and scooped up the stone.

"Bou-sehk—"

"Father, a thousand pardons for interrupting you but it seems that I have seen this opal before." With an effort, she lifted her gaze from its heavy fire. "I overheard you asking Danny to find out where this was bought. Is it important?"

For a moment, Three Oaths considered lying to her for her own good. He was worried about her but felt unable to come to a decision as to how to help her. Now, seeing the look in her eyes he knew so well, he did the only thing he could: told her the truth.

"Jake gave it to me before he left for Japan. He was followed by an operative who delayed him from reaching the junk when he had planned to, the night Zilin was murdered."

"Did Zilin know of his arrival?"

"I think so, yes."

Bliss staring into the face of the opal, turning it over and over at the slender tips of her fingers. The fire broke apart and coalesced. In its aqueous glimmering she thought she could see the countenance of the Jian.

"Bou-sehk . . . ?"

"Father, I would like to—"

"It is out of the question," he snapped, afraid for her. "It is for Danny to do. He—"

"Would you keep me here like a prisoner?"

"What nonsense!" Three Oaths protested. "You are free to go when and where you wish."

"As long as my sister, Ling, accompanies me," Bliss said. And when he made no reply. "Like a patient, then."

"I do not—" He broke off, turned to his number three son. "Danny, please leave us."

The young man nodded and when the door had closed on his back, Three Oaths said, "Bou-sehk, bou-sehk, what would you have me do? Send you into known danger when I am uncertain of your physical state?"

"The only danger," she said angrily, "is that I will die of inaction and worry over Jake. This is what you have consigned me to."

Three Oaths shook his head. "I do not think that you yourself are aware of what is wrong with you."

"Nothing is wrong with me." Roar of *da-hei*'s inchoate power. "But you are right, I am not the same as I was before . . . my godfather died." She sat down on the chair that Danny had vacated, ran a hand through her hair. "Shi Zilin was my last link with my past. His mentor, the first Jian, was my great-grandfather. It was to Shi Zilin that my mother came in her time of greatest need. Without him I might never have been born. Certainly I never would have come to Hong Kong, never had you as my father.

"Yes, I am different and I don't deny it. There is a Void where before there was energy, a connection. I accept his death, Father. Buddha willed it. *Joss*. But I cannot be unaffected. I am not the same and I cannot pretend that I am."

"No one is asking you to be," he said softly.

"Well, then."

Three Oaths contemplated this young woman whom he had raised and wondered at the boundlessness of his love for her. "I will not sacrifice you to the service of the *yuhn-hyun*."

"It has already been done," she said. "You made that decision long ago, Father. You have trained me. Now please allow me to do what I was molded for."

"I regret—"

"Too late for regrets, Father."

And Three Oaths knew the wisdom of her words. Thus he capitulated and gave her all the information Jake had passed on to him regarding the fire opal.

When he was done, Bliss smiled and, leaning over, kissed him on the cheek. At the same time, she closed her fingers over the stone.

Jake heard voices. The dead were shouting in his ear. Their bones rattled, setting his teeth on edge; their naked jaws clashed together with an alligator's snap; their bony fingers pointed, clicking like insects' mandibles.

Their message seemed important, which was why, he supposed, they continued to shout. Jake said nothing; their tirade persisted unabated.

He wondered what it was that could be so damned vital. The cacophony was beginning to annoy him. If he was dead, nothing was that urgent. If he was not dead . . .

Blackness mutated into charcoal, a whiff of grit blown into his face. He began to choke on the smoke as the gray began to swirl, coalescing light.

Blood and skin, flecks of flesh made bright by the quick gush of crimson the result of the Bison's invasion of Mikio's house. The percussion . . .

Opened his eyes.

. . . throwing Mikio's body into him, ribbons of skin in gaudy, gauzy patterns with the kimono, the great three-lobed wheel *kamon*, the Komoto crest, bursting apart. The percussion . . .

Opened his eyes and saw that he was lying in a room made all of polished cedar.

. . . mangling Mikio's body, tangled up in his, the heat already forming, a sheet of screaming fire, and in the end, just before consciousness was extinguished, the horrendous sight of what was left of Mikio's face, only blood and bloody bone, pink and shiny, a grinning death mask.

Saw a line of *shoji*, partly open—the green of trees beyond?—and on the other side of the room a closed *fusuma*, a wooden door with an opaque center panel of brocaded silk. As he watched, it slid silently open on its track. Heard a bird begin trilling—from the trees outside?—he could be sure of nothing, senses still filled to overflowing with the percussion, the weight of Mikio hard against him, a human body coming apart beneath the strain of forces too great to bear.

Mikio, my friend!

A corridor of shadows opening up in front of him and Jake squinted as a figure entered the room. On silent, *tabi*'d feet it approached and bent over him.

Jake looked up, willing the ghosts of cordite and smoke away, the white noise of the percussion from his burning ears, up into the face that he knew so well.

"Mikio-san!"

The first thing Andrew Sawyer thought of when it began was: I've got to find the *Zhuan*.

Then, knowing that was impossible since he had no idea where the *Zhuan* was, he grabbed the phone in his cubicle and dialed Three Oaths' number. Far below him, the floor of the Hang Seng, Hong Kong's stock market, was a maze of activity. Like a pit of writhing snakes, the motion was nonstop and frenetic.

Sawyer reached inside his suit jacket, peeled his expensive silk shirt from his clammy skin. It was stained, soaked through with sweat. Damn, it, he thought anxiously as the phone rang at the other end of the line, where the hell are you?

His nervous gaze swung like a pendulum from the numbers on the high board to the hive of activity surrounding Peabody, Smithers and Tung Ping An, two of the largest investment brokerage firms. The signs were unmistakable from both quarters.

At last the burring stopped and Sawyer gasped in a breath.

"Weyyyy."

"It's begun," he said. "The worst is happening."

"Where are you?"

"The Hang Seng." The Hong Kong stock exchange.

"It's bad?"

"Worse than bad. Today I'd gladly take bad home to bed with me."

"I'll be right over," Three Oaths said.

"Dear God," Sawyer said into the already dead line. He replaced the reciever with a hand already numbed by shock and fear.

Next to him, his assistant was continually passing slips of paper over to him with fifteen-minute updates on stock transfers and movements.

They all pointed to the same thing and had done so since the opening of the trading day: blocks of ten thousand shares of InterAsia stock were being bought up at sporadic intervals by the two brokerage firms, Peabody, Smithers and Tung Ping An. What was odd about that was that the blocks were not being disbursed.

Because InterAsia was a relatively new issue and because of the volatility of the Hang Seng, great fluctuations in price and selling and buying patterns were not uncommon during the course of the day's trading. It was also usual for Sawyer, who was nominal market caretaker for InterAsia, to monitor all purchases of blocks of over one thousand shares. His network ran checks of who the trading firms were buying for, even if that often led back to nothing more than dummy corporations.

Disbursements as much as buy and sell orders gave Sawyer and the other senior members of the *yuhn-hyun* the pulse of the market, kept the multiarmed corporation running smoothly.

Today, though, between them the two brokerage firms had bought up close to seventy-five thousand shares of InterAsia stock, yet there was no record of any disbursement whatsoever. This fact, more than any other, had set Sawyer's nerves to twanging uncomfortably. InterAsia was under corporate attack.

But by whom?

He heard a disturbance behind him loud enough to bring him out of his nervous musing. He turned around and his jaws clicked shut with a painful resound. Three Oaths was hurrying up. The elderly Chinese was pasty-faced. Beads of sweat stood out along his wide forehead.

"Bad news," he said, gasping as he entered the cubicle. Sawyer's assistant had to give way in order to make room for him in the tiny space.

"More than this?" Sawyer's hand spread out to take in the crowded floor below. "I don't think you grasp the gravity of—"

"Southasia," Three Oaths interrupted. "The news of the scandal is all over the Colony."

"Oh, mother." Sawyer collapsed back into his chair. In a moment he had begun to shake. "The bank?"

"The run is on," Three Oaths said. "And unless it can be stemmed right away we're not going to have sufficient funds to cover it."

"God-bleeding-damn it!" Sawyer had visions of his entire life going to waste, all the work, sweat and dedication to building Sawyer & Sons into one of the preeminent trading houses in the Far East. And what for? he asked himself. To have it all end in disaster? Christ, no! His blazing eyes locked with the other man's. "We just may lose Southasia and InterAsia in the same week."

"Fornicate unnaturally all our enemies!" Three Oaths rumbled. "That means we'll lose control of Pak Han Min and Kam Sang. Just what my Elder Brother warned we could not allow."

"Kam Sang?" Sawyer cried. "Who in the name of the Holy Trinity cares a pox-ridden dog about a project six hundred miles away that we know nothing about anyway? It's our own trading firms that're on the block now. If InterAsia is successfully raided we'll have worked all our lives for nothing. Do you understand, Honorable Tsun? Nothing at all!"

"You gave us quite a start, *yumi-tori*."

The holder of the bow. It was an honored title given to a warrior of rank, a master archer. Who was calling him *yumi-tori*? "Mikio-san?" Who would know that he was a *kyujutsu sensei* other than . . . "Is it really you?" He started upward in order to see the face more clearly in the room's filtered light and a shaft of pain seared through him.

"Easy, Jake-san." Mikio's soothing voice. "Yes, it is I. But, please, you must take it easy. You've had a bad time of it."

"But how?" He felt a pressure on his shoulders, holding him down and, turning his head, saw a young woman in a

293

persimmon-colored kimono. Beneath, she showed just a line of underkimono the color of flame.

He turned his attention back to Mikio. His head was reeling. "How?" he whispered. "I saw you die in your study. I was there when your enemies fired the Bison. I felt the explosion tear your body apart."

"That body is what saved your life." Mikio Komoto smiled down at Jake, but behind it there was a great deal of strain. "I tried to warn you, Jake-san. I tried to keep you away. It had to be done in an oblique way since I suspected that all my communications were being monitored by my enemies.

"I deliberately did not answer your calls. I thought perhaps you'd understand and accept the difficult circumstances. I bade Kachikachi send you back to Hong Kong when I received news of your arrival here. Hong Kong is where you belong, *neh*? Not here in the midst of my war.

"But it was my error, my friend. I forgot just how persistent you can be. I am eternally grateful to the Amida that you were not seriously injured."

"Tell me," Jake said, "what happened?"

"It was a ruse," Mikio said. He wiped the flat of his hand through the short bristles of his salt-and-pepper hair. "It fooled you; well, then, it fooled my enemies as well. As you may have already surmised, that was not me who you tracked from Jisaku back to my house."

"Kachikachi!" Jake suddenly remembered the diminutive Yakuza's treachery.

"All part of the ruse, Jake-san. Do not fear. My Kachikachi is still loyal to me. Still and always, my friend. But his role-playing seduced the Kisan clan into believing they could make one preemptive strike against me and end this bloody battle once and for all. Without an *oyabun* who will command the respect and allegiance of all the clan a war cannot be carried out."

"Then who died in your study?"

"A brave man," Mikio said. "A hero of the clan. He volunteered. It was a *samurai*'s death and while I mourn his passing, I rejoice in his good fortune. His *kami* will be exalted . . . and now I have my edge over Kisan. In their eyes, I am dead, the position of my clan is untenable. It is the end for us, they believe."

"I almost screwed the whole bloody brilliant scheme up," Jake said.

"I should have understood your desires more completely. I should have anticipated this."

"You could not have anticipated my father's murder."

"Shi Zilin dead? Amida! But do you know who?"

"Yes," Jake said and Mikio noticed that his voice turned bitter. "A *dantai* assassinated him, Mikio-san. A Yakuza *dantai*."

"But that is absurd," Mikio said quickly. His utter dismay was evident on his face.

"I fought them," Jake said. "They killed my father and seriously injured Bliss, who's in hospital now. There can be no mistake. I saw their tattoos myself. *Irezumi*."

"*Irezumi*," Mikio breathed. He sat back on his haunches. "But who would send Yakuza to Hong Kong? No *oyabun* I know of would dare risk so open a strike on foreign territory."

"Yet Yakuza only take their orders from *oyabun*," Jake said. "That is one reason I had to come here, Mikio-san, one reason why I did not use the ticket Kachikachi gave me. It is imperative that I find out who is behind my father's murder. His entire ring is under attack and there is no defense I can take without first knowing who my enemies are."

Mikio nodded. "I see. You did the wise thing, Jake-san. The only thing possible." His eyes were far away, filled with thought. "But the Amida watches over us. He has protected you and for that we should all be grateful. Now—"

But at that moment, the kimono'd woman touched his arm, directing his gaze back down to Jake whose eyelids were fluttering closed.

"I see that it is best to let you rest," Mikio said gently. "When you awake, there will be food and something to drink if you wish it. Time enough then to talk."

No, Jake said, *I want to talk now*. But it was only in his mind. He was already asleep, falling fast through the layers into restful delta.

Tony Simbal had been in Miami Beach a little over three hours when he spotted the Cuban. It was in a splashy joint called La Toucana. Pastel blue-green walls, mirrors, and a long bar built out of translucent glass blocks, lit from inside by neon strips. Rattan chairs, glass-topped tables, the place was some zonked-out South American's dream palace. It made Simbal want to throw up.

Dressed in a lightweight white suit beneath which he wore a royal-blue T-shirt, he sat at the bar and had to keep his sunglasses on because of all the neon. He ordered an Absolut on the rocks. He had pushed the sleeves of the jacket up his arms mainly because that was the style and he needed to look like he belonged here.

The Cuban came in a little while later and his presence surprised Simbal. The Cuban's name was Martine Juanito Gato de Rosa. With a name like that it was no wonder he was simply known around the Campus as the Cuban.

The Campus was SNIT headquarters; the Cuban was one of SNIT's expert operatives, so it should have been no surprise for Simbal to find him here. The fact that Edward Martin Bennett was also in Miami was what caused the alarm to go off in Simbal's head.

There were plenty of other places around the world for the Cuban to be at this moment—in fact, the CIA was always sounding off about him and his effectiveness in "the Subcontinent" as they so quaintly called South America.

This was a coincidence of large enough proportions for Simbal to question it immediately. Bennett and the Cuban. How many scores had they been on together? How many times had Bennett claimed the Cuban saved his life and vice versa? Plenty on all counts. Simbal had memorized Bennett's SNIT file filched via the DEA computer with Monica's help.

Monica. When he thought of her now it was with an uncomfortable tightening in his lower belly. What were Monica and Max Threnody up to? What was it Max wanted from him? Simbal wondered for the hundredth time since he flew out of Dulles whether or not he should inform Donovan of his own suspicions. He had opted not to. It seemed enough for the moment that Donovan harbored his own doubts about Max's immediate maneuverings. He did not want things to get out of control while he was away from Washington. Better, he felt, to play along with his former boss until he got deeper into the situation. There was always time to make his report to Donovan and bring in the cavalry.

Or was it just that deep inside him he could not bring himself to believe that Max could be working against him. If he *were* working against Simbal, then who was he working for? That was another question that Simbal preferred not to have answered. Finally, on the plane, after going through Bennett's file for the third and last time, he had decided, fuck it, if he was procrastinating in making a decision regarding Max, so be it. He'd just have to take the consequences of his action—or inaction—when the time came.

Martine Juanito Gato de Rosa cut a dapper figure in a pale peach suit that set his coffee-colored skin glowing. His wavy hair was slicked back from his wide forehead, shiny and form-fitting as Lycra. There was a dusting of freckles on his cheeks that gave him a deceptively boyish air.

Simbal knew that he was far from boyish. In fact, Simbal had crossed paths with the Cuban twice during his tenure in the DEA. Once was on assignment in Colombia and he had seen this slim, handsome man with eyes the color of topaz slit open the throat of a cocaine smuggler with the ease and precision of a master surgeon.

It had been the Cuban's attitude while performing the act that had stuck in Simbal's mind. If he wasn't exactly enjoying the task he certainly showed no repugnance.

Simbal was always suspicious of people—even the ones in his line of work—who showed no adverse reaction to killing. It wasn't natural and it was dangerous. So he had marked the Cuban down and some months later when they had met at a party on Campus, he was stunned to see how urbane, witty, relaxed, how utterly civilized the man was. He bore no resemblance to the bloody killing machine Simbal had witnessed in South America.

There was some kind of voodoo going down, something very odd indeed about the Cuban. These thoughts had reignited when he had come across the name so prominently in Bennett's file. Now that he saw him here, the flames were burning.

It was no accident that Simbal had come to La Toucana on his first night in Miami. According to both DEA and SNIT files, this was one of the new hotbeds of *diqui* and drug movement in the area. He had been to the other two earlier in the evening. Lots of deals went down under its spangled roof, all high-level. Heavy money that allegedly ran all the way up to the mayor's office kept the place clean of narcs and adversary types.

The monsters all seemed comfortable here, eating long, voluminous dinners laced with the kind of overpowering California wines that were all the rage. And while they ate and drank they built their individual empires. In this manner, the wholesalers kept themselves in shiny imported sports cars, luxury yachts, terrazzo-floored villas and deep-cleavaged women whose only real interest was in staring at their own painted faces in the column mirrors.

The Cuban fit right in. He was flashy in the way only Miami

understands and appreciates. A mixture of the hip, the Latin and the gaudy. It was an interesting and potentially deadly mix.

He sat at a table at which a couple were already having drinks. Simbal searched the catalogue in his mind and came up with a name for the man: "Mako" Martinez, a heavy hitter on the cocaine wholesaling circuit. The most interesting thing about Mako, what set him apart from the majority of his colleagues, was that he was also an arms dealer.

Simbal thought it curious that the Cuban should be sitting down to dinner with this particular monster. Now he had two questions to answer: Why was the Cuban in Miami? Why was he making contact with Mako Martinez?

To his knowledge arms smuggling was right out of Martine Juanito Gato de Rosa's bailiwick. Of course arms could have no place in their discussion tonight. But it seemed like another coincidence and Simbal didn't like that.

He finished his Absolut, ordered another and signaled the maître d' he was ready for a table. In a moment, he was being led right by their table. Simbal looked into the woman's face and smiled. Her gaze was icy, incurious. He thought that in a fight with Monica she could have knocked Monica out with her makeup case.

The maître d' sat him two tables away and Simbal chose a seat with an oblique view. The second vodka on ice was brought and he ordered soft-shell crabs, a Caesar salad and asparagus vinaigrette despite the fact that the maître d' extolled the virtues of the char-broiled steak.

Brazilian music was blaring through loudspeakers and, to one side, there was a dance floor made out of Lucite. Water seemed to be running in colored rivulets beneath it.

The meal was mediocre but then Miami was not noted for its culinary level. It didn't matter much anyway since he had his eye on the Cuban's table. The men were deep in discussion; the woman was staring fixedly at something in tight pants reflected in the mirrored columns. The men spoke in desultory bursts. Simbal could just make out the language: Spanish.

It happened in the way Simbal wanted, Mako dismissing his woman as the conversation got around to business. The Cuban had to shift his position in order to facilitate her egress and he caught sight of Simbal.

Pinlights rotated above the dance floor and now there were several couples, moving sinuously to the Latin beat. There was something here that reminded Simbal of the jungle, or, perhaps more accurately, of something that put aside civilization. There was more than a bit of the ritualistic splendor of cultures more primitive and therefore, in his opnion, more valid than this one.

Simbal called for the check. He was aware of the Cuban's eyes on him but he would not look up. He took his time paying the bill, then sauntered out of the restaurant. Plenty of time for the Cuban to follow him.

The valet brought his rented Corvette around and Simbal had no choice but to get in; there were others in line, the place was just heating up. But no Cuban. Simbal looked from the main entrance to the street beyond. Neon spangled the pavement, the enormous lighted bird above La Toucana's name moving its head up and down in a mindless cycle. No Cuban. The beeping of horns became more insistent behind him. He put the car in gear.

Was it his imagination or had he seen one of the valets hurrying inside as he drove off?

"There are approximately twenty-five million shares outstanding of InterAsia," Andrew Sawyer said. He wiped the sweat from his forehead with a linen handkerchief. "Peabody, Smithers has in their possession four million unassigned shares. Tung Ping An has one-and-a-half million, including what they bought in today's session."

"*Dew neh loh moh* on going public," Three Oaths fumed.

"It's usually the best way to raise great sums of capital," Sawyer said.

"By the spirit of the White Tiger, I sometimes think I would have been better off staying in the opium trade!"

"Surely you don't mean that."

"By the pox-ridden, dung-eating offspring of our enemies, I do!" Three Oaths thundered. "There at least you know who your enemies are. There's no chance at dummy corporations and lice-infested whore's sons investment brokers acting as shields."

The two *tai pan* were still in Sawyer's cubicle. Though the Hang Seng had closed for the day hours ago, they had remained in their command post awaiting confirmation.

Sawyer knew the Chinese was merely venting his rage at the thought that they might lose control of InterAsia. Virtually all of their own personal fortunes were tied up in the *yuhn-hyun* corporation. Shi Zilin had insisted that they give

299

the *Zhuan* power of attorney over all assets, liquid and otherwise. Now there was precious little left with which to fight off this takeover bid. If he had not owed such a debt to Shi Zilin. If they had not gone public. If, if, if. Bile rose in his throat at the thought that all his years of hard work would collapse about him in a week's time.

"We've had to close Southasia Bancorp's doors," Sawyer said morosely. "There was no way we could keep up with the demand for withdrawals. Once the word got out about the fiscal shortfall, Southasia was doomed." He slammed his fist onto the paper-littered table. "Damn it all, I don't know how it leaked out! We were so careful!"

Three Oaths spat. "I have spies at Tung Ping An, many of the other trading houses. Why do you think that we are free of informers? The *h'yeung yau*, the fragrant grease, works wonders in the Crown Colony. It always has. Money passes hands in return for information not readily available. It is the way of life."

"Not in my company!" Sawyer said.

"You are above all the rest, then."

"I'll find the informer."

"Better by far to concentrate on solving the problem he has created for us."

Sawyer turned to the other. "And the next time? We will be caught in the trap again."

Three Oaths was silent at that.

"Where is he?" Sawyer said, looking at his watch. "He was supposed to be here an hour ago."

"Are you worried that he won't come?" Three Oaths said. "He will be here when he can. There is no point in arousing suspicions at Tung Ping An at this late date, *heya*? Give Bent-Nose time. He is a good man, an honest spy." Three Oaths had a good laugh at that. "If there is such a thing."

"I didn't think there was," Sawyer said sourly.

"Bent-Nose is my brother-in-law," Three Oaths said. "His loyalty is beyond question." He laughed again. "Besides, I pay him more than enough to keep him happy."

The silence of the space below them was awesome in contrast to the bubbling babble when the Hang Seng was open for business. In that vast echoey space, now unnaturally quiet, the footfalls, though soft, rose clear to their ears.

"He's here," Sawyer said.

Three Oaths turned as a middle-aged man appeared. He was unprepossessing in appearance and would have been altogether forgettable had it not been for a nose that had been broken several times early in life.

"What news?" Sawyer said.

Three Oaths poured his brother-in-law tea. It was by this time tepid but the man accepted it thankfully. He drained the cup and said, "I have the information. It took a lot of work and I did not obtain it until just moments ago. The office has been inundated with paperwork from the transactions on all the buy orders for InterAsia."

"Who has Tung Ping An been buying the blocks for?" Three Oaths asked.

"Sir John Bluestone," Bent-Nose said.

"Bluestone!" Sawyer said, shocked.

"But that is impossible," Three Oaths said. "There must be some mistake. When we baited Five Star Pacific with Pak Han Min nine months ago, we made certain that its short-term capital was depleted. That was Shi Zilin's plan in implicating his enemies in Beijing who bought up Five Star's notes." He shook his head. "No, no, Sir John has too much debt to be behind all this buying."

"But it is him," Bent-Nose assured them. He thrust out a handful of Xerox copies. "Take a look."

The two *tai pan* read the flimsies. They confirmed what Bent-Nose had said.

"Where's he getting the money to sink into InterAsia?" Sawyer said.

"I wondered about that myself," Bent-Nose Su said. "So I rang a friend of mine at Peabody, Smithers. A consortium has been formed, Brother-in-law. I checked our own recent records. Tung Ping An has been selling large chunks of illiquid holdings—real estate, businesses and the like—for these people. Here are the names."

Three Oaths read them over, handed them on to Sawyer. "We know them all," he said. "Bluestone's mates, business associates. Men who owe him favors. He's called in all his markers."

"The proceeds from the sales are being used to finance the InterAsia purchases," Bent-Nose Su said.

"Jake and Shi Zilin never could have anticipated such a thing," Three Oaths said, stunned.

Sawyer crumpled the paper in his fist. "That tears it." Despair was evident in his voice. "Bluestone means to get control of InterAsia and because of how Jake and Shi Zilin set up the firm I don't think there's a whole hell of a lot we can do about it." His balled fist slammed down onto the polished desktop. "God damn his eyes!"

Bliss took the opal to the Monkey Man. His name was Chan—she knew of no one who could tell her his first name. In any case, to her knowledge no one called him anything but the Monkey Man.

He had a shop on Yat Fu Lane in Kennedy Town. It was a dusty, ramshackle affair from which he sold just about anything one could imagine. On one side was an apothecary dispensing mandrake root, whole ginseng and powdered tiger's teeth to an avid Chinese following. On the other side was a large rug factory.

As she passed, Bliss could see the young women—little more than girls, really—hanging the patterns for the men on bamboo scaffolding who wielded electric shears to perform what was euphemistically called "hand cutting" by dealers anxious to fleece the *gwai loh* tourists.

Chan was called the Monkey Man for good reason. He had a face like an orang-utan. It was part of a head too large for the small, stooped body. This posture, perhaps, was what caused him to seem to have arms longer than any human should.

The Monkey Man's physical oddities never bothered Bliss as they had many children of her acquaintance when she was growing up. Now he was old, venerable in a way that transcended even the manner in which most elderly Chinese are treated.

He was, of course, delighted to see her. The skin around his button eyes crinkled all the more as his strange face broke into a wide smile. He called her *tihn gai-jai*, little frog, because, when she was a child, he used to take her to a pond in the New Territories to listen to the tree frogs singing their song of summer.

When he was finished with his customer, he locked the front door and took her into the back of the shop. This was where he lived and its contrast to the dismaying plethora of stacked items in the store was remarkable. Here every thing had its place, free of dust, sparkling like cut crystal.

He puttered around, making tea for them, bringing out sweet cakes. Bliss did not deter him; he had always liked to make a fuss over her. She watched him as he worked, overcome with emotion.

In time, they came to the reason for her visit. The Monkey

Man knew from the moment she walked into his shop that it was for a specific purpose but it would have been bad manners to inquire what it was right away.

Bliss pulled out the opal and the old man hefted it in his leathery palm. He produced a jeweler's loup, dragged over a table lamp and switched it on. Took a look.

"Excellent," he said softly. "Exceptional fire. Furthermore, it is thick and has been cut by a master." He looked at her, swept the loup off his face. "How much did you pay for this?"

"Nothing," Bliss said, and told him how it came to be in **her possession**, what she was searching for.

"Uhm, not so easy," the Monkey Man said ruminatively.

"But you said that it was cut by a master. Isn't there a way to tell from that?"

He shrugged. "I suppose, yes. But whoever cut it, might not have been the one to sell it. For all I know this was cut in Australia where it was dug out of the earth."

Bliss felt her heart sink. "There must be a way."

The Monkey Man weighed the opal in the center of his palm, nodded. "Perhaps." He got up and went to a phone. Dialed a local number and for several minutes spoke into the receiver in low enough tones so that Bliss could not hear what he was saying.

Thoughtfully, he put down the phone and came back to the table where she was sitting. "There is a way," he said.

"Good."

"Maybe." He shook his head. "I'm not an expert in opals. I don't sell them, you see, as a rule. If one comes my way, well . . ." He shrugged again. Rubbed his fingertips over the smooth face of the opal. "I called an acquaintance." Bliss knew better than to ask who it was. The Monkey Man was connected with a strange and varied assortment of types throughout the Colony. It was why she chose him to begin her search. "I was given a name but . . . I hesitate to give it to you."

"Why?"

"Have you ever heard of Fung the Skeleton?"

"The smuggler?"

The Monkey Man nodded. "Most of the opium that flows through here is handled, in one way or another, by Fung." He looked at her. "As it happens, he's also interested in gemstones. Something of a personal hobby. Got a collection,

I'm told, that would make any national treasury weep with envy."

"Then Fung's my man." Bliss reached for the opal but the old man closed his fingers over it.

"He's a dangerous man."

Bliss laughed. "Look at me. I'm not a little girl anymore."

"*Tihn gai-jai*, this is not a joking matter. A man who trades in the tears of the poppy has no scruples, no morals . . . no soul. He might just as soon kill you as look at you."

"Is he the man I must see?"

When the Monkey Man said nothing, Bliss took this for assent. "Then tell me where I can find him." She paused. "I have other ways. You cannot stop me by not talking."

At last the old man's fingers uncurled and Bliss took the opal from his palm. It was warm from his heat. "Do you know where the Container Terminal is?" he said.

"Along Hoi Bun Road? At Kai Tak." Kwun Tong, a mainly industrial district near the airport in Kowloon.

The Monkey Man nodded. "The best time's just before dawn, I'm told." He looked so morose that Bliss reached out and stroked his unlovely cheek. "If you're hurt, your father will kill me."

Bliss laughed again. "You were always a worrier. I am my father's daughter. What will Fung the Skeleton dare do to me?"

The Monkey Man said nothing, but as she left Bliss noticed that he had switched from tea to Johnnie Walker Red.

Mikhail Carelin lay in his bed and stared at the ceiling. It was an unlovely sight, being as it was water-stained, uneven, the paint so old it was patinaed. Plaster peeled in abstract patterns. When he contemplated this ceiling what he saw was a landscape: the abstract patterns of peeling plaster became continents rising up from a sea of spiderweb cracks and whorls.

Though the bed was comfortable, though there was a well-supplied bath through a partially opened door not five meters away, he was not in his apartment. Rather he was within the crenellated walls of the Kremlin in a suite adjacent to his office, a steamy, noise-wracked space in winter. In the summer it was stifling. It was next to the great corner office in which Fyodor Leninin Genachev conducted much of his business.

Genachev liked the night. *In darkness*, he would say, *is peace. The peaceful times, Mikhail, are for working. Even in the middle of the most atrocious cacophony one has time to dream.*

Carelin, too, preferred the night. But for other reasons. Nights were a time for listening. In the semidarkness of the Kremlin's labyrinthine corridors one could hear the cipher machines, the pockets of night crews manning the worldwide networks of power. Genachev, who was unusally not fond of clichés, was guilty of using one: *Somewhere in the world*, he would say, *it is always daytime. Therefore, there is work to be done.*

The night, Carelin knew, was the time for clandestine assignations, suborning of *apparatchiki*, bribe-taking. Venality was spawning in the darkness and there it fed like a city rat gorging itself on garbage and excrement.

Selene.

Always he was brought back to *Selene.*

His activation code. He had required nothing more of his source. His mission had been preset, the contingencies outlined, the objective absolutely clear.

And yet . . .

So many things had changed since he had been given the mission's parameters. So many years in the darkness. He had a fondness for the nighttime, looking out windows, so many different windows, but mainly the one in his pink stone house on Gorky Street. There, in another room, his wife dreamed while his world was just awakening. Treachery, deceit, the calm face of the ferret sniffing down holes filled at their far ends with sensitive secrets.

The lights of Moscow at night, winking and glittering, as far off as stars. Like the ceiling at his Kremlin office, he created out of those lights his own landscape.

No man, he had found, was content without a country. He had been deprived of one almost all his life so he played a game with himself, a game of deadly seriousness. He had built his own land, out of the darkness and the strings of lights arcing across the Moskva or along Kuznetsov Prospekt. Muscovites snug in their beds, exhaling the fumes of vodka and cabbage, creating fat, laughing women out of dreamstuff. While Carelin returned to the land of his own creation. Like Dracula rising each night to live again a certain kind of life.

So it was with Mikhail Carelin.

Until his source had beamed him the one word code: *Selene*, and everything had changed.

He had been trained to lie in the darkness and wait, to take

305

in the night that which did not belong to him and to transmit it far across the sea. He had been trained to kill as well.

With a grunt, Carelin levered himself off the bed. In bare feet he padded across the cold floor. In the bath, he ran the cold-water tap and put his head under the gushing water.

Snorted as he dried off, slung the towel across his bare shoulders. He glanced at his watch. Three thirty-five in the morning. Genachev was still on the phone with Washington. Carelin knew this because Genachev would buzz him as soon as he broke the connection.

At the window, he looked out at the onion domes of St. Basil's, pale and golden in the illumination from the floods. It was not enough, he thought, to say that everything changed when he received the *Selene* code. It had altered drastically afterward, too. When he had discovered that his source had been killed.

Carelin had only been under discipline to one man. When he was gone Carelin found that he was in limbo. Who could he contact? There was a mole in the organization to which he reported; a mole in such a position at Central that he could not take the chance of contacting anyone else there.

He thought fleetingly about getting out. Letting *Selene* crumble into dust alongside its creator. But he held no abiding love for Russia though he had been born there. It was only his work that made life bearable. He had understood then that he had no choice, that he must continue as a ferret or he would dry up and blow away like a paper bag.

But a ferret without a Control was nothing.

Who then to contact?

Jake Maroc had been the logical choice. The *only* choice open to Carelin. As an ex-operative, Jake knew the Quarry inside and out. Based in Hong Kong, no longer connected to Central, he was safe from Chimera, the only man in the world Carelin could trust.

And there was one more thing. Maroc had been Henry Wunderman's best friend; more, Wunderman had been his mentor. Maroc deserved to know the truth. So Carelin had made contact and that had been that.

Until, of course, he realized that he had fallen in love with Daniella.

Now he was God. To destroy or to create, that was the question. And until this very moment, he had not understood how agonizing the decisions God must make could be.

From the open door to his office not far away he heard the

strident sound of the buzzer. Genachev's call to Washington was over. He was wanted.

Took one last look at the nighttime lights of Moscow. If the answer was not there, where would he find it?

The buzzer sounded again and he got out of there. But his mind would not let him be.

Jin Kanzhe was on his way through the portals of heaven when it hit him. He was with the Acrobat. She had a name, of course, but it was more exciting in his mind to think of her as the Acrobat.

He had met her backstage after a particularly compelling performance of the Dazhalen Acrobatic Troupe to which Huaishan Han had dragged him. The old man had fallen asleep in his seat almost before the lights had dimmed, a not uncommon occurrence and one which Jin Kanzhe could predict with frightening accuracy.

Nevertheless, he had quite enjoyed himself. The troupe was nothing short of spectacular. They liked, rather artily, he thought, to title each routine. During one called "Straw Houses," he noticed the suppleness of body, the feline face that spoke of Northern climes. One woman among many darting about the stage. Yet something about her cut him to the quick. She had, in retrospect, a way of moving over the stage that transcended grace. She moved from her hips; this excited him immensely. He found, in fact, at the end of "Straw Houses" that he had a rather painful erection.

At intermission, he had the car take the somnolent Huaishan Han home. At performance's end he used his official I.D. to get backstage. That made him something of an instant celebrity, which he liked.

He did not see the Acrobat right away. Lights and sweat, rounds of tea and champagne—which someone tried to keep him from seeing; he laughed inside at that. A sea of faces, half-shadowed in the odd, overhead theatrical spots turned into corners. Nothing of much interest, really.

He had just about made up his mind that she had beat a hasty retreat when he found her. His heart rolled over, and he could not catch his breath. News of his presence had already spread throughout the backstage area. She seemed prepared for him, flashing that smile he had seen from the other side of the footlights, and he was lost.

Now, as he entered the soft, moist portals of heaven he heard her groan beneath him. She liked to be vocal and Jin

Kanzhe, unused to such a thing in anyone, let alone a female, could not stop himself from coming when she let go like that.

The Acrobat was in the most extraordinary position beneath him. Her oiled flesh, so firm and smooth, rippled like the sea. He watched her ankles part as she moved again, her long legs high in the air near her shoulders. This did something to the contours of her jade gate, raised, presented to him like a sacred offering, that increased their pleasure tenfold. The sides of her calves grazed his neck; his loins began to melt.

He was all the way inside her. Her heat was incredible; he felt as if he had walked into a furnace. He was engulfed in a pool of liquid fire. Her depths, too, were prodigious; she took him in and in and in. Jin Kanzhe felt so inside.

Her hips were dazzling in their movements. She was a human rubber band. He could not believe what his eyes told him was real. He gasped air out of his lungs and she groaned.

He began to shoot heavily inside her and this increased her vocalizing. She heaved like the ocean, the sounds of ecstasy were like the wind in his ears. The smell of their mingled musk was overpowering.

They had been making love for a long time. To Jin Kanzhe it was like walking across rooftops: delicate, dangerous, terribly exciting; in the air, above the hurried stream of everyday life; apart; beyond.

Spurted and spurted into her. And thought of Huaishan Han.

Well, not exactly the old man. It was so odd, he shivered. Abruptly, he felt the strain of their contorted position on his arms. His biceps began to jump and quiver. Sweat ran down the center of his forehead, dripped from the end of his nose onto the burnished flesh between her small firm breasts.

The Acrobat, herself in the midst of the clouds and the rain, was oblivious. Her face was contorted; she ground up against him, sealing her jade gate onto the base of his still rigid member. Flipped her hips, once, twice, three times. And gave a little yelp.

Jin Kanzhe was unmoved. The image that had risen to the surface of his mind expanded by pleasure clamored for his attention. He could see the study in Huaishan Han's villa. It was night—precisely which night he could not remember. They had gotten drunk together, talking about old times—the old man running on about Shi Zilin, Jin Kanzhe immersing both of them in the hell that was Cambodia.

He must have dozed off. In his dreams he heard the sonorous ticking of the old man's clock. Heavy lids, grainy with alcohol, opened to slits. Enough to see the old man staring at him. A shaded lamp caused the hard glitter of those eyes to strike Jin Kanzhe like a physical blow.

Then the old man reached out and pinched Jin Kanzhe. "Are you awake?" he whispered.

When Jin Kanzhe made no move, Huaishan Han nodded and moved away into the semidarkness of his study. Jin Kanzhe was very tired. The surfeit of alcohol still pulsed through his veins, throbbing like venom. His eyes closed and he slept.

At least that is what he had thought until just this moment. Then the image had surfaced, brought to consciousness by his orgasm. The ejaculation, to be more precise.

Image of Huaishan Han urinating in the bath adjacent to the study. He squatted, so old that he needed support. The door ajar, the old man reaching for the niche where the toilet paper lay. Toilet paper to urinate? Perhaps he was semi-incontinent, not unheard of in old people.

But why then was he reading it instead of using it?

Jin Kanzhe disentangled himself from the Acrobat's limbs. In the process, he slipped out of her jade gate and she gave a little cry of disappointment. She wanted him in until the last possible moment. He rolled away and began to dress.

It was very late. She said, "Aren't you going to stay the night?"

"I'll be back," he said, holding his hand out for the key.

She curled her amazing body into a ball and lifted her face toward him. Between her lips was a glint of metal. The key to her apartment.

"Kiss me," she said, having no trouble enunciating with her mouth full. Jin Kanzhe bent down, closed his lips over hers. Slowly, her tongue pushed the key past his teeth. Then it swabbed the inside of his mouth.

She smiled as he straightened up. "That's how Houdini did it," she said. She was proud of her knowledge of arcane things. "His assistant passed him the key to his chains when she kissed him just before he was lowered into the water or the sealed coffin."

It was no good asking her where she obtained such odd bits of information. Hers was a mind Jin Kanzhe could not fathom.

The car outside her apartment took him out of Beijing, into the northern suburbs where Huaishan Han lived. There was no traffic to speak of, just the rumbling of truck convoys:

foodstuff instead of soldiers being delivered, but it sounded the same.

Jin Kanzhe lowered his head. He missed Colonel Hu. The war in Cambodia had linked them closer perhaps than brothers. What they had endured together! When two men are in desperate danger each day, when with their bare bloody hands they kill an enemy in alien territory, their bond is immutable.

"Jin *tong zhi.*"

He started. He had the feeling this was not the first time the driver had spoken his name. "Yes?" Voice thick, as if he just wakened from a dream. He could smell the Acrobat's musk upon him. His flesh felt sticky, coated with their lust.

"We have arrived, Jin *tong zhi.*"

He could see the driver looking at him in the rearview mirror. "Go relieve yourself," Jin said.

"I'm fine, comrade."

"Do as you're told and take a piss," Jin barked.

He sat alone in the car for some time. Heard the engine ticking over as it cooled. His tongue moved in his mouth, tasting the odd metallic tang of the Acrobat's key. He thought of Houdini with some admiration.

Slipped out of the car and did not close the door all the way. The night was exceptionally mild, a taste of better days to come, the brief respite between the bitter winter and the broiling summer. A nightbird twittered for a moment just above his head.

Jin Kanzhe went from tree to tree. The old man always left a light burning in his study. He was at an age when his sleeping habits were erratic. He could sleep all day and be up most of the night.

Cautiously, Jin Kanzhe stepped up onto the wooden porch and, fitting his laminated I.D. card into the narrow space between the study door and its ancient frame, he worked a trick Houdini would be proud of. The Acrobat as well.

He peered in, saw the study was deserted. Took off his shoes, leaving them just outside the door. Crept soundlessly across the Deco carpet, swirls of silver, slate gray, amethyst on a sapphire field. Stumbled over something and went down on one knee, cursing under his breath.

A slipper. He pushed it out of the way, remained motionless for a long time. Listened to the clock ticking away the seconds. Wiped sweat off his brow.

Went on across the study, pulled open the door to the bath. Here he knelt beside the niche and examined the paper. It was a normal roll. It was dark in here and he dared not turn on a light. Stuck his hand into the niche, fumbled a bit, found with accelerated pulse that there was a false back. Took out what was secreted behind it.

Back in the study, he hunkered down by the one lamp with a sheaf of papers. They looked like contracts but they were all handwritten. These must have been what Huaishan Han had been reading while he thought Jin Kanzhe was asleep.

Jin Kanzhe began to read. Soon the hackles at the back of his neck began to stir. He felt a sickening lurch in the pit of his stomach. The more he read the more the terror built, the faster he read, the more feverish he became to reach the end.

It was unbelievable, beyond reason. He had suspected that Huaishan Han was half-mad; now he had proof. Now he knew what lay behind the old man's seemingly limitless power. He remembered what Huaishan Han had said, *Money is no problem. It flows through my hands like an endless river.* Now Jin Kanzhe knew why. His wealth must be staggering, almost limitless. But at what a price to China!

"Have you read your fill?"

Jin Kanzhe started, his eyes rising, as frightened as a deer caught in the spike of an automobile's headlights. Huaishan Han stood in the black doorway to the corridor. By his side was the great guard dog, and Jin Kanzhe's driver. In the young man's hand was a pistol.

Jin Kanzhe rose. "What have you done to us?" His voice was clotted with rage and disbelief. He waved the damning documents. "You will destroy us all."

"Hardly," Huaishan Han said. "But I mean to gain my vengeance over Shi Zilin and his entire family. This was the only way."

"The only way!" Jin Kanzhe was incredulous. "Your obsession has put this entire country at risk. Do you understand what you are doing?"

Huaishan Han laughed. "Oh, yes," he said. "I am killing you."

As if in a dream Jin Kanzhe watched Han's ancient crab's claw reach out and pinch the great dog's brindled neck. The dog growled deep in its throat, and leapt unhesitatingly into Jin Kanzhe's face.

The metallic taste was back in Jin Kanzhe's mouth. He felt the alien presence of the key between his teeth, the sexual probing of the Acrobat's hot tongue that came after.

As he felt the fangs sink into his neck, he wondered in a gray haze how Houdini would have gotten out of this.

Huaishan Han blinked. He held out his withered hand for the weapon and the driver deposited it. "Make sure he's dead," the old man said, whistling the creature back at his side.

When the driver had carried out the command, Huaishan Han shot him once through the heart with the kind of accuracy that, once learned, never fades.

At the appointed time, Three Oaths sat down at the old shortwave radio and, checking the series of codes Jake had given him in order to reach Apollo, began the long, complex process of call and recognition. If the truth be known he was immensely excited. This transceiver held many poignant memories for him. It was with this set, salvaged from his previous junk, that he had kept in touch with Shi Zilin in Beijing during many of the long years of their difficult but necessary separation. For decades, then, this piece of well-run machinery was all that kept the two loving brothers in touch with one another.

Now, all those memories swept over Three Oaths with the force of waves. His eyes were wet with tears. He missed his eldest brother fiercely. All his life Shi Zilin had been there. For seventy years they had been—figuratively and literally—putting their heads together. Scheming for the future. Piecing together the great *ren*, the harvest that China was now on the verge of reaping.

Three Oaths' loss was immense. His heart shuddered with the pain as he confronted the emptiness that Shi Zilin's death left inside him. He was unused to such deep introspection and nostalgia. Perhaps that was why he did not hear Neon Chow come up behind him.

And why, when she put her arms around him, put her face alongside his, kissing him, he did not give her presence much thought. Strictly speaking she should not be belowdecks when he was at the shortwave. It was an ironclad rule of the junk, so to speak, and it extended to all of Three Oaths' family.

"I see the sadness in your face," she said, using her softest tone. "I see the heaviness of grief in your gait." She hugged him gently. "Here is what little I can do to help. I know that it is inadequate compared to your grief."

"No, no," Three Oaths said. "Far from insignificant." He was grateful for her warmth. It eased the emptiness that gnawed at him. He did not think of why she was here where it was forbidden to be.

Close behind him, Neon Chow opened her eyes. On the shallow table that swung down by two brass chains from the bulkhead she saw a sheet of unfolded paper. On it she recognized the writing of the *Zhuan*.

"Who else have you now to comfort you, to throw their arms around you, to love you all through the night?" she whispered while reading what was on the sheet. Her pulse rose up into her throat and she felt the onset of a blinding headache. She fought for control as the words Jake Maroc had written for his uncle began to make sense to her. Dear God in heaven, she thought, as she read the identity of Apollo, the Quarry's mole inside the Kremlin, I must ask for an emergency rendezvous with Bluestone. She did not of course know that Apollo was a Quarry mole—that fact had been communicated to Three Oaths verbally. But she did know that this was the man who Three Oaths was contacting for Jake. Hadn't he boasted to her just yesterday of the great honor the *Zhuan* had accorded him? Hadn't he made certain she knew that she had been wrong about the *Zhuan*'s motives? Hadn't he needed to show her that he still possessed as much power within the *yuhn-hyun* as he had when Shi Zilin was alive? Yes. Yes. Yes. A contact in Russia, he had told her. *Inside the very Kremlin.* Now she had more than enough to piece it all together.

"You," he said now. "Only you."

It took Neon Chow a moment to realize that he was responding to her own words, so enthralled was she by the import of this fantastic piece of intelligence.

"This evening," she whispered, licking his ear, "come to bed early. I feel that you are in need of nightlong comfort." Her hand snaked down between his legs, squeezed inward. She felt him give a little shiver and she laughed, leaving him then, forgetting him immediately, her mind filled with the accolades she would receive from Bluestone when she delivered to him this fantastic prize.

The young woman, her head bowed to watch her tiny feet in traditional *tabi* and *geta*, came silently toward them. She wore a kimono of pure white, embroidered with pale peach peonies. Clutched to her breast was a small wrapped package. As they watched, she knelt before a vault where the image of Kannon reposed, an object of such extreme sacredness that it was displayed to the penitents only once every thirty-three years.

The sad-faced young woman bowed in obeisance to the goddess of mercy. Around her, dishes of food and flowers spread color and scent in profusion. Her lips moved in silent prayer, to what *kami* they did not know until she slowly unwrapped the small package and reverentially placed the tiny girl doll amidst the white and yellow camellias arranged on a fired clay plate.

Then her sadness became as clear to them as the sunlight that spread itself over the valley below them. This woman's young daughter had recently died and the doll she had brought to the goddess of mercy was the little girl's most prized possession.

Jake and Mikio Komoto sat side by side, their eyes filled with the woman's delicate features, her dark eyes brimming with pain. And then, as she rose and took one last look at the perfect features of the doll, a solitary tear slipped down her cheek.

"This is where they all come," Mikio said, "the women of Kyoto. To Kiyomizu-dera." The two of them were here alone without Yakuza soldiers because of the attention the added men would bring. Besides, Mikio was supposed to be dead. "Oh, they come from all over, really, to petition Kannon for a safe childbirth or in the case of this one to protect the *kami* of their dead child."

Jake said nothing. Instead, he savored the seemingly limitless view from this mountain Buddhist temple of all of Kyoto, the verdant forest slopes up the mountain thick with burgeoning greenery and, beyond, the precisely ordered geometrics of farmland through which tiny figures, black with distance, made their way.

"My wife used to come here quite often."

Jake listened carefully. He had not known Mikio's wife and, in any case, for a Japanese to embark upon such a personal topic commanded respect and a special attention. He closed his mind to his aches and pains. Concentrate, he demanded of himself.

"She came," Mikio went on, "to petition the Compassionate One to allow her to have a child. It was . . . difficult for her. The doctors said that her uterus was tilted in such a way that it made conception unlikely." Mikio put his hands together almost as if he were praying. "They recommended artificial insemination but we found that somehow . . . distasteful. So she came here and prayed to Kannon. On this exquisite promontory where this temple was dedicated in seven ninety-eight, she felt the goddess resided. She felt that here the goddess would hear her."

They were on the temple's vast cantilevered veranda, which had been designed and built to view sacred dances. Nearby was melodious Otawa, one of the most renowned waterfalls in all of Japan.

Abruptly, Mikio rose and went to the edge of the veranda closest to Otawa. Jake followed him and they both looked down upon the white-clothed pilgrims, their mittened hands raised as, drawn within the protective barrier of the water spray, they prayed to Fudo-Myo-o to guard against the deeds of their enemies.

"We should be down there," Jake said. "We both need a lot of protection these days." After a time, he said without looking at his friend, "Did Kannon answer your wife's prayers?"

"You see me as I have always been, Jake-san, sadly childless."

It was not enough to say he was sorry so Jake said nothing.

"Perhaps," Jake said after a time, indicating the supplicants within the rain of the waterfall, "they know something that we do not."

"If so," Mikio said, "then we'll never know it."

Out of the corner of his eye, he saw a single tear sliding down his friend's cheek and he thought of the young woman and her parting from her child's cherished doll. He knew now why Mikio had brought him here. He still felt that he was responsible for Jake's almost having been killed in Tokyo. It did not matter to him, Jake knew, that it had been Jake's pig-headedness that had been responsible. Jake knew that Mikio had done all in his power to remove Jake from the red sector. Jake had simply not paid any attention to the repeated warnings.

In Mikio's mind when Jake was in Japan he was the *oyabun*'s—the Yakuza boss's—responsibility. Period. It was that simple. And that complex. Now Mikio owed Jake a debt that he could never realistically repay. *Giri* as much as friendship—*giri* entangled in friendship—was what bound them so intimately. *Giri* was what obliged Mikio to open up a most personal and undoubtedly painful part of his past to Jake. That had been an extraordinary moment and it was not lost on Jake.

"But love endures, Mikio-san," Jake said. "Like the mountains and the seas, love never dies." He watched the pilgrims, purifying themselves in Otawa's shower, covering themselves with the glory of God. "Perhaps that is all that keeps us going at times, *neh*?"

Mikio, never taking his eyes from the falls, nodded wordlessly. He understood.

Silence—the silence of natural sound—covered them as completely as if they were standing at the bottom of Otawa, immersed in water. Within that camouflage Jake saw a gray plover lift off from one branch to another. Without thinking his eyes followed the graceful line of the bird's flight as it lifted and fell across the weight of the dark green forest, rising ever upward until it crossed over their heads and disappeared behind the burnished façade of the bell pavilion.

The plover's motion remained, transmitted to the two men in dark suits who came down the wide steps on the east side of the pavilion. Both had closely cropped hair, angular faces. They wore wraparound sunglasses with mirrored lenses. They made no secret of the objects of their interest.

"Mikio-san," Jake said softly but urgently, "I fear the war has found us."

Speeding down Miami's Intracoastal Highway in his rented black Corvette, Tony Simbal did not hear the noise until it was almost too late.

Doing eighty-five with the windows down, the rush of the wind almost drowning out the rock beat of the Stones coming over AM, turned up to deafening volume, it was perhaps natural. Natural but inexcusable.

Because it was the Cuban calling to him, Martine Juanito Gato de Rosa in a fire-red Ferrari, coming up alongside the 'Vette, screaming his lungs out.

One hand was on the wheel, the other held straight out the open passenger's window a Magnum .357 that could blow a man's head open like a ripe melon. The gun was aimed at Simbal's left ear.

"Pull over! You goddamned sonofabitch! *I said pull the fuck over!*" Snapping back the Magnum's hammer.

The valet at La Toucana had done his work, reported to the Cuban the make, model and license number of Tony's rented Corvette.

Pastel high-rises, pink, powder blue, seafoam flashing by, interspersed with clawed marinas where glossy white-and-blue yachts and fishing boats swung in lazy arcs, sending bubbling wakes, little clouds of diesel running after them. Girls in string bikinis, cool sun visors over their pulled-back hair, Nivea cream massaged into their sunburnt shoulders, laughing with silver-haired millionaires, Hawaiian shirts open to the navel to display 24-carat chains, white ducks, glossy white shoes anyone in New York City or Washington would sneer at. They hadn't a care in the world but Tony Simbal was being forced off the road by an animal Ferrari and the black hollow muzzle of a hand cannon.

The quiet of the landscape seeped into the open windows of the 'Vette, the engine ticking over and, to his left, the traffic whizzing by at hummingbird's speed.

The red Ferrari, sun spinning off its long hood, crouched just behind him as if it were manned by a traffic cop.

Heard a car door slam and the crunch of shoe soles over the composition of the verge. Then the sun was blotted out as the figure of Martine Juanito Gato de Rosa leaned into the Corvette. Simbal felt the cool muzzle of the Magnum pressed against his temple.

"You little piece of wormshit," the Cuban said in his clipped, slightly skewed English, "I ought to blow your motherfucking brains out but I got too much respect for the interior of this automobile."

"Down, boy," Simbal said. He was careful not to move his head toward the Cuban. "Let's have a chat and—"

"I wouldn't *shat* with you on a bet, Wormshit."

"—cool down."

"You got some fucking nerve, uh, coming down here, putting your nose up my business."

"I don't even know your business."

Magnum jammed painfully against this temple. He could smell the Cuban's musky cologne, a bit of his sweat; was he frightened of something? Of Simbal?

"You think you're gonna scare the shit out of me? *Hijo de puta.*"

"I'll have you know my mother was quite a lady, Martine," Simbal said. "The only whore I ever knew was your sister."

The Cuban ripped open the Corvette's low door. He growled low in his throat. "Get the fuck out of there."

Simbal did as he was told. "What are you going to do," he said, "shoot me with a score of witnesses passing by every thirty seconds? Listen, we can trade insults all day, if you want. Me, I've got more important things to do."

"Like poach on my property."

"Mako's all yours, buddy." Simbal raised his hands. "Hell, I could've walked up to you in La Toucana. I knew if I did that I'd blow everything."

"What kind of everything?"

"Come on, Martine. This heavy shit that's going down with Mako and Eddie."

The Cuban's hazel eyes narrowed. "What the fuck do you know about it? And what the fuck are you doing here, anyway?"

"Quarry sent me down," Simbal said. There was no point in bringing the DEA into it at this stage. "There was a *diqui* hit in Chinatown last month. Big one. Their main man, Alan Thune, got blown away by party or parties unknown. Then one of the DEA hounds by the name of Peter Curran gets his limbs separated from his torso in Paraguay and the Nazi subculture is blameless. *Diqui* again. Now I'm interested. So's my boss, the head honcho. The Big Kahuna. So here I am."

"Why here?"

"Let's go somewhere nice and quiet and discuss this like men. Over a stiff drink."

The Cuban lifted the .357 so that the muzzle was aimed straight at Simbal's face. "Why here?"

Simbal sighed. "Because this is where Edward Martin Bennett is. Isn't that right?"

The Cuban directed them to a little place on Key Biscayne with a spectacular view of downtown Miami, if one was fond of watching the decay that follows greed setting in. Great granite, marble and smoked-glass towers rose up in the same profusion that hen's teeth sowed into the ground produced an invincible army. Hotels built almost overnight during the feverish years when it was thought gambling would be legalized in Miami. Multimillions sunk into lumbering leviathans that now stood nearly empty, silence filling up their cavernous interiors, all in receivership, functioning like limping men old before their time.

But beneath the shade of a faded striped umbrella, the bay was bright and sparkling, the powerboats streaking its surface like water spiders, setting a low background rumble.

The Cuban sipping at his rum and Coke and saying, "You know, I think they were insane, man, to change this thing, this great American thing."

"What thing?"

"Coca-Cola, dude." The Cuban looked at Simbal as if he were an idiot. "An American tradition, uh? What the fuck they have to go and mess with that, tell me? Now none of that shit tastes right, no matter what they call it. I mean, what's tradition for, anyway?"

Simbal went at his vodka tonic judiciously. "Murder has a habit of making me a little testy, Martine," he said. They both wore dark glasses because of the sun and the glare off the bay. That was bad for a negotiation but, thought Simbal, it was a damn sight better than having a Magnum .357 pressed against the side of your head. He counted his blessings and was grateful for progress.

"Murder happens every day in our line of work, don't give me any bullshit here, uh."

"It doesn't always trace itself back to a SNIT," Simbal said. "A member of one agency wiping out a member of another is very likely to get me bent." Simbal leaned forward. "See, Martine, Curran's demise has gotten me a little pissed off."

"So go kick a trashcan around the block."

"I tried that with your sister."

The Cuban got red in the face. "You fucking piece of wormshit, I should've smeared you all over the highway while I had the chance."

"Maybe you should've," Simbal said, "but that's all over and done with. I'm sitting here with you now and we've got some business to get done.

"Anyway, killing me's not going to do you a whole helluva lot of good. I'm not with DEA anymore. The Quarry's got its teeth into the *diqui*. Right now I'm the rabid dog that's chomping away but there's plenty more where I came from. My Kahuna answers to only one man and that's the President of the United States, buddy. The Quarry's got power the SNITs only dream of. I don't think it's to your advantage to get your bowels in an uproar with me. Not when I could be your friend."

The Cuban said nothing for some time. The maître d' led a family of three past their table and nothing was said until there was empty space around them.

"Then you'd best tell me more about it, dude. I don't think I'm ready to believe you're down here because of a murder. Got the Fat Boys Institute for that, man."

"The FBI couldn't solve this one if I handed them a map and said Professor Peacock in the drawing room with the knife."

But the Cuban was already shaking his head. "You a heavy hitter, dude. You get sent in when things is all fallin' to shit." He had ceased to drink, Simbal noticed; merely rolled his glass around on the table. "That what's happening here?"

"You and Mako," Simbal said.

The Cuban shrugged. "He and Bennett've hooked up together. That's what I'd heard, so I needed to get it firsthand."

"And?"

"What did Mako tell you?"

The Cuban turned his attention back to Simbal. "He and I, we moving boatloads of shit in and outta coves all around Miami. What more d'you want?"

"I want to know what he and Bennett are up to."

The Cuban grunted. "Why don't you ask him right out then? I'm sure he'd oblige you." He shook his head.

Simbal took a conversation pace backward. "What do you suggest?"

The Cuban feigned astonishment. "You askin' *me*?" His eyes got big around. "*Madre de Dios!* What could us po' folk stuck in the trenches with our noses in the mud these guys rake up tell *you,* the Great White Hunter?"

"Cut the comedy, Martine."

"Jesus, you really got a nice pair of *cojones* on you, dude." Simbal ignored him.

"What're Bennett and Mako up to?"

The Cuban shrugged. "I don't know. You tell me."

"You'd better let me in on it,' Simbal said.

After a time the Cuban said, "Shit," took a swallow of his drink. "He's got a party going later tonight, after midnight. Real exclusive bash. I'm supposed to hook up with the two of them there. Dealing with Mako's been strictly dust city."

"Bennett," Simbal said reflectively.

"I suppose if you're in I'd better brief you," the Cuban said a bit sourly.

"I've already read Eddie's file," Simbal told him.

"That means there's a lot about Eddie Bennett you don't know."

"Oh?"

"You don't know this *hombre* personally, you don't know shit about him."

"Meaning?"

"Edward Martin Bennett's one mean motherfucker."

"Tell me something I don't know."

"I'm tryin' to, dude." The Cuban reached for his drink,

320

took another healthy swallow before he said, "It was this way: Eddie and Peter Curran had a falling out."

"You mean they were on a joint DEA-SNIT mission together?"

"No, man. Nothin' like that."

Simbal tried to discern from the Cuban's expression what he did mean. Whatever it was, wasn't good, that much was clear. "Don't tell me they were in business together?"

"No business," the Cuban said, downing the rest of his rum and Coke. "Pleasure."

"Oh, Jesus." Simbal thought for a minute. "You're not telling me that all of this—shit—happened over a lovers' spat."

The Cuban fiddled with his empty bottle. He seemed to want another. "I believe it began that way, yes. See, they couldn't live together, be seen in public together, none of that shit, man. It was very bad for them. Once that kind of thing gets into your file, Madonna, there's nothing more you can do in our line of work. The field's out and forget about handling any classified shit. They send you off to the Leper Colony. That's what Eddie used to call it. Learn to be a clerk, pushing papers, real important stuff like promotions, raises, requisitions, shit like that."

"You said nobody knew about them," Simbal said. "You know."

"Sure I know. Eddie and I worked together more than a couple of times. You know that much from his file. But like I said before, that file, at least in Eddie's case, ain't worth piss."

"To know Eddie Bennett is to love him," Simbal said. "That it?"

The Cuban screwed up his face. "You think you're pretty cute, uh? Work for the Quarry, you got power up the yin-yang, look down your nose at us country folk now, that it?"

"It was my only way in, Martine," Simbal said. "This was a closed shop, I was quick enough to spot that. I didn't have time to finesse my way to see you. Don't get your nose out of joint, it's nothing personal."

"That's where you're wrong, *hombre*. This whole boatload of fish is personal from the bottom to the top."

"Then you'd best tell me about it."

The Cuban nodded. "For Eddie, there was nobody else on the beach besides Peter Curran. They were in school together."

"Yeah, I know. Yale. Same frat, same club."

"Hellfire Club," the Cuban said. "Some heavy shit going down there. Same drunken night Eddie told me about Curran, he told me about the initiation into the Hellfire Club. He and Curran pledged together." The Cuban shrugged. "I guess men can fall in love, too." He signaled the waitress for another round. "Can fall outta love just the same."

"Is that what happened to them?"

"It was like any marriage that falls apart," the Cuban said. "That's the funny part. One of them changed, the other didn't."

"That must've been Curran," Simbal said. "Curran'd been floating around with a female operative at the DEA."

"Yeah, that seemed to piss Eddie off all right," the Cuban admitted, "but the cut came because of Eddie. He was sent out into deep water." That was SNIT-speak for long-duration undercover work.

"Let me guess," Simbal said. *"Diqui?"*

"Right." The Cuban took his drink off the girl's tray. He seemed inordinately thirsty and Simbal remembered that feeling of fear he exuded. "He's been out a long time. A very long time."

Simbal picked up the undercurrent. "Meaning?"

The Cuban made a face. "See, that's the reason I'm here. That's the reason I got so bent when you showed up on my doorstep. Eddie's not coming back. He's gone over to the other side."

And in the shocked silence, Simbal thought, Dear God, what we're dealing with is a voodoo spook.

Sun Tzu said that the most effective manner for a general to deploy his troops was to ensure that they had no identifiable shape to the enemy. In that way, no defense against them was possible even from the most brilliant military tactician.

That was written in 500 B.C. but such was the incisiveness of Sun Tzu's strategy it was as true today.

This is what flitted through Jake's mind as he and Mikio turned the corner of the scriptures hall. They had begun their run along the temple's vast veranda. The two sunglassed Yakuza had guns; there was no point in heading toward them or even in holding their ground. Jake and Mikio were unarmed; any form of weapon was strictly forbidden within the temple's grounds. Besides, Mikio had "died" the day before in Tokyo. There was no reason to expect any form of pursuit here.

But they had their superbly trained bodies and Sun Tzu had counseled to find the proper battleground. So Jake and

Mikio took off along the edge of the veranda. They hurried down a flight of stone steps, brushing past a long line of women supplicants.

Passing the open doorway to the scriptures hall they could hear the rhythmic *pok, pok, pok* of the hollow wooden fish being struck to keep the tempo of the priests' chanting.

They skidded to a halt. "Oh, Buddha," Jake said softly. Sun Tzu's strategy became uppermost in his mind as he saw four more Yakuza making their way toward them. Then he knew. The first two with the guns had been stalking horses. Cursed himself mightily. He should have suspected something of the sort when he saw the pair draw their guns. In a place like this where much of the structure had been designated a National Treasure by the government of Japan, there would be no question of gunplay. Other, more silent—and discreet—methods would have to be used.

"Into the garden," Mikio hissed and, bent almost double, they scuttled into the large forested area between the scriptures hall and the bell pagoda. They stepped off the wooden walkway onto a large flat river rock. Stepping stones led a way through pebbles, haircap moss, moso bamboo. On their right they passed a gigantic rock rounded by centuries of rushing water. It was the Benevolence stone, one of five such enormous rocks that studded the garden. Each one represented one of the five Confucian Virtues.

Aspidistra and ostrich fern floated in the breeze of their passage. Jake already felt a shortness of breath, a pounding behind his eyes.

It was very still. They could hear the whisper of water somewhere close at hand, hidden by the bands of meticulously barbered greenery, even now and again the chanting, the *pok, pok, pok* invoking the rhythm from the scriptures hall.

They both became aware of the men at the same time. Mikio touched the edge of Jake's sleeve and the two of them moved off. Deeper into the garden, moving along a narrow, serpentine path of moss-encrusted stepping stones artfully arranged to suggest to the stroller a rushing stream.

They crouched down beneath a cryptomeria whispering ancient secrets of the timeless place. To their left twined the red-gold leaves of a dwarf cut-leaf maple. Directly ahead reared the Justice stone, its enormous body a series of roughly concentric plateaus built one upon the other like the rings of a rent redwood. Confronting it, one was thus inexorably reminded of the passing eons, slabs of time that dwarfed any human's lifetime.

This was the stunning effect of the stone—said to have taken the garden's designer ten years to find—to place the viewer in perspective, to remind him or her of the timelessness of this place, the immutability transmitted to and from the Confucian Virtue of Justice, itself an extension of nature.

"I do not understand this," Mikio said in a whisper. "To the Kisan clan I am dead. Yet they have picked up my trail so quickly."

"A traitor?"

Mikio shrugged his heavily muscled shoulders. "Anything is possible, my friend. But I prefer to look for another explanation."

A whistling brought Jake's head around just in time to see the beginnings of *shohatsu*. He kicked out reflexively, deflecting the weighted end of the Yakuza's chain. The *manrikigusari*—which meant literally "chain with the strength of ten thousand"—rattled as the sunglassed man brought it back toward him.

Jake extended his hand in a feint. This brought the expected response, the *uchiotoshi*, a striking drop attack which missed as he drew back his wrist at the last instant.

Grabbed hold of the chain and twisted. They both lost their footing and crashed into a carefully manicured bed of spidery ferns.

The man was not big but he was unusually powerful. As he sprang back to the balls of his feet, Jake saw that he seemed to have all his energy concentrated in his upper arms and torso, which was unusual in a Japanese, who prized big *hara* so highly—the centralization of intrinsic energies in the lower belly. That was why *sumo* wrestlers were so heavy.

Used a *tenkan*, bringing both their bodies around to his left, making it the low turn because the Yakuza's hands were reaching for his wrist to free the *manrikigusari* and Jake thought, This is what happens when your mind relies on weapons: they become more important than your own body.

By grabbing for Jake's wrist the Yakuza had sacrificed position in order to regain full control of his chain. This allowed Jake to flow his own body with the Yakuza's momentum, bringing both his arms up and out while Jake's free hand pulled downward at his neck.

In a moment, the Yakuza had arched backward, crashing onto the mossy stones. Flicked the *manrikigusari* and it curled around Jake's extended left ankle. The Yakuza pulled hard and Jake lost his balance.

The breath went out of him as he hit on his side. Turned in time to see Mikio apply a liver kite with vicious accuracy. The Yakuza's lips pulled back from his teeth in a grimace of agony. He let go the chain, clutching at himself as Mikio repeated the blow. Jake smashed the heel of his hand flush on into the Yakuza's face and his sunglasses burst apart. He went limp.

Jake took a deep breath and Mikio extended a hand, grunted heavily. The whites of his eyes showed all around and his mouth opened silently. He collapsed onto one knee and Jake leapt to catch him, pulled out the *shuriken*, the honed steel throwing spike.

Blood gushed and Mikio put a palm over the wound. Jake heard a whirring and, simultaneously, felt Mikio crash into him. A second *shuriken* embedded itself with a *thwok* in the trunk of the cryptomeria.

Jake crawled on his elbows and knees through a low copse of boxwood, pulled up behind a swaying mass of azalea. He glanced back, saw Mikio ripping his shirt with his teeth, applying a tourniquet to his arm, grunting with the effort. In a moment the white cotton was dark and wet with blood.

Jake returned his attention to the *shuriken* thrower. Tried to ignore the bees moving busily through the field of flowers beside his head. He kept himself very still. When he decided to move he did so with extreme caution and slowness.

The garden had about it a certain tempo as the light breeze took leaves, certain small branches and set them to moving. Any deviation in that tempo would, he knew, bring instant attention to himself. The idea was to sink in to his surroundings, *chahm hai*, as Fo Saan had taught him. Yet all his training revolved around *ba-mahk*. If Jake could no longer reach out and be in touch with the eternal cosmic pulse of things then all avenues were closed to him.

Still, he did what he could to blend in with his surroundings. It wasn't enough. The slither of the chain caused him to turn his head but the *manrikigusari* was already around his neck in *makiotoshi*, the terminal strangle attack.

The first thing was to keep the hands down, away from his neck. The organism's first jibbering response would be to get its hands up to free the neck. This would be a mistake because there was no way for bare hands to break the drop-forged steel chain. Precious seconds would be wasted while the attacker applied even more pressure. Death would surely follow.

Took a deep breath. Used the boar, a rib *atemi*, an edge-of-the-hand percussion blow that required him to perform a quarter-turn twist to his left. This severely restricted his windpipe. But the breath was already inside him and he used his full strength, aided by the organism's knowledge that death was near. Used the animal fear, rearing its head like a spur, as he had been taught, letting it pump excessive amounts of adrenaline into the system.

Twisted now to his right, delivering a boar to that side, and quickly, again, feeling three ribs give as the heat on his face became almost unbearable, the chain beginning to stop the blood flow to the brain and Jake knew that this was strictly shunt-ended, very little time before the sparkling lights sprang up before his eyes and the lack of oxygen clouded his judgment or, worse, affected his coordination.

The Yakuza slipped to his knees, bringing Jake down with him. But his training was extraordinary and even with three ribs shattered he would not let go, he was still positioned directly behind Jake where it was very difficult to get anything done against him.

Time was critical now. Lungs burning and he was experiencing consciousness slippage, aware of the sunlight filtered onto one leaf, suprareal; the sighing of the breeze like the chattering of animated spirits, playing hide and seek amid the trees; cloud, blue-gray, in the shape of a samurai at the charge and . . .

I'm not getting any air!

Stop daydreaming and get on with it! he berated himself. Tried four different types of leg *atemi* but the Yakuza slipped away each time, doggedly keeping his strength in the tautness of the *manrikigusari*. Jake suspected that he was slowly drowning in his own blood. But that would be little consolation if he was able to hold on long enough to keep the air out of Jake's bursting lungs.

Seconds now rather than minutes and Jake did the only thing he could, arching backward, putting all his weight excruciatingly on his neck for the instant when it became the fulcrum for the back somersault.

Used an elbow *atemi* with both fists clenched together, consciousness wavering in and out of focus, jamming down, down in a sharp motion that shattered the Yakuza's sternum.

The man arched up, his fingers white as bone as they slid

along the wet links of the chain and Jake, slamming his left elbow at the side of his neck, smashed the flat of his right hand against his adversary's cheek. Heard the sharp snap of the cervical vertibrae as they gave way beneath the enormous pressure.

A nacreous blackness and he saw the ant making its laborious way through a field of stalks.

Then he became aware that the field of stalks was the hairs on the back of his hand. Head hanging down, the *manrikigusari* hanging around his shoulders like the weight held aloft by Atlas.

"Jake-san!"

Mikio by his side. "Are you all right?"

It hurt too much to nod his head and his tongue was so dry it felt swollen enough to fill his mouth.

At Mikio's silent urging, they moved off, edging around to the far side of the Justice stone. Surrounded by box tree and silver juniper.

"There are four more," Mikio said. He kept looking at his watch as if he were late for an appointment. "We must hold them off."

Jake noticed that he had taken the *manrikigusari*. "How good are you with that?" He was testing the raw flesh around his neck.

Mikio gave a grim laugh. "It depends on whom you speak to." He gave Jake a look. "Don't worry, *kyujutsu ka*, we'll be drinking Kirins at my favorite bar in the old quarter of Kyoto an hour from now."

Jake said nothing but he wondered if that was going to be so. He badly needed some rest and there was no telling how badly Mikio was wounded. He watched their immediate environment. He listened.

He heard a sharp clack and jump slightly. Mikio put a hand on his knee. "It is only the *shishi odoshi*."

Jake looked around, saw the bamboo and stone "deer scare" not twenty meters away. Originally created by farmers to keep their crops from being eaten by animals, the *shishi odoshi* was now a common element in the modern Japanese garden. A wide length of bamboo filled part way with water and as the liquid's weight tipped it over, its end would strike a stone, making the loud clacking noise. Emptied of water it would rise back up again to be refilled and strike the stone once more.

In the changeless harmony of the eternal garden, the *shishi odoshi*'s metronomic sound might be the only outward manifestation of the passage of time.

To Jake, every clack that reverberated through the foliage brought them that much closer to the end of the overwhelming peace of the garden. Here beneath the willowy branches of the evergreens, the Chinese Judas, amid the aspidistra and plantain lily, the lacy ostrich fern, the okame bamboo grass, he was never more acutely aware of the beauty of the world. Wiping the sweat from his face, he was determined that they would not die here, not today, not for a long while.

Clack, clack, the *shishi odoshi* spewing out the water on the back of the striking stone. The changeless western face of the Justice stone, bulging out toward them, then running away in a wide arc down toward the Japanese maple and the cryptomeria.

Glimpse of black, pin stripe, a suit sleeve? and Jake saying, "Brace yourself, Mikio-san, here they come."

Mikio used the *manrikigusari* on the leading man, tumbling him so that the *shuriken* he was about to release clattered to the stone path.

At the same time, Jake was up and running toward the breadth of the Justice stone. It was imperative to split these four up. In a bunch, Jake knew, they'd have little chance against a massed assault.

Took three with him—obviously with Mikio wounded they figured Jake was the most dangerous. They came at him from three different directions at once. Expected him to run but he stood his ground. Deliberately made himself appear confused; he was careful not to move so that when he did it would come as a shock, gaining him a fraction more time.

And when the one on the left was close enough, he began his attack, a flat-handed *atemi* that Jake watched come at his face. At the last instant, he dropped to one knee, swiveling his body to his left as he did so. With his right hand he reached up, caught the cuff on the man's extended right sleeve and, using his own forward momentum, pulled hard across his own body and down, throwing the Yakuza into his companion, rushing Jake from the right.

Now, as Jake rose to his feet, the man in the center grabbed him from behind over Jake's shoulders. Jake kept his body moving to his right, jamming his left hand upward under the Yakuza's armpit, and threw him off.

The first man was on him again and Jake, seeing the *shuriken* in his hand, allowed him to stab forward with it. His left hand flashed out to meet the blade, bypassed it, locked around the Yakuza's wrist, pulling toward him using his own momentum combined with his strength to pitch him forward.

As the Yakuza stretched out, bending, Jake's right hand came up, slashed down onto the back of the man's exposed neck. He collapsed into a heap.

Jake kicked out at the third man, rocking him back, while eying the short sword the second man had unsheathed. He rushed at Jake, the sword extended in front of him. He began to *kiai* shout but Jake slammed the heel of his hand into the Yakuza's chin. His other hand blurred up, deflecting the blade away and down.

But the Yakuza had kicked out and Jake felt a searing pain along his hip. His left leg went numb and he collapsed against the curving face of the Justice stone.

The Yakuza slashed down and Jake rolled. Heard the scraping crash as blade encountered rock, saw the bright blue sparks.

Jake reached out, curling his fingers into the front of his adversary's jacket. In close quarters the sword was no good at all, neither would be the man's potentially lethal foot *atemi*.

Surprising Jake, the Yakuza immediately dropped his weapon, landed a double kite just above Jake's heart. Jake doubled over, had the presence of mind to roll out of the way of the *atemi* he knew would be aimed at the back of his neck.

The Yakuza followed closely, sensing victory. The edges of his hand were extended and Jake could see that his karate training had been extensive. He struck and Jake used a *ten-kan*, jamming the heel of his hand against the Yakuza's elbow. At the same time Jake twisted his torso, giving him the added leverage, swinging himself and the other man around, slamming him to the ground.

The Yakuza, half-stunned, nevertheless grabbed up the hilt of the short sword and, in the same motion, slashed upward. The blade came within a hair's-breadth of severing Jake's neck.

Used his feet to take the Yakuza down but his position was bad and the man was wielding the sword with deadly force. So Jake did the only thing he could. Using *irimi* to bring the man toward him down and, at just the right angle, smashed the top of his head against the immutable face of the Justice stone.

He was staring at the limp form when the blow landed on

329

the side of his face. Jake reeled, sliding down the side of the stone. He blinked several times, trying to clear his vision, but nothing would quite come into focus. His depth perception was gone. His arms felt weighed down with lead, his leg was burning with the pain inflicted by the foot *atemi*.

The last of the Yakuza stood over him with his fallen compatriot's sword in his hand. He lifted the gleaming blade and Jake knew there was nothing he could do to stop him. He saw his own death reflected in the shining perfect blade of the *wakizashi*, felt the cold pressage of the flat, arcing blow that would sever his head from his neck.

The blade began to blur, picking up momentum. At the moment it struck through his skin, flesh and bone, he knew, it would be at the height of its speed.

It was so close now that Jake could see the meeting of the two planes of the blade—or thought he could—a hairline so intensely white as to be blinding. It was like looking into the face of God.

Then something funny happened to the Yakuza's body. It ballooned outward at its center, perhaps six centimeters above the heart, and Jake was covered with a heavy, wet heat. A stench like that of a charnel house suffused him so that he began to gag.

Then the full weight of the Yakuza crashed into him, into the Justice stone, smearing its face with blood, guts and shards of shattered bone. The stink of steaming feces was overpowering and Jake, without conscious thought, began the difficult process of crawling away from it. He felt buried in filth. It was difficult to breathe and he began to pant.

He felt someone begin to pull him away and he rolled face upward. A cloth passed across his face, wiping away the flecks of blood and flesh. Jake looked at the dead Yakuza, saw the rear end of a black anodized steel bolt stuck through what remained of the man.

He raised his gaze, saw the beautiful woman in the exquisite persimmon-colored kimono who had helped tend to him at Mikio's house, kneeling beside him, a bloody cloth in one hand.

It was only after a stunned and silent moment that he realized she carried in her other hand a Mitsui Jujika-1000 compressed-gas powered crossbow.

Bliss knew what it was like to be in the arms of Buddha. As she approached the Container Terminal at Kwun Tong she saw that Fung the Skeleton was not present. She saw this not with her eyes but with her mind.

Her *qi*, part of which was now always within *da-hei*, the great darkness, made her aware of this fact. Spread upon the sea of quickening night, her spirit tapped into the vibrations of the universe.

Who was that crying in the street? She was forever aware of the wailing of the dead, massed, an army that took up a continent. Who were they? Her countrymen, the dead of China, calling to be free.

How did she know this? What was it like to be in contact with a spirit? Bliss, in the bow of the *walla-walla* she had hired, closed her eyes, listened to the voice of Shi Zilin. It was in the whisper of the wind fluttering the tendrils of her hair, in the lapping of the waves against the small craft's sides, the bubbling of its wake. It was in the cries of the sea gulls, greedily circling a fishing trawler.

The earth moved and Shi Zilin spoke. They were one and the same, interchangeable. The *qi* of the planet rose and fell as it inhaled and exhaled. She felt this as she heard him speak. There were no words but rather impulses akin to the way one's brain automatically sent messages to one's extremities to move. One was never aware of the process, only the end result. It was mysterious, magical, awesome, even. Therefore, it was not something one could share with another human being. Often, Bliss wondered what she would do when Jake returned to Hong Kong. What would she tell him? How would he perceive the changes in her. How would they affect him?

She gave a little shiver in the predawn darkness. Already, in the east, a line of palest pink had begun to color the oyster gray as night paled.

"Tell me where, miss," the boatman said. "Exactly."

Bliss pointed and when there was no reply, turned around. Caught him staring at her with a kind of fright. What is it that he sees? she wondered. Perhaps I am branded, a scar struck along my cheek. And, unconsciously, she put fingertips to flesh, ran them along the smooth surface. She laughed at herself but it was an uneasy sound, itself making her shiver all over again.

She wished Jake were here beside her. Not to tell her what to do or even to reassure her. For the first time since their reuniting, doubts about the two of them lay like clouds across the horizon.

His history haunted her. She knew of his first wife's suicide, the death of Lan at the Sumchun River; knew, too, of Jake's second wife, Mariana. Her murder in the Japanese Alps had brought Jake back to Bliss for good. But neither of his marriages had been particularly happy ones.

Jake was married to his work, whether that be with the Quarry, in the past, or the *yuhn-hyun* in the present. His was a wholly obsessive personality and this very obsession had caused, his closest friends felt, his estrangement with those he loved most in the world.

Bliss knew this to be only part of the story. She thought of Jake's specialness. She had trained with the same martial arts and philosophical master Fo Saan, who had trained Jake. She therefore knew with great intimacy the extraordinary talents Jake possessed. It was his heightened *qi*, his ability to enter into a semimystical state known as *ba-mahk*, she believed, that set him apart from most people. It was this, she believed, that was most responsible for estranging him from his family.

Now Bliss wondered how their relationship would be affected. Her own *qi* was expanded within *da-hei*. It was here that Zilin spoke to her. She wondered if she were the guardian of the Jian's spirit, or if his *qi* had become hers. She wondered if he were guiding her in some way and, if so, to what purpose.

"Here, miss," the boatman said as they touched the pier. But he would not take the money they had agreed on before setting out. He would not even meet her eyes nor answer her questions. Clearly, all he wanted was for her to get off his boat.

This Bliss did, gaining access to the dockside via a rusted metal staircase that ran up the concrete bulkhead from the lower quay. She could smell the diesel fumes from the airport. To her left was the Container Terminal itself and, beyond, a seemingly endless line of godowns—warehouses filled with all manner of licit and illicit goods awaiting transshipment to virtually every country on the globe.

Fung the Skeleton's boat lay at anchor perhaps three hundred meters down the quay. It was a slim, sleek-looking craft with enough horsepower to outrun the most modern of the police launches. It was painted the color of deep water at night and was almost invisible.

Its captain, she learned by questioning a crew member, was known only as the Malaysian. She had been there less than twenty minutes when he appeared. He was a dark-skinned man with an athletic build running to fat. He had a great, curling mustache shining with wax.

He was young, no more than his mid-thirties, Bliss judged. He wore a pair of knock-off Guess jeans, a muscle T-shirt that looked ludicrous on a man of his bulk.

The same man whom Bliss had questioned stopped the Malaysian, spoke to him for a minute. The Malaysian nodded, dismissing the man. He came across the pier to where Bliss was waiting.

He squinted into the sunrise, said, "You looking for the captain of this boat?"

"I'm looking for Fung the Skeleton."

The Malaysian took a hand-rolled cigarette out of a pocket of his jeans. It was half-crushed. He spent some time trying to straighten it out, somewhat more lighting it. He sucked in some smoke, then said, "We have nothing to talk about," as he exhaled.

"I've got something to sell," she said.

"You?" He gave a laugh and shook his head. "You've got nothing I'd be interested in buying. Unless . . ." His eyes swept over her body.

"Opals," Bliss said.

"You're wasting my time." He began to turn away.

"Fire opals from Australia," she said. "Are you familiar with them?"

He took another drag on the cigarette. "Sure. Everything's got a price and I know 'em all."

She noted his attitude. He liked to feel superior. "Familiar enough to know what this's worth?" She handed over the opal.

The Malaysian grunted, took a look at it. Turned it over. Held it up to the light. Then he turned his head and spat. Dropped it back into her palm. "That all?" he said. "Go on. Get outta here."

"Not just this one," she said, unfazed. "One hundred more just like it."

"Same quality?" She noticed that he wasn't so eager to leave now.

She nodded.

"You got a price in mind?"

Bliss looked at him, saw what she needed in his face. If he saw even a tiny chink in her front now, he'd roll right over her. "I've got a price." Put an edge into her voice.

"Let's hear it. If it's—"

But she was already shaking her head. "Not you," she said. "I'll tell it to Fung the Skeleton."

"Who?"

"Are you interested in the opals?"

"Only if the price is right."

"What are you going to tell Fung when I sell these to his competition."

The Malaysian said nothing.

"Opals are Fung's specialty."

The Malaysian contemplated the dying end of his cigarette. "I don't know you." His icy eyes met hers.

Bliss held the opal out to him. "Take this to Fung," she said. "Maybe that will ease your mind."

The Malaysian flicked his butt into the water. He seemed to have made up his mind. "Get on board," he said, ignoring the jewel. "We sail in three minutes."

When they were on their way he took her arm. "You're either very smart or very stupid," he said. "I wonder which one it is."

Daniella had never been to Zvenigorod but it was no surprise to her that it lay nestled on the banks of Maluta's beloved Moskva. Great fir forests rose upward through steep ravines on either side of the rolling hills upon which the town was set.

But she had heard of the Sobor na Gorodke, the Cathedral of the Assumption, built of gray stone almost five hundred years ago. What seemed odd to her as the heated Chaika took her past its gates was its slit windows, its single austere central dome, so much more like a medieval keep. Its appearance was less like an edifice of God than of war. Sometimes, she thought, they were one and the same, at least in the hands of imperfect and often venal mortals.

Daniella had thought that she would be safe from Maluta over the weekend. After all, he was away at his *dacha* in Zvenigorod and she was in Moscow. It had been early morning and she had thrown the windows open in her office so that she could hear the first birds of spring as they flitted from branch to branch in the firs outside. Traffic on the Ring Road was minimal and the forest dominated.

She had been poring over the latest intelligence from Mitre, her heart surging with the news that they were now so close to taking the whole thing: InterAsia, the *yuhn-hyun.* Kam Sang! More than anything, Daniella wished to penetrate to

334

the hidden core of that Communist Chinese project. She did not believe that its real secret had been revealed to her via Zhang Hua, Shi Zilin's assistant in Beijing. Perhaps part of Kam Sang revolved around the new-design nuclear desalinization plant to alleviate Hong Kong's perpetual water shortage problems. But only part.

The Chinese army was heavily involved, their top minds invested in Kam Sang. Why? She suspected now as Mitre amassed for her more and more data that Zhang Hua had either been incompletely informed about the project or—and this possibility chilled her—he had been a double agent, ostensibly her mole inside Shi Zilin's office but in reality relaying to her just what Shi Zilin wanted her to know.

Well, she'd never know now since both Zhang Hua and Shi Zilin were dead. But Jake Maroc Shi, Shi Zilin's son, survived and it disturbed her that Mitre had no idea where he was. Maroc should have been in the center of *yuhn-hyun* operations in Hong Kong. Yet he was nowhere to be found in the Crown Colony.

Daniella sent a cipher to Mitre instructing him to begin a full-scale trace of Jake Maroc's whereabouts. She was sending it when the phone rang. Assuming that it was Carelin calling to confirm their date for lunch she answered immediately.

"I tried you first at home, Comrade General." Maluta.

"A woman's work is never done," she had said, and he laughed.

"Which is why I called." He paused. "I want an update on your progress."

"Monday morning first—"

"Not Monday," he interrupted. "Now."

"But I have lunch with Carelin."

"Break it. I need you here. And while you're at it you can give your report on your liaison with him."

"You make it sound like filth," she said, abruptly angry—at being intruded upon, ordered around like a wind-up doll; at being pulled away from Carelin.

"And perhaps it is," he said shortly. "But it's not for me to judge."

"You're a prick, do you know that?"

"You bandy Western curses about as if they were your first language. I find that somewhat suspect, Daniella Alexandrova."

He had that capacity to turn just about any insult around like a boomerang; she began again to burn.

"Why are we suddenly speaking of loyalty?"

"Is that what you think, Comrade General? Loyalty?" His voice was mocking. "How interesting! I wonder what a *sluzhba* psychologist would make of that comment. Uhm. Perhaps we should schedule you for a session at the Serbsky Institute."

"What an idiotic notion!" But she knew he had the power to implement even such an absurd suggestion.

"Are you beginning your menses?" he asked. "Your attitude is so antagonistic."

Daniella shut up. She knew why she was doing this and it only raised her anxiety level. In Zvenigorod, at the *dacha*, there could be no escaping him. The black hole of Oleg Maluta would be staring her in the face and she was terrified. Therefore, part of her was attempting to run away.

She heard Carelin telling her, *You'll find a way. I know it.* A way to bring Oleg Maluta down. Wasn't it Maluta himself who had said, *Termination is not the only way to remove obstacles from one's path.* Yes. Yes. She thought of her *wei qi* board, a string of strategies, springboard to . . . to what?

She so wanted to dispel this debilitating terror that Maluta's power produced in her.

Opened her mouth and said, "What time do you want me at the *dacha*?"

"My Chaika will be downstairs to take you home within a half-hour." Did she detect some disappointment in his voice that she had not risen to his baiting? "Don't take too long packing, I want you here for lunch."

Now, several hours later, she was here. Oleg Maluta's *dacha* was at the foot of one of the farther hills. It was elevated above most of the town so that from almost every spot in it one had some kind of view of the Moskva.

The place had an aspect about it of a hunting lodge. Daniella could not think that this was the same design as the one that had burnt down; no female she knew would be comfortable for long in this wholly masculine environment. Inside, it was seemingly all wood—floors, walls, ceiling; the heaviness was oppressive. The furniture, at least, could do with some floral chintz, she decided.

Maluta, in smoke-gray mohair slacks, hand-stitched loafers and a cashmere pullover, greeted her at the door. The driver went past them with her bags. Maluta looked at the attaché case Daniella carried and nodded approvingly. Only then did he move aside for her to enter.

A rather old-fashioned squarish vestibule gave out on one

side to a library, on the other to the living room. The bedrooms and his study, he told her, were up the wide, mahogany-banistered staircase to a second floor which dominated the rear half of the villa. The kitchen and dining areas were in the rear on the first floor.

All the rooms seemed vast to her, even cluttered with the thick-legged furniture, most of which was layered with the accumulated mementos of half a lifetime. Too much from one man or even a couple. As Daniella went around the living room she saw pictures, frames, medals, commendations, even grisly souvenirs of the war, that had to have belonged to Maluta's father. Maluta had moved all of this from his Moscow apartment after the first *dacha* had burned.

He poured them both drinks and, without asking her what she wanted, handed her a glass of white Rhine wine. It was a bit too sweet to suit her taste but she smiled and, after the first sip, made a complimentary remark.

"What do you have for me?"

It was typical of him, this total lack of courtesy. But Daniella was beginning to see his strategy. It was as if he felt that he must shape entirely his immediate personal environment. He liked disconcerting those in his presence, believing, perhaps rightly, that this gave him a certain tactical advantage.

With an inner start, Daniella perceived just how well it worked in her case. That was why she thought of him as a dark star. Maluta worked at having his own laws in his personal universe; and this he carried around with him wherever he went. She was, consequently, never herself when she was with him. For Daniella especially this was a great hardship. It was why she was never able to face him equally: she was never sure of her footing.

With a deliberate gesture significant only to herself, she snapped open the attaché case. It was of hand-tanned wild ostrich hide, one of many extravagant presents Yuri Lantin had bought her from the Beryozka. She produced several pages of pink flimsies, proof that they were Kremlin departmental originals.

"Here is what my asset in Hong Kong has accomplished—"

Red-faced, Maluta came across the Oriental carpet toward her. Daniella, though she felt the rage inside him as a physical force, held her ground. "What shit is this?" He batted the flimsies away so that they fluttered to the carpet. "Jake Maroc is still alive and Kam Sang is still as much a mystery to me as it first was."

"My asset is very close to gaining complete control over Kam Sang, Comrade," Daniella said calmly. "This is the way."

A long blue vein pulsed at the side of Maluta's forehead. His great knuckled fingers curled and clutched at air, making hairy fists. "Is that so?" he gasped in such a strangled voice that Daniella knew he was having difficulty controlling his emotions. "Perhaps we should just overfly the Kam Sang project and 'accidentally' drop a bomb on it!"

Daniella watched him as if he were some poisonous creature. "That is foolish talk and you know it," she said.

Maluta glared at her in silence for a long time. Then he turned on his heel and stalked to the bar. With a clatter, he threw ice into a wide-mouthed cut-crystal glass, slopped vodka almost to the brim. He downed half of it in one gulp. "You know what this means," he said with his back still to her.

When Daniella said nothing, he barked at her, "Tell me!"

"I'm not sure what you're getting at, Comrade."

He swung around and his gaze was baleful. "Stupid bitch!" he shouted. "You cretinous cunt, I'll have to spell it out for you then. Fucking idiot! I have nothing but fucking idiots around me." He gulped the last of his vodka, threw the glass onto the bartop, took some gratification at its shattering.

He came close to her and said, "It means one of two things, Comrade General. Either you are incompetent or you have been lying to me." He glared at her. "Now which one is it?"

"You do not know Maroc," she said, restraining herself from hitting him. "He is my nemesis. He is not so easily destroyed. One does not snap one's fingers and make him disappear."

Her calm tone, perhaps, had some effect on him. She realized that he enjoyed baiting her to get her visibly upset. In this way he could continue to throw up to her her inherent weakness as a female of the species.

"All right, all right," he said in a more normal tone of voice. "I concede that Jake Maroc is not the normal objective. But on the other hand he is not invincible, Comrade General. No one is. He must have a vulnerable spot and it is up to you to find it, exploit it, and terminate him with all due dispatch. Is this clear?"

"Perfectly," Daniella said, despising him more than she had despised anyone in her life.

McKenna drew his Magnum .357 and shot them each once through the center of their foreheads. They pitched forward, covering the steer they had so recently slit open.

That was how he thought about the incident now, even how he dreamed it, sometimes. But that was not how it had happened.

Bundooma. The Northern Territories of Australia. McKenna and Deak Jones on the trail of the trio of abos who had stolen six head of steer. The trail had led into the Simpson Desert.

The Simpson in January. It was a bleak, godforsaken place at the best of times. But in the height of summer it was something else again.

It was true that Deak had argued against going after them: *Not in there, mate. Let the buggers go. They'll fry anyway in there.* Squinting against the unrelenting sunlight reflecting in intense waves off the desert floor. *They were starving. They stole in order to live.*

But McKenna was the senior in rank and time of service. If he said, Go, they would.

It's our job, Deak, m'lad. If we don't have that, we don't have a bloody thing.

And afterward, Deak Jones had asked for a transfer. He could no longer bear to look at McKenna's face. Because McKenna had shot three thieving abos? Not bloody likely.

Sometimes, when McKenna dreamed of the incident, he dreamt the truth:

It took them two days to get the scent and overtake the abos. Near dusk they topped a rise and found the trio and what was left of the cattle. By then they had been in the Simpson for close to fifty hours and it had taken its toll. Toiling mile after mile of scrub and thornbush, dry-backed lizards, piles of rocks like cairns, marking the resting places of those unfortunates who had traveled this path before.

Let's take them, Deak said through crusted lips. McKenna had headed down the slope, silent as a dog.

The aborigines looked up at the policeman's approach. As McKenna had predicted, they had slaughtered a steer. Its blood was pooled at its open belly.

Nothing was said. The aborigines made no move; there was no animosity on their faces, no remorse even. This inflamed

339

McKenna. If they had sinned—and he was convinced that they had—they should be made to feel remorse for their crime. Their absolute placidity filled him with unspeakable rage.

At other times, in other dreams, the trio was composed of three men. This was a function of McKenna's superego imposing itself on his id. The fact was that the trio was a family unit: a father, a mother and their eleven-year-old boy.

It was the boy who was holding the knife. The steer's blood dripped from its keen edge to the thirsty ground. The father, McKenna supposed, had been teaching his son how to survive in times of drought.

All right, Deak said. He had pulled out his pistol and was aiming in the direction of the family of abos. They said nothing. None of them looked directly at the weapon. It was as if it did not exist for them. He crouched in the universal marksman's stance. Both hands were white around the Magnum's grip. But he did not move. It was as if he were waiting for the abos to move first, or that he was afraid to get closer to them.

For McKenna's part, he saw only the boy. He crept closer, his hand on his holstered Magnum. He blinked the rolling sweat away from his eyes. His gaze swept the face of the boy, certain now that this was the one. McKenna had seen him in Bundooma several times. But ever since the first glimpse, that face had haunted him until, eventually, sleep was but a memory for McKenna.

This was what had brought him into the Simpson in January. The criminal act was but a secondary thought. What was one more criminal act among many?

It wasn't until McKenna touched the boy that any emotion registered on the father's face. The man leapt up, cocking his arm to strike McKenna. That was what McKenna had been waiting for. He drew his Magnum and shot the father once through the center of his forehead.

The abo's mouth made an odd, clacking sound. Reflexive motion caused him to bite off the tip of his tongue, though he was beyond pain, beyond knowing.

His body leapt into the air, dancing a jig in the air, crashed to earth, head first onto the carcass of the steer.

His wife screamed, her eyes opened wide with horror and fear, but McKenna showed her the working end of the Magnum and she shut up. Her hands trembled in her lap.

It seemed as if Deak were shouting directly into his ear.

Christ Jesus! We were meant to take them back. Alive, mate. A—bleeding—live!

Shut up, McKenna said, without turning around. *Just shut up. If you can't take it, you shouldn't've come into the Simpson in the first place.*

I didn't bleeding want *to come. If you remember.*

Now you're here, make the best of it. Who knows? Maybe you'll get a medal out of it. McKenna had laughed at that. He had not taken his eyes off the boy and, in the process, he had grown hard. *Keep your gun trained on the woman*, he said with a thick voice.

Christ, why? Deak said. *What d'you think she's gonna do, jump two policemen with drawn Magnums?*

Just do as you're fucking told, mate! McKenna said, swinging around and training the muzzle of his gun on Deak. Then he swung back, holstered the gun. His hold on the boy tightened. He half-walked, half-dragged him away from the fire's flickering circle of light.

Where you taking him?

McKenna ignored Deak. In the semidarkness, he could hear the chittering of the desert insects. There was nothing else in the world. The bowl of the sky was enormous, containing all things and nothing at all. McKenna felt liberated, free of the fires churning inside him. He began to laugh.

Then he opened the buckle of his belt, unzipped his pants. They fell away from him, pooling around his ankles. With a fierce jerk, he turned the boy until he was facing away from him.

Take down your pants, McKenna said in English. When he repeated it in dialect, the boy complied.

His heart bursting, McKenna stared down at the bare buttocks. They seemed white, virginal, full of promise.

What—!

His flesh lurched forward as if of its own volition.

—in the name of bleedin' Christ are you doing!

He closed his eyes. The desert breeze fanning his cheeks. He began to pant.

Something slammed into him. He took one stumbling step, his big hand on the boy's shoulder. Half-turned and lifted the Magnum, shot the boy's screaming, clawing mother once through the center of her forehead.

When he was done, the shudders going on and on like echoes through his body, he pushed the boy roughly away from him. He felt nothing but revulsion for the eleven-year-old. He was dirty, polluted.

The boy sat where he had landed. He stared up at McKenna and still—still!—nothing registered on his face. It was as placid as it had been when McKenna had come upon it.

React! McKenna screamed, and shot the boy once through the center of his forehead.

Have you gone stark staring bonkers? Deak cried.

McKenna said nothing, pulled up his trousers, buckled his belt.

Answer me, you bloody pig! Deak screamed.

We got what we came for, McKenna said as he went past him to where the rest of the steers were waiting with bovine patience . . .

Was it any wonder that Deak Jones had asked for a transfer the moment they got back to civilization? That he did not want to look at McKenna's face ever again?

But that was hardly the worst of it. Though the incident itself would be enough for a haunting, there was more. There was the image of the great green-headed fly, bloated with blood, crawling across the boy's open eye. There were the nights in Bundooma when he could see the fires flung like giant eyes across the face of the Simpson, skyscrapers of sparks shooting upward into the black, starless sky.

And the chanting of the tribes. He could hear the chanting even in his bed, even with the curtains pulled, the covers over his head. The chanting had a power that could not be interfered with.

Because, McKenna knew, the chanting was directed at him. For what he had done on the bleak back of the Simpson. The aborigines possessed a kind of primitive magic. McKenna had seen it at work, though he had never believed in it. Not really. He had thought of it, rather, as clever illusion, a prestidigitator's trickery.

Until the chanting had come, infiltrating his nights, making him start, gasp, sit up in bed covered in sweat. Thinking of that fly with the metallic green head, crawling over the milky arc.

What right had creatures little more than animals to do this to him? Rage and terror battled for supremacy within him. He wanted to commandeer a jeep and race out into the Simpson, pump them all full of lead. He had seen the "Mad Max" films.

He would do no such thing.

And in the end he left his command; left Bundooma, the edge of the brooding horror-filled Simpson, the Northern Territories, Australia itself. Came to Hong Kong to make a new life for himself. But here he was amid the bloody wogs again.

And the chanting had followed him all this way. He had to stop the chanting. He had to do *something* or go completely mad.

McKenna rose, pale as a corpse, and hunted through his beaten footlocker. Dressed in the clothes he had worn in the Outback, neatly folded, stowed away for, perhaps, just such a time.

Picked up his Magnum .357 and checked the action. Slowly, methodically, he loaded the chambers. Then he went out the door of his apartment.

He was looking to kill or be killed. He did not know which.

Imagine! They would have gone to the ends of the earth for you. They sold their souls for you.

Daniella before the mirror that was part of a massive oak armoire that dominated the bedroom assigned to her at Maluta's *dacha*. It had a beautifully beveled edge but here and there dark patches like oil stains on limpid water bespoke the wear to which it had been subjected.

The black Dior gown that Yuri Lantin had bought her dropped to the carpet. Daniella stood, watching herself immobile in the mirror. It was almost as if, for this interminable instant, she were gazing at a sepia-toned photograph, her own daughter or granddaughter, perhaps, flipping through the family album, coming upon the image of Daniella Alexandrova Vorkuta.

It was at this instant that, in the same manner a flash of lightning will illuminate a nightscape, she saw how distorted and unpleasant her life had become. Why, she realized, there is nothing at all normal about it.

Perhaps it was the thought of a daughter—a child she might never bear—or the granddaughter who would never exist. She had, in fact, no personal life whatsoever. She belonged to the *sluzhba* body and soul. Even the small pleasure she derived from being with Carelin was illicit, forever consigned to clandestine shadows, laced with the bitter taste of fear: that Maluta would expose them, or that someone else within the *sluzhba* or the Politburo would find out and use the information to suborn or destroy them.

For years she had been far too busy constructing a career on the back of her stretching ambition to think about what it was she was sacrificing on this terrible altar.

Mother of God, she thought, if someone had mentioned children to me even three years ago I would have laughed in her face. Children? For someone whose ambition was limitless?

For the first time in her life, Daniella contemplated the hollowness of power. Locked within her hideous psychological struggle with Oleg Maluta, she felt nothing but fear and loathing. Should she by some miracle defeat him, she knew that she would feel no sense of triumph.

Bowed their heads before you, conferred to you on bended knee all that made them powerful.

It was true what Maluta had told her that frigid night by the bank of the Moskva. She had been greedy for power. Like a vampire, she had feasted off it and then killed them all, all the men in her life who had tried to use her and had, in return, been used by her. They trooped through her mind like beloved actors asked to take a curtain call by their admiring audience.

Now, staring into her own cool gray eyes, those same eyes that had bewitched so many powerful men, she stumbled upon an astounding notion. She found what would make her happy. It was not the defeat of Oleg Maluta; it was not an elevation to head of the KGB or even to the head of her country. It was, simply, to feel Mikhail Carelin's seed flower inside her. She wanted his baby more than she wanted anything.

She lost her balance for a moment, falling into her own image, their lips meeting in cold gesture. When she pushed back, there was a dead spot on the mirror where her perspiration occluded the reflection.

In a moment, Daniella bent to pick up her Dior gown. It was all wrong for this evening. Putting aside the dress, she looked at herself in the mirror one more time. Her uniform with the blue shoulderboards was holding its press well. There was nothing wrong with her, she decided, the way she was.

There was even the possibility that this was the correct way to go about it.

She had never seen Maluta drink—that is, seriously drink. In Moscow, he drank an occasional shot of *zubrovka* at dinner. That was all. But here in the *dacha* he swallowed *ry-*

abinovka—the vodka flavored with ashberries—as if he owned a piece of the business.

He was already well into the vodka when she came downstairs, where caviar and hot blini were waiting, piled on a chased silver salver. Before going in to dinner, he opened another bottle, bringing it in with them. Someone had obviously spent a great deal of time in the kitchen but it was Maluta himself who served the meal. If anyone else was in the *dacha* Daniella failed to see him.

The meal began with *kulebiaka*—baked salmon surrounded by a multilayered wrapping of flaky pastry. Then *rassolnik*—a steaming, rich soup made with a variety of pickled vegetables, many not readily available in the beginning of spring. The main course was an excellent chicken Kiev that shot a geyser of melted butter across its golden flank when Daniella pierced it with her knife.

For dessert, they feasted on *vareniky*, sweet dumplings filled with a delectable cherry conserve.

Over *chai*, Daniella said, "Do you always eat this well, Comrade?"

Maluta, who was busy sugaring his tea, said nothing. He placed three cubes in his glass at once, using the curved end of his spoon to tap at them until they broke apart. He'd stir the tea a bit, then add three more lumps and repeat the process.

At length, he said, "My wife was an exceptional cook." But his tone told her that he was speaking more to himself. "At home, I am used to eating in a certain manner. Some things should never change."

Abruptly, he got up and went out of the dining room. Daniella spent a moment stirring her tea until she saw the sugar dissolve. Then she rose and followed him out.

He stood by one of the great paned windows in the living room that looked out on the Moskva far below. He sipped his tea absently, his free hand behind his back. He seemed uncommonly melancholy tonight, a side of him Daniella had never before witnessed. She had seen him calm and almost hysterically angry but never withdrawn and brooding.

"The Moskva survives," he said, and again she had the eerie sensation that he was not talking to her at all, perhaps not even to himself but to some unseen presence. "The mountains endure. But life must ebb and flow."

He turned around to face her. "Isn't that so, Daniella Alexandrova?"

She nodded. "It is a law of nature, is it not?"

His dark eyes watched her from the shadows cast by the heavy brocaded curtains. "Perhaps, yes. And we should know, eh? We who concern ourselves during each waking moment with the law. Is it man who makes the laws in this world, Daniella Alexandrova? Or is it, as you have said, nature?" He lifted his glass of *chai*, sipped at it without taking his eyes from hers. "Is nature, I wonder, another name for God?"

The short hairs at the nape of Daniella's neck began to stir. Oleg Maluta talking of God? It seemed an impossibility for such a rigidly pragmatic believer in the Party. She did not understand the territory to which he had brought them, so she said nothing.

"Who made the world, Daniella Alexandrova? Was it created in a burst of incendiary star-matter? A trillion-year swirl of cosmic detritus? Or can you observe a divine hand in the molding of virgin clay?"

"Are you asking my opinion?" Daniella asked. "Or merely listing options?"

He came away from the shadows of the brocaded curtains. "I am curious about what you believe in." They stood not a meter apart. "I am curious to know if you see a, what shall we say, a higher intelligence at work—at the beginning of all things."

"Yes," she said without hesitation. "And God was a Communist."

He did not laugh as she expected he would. Instead he frowned. "I am serious, Daniella Alexandrova." She wondered what he was getting at; what new trap he was about to spring on her. "I want to know if you believe. You know what I mean. I want to know—if you do—whether this belief affords you any measure of solace."

"I was lying before," she said. "God doesn't understand Communism."

He moved closer. "Then you *do* believe."

"I am a Communist," she said. "God doesn't understand me either."

Now he did laugh. "If He exists, which I doubt, I can't imagine that He'd understand any of us." In a moment, his gaze broke away from hers. He stared down at the russet surface of his tea. The melancholy had returned, shrouding him. "Daniella Alexandrova, I must ask you this. Did anything happen in your life that you could not explain . . . that you did not fully understand."

"I'm not certain that I follow you, Comrade."

Maluta lifted his head and his eyes grabbed hers again. "I am speaking now about tragedy."

And in a flash, Daniella knew what he was alluding to: his wife's appalling death. And because she knew he wanted a certain answer from her, she lied. "Yes."

"And?"

"Yes, and?"

"Did you—" He broke off, perhaps embarrassed. "Did you witness the hand of God in this—tragedy?"

"If you believe, Comrade, then the hand of God touches everything . . . and everyone."

"Then how is the inexplicable . . . the tragedy of a lifetime explained."

"It is never explained," Daniella said, thinking now of something Uncle Vadim told her when her mother had died. "That is an impossibility. It is, rather, resolved."

"Resolved?" He said it as if he had never heard of the word before.

"Yes," Daniella said. "In one's own mind. A kind of inner peace. An ending to the hurt."

Maluta closed his eyes for a moment. His lips seemed to move as if he were murmuring a prayer. Or perhaps it was only a momentary trembling. "I see," he said at last. "An inner peace." This last was said in the peculiar tone of voice reserved for uttering such concepts as "A hundred billion rubles," that were both personally unobtainable and difficult to grasp. "Then you sleep at night."

"What?"

"Do you sleep at night?" Maluta asked.

"Yes."

"And do you dream?"

"Sometimes."

"Only sometimes," he said wistfully. "I dream all the time." He turned away, put on music. Tchaikovsky. *Swan Lake*.

Clouds had broken apart and there was moonlight on the Moskva. Daniella could almost imagine the alchemical transformation of animal into human that had so bewitched Tchaikovsky's hunter. *They sold their souls to you.*

Daniella crossed to the sideboard. The record player, an outdated affair so different from the one Lantin had bought to play his black-market foreign pressings, was crowded along its top with framed photographs of Maluta as a young man, as a boy with his mother and father, with his mother alone, lifted onto her broad shoulder as she laughed into his startled face. Behind them, two rows of well-bound books, foreign editions.

In a sterling-silver frame, a young woman who might have been his sister except for the obvious age of the photograph, looked at the camera, wide-eyed, unafraid, even with a bit of aggression to which Daniella could relate. Beside this studied portrait was a snapshot in a similar silver frame. It was of a dark-haired Georgian beauty with the typically wide, flat-planed face with powerful cheekbones and jawline. Her coal-black eyes dominated an already strong, almost haunting face. Daniella had never seen a picture of Oleg Maluta's wife but she was certain that this was the woman.

"Oreanda," she said, quite without thinking.

Maluta snatched the photograph out of her hand, tilted it away as if even by looking at it she would sully its pristine nature.

"She was quite a handsome woman," Daniella said, wondering how far she could take this.

Maluta grunted. He put the photo face down beside the bar as if it meant nothing to him. "It is late. Time we were saying our good nights." But he did not move and Daniella remained where she was. All she need do was reach out and pick up the snapshot of Oreanda Maluta, burnt to a crisp in a conflagration of mysterious origin that ravaged the first *dacha* built on this parcel of land.

Daniella saw in her mind the woman's countenance, so full of strength and an almost regal bearing. One saw that rarely in Russian women. She wondered again whether Oreanda was the key to Oleg Maluta.

"I'm not tired," she said. "If you don't mind, I'd prefer to stay here and read for a while."

"Do you wish a book? I have an extensive library of Russian authors."

"I brought my own, thank you," Daniella said. "The Marquis de Sade." She put aside her tea. "Do you know his creation, Justine?" She watched his face carefully. This was one of the volumes she had seen on the shelf here. She could hardly believe it was his kind of reading; *Crime and Punishment* was more his style. Had it been Oreanda's?

Maluta's eyes had narrowed. "What do you know about me?" *They have conferred to you on bended knee* . . . "You picked that title. I do not believe in coincidence." . . . *all that made them powerful.* "Who have you been talking to?

There is no one who knows about Oreanda. No one but myself."

"Then that answers the question." Daniella kept her voice light, a small smile on her face. She was on the right path, she saw it in his breathing. "I have spoken to no one about your wife."

"Yet you know!" Grabbing her wrist, as if by this gesture he could wrench the knowledge out of her.

"I know how beautiful Oreanda was. How strong—"

"Strong, yes. Strong. So unlike a female personality."

She had only meant her face but had allowed him to finish the thought she had begun. This was turning into a psychological interrogation. It was a matter now of feeding him the right cues, of fanning the fire that had already begun.

"There could never be another woman like her," Daniella said softly. She was very close. They key was to remain near him, proximity equaling intimacy in this equation. "She was special. So special."

"Special." His eyes opened wide. "Oh, yes, she was special. She was a world unto herself. She was like Justine." A fierce, cold light emanating from his face that Daniella struggled to decipher. "Everything changes when I return to Moscow. I can breathe again. After her tears flow, after the moonlight disappears from the Moskva, after the air clears and the rain settles the dust onto the pavement."

She recalled his earlier questions concerning faith, God. "Your love for her will never die."

"No, no, no!" He was suddenly wild, his grip on her wrist painful. "Oreanda!" Calling her name. Not in love and remembrance but rather in anger and in fear. "It is *she* who will never die. Never, never, never!"

"But she *is* dead, Comrade. Oreanda is nine years dead."

Those eyes fevered even in the brightest light. "Burnt up, black as night. I saw the corpse, even as they pulled it out of the wreckage, the skeletal arm falling away at the socket, the eyeless skull staring up at me, mocking. Was it her? Was it Oreanda?"

"The coroner's office must have checked. There had to be a positive I.D. for the death certificate to be issued. Dental records."

His head bobbed. "Dental records, yes. That was how it was done. It was Oreanda. The coroner had no doubt."

"Then she is dead, Comrade. What—"

"No!" Maluta shouted her down. "She is here! I built this

for her. She made me build it for her, on the same spot!"

Then Daniella knew, it all fell into place: Maluta's almost schizophrenic behavior, the uncontrollable bouts of rage, the malicious hatred of women, of her, his torturing her, his saying, *They sold their souls to you, bowed their heads before you.* How wrong she had been!

This was the magic he had conferred upon her: the power that had resided in Oreanda, the power that made him hate her fully as much as he must have loved her; the power that had chained him, *Everything changes when I return to Moscow. I can breathe again.*

Had he set the fire that had killed her? Had Oleg Maluta murdered his beloved wife? She was determined to find out.

Took his hand, saying, "You're wrong, Oleg," the first time that she had used his given name. "Oreanda is gone, gone, gone." Drew his hand inward to the juncture of her thighs. "This is what remains." Then to the bulge in his groin. "And this." Felt it growing and put her thumb and forefinger around its tip. Twisted her wrist and his hand fell away, freeing her.

Slipped to her knees, deftly undid his trousers. Took him out, slipped her lips over the semihard member. Bathing him in warmth until she felt his own heat rising. Then she began to use her tongue, swiping it along the length, curling it as she went. Fluttering it against the underside of the head until she felt the powerful muscles along the insides of his thighs begin to jump and convulse. Then she stopped.

Stood up in front of him.

"What—" he said, almost gasping. "What are you doing?"

"Starting?" she said. "Or stopping?" Her half-open lips were wet, shiny with saliva and his own precoital fluids.

He gave a shiver. Of anticipation or of fear?

"Stopping," he said in a shaky voice.

She put the flat of her hand over his heart, could feel the thunder of its beat. "I can't go on," she said. "Oreanda wouldn't like it. You're her husband, her lover. You're hers alone."

He shivered once more, his eyelids fluttering closed. "I can breathe again," he whispered.

"The moonlight on the Moskva," Daniella said in his ear, then licked it with the tip of her tongue. All the while the tip of his penis was grinding into the palm of her hand. Grazed her fingernails at its base.

"I can breathe again," he coughed.

"Oreanda . . ."

He put his hand on her shoulder, pushing her down. Daniella had clandestinely unbuttoned the uniform's skirt. Now as she began again to kneel, it slithered off her and she stepped out of it. She was naked beneath.

Oreanda! his mind screamed. She had enslaved him with her sexual demands. Something inside of him had offered her the power and she had swept it from his opened palm. It was cruel and vicious, this cycle of Oleg and Oreanda. The more power he obtained in his professional life, the more he granted her in his private life—or the more she took from him. He did not know which gave him the most pleasure. The specter of her sex moving him from place to place within the *dacha* haunted him still. So much so that now he felt his insides melting helplessly in the furnace of Daniella's sexual aggression. He had not felt such pleasure since . . .

Maluta gave a sharp cry, his fingers clutching at her jacket. "Uh, uh, uh," as her hot mouth engulfed him again. All his insults, his sneering at her sex, had masked this hunger. He burned for her, hated her for what Oreanda had done to him. Feared her as well, terrified that the enslavement that had haunted him for nine years would begin anew. *Everything changes when I return to Moscow. I can breathe again.*

In the end, he worshiped her as he had worshiped Oreanda before her.

Daniella took all of him inside her, opening her throat and relaxing the reflexive impulses. Above her, Maluta gurgled deep in his throat. The tip of his penis expanded and began to pulse.

Daniella withdrew her heavily sucking mouth and pulled him down until he was lying on the carpet. She knelt over him, holding his quivering member in the palm of her hand.

Her knees were on either side of him. She guided him to her. "This is what you want, don't you?"

He groaned.

"But you've told me that you never want it." She bent over him. "Never ever. So now you can't have it." She pushed his penis away from between her thighs.

Maluta reached up to grab her but Daniella used the edge of her hand to slap him away. "No, no," she said. "Not that way. Not any way."

Perhaps he could have overpowered her, perhaps not. In any case, that was not his desire. "There must be."

Daniella took the tip of him and again brushed it along the silken flesh between her thighs. Immediately, it began to pulse and throb and she released it. She did not touch it, would not allow him to, either.

"What?" It was an almost strangled cry.

"I want it."

"What?"

"Say it," she coaxed. "Say, 'I want it.' "

"I want it," Maluta said.

"I want to know that you mean it."

"I *do* mean it. I want it."

"Here," she said, lifting him up and settling herself down. "It's yours."

He let out a long, ecstatic groan, as she slid all the way down him. She rocked back and forth when only the base of him remained unsheathed, and he gasped, arching his buttocks off the carpet.

His penis began to convulse, shooting heavily deep inside her. At the same time, his hands reached up, cupping her breasts through the thick cloth of the uniform, pulled her down against him while he emptied himself inside her.

When, sometime later, he slipped out of her, she was still astride him. Her breasts were against his chest. His breathing was becoming deep and regular; he was nearing sleep.

She put her fingers around his neck. Put her lips against his ear until she felt him stir. "I should kill you now."

He gave a tiny indrawn breath and she reached down, grabbing his flaccid penis. Gave it a painful twist.

"That's what Oreanda would want, isn't it?"

"What do you mean?"

"You killed her, Oleg."

"What?"

"That's right. You set the blaze. You were clever, doing it so that there would be no suspicion of arson. But you murdered Oreanda just the same."

"No, no."

"Don't lie to me, Oleg. I know when you're lying."

"I'm not lying now!" he cried. "I had nothing to do with the fire here. Nothing! I swear."

Daniella took her hand away from his penis but not from around his throat. "I want you to know something, Oleg," she said, putting all the contempt she felt into her voice. "When you were inside me, I felt nothing. And when I had you in my mouth, it was all I could do not to vomit for the thought of it."

"Why do you tell me this?" he said, his face averted from hers.

"Because it's important that you know the truth."

Maluta pushed her off him and, clutching his trousers frenziedly, pulled them up over his nakedness. His face was filled with shame and this gladdened Daniella's heart.

Now, she thought, I have gained a measure of power over him. Perhaps at last we face each other as equals.

"We are almost there," Kazamuki said.

Jake, sitting beside her in the Mitsubishi sports car, watched the play of her persimmon-colored kimono as she drove. There was not one spot of blood on the lovingly woven silk.

Mikio lay on the back seat, holding his wounded arm. "It is nothing," he said into the air in the back of the Mitsubishi. "The blood has already coagulated. There is almost no pain."

"Please," Kazamuki said softly, as she fired them into a turn. "An *oyabun* should conserve his energy."

Jake closed his eyes, dizzy with exhaustion. He thought of the scene back at Kiyomizu-dera. Mikio Komoto sat with his white fists still wrapped around the chain of the *manrikigusari*. The Yakuza who lay sprawled at his feet, his white face at an unnatural angle, had the end of a black anodized steel bolt protruding through the center of his chest. The wicked triple-serrated barbed point had come out the other side. The force of the missile's impact had broken his spine.

Kazamuki had made sure her *oyabun*'s life was not in danger before felling Jake's last adversary.

Waves of vertigo assailed him as the Mitsubishi hurtled out of Kyoto. Heading northeast, back to Tokyo. Abruptly, he was swept by a blackness that could not be denied. He asked Kazamuki to stop the car and, at the side of the road, he got quickly out and vomited.

Without *ba-mahk* he was just an ordinary man.

Wearily, he climbed back into the car. Kazamuki had the good manners to be watching her side mirror so as not to be witness to his shame. They continued their high-speed journey.

Psychological fatigue as well as physical fatigue brought about by extreme fear. Mikio Komoto sitting with the *manrikigusari* wound around the young Yakuza. The wraparound sunglasses shattered, the face, though grotesque in death, apparently recognizable to the *oyabun*.

"Jake-san," Mikio had said warily, "I am afraid there is

some extremely disturbing news. These Yakuza are not part of the Kisan clan." His keen ebon eyes looked up at Jake. "Do you understand what that means? My security is still intact. These men were not after me; they were not part of the Yakuza war at all."

Woodenly, Jake had said, "Who are they?"

"Members of the Moro clan. Have you heard of them, Jake-san?"

Shook his head. "No."

"Are you certain? No dealing with them at all when you were working at the Quarry?"

"Not that I am aware of. Why?"

"Because, my friend, this attack was not directed at me. *You* were the objective."

The Mitsubishi hit a bump in the road and at 140 kph it was enough to make Jake groan.

"Are you unwell, Jake-san?" Mikio's voice from the back seat.

Jake said nothing, squeezed his eyes tighter shut. They had stopped in Kyoto long enough to see a doctor of Mikio's acquaintance. *Yakuza.* The damage was minimal.

"Now we go to Karuizawa," Mikio had said. "That is where the Moro clan is headquartered."

"Jake-san."

Opened his eyes, caught the flick of Kazamuki's eyes.

"Is the *oyabun* awake?"

Jake listened to the softness of her voice, turned carefully around. Mikio's eyes were closed, his breathing deep and regular.

"Asleep," he said. "Is there a problem?"

"That depends," she said, glancing again in her side mirror. "For the last twenty kilometers or so the same Toyota truck has been two cars behind us."

"Are we being followed?"

"I think we must find that out, *neh*?"

She turned the wheel hard over and the Mitsubishi slewed into the far left lane. She stepped on the accelerator until they were doing upwards of 160 kph.

Jake glanced in his side mirror, saw the black Toyota immediately. It was one of the futuristic-looking vans. The windows were completely blacked out so that it was impossible to see inside.

He watched for some kind of movement on the part of the Toyota: an acceleration to match their own or a change in lane. There was nothing. The van was now four cars behind.

"Now we'll see," Kazamuki said. Accelerated again and now, with a high squeal, pushed them back through the lanes. Horns blared, the screeching of brakes behind them and then they were onto the off-ramp.

Jake took another look in the mirror, saw the black van's ballooning image. "Here they come," he said.

Kazamuki downshifted, weaving in and out around two slowing cars and a truck. The moment she was beyond them, she stamped down on the accelerator, running a light. Three blocks later she slowed until they were almost drifting.

The Toyota blew out of the traffic pattern they had left behind. It slowed as soon as its driver picked up their change in speed. With a shriek of tires, Kazamuki brought the Mitsubishi back up to fourth gear. The Toyota came on.

Now it was not directly behind the Mitsubishi but rather off to one side. It blared its horn at an oncoming car, which slewed out of the way, running up on the sidewalk.

The black van closed the distance between them. Jake could see that the off-side window had scrolled down. He saw the machine-pistol muzzle poke itself out like the snout of an ugly dog.

"Out of the way!" he shouted as he pulled heavily on the wheel.

"What!" Kazamuki cried in alarm as the Mitsubishi went hurtling toward a wall. Heard a series of explosions behind them and Kazamuki straightened their run.

She looked at him briefly. "They've got more than *katana* in that van," he said.

Kazamuki concentrated on her driving. The Toyota had lost some ground during Jake's impromtu evasive maneuver but it was gaining on them. They had obviously done something to the engine because it was performing like a rocket.

"They're very close," he said, and she nodded.

Took the Mitsubishi into an acute left turn, the speed so great that the two right side tires went off the macadam. Almost hit a trio of pedestrians who scattered, screaming. Three blocks later, she made another left.

They could hear the squeal of the black van's brakes behind them but could not see it. She had them at an unsound speed but that could hardly be helped. It was the rush of wind now or the steel-jacketed bullets from the machine pistol twisting the Mitsubishi into junk.

One more left and they were almost home. Now Kazamuki

355

accelerated and Jake's teeth began to chatter. Outside was just a blur and he prayed no one would get in their way.

The wheel hard over and they had completed the circuit. The Mitsubishi righted itself and took off. Now they were directly behind the black van. Not a maneuver for the faint-hearted, Jake thought.

She ran up their tailpipe and, just before a light turning off the green, she tramped heavily on the accelerator. The Mitsubishi obediently shot forward and, with a thunderous lurch, slammed into the black van.

The speed was sufficient that the collision sent the Toyota careening into the intersection. The light had already changed, there were cars moving. The black van hit two of them broadside and flipped upward.

It began to roll like an acrobat performing the last, electrifying stunt at the climax of the circus. The Toyota came down hard onto the macadam rear first. The gas tank ripped open along with the left side. Sparks from dragging, exposed metal caught the fumes and there was an oddly muffled *whump*!

Kazamuki cut a hard left and began to accelerate.

He was known as Fung the Skeleton because of the tattoo, a dancing man composed all of bones that was animated by the rippling of his muscles. Usually he went shirtless on the job so that everyone could see the tattoo embedded in the layers of skin across his right shoulder blade. Here, it was important that he keep the name alive.

This was Mong Kok, the northern end of the massive typhoon shelter at Yau Ma Tei, on the western side of the Kowloon peninsula. A veritable sea of boats were moored here, encompassing almost every size and shape. A city of people lived and worked in this space, an extension of the land itself.

It was easy to get lost here, to secrete a treasure even when others were searching for it. Fung the Skeleton possessed such a treasure and, certainly, there were many who would gladly give up a year's salary to discover its whereabouts.

Many had tried with little or no success. Not because Fung the Skeleton could not be found—anyone in Hong Kong could be found for a price; not because he was a criminal of such stellar magnitude to command sufficient muscle.

The fact was that Fung the Skeleton was a legitimate businessman. Not on board any of his drug-running fleet of boats, which he visited in the early morning or late at night.

From nine to five, dressed and acted like all the other upwardly mobile *tai pan*. He did not show off his tattoo. Neither was he known as Fung the Skeleton.

Ian McKenna would have recognized him immediately as Big Oysters Pok.

That he was able to lead this rather dangerous double life in the claustrophobic and rumor-hungry Crown Colony was a tribute to his skill and ingenuity. The very fact that Special Branch Inspector Ian McKenna knew him only by his legitimate identity bespoke Fung the Skeleton's inordinate cleverness.

Legitimate was an approximate word, considering that Fung the Skeleton had gone out of his way to build this third identity for himself as a trader in flesh. It amused him to hang out in Wan Chai, one gorgeous woman after another by his side. He liked to see the policemen's eyes bug out, their mouths water for a taste of what he obviously dealt in.

In a way, it was a real joy to play the sleazoid to whom everyone came for information. In another life, perhaps, Fung the Skeleton would have been an actor—and a damn fine one at that. But he was, alas, Chinese, and the market for Chinese actors was, as it had always been, at a standstill.

There was of course an extensive police file on Fung the Skeleton; but like many such dossiers it was thick with a hodgepodge of unsubstantiated rumor and useless hearsay. There was not one solid fact about the subject, certainly no photograph or any such piece of evidence that could lead the Special Branch to an arrest.

The simple fact was that too many people got rich off Fung the Skeleton's business for the police ever to hope to rope in an informer. Besides which, it was common knowledge that anyone hindering his affairs would be a dead man within twenty-four hours.

Such was the man's power. In a land where modern legends were commonplace, he was talked about in the most reverential tones.

When the Malaysian brought Bliss to him, he was going over backup trade routes with one of his captains. All his boats had primary routes, and backup should they run across police interference. All the routes changed daily and were known only by Fung himself and the captains. That way there was no chance of a leak. Responsibility weighed most heavily, Fung the Skeleton often said, when it was borne alone. And he was quite correct. His security was one hundred percent, as it always had been.

The Malaysian held Bliss aside while Fung the Skeleton finished his business with the captain. He stood partially between her and his boss so that even if she could read lips she would have no opportunity to do so.

At length, the captain departed, shouting to his crew. Fung the Skeleton nodded and the Malaysian brought Bliss over.

"I know you," Fung the Skeleton said immediately. "You're Jake Maroc's woman."

Bliss said nothing. She wondered whether she had met this man before. She had never had anything to do with drugs so she knew only the name. But she knew about her father's past and suspected that the two had met at one time or another. Fung the Skeleton was younger than Three Oaths by at least two decades but his contacts were so extensive that she could not believe the two had lived their entire lives without their paths crossing.

"On the contrary," she said, taking a chance, "I believe you know my father, Three Oaths Tsun."

Fung the Skeleton lounged against the taffrail of the boat. "Is that so? Was it he who sent you here?"

"No. It was the Monkey Man."

Fung the Skeleton grunted, held out his hand. "Let's see what you have."

Bliss dug out the fire opal, dropped it into his hand.

Fung the Skeleton took an inordinately long time examining the jewel. At last he looked at her and said, "Where did you get this?"

By his tone alone Bliss might have guessed it, but the part of her *qi* that resided in *da-hei* warned her quite clearly that she should not lie to this man. So she told him what her father had been told by Jake.

"Now I know why you are here," Fung the Skeleton said. "It has nothing to do with selling me Australian fire opals. It has to do with this particular stone."

"Do you know the young woman in question?"

Fung the Skeleton stood up from the rail, moved forward along the side of the boat until he was at the bow. Bliss went after him. The typhoon shelter was live in the early morning with cooking fires, children scampering up ratlines, *walla-wallas* moving slowly down sea lanes, junks putting out to sea or returning, laden with unknown cargo. Far out at the western edge of the shelter she could make out the sleek predatory outline of a police launch, lazily patrolling like a shark along a reef.

"Somewhere," Fung the Skeleton said, "out there is the dream of riches beyond comprehension. Everyone thinks about it: cashing in on the one great deal of a lifetime. Sometimes I think people—some people—are willing to take any risk, no matter how dire, for the prospect of such riches. What do you think?"

"I think there's a sucker born every minute," Bliss said.

There was silence for a time. Then, abruptly, Fung the Skeleton roared with laughter. His captain, alerted for bright sharp sounds, lifted his head from his charts, saw that everything was all right, and went back to work.

"I used to believe that the *loh faan*, the foreign devil, were the only suckers in this world." He turned the opal over in his fingers so that the sun struck the crimson fire, dazzling them momentarily. "Now, of course, I am older, wiser. I know different.

"To answer your question, yes, I know the young woman from whom Jake took this stone. It is my stone. She appropriated it from me under, let us say, delicate circumstances."

"I hope she was worth it," Bliss said.

Fung the Skeleton smiled. "No single woman is worth the price of this jewel. If you knew anything about opals you would understand that."

"Why was she following Jake?"

Fung the Skeleton looked out to sea. She knew he was following the progress of the police launch; it was habit with him. "Perhaps for the same reason she stole this from me."

"Meaning?"

"She was crazy to do that. She knew what would happen to her. The only reason I did not have her killed was that Jake beat me to it."

"She wasn't crazy," Bliss said. "Jake would have known that."

He turned to her. "Then do you have an explanation?"

"She wasn't stupid," Bliss said. "She was very smart. Smart enough to keep Jake away from his appointment with his father, to keep the path clear for those who assassinated Shi Zilin."

Fung the Skeleton looked from Bliss's face to the flash of intense color between his fingertips. "Why do I have the feeling you know why she stole this?"

"I have a feeling about it," Bliss admitted. *Da-hei*. Shi

Zilin. "I think she saw the stone, knew its value and decided to take the chance."

"But she knew I'd have her killed within the day."

"Then obviously she knew that she would be out of Hong Kong within hours."

"Jake stopped that."

"Yes."

Fung the Skeleton studied this woman more carefully. She was very sharp. He wondered just how sharp she was. "I know she was seeing someone else while she was—at my house."

"Do you know who?"

He glanced at his watch. "I'm late for an appointment I cannot postpone. Will you meet me later for dinner?"

"Where?"

"I usually go to Star House, do you know it?"

"In the Causeway Bay? Yes."

"Eight o'clock all right?" He signed to the Malaysian.

Bliss wondered whether he knew anything more. She had seen his face, read his mind as the Malaysian had brought her over. She knew when she was being mentally undressed. But what choice did she have. He was her best—and only—lead to the mysterious woman who had followed Jake. She had no choice.

She shrugged. "Eight o'clock."

The storm caught up with Qi lin just after she had crossed the southern frontier. It might have gotten to her sooner but she had in her mind something the old doctor at Jiao zhuang hu had said to her, *Remember the rivers that flow to the sea* and she used the great trees that grew by the plateau's wide, muddy river for protection.

Now, high above sea level, Qi lin knew that she was at last out of danger. She was in the mountains of northern Burma.

The Shan States. Where there was no law, and even the Chinese army lived in fear.

She knew that she was within the Golden Triangle, an area that encompassed not only a section of the Shan States but areas of Laos, Thailand and her own country's Yunnan province as well. She knew that the business here was opium or, as it was locally known, the tears of the poppy.

The Communist Chinese government had been trying for years to stamp out the illegal but enormously profitable opium trade, as had the rather ineffectual Socialist regime in power in Burma. But the Shan States were a universe unto themselves. These mountains were riddled with ancient tribes, commanded by ferocious and imposing warlords, well-armed and -trained private armies that, along with the terrible terrain, assured a permanent continuance of the lucrative trade.

America and Russia, the most powerful of the world powers, Qi lin knew, had accepted this fact and, for years had tried to infiltrate these mountains with the intention of gaining control over the opium trade and its billions-of-dollars-a-year profits.

Both the CIA and the KGB had had so many setbacks in these mountains that Qi lin had heard a rumor that there were separate appropriations set aside by both governments to handle the losses.

The moment she crossed the frontier into Burma, Qi lin became more cautious. This was no longer China; her documentation was useless here. In fact she had stuffed the papers into a pouch and buried it on the Yunnan side. In the Shan States, the Chinese government was active in trying to destroy the trade; thus a Chinese citizen there would be subject to hard scrutiny and heavy suspicion. But a fugitive newly escaped from prison, that was another matter entirely . . .

Especially if her story was that she was looking for her sister who had fled China just days before her.

Shan means "free people." This same basic meaning can be applied to the words *Siam* and *Assam*, the names of peoples who have settled over a wide area of Southeast Asia. From perhaps the fifteenth century to 1959, the Shan were ruled by thirty-four *sawbwas*, lineal princes whose individual fiefdoms were passed down in true feudal hereditary manner. Nowadays, the Shan warlords who ruled the Golden Triangle were often hybrid offshoots of those original ruling families.

But there were other—and no doubt to her—far more dangerous warlords. These few were rogue generals who had defected from the Chinese Communist army. Greed, avarice, the lure of power beyond most men's wildest dreams, these warped ideals were what drove them. These few, even more than the Shan princes, would be more suspicious of any Chinese crossing the border. More than anything else, Qi lin did not want to run into one of these.

Quite near the frontier, she was picked up by Shan soldiers. They wore the red headbands, floppy white trousers, fatigue blouses and peculiarly heavy quilted jackets traditional of the Shan people. She did not know their dialect but, when prompted, one of them spoke an atrociously accented form of pidgin Mandarin.

Qi lin allowed herself to be searched and questioned. At length, she produced the photograph of the old doctor's daughter. "Sister," she said, pointing to her. "My sister."

Mok, the one man who spoke the vile Chinese, passed the photograph around. There was a conference among all the soldiers. Then Mok turned to Qi lin, said, "You wait here." His face grew fierce. "If you move, orders shoot, kill." Qi lin nodded docilely.

Mok left her surrounded by the others. Behind them was a concrete bunkerlike structure. Qi lin could scent a peculiar odor, sweet and, at the same time, sharp, at the back of her throat. She coughed, raising her hand to her mouth, and one of the soldiers leveled his AK-47 at her. Qi lin lifted both hands, palms toward the soldier. "It's all right, you motherless turd-sucking pox-ridden dog," she said in her most servile tone of voice. "I've got nothing up my sleeves." She smiled and the young soldier bared his teeth in response. They were as black as night.

Qi lin could see more soldiers trudging with backs bowed by burlap sacks in single file through a door to the concrete building. Other soldiers guarded them with AK-47s. Qi lin had not seen such a massed display of firepower in her life, even when she was a member of the *Gong lou-fu*, the Steel Tiger Triad.

In the distance she could see the mule train from which soldiers were off-loading the burlap sacks. Now she recognized the smell. It was opium "cooking." This was a "factory" where the raw opium was refined into Number Four or Double Ouglobe, a form of heroin that was so concentrated it took up about one-tenth the space of a pound of the raw product. In that way it was far easier to transport over difficult terrain, and to smuggle into civilization.

Mok was coming back and Qi lin redirected her attention. "None see her," the soldier said. It was all Qi lin could do not to wince as the man single-handedly destroyed the language.

"I want to see the head man anyway," Qi lin said, careful not to move; she was all too aware of the AK-47s trained in her direction.

"Uh?"

"The head man."

"Head man?" The puzzled look remained on Mok's face

for a moment. Then he brightened. "Ah Ko Gyi," he said. "Go see him."

"Yes," she said. "That is what I want. Now."

Mok nodded. "Go now." Mok signed to the other soldiers and they closed ranks around her.

Qi lin watched Mok's eyes. They were flat and wholly opaque. Something had happened while he was away. What?

By sunset, Qi lin and her escort had traveled perhaps seven kilometers in distance. Also they had ascended just over four thousand meters. By then she was shivering with the cold. No one offered her a jacket.

On a narrow plain high in the mountains, they came upon a village composed of bamboo latticework houses grouped around a central clearing.

"Is this where the Ah Ko Gyi is?" Qi lin asked.

Mok ignored her. He had said nothing during the entire trek. Qi lin felt a shiver of a dark premonition. But it was too late to turn back. And, in any case, where would she go?

Within the Shan village, the other members of the escort melted into the twilight. Mok took Qi lin by the arm, directing her to a bamboo-and-mud house somewhat larger than the rest. The local warlord's residence, Qi lin reckoned.

Someone must have passed on the news of their arrival because as they approached the beaten-down staircase to the wide veranda several figures emerged from the house.

As if this were a prearranged signal, Mok pushed Qi lin forward. "The intruder," Mok said in quite excellent Mandarin. Qi lin gaped at him as Mok repeated the story of who she was and why she was looking for the woman.

"Your name?" the warlord barked.

Qi lin lied without thinking, an instinct for self-preservation. She took her first good look at the man, who was exceptionally short, as round as a vat, with the most powerful arms and shoulders Qi lin had ever seen. He was wearing army fatigues, a sleeveless shirt of a dark indeterminate color to which were affixed several gold and silver pins as if they were medals. Around his waist was a webbed ammo belt with a black leather holster containing what appeared to be a U.S. Army Colt .45. He wore soft leather boots all the way up to his knees. He seemed totally immune to the biting cold of these high altitudes.

"Is this the one?"

Qi lin did not understand the question, and was about to say so when she realized that the warlord was speaking to a shadowy figure behind him. The figure moved slowly, almost, Qi lin believed, painfully forward.

"Yes," the old man said. "That is she."

Qi lin goggled. Buddha! She had seen that old man before! Her heart sank. All the miles since her incarceration at the hands of Colonel Hu raced in upon her. She felt as if she had been traveling in a circle.

"Huaishan Han?" she said bewilderedly. "Is that you?"

You were nothing in Miami unless you lived overlooking the ocean. Mako Martinez lived in a condo duplex so vast Simbal figured the whole top floor of the Quarry offices could have fit nicely into its layout with room to spare. It was on the thirty-third and thirty-fourth floors, accessed by an elevator that rose fast enough to give you a nosebleed.

The hallway was wide and plush as a thousand-dollar-a-night whore. It was decorated in modern Miami pastel, padded wallpaper in a ribbon pattern reminiscent of water. There were real paintings scattered here and there, and expensive-looking rattan furniture flanking the bronze doors of the elevators as if the designers thought this might be a comfy place for a late-night chat. Every few feet brass-edged translucent glass wall sconces drifted light up at the pale salmon-colored ceiling.

"This place reeks from money," Simbal said.

Martine Juanito Gato de Rosa grunted. "There are three more towers like this scheduled to be built. If it weren't for the cash Mako and his pals poured into this place to keep it afloat, it would've been just a rusting skeleton by now. The condo business down here stinks. We got so many they're coming out've our asses."

"You sure Bennett'll be here?" Simbal asked.

"Nothing's ever for sure in Miami, dude," the Cuban said. "Don't need me to remind you of that."

Double doors at the end of the hall opened and they were in. Simbal had seen many a palace before but, really, he thought, this takes the cake. The whole of the south face of the living room which, Simbal estimated at no less than sixty-five feet long, was a wall of glass which looked out over the Intracoastal waterway, islands spangled with night lights. Off to the right rose the distant high-rise hotels of the Beach, as it was locally known.

Near the eastern end of the room, a great floating spiral staircase made up of Lucite wedges lit along their front edges with tiny sparkling lights wound its way up to the second floor.

Otherwise, the expanse was filled with lengths of sleek slate sofas, oversized curved chairs of supple umber leather that had that man-eating look indigenous to so much ultramodern furniture. Taupe sand-painted walls upon which enormous, eerily amorphous abstracts in smears of mauves and pinks floated. Potted fiddlehead ferns, sprouting corn plants, feathery horsetail palms strewn about. There was even a natural hemp hammock strung between architectural columns. A model of grotesquely inhuman proportions was stretched out on it, exhibiting her bone structure.

The place, Simbal decided, would have given the Shah of Iran the willies. He edged away from the Cuban and went through the crowded living room. Rock music was blaring. The Police. Simbal was amused.

There were so many men wearing unconstructed linen and silk jackets, sleeves pushed up their hairy arms to call all the more attention to the T-shirts they wore underneath that Simbal thought, Good Christ, are they filming "Miami Vice" anywhere near?

He went up the spiral staircase, which was narrow enough so that when he had to pass a woman in a crepe gown and a Martini coming down, things got interesting. For a moment, Simbal thought she was going to ask him to do it right there but she only licked her lips and said, "I'll be sure to see *you* later."

Upstairs the polished honey parquet floor gave way to thick pile wall-to-wall the color of clotted cream. It made you want to take off your shoes and run through it barefoot. Which was just what a young woman with long red hair was doing. She had lifted her full Mexican peasant skirt up with both hands so high not only her sleek thighs gleamed in the lights but the smallest pair of panties Simbal had ever seen. The sea of hair in which the minuscule swatch of fabric was buried was the object of everyone's attention.

Simbal looked around, found the portable bar. He asked for an Absolut on the rocks and took a sip. Wandered off.

There was a balcony up here as well. Not as wide, perhaps, as the one on the first floor, but it was adequate enough. Simbal peered out through the glass at the motor launches moving lazily along the Intracoastal. A tiny uninhabited island had been festooned with colored lights so the lush unspoiled foliage could be admired at any hour.

His eye caught a movement and the multicolored illumination revealed the flat planes of a face with which he was familiar. Run-Run Yi. New York's *diqui* honcho and, by all reports, Alan Thune's strongest supporter into the organization's higher echelons. Who was he talking with?

Simbal drifted some more. Darkness and then the light. Bennett! The voodoo spook himself. Simbal took a long look and then, as Bennett suddenly turned in his direction as an eruption of noise came through the open window-doors, stepped quickly back.

When Simbal looked again Yi was alone. Cursing, he put his drink aside and went out along the terrace. Movement, shadows and light, blending. Couples swaying to the rich, soaring voice of Nona Hendryx, funky, jazzily complex.

Pushed his way through the throng, passed right by Run-Run Yi, who was leaning on the rail, staring down. Simbal paused, did the same. Saw Bennett on the floor below.

Inside, the woman with the long red hair had lifted her peasant skirt all the way over her head. Already three Latino types, dripping grease and nine-hundred-dollar Armani suits, were beginning to close in, the hungry look of the predator on their shiny faces.

An egg-shaped cocktail table had been cleared of its carefully arranged array of crystal bowls, thick verbena-scented candles, a stark Japanese-style arrangement of bird of paradise, and now four kneeling couples were taking turns slurping lines of white powder off the glass top with a golden straw.

Jesus, Simbal thought as he brushed hurriedly past them, all this scene needs now is Lot's wife.

His progress down the shimmering spiral staircase was impeded momentarily by a macho man with too much hair and gold on his chest who was drunk or high or both. Simbal finally pushed him in the direction of the egg-shaped table.

As he raced the rest of the way down to the lower floor, he wondered what had happened to spook Bennett. Had he caught sight of Simbal? If so the recognition factor had been instantaneous. Then Simbal remembered a note from Bennett's accessed U file. That was the confidential shrink personality-evaluation section. Bennett had an eidetic memory. His recall of visual data was absolute. Then it was a sure bet he had caught a glimpse of Simbal.

Talking Heads were singing about a psycho killer as Simbal got a visual fix on Bennett. The Cuban had picked him up as well, knew from the look in Bennett's eyes that a wheel had come loose somewhere. He and a young Mexican woman were standing between Bennett and the front door.

Simbal headed their way. There was some heated talk but David Bowie singing something about Templars and Saracens made it impossible to make out what, even though the two of them seemed to be shouting.

Bennett raised his fists first and the Cuban tramped hard on his instep. Bennett used his elbow, ramming it into the Cuban's ribs. Then his ham fist, already cocked, struck down at the side of the Cuban's face.

Gato de Rosa was reeling as Bennett grabbed at the Mexican woman, spun both of them out the door. Simbal caught the Cuban as he was about to fall, lifted him up. His head came around, his eyes uncrossing slowly.

"Martine?"

"That you, dude?"

"Yeah. Bennett's a little high-strung these days, wouldn't you say."

"He's got Maria. She's a local contact I've been working." The Cuban hawked into a linen handkerchief. Stared at it as if he'd never seen his own blood before. "Goddamn it!"

"Let's get the sonofabitch," Simbal said.

"You watch that dirty temper of yours, dude," the Cuban said. "That's my *corazon* he's got with him."

The sconces of light seemed like empty smiles, mocking them. Gato de Rosa swabbed at the side of his mouth with the bloody handkerchief as the descending elevator tried its best to burst their eardrums.

"No one's ever done that to me," the Cuban said. He seemed more concerned with the loss to his peculiar brand of personal honor. "*Hijo de puta!*"

"What'd he say?"

"He said to me, 'What's that goddamned fucking pig, Tony Simbal, doing trying to shove his snout up my ass?' I told him he must be hallucinating. And he said, 'Simbal's fucking here and you'd better believe that I know who he's looking for. He's a goddamned one-man terminator.' "

"I resent that!" Simbal said hotly.

"Don't knock your rep, dude."

The doors slid open on the ground floor and they stepped out. Simbal took a step toward the lobby but the Cuban said, "Hey, man, *this* way."

They went out the back, down a wide bluestone path lit by brass ground lights with a vaguely nautical motif. Palm fiddlehead swayed and insects buzzed, flinging themselves suicidally against the hot lights.

Ahead of them Simbal could see the boat slips that, along with the famous but faded Australian tennis pro, was one of the condo's main selling points.

"He didn't come in a car," the Cuban said as they began to sprint down the path. "Cars make Bennett nervous. He doesn't go anywhere he can't get to by boat." He pointed as they turned along the quayside. "That's his cigarette there. The black one with white trim."

Cigarettes were common in Miami. Slim power launches that were almost all engine, they were manufactured primarily as racing craft. In Miami they had been adapted for use by the drug smugglers who plied the ten thousand waterways, covelets and tiny beachfronts that beribboned the coastline.

"Don't come any closer!"

Bennett's shout brought them up short. They were not more than one boat's length away from the stern of the black cigarette.

"This's the end of the line for the two of you!"

"Eddie, I don't know what's gotten into you. I—"

"Shut your fucking lying mouth, you Cuban cocksucker!"

"Now, look!"

"No, *you* look, pimp-face!" Bennett emerged from the shadows of the cigarette's cowling with a figure held tight to his front. Simbal could see the Magnum .357 pointed at Maria's temple. "You look at this. Wanta see her brains splattered all over the dock, hotshots?"

Simbal and Gato de Rosa said nothing.

Bennett laughed and his heavy face twisted in a sneer. "Look at you! I wish I could play you a video tape of your faces. Jesus, you look stupid! What a couple of fucking Boy Scouts."

"Let her go, Eddie," the Cuban said. "She's only a skirt. You don't want to do nothin' to her."

Bennett sneered. "You better pray I don't, dude."

"I don't know what you're up to, Eddie," the Cuban said.

"I know," Simbal said. "He's joined the lunatic fringe."

"Watch your mouth, Boy Scout!" Bennett pushed the muzzle of the Magnum so hard against Maria's temple, her head canted over at an angle. "You think I won't waste her? You're fucking jerks. They sent me up to New York to do a number on Alan Thune. You heard about that one, I know, every-fucking-body heard about it. That was the point of it."

368

"What the fuck're you doin'?" Gato de Rosa said to Simbal under his breath. "I warned you about this."

The thing was, Simbal knew, to break the deadlock. This was not a siege situation where time was almost always on the side of those who waited longest. This was what Simbal called a flashburn, a short-fuse situation that was going to be resolved quickly one way or another. The person who thought the fastest would come out the winner. He looked for a minute into Maria's liquid eyes, saw to his surprise no fear or panic. That was good. Perhaps there was a chance, after all.

"You know what you've become, Bennett?" Simbal deliberately raised his voice. "You're a pariah!"

"Martine," Bennett said, "what's he talkin' about?"

"You ain't got a home, buddy," Simbal continued. "You're a rolling stone nobody wants."

"You're fucking out of your mind!" Bennett called back. "Looney tunes!"

But Simbal had his attention. "You've been put on the hit list."

"Fuck the DEA!" Bennett said, laughing again. "I got myself a better home. I make more money than you poor dumb shits could ever dream of."

"I'm here to put you out of your misery, Bennett."

"Yeah, I figured. The Company hitman."

"No, no, you've got it wrong, Bennett. The *diqui* hired me."

"What?"

Reaction time was everything. Under normal circumstances one had only one's training to rely on. And one had to hope one's own training was the better. But there were times of extreme peril when that kind of thinking was inadequate, when one needed an edge.

It had been Simbal's experience that the only advantage to be sought in such times was that of surprise. The body responded instinctively to motion, so this had to be discounted. The mind was the target. The mind had to be frozen that infinitesimal instant so that the impulses to the nerves and muscles were delayed the fraction needed to gain the advantage.

The words were not entirely out of Simbal's mouth when he was already pushing his body on its way. One, two, three strides and then leap, you bloody bastard, leap into poor Maria's torso, knocking her and Bennett backward.

The three of them tumbling to the deck, everything happening in a blur, bad luck handcuffing him, the edge of Bennett's cowboy boot rising in reflex, catching Simbal over the right eye, the Magnum discharging, Maria's chest exploding.

Bennett charging while Simbal was still recovering, the muzzle of the Magnum landing alongside Simbal's nose, making breathing impossible, the nerves in his face going numb.

Simbal fighting back now out of pure instinct, the organism, in terror for its own life, cared nothing but to wrest control of the gun from Bennett. It had seen what one hollow-nosed bullet had done to a human being and it wanted nothing more to do with the working end of the Magnum.

Still on the dock, the Cuban had his pistol out. He could see Maria but he did not know how badly she had been hit. The shots had stayed him from leaping onto the cigarette. The three of them were so entangled that he feared his intervention would get Maria or Simbal shot.

A knee in Bennett's groin brought the pistol down far enough for Simbal's bloody fingers to slip over its slick metal surface. Simbal chopped blindly down, made another grab for the Magnum. It flipped over the side, making a heavy splash.

Bennett used his ham fists, locking the fingers together, bringing the combination down like a cudgel on the back of Simbal's neck. That was the end of it. Simbal had absorbed too much in too little time to recover. He went down in a heap and Bennett kicked him savagely once, twice.

Fumbled in a locker, drew out a Mack 10, trained the mini machine pistol on the Cuban who had started forward with the sound of the Magnum going into the water. "Sorry about the skirt, brother," Bennett said. "But you've only to blame this shit-for-brains for that." He let off a quick burst as the Cuban made an abortive move. "You're not as stupid as this one here," Bennett said. "So throw down the gun."

With one eye on Gato de Rosa, Bennett undid the mooring lines, then started the engines. A rumbling, liquid roar and he guided the black cigarette out of the dock.

When he deemed it far enough he put the boat into neutral, went back along the deck to where Simbal and Maria lay unmoving. Bennett reached out and lifted Simbal onto his shoulder. With an animal grunt he threw him overboard, said to no one in particular, "Don't pollute this rat-infested place too much." He spat into the place where the body had sunk.

Back at the helm, he turned the wheel hard over and, in a thick plume of phosphorescent spray, was gone.

The Star House in Causeway Bay was the kind of restaurant Bliss usually avoided. Great multifaceted crystal chandeliers floated above circular tables for eight or ten people. Ornate carved dragons rippled in lurid bas-relief along the gilt-flecked walls, and columns in the form of crimson-and-emerald phoenixes studded the interior.

In all it was the kind of out-of-the-way place that tourists flocked to simply because it wasn't in the Hong Kong Tourist Association guidebook and, because of its rather awesome décor, was believed to be frequented by the locals "who really know good food."

The two or three times Bliss had come here the food had been solidly mediocre. But this time was different. Each dish put before them was sparklingly fresh and absolutely delicious. When she commented on this, Big Oysters Pok laughed and said, "They all say that, everyone I take here. I like to see the looks on their faces when they walk in and when they take their first bite of *faahn*. The answer's quite uncomplicated. The chef is my brother-in-law. He cherishes my sister like no one else in the world. Therefore, he says, he owes me everything."

"How is that?"

"My parents are dead," Big Oysters Pok said.

"I see." As the head of the family, it was up to him to approve of the marriage. Obviously he had.

Tonight he was Big Oysters Pok, not Fung the Skeleton: pale oyster-gray linen suit, pin-striped shirt with a pastel blue background, midnight-blue raw silk tie. He was very dapper, difficult to recognize as the muscular, bare-backed smuggler she had met earlier in the day.

He said something amusing and Bliss laughed. He nodded his head, smiling almost shyly. He found himself liking her. She was unlike any woman he had ever met. She had the mind of a man and that intrigued him. He saw no weakness in her, only a shrewdness that made her flexible.

Occasionally Big Oysters Pok had run across the new breed of Western woman, tough as steel and about as appetizing. In pushing themselves into what was essentially a male arena they had hardened their souls. Male strength—the pattern which they followed with slavish devotion—had made them inflexible because they had mistaken an essential quality of

371

this nature. One learned strength in business by watching the work of the ocean against the rocks along the beach. The sea endured while the stones, over time, became smaller and smaller.

Bliss was so unlike these new Western mistresses of corporate entities it was startling. It was unlike him—so untraditional!—to find such strength in a female attractive. Yet he did.

Across the table, Bliss was not unaware of his change in attitude but she was unable to address herself fully to the shift. Part of her had slipped into *da-hei*, her *qi* strung out across the bosom of the South China Sea. Moonlight dappled the waves; the whine of powerful diesels far off yet carried in the water along with the long, drawn-out notes of the whales conversing pack to pack.

Annoyed at being drawn away from her mission, she made an effort to turn her back on *da-hei*. If she was to get the name of the woman who followed Jake, who knew of his appointment with Zilin, she knew she would need all her concentration. Big Oysters Pok was not just another smuggler of the tears of the poppy. He was a complex man. She needed to know what his quid pro quo was going to be for the information she sought—before he asked his price. That was the only way to deal with such a shrewd businessman.

"You seem to change personalities as easily as you change clothes," she said.

Big Oysters Pok smiled. "It is only a modest quality, not even a talent really. If I live many lives, I can have many loves."

So that is what he wants, Bliss thought. Me.

"I imagine it can be dangerous as well," she said. "Being so many people brings complications, doesn't it?"

He shrugged. "Perhaps that is one of the reasons I pursue such lives. Like smuggling there is a high degree of risk. I find that life has no meaning without such an element. Like Sichuan peppers, risk imparts an undeniable piquancy that is instantly identifiable."

"You could put a revolver to your head and play Russian roulette," Bliss said.

Big Oysters Pok laughed. "I've done that as well. On a bet. Or a dare. I got one of my boats that way. Very easy." He laughed again.

"About the woman who stole this opal," Bliss said.

Big Oysters Pok looked at her. "Do I get it back?"

She slid it across the table.

Big Oysters Pok said, "She was my mistress. Until I found out that she was meeting a Communist agent from the mainland."

"She was a Communist spy?"

"Yes."

Her eyes losing focus, night turning to day, the moonlight shimmering, a pathway leading her on, *da-hei* engulfing her, *Not now! I'm almost there!* The strange calling of the sea creatures blending into the pathway of light, intensifying the illumination until it transmogrified into a voice, calling to her . . .

—*Coming, he's coming*—

Who's coming?

—*He's coming, coming now*—

Big Oysters Pok turning his head, chopsticks clattering off the edge of the plate as he let them go. Big Oysters Pok trying to rise as Bliss sat enraptured by the ethereal voices in *da-hei*. Big Oysters Pok opening his mouth, saying, "*Dew neh loh moh* on y—"

Then the explosions, one! two! three! four! five! six! as the bullets landed.

Out in the night the fires were burning. In the Outback. Behind Ian McKenna's eyes. The green-headed fly tap-tap-tapping on the convex surface of the buggered boy's milky eye. Staring blindly up at the winking stars. In the desert. In the death of innocence, in time out of mind. When Ian McKenna went mad.

The string had been pulled then but his mind refused to believe it, to accept any responsibility for its own agonizing predicament. Rather it was the magic, the magic of the sparking fires ringing the Outback, the runic chanting that had ensorcelled him.

The wogs, McKenna had decided. It was the bloody wogs who wanted him dead, who insisted that he pay for his sin, his crime against nature. Aborigine or Chinese, it no longer mattered to McKenna. One and the other was blended in his mind in a kind of hideous amalgam, a larger-than-life figure that sought to humble him, to take from him his superiority, his very manhood.

The mind twisted by such torment sought the nearest target, the one who had most recently humbled it.

Big Oysters Pok.

Ian McKenna had been searching for Big Oysters Pok in every dive in Wan chai. Then someone in the Pink Teacup had reminded him that Pok invariably ate dinner at the Star House in Causeway Bay.

McKenna had walked in, his red-brimmed eyes staring wildly. He was quite mad but since they considered all *gwai loh* mad, the Chinese scurrying back and forth along the crowded aisles with food-laden trays held high paid him no attention. Even when he approached Big Oysters Pok's table at full speed.

Until he pulled out the Magnum .357 and, squeezing the trigger six times, emptied it.

And all hell broke loose.

"I have made all the necessary calls."

Eyes closed, his mind was floating in darkness, in nothingness.

"Jake-san, did you hear me?"

"*Hai*, Mikio-san," he said wearily. "I heard you."

Mikio settled himself across from Jake on the *tatami*. Across the room, Kazamuki, standing by the window, waited for Mikio's sign. He gave it, just a slight flick of his hand. She bowed slightly and left the room in such utter silence that Jake, tired to the bone, was not aware that she had gone.

"I have spent some time speaking to my contacts in the prefecture police," Mikio went on as if nothing had transpired. "You have nothing to fear from them, believe me."

"How did you manage that?" Jake said without humor. "We've left rather a mess in our wake."

Mikio ignored the impolite question. He was more concerned to see his friend in such emotional anguish. Jake's tone made it clear that he was immersed in self-pity. Mikio thought that was quite unlike him.

Mikio grunted. "It's been nothing compared to the war I've been waging the last few weeks. Do not concern yourself." Clandestinely, he peered at his friend, wondering whether the death of Jake's father was the cause of this despair.

They were in a large room by Japanese standards, in a large house by Japanese standards. But this was Karuizawa, the elegant resort so dear to the hearts of Tokyo's upper crust. Here amid wide larch-lined streets, within estate villas set back by exquisitely groomed lawns, the traditional elite of Tokyo came to relax and have fun.

Karuizawa was a resort with a split personality. Here in the old section, the Imperial family stayed, along with poets and artists, the older corporate heads. Not a kilometer away was the other side of the coin, where the new rich—the sons and daughters of the old monied class—strolled, dressed in the latest Fila and Ellesse tennis togs, swinging Prince Graphite racquets over their shoulders, splurging between sets at the trendiest boutiques. Here, the life-style revolved around the concept of see and be seen.

Only two hours north by car from the center of Tokyo, Karuizawa sat cool, clean and beautiful along the ridge of the Japanese Alps, the central spine of Honshu.

"We are close to the core of the Moro clan, Jake-san," Mikio said now. Concern darkened his face. Jake's eyes remained closed, his lips unmoving. "Jake-san."

"Have you any *saki*?"

Mikio considered a moment, then rose and fetched a bottle from the cedar sideboard. He returned with two tiny cups on a red lacquered tray. Only when he heard the trickle of the rice wine did Jake open his eyes.

Mikio handed him the cup. "I regret it is not hot."

Jake downed the *saki* in one convulsive gulp; Mikio, thoughtful, sipped at his.

"Pain," Mikio said carefully, "always seems hardest to bear when it dwells solely in the mind. I have been injured many times in my life, some badly, some not so. But the pain of all my wounds was nothing in the face of the pain I suffered when my wife, Kaziko, died."

He had never said how it had happened and Jake had had the good manners not to ask. As Jake refilled his cup, Mikio said, "I think because she died in childbirth, because both of us had labored so long to have a child, because, in the end, neither of them could be saved, their passing would not let me be for a very long time."

Jake was silent. His respect was more eloquent than a hundred thank-you's.

In a moment, Mikio resumed. "I tell you all this, Jake-san, so you will understand that I have had much experience in the matters of pain. So you will not take offense when I say that I see a similar kind of pain binding you."

Jake looked away into the distance. The immutability of the wooded hills was a comfort.

"You may have come here to find out who killed your father, Jake-san," Mikio said, "but it seems clear to me that you had another reason—just as personal. And, perhaps, even more urgent."

Jake finished off the rice wine and put his cup onto the lacquered tray. He did not reach for more. His hands, folded in his lap, were quite still. "I have lost more than my father, Mikio-san. I have lost—the center of myself. I can no longer enter *ba-mahk*. I cannot feel the pulse, as I have been taught to. Without *ba-mahk*, my entire life has changed."

"When the ocean's tide turns," Mikio said, "the world is altered. This occurs twice a day, many, many times in a lifetime."

"It is not the same."

"On the contrary, Jake-san, it is just the same. The tide is mighty. Even boats dare not sail against it. But as the tide changes, so do circumstances. Whatever changes must change back again."

"I do not think that my ability to enter *ba-mahk* will return."

"That may very well be, Jake-san. If so, it is your *karma*. *Joss, neh?* You must accept whatever has befallen you. You must accept it and go on. Because strength of spirit, unlike the strength of the tide, must not be allowed to ebb. Strength of spirit is all that makes a man. It is all that differentiates him from the animals. It is by this alone that man may consider himself civilized. This, solely, must be the focus of your thoughts. Even though the pain you feel hinders you—*especially* because of that. Because the spirit must remain strong always." He put down his cup. "Always, Jake-san. Or all is lost."

Jake was thinking of the mountain his father had spoken of a lifetime ago, or so it seemed, when they had sat on the shore of the South China Sea. Zilin had said that it was on the mountain that he would be tested; there it was dark and Jake was alone.

Jake knew that Mikio was right. Jake might have arrived in Japan in order to ferret out the identity of his father's murderer; to protect the inner circle; to help Mikio, his friend. But these were practical matters. There was the spritual side, as well. This, really, was why he had been so determined to return to Japan, the place where he had been educated. The baffling loss of *ba-mahk* had caused a crisis within him. He had needed a renewal of spirit, and sought it in the ancient, mystic hillsides of Japan where the true essence of his youth resided.

When he looked up, he saw Kazamuki standing just inside the door. She wore an oversize black blouse, loose black trousers, what appeared to be black thin-soled dancer's shoes. Her thick black hair had disappeared within a tight black cotton headband. Her face was streaked with lampblack.

"We are ready, *oyabun*."

"Good." Mikio Komoto rose and took the canvas bag from Kazamuki. He bent, opened the zip top, pulled out several items. He turned back to Jake and said, "No matter what has happened, you are still *yumi-tori*." The holder of the bow. He stretched out his arm. Jake saw that he held an *ouruma* wood war bow. "It is time that you took up your weapon."

Their eyes met. Gratefully, his heart filled up again, Jake took it from him.

The Burmese rain forest at five thousand meters closed over their heads like a vast cathedral. The triple canopy was brilliant with life, a teeming flow as rich as that of the ocean.

Sir John Bluestone said, "We have them now." His red face was aglow with good humor. "We've broken the *yuhn-hyun*!"

He sat behind a battered bamboo desk. It was a far cry from his own intricately carved Bangkok rosewood desk at Five Star Pacific. But that did not matter to him. This moment was special; to be savored like a wine of the finest vintage. The knowledge that he was close to controlling his enemies' business interests made him tremble, so that he was obliged to press his hands hard against one another beneath the desk.

"Now we have begun our run on InterAsia Trading." He was speaking of the *yuhn-hyun*'s umbrella corporation. "With the disaster of Southasia Bancorp nagging at our enemies, our move on the Hang Seng has had its maximum effect."

White-Eye Kao was not impressed. He went across the faded blue-and-gold Hereka rug and fixed himself a drink from one of several bottles scattered atop a half-open crate.

The view out the dusty windows, partly covered by tattered, yellowed newspaper, was full of Shan soldiers carrying AK-47s and burlap bags of opium. The sickly sweet stench of the refining of the tears of the poppy hung heavily in the air.

White-Eye Kao downed some Scotch, poured more amber liquid. He was waiting for the word.

"The idea is to gain fifty-one percent of InterAsia Trading before they have a chance to know what's happening," said a voice from the shadows.

It had come. White-Eye Kao turned into the recesses of

the room. He watched the small figure with the kind of avidity the other man could neither pick up nor understand.

"If Sawyer or Three Oaths Tsun get an inkling of what's going on before we have bought up a sufficient number of shares, *tai pan*, they could cause us discomfort."

Though he spoke only in the most deferential tones, Bluestone listened intently to the third man. He was Chinese. His age could be anywhere from fifty to seventy-five. His skin was smooth except at one corner of his mouth where a pale, puckered scar turned it down into a perpetual frown. Yet, despite this, he was a handsome man. He had the eyes of a twenty-year-old, undimmed by either time or ennui. He possessed, as well, a singular kind of electricity. He was not a man to cross. One disagreed with him only at great peril or when absolutely certain of the correctness of one's position. Chen Ju was a most implacable enemy.

"We are at a critical stage," he went on, "and I must reiterate: there is no room for a mistake. The cards we hold are fragile at best. At this moment, they give us a tremendous advantage over the *yuhn-hyun*, that is certainly undeniable. We must be vigilant to ensure that we maintain the advantage."

Bluestone unfolded himself from the scarred wooden chair. He felt obliged to show off every inch of his height in front of this particular Chinese. Bluestone, who was among the most pragmatic of men, nevertheless felt acutely uncomfortable in the presence of Chen Ju. Bluestone thrived on control, and control was the one thing he was unsure of with this man.

Chen Ju possessed more power than any other man Bluestone had met. In fact, for a man who clung to secrecy with such tenacity, Chen Ju's influence was staggering. Not one ounce of opium, Bluestone had learned on linking up with him, moved in or out of Hong Kong without his knowledge, consent and assistance.

What I could do with such an awesome shadow network! Bluestone thought greedily. How can I turn this partnership to my own advantage. I want what Chen Ju has; now I must see how best to wrest his power from him.

With an effort, Bluestone grinned broadly. "There is no reason to be so gloomy, my friend. We are almost home." He clenched his fist. "I can feel the noose tightening around that bastard Sawyer's neck. Have no fear, Chen Ju."

White-Eye Kao smiled but he was enmeshed within bars of shadow and therefore quite safe. It was a most secret smile.

It was Chen Ju who had trained him, set him on Sir John Bluestone as a spy.

"I have no fear," the scarred Chinese said. "Have a care." He stared at the tall Englishman and thought, Never in my wildest imagination would I have believed that I would be in league with a *gwai loh*.

It was hatred that bound these two men together—hatred for Andrew Sawyer. Once Chen Ju had been Barton Sawyer's most trusted comprador. Andrew's father had been an extremely talented businessman. It was his expertise as *tai pan* of Sawyer & Sons that had made the trading company flourish. His expertise and Shi Zilin's.

Chen Ju clenched his teeth at the memory. If not for Shi Zilin's intervention, Chen Ju himself would have eventually become *tai pan* of Sawyer & Sons. Shi Zilin and Andrew Sawyer had taken from him that which had been rightfully his. Before Shi Zilin's coming, Andrew Sawyer had been totally unfit to become *tai pan*.

The Sawyer & Sons name was a total misnomer. Though Barton's *tai tai* had birthed him three sons before she had died, the eldest had died in a boating accident, the youngest had been born an idiot and had mercifully failed to live beyond his fifth birthday.

That left only Andrew, despite his father's great dream of founding a dynasty of Sawyers. Seeing that Andrew was obviously unfit to carry the burden of the trading house on his shoulders Chen Ju had gone to his *tai pan* to suggest an alternative.

"If I had no sons at all," Barton Sawyer had said, "you know that you would have to carry on after I'm gone."

"I am only thinking of the house, *tai pan*," Chen Ju had said.

"I know that."

But Chen Ju had also been thinking of himself. He wanted to be *tai pan*. After years so close to the power source, after all that time whispering advice in Barton Sawyer's ear, he craved status above that of comprador. He craved, too, to turn Sawyer & Sons into an Asian trading house. It was only in this way, he believed, that the company could compete effectively for the spot of the emperor's house—the name traditionally given Hong Kong's most respected trading company.

In Chen Ju's mind Andrew Sawyer as *tai pan* would take Sawyer & Sons from the running for all time. Therefore, he set out to prove to his *tai pan* that he had been correct about Andrew's unfitness.

He conceived a plan to introduce Andrew to the daughter of Jiu Ximin. This was very amusing to Chen Ju since the girl's father was a labor organizer and fully seventy percent of Sawyer & Sons' labor force came under his jurisdiction. He was not a man with whom Barton Sawyer could afford to be at odds.

Yet that was surely what would happen if Andrew were foolish enough to start seeing her. It was one thing for the son of a *tai pan* to visit a brothel and there have his needs assuaged by women of the pillow world. They might even be Chinese. But to see a Chinese girl in the open without having an intention of marrying her was unthinkable.

It was Andrew Sawyer's ultimate test, and he failed. The eldest daughter of Jiu Ximin was an exquisite flower indeed. Chen Ju had chosen well. She had a face that would have set a blind man on fire.

All went as the comprador had planned until Shi Zilin had once again stepped in. Unbeknownst to Chen Ju, Andrew had gone to Shi Zilin seeking aid. And Shi Zilin had provided it. He had mediated with the girl's father and had gotten Andrew off the hook before Chen Ju had been able to go to Barton Sawyer with the sad news about his wayward son. Suddenly there was no news to bring and, to boot, Shi Zilin was tutoring the young man in the ways of the *tai pan*.

Chen Ju never found out what precisely Shi Zilin had exacted as payment but it must have been substantial, for the debt was large.

In any case, that was the end of the road for Chen Ju at Sawyer & Sons. He would never be *tai pan* now and, increasingly, Shi Zilin was usurping what power remained to him. He left.

"Have a care," Bluestone echoed now. He grunted. "You sound like my grandmother. I know enough to take a scarf when I go out in winter."

"Yes," Chen Ju said, "but do you wrap it around your throat?" He clasped his hands on his rounded stomach. "I have waited a long time to exact my revenge. Do you suppose that I will allow someone else to assure me that everything is all right?"

"What could go wrong now?" Bluestone wanted to know. "The old man, Shi Zilin, is dead. His son, Jake Maroc, is God only knows where. Three Oaths Tsun is busy with the mare's nest of the takeover threat we've given him. With Neon Chow we have a direct pipeline into the *yuhn-hyun*. And the only other *tai pan* we need fear, T. Y. Chung, has just negotiated a partnership with me." He spread his hands as if to say, What more could you want?

Yes, Chen Ju thought, T. Y. Chung. You seek to subvert him just as you will seek to subvert my own power. But you are nothing next to me, *tai pan*. I have contrived to reveal to you only a fraction of my power. It would dazzle you if you ever caught a glimpse of its real extent. "Maroc may be out of our sight," Chen Ju said, "but I for one do not see that as a cause for celebration. Just the opposite, in fact."

"Have a care," Bluestone said, mockingly.

"Precisely, *tai pan*," Chen Ju said, as if he were too dense to have caught the other's tone. But inwardly, he thought, This arrogant *gwai loh* needs to be shown his place in the world. "Jake Maroc is Shi Zilin's son," he went on. "He is the *Zhuan*, the chosen one. Do you think that means nothing?"

Bluestone shrugged. "It is a name only."

"In China, *tai pan*, I need not remind you that there is power in a name," Chen Ju said evenly, reining in his temper. "Jake was given that name by Shi Zilin. Do you think the old man was a fool? If so you have already embarked upon a dangerous course."

"I have nothing to fear from Jake Maroc," Bluestone said, thinking of Neon Chow at the center of Shi Zilin's *yuhn-hyun*.

Chen Ju was out of the chair and at Bluestone's side in a blur of motion. The look in those black, predator's eyes made Bluestone's mouth go dry. "You are in partnership with me now." Chen Ju's whisper was like a serrated blade at the *tai pan*'s neck, so much menace did it hold. "I will not tolerate stupidity. You have underestimated Jake Maroc in the past. If you cannot learn by your mistakes, you are of no use to me."

The rage Bluestone now felt—that of the civilized Westerner against the primitive Easterner—threatened to overwhelm him. White-Eye Kao felt it and tensed, rising on the balls of his feet, ready to spring into action. One blow would be sufficient to fell the tall Englishman.

Chen Ju, aware as well of how deeply his words had cut into Bluestone, waited a moment, then made a clandestine hand signal. White-Eye Kao relaxed.

"You control your emotions almost as well as a Chinese," Chen Ju said to Bluestone. "That is one lesson you have learned well." His eyes bored into Bluestone's. "Can you learn this one as well, I wonder?"

"Maroc." There was a thickness to Bluestone's voice. "I will not underestimate him."

Chen Ju cocked his head. "Remember what you have pledged here, *tai pan*. When you walk out this door, there will be no one to remind you."

"InterAsia will soon be mine to run. This is *your* pledge to *me*," Bluestone said, pulling himself together with an effort. "That knowledge alone will break Jake Maroc."

"Yes," Chen Ju agreed. "InterAsia for you, Kam Sang for me." Oh, but he is greedy, he thought. And that greed blinds him to the truth. He is too stupid to see where the true power lies. Like all *gwai loh*, he is attracted to that which glitters, not that which abides.

"Equal partners, eh? A fair split of the spoils," Bluestone said, thinking, I can afford to be generous, I've got the better of this deal.

"Exactly, *tai pan*," Chen Ju said. Without me, he would be no closer to control of InterAsia than the man in the streets of Hong Kong, he thought. It was I who maneuvered South-asia's comptroller into embezzling the corporation's assets. The man gambled incessantly. He was a chronic loser. It was easy to direct him to people in my employ. Easier still to threaten his wife and children so that he would see that he had no choice at all. He did what I wished. I gave the information to Bluestone and now after he gains his fifty-one percent control of InterAsia Trading, he will be content. The fool! The world is in the palm of his hand and he is not aware of it.

"As long as I know what Kam Sang is all about," Bluestone reminded him. This is what General Vorkuta is dying to learn, he thought. What a coup for me to get it for her. Chen Ju knows nothing of my connection with Moscow Center. And I must ensure that he never does. Knowing the Chinese, he would turn on me instantly were he to find out that I am the KGB's top operative in Hong Kong.

Chen Ju smiled. "Rest assured when I know Kam Sang's secrets you will as well."

"We both desire the destruction of Andrew Sawyer," Bluestone said. "Without Sawyer and Sons, Five Star Pacific will become preeminent among Western-directed trading houses in Hong Kong."

But I desire much more, Chen Ju thought. Already I look beyond Hong Kong, beyond all of Asia even. My mind encompasses more than any other Chinese before me. And Kam Sang will deliver it all to me.

I wonder what this *gwai loh* would think if he knew who I really was and what I have been doing all these years since the war. He laughed inwardly. In a way, it was the war which shaped my direction. Ironic, isn't it, that the war which brought so much destruction upon China and Chinese should have provided me with the basis for my future. But then, I wasn't in China at all in those days.

Bluestone's desire to see Andrew Sawyer toppled precluded his looking carefully at my own motives. My *joss* is good in that. He wanted to believe in me—in what I could provide him—and so he did. Better for the both of us in the long run, at least as far as I am concerned.

"Well," Chen Ju said now, "all the wheels have been set in motion. Tomorrow or the next day perhaps Southasia will collapse. Our buying of InterAsia shares will continue as the price falls on the Hang Seng. Then the entire *yuhn-hyun* will be ours." He stood. "For now, there is nothing more to do." He smiled amiably. "Would you care to join me for dinner, *tai pan*?"

"Of course," Bluestone said. "It will be a delight."

Shadows in twilight. Three black ravens caught up in the darkling lane. Past two long Mercedes limousines that Mikio whispered had been especially manufactured for Hige Moro, the *oyabun*, with half-inch armor plate and built-in tear gas dispensers. Quite illegal, of course, Mikio whispered, raven to raven, but who was to stop him. Not the police, surely.

Three swaying cryptomeria, one for each raven, the shadows beneath deep enough to shield them in their black garb from even the most vigilant eyes.

"Hige Moro runs the clan," Mikio had said, "but he has three brothers, all younger than he, to whom he has parceled out sections of the Moro territory. This was the express wish of their father who, it is said, before he died, detailed this unorthodox method of organizational design 'so that like the legendary Hydra the Moro clan will have many heads, many lives; so that it cannot be destroyed by willful enemies.' "

Three black ravens creeping through the shadows of the

underbrush that surrounded the huge, tiered villa of the Moros.

"But it is Hige Moro whom we must confront. Only he will know the truth of why you are being hunted here. The others are useless to us."

"I think it would be better if I went myself," Jake said. "I am affiliated with no clan and therefore my attack can engender no retaliation. You already have enough to think about with your war with the Kisan clan."

"On the contrary," Mikio replied, "Hige Moro has broken faith with the Yakuza code several times. He has attacked you, my friend, on my territory. He has also tried to kill Kazamuki and myself in the bargain. Hige has only himself to blame for what may befall him now. None of the other clans will lift a hand against me or even you."

Night enveloped the villa like the hand of Buddha. Fireflies darted here and there, bobbing above the vast manicured lawn like tiny fishing boats upon the ocean. The ravens moved through them like gargantuan wraiths, silent as gods.

Mikio held his *katana* before him. Its scrollworked sheath had been left behind in their car. Tucked within the crook of her elbow, Kazamuki carried a Hado miniaturized machine pistol. It was capable of spewing out a hundred rounds per second and was air-cooled with a boron muzzle to prevent overheating.

"This must be done very fast," Mikio had said as he spread out the floor plan of the Moro villa, "if we are to get at Hige. The longer it takes us, the higher the odds become. He will be here, in the center of the house, which was constructed for his father and is something like a maze."

"Are we certain of Hige's exact location?" Jake had asked.

Mikio had nodded. "Kazamuki has seen to it."

The first line of defense was the dogs. Jake saw the gleaming black backs of the Dobermans as they came bounding over a copse of azalea, pruned into a massive hedge. He drew back on the war bow and let fly, allowing his mind free reign, moving effortlessly through *kata*, the phases of *kyujutsu*: *ashibumi*, the balanced archer's stance; *dozukuri*, the centralizing breathing; the raising and lowering of the bow with the draw of the arrow, *uchiokoshi*, *hikiwake*; *kai*, the sighting of the target; *hanare*, the release. And the final *zanshin*, the most critical aspect as the archer's spirit follows the arrow's humming flight.

The lead Doberman went down without a sound and Mikio

stepped forward as the second one, growling deep in its throat, leapt upward. The *katana* flashed, its fearful shades of steel cleaving through the neck of the careering animal in one clean stroke.

They moved on, past the hedge of azalea. The heady scent of roses and jasmine laced the air. Mikio signed to Kazamuki, who moved off toward the rear entrance. Ninety seconds later he glanced at his watch. A night bird called, then again, and he said, "It is time. She is in place."

Jake removed a steel-tipped arrow known as *tsubbeki-ne* because of the odd, chisel-shaped head. He notched it. "Now!" Mikio said softly and Jake released the tension.

The arrow struck the front door, splintering wood, shattering the old-style iron lock. Mikio was already running up the front steps, crashing through the broken door. Jake was just behind him, his hand reaching back, notching another arrow, letting fly in almost the same motion the *rinzetsu*, the dragon's tongue, piercing the heart of an oncoming Yakuza guard.

There were three more. Mikio felled two with upward, downward strokes of the razor-edged sword. Another dragon's tongue punctured the neck of the third Yakuza.

They heard the unmistakable *burt-burt-burt!* of the Hado and knew that Kazamuki was in. She would not penetrate to the heart of the villa but stand guard to assure that Hige could not escape out the back.

Jake and Mikio went quickly through the rooms. It was imperative that all the Yakuza in the villa be accounted for and dispatched. None left alive would tolerate an attack on their *oyabun* so there was no choice.

The click of a safety being thrown off and Mikio whirled, slashed up and out. A young man, half-dressed, screamed as his extended arm was cut in two. Mikio struck again and the Yakuza collapsed.

Two bare-chested men, their *irezumi*—tattoos—rippling in the low light, rushed from the right side. Jake loosed two arrows in a blur and the men were flung sideways, *katana* clattering away.

They rushed through the villa. The *burt-burt-burt!* came again, this time in a longer burst. Mikio had shown them the best route to Hige's quarters but it was essential that they check every room.

There was one arrow in Jake's quiver kept apart. This looked like none of the others; its tip was three times the size. It was known as *watakushi*, the flesh-tearer. Such was the destruction its tip caused, even an inexpert marksman could kill his foe with it. In the hands of a *kyujutsu sensei* such as Jake, the *watakushi* was a weapon of appalling proportions. This terrifying missile was for Hige Moro.

They found him in his quarters, along with four of his guards. Mikio, using the seven stones cut, struck two of them down immediately. The third convulsed in the attack stance with a dragon's tongue through his belly.

The fourth man struck at Mikio, parried Mikio's blows in expert fashion. He began his own counterattack and with every blow it seemed the tip of his *katana* came closer and closer to piercing Mikio's flesh.

In this manner, his confidence grew. Fed by his success, this confidence grew into aggression and, then, the beginning of triumph as he saw his blade flick against his foe's skin, drawing blood.

He redoubled his attack, which was precisely what Mikio had been waiting for. Mikio performed the air-sea change, abandoning one strategy for another. In that breathless moment when Mikio's strategy was hidden from him, the Yakuza was made vulnerable.

Using the red leaf cut, Mikio penetrated his defense and, deflecting his *katana* away with a clang, stabbed forward with his entire spirit. The man was dead before he hit the floor.

Now there was only Hige Moro, a bullet-headed man with salt-and-pepper hair in a crewcut so short his scalp shone through, and the tip of the flesh-tearer, drawn to the edge of the *ouruma* wood war bow.

Mikio Komoto said, "This is the man who you have been set to kill. I think he wants an explanation, Moro-san. An explanation for why you seek his death, for why a *dantai* of your clan murdered his father, Shi Zilin."

Moro looked from Mikio's face to the shining tip of the *watakushi*. "He is *iteki*, a barbarian. He is nothing," Moro said.

"This man is *kyujutsu sensei*, Moro-san," Mikio said with an edge to his voice. "He is *yumi-tori*, a warrior of rank. I urge you to reconsider."

Moro spat.

"You must be prepared to kill Hige Moro," Mikio had said to Jake. "Torture, humiliation will mean nothing to him. If we invade his home, kill his men but leave him alive, he will laugh in our faces and spend the rest of his life hunting us down."

Jake loosed the flesh-tearer and Hige Moro screamed. He jumped or, rather, his body flew backward. He was literally lifted off his feet as his breastbone cracked. Impaled on the spike of the arrow's haft, Moro was slammed against the back wall.

Jake threw down the bow, crossed the room to where Hige hung, suspended in agony. He grabbed his jaw, slapped his cheeks to get the blood back into the white, white face.

"Why did you kill my father! Tell me! Why!"

Hige coughed. There was blood in his mouth. "I was paid," he whispered.

"Who? Who paid you to kill my father?"

"A man . . . a man named Huaishan Han."

Jake thought, A Chinese? "Who is he?"

"I don't—" Hige coughed again and this time blood fountained from between his lips. "Someone on the Mainland. A minister of the first rank."

"A *Communist* Chinese?" Both Jake and Mikio were incredulous. "You were in the employ of the Communist Chinese? But why?"

"I told—told you." Hige's head lolled, his eyelids fluttered closed so that Jake was obliged to pinch his earlobes to get him to regain consciousness.

Jake repeated his question.

"Money," Hige said. "The money they . . . paid made my clan the wealthiest in Japan."

"For our deaths?" Jake was shouting now. He felt the texture of the mountainside sliding away from him. Darkness rose up on all sides, an unearthly chill rode down his spine. "I know the Communists. They wouldn't pay that much for our deaths."

"Oh, no," Hige said, and now he was making a peculiar kind of sound that seemed like that of a barking dog. In a moment, Jake was appalled to discover that it was laughter. "No. Not that at all. They paid us more money than you could ever imagine."

"For what?" Jake screamed into his face. Covered in the Yakuza's blood, he grabbed Hige's shirtfront, butting their heads together. So close to lifting the darkness from the mountainside his father had told him it was his *joss* as *Zhuan* to climb. The *shan* was shaking from the impact of what Hige had revealed. Jake thought of his father, of the time they had

387

spent together. So little time! Death and the end of that contentment, to sit beside the old man, to absorb his genius, his love, his humanity. It was a grief too much to bear. Tears in his eyes. Of rage, frustration and despair. "Tell me! For what?"

"Only the mountain . . . the mountain knows."

"What!" Jake's hair stood on end. The mountain? What did this Yakuza *oyabun* know of the mountain? "What mountain? What do you mean?"

But now even that hair-raising laughter had ceased. Hige Moro's eyes stared unblinking at Jake. The spirit, already released from the cooling flesh, held greedily to its last enigmatic secret.

Huaishan Han returned from Hong Kong a hero. At least Hong Kong is where he told Zilin he had been. If he had been, as he had intimated before his departure, as far as Taiwan, he gave no indication of it.

Though he had seemed intensely concerned with Senlin's health before he left, he did not ask how she had been when he arrived home. Neither did he thank Zilin for taking care of her. In fact, he seemed to have forgotten that he had asked a favor of Zilin at all.

He had been in Peking some hours already, having reported first to Lo Jui-ch'ing and, then, to Mao. He showed them the medal that Mao himself had presented in what Huaishan Han called "a small, elite ceremony."

Privately Zilin wondered why he had not been summoned to the ministry to be present at this "small, elite ceremony."

Senlin wanted to know what her husband had done to deserve this signal honor; Huaishan Han replied that he was not at liberty to say. But after dinner, when the two men took a stroll in the garden, he told Zilin.

"I saved Mao *tong zhi*'s life." He was bursting with it. He fairly shouted it out. To Zilin, it was like getting slapped in the face. Confucius said that pride was held dear only by the wicked. It was antithetical to his Five Virtues: Justice, Benevolence, Politeness, Fidelity and Wisdom.

"This is not a matter to be trumpeting in public," Zilin said.

"Why not?" Huaishan Han said. "How many men can say they performed such a deed, eh? Precious few."

Zilin had noticed that over the past six months Huaishan Han had begun to answer his own questions. "That is an even better reason to keep such knowledge to oneself."

"No, no. That is precisely the attitude we must do away

389

with. The atmosphere is filled with patriotism. We are marching on Korea, you know. 'Resist America and Aid Korea' is our new national campaign. It is sure to catch the spirit of the people, don't you think?"

Zilin said nothing. He knew when he was being asked a rhetorical question. He thought of the people of China, tired, sick, still nursing their wounds, burying their dead from the long, arduous years of war. There wasn't one of them, he'd wager, who wanted this war. But, he reminded himself, he himself had argued for it. It had become a political necessity. But that did not mean that he liked what he had to do. He saw the overriding need for it, how the future good of China would be served by it. But that did not negate the deaths and suffering that would be engendered by it. He shuddered inwardly and, not for the first time, wondered how long his conscience could bear the weight of the wailing spirits.

Already the dead rose up in his dreams, wrapping their skeletal arms around Athena and Mai, keeping them from him. He was used to speaking to the spirits of his wives in his dreams. Like a balm smoothed on the wounds inflicted during his long days, these conversations served to, at least temporarily, soothe his own tortured spirit. But for some time even that little surcease had been denied him.

Babbling wraiths and cackling demons conspired to haunt his nighttimes until sleep itself began to fill him with dread. And when at last, exhausted beyond endurance, he did fall asleep, sitting up, an open book in his lap, he dreamt of the spring night, four twenty-four, at the lip of the spirit well. *Die and die again.* To awake with a start, a heavy lurch of his heart, his eyes wide and staring about as if to pin some intruder to the wall.

But there was no one in the villa. No one but himself.

"The people need direction, a renewed energy," Huaishan Han was saying. "They need to put their hearts and minds into winning this war in Korea, the war here at home. There is much to do, Shi *tong zhi.* We are out to change the world, after all. That can be no easy task. We require unswerving dedication from every comrade."

"We need money as well," Zilin said soberly. "All the good intentions in the world will avail us nothing unless we find the capital somewhere to fund Mao's reforms. It will not come from our economy. As of now, we have none. We are barely able to feed our own people, let alone finance the industry we must have in order to survive." He was wondering, if they were successful in Korea, how Stalin would choose to pay the enormous debt he would owe them. It occurred to him that perhaps they would get less than they anticipated.

"Money, yes," Huaishan Han said, meditatively. "There is much talk of money at the ministries."

"So much," Zilin said, "one might almost think we were turning into capitalists." He laughed but his friend did not follow suit.

"There is nothing amusing about such a thought," Huaishan Han said somberly. "There are powerful enemies who seek to infiltrate our new power structure. They are all capitalist-roaders, or are you so unaware of recent developments."

"Oh, I still keep in touch," Zilin said somewhat ironically. "I have not retired in your absence." But he was thinking of the Soviets. In the future, he believed that Moscow, not Washington, would stand as China's implacable enemy. For Stalin—as for the Soviet leaders who would follow his iron fist—there could only be one form of Communism. He saw how any deviation from the Moscow line would be viewed as heresy, a potential threat to its design of world hegemony. In Moscow's view, there could be only one eventual winner in world ideologies.

And, in a way, Mao's road was more dangerous to the Soviets than capitalism. At least with Washington, they could point the finger at the rich man's exploitation of the working class, the poor. But the same could not be said in China. Here, the differences were more subtle, and therefore, more difficult to dismiss or deal with. And the Soviets' strong suit, Zilin well knew, was not subtlety.

In the stifling night, a cuckoo sang and then was still. Strings of lights could be seen over the top of the wall that enclosed the garden. The cicadas droned, an all metallic symphony. The thick bed of peonies that Senlin happily tended each day perfumed the thick air.

"It is good to be a hero," Huaishan Han said. "It is important to have heroes in a country in transition." He sounded as if he were trying to convince himself. Self-importance had become more and more precious to him ever since he had joined the State Security Forces. Zilin remembered the conversation with Mao. *We will be forced to depend more and more on the Ministry of Public Security*, Mao had said. *The secret police*, Zilin had corrected. *If you would call them that, yes.* And Zilin had said, *I cannot condone a reign of terror.*

Was that why he had been excluded from that small, elite ceremony?

Abruptly, he said, "How did you save Mao's life?"

Huaishan Han took a cigarette out of a chased silver case, tamped its end on the burnished top. The case was not Chinese, Zilin saw, but rather of Western manufacture.

"Where did you get that?"

Huaishan Han either did not hear the question or preferred to ignore it. He pocketed the case and lit up. He smoked for a while. When he had assured himself that he was in control of the conversation's pace, he said, "In Hong Kong, I discovered a plot on Mao's life. That, in fact, was why Lo Jui-ch'ing dispatched me on this mission. 'You are the only one,' he said, 'who we judge capable of successfully carrying out such a difficult assignment.' "

Zilin was not impressed. He knew Huaishan Han was lying since Mao had already told him that it had been Mao himself who had been sending Huaishan Han on his last several missions. Including this one.

Zilin wondered why his friend was standing here, lying to him when he could have been inside with his wife, whom he had not seen in almost two months.

Huaishan Han continued to puff on his cigarette, the smoke drifting from his half-open lips. "Our intelligence was correct," he went on after a time.

"And so you returned home, the triumphant warrior," Zilin said with an edge to his voice, "to claim your prize."

"But not alone," Huaishan Han said with a little smile. "I brought with me the enemy."

"The enemy?"

"The capitalist who was masterminding the operation to assassinate Mao *tong zhi*. He is my prisoner."

"Can you see it? The ocean. I can see the whole expanse of it, the moonlight shining on the surface, the motion making tiny pinpoint spotlights that I can feel as well as see. They're hot as an open fire."

Senlin opened her eyes, stared into Zilin's face very close to hers. "Do you see it? The ocean, I mean."

"No."

"Why, I wonder?" She peered down through the shadows the stand of moso bamboo cast them in. She turned their hands over. "I thought if we touched . . . if we were linked in some way . . . you would be able to see it too."

392

"But I can't," Zilin said. "This is your talent, Senlin. Not mine."

"No," she said firmly. "It is ours." She recalled the opening of her spirit at the moment of the clouds and the rain, when he was deep inside her. She wondered if she was wrong, if, indeed, a more intimate connection of the flesh was required. "I am certain of it. I had no sight—at least a sight of this kind—before I met you."

"You mean before I took you to Fazhan."

Her eyes fluttered closed at the mention of the Black Hat *feng shui* man. She was so exquisite, he thought. So frail of body, so strong of will. The combination recalled to mind the translucent vases from out of his country's past. And he thought, Beauty is its own strength.

"No," Senlin said now. And that was another thing. She knew her own mind. "I would not try to deny what happened to me that night. I know better than anyone what was pulled out of me by Fazhan's incantations. The spirit of Hu chao, consort to the last of the Ming emperors."

"Evil may be called by many names."

"You think Hu chao was only evil?" Senlin sighed. "Her spirit was a twisted, hideous thing. Made so by the evil that had been done to her. Evil entered her and she was consumed by it. Evil destroyed her body but it also corroded her spirit."

"And how came this evil spirit into you?" Zilin said, half mocking.

"The Soongs have a long history," Senlin said steadily. "Perhaps Hu chao was my great-great-great-great grandmother."

"It is not even certain whether she had any children," Zilin said.

"Then she was reborn in me."

This talk of spirits and possible reincarnation disturbed him. He was a Buddhist; he was in tune with the land, with the rise and fall of *qi*. These were no mysteries to him; neither were they magic. They merely were.

Feng shui—geomancy—was one matter, this was another entirely.

"Either way," he said, "the evil is gone."

Senlin, hidden within the bower made by the rustling of the high bamboo, was struck by slivers of dark and light. "The evil, yes." They moved across the exquisite planes of her face. "But something remains." Like moonlight across the face of the ocean. "Something calls." Brilliant pinpoints, sparking like lightning play in the crests of the endless waves. "Can you tell me what?"

He could feel their heat upon his flesh, ten thousand minuscule fires burning. Appearing, disappearing, reappearing, the sprinkle of stardust.

Calling?

Opened his mouth but no sound coming out, vibrations that carried from him to her and, thence, outward onto the spangled bosom of the ocean.

Where are we?

Beneath the rushing water, the deep cool currents running, scissoring each other, whirling, carrying along the universe of diverse life that breathed water instead of air. The songs of the whales, calling, calling, the echoes reverberating upon them, rippling flesh that was no longer flesh, playing upon skin that was invisible.

And then Senlin and Zilin came together in a way that was wholly different from the way they had merged before. And far more intimate. In that moment of ultimate fusion, he knew that she was right. Somehow this was not she, not he, but a result of both. The music they heard, saw, scented, felt, was the harmony of their *qi*, playing one upon the other, twining . . .

. . . becoming whole.

The war in Korea ground on. The first fantastic swell of early Chinese victories brought a kind of euphoria, elevating the internal morale of a country that had taken a beating in the war and now, suddenly, found for itself a kind of world-wide prestige. Where before, the Chinese soldier was an object of ridicule after suffering one defeat after another, suddenly the nations of the world were tendering a measure of respect for China's new-found military prowess.

As China's fortunes in Korea blossomed, so did the young career of Mao's elder son, Mao An-ying. Whether it was the boy's talent or, perhaps, some canny commander's subtle plot to advance his own career, Mao An-ying was promoted to serve at the field headquarters of the Second Chinese Army.

American bombers overflying the perimeter unloaded on the encampment like squatting beasts, destroying all who plotted their defeat there. Mao An-ying was no exception.

The news was brought to Mao as quickly as possible. But, as one may imagine, there was some delay as soldiers under frantic orders combed the stinking, smoking debris for signs of life. A general at last made the identification of Mao's elder son.

"War," Mao would tell Zilin sometime later, "is like bitter tea. The fortification it brings is tempered by the taste of ashes it leaves in one's mouth."

"This is evil, what we do."

"Does it seem so to you?"

"Yes."

"Then we must end it."

She let out a deep groan, her forehead pressed against his chest. "I cannot."

Zilin stroked the raven's-wing cascade of her hair. In the moonlight, it appeared as if silver thread were laced through it. He thought of the boundless energy of the sea.

"Your husband," he said. "Does he ask questions about your health?" He never used Huaishan Han's name when he was with Senlin.

"He sees me eat, he sees me go outside," she whispered. "That is sufficient for him."

"Do you talk?"

"Sometimes, yes."

"And . . . touch?" Now it was his turn to whisper.

"Do you mean are we intimate?"

He nodded, wordless.

Senlin put the palms of her hands on his chest, pushed her head away from contact with him. Her black almond eyes peered at his as if they could pierce the shadows of their enfolding bower. "My answer, I think, is more important than the question, *neh*?"

Women, Zilin thought, are so much wiser than men in ways their male counterparts do not even know exist.

"Would you believe me if I told you that whether I tell the truth or lie to you it is the same?"

"No."

"But it is." She put her palm along his cheek. "There is no difference."

"The truth," he said, "differentiates itself from all else. There is no ideal in this imperfect world but that. The truth."

Senlin spread her arms wide. "But the truth does not reside here, in the world around us. It is in *da-hei*, in the great darkness within which all spirits reside. The only truth is what occurs when we are together in *da-hei*."

"Then you *are* intimate with him."

"You have no right to ask the question."

"No right?"

"He is my husband, not you."

"Cruel to say."

"But it is the truth." She looked at him. "The truth is your god, not mine." Her fingers stroked his face. "I do not want to hurt you. Instead, you have hurt yourself."

Zilin closed his eyes. "It could not be avoided."

"No," she said. "Not if you were determined to unearth the truth."

The truth, Zilin thought. She was quite right. It *was* his god. It was no good blaming her for his own frailty. He searched inside himself, cleansing himself of his anger.

When he opened his eyes, he thought of Huaishan Han's cigarette case. Not for the first time. He had only been afforded a glimpse but he was certain there was something about it that was familiar.

He took hold of Senlin's hand and, thinking of the truth, his master, he said, "I want you to do something for me."

More than a week passed before she was able to bring it to him. For one thing, Huaishan Han was out of the city for part of the time and he took it with him. For another, he was covetous of it, even at home. It took some doing, then, for Senlin to spirit it away and then it was only for a couple of minutes.

The cigarette case of Western manufacture.

Of course Zilin had had to convince her. "He is my husband," she said. "You are asking me to plot against him."

"You are already involved in a plot against him," he pointed out.

"He is your best friend," she said. "Why are you doing this? Friends do not plot against one another."

Zilin looked out at the larch and pines beyond the perimeter of their stand of bamboo. A crescent moon much like the one that had risen that night on the four twenty-four rode thin cumulus, breaking them apart upon its sharp horns like gossamer.

He thought about what the Communists had done to Senlin. He wondered if Huaishan Han knew what had happened to her at his former master's hands. He thought not. Why would she have told him? And Huaishan Han would never have asked.

"It is not friends I think of now," he said. He spoke as

much to himself as he did to her. "It is China. You told me some time ago that you thought the truth was my god. Well, perhaps that is so. But it is China for which I toil. I would gladly give my life to ensure its future."

"Why do you fear for China's future?"

How to explain it all to her? How to make her see that he was a celestial guardian of his country? "Who controls China," he said, "may one day control all of Asia. If China makes a mistake, if it falls into the wrong hands or comes under evil influence, there may well be no turning back. China is so massive, its peoples so multitudinous that once policy is set, it is difficult to change. China has its own momentum, and it is the momentum of a behemoth.

"China needs a guardian. Someone to ensure that it first survives, then prospers, and finally, becomes powerful. A *Jian*."

Senlin stared at him for a moment before she said, "You?"

"I do only what must be done."

"But how can you?" she asked. "You cannot see the future."

"No," he said. "Mostly I work in the dark."

"Then you must make mistakes, you must regret some actions."

"Some, yes, perhaps," he conceded. "It is regrettable but, I fear, unavoidable."

Her fingers stole along the inside of his wrist until they wrapped themselves around his forearm. "But no more." Her voice was only a whisper. "No more."

"What?"

Her face was very close to his. He could smell the sweet scent of her, like jasmine and honey. "You have *da-hei* now. *We* have *da-hei* now. The great dark."

"What are you saying, that it is possible to see the future there?"

"Perhaps, yes," she said, softly echoing him.

He gave a little laugh. "Then surely *da-hei* has foretold that you must bring me your husband's new silver cigarette case."

"Yes," she said seriously, "it has."

"That is preposterous, Senlin."

Suddenly her grip upon him tightened. "Listen to me." Her low voice was urgent. "I ask you not to do this. I plead with you not to ask me."

"I don't see why. You can always refuse."

"I cannot."

He contrived to laugh again. "You can resist me nothing?" But it had a hollow ring to it.

"Only partly," she said. She pressed herself against him so that he could feel the triphammer beating of her heart. Instinctively, he put his arms around her as if to protect her. From what? "You seek the truth," she said in his ear. "I must bring it to you."

"And if you do?"

"It would be better—far, far better—if you would leave the truth unearthed this time."

"Why? What do you know about that case?"

"Nothing," she cried suddenly, and clung to him. "I see."

"What?" he said. "What do you see?"

She was weeping openly now, her tiny white teeth biting into the flesh of his shoulder.

"Senlin," he said, "what is it you see?"

She gave a great shudder and said, "The end."

But, true to her word, she obeyed him. And once again betrayed Huaishan Han. She brought Zilin the cigarette case.

"There is little time," she said, as she hurried up to where he was waiting within the bower of bamboo. "Huaishan Han has just returned from Buddha only knows where. He sleeps now before dinner. But soon he will awake." By her tone as well as her words she made Zilin feel that he was enmeshed in a children's fairy tale. He could remember such an American story he had read in English class at the university in Shanghai. "Jack and the Beanstalk." Hadn't there been a character in the tale like Huaishan Han? The ogre.

Zilin took the case from her, looked at it carefully. Its chased silver filigree caught the watery light of the waning day. It was familiar, he was certain. But why?

He turned it over, saw the silversmith's frankings, saw that it was made in the United States. Ripple of shock, like ice water in his face. He had suspected it of being English.

Turned it back right side up and opened it. A tiny worked-silver spring lever kept Huaishan Han's vile black Russian cigarettes in place. Something on the inside of the lid caught Zilin's eye and he angled the case away from him to pick up what light was left in the umber sky.

Saw initials carved into the silver in masculine serifed English letters: R.M.D.

And—perhaps it was *da-hei*—knew it all: why Huaishan Han had lied to him from the first about his mission, why he had refused to answer Zilin's question about where he had gotten the cigarette case. Most terrifying of all, he knew who Huaishan Han had brought home, trussed like a pig to the slaughter, the mastermind behind the plot to assassinate Mao.

Zilin felt the pain in his heart and slowly, slowly, brought his forehead down until it touched the shining, chased top of the cigarette case of Western manufacture.

In the streets of Peking, Shanghai, the communities of Canton and Hunan, in the endless paddy fields, bamboo forests, along the banks of the twisting Yangtse—throughout all of China—the tramp of uniformed, booted feet could be heard.

The nights became a time for listening. For the scrape of the metaled heel on hallway boards, the sharp rap on the front door, the shouted commands. Confusion and the trickle of fear as one's neighbors were pulled from their beds and without explanation were spirited away into the heavy mist, the rumble of the engines fading slowly, held in the air by the fog.

Without its inhabitants ever having felt the transition, China had become a land of repression in which a reign of terror swept across its length and breadth in an all-encompassing net.

In every city, Huaishan Han had devised the creation of urban residence committees, consisting of groups of perhaps one hundred households. The same was true in the countryside, where each *hsiang* or agrarian administrative committee oversaw the daily control of paddies and farms.

These units, Huaishan Han argued, were essential for controlling the vast population. Further, they were easily infiltrated by members of the State Security Forces apparatus. Thus, in every level of Chinese society dwelled spies for the Ministry of Public Security. And, thus the tramp of the booted foot at night, the sharp orders, the unexplained disappearances.

"We have only to look at the French Revolution," Mao said to Zilin. "Or, if your prefer, a more Eastern reference, the Marxist Revolution in Russia, to find your historical antecedents.

"We are in a period of infancy. We have torn down the old, the corrupt, the degenerated. In its place we are building a new country from the roots up. Our first order is to build the power of the state machine because it is the engine without which China will lie dormant.

"The traditional enemies of the forces of restoration are historically civil war from within and foreign invasion from without. It is the Americans we have to fear the most, Shi *tong zhi*. It is the Americans who we oppose in Korea, the Americans who continue to pour money and war matériel into Nationalist coffers, the Americans who have made a protectorate of Taiwan.

"They do all this, Shi *tong zhi*, because they fear me. And because they know that their protectionism binds the Nationalists to them. Without American aid, the Nationalists are nothing. Yet they fail to see that, either way, they are nothing. For now, with the American aid, they are merely capitalist puppets. They do the American president's bidding in every way or they are threatened with a cessation of aid."

Mao paced the small room like a caged tiger. "The counterrevolutionary foment has already begun, fueled by the Nationalists and the Americans. If the Americans can invade Korea, the next step could very well be China. This we must ensure never happens."

"And repression is the only way?" Zilin asked.

"Read your history, Shi *tong zhi*," Mao said shortly. "It is the only sure way." He grunted. "No one takes kindly to reeducation. People often do not know what is best for them. That is for leaders to decide."

"It is for leaders to impose."

"Yes, indeed," Mao agreed, apparently oblivious to the sarcasm in his adviser's voice.

Zilin called for tea to be brought in and, when it had been served, sipped at it meditatively. "What is being done with the prisoner Huaishan Han brought back from Hong Kong?"

"What?" For a moment, Mao appeared confused. To cover, he made an elaborate show of pouring himself tea, staring into the swirl of tiny leaves at the cup's bottom. "Uh, oh. Yes. I forgot for a moment that you and Huaishan Han were so close. Yes, well." He downed some tea, frowned as if he did not care for the taste. Nevertheless he poured himself some more. "Nothing has been officially decided as yet. I am considering how best . . . to use the spy. We must make an example of him, of course."

What was most odd, Zilin thought, was not so much Mao's uncharacteristic beating around the bush, but that his eyes had not lifted to meet Zilin's once since the topic had begun. Mao, who had a most direct manner about him, who used

400

his piercing gaze as a weapon to disarm those who sought to oppose him even in the most incidental of matters.

"Why are you so interested in this man?" Mao asked.

"I want to interview him."

"I don't think that would be wise," Mao said. Something in his cup had his undivided attention. "He is the property of the State Security Forces. This is not your province."

"It would be if you gave the order."

"That would not make Lo Jin-ch'ing happy. It would, further, come under review by K'ang Sheng." Mao was speaking of the Chinese Communist Party's chief of secret police. "How would I explain such a thing to them?"

"Since when did these people wield such power?" Zilin felt anger rising within him. "I am your personal adviser. I have always gone where I wanted, when I wanted."

"Times have changed, my friend," Mao said.

"Then I, too, am under scrutiny."

Mao shrugged, acceding the point.

Zilin was appalled. *Times have changed, my friend.* How had they changed so far, so fast without him being aware? Then, with a great sadness, he understood that none of these changes had happened without his being aware of them. They had been incremental, yes, but he had been there at their inception. He could have opened his mouth to protest; could even have insisted that there was another way besides the institution of the vast network of informers, harsh-minded policemen who ventured out at night like spirit demons to pull in unsuspecting citizens because they were too well educated or had the wrong family name or perhaps spent one solitary hour beyond the prying eyes of the Ministry of Public Security.

Zilin was all too familiar with Beria and the NKVD. He abhorred the Russian's devotion to iron discipline and repression, an apparatus that went beyond interfering with one's choice of religion, way of life—to the very thoughts one had locked inside oneself.

He was to blame for this fully as much as Mao or Lo or Huaishan Han. So much suffering for a people who had suffered for so many years, first at the hands of its own emperors, then its secret societies, and lastly, the long invasion by the foreign devil. By now one would think that the people of China were well used to being exploited. Perhaps it was their *joss*.

No! No! How could he think such a thing. But the future

was bleak, indeed. He felt as if he were on a vast mountain-side, struggling up its face in the cold and the dark. It seemed that he no longer could remember what lay for him upon its snow-rimmed summit.

"I must interview the prisoner," he said.

"Why are you insistent on wanting something that I cannot grant?" Mao wanted to know. He looked wounded.

"I ask out of our long-standing friendship," Zilin said. "I do not ask that you remember what I have sacrificed for China or, even, how I have helped you over the years. This is not a matter of politics or of power. I stand before you only as your friend. In this light I beseech you to allow me one hour with the prisoner."

Mao turned away and, as he went across the room, Zilin noticed for the first time how bowed his shoulders had become. Mao stood looking out at Tienanmen Square, where the machines of war sat idling, prepared for the dreaded counterrevolution that rode above all their heads like a barbarian's sword.

"Soon," Mao said, "it will rain." He watched the fat black clouds scrolling across the low sky, and closed the window a little even through the heat. "Tonight," he said, "the sky will open." And then, without a change in tone, "You'll have half that time."

"They picked me up in the mountains," Ross Davies said, "a tiny encampment on a plateau a mile-and-a-half up in the Shan States." The Shan States. Burma. Not Hong Kong, as Huaishan Han had said.

"I had been there six months or more. It was the poppy fields that made us think of it."

"Us?"

Davies's cracked lips split in a smile. "You don't expect me to tell you that, do you, old friend?"

"Why not?" Zilin said. "I'm dead, aren't I?"

They both laughed at that, remembering the lengths all of them—Davies, Huaishan Han and Zilin—had gone to ensure Shi's "death" would be convincing to Chiang and his lieutenants.

Inwardly, Zilin was appalled. When the pass that Mao had written out for him had let him into the State Security Forces prison, he had been expecting to find his old friend—R.M.D.: Ross Marion Davies—with his long shock of curly reddish-gold hair, bright blue eyes, boyish face.

What he confronted was, instead, a thin, lanky, leather-faced man with eyes so bloodshot and swollen Zilin could see only the barest sliver of washed-out blue in their midst. Gone entirely was the open boyish grin, and the nose that had been patrician straight was chopped and bruised, so swollen it covered fully a quarter of his face.

"I was in the Shan States because of the poppy fields." When he spoke, Zilin could see how many teeth he was missing. "The thought was to infiltrate and to gain control."

"Of the refining."

"Yes."

"What would that bring you?"

"Money, for one thing," Davies said. "Great gobs of money." He sat on a rude wooden stool that was bolted to the floor. He gripped the bars that rose between them with fingers swollen by disease or torture, it was impossible to say which. "For another, we felt that eventually it would give us control of the entire area as well as a way to infiltrate further afield."

"To assassinate Mao."

"What?"

Zilin watched Davies's face very carefully. Without being fully conscious of what he was doing, he dissolved a portion of himself into *da-hei*. In that night-black space, he found that he could distinguish truth from the lies. There were "colors" attached to both, separate and distinct colors that he could see.

"That is what I have been told. By Huaishan Han. That you were preparing a plot to assassinate Mao."

"That's not true."

Davies was telling the truth. Zilin nodded, took out a pack of cigarettes, passed them through. He lit one for his friend, watched as his face relaxed as he puffed.

"Christ, I haven't had a decent one of these since Hector was a pup."

"I am sorry they're not the brand you are used to."

Davies waved away the apology. The smoke drifted through his scabbed lips, seeping through the bars, seeming to dissolve them in undifferentiated grayness.

"I was there a long time," Davies went on as if they had not gotten off the topic. "A lifetime." He exhaled slowly, luxuriating in the tobacco. "Got to know the local honchos real well. Well enough to know that we'd never be able to take control."

"The Shan hate the Americans, the Russians as well."

Davies looked at Zilin oddly. "Let's cut the crap, okay?" he said suddenly. He dropped the butt, ground it out under his horny heel. He had to slip off the paper slippers he had been issued to do it. "We both know why it's impossible for the Americans—or anyone else for that matter—to get a toehold up there in the mountains."

"Tell me," Zilin said.

"Don't insult my intelligence," Davies said disgustedly. "I thought that you, at least, I could trust."

"Then humor me." They stared at each other for what seemed an eternity. "Please."

"Because, old friend, you control it all: growing, harvesting, refining, distribution."

"Me?" Zilin was startled, and showed it despite himself.

"You, Mao, Huaishan Han. You goddamned Chinese."

"That is idiotic!" Zilin said, stunned. "I don't believe you." But of course he did. He had to. In *da-hei* he saw the color of truth. Then, concern wrinkling his face, "I know nothing about this."

Davies watched his face as before Zilin had studied his. "Yeah, well." He turned, put the pack of cigarettes carefully away beneath the corner of his bare straw mattress. "You mean you don't know which one is behind it? It's not Mao?"

"I do not know," Zilin said. But he was hearing Mao telling him, *We must make an example of him, of course.* That would be Huaishan Han talking. His power was growing daily with that of Lo Jui-ch'ing and K'ang Sheng. Was this the source of their power? Or was it Mao's? Buddha! "Tell me," he said now, "were you able to find out the name of the man who runs the poppy fields in the Shan States?"

"He calls himself the Naga, you know, the Burmese mythological serpent. His organization is known as the *diqui*. The rest, I'm afraid, you'll have to divine for yourself." He gave a little rueful smile and a hint of his former self shone through the blackened skin of his recent travail.

Zilin heard a rustling behind him. The guards were coming, his time was up. He began to rise and Davies reached out a hand. There was some fear in the American's eyes as if he felt that with Shi beside him nothing untoward could befall him.

"What will become of me?" he asked.

"I do not know, my friend," Zilin replied. But he did know. *We must make an example of him, of course.*

"Will I see you again?"

Zilin looked down at Davies, who was still seated on the wooden stool. He seemed not to have strength left to get up and Zilin thought, What are they doing to him here? He remembered what the Communists had done to Senlin and wondered whether these people, those under Huaishan Han's command, were any different.

"Tell me," he said, "were you with the American Secret Service years ago, when we first met?"

Davies put his head against the bars and Zilin could see the patches of bald, discolored scalp, as if in these places his thick, richly colored hair had been burned away. "Does it matter?"

Zilin shook his head. "No," he said truthfully. "Not at all."

"He knows!"

She was like a frightened doe, trembling in fear.

"It is important that you be clear about this. Does your husband know or does he suspect?"

"He knows. I think he knows."

Sinuous stratus, tinged with the pink-orange-sienna of reflected light, the sun sinking into the cool blue mountains to the west. A pair of plovers winging their way across the dusty strands of sunlight, their feathers burnished gold for a moment, before they were gone. The scent of almonds in the air, reminding him of cyanide. He had seen a man die of cyanide poisoning once, a spy who had failed, his operation compromised, capture imminent. Not only capture but torture and, finally, a longed-for death. Bit through the capsule in his mouth.

Zilin looked away, to the cyan hills. "If you believe that, then you must leave."

"Leave?" She seemed bewildered. "Where shall I go?"

"I will protect you."

"He is my husband. I cannot leave him."

"On the contrary, Senlin," he said. "You left him long ago."

"Hold me," she whispered. "Will you hold me?"

Zilin put his arms around her and she ducked her head inside, lay her cheek against his chest. Her hair swept down across her face so that she seemed lost to him. He wondered now why he had begun this affair. He had known—always known—that it would come to this one day. Such liaisons ended this way without fail.

But he knew that he did not want it to end. With a tiny

start he realized that he was not prepared to give Senlin up. He wanted to make her happy. At this moment, that wish was extraordinarily important to him. It was as if by doing this he would be expiating all his sins. He would ease a conscience made dull and heavy by the wailing of all the dead, all the injustice, all the terror. And he might even atone for the necessity of leaving Athena, his second wife—Jake's mother—and Sheng Li, his mistress, to fend for themselves during the war.

He knew he was putting much weight on one act, the happiness of one human being. Perhaps too much. But Senlin was special. Was he the only one who saw that? Certainly Huaishan Han did not.

Huaishan Han. This had to do with him as well. Zilin's conscience was burdened by Huaishan Han. Without Zilin, the man would not be here now and perhaps this hideous reign of terror might not be happening.

But even as he thought it, Zilin knew it for a solipsistic thought. This reign of terror had not been thought up by Huaishan Han, and he knew deep in his heart that it would have occurred with or without the man.

Still, the evil that Huaishan Han perpetrated was plain enough. And there was the matter of the Shan. Perhaps only the mountain knew who was organizing the reaping and distribution of the tears of the poppy, but Zilin could not believe that Mao was involved. Mao longed only to be out from under the thumb of Moscow. The war in Korea, as Zilin had argued, was a difficult but definite way out. If Mao was raking in such enormous amounts of capital from the sale of opium would he have needed to involve his country in a dangerous war? Zilin thought not.

On the other hand, Lo Jui-ch'ing, K'ang Sheng and Huaishan Han had most recently emerged in the power hierarchy of the new government with an appalling amount of influence. How had it happened? Was the mountain, the Shan, partly the cause? Zilin thought it reasonable to think so.

Against him, Senlin was weeping. "It is ending," she said, "just as I saw it would."

"No," Zilin said. "This time you're wrong." But the scent of almonds was still strong on the air.

He reached upward and snuffed out the moon. Now the velvet night enfolded him. Thick clouds rode across a wheat-colored moon that was almost full. Rain was in the air, coming from the southeast. The barometer was falling, the indolent air becoming heavier still.

Zilin used the pass Mao had signed for him. He had spent an hour-and-a-half reworking the date and the result, he felt, was more than adequate. The State Security Forces prison loomed dark and forbidding. It was off the square, in a new building whose design and construction had been supervised by the Russians. Consequently, it squatted ugly, already dilapidated, old when it should have been young. It was surrounded by a phalanx of newly planted plane trees. There was an army tractor and two troop transports parked in front. All the vehicles were empty. At this time of night, the square was deserted. He pulled his official car over and parked.

He was passed through by three sets of guards without incident. But it wasn't getting in that concerned him; it was getting out.

At night, the prison staff was cut by two-thirds. That was principally because the upper floors were currently being used for administrative purposes and high-level staff meetings.

The prisoner was not in his cell, he was told by the cellblock division leader. He was being interrogated. Was this usual? Zilin wanted to know. The division leader, whose name was Chu, said yes. It went on all night.

"When does the prisoner sleep?" Zilin asked.

"He does not sleep," Chu said without much interest. "This is part of the interrogation process."

Zilin shoved the paper signed by Mao in Chu's face and said, "Take me to him."

"This is most irregular," the division leader said. "Perhaps I should check with Huaishan *tong zhi*."

"I come from Chairman Mao. Why don't you do it right and call him," Zilin said with heavy sarcasm. "I'm sure he would appreciate being woken up to answer such a pressing procedural question."

Chu looked doubtfully from the slip of paper to Zilin's face. Then he nodded. "This way," he said.

The hallway smelled chokingly of disinfectant. It merely masked the stench of feces and urine. Bare light bulbs set in wire cages hung from the concrete ceiling, providing mean illumination. Their shadows flickered in front and in back of them as they moved down the hall.

Chu stopped and rapped on a metal door with a wire grille set into it at head height. After a moment someone spoke to him through it. They were let in.

407

The vile smells assaulted him. Three uniformed men were taking turns with Ross Davies who was squatting, naked, in the middle of the square room. A battery of lights were trained on him. There was an odd, vitriolic buzzing in the room and Zilin looked around. One of the interrogators was holding an electric prod. As Zilin watched, the man pressed the tip of the prod against Ross Davies's pale flesh. There was a blue-white arc, a strangled gasp of pain, and a whiff of smoke, stinking from charred flesh.

"That is enough!" Zilin commanded. "I have come for the prisoner."

"By whose authority?" the man with the electric prod said defensively.

"Mao *zhu xi*," Zilin said.

"It is true," Chu said, waving the paper with Mao's name affixed to it. "This minister is on the Chairman's personal staff."

"Give him his clothes," Zilin said, knowing that this had to move fast now, very fast or they would spot the flaws. "Get him dressed. Not in prison attire. Mao *zhu xi* wishes to interrogate the prisoner himself."

Two of them had to help Davies on with his clothes. His hands trembled and he did not trust himself to look in Zilin's direction.

"Do you need any assistance, Comrade Minister?" Chu asked when Davies was ready. "I can spare two of my men."

"No," Zilin said, "that's quite all right, Chu *tong zhi*. I can manage him."

"Are you quite certain, Comrade Minister?" Chu inquired, holding the door to the interrogation room open as they passed through. "I do not want to think of what would happen should the prisoner escape."

"Look at him," Zilin said, supporting Davies. "The man can hardly walk a straight line let alone attempt to overpower me. I take full responsibility."

"As you wish, Comrade Minister."

Three checkpoints and they were passed through each one. Outside, in the still night, Davies let out a tiny sigh. His head rested on Zilin's shoulder just as Senlin's had earlier that night.

"Just a few steps farther, old friend," he whispered in Davies's ear. "We're at the car now. Can you get in?" Davies nodded, disentangled himself from Zilin's embrace, slid himself painfully onto the passenger's seat.

Zilin went around and climbed in. He started the engine and pulled away from the square.

Even years later, when the memories still haunted him, he was unable to say just what it was that led him to Xiang shan. The huge park was nestled into that area of Peking known as the Fragrant Hills. It was only afterward that Zilin remembered the old name for the place: Hunting Park.

Perhaps it was because Zilin always loved this park. It had a stream running through it which originated in a limpid pool high atop Gui jian chou Shan in the west.

In the twelfth century there was so much game in these forests that the emperors made it their personal hunting ground. But by the middle of the eighteenth century the greedy emperors had depleted the stock so completely that Manchurian *ma lu* had to be imported so that the hunting could continue.

The place within Xiang shan where Zilin brought Ross Davies was Shuang jing, the Villa with Two Wells, in the southern end of the park. Here there was both shelter and water, though one of the wells, the deeper one by far, was covered over with a rusting corrugated iron cap.

Zilin stopped the car at the entrance to the park and they got out. With Zilin's assistance, Ross Davies limped past the bronze lions, guardians of Xiang shan, on what used to be known as Mai mai jie, Tradesmen's Street. There were still remnants of the shops that once proliferated here.

It seemed an inordinately long way to the Villa with Two Wells but it was well screened even from within the park. This was only a temporary resting place. In the morning Zilin would have to move Davies on. But where? First things first. *We must make an example of him, of course.* He could not let that happen. Spy or no spy, Davies was his friend. His life meant more to Zilin than a dress espionage trial ever could to the new China. The present regime would soon forget that Ross Davies had ever existed; Zilin could not.

He set Davies down, gave him water, made him as comfortable as was possible.

"Why have you done this?" Davies said. His face was streaked with dirt which had run in the runnels of his sweat and blood. "I was certain I'd never see you again."

"You are a barbarian," Zilin said softly. "What do you know."

Davies smiled and closed his eyes. "I thought the Shan was bad," he said. "It was worse in there," he said. "Much worse."

Zilin said nothing as he squatted next to his friend. Perhaps, he thought, it is important for him to talk now because he could not before.

"I thought that they had prepared us well for . . . all eventualities. But now—now I think that even they did not know what would happen to us if we were captured."

There was a deep-throated rumbling from the southeast. The rain was on its way. Zilin looked up, past the tiled roof overhang. There was no illumination in the low sky save a dull electric reflection from the lights of the sleeping city. He thought of the brilliant blue-white electric arc of the prod, the smell of cooking flesh, Ross Davies's flesh, and was glad at what he had done.

"I don't know," Davies said as the first drops pattered onto the villa's roof, "how I got here. This is a long way from Virginia. A long way from home." He put his head down between his drawn-up knees. "I feel like I'm on another planet, and I think—I think, absolutely, that is the worst part. Dying so far from anything familiar."

"You're not going to die," Zilin said, shifting a little to get out of the rain, which was coming down harder now. He remembered the wild ride they had taken along the Jinyun Shan. He took out a cigarette, lit it, put it between Davies's lips. He thought it was good that Davies's parents wouldn't see him this way.

"I am afraid," Davies said, not smoking at all. "I am afraid to die. I would have tried to kill myself in my cell between interrogations but for that. It is a mortal fear. What will happen to me afterward? Will I drift in nothingness? Will I feel the cold? Will there be anything at all?"

"I am a Buddhist," Zilin said. "There is no heaven, no hell."

With an uncoordinated jerk, Davies turned his head. "Then what?"

"A beginning," Zilin said. "Life—our life—is only the beginning of a cosmic journey. And who may say where it will end. Life is to be fought for. Every moment. But death is not to be feared, my friend."

He reached out, took the faltering cigarette from between Davies's lips, sucked in some smoke. He exhaled, gave it back.

Davies looked at him. "I am so far from home."

"Forget about America," Zilin said. "China is your home now."

Davies put his head back, took a long drag of the cigarette.

A noise, a sharp sound from the shadows beyond the well, and Zilin lurched to his feet. Saw a figure staggering toward the villa. Took a step forward, rain cascading over him, then another and another until he was near the covered well.

"Senlin!"

She hurled herself over the last few meters, into his arms.

"Ah, the lovers!"

Zilin knew that voice well. Huaishan Han. He appeared from out of the copse of trees, the hunter bringing his prey into the killing ground.

"The loyal Chu called me after you left," Huaishan Han called as he advanced on them. "He is a very thorough man, Chu *tong zhi*. Suspicious as well. I told him to keep you under surveillance until I arrived." He smiled but there was no humor in his face. "Now I am here."

Zilin looked down at Senlin, who was shivering uncontrollably against him. It was very dark and the rain swept away what clear vision there might be. A clap of thunder, darkness and then a spit of lurid lightning illuminated her bruised and battered face.

"Senlin, what—!"

"I told you he knew," she sobbed. "This is my punishment. He hit only my face. I think there are broken bones. That is what he wanted. 'Everyone must know your shame!' he shouted as he beat me. 'For the rest of your life, you will be known by what you have done!' "

Zilin, speechless, hugged her to him. He kissed her face while she whimpered.

"For this?" he said, in time. "For this?"

"Not only for my infidelity," Senlin said. "But also because I carry a child in my belly. It is your child."

Stunned, Zilin watched, detached, as Huaishan Han gripped Senlin's wrist.

"Give her up, traitor!" His eyes blazed. They had the flat, opaque quality endemic to ideologues. Once Zilin would have bet on Huaishan Han's conversion to Communism. That was what motivated him to change sides, wasn't it? No, no. Now Zilin saw Huaishan Han for the clever opportunist he was. Moving from Nationalist to Communist served Huaishan Han well, and that was all he cared about. That was why he had involved himself with the tears of the poppy. Money and a widening power base: these comprised the ideology to which Huaishan Han subscribed.

Huaishan Han placed the blade of a knife at the side of

411

Senlin's neck where the carotid artery pulsed. "Give her up unless you want to see her die."

Zilin unwound his arm from around Senlin. Watching for that split instant of relaxation in Huaishan Han, he ducked down and forward, butting his head against the other man's stomach, bulling him backward.

Huaishan Han grunted as his spine was jolted by the edge of the iron-capped well and the knife spun from his nerveless fingers.

Zilin put his hands together, slammed them down onto Huaishan Han's sternum so that the other doubled over in pain. Lifted him by crotch and hip, the rage, long held neatly in check, boiling over in a fever. Threw him upward.

Huaishan Han landed heavily on the center of the iron lid. Already rusted through by the elements and decades of neglect, the cap gave way. Huaishan Han shouted and, reaching desperately out, regained his hold on Senlin. She went down with him.

Shouting into the storm, Zilin scrambled atop the well, shaving skin off his knees and shins. The odor of the ages assaulted him. He could see nothing, only feel a hand, fingers grasping for his. Reaching to his limit, he held on to skin made slick with sweat and slimy condensation.

Whose hand was it? Huaishan Han's or Senlin's? In the darkness and the storm he could not tell.

Then the bosom of the moonlit ocean opened up to him and he was within *da-hei*. He heard the calling.

I will destroy him. He felt the voice. *I must destroy him. Let go. Let go.*

No! He cried silently. *No!*

There is no other way. He is killing me.

Hauling on the hand. *No!*

I will not let him kill you as well. Let go, I beg you.

Senlin! Stars dancing in weir light off the bosom of the ocean. *I can save you!* And he reached out, not with his hand or even his mind but with his *qi*, his extraordinary *qi*, until he found her, grasped that essence of her with which he had merged so many times.

And merged with it one last time.

Senlin.

It is the only way!

Then he let go of the hand.

* * *

412

Time out of mind. Minutes—or was it years—later he crawled down from atop the ruined well. Beneath the dripping villa's overhang, Ross Davies was sleeping. Zilin crawled inside, out of the cold and the damp and the utter blackness. He put his arms around his drawn-up legs and shivered violently.

It was only then that he smelled the nauseating scent of bitter almonds and, turning his head, saw the top of the bitten-through hollow tooth, saw his friend's torn, breathless lips a deep, unnatural shade of blue.

IV

EXISTENCE
VIVARTASIDDHA

MIAMI/MOSCOW/HONG KONG/
SHAN/WASHINGTON

"He's ghosted."

"What?"

"Ghosted, dude. You know, gone. The motherfucker's gone."

"Bennett?"

Martine Juanito Gato de Rosa cocked his head. "You think I got all the water out of your lungs, dude? Maybe I missed some."

"Whoa! Any more mouth-to-mouth," Tony Simbal said, "and I might fall in love with you."

It was dark down there, and cold. Simbal had never been so cold in his life. But thank Christ for the cold; that was what had revived him. Without the cold he would have dropped like a stone to depths that the Cuban could not reach without a set of artificial lungs. Simbal shivered, still feeling the effects of the cold and the dark.

The Cuban's topaz eyes opaqued. "What a fuckin' waste." He sat with the gray blanket emblazoned with MIAMI METRO POLICE in black stenciled letters. He'd flashed his credentials at the cops who had come in response to some citizen's irate phone call and, after taking cursory statements, they had left, sirens screaming to the site of a real disaster, a hotel fire downtown. The paramedics had worked on Simbal's cuts and abrasions. They had wanted to take him to the hospital for tests and observations but he had refused. "Maria wasn't like the mean bitches you usually find down here, holding on to the fringes like dogs to a bone. She had a useful mind."

In the cold and the dark there was no breath. That was the thing that gnawed at Simbal's mind still. No air, no life. He imagined the lungs ceasing to work as the cold and the dark crept in, trickling down the nostrils, between the tightly clenched teeth until it became a tide. Drowning. He shivered heavily again and pulled the rough police blanket around him more tightly.

"Look at my suit," the Cuban said. There was real mourning in his voice now. "I might as well throw it in the incinerator, all the use I'll get out of it now. You know how much this bastard set me back?"

"Shut up."

"What?"

"I said shut up. The Company paid for that item, didn't it?" He meant the CIA.

"Well, yeah."

"So stop bitching."

The Cuban put his head down. "It's not the motherfucking suit, dude. Shit, man."

Simbal was trembling, aftershocks following the quake.

"That *hijo de puta* turned his gun on her and blitzed her out. Just like that. It takes a cold, cold heart to do it, I'll tell you. A voodoo spook is right."

"Martine, shut up." But he was listening to the Cuban very closely now, trying to interpret a feeling.

"Why for you tell me to shut up, man," the Cuban said in an aggrieved voice. "Who d'you think dived in, with all the sharks and shit, and pulled you out."

"No sharks that close in, Martine."

"You never heard of poetic license, dude? *Madre de Dios*, I save your unbelieving hide from a watery grave."

"And I appreciate it, Martine, really I do, but will you kindly, for Christ's sake, keep your yap shut for a minute."

The Cuban looked out at the lights bobbing across the marina. "That's no way to show your appreciation, man."

"You say Bennett's disappeared."

Gato de Rosa was watching the water. "Ghosted, dude. Like the tide."

"Maybe not," Simbal said.

The Cuban turned to look at him. "What do you know that I don't."

"Run-Run Yi."

"The Chinatown Yi? One of the three brothers who run the *diqui* in New York."

"The same. I spotted him at the party. He and Bennett were talking."

"So?" The Cuban shrugged. "Ain't that what parties're all about?"

"Not this one," Simbal said. "Remember what Bennett

said? He wasted Alan Thune. Run-Run Yi was Thune's big booster within the *diqui*. Word I got was that Yi was putting Thune up for a big promotion."

Gato de Rosa's topaz eyes opened wide. "And you think . . ."

Simbal nodded. "If something was wrong with Thune, chances are that same thing is wrong with Yi. Who knows, maybe the two of them were skimming or, even, planning to go into business for themselves."

"If you're right," the Cuban said, "we find Run-Run Yi and we'll find Bennett as well because Bennett's here to ice him."

"My thought precisely."

The Cuban rose, shed his blanket. "Let me make a couple of calls. Someone's gotta know where Yi is staying."

Someone did.

"The Yak says Run-Run's booked into the Trilliant on the Beach."

"The Yak?"

"Listen, *hombre*, if you had as much hair as this dude, they'd call you the Yak as well." His fine cream-colored silk suit was an unholy mess, crinkled and bagged at knees and elbows. "Let's get us some dry duds." He held out his hand. "Then find Yi." He pulled Simbal to his feet. They were standing very close. "Wherever this bastard goes now, I'm going with him."

"Bennett's my objective."

"Not anymore," the Cuban said. "Not after this."

The Trilliant lived up to its name, a fiery jewel of a place, so modern its triangular pyramidal shape was dizzying. Between its melon-colored sloping façade and the ocean, an enormous triangular lagoonlike pool with a central island dotted with palm trees was lit up like an airport runway.

Gato de Rosa grunted as they pulled up and a uniformed attendant took over the fire-red Ferrari. "Wait'll you get a load of their golf course," he said. "The back nine packs quite a kick. The trap on the seventeenth hole's got more than water in it. It's got a fucking croc, too." He laughed shortly.

Emormous pale pink flagstones led up to the glittering smoked-glass and brushed-bronze entrance. Plantings of palm, azalea and bougainvillea flanked either side.

"First class," Simbal said.

"Yeah," the Cuban said, "if you can stand this shit for more than an hour."

Inside, the air conditioning took their breath away.

"Jesus," Simbal said, "where's my parka?"

"Whassamatter," Gato de Rosa said, "you got something against freezing to death?" He went over to an industrial-size marble-topped credenza upon which were sitting a line of pink dialless telephones. He picked up a receiver, asked for the number of Run-Run Yi's room. The operator would not give it to him and he did not want her to ring the room.

He sauntered over to the reception desk, waited for the swarthy-skinned concierge to get off the phone. Gato de Rosa called him softly over, transferred a twenty into the man's waiting hand. The bill passed between them with the kind of mysterious adroitness shown at a magician's convention. They spoke in Spanish for less than thirty seconds.

In a moment, Gato de Rosa was back. "What d'you expect," he said in a moment. "Thirty-seven-oh-one-and-two. Top-floor suite. That's five bills a night."

"Who said crime doesn't pay," Simbal said as they headed for the bank of burnished-bronze elevator doors. Each was emblazoned with the triangular pattern that was the hotel's logo. It was woven into the custom carpeting along the lobby floor.

"Your paisan say whether old Yi was in?" Simbal asked.

"He thought yes."

"Any visitors?"

The Cuban looked at Simbal with some skepticism. "Come on, he's the concierge not Superman. The Trilliant's a goddamned big place. A truckload of Marines could come in and he might not know it."

"But at least you determined yours was the first bribe he'd taken tonight."

Gato de Rosa laughed.

The sight of Bennett stepping out of one of the elevators cut it short. *"Hijo de puta!"*

The lobby was jammed with guests in glittery outfits. Music was blaring from off to the left and the general flow of the people was in that direction. A late floor show at the nightclub. The amount of diamonds on display would have made even Murph the Surf salivate.

Bennett was making his way against the flow of the crowd. He seemed in no hurry and hadn't bothered to look behind him. Like most madmen he was very confident. Simbal and the Cuban started after him, shouldering their way through the Nipon and Ungaro dresses, the After Six tuxes. Clouds of Norell and Chanel No. 5 clung to them.

Bennett disappeared through a side door and they picked up their pace. Through the doors they found themselves in a concrete corridor. The floor was covered with Astroturf. Affixed to one wall was a sign that said: NO SWIM SUITS ALLOWED IN THE LOBBY and Simbal said, "Shit!," breaking into a sprint. He remembered what the Cuban had said, that Bennett never went anywhere not accessible by boat.

They went through glass doors that opened at their approach, skirted the lighted swimming pool. It was as large as a ballpark. Past the lip of the vast concrete apron on which over a hundred lounge chairs were neatly arrayed in precise rows, were set a flight of wide stairs. They were dusted with sand and they went down them three at a time.

In the glow from the pool lights they could see Bennett already at the water's edge. As Simbal watched, he plunged into the surf and came up with a twist of his head. Hard, powerful strokes took him past the crash line. The Cuban went into the water after him.

Moments later, Simbal caught sight of the sleek black cigarette bobbing at anchor.

"Goddamn it!" he said and began to run back toward the hotel.

The double mahogany doors to the suite were unlocked. Run-Run Yi lay on a sea-green sofa that wrapped around the living room. His flat Cantonese face was white as rice paper. His chest fluttered inconstantly and his eyes were closed.

Simbal knelt, felt for a pulse. "Elder Uncle," he said in Cantonese, "you're going to be fine. Bennett did this to you. Edward Martin Bennett. Why?"

Run-Run Yi's eyes opened but Simbal knew that he wasn't seeing anything except what was in his mind. "Bennett needed me dead," he said slowly, softly, painfully.

"Like he needed Alan Thune dead?"

"Yes."

"Why?"

Yi said nothing. His eyes rolled in pain.

"Why, Elder Uncle? Why did Bennett need you and Alan Thune dead."

The Chinese murmured something and Simbal, desperate, said, "What?" very loudly.

And when he heard it, it did not compute. "Arms?" he

said. And then with more urgency, "Elder Uncle, did you say arms?"

Yi's eyelids fluttered. "I'm dying," he said in a guttural voice, thick with his own fluids. "You must inform my brothers."

"Yes, yes."

"All gods bear witness," Yi whispered. "I curse my murderer to sixteen generations."

"Bennett wanted you and Alan Thune dead because of arms?" Simbal said. He was very close to the other man now and could smell the peculiar odor of death stealing over him.

"Yes." Yi's lips were trembling. "Is it cold in here?"

The arms, Elder Uncle."

"That is the province of the new generation, it seems. Bennett, Mako, the others."

"What others?"

Consciousness was coming and going. Yi's eyes fluttered closed. He seemed to be marshaling his energy. "Arms, antipersonnel weapons—Blackman T-93s—we are told, are what we must now transship. But there is no profit in these arms. We are not selling them."

"What then?"

"Stockpiling."

"In Asia?"

"Asia, South America, Europe, America. All places."

"But why?"

A pink bubble formed between Yi's trembling lips. "Thune was against it. I was against it. We should have known better. But it is dangerous. So dangerous for the world."

"What kind of danger?" Simbal urged, his face close to the other's.

"The worst kind."

"What do you—"

"These weapons—will have the power to destroy the world." The cold sweat was rolling off Yi's flat face. His skin had taken on an awful pallor. "When Bennett—"

Simbal waited, breathless. He could hear his pulse hammering in his ears. Mother of God, he thought. What have I fallen into? " 'When Bennett,' " he repeated.

"Bennett is the jinn who opens the door."

What did that mean? "Where has he gone?"

"To the Shan," Yi said, and shuddered. "The source."

"Elder Uncle?" Simbal reached out, felt for a pulse that was not there. In a moment, he sat back.

The *diqui* into arms shipments? he wondered. Antipersonnel weapons, specifically Blackman T-93 one-man rocket launchers. Why? And how could those small arms cause the destruction of the world? Simbal found himself shivering. He felt as cold as the dead.

"What was that all about, man?" Gato de Rosa said, coming into the room. He was making puddles on the thick carpet.

Simbal did not look at him. "Bennett?"

"The cigarette," the Cuban said. "It was waiting for him."

Simbal sighed. "I'm tired," he said.

"Hey, don't bullshit me, dude," the Cuban insisted. "You were talking to the Chink. I heard you."

"He was ranting," Simbal said. He felt as if he had the weight of the world on his shoulders.

"Bullshit!"

"Damn-fucking-right!" Simbal flared. He stood up. "You let me handle Bennett."

"Fuck that!"

"You've got no choice. It's out of your hands now."

"You think so?"

Something in his tone sent a warning bell through Simbal. He remembered the feeling he had tried to interpret from the Cuban's words while they were at the marina.

Abruptly, he began to walk across the room. When he got to the front door, the Cuban said, "Where you going, dude?"

"See you around sometime, Martine."

Gato de Rosa jumped up. "Hey, hey, you can't do that. Hey, dude!"

Simbal turned around. "What are you going to do, shadow me?" He gave a ghostly smile. "You know better than that."

There was silence for a time. They stared at each other.

"Hey, man, this suite's gonna begin stinking like a tuna boat any minute."

"You going to tell me who it was you called from the marina, Martine?"

"I told you, dude."

"Yeah. Right."

"Oh, shit." Gato de Rosa came across the room. "He told me to keep an eye on you. He told me to go where you went. I don't think he trusts you, dude."

"Who's that?" But he already knew.

"Max," the Cuban said. "It was Max."

Max Threnody, Simbal thought. First he got to Monica and now the Cuban. But Gato de Rosa was a SNIT and Max was

423

the head of the DEA. Just what the hell is Max up to? Simbal wondered.

"You tell Max that if he wants me shadowed he can god-damned do it himself. I know where Bennett's off to and that's where I'm going." With each word getting closer to the Cuban.

"You're going to have company, then, *hombre.*"

"Bullshit," Simbal said. Moving very fast he went beneath Gato de Rosa's suit jacket. Pulled out the tiny snub-nosed .22. "A woman's weapon," he said, "but you know better than I do the damage it can do this close in."

"Hey, dude, hey. You crazy?"

"Nothing personal, Martine." Simbal leveled the .22. "Get over to the couch."

"Hey, for Christ's sake, man, lighten up, uh?"

"Just do as I say," Simbal said low in his throat.

He used the belt from Yi's silk robe to tie the Cuban's hands behind his back. "I don't mind letting you walk around," he said. "The police will be here before you can get out of that. I'll be long gone by then."

"Gone where, dude? Where you off to?" The Cuban's eyes had turned the color of coffee.

Simbal took the bullets out of the .22 and threw them at Gato de Rosa's feet. "Tell Max when he gets here." Tossed the gun after them. "Tell him I've gone to the Shan."

Qi lin slept.

"You see how marvelous the human brain is." Huaishan Han stared down at the supine form with such hunger in his eyes that Chen Ju was momentarily appalled. "You see how fantastically complex a machine it is." Huaishan Han's odd, bowed gait was exaggerated by the bare-bulb lighting, turning him into some truly grotesque figure. "Colonel Hu knew and appreciated that."

Chen Ju grunted. "Colonel Hu is dead."

Huaishan Han smiled and again Chen Ju felt a little thrill go through him. That smile was the kind used by those more than a bit mad. "Always the pragmatist, my friend, eh?" Han nodded. "But I divine your message." His hand moved out, stroked Qi lin's unlined brow. "Yes. She killed Colonel Hu, and she escaped his compound. A heavily fortified military complex, I might add."

"It seems to me," Chen Ju said, "that whatever it was Hu did to her, didn't take."

"Is that so?" Huaishan Han gave off that smile again, as a lambent sun throws off heat. "The war in Cambodia had marked Colonel Hu irrevocably. He was a master at his trade, true enough. But he drank himself into a stupor almost every night. The men had begun to question his commands, his leadership.

"You know what that meant. His unit was hand-picked to accept orders unthinkingly. That was essential, especially if they were going to march into Kam Sang, disarm the members of the army guarding the installation, imprison everyone within—including members of the intelligence service—and take what we require."

Huaishan Han sighed. "In short, my friend, Colonel Hu had become a liability." He reached out, stroked Qi lin's brow once again. "My precious *lizi*, my plum did just as I asked. Do you think it was *joss* that brought her within sight of General Kuo's soldiers? No, no. She was programmed for all of this. To kill Hu, to escape and come here."

Chen Ju looked doubtful. "But how?"

"With this." Huaishan Han produced a bottle of alcohol, a wad of cotton. He took Qi lin's arm and turned it so that the inside of her elbow was facing him. Using the cotton, he swabbed down an area of her skin. In a moment, he had a syringe in his hand. He uncapped it, squeezed a bit of the clear fluid out its tip. Then he inverted it, plunged it into Qi lin's vein. "A steady supply of this drug. It was Hu's own discovery. It works directly on the central cortex, inhibiting ego and superego. In effect, it stimulates the primitive emotions. Hate, fear, desire become matters of life and death. In this unbalanced state, the subject is akin to a piece of clay, ready to be molded by the artisan's fine hand." He put the materials back in his pocket.

"And she knows nothing of this?"

"There is a consciousness-blocker," Huaishan Han said. "She is mine from the inside out. Mine forever. By coming here, by escaping, she proved her skills to me. Now she has a most difficult task before her."

Huaishan Han looked at Chen Ju. "Many before her have tried to kill Jake Maroc Shi. All have failed. *Joss*, eh? But I have found that *joss* is like the tide of the ocean. It flows, it ebbs. You see?"

I want to control the world, Chen Ju thought, and this old, broken man is concerned with nothing more than warping a young girl's mind. It is shameful. He seeks only personal revenge, a petty and foolish undertaking at best. The fall down the well did more than disfigure his body, it scarred his mind as well. Once he would have understood the grand design that I am weaving; once he would have joined me.

Chen Ju shook his head. Perhaps his many years in the Shan had changed him subtly. There wealth meant nothing—warlords strolled their compounds with handfuls of rubies, sapphires, Imperial jade in their pockets. They guided the distribution of the tears of the poppy and thereby reaped enormous profits. But their power was over people. Material wealth in the Shan was secondary. The reason that the Americans and the Russians had been locked out of the Shan was that they had no mastery over the people. Their CIA and KGB, respectively, had invaded the Shan using basically the same methodology: handing out money to everyone they met.

The Shan laughed at the Westerners; their warlords sneered at them and turned them away. Power was distribution. Control of the farmers who grew their fields of poppies; control of the armies who guarded the factories where the raw opium was refined, and guided the mule trains down the steep sides of the Shan to where greedy wholesalers waited.

And if Chen Ju had learned anything during his long exile from Hong Kong it was this: that true power resided in man's mastery over his fellow man. Those who wielded only wealth possessed an illusion.

Huaishan Han, so long deprived of true power, had filled his villa with the accumulated archaeological wealth of the centuries. But what meaning did it have? When he died, that wealth would be reapportioned, broken up, dispersed like so much sand. What would be left? Nothing. Nothing at all to mark his passing.

But Chen Ju knew that what he himself had embarked upon would surely change the world for all time. Like the pharaoh Cheops he was building an eternal monument to mark his brief time upon the earth.

Greed I leave to lesser spirits, he told himself. And he recognized greed in Han's face as he gazed down upon the slumbering countenance of the young girl who was so important to him. He longs for what he can never have, Chen Ju thought, and that is an apt definition of greed; he longs for a child. It is from this loss that his burning hatred of Shi Zilin stems. And perhaps that is the root of his obsession with this poor girl; why he openly adores her so, why he cannot understand how he tortures her.

Looking at Huaishan Han, Chen Ju was struck by the damage that time can do to mortal mind and body. All the more reason, he told himself, to get on with what I have to do. The world is about to enter a new age.

Daniella Vorkuta received her intelligence reports from Mitre—Sir John Bluestone's KGB code name—on Thursday mornings. They came coded, by special courier, and it was Daniella's habit to set aside an hour just before lunch to pore through the progress her most active asset was making toward burrowing inside Kam Sang.

However, this particular Thursday was a nightmare. She was woken out of sleep by the duty officer. Army intelligence required liaison with her people in the field in Afghanistan. That crisis was handled as she was dressing. At the office, she found wheels had come off no less than four separate operations, two of which were in their final phases and therefore needed her undivided attention as she guided the respective case officers through harrowing twists and turns in order to keep their field agents alive and ticking.

Lunch brought no respite since the frantic morning had required the administrative meetings be held in abeyance until the missions were past their crisis phases. A dozen department heads were kept waiting for her appearance so an entire round of morning meetings had to be crammed into the lunch hour.

And the afternoon was even worse. News was brought to her that despite her best efforts one of her agents in the field had been overrun by the opposition. Even worse, he had been captured alive. Daniella was required to begin sensitive and humiliating negotiations to try to bring him home.

That night, she and Carelin did not go back to her place. Instead he took her to a small apartment on the top floor of a red-brick building on Solyanka Street, just off Pokrovsky, one of the Green Boulevards, so-called because of the grass and parklands that are part of their makeup. From one of the tiny windows, one could see the Ustinsky Bridge and lights glinting off the dark face of the Moskva. The view, Carelin told Daniella, had been better before the tractors and road-rippers had come in, part of the municipal plan to turn this cul-de-sac into the Internatsionalskaya and the Ulyanovskaya which would eventually link the boulevard to the south bank.

They were here because of Carelin. Or, more accurately, because he could no longer suffer the vigil Maluta had on her. This was a place no one knew about. "I am tired of making love to you," he had said, "while Maluta's soldier watches from the shadows."

Too exhausted, physically and emotionally, to eat, Daniella had stripped off her clothes and had stood under a shower so long that Carelin was obliged to hammer repeatedly on the door to ask her if she was ever coming out.

Eventually she emerged, unsmiling, wrapped in a thick American-made towel. Her gray eyes met Carelin's and he leaned forward, kissing her tenderly on the cheek. He went into the bathroom, closed the door. In a moment, she heard the sound of the shower.

Daniella, on the bed, listened to the drumming of the rain, watched the lurid splashes of electric-blue lightning pierce the shades like knives. She closed her eyes and remembered the unread report from Mitre. She was so tired she thought fleetingly of leaving it for the morning. But, in the end, her desire to read about any progress on Kam Sang broke through her lethargy. She rolled over, dug it out of her bag. There was no danger in reading it here. The code made it indecipherable to anyone but Mitre and herself.

She propped herself up against the pillows, slit open the envelope and began slowly to read.

In a moment, she put down the sheets of flimsy and stared at the closed bathroom door just as if she had acquired x-ray vision. She sat up fully and read through the report again. It was absolutely revelatory. It contained the intelligence Neon Chow had given to Bluestone regarding the Quarry asset Apollo. The last line contained Apollo's identity: Mikhail Carelin.

When Daniella came to his name written out in code, her stomach gave a lurch and she gagged, for an instant overwhelmed by nausea. She put her head back against the pillows and did nothing but breathe deeply for a long time.

Mikhail Carelin was an agent working for a foreign power—for her most powerful enemy!

Now that she knew this, she should begin devising ways to find out what his assignment was. She should be thinking of ways to turn him. Or, alternatively, to bring him to justice. He was a traitor, after all.

But she was thinking about none of these things. With a kind of jolt, she realized that it did not matter to her. Traitor or patriot, there was absolutely no difference. Carelin was still the man she loved. And she knew that she was going to do nothing that would jeopardize her relationship with him.

Daniella Vorkuta, trained and bred in the elite Soviet underworld of the *sluzhba*, was now nothing more or less than a human being. Her rank of general meant as little, she realized, as her elevation to the head of the First Chief Directorate or, even, God help her, the Politburo.

Her career, her life within the *sluzhba* meant nothing. What mattered was this. How could that possibly be? she asked herself. She put her fingertips against her lower belly, and then further, pushing them through the fur between her thighs. She probed into the heat between her legs until she was certain of her previous findings. The mucus was there; that meant her time of the month was now, her egg was ready and waiting. Her hands, when she took them away, were trembling. Had she gone mad? There was no other rational explanation. But, she knew, there was nothing rational about this decision. It was purely emotional. It was the true difference between a woman and a man.

In time, Carelin padded into the bedroom. He saw that she was not reading, was perhaps even asleep, and she had turned off the lamps. When he was next to her, she stretched, as if in sleep, and turned her long, naked body against him. Her fingers cupped him, began to massage him.

After the longest time: "Danushka?" he whispered. "Are you awake?"

She brushed her breasts against him, trailing her nipples over his flesh. When they reached his belly, they were hard. Her lips opened, enclosed him in exquisite heat. Her tongue rose up his stem, lashing his expanding tip. When he was hard and quivering, she replaced her mouth with her mons.

She scrubbed him with it until he was groaning, until his own hands guided her onto him. He went in with a rush and when he arched up, bringing her with him, when he felt his hot seed jetting high into her, he heard her crying, "Mikhail, Mikhail, Mikhail!" And felt her face wet with tears.

Bliss felt the bullets going in—one, two, three, four, five!—like slices of silver, a hungry civet's slashing grin in the emerald jungle. White on black, their brief, whirring journeys were broadcast to her through *da-hei*, the great darkness.

As they entered the man sitting at her left elbow, the empathic flow caused her to cry out with the agony that he was sustaining. Big Oysters Pok jerked up and back with each hit, as if he was a marionette whose strings were being pulled by a madman or a drunkard.

Even before that, however, Bliss had upended the table, crashing dinnerware, glasses, the piled remains of their meal. Now three good inches of solid wood and iron braces were between her and the sixth shot that embedded itself into the center of the table instead of in her heart.

From her vantage point she could see the lower half of Big Oysters Pok's sprawled figure, his legs tangled up in the overturned chair. Blood was running darkly along the floor.

She turned away from the assassin who had spun and was loping away, shouldering roughly past the Chinese waiters and the screaming, cringing *gwai loh* patrons. Slipping in the muck as she scrambled on her knees to where Big Oysters Pok lay.

Five shots point blank and *da-hei* showed her the ending of life. But she put her fingertips against the side of his neck anyway because she needed the physical assurance. There was no pulse. She bent, put her lips near his. No breath, either.

She had been so close. Bliss closed her eyes and sighed. Now she had nothing to go on. Her search for the murderers of the Jian had hit a stone wall.

The only thing Huaishan Han could see when he looked into her face was the well. He stared into Qi lin's face and saw madness. The well was madness.

Echoes. Wet echoes, slime, mold, rust and mud. The slide of viscous substances across his goosepimpled flesh. The exquisite agony of being on the rack, of one's numbed fingers supporting one's entire weight for—how long? Buddha, how long! An eternity. Not a moment less.

Now as she looked upon Qi lin and saw the madness, he no longer knew whether it was hers or his own. He thanked Buddha for his great good fortune. Oh, his *joss* must be powerful indeed!

Colonel Hu's mind sculpting had done its work. Chen Ju had advised him and he had passed the information on to Hu. The best place for a fugitive from the Chinese government to cross over was this section of the China-Burma frontier.

The Shan States were a wild and, at best, unfriendly place. The ethnic tribes of the region—the Shan, Wa, Lahu, Akha, Lu, Lisu—migrated here during the fifteenth century. Fiercely independent, they had resisted all efforts by various Burmese regimes to incorporate them into the nation as a whole.

Today, many of the warlords who ruled tribal armies and fiefdoms of medieval splendor, are descendants—or claim to be—of the original *sawbwas*, the hereditary Shan princes. Other warlords are renegade officers from the Chinese army, lured into the Shan by the promise of power and riches beyond imagining.

And of all the warlords here in the Shan States, it was General Kuo who was the most powerful.

He commanded by far the most men, armed well enough to dissuade the Chinese army from invading his territory. How then could she fail to be stopped by one of his border patrols?

Her beauty struck him like an arrow through his heart. Now that she had come back he was aware of how much he had missed her. She was the granddaughter of his enemy. Shi Zilin lived on through her, as he did through Jake Maroc. There was a certain exquisite irony in using Shi Jake's daughter to assassinate him. That thought made laughter bubble up in Huaishan Han's throat.

General Kuo disliked the sound of Han's laughter. It was unwholesome and peculiarly obscene, like an old man peeping under a little girl's skirts to catch a glimpse of something pure and pink.

General Kuo said nothing of this, however. He was paid a king's ransom to supervise the harvesting and the refining of the tears of the poppy, not to render his opinions on the personalities involved. Number Four opium was his first priority. His second priority was keeping the American CIA, the Russian KGB, the Chinese and Burmese armies at bay. After that, no one gave a damn what he did or did not do. He had admired Huaishan Han more than any other man alive.

General Kuo knew that he could line up twenty men right now and order them shot and Huaishan Han would not even turn his head in the direction of the shots. The high Shan plateau was General Kuo's territory, pure and simple. And Huaishan Han knew it.

But then it was General Kuo who had saved Huaishan Han from the hideous depths of the stinking well in Fragrant Hills Park, so long ago. Kuo had been no general then. But his quick, shrewd mind had already set him apart from his contemporaries who seemed content to bury their heads in the sand blowing in off the Gobi.

General Kuo had disliked taking orders. He was in the military because to him the army was synonymous with power. He craved power in the same way that most people needed food and sleep. Kuo could never remember sleeping for more than three hours a night; he had never needed to. What he required was power.

He was no politician. He had an incredibly ordered mind. Discipline. He was born with a disciplined mind. He was natural for the army—except that he resented taking orders from superiors who were that in rank only.

General Kuo had discovered *wei qi*, the board game of master strategy, at an early age. He learned to play by observing an old man who took on all challengers every day in the park. Kuo had been involved in *wei qi* now for close to sixty years and he had never encountered a better player in all that time than the old man in the park.

It was *wei qi*—or more accurately the strategy learned in its pursuit—that allowed Kuo to see an opportunity of a lifetime when he discovered the well and its contents.

By that time, Shi Zilin had gone to Mao, revealing what he had learned regarding the personal use of funds from the nefarious opium smuggling. A full-scale investigation was immediately launched in the course of which both Lo Jui-ch'ing and K'ang Sheng were exonerated. Huaishan Han, however, presumed dead, was discovered to have devised and run the scheme.

Kuo had heard of all this, of course, by the time he was in Xiang shan. It was a week after the incident in the park and, after dinner, the weather being mild and comfortable, Kuo had taken his young lady for a stroll in the park.

In truth, he had picked this park, and even this spot, Shuang jing, the Villa with Two Wells, quite deliberately. He had been involved in parts of the investigation and therefore was privy to a great deal of information unavailable to the general public. He had meant to describe in grisly detail the events of the week before and his part in the subsequent inquiry in order to impress his young lady.

As it turned out, he never got the chance. She screamed even before he had begun his carefully prepared recitation. He turned. Moonlight glinted like metal off the two wells. His ladyfriend pointed, her hand over her mouth, and Kuo went to investigate.

What he had at first taken for shards of the ruined iron cap were, on closer inspection, clawlike fingers, the flesh white with tension and a kind of semiparalysis.

Kuo, peering over the wide stone lip of the well, could

make out a pair of eyes, brightly burning like those of a nocturnal animal, glaring at him from the fetid murk.

It was Huaishan Han, battered, bruised and swollen almost beyond recognition. His back was broken or at least vertebrae in the spine were cracked. He was like a hunchback when Kuo pulled him out of the private hell he had been clinging to for a full week. Kuo was astounded that any human being could live down there for any length of time with only rain water to ingest. Because of this he held Huaishan Han in a kind of awe, as if he were somehow something more than human.

It was Huaishan Han's great good fortune to be rescued by Kuo. And Kuo's great good fortune as well.

Virtually any other military man would have informed his superior and Huaishan Han would have been taken to the military hospital where, after he had recovered, he would have stood secret trial for his crimes. His punishment would have been terrible indeed.

But Kuo saw in this situation the seeds for his escape from the military. He recognized in Huaishan Han's scheme a lifetime of power and riches beyond even his wildest dreams. Therefore the preservation of this man became paramount to him. Kuo knew that he not only had to keep Huaishan Han safe but also undiscovered by the government.

With his ladyfriend's assistance, he took the injured man to a military staff car. He would have to take the girl with him, he knew, in order to keep security at one hundred percent. That was all right with Kuo but he was not so certain of the girl so he lied to her. He was good at that. Part of the strategy in *wei qi* involved spurious forays into enemy territory in order to shield one's real strategy until it was too late to counteract.

Kuo drove all night. He needed to get as much distance between him and Peking as he could before first light. In the south, there were people he could trust, and others, he was certain, who would aid Huaishan Han in return for becoming a part of the opium network.

As it turned out, Kuo was right on target. The injured man was admitted to a hospital under an alias. He was one of many war casualties who were streaming in from the Korean War. It was easy to lose his identity and no one this far south would recognize Huaishan Han's face.

Now, General Kuo, standing on the front steps of his hut high on the Shan plateau, took in the triple-canopied forest.

The purple and white mountains of northern Burma rose into the night sky all around him. He thought of them as part of his army, great natural sentinels which he had learned how to use.

That was the beginning, he thought. A young man's desire to impress his woman; a wild ride south in a cloud of dust. A dream he had turned into reality. For this was the goal. He was ultimate master over thousands of people; his pockets were bulging with rubies, sapphires as big as his knuckle. He could buy the business of any *tai pan* in Hong Kong should he choose to do so. He knew he never would, however. This was his home. This was where he was emperor. More, he was god.

The Shan.

Only the mountain knows . . . Hige Moro's last words echoed in Jake's mind all the way back to Hong Kong. What mountain? Surely the Yakuza *oyabun* couldn't know about the personal mountain upon which Jake toiled. The mountain of Shi Zilin, Jake's father, the mountain of the Jian, of the *Zhuan*.

What mountain could link a Communist Chinese minister and an overlord of the Japanese underworld?

Mikio Komoto had not known and neither did Jake. Mikio had been stunned by Hige Moro's revelations and, he said, if Moro hadn't been on the point of death, he would have been inclined to dismiss them out of hand. Privately, he might believe that Hige Moro had been making fools of them. But Jake was not so sure.

For one thing, the story was just too improbable to be a last macabre joke. For another, Jake had been looking in the *oyabun*'s eyes when he said it. Jake was willing to bet that he had seen the truth there.

The 747 Jumbo hit the tarmac at Kai Tak without his having made any headway with the problem. He had been hoping to get some sleep on the flight but he had been unable to tear his mind from its frenzy of thinking.

Consequently he returned home tired, his body aching over virtually every square inch. He came out of the terminal into a day dark and rumbly with thunderheads. Their bruised purple dominated a fulminating sky. Victoria Peak was wreathed in darkness and every now and again pale lightning flickered like an adder's tongue.

His apartment at the Cloud Levels on the Peak was as dark

as night. Without Bliss it seemed desolate and chill. He dropped his bags and went straight into the bathroom. Forty-five minutes later, with a tiny cup of saki in his hands, he felt halfway human for the first time in days.

Staring out the windows at the billowing electrified clouds, he picked up the phone and dialed his uncle. The precipitation that slid down the panes of glass bore only a passing resemblance to rain. The sky seemed to be weeping bitter tears.

Said hello to a young voice, one of his nephews and, in a moment, Three Oaths came on the line.

"I'm back, Uncle," he said. "I know who killed my father."

"Do you know why?"

"Only partially. The full answer was not in Japan."

"Are you well, Nephew?"

"It depends on your definition," Jake said. "Well enough. How is Bliss?"

There was a slight pause. "She is out of the hospital, Nephew. But I think you had better come down to the junk immediately."

Jake felt a return of tension, a knot of worry in his stomach. "Is she all right, Uncle?"

"Someone tried to kill her."

"Who?"

"Someone," Three Oaths said, "you know well. Great Pool of Piddle."

"McKenna? *Ian* McKenna? Why?" Jake knew that he was shouting; he didn't care.

"My daughter insisted on following up the lead of the opal, Nephew. The trail led to Big Oysters Pok. She was having dinner with him when Great Pool of Piddle shot him dead. And, almost, Bliss."

"Is she injured?"

"Physically, no," Three Oaths said. "I ask you again, Nephew, to come to the junk. There is much more to— Nephew? Nephew? Jake, are you there?"

Jake wasn't.

At seven thirty in the evening, Rodger Donovan took the call on the powerful shortwave he had built and installed himself in a corner of the converted attic at Greystoke. He had just come back from a long, exhilarating drive in his '63 Corvette. Donovan loved the car, cherished it, really, as he had longed to cherish Leslie, as he longed to cherish Daniella Vorkuta.

435

He knew every square grease-coated inch of the 'Vette's insides, which was more than he could say for any woman he had ever known. Donovan, who was such a genius with machines and men, could never fathom the arcane workings of the feminine psyche.

This was a deficiency that, had he thought about it, he would have seen Daniella had discovered and used with ruthless proficiency years ago. During their months in Paris she had been able to recruit him as much because he thought he understood her and did not as because she found in him a more general deep and abiding antipathy for the elitist class system that had spawned him.

"Three-four-seven-eight," he said, into the opened frequency.

"I'm here."

"Daniella," he said. "Are you still hip-deep in snow?"

She stopped his bantering tone when she said, "What do you know of Apollo?"

"Apollo?" His mind was like a computer and he reviewed the name quickly. "Nothing."

"Are you certain?"

"Absolutely. Are you going to clue me in?"

"What?"

"Give. Who or what is Apollo?"

"A mole," she said, "inside the Kremlin. A Quarry asset."

"Impossible. I—"

"He was strictly Henry Wunderman's brainchild."

"Oh, Christ." He stared out the window. The rolling hills were black against the setting sun. "Do you know who he is?"

"Mikhail Carelin."

He blinked. "Genachev's adviser?"

"Just so." There was an unnatural pause. "Listen to me. Apollo was Henry Wunderman's asset. That means he knew Wunderman wasn't Chimera."

"Jesus!" Donovan gritted his teeth. Pushing his anxiety aside, he began to think furiously. "Do you know who Apollo's new control is?"

"Yes," Daniella said. "Jake Maroc."

"Maroc again." The adrenaline was rushing through Donovan's veins. The verdant Virginia hills were fired along their tops now. "Somehow I knew I hadn't heard the last of him. I tried to recruit him just after he killed Wunderman. I thought, psychologically, it would be the advantageous time. He wasn't interested in anything to do with the Quarry."

"He's going to be now," Daniella said. "As soon as Apollo tells Maroc that he was wrong about Chimera's identity. What do you think Maroc will do to you once he figures out that it was our disinformation that gave him cause to kill Henry Wunderman? Wunderman was Maroc's mentor; Maroc loved him like a father."

"Christ, you don't have to tell me that." Donovan's eyes had gone blank as he thought the problem through. He conjured up, then discarded option after option. "I don't think we have any choice," he said carefully. "We'll just have to take care of Mr. Maroc once and for all."

"Frankly," Daniella said, "I don't think you've got an operative who's up to the job, and this is not an assignment that can be given twice."

Donovan thought about the long afternoon, putting the Corvette flat out for the sheer excitement of it. "Don't worry about that." The mind appreciated being on the precipice of danger. "Even if there was, there isn't anyone here I'd trust with this, anyway. It would give rise to too many awkward questions." The mind liked to be fooled this way every now and again; it gave the thought processes a jolt, set them running full out again.

"Do you know where Maroc is at this moment?"

"At the moment, Hong Kong," Daniella said. "Mitre's people are monitoring his movements closely."

"Good," Donovan said. "Just keep me updated." He brought back the memory of the severe S-curve, how he had taken it at eighty-five. And in front of him the hill, an emerald blur, looming. "I'll take care of Jake Maroc myself."

Ian McKenna lived in a battered, peeling house along Dragon's Back, an area in the southeast of the Island bounded on the north by Mount Collinson and on the south by the D'aguilar Peak peninsula. It was, for the most part, a desolate place, quite unlike the rest of Hong Kong. There was, for instance, more than a touch of Australian topography there. Which was, Jake supposed, why McKenna had chosen it.

Jake pulled the Jaguar over onto the rocky dirt verge and killed the engine. He was still a thousand meters from the house. He had been traveling for the last mile-and-a-half without lights. The road had too many switchbacks that, at night, would send his car's headlights far ahead. He had passed no other vehicles and he did not want to give Great Pool of Piddle any warning.

Got out of the car, leaving the door open. Sounds, as well as light, traveled far here. Behind him, the lights of the Peak and to his right, Aberdeen, were awash with rain. Everyone in Hong Kong rejoiced when it rained. Until Kam Sang's desalinization plant came on line, the Crown Colony still had a chronic water shortage.

McKenna's eyes bugged out when Jake came through the door. He was sitting in a corner with his back to the bare walls. All the pictures and paintings had been torn down and now lay, ragged as battle pennants in a welter of broken glass and shattered frames. Shards of mirror glittered at McKenna's bare feet. No lights were on, and the shutters and blackout curtains were drawn across the windows. McKenna steadfastly faced them as if manning the battlements at Armageddon.

"Hello, McKenna."

"Maroc, what the fuck're you doing here?"

"Came to pay a debt." He was grinning like a hungry wolf.

"Huh?"

Jake looked around. "Got any little boys here, McKenna?" The big man started. "What d'you know about him?"

"Who?" He saw McKenna's eyes as big around as saucers.

"You're not supposed to know. No one's supposed to know." There were beads of sweat trembling on McKenna's face. "But it's too late for that, isn't it? They know, don't they? *They* know."

This was getting interesting, Jake thought. "Who knows?"

"Don't play games with me, Maroc. You know who. You know. They know." His head whipped around and the sweat flew from him like rain. "I know it because I can hear the chanting."

"The chanting," Jake said, coming closer. "Sure, McKenna, I hear it."

The big man nodded. "The abos think they can break me by keeping me awake at night." He gave a little cackling laugh. "They're underestimating me again."

"Sure they are, McKenna," Jake said, coming on. "What about Big Oysters Pok. Why did you kill him?"

"Kill him? I did? Well, then, he deserved it." Jake could see now that McKenna was naked. He held a blanket over part of him, but his thick pale flesh shone here and there. As Jake watched, McKenna took one hand from beneath the

438

blanket. It was filled with a Magnum .357. "Did him with this, Jake. But then, he deserved it."

"He did, huh?" It was important to be careful now, very careful. "He fuck with you, McKenna?"

"Nah!" That cackling laugh again, just this side of hysteria. "Nobody bloody fucks with me, Jake, you know that. But he was a wog, see, a wog! Bloody wogs've been after me since, well, you know."

Jake had no idea but he nodded just the same. The thing was to keep McKenna talking. He was obviously as mad as a March hare but somewhere in that confused mind of his Jake suspected there was a sane reason why he had shot Big Oysters Pok. "You killed Pok because he was Chinese, that it?" The thing was to tune in to McKenna's batty level.

"You got it!" McKenna grinned savagely. "I always pegged you for a smart one, Jake." He was waving that gun around. "I'm glad I was right about you." The expression changed with appalling quickness. The gun leveled at Jake's midsection. "But don't come so bloody close, mate. You never know."

Jake froze. "Never know what, McKenna?"

The big man stared at him as if he had lost his mind. He pointed the gun at the windows. "About the abos, of course." His tiny eyes got canny. "They could have got to you, you know. They have their ways."

"They certainly do," Jake said, fighting to keep his voice even. He wanted to leap across the several meters still separating them and shake the truth out of McKenna. "But they haven't contacted me. Yet."

McKenna's eyes filled with fear. "Yet? What do you mean?"

"Well," Jake shrugged, "I've heard the chanting, of course."

"It never stops. Never," McKenna said. "It used to, you know. But now there're just too many of them. Abos. They can keep the chanting up forever. Forever."

What sin, Jake wondered, did McKenna commit in Australia to have driven him this far over the edge. "Is that why you wanted to kill the girl too?"

"Girl?" McKenna's face was filled with bewilderment. "What girl?"

"The one with Big Oysters Pok when you shot him."

The big man's eyes were far away. "Was there someone with him? I don't remember."

"You must remember the girl, McKenna," Jake said. He described Bliss.

"Did I kill her too?"

"I don't think so, no."

"Pok's always with one," McKenna said sorrowfully. "His oysters aren't so big now, huh? Bloody hell. He liked to talk big, like he wasn't a wog. He didn't know his place, what with his beautiful women, his high living. He's not living so high now. Bloody right he's not."

So it wasn't just that Pok was Chinese, Jake thought. There was some personal connection. "You showed him," he said. "You had the last laugh."

"Laugh," McKenna said. His voice was eerie, skittish, swinging through the emotions. "He laughed at me. He looked down on me. But he got me the information, didn't he?"

"He sure did," Jake said, knowing that he was close now. "What information?"

"Oh, you know," McKenna said, "confirmation of the rumor that there was trouble—big trouble, huh, Jake?—at Southasia Bancorp."

"Where'd you hear that one, McKenna? That was top secret. No one was supposed to know but the directors of InterAsia."

"Don't I know," McKenna said happily. "I—"

But the front door was swinging open and McKenna, his head whipping around, had returned with frightening swiftness to his hysterical state. The muzzle of the Magnum swung in a blurred arc and he screamed, "They're coming! They're coming!"

Jake saw Bliss in the brilliant illumination of her car's headlights, coming through the half-open front door, and he leapt at McKenna. The first shot went high as Jake crashed into his outstretched arm.

McKenna grunted and rolled, freeing one hand. He lifted a ham fist, slammed it down on the back of Jake's head. The blow made Jake's head swim but he had no time to stop it and the successive ones that landed in the same spot. His main concern was the Magnum. With that caliber size, one shot was all it would take to put him down permanently.

But McKenna was not letting go. He had the strength of madness about him and it was impossible to wrest the weapon from him. Then Jake knew why. He had been gripping it before Jake even arrived. He saw it as something magical, his only protection from the abos.

Jake used his foot, pressing down on McKenna's wrist to keep the Magnum at bay. At the same time he used a liver kite, a purely percussion blow, an *atemi*. The big man grunted and jerked his knee up. It smashed into the back of Jake's head, making him see stars. He wavered and McKenna, with superhuman strength, pulled his wrist free. Pointed the Magnum into Jake's face.

"Bye-bye, baby," he said thickly.

And Bliss kicked him hard in the side of his head.

He began to gag and Jake, recovering, used his elbow in a series of *atemi* that would have put any normal man out. Not McKenna. He came on, flailing with the gun and his balled-up free hand so that Jake had no choice. The Magnum was very close and impossible to control. Used the *jut-hara*, the killing blow, the heel of the hand striking the fifth and sixth ribs at such an angle that the shards of bone pierced the heart.

McKenna screamed, his eyes bugged and he arched upward like a speared fish. The corpse, already dead, juddered reflexively.

Jake, still groggy, lurched to his feet, took Bliss by the hand and went out on the patio. The waves far below crashed and hissed against the black crags, the last of the rain beat softly against them, the night wind sought to cleanse them.

He tried to catch his breath, couldn't and stood, bent over, while Bliss held his thundering head. After a long time, he heard her whispering, "Jake, Jake, Jake."

"Stupid of you to come here," he said. "Just plain stupid."

"I could say the same for you," she told him, close beside him. "I begged my father not to tell you anything until you got to the junk. I knew you'd do something like this. Oh, Buddha, I was so frightened for you!" She shouted this into the night, then fell against him, sobbing. "Where were you?" she whispered. "Why didn't you call? I was so worried."

Jake put his arms around her at last. He wanted to tell her everything: what he had found out in Japan and why, finally, he had gone. But he could not. He felt as if he were in a dream where one cannot find one's voice. Why did he remain mute?

Instead he kissed her, thinking of them as a movie poster, he the all-powerful hero embracing the softly vulnerable leading lady. It gave him a measure of solace and briefly he wondered why.

He felt her heart beating hard against him, her warmth seeping into him and he realized just how much he missed her, and how worried about her he had been. He had wanted to call her many different times, when he was in Japan. Each time he had stopped short. Why? It wasn't for lack of caring. Perhaps, then, he cared too much. The situation had been dire enough in Tokyo and then in Kyoto without his being distracted by his emotions. During that compressed time it had been far better to keep her at arm's length.

But he realized now how cruel he had been to her. "I'm sorry, Bliss," he said. "It was a bad time for Mikio. There was death all around and I didn't want to share that with you." He kissed her neck. "And I know you. You would have picked it up the minute I said hello."

"It's all right, Jake," she whispered. "As long as you're back, safe."

She kissed him. "I found out about the woman with the opal," she went on quickly. "She was Big Oysters Pok's mistress. She was also a Communist spy."

"Then I was right," Jake said. "She was tailing me to keep me away from the boat. So I couldn't interfere with the *dantai*'s work."

"But—"

But he put a hand over her mouth, made a silent ssh-ing sound with his lips. Their faces were very close and he saw the puzzlement in her eyes.

Car, he mouthed silently to her, then, in her ear, whispered, "Go to your car and move it from out front. Don't forget to turn off the lights. Then come right back here."

"But, Jake—"

"Hurry, now!" he said urgently, and watched her disappear into the shadows wreathing the side of the house. She made no noise and in a moment he was straining to discern where she had gone.

When she returned, she seemed almost to materialize out of those same inky shadows. She came toward him in a scuttling half crouch.

"Did you see anything?" Jake whispered.

She nodded. "Car coming. I could see its headlights."

"Right," he said. "Let's find out who's visiting Great Pool of Piddle at this time of the night."

It meant going back in there. The stench was already overpowering and Jake knew they would have to be quick, so he set them up just inside the front door. They waited uncomfortably. Even breathing through their mouths didn't help enough.

In time they heard the throaty rumble of exhaust. The rain

had ceased completely by then and it had grown very still. They could hear the crunch of the gravel and the noise of someone walking up the steps.

There was a knock on the door and Bliss opened it while Jake lunged forward, pulling the figure on the doorstep over the threshold inside. Bliss kicked the door shut and turned on the light.

The Chinese looked at them from his one good eye. The other, milky white and unseeing, glowered like an angry winter's sun.

"I don't want to see him," Sawyer told Sei An. "Under no circumstances—"

"But I'm already in," Sir John Bluestone said, opening the door into Sawyer's office.

"I'm terribly sorry, *tai pan*," an apologetic Sei An said, peeking in around the tall *gwai loh*. "He took me by surprise."

"That's all right, Sei An," Sawyer said.

"I've sent for Security."

Sawyer saw the wide smirk on Bluestone's face and knew that he couldn't live with that. "No, no, Sei An. You tell them everything's all right." Ignoring the loss of face it caused him.

Sei An looked at her *tai pan*, saw his predicament and, not wanting to lose him more face, nodded wordlessly, pulling the door shut behind her.

"Sit down, *tai pan*," Sawyer said with a forced smile. "To what do I owe this honor?"

It was late in the day. The sun hung in the sky like a swollen bruise, washing the city in dusty, russet light. Victoria Harbor was filled with vessels of every description from old, seemingly decrepit junks, their faded orange sails spread wide, to sleek, modern cruisers, their diesel exhausts bubbling; from stained cargo vessels registered in lands halfway around the world, to crisp naval-gray aircraft carriers in for R & R.

"The view from these windows," Bluestone said, ignoring Sawyer, "is quite extraordinary. It makes one feel as if one owns all of Hong Kong." He turned with a grin on his face and, without asking, went over to the granite-topped sideboard and poured two drinks into wide-mouthed cut-crystal glasses. He put one on the desktop in front of Andrew Sawyer and sipped at his own. "Ummm, single malt. Excellent."

Sawyer did not touch the glass of Scotch. He kept his hands folded together, the fingers laced, in order to conceal their trembling. He did not know whether it was in rage or in fear.

"Not thirsty, *tai pan*?" Bluestone gave another wide grin. He was wearing an impeccably cut tropical-weight chalk-stripe suit, pure white Turnbull and Asser shirt with a regimental tie, gold nugget cuff links and tie tack, polished oxblood wingtip shoes.

"Is this a social visit?" Sawyer said finally, exasperated.

Bluestone smiled at another tiny victory. He knew that they added up. He looked down at the Scotch, swirling the amber liquid. "Social? Ah, no, *tai pan*. I don't believe I could spare the time for that."

"Of course not," Sawyer said archly. "You've been busy lately, haven't you?"

"And you'd like nothing better than to swat me down, *tai pan*." Bluestone's head rose until he was looking directly at Sawyer. "But you'd better beware."

"Is that a threat? Do you think you can frighten me?"

"It would be an awfully stupid man," Bluestone said with some edge, "who was not frightened at the prospect of losing his entire empire."

"I see why you've come here," Sawyer said. He stood, conceding another minor victory to Bluestone. He could no longer bear being physically looked down upon from Bluestone's regal height. "It's to gloat. You think that you've already won, that all of InterAsia belongs to you."

"Doesn't it?"

"Not by a fair margin," Sawyer said firmly.

Bluestone came over to the desk, leaned over it. "We own thirty-eight percent of InterAsia now. Today alone we picked up another eight percent. The stock is plummeting and our brokers are flooded with offers to sell shares at the price we are offering, which remains a full ten dollars over current value on the Hang Seng. Do you really think you can stop the takeover at this late date."

"Get out of my office!" Sawyer shouted, losing more face now but not caring, his cheeks flushed with anger and resentment.

Bluestone looked leisurely around the great room. "I always coveted this office, this building. Its location is superb."

"It's mine!" Sawyer thundered. "And as long as it is, you're barred from the premises!" He picked up the phone and asked for Security to come up on the double.

"As long as it's yours, that's your privilege." Bluestone thumped his glass onto the center of a pile of papers. "But realistically we both know that won't be very long." He tapped his forefinger against his lips and said meditatively, "You know, I think I have just the right decorating scheme to maximize the drama of this view." Two armed uniformed men came into the room and he said, "Well, I see that you're busy, *tai pan*. And I have a great deal to do." He lifted his arms. "All of this has to be replaced, of course, and that's rather a tall order, so I know you'll excuse me." And went quickly out the door.

The senior of the uniformed guards said, "Sir?"

"Nothing," Andrew Sawyer said, his head in his hands. "There's nothing you can do."

When Oleg Maluta summoned her to his office, she went willingly. Now that she was well into the game, now that she had slipped the knife between the plates of his armor and found the soft spots, she no longer feared him.

Oleg Maluta no longer seemed seven feet tall, filled with an inexhaustible power, possessed of an endlessly clever mind that could trap her at every turn.

She remembered the gun he had with her unsmudged prints embossed by her own oils into the grip. The photographs he had of her weeping in the winter night when he had happily trapped her into murdering Alexei. The smutty photographs he had paraded before her that reduced the love she and Mikhail Carelin felt for each other to grasping, a fluid-filled animal coupling.

Photographs like that should not be allowed to exist, she thought. They were an affront to God as well as to the sanctity of emotion. Whores and screen actors could be caught thus in the intimacy of a celluloid moment since no real emotion passed from person to person in the reality of the scene. The viewer—the voyeur—was required to participate by adding elements from his or her own imagination in order for it to take life. But here, the nakedness of Daniella and Carelin was appalling. It was the capturing of what they felt for each other that was the true obscenity.

The Ring Road was filled with traffic and Daniella was obliged to roll up her windows against the cement dust which rose so high it turned the watery sunlight into a pointillist's brush.

She didn't mind any of it. She was, by this time, thoroughly fed up with a day crammed to overflowing with meetings concerning budgets, personnel, ongoing project evaluation, central staff evaluation, expense record overviews and, of course, the chronic maintenance problems plaguing the new offices.

The weariness of inertia coated her like grime. It was endemic to the Soviet bureaucratic structure but that, somehow, today, made it even harder to take. Her department—the entire *sluzhba*, it seemed—was mired in inefficiency, boredom and stupidity. The humdrum had claimed them all, making of them nothing more than dull-witted slugs squirming blindly through rock-strewn soil.

After more than a decade and God alone knew how much money, Africa was turning further and further away from Communism. The coordinated protests throughout Western Europe were now no more than an insignificant trickle, and Russia's hold over Eastern Europe, though steadfast, only served to make clear to her her own country's lack of vision and global inspiration.

Only the Soviet-backed terrorist training centers were an unqualified success, but while many of Daniella's colleagues applauded their work and clamored for even more recruits from the Middle East, she saw what they did not: that arming the Arabs was one thing, training them in this way was quite another.

The absolute danger of fanaticism had faded in Russia as the government rewrote the histories of Stalin and Trotsky. Ideological fanaticism is bad enough, Daniella thought. But religious fanaticism was a lethal bomb of quite terrifying proportions. She wondered now, as her Chaika rolled through the Borovitsky Gate, if any of them within the *sluzhba* knew just what it was they were helping to spawn.

Oleg Maluta's office was actually a suite of three rooms inside the Kremlin. It was on the fourth floor of an unremarkable building near the theater, its ancient windows affording an excellent view across tourist-laden Cathedral Square to Tainitskaya Bashnya, the Tower of Silence, built in 1485 and the oldest of the Kremlin's outstructures.

Velvet drapes hung on either side of the casements and a massive desk of solid mahogany was set just in front of this. In this way the light was always behind Maluta and in the eyes of his visitors.

Daniella closed the oak door behind her and went across the Isfahan carpet, threading her way between the two velvet-covered highbacked chairs. Portraits of Lenin and Stalin, oversized, definitely not standard issue, hung on either side

446

wall. The end of a leather sofa peeked out from behind a partly open door.

Maluta was on the telephone, half-turned away as she delivered the two manila envelopes onto his desktop: her latest report on Carelin and Genachev. She looked out the window. Beyond the Italian-inspired crenellated wall, beyond the Tower of Silence, boats upon the Moskva moved with the alacrity of snails crawling up a hill. From this distance, the water appeared as dense as lead. It was the color of zinc. The windows were closed against the stink of diesel fumes and the noise of constant construction. Still, she noticed the seepage of grit along the sills.

Maluta motioned her to a chair but she ignored him. She went around the side of the desk and put one booted foot up on his chair. With a shove, she swiveled his leather chair around and flexed her knee. The thick brown fabric of her uniform skirt drew back as if by accident, revealing the flesh of her thigh.

Startled and angry, Maluta lifted a hand to strike her but Daniella caught it by the wrist in her two hands. He opened his mouth but she put her face very close to his and slowly, slowly drew his hand downward. Their eyes locked and this time Daniella saw the vulnerability behind the carefully groomed façade. He was a child just as all men were children deep down in their souls. That was the essential difference in the sexes, Daniella thought: men, at their cores, are children; women are mothers.

Daniella cursed into his face while she brought his reluctant hand within the hem of her skirt, into the darkness.

"This is what you want, bastard," she hissed at him. "This is what you're afraid Oreanda will punish you for having. Isn't that right, Oleg."

"Don't call me that here." His face was flushed and the hand holding the receiver was white.

"Put the phone down, Oleg."

"I told you . . ."

She gripped his hand hard, guided his fingertips until they grazed the humid bush of her pubic hair. As soon as she felt the tremors begin she pushed his hand away along her thigh.

Maluta's brain was on fire. Through the conflagration he saw the visage of Oreanda. Her full sensual lips opened and she spoke to him. He felt rather than heard her words. They fell like drops of dew onto his imprisoned fingertips.

447

His tongue came out, swiped at his dry lips; he began to tremble in earnest.

"It *is* what you want, Oleg." Her voice was silken whisper.

"Not here," he rasped thickly. "Not now."

"Oh, yes," she said, her lips against his ear. "Here. Now."

"No!" he shouted, beginning to rise up out of the chair. But Daniella drew his palm forward until it cupped her. She pushed the fingertips inside her and she said, "There," as she would to an infant whose constant crying she wished to end.

Oh, God, God, God, Maluta thought, shivering. He felt the sweat trickle from under his arms. With a stifled groan, he hung up without ending the conversation. There was an odd, sweet taste in his mouth.

"Are you crazy?" he said but he knew it was likely not she but he who was crazy; knew that if he had to take his hand away now he could not. "Why are you doing this?" he whispered. He could not take his eyes off her hips as they made sharp little circles. "Is it to humiliate me further? To tell me how much you despise me, how you hate making love to me, how it disgusts you?"

"I'm going to come," Daniella said, arching herself into his probing fingers. The gaze from her gray eyes seemed to caress him. "Right now." And reached down to twist the bulge inside his trousers.

Felt him lurch, then spurt heavily and said, "There. Oh, there."

The phone began to ring. He was panting, his face slick with running sweat that trickled down into the starched collar of his shirt. He jerked a little, as if with tiny electric shocks, as she continued to rub him through his sopping trousers. In a moment, the ringing ceased.

"I hope you have a change of clothes here," she said, laughing as she took his hand from her and put her leg down.

"Did you enjoy it?" Maluta's eyes never left her as she walked around the desk and sat, finally, on one of the velvet-covered chairs. She sat with her back very straight, her legs demurely crossed, a soldier's posture. Her head was back, a strand of her thick, honey-colored hair curling down over one cool appraising gray eye.

"I want to know," Maluta said. "It is important that I know." He had not moved an inch since she had left him.

"Why is it important to you, Oleg?"

"Because," he said. And stopped.

"Because you fancy yourself a great lover?"

"Because Oreanda never . . . enjoyed it!"

He had blurted it out and Daniella suppressed a smile of triumph. She had known that he could not fancy himself any kind of lover at all, the celibate all these years since Oreanda's death. But she had wanted to provoke a response in him, knowing that if she stung him deep enough the truth would inevitably emerge. And in this she had been successful.

"Now you must know whether I am like her in this," she said.

"Yes."

"Oleg, Oreanda never came into your office and did that to you."

"It never would have occurred to her," he admitted.

"What did she enjoy?"

His eyes were closed, his arched fingers massaging his forehead. "She read de Sade. You know that."

She had not, she had only suspected it until he had told her at the *dacha*. "And she practiced what she read." She watched him. "Yes," she went on eventually, "I imagine she *was* a cunt."

"You know nothing about her," Maluta said, but there was no conviction left in his voice.

"On the contrary," Daniella said, deliberately ending the thought there.

"Well?" he said. "You didn't answer my question."

"I thought I had."

"I don't understand."

"Oleg," she said, "it's all the answer you're going to get." She stood up, smiled. "I hope you don't have an imminent meeting. You're all wet."

He looked down at his lap as if first becoming aware of the mess there. "Look what you've done to me."

"I want the photos of Mikhail."

"No," Maluta said.

"What do you do," she said contemptuously, "spill your seed all over them?"

He was abruptly offended. "What are you thinking of? You cannot shame me into giving them to you."

"I have no need to, Oleg," she said earnestly. "You have already shamed yourself."

"How easily the lies fall from your mouth, cunt."

"No, Oleg," she said. "Oreanda was the cunt, the controlling bitch who made your life a hell."

"I loved her!" he shouted and she thought, Yes, the wound

449

is still as fresh as if it had been inflicted yesterday. "I loved her with all my heart."

"You couldn't have," Daniella said assertively. "Otherwise she would not have died."

His face was white. "What do you mean?" But he knew perfectly well what she meant.

"You protest that you didn't set the fire," she said. "Why? Do you think that you can hide it from her? Do you think that you can escape her retribution?"

Maluta was gripping the arms of his chair.

And then in a softer voice, "She's listening now, isn't she, Oleg?"

His eyes were wide and staring. "You *are* crazy!" He was shaking now. He knew that he must fill up the hissing silence or he would go mad. This was what he had been fighting with since Oreanda's death. Now it was coming out, leaking through the fine seal he had set up at the dark edge of his mind. "She's dead. Dead and gone!"

Daniella shook her head, sensing victory. His eyes, with the whites showing all around, had the aspect of a panicked animal's. "She's inside your soul, Oleg. You must know that."

She leaned over his desk, her eyes glowing, feral. "She knows who set the fire. She knows who killed her."

Then abruptly, Daniella came around the desk. Her aspect softened along with her voice. "But I'll protect you, Oleg." Her hand rested on his crotch. She felt the stirring there. "I'll protect you from Oreanda. Her power is mine, isn't it, Oleg. The magic has been transferred. It is mine to use as I wish." Her voice had turned into a croon. "Yes, I'll protect you."

Maluta, giving a great shudder, dug frantically inside the collar of his shirt. He produced a tiny, odd-looking key on a gold chain and, rattling it against the lock in the desk's lower drawer, finally inserted it. He pulled out the drawer and fumbled there for some time out of Daniella's line of sight.

"There," he said, finally. "All right? There."

Daniella looked at the packet he had thrown on the desktop, her heart beating fast. She tried, unsuccessfully, to catch her breath.

"You and Mikhail Carelin," Maluta said through tense lips. "In there like characters from a film. A pornographic film." He looked away, as if he could not bear what he was doing. "The prints and the negatives. Everything is there." A pulse beat erratically in his temple. He appeared inordinately tired, as if giving up the photos somehow robbed him of energy.

Daniella lifted her hand, mopped at his sopping brow. "Poor darling," she whispered. "Rest now. Sleep."

Oleg Maluta nodded. He closed his eyes.

Slowly, with the kind of reverence her mother had approached the image of Christ on the cross, Daniella put her hand over the packet.

Jake hit White-Eye Kao very hard in the center of his nose. The flesh rent, the cartilage split and a torrent of blood gushed forth. Jake held the Chinese's hands, preventing them from stanching the flow.

White-Eye Kao's good eye was red-rimmed and his cheap suit was stained red. "I know you're not here to be buggered," Jake said. "You're too old for McKenna, for one thing." He hauled on the Chinese, dragging him across the brightly lighted room. "For another, you're a bloody wog. That's what McKenna called you, know that? Did he ever say that to your face, I wonder? No, he didn't have the guts for it. But he thought it every waking moment. You were nothing but a running sore to him."

Took White-Eye Kao by the scruff of his neck and, as if he were a pet who had soiled the carpet, shoved his face into McKenna's bloated one. The stench was horrific.

"Gr-Great Pool of Piddle!" White-Eye Kao finally got out. *"A mi tuo fo!"*

"That's right," Jake said, "call on the Buddha. But he won't be merciful tonight. Not to you, anyway."

He hauled back on the Chinese, kept him standing. It was important to keep him as uncomfortable as possible.

"Water," White-Eye Kao said. He turned his head in Bliss's direction. "Buddha's mercy, some water!"

"Oh," Jake said, "you want her to take care of you instead of me? All right. It's a mistake you won't make again, I guarantee that."

White-Eye Kao's bloodshot orb stared at him, uncomprehendingly. Jake smiled into White-Eye Kao's face and at the same moment, his arm shot out and his clawed hand grabbed his sacred sac, squeezing it so hard that White-Eye Kao's good eye bulged in its socket with the exquisite agony, making him tremble and jerk. Beads of sweat formed on his eyebrows. His lips were pulled back in a rictus of pain.

His chest fluttered, heaving, as Jake let go. He groaned deep in his throat and his head sank down.

"Jake . . ." Bliss took a step toward him but Jake waved her back. He ignored the concerned look on her face.

"You see now how unwise you've been," Jake said softly in White-Eye Kao's ear. He waited until the Chinese nodded before going on. "Now tell me what you're doing here."

"Vis-visiting."

Jake used his hand again. This time White-Eye Kao's body arched, his legs kicking uncontrollably. "Ah, Buddha!" he hissed through gritted teeth.

"He won't help you now," Jake said. "No one's going to help you. Now tell us what you were doing here." He gave a tentative little squeeze and the Chinese made a high keening in his throat, trying to shrink away from him.

"I know who you are," Jake said softly in his ear. "I know you work for Sir John Bluestone. And I know who Bluestone is. Now what does that make you?"

White-Eye Kao, staring in terror into Jake's face, said, "A Communist."

"And what does a Communist want with Great Pool of Piddle McKenna?"

"He—" The Chinese gulped, swallowing his own blood. "He was a conduit. A conduit through which Bluestone was able to spread the news of trouble at Southasia."

"And you were Bluestone's messenger boy?"

"Yes."

"McKenna suspected nothing?"

"Suspect what? He thought I was from a Triad. Green Pang, maybe. Who knows."

"Bluestone was behind Teck Yau's embezzlement of Southasia funds."

"Yes. Of course."

"Who else was involved?"

"I don't know."

Whirled him around, pulled him erect with a hard jerk. "Listen, you pox-infested piece of dogshit," Jake said menacingly, "my father's been murdered, this lady's been shot at and someone has been trying to kill me down every street and back alley from here to Kyoto."

"Jake, he's had enough," Bliss said reasonably.

"No," Jake said so fiercely it frightened her. Then to White-Eye Kao, "Tell me what you know."

"I've told you. Ohhh!" He vomited, retching dryly at the aftermath of Jake's liver kite.

"Jake." Bliss put her hand on his shoulder. "Maybe he's telling the truth."

"Listen to her," the Chinese gasped, on his knees. His forehead was pressed against the threadbare carpet. "Buddha, what do you want from me?"

"You've got a smart mouth," Jake said, bending down over the Chinese. "I want to know who trained you."

"Bluestone."

Jake lifted his head, looked at Bliss. "He's got the same answer for every question." Saw that look on her face as she shook her head in a negative. The Chinese was lying.

"*A mi tuo fo*, it's your questions, not my answers!"

"A master," Jake said seriously. "I told you he had been taught by a master."

He left the Chinese curled on the floor, watched over by Bliss, and rummaged around the kitchen. He returned with a small knife and, bending over, took White-Eye Kao's sweat-slick hair in his fist, pulled back his head. "Since you've got a smart mouth we're going to do something about it."

"Wha-what d'you mean?"

Jake grinned down into his face. "You've got a lot of teeth." The grin was fierce and utterly merciless. "They're going to come out one by one."

"*Dew neh loh moh*, are you crazy?" White-Eye Kao's gaze was fixed hypnotically on the shining point of the blade. He smiled then, canny as a fox. "That's good. Very good. You know what? You almost made me shit my pants. But I know you wouldn't—"

"Jake, for the love of Buddha, no!"

White-Eye Kao screamed as Jake stabbed the knife downward, digging into the soft pink gum beside a lower molar. Twisted the blade, scraping against the enamel, levering the tooth out.

"Jake, what's gotten into you?"

It popped with a gush of blood. White-Eye Kao gagged and gurgled. His fists beat at his own head to stop the pain.

"Oh, oh, oh," he moaned. "He didn't tell me it would be like this."

"Who didn't tell you?" Jake was very close to him.

"He said I wouldn't get hurt. I wouldn't . . . Ah, Buddha, it hurts!"

"Imagine how much worse it'll be when I go in on the other side of your mouth," Jake said, getting the blade set.

"*A mi tuo fo*, no!" White-Eye Kao tried to crawl away but

Jake held him fast. Tears were in his eyes and he spit out more blood. "It's not worth it! Nothing's worth it!"

"You weren't trained by Bluestone," Jake said. "Who then? Daniella Vorkuta?"

"A fornicating woman?" White-Eye Kao said with some contempt. "Buddha, no." It was the pride that stopped the flow of tears. "I was trained by Chen Ju."

Jake laughed. "That old bastard has more legends about him than anyone else I know. Now you'd better come up with the truth."

"It is the truth! Buddha, do you think I want any more of that?"

"Easy to talk about Chen Ju," Jake said. "The old man's long dead."

"Dead?" Now it was White-Eye Kao's turn to laugh. "What do you think this is all about? Bluestone?" The Chinese spat again. "The *loh faan* is the only one who believes himself so clever." He wiped blood off his face with his sleeve. "Who came to the *tai pan* with the thought of penetrating to the heart of Southasia?"

Jake took the Chinese up by the front of his jacket, already stiff and stinking with dried blood. His knuckles were white with tension because Bliss, able to intuit the truth, had passed her knowledge silently on to him. "What are you saying?"

"If Chen Ju is dead," White-Eye Kao said, "then I have come face to face with a ghost."

Mandalay, the Golden City, was the center of the world. At least the Royal Palace that the Burmese king, Mindon, had built all of solid teak in 1857 was its site: the mystical Mount Meru so dear to the Brahmin-Buddhist cosmology.

By Burmese standards, Mandalay, just over a mere century old, was a recent city. Yet, lying athwart the upper Irrawaddy in the north, it had quickly become the center of all trading, being in the midst of the rice-growing districts. Still, its climate was often so dry that the sky was turned ochre by plumes of dust kicked up by ancient vehicles.

Mandalay nevertheless held a magic incomparable in the Burmese heart. It was said that it was to Mandalay that Gautama Buddha journeyed in order to announce that on the twenty-four-hundredth anniversary of his death the world's largest center of Buddhist teaching would spring up at the foot of Mandalay Hill.

This legend was the kind of thing the British dismissed

out of hand as so much Asian mumbo jumbo. When they took over the city in 1885, they renamed the Royal Palace Fort Dufferin and made barracks of the sacred chambers. Mustachioed batmen diligently polished their officers' boots in lemon-scented corridors where, before, holy voices had echoed. The commandants unsheathed their Wilkerson swords, touching tips and shouting Hallelujah! Another outpost of the Empire had been secured.

In the early spring of 1945 the British shelled the fortress—then defended by a handful of Japanese and Burmese soldiers. The gunners did such a thorough job that today only the outer walls and the moat remain.

This is what Tony Simbal was thinking of as he looked down upon the ruins of the Royal Palace, a perfect square whose walls faced in the four cardinal directions. He was studying the spot he knew to be the Lion's Room, the central throne room where the British general Prendergast led his horse when King Thibaw was forced into exile in the winter of 1885. The nervous animal's steaming droppings soiled a carpet many hundreds of years old brought to Mandalay from the ancient capital of Amarapura. The general thought it just as well. The weavers' detailed depiction of the Theraveda *arhats* or saints made him uneasy and he had it burned without a pang of remorse.

If one faced the Royal Palace today, Simbal thought, one could still catch a whiff of burning material.

To the east, the umber sky withheld its promise of rain. The achingly dry ground was cracked beneath a glaring sun, so many mouths crying silently for moisture. Simbal, in white sea-island cotton shirt, bush shorts and sturdy, high-topped leather hiking shoes, waited while Max Threnody laboriously climbed the hill.

The heat was intense and by the time Threnody made it up, his khaki shirt was soaked through. He wiped at his brow with an oversize handkerchief already darkened by many such moppings.

"Christ," he said, "but this is a godforsaken place."

"On the contrary," Simbal said, still staring at the palace ruins, "it is quite near the place where God dwells."

"And where might that be?" Threnody said sarcastically.

"There." Simbal pointed to the northwest, where the purple mountains rose upward from the vast Irrawaddy plain.

"The Shan?" Threnody snorted, shifting on his feet. He

wished desperately to get out of the sun. "Christ, the only thing worth anything up there kills people."

"Really?" Simbal was in no mood for his former boss's monodirectional thinking. "There's power up there. Real power. The kind people like you can only dream of. The mountain knows that secret better than any of us."

"I suppose," Threnody said, "that people like you don't covet such power."

Simbal turned to look at him. The heat somehow made his eyes seem to pop even more. As a child, Simbal had once had a tropical fish tank. His uncle had brought him a pair of beautiful velvet-finned goggle-eyed goldfish. Simbal had loved them but one night he had gone out and inadvertently left the grow light on over the tank. When he returned, the goldfish were dead, bloated grotesquely, parboiled in the heat. Threnody reminded him of those fish now. "I'm surprised you came."

"Frankly, you didn't leave me any choice." Threnody thrust his hands into his trousers' pockets. "By the way, the Cuban's pissed as hell at you."

"I'll try not to cry," Simbal said. "He'll get over it."

Threnody peered at him through his thick glasses. "Do I detect a bit of hostility, Tony?"

Simbal reached into one oversize shirt pocket, deposited three photographs into Threnody's hand. They were black and white with the kind of grain brought about by blowing up a section of a negative. Also, they had the absolutely flat aspect produced by a long lens. They were surveillance photos Simbal had taken of a handsome man in his mid-thirties with clear, intelligent eyes, an all-American nose, a sensitive mouth. The bit of slightly out-of-focus background made it clear that the subject was photographed just outside the Royal Palace.

"So this is where he is," Threnody said.

"Just like you, Max," Simbal said shortly. "Not, 'My, he's still alive.' " His eyes burned bright.

"What earthly good would that serve," Threnody said. "The fact is, Peter Curran is alive." He glanced down at the photos Simbal had handed him. "We'd better put whatever surprise we may feel behind us. I want him and you're going to get him for me."

"Just like that?"

"Don't take that righteous tone with me," Threnody said sharply. "What kind of business do you think you're in, Tony? Do you suppose we're all gentlemen here, meticulously saying 'please' and 'thank you' and not getting in each other's way?"

"You used me." Simbal's tone was accusatory. "You used Monica and Martine to keep track of me."

"Congratulations," Threnody said, "you've deciphered the language of your trade. Better late than never, Tony. Yes, I had a job to do. I used all the resources—you, Monica, the Cuban—at my disposal. That's what the government pays me to do."

"A fucking dirty job it is."

"Should I say, 'But someone's got to do it'? It's true." He put the photos of Curran away. "You have no legitimate complaints, you know. It's your job, as well."

"But you're DEA, Max," Simbal said. "In case you've forgotten, Martine is a SNIT. That's CIA. The Company and the DEA are always miles apart on everything. You'd better tell me what I'm missing."

"All in good time," Threnody said. "Now that we're both here you'll hear the whole nine yards."

Simbal watched a line of saffron-robed monks moving slowly past one of the palace's twelve gates. Their shaven heads gleamed in the dusty sunlight. He thought of what the British had done to the Golden City, shit all over the rug from Amarapura.

"The Burmese," he said after a time, "practice a certain form of Buddhism. In Theraveda, there is no all-powerful god. One cannot even pray for the benevolence of Buddha. There can be no divine intervention. Salvation is entirely in the hands of the individual.

"All life is suffering, the Theraveda Buddhists believe. Life and death are opposite sides of *samsara*, the rebirth. There is only one way out of the perpetual cycle of misery and that is strict adherence to Buddha's sacred teaching, the Dharma. One must diligently follow the paths laid out by the *arhats*, the saints and the *boddhisatvas*, the Buddhas-to-be. Only then may one reach nirvana.

"Today, even here at the center of the world, perhaps it is only the monks who practice such a pure form of Theravada Buddhism."

"And you are one of them, aren't you, Tony?" Threnody wiped at his face again. "You're high above the masses. You're on the Shan, on the mountainside, looking down at all the pathetic little ants crawling slowly along, going about the daily routines by which they must live."

"Is that what you think of me?"

457

"Oh, come off it, Tony. You're a goddamned elitist. Do yourself a favor and admit that much, at least."

The monks were turning a corner. They were all in step, the many with one mind.

"Do you know who Peter Curran came here to meet at dawn?" Simbal said.

"Surprise me."

"Edward Martin Bennett."

"Well, well," Threnody said, "there's something the vetting department failed to turn up."

"What does the *diqui* want with them?"

"Are you kidding, Tony? With what they stole from the DEA computer the *diqui* will have clear drug runs for months until we rearrange all our Asian networks."

"I don't think this has anything to do with drugs, Max."

"I don't care what it has to do with," Threnody said. "Terminate them and be done with it." He waited for Simbal's head to swing around, the eyes to contemplate him. One thing you had to say for the bastard, Simbal thought, he had great timing. "It's time for us to have a little talk, Tony. Heart to heart, so to speak."

"I don't think Chen Ju is our most immediate problem."

Three Oaths lumbered across the teak deck of his new junk, delivering tea that Neon Chow had made.

"As of this morning Bluestone has increased his share of InterAsia to just over forty percent."

"I wonder where he's getting all that capital?" Jake said as he took a meditative sip of the steaming tea.

Three Oaths recited the list of investors given to him by Bent-Nose Su. "There's enough money in there to buy all of Hong Kong if necessary."

Jake was aware of the anxiety in the other's voice. "Bobby Chan, Six-Toe Ping, Sir Byron Nolin-Kelly, Dark Leong Lau. Impressive. Still," he mused, "there has got to be a limit to the amount of liquid assets even Bluestone's combine can sink into one project."

"They only need nine percent more to gain control," Three Oaths said.

"That would make it thirteen million shares, give or take. What's the current price on the Hang Seng of InterAsia?"

"Let me check." Three Oaths went down the companionway. Jake took a look around. He saw Bliss talking with Neon Chow. Both were engrossed in their conversation but every now and again he saw Neon Chow glancing in his direction. Out of the corner of his eye it was impossible to decipher her expression. He made a mental note to ask her what progress she had made with Bluestone.

"Twenty-two-and-a-quarter," Three Oaths said, returning. "We took a terrible beating when we were forced to close Southasia."

"They've still got to put up, what?, two hundred ninety million dollars," Jake said. "What have they anted up already?"

Three Oaths did some fast calculating. "I'd say close to three-quarters of a billion. To do that they've had to liquidate some holdings, of course. But what's the difference? As soon as they take control of InterAsia, they'll have effectively sewn up the entire Crown Colony. A billion dollars is a cheap price to pay for all of Hong Kong."

"Cheap only if you can afford it," Jake said thoughtfully.

"So what shall we do now, *Zhuan*? How are we going to prevent the *gwai loh tai pan* from taking everything from us?"

Again Jake was aware of the edge in the other's voice. He knew that he was being shut out of momentous business decisions and he resented it. This had not been his relationship with Zilin. But Jake was not the Jian; he was *Zhuan*, and these were different times. *Trust no one with this, Jake*, his father had told him. *No one. Not until you find Bluestone's conduit into the* yuhn-hyun. Jake said, "I want you to tell Sawyer to call our broker and float the du Long bonds."

"What?" Three Oaths cried. "Those are junk! High gain— triple the interest available on the market—for high risk. They'll increase InterAsia's debt tremendously. And for what? Yes, they'll drive up the price of the stock but for now long? And for the piddling amount of cash they'll add to our depleted supply of capital, they'll make us liable to pay back sums that could break our backs."

"If we're still here, we'll be glad to pay," Jake said evenly.

Three Oaths turned thoughtful. "A moment. Are you doing this for Bluestone's benefit? That added debt would make InterAsia less desirable for a takeover as well."

But not enough, Jake thought. Not nearly enough. "How much do you think the stock will rise?"

Three Oaths considered this. "Seven points. Ten, if we're lucky."

Will even that be sufficient? Jake wondered. So close to the ultimate abyss now, he could feel the edge of the sword

Bluestone, Daniella Vorkuta and Chen Ju had manufactured hanging over him. He wondered whether he had been right to trust so completely in his father. Zilin had been merely human, after all. He was prone to making mistakes. Trust sometimes could not withstand the rigors of time.

But, he knew, it had been he, as *Zhuan*, who had made the final decision. It was, in the final analysis, his judgment. No good to blame the dead if it all fell apart now.

Three Oaths's fist enclosed his tiny teacup. "*Zhuan* I was against going public with the new company from the first."

"I am aware of that, Elder Uncle."

"By the Spirit of the White Tiger, if you had heeded my advice, none of this would have been possible! I would not be watching everything I have worked for since I journeyed here from Shanghai being taken away from me by a fornicating *loh faan*!"

"Do not forget, Elder Uncle," Jake said, "how it was you came to Hong Kong in the first place. My father sent you here in the employ of Andrew Sawyer's father, Barton, to begin your work for the *yuhn-hyun*. The decision to go public with InterAsia was made by me with my father's blessing."

For a moment, Three Oaths did nothing. He peered into Jake's hooded copper eyes. "I wonder where my nephew has gone to?" he said softly. "Where is the young man who used to confide in me, with whom I shared secrets, I wonder?"

"That was a long time ago, Elder Uncle. The difference is day and night."

"I can see as well as anyone," Three Oaths said. "I am not yet that old."

"Please do as I have asked," Jake said gently but firmly. "I want those bonds on the market before day's end."

He stood by the railing for a long time. He preferred not to watch the old man's painful progress down the companionway. Beyond the junk's berth, *walla-wallas* were busy taking wide-eyed, camera-laden tourists to and from Jumbo, the gargantuan, multitiered floating restaurant that, along with two others, was permanently anchored in Aberdeen Harbor. The riders took in the teeming waterfront with a mixture of fascination and apprehension, as if they anticipated coming across a real-life smuggler or Triad assassin.

He joined the women and they broke off their conversation. "Don't stop on my account," he said.

"We've finished," Bliss said.

Neon Chow smiled. "Are you done with your uncle now?" she asked.

It occurred to Jake that she had missed her calling. Only an excellent actress could smile so winningly while being so verbally acerbic. He chose not to answer her. Instead, he said, "How are you proceeding with Sir John Bluestone?"

"He's urbane and witty."

"He's also a Communist spy," Jake said drily.

"Did you expect him to come out and confess that to me already?"

"I expected some progress."

"Whores," Neon Chow said, "do not make progress. They merely sink deeper and deeper into an abyss." That smile again. Now he could see its sharpness, like a stiletto's shining blade. "And that's what you've made me through your directive, *Zhuan*. A whore."

"Well, what do you know," Jake said. "I didn't think Bluestone had it in him."

Neon Chow slapped him across the face, saying, "Bastard! Do you know how hard this is on your uncle?"

Jake did not move. His copper eyes glistened.

"Go on," she said. "You may terrify the rest of them. *Zhuan*." She spit it out as if it burned her tongue. "I'm not afraid of you."

"All I ask is that you do as you are told," Jake said reasonably. "If that's too much, say so. You're my uncle's mistress, not mine. You have other things to occupy your time, I imagine."

"You really are a bastard, aren't you?"

"I think you ought to stop seeing Bluestone," he said abruptly.

Her eyes widened. "Why?"

"It was a mistake," Jake said. "Let's call it quits."

"I don't want to. Are you saying I can't do it?"

"I told you it was a mistake, that's all. Besides, you said yourself that it's hurting Three Oaths. I don't want to do that."

"You want Bluestone's secrets, don't you?"

"There's always another way." He did not want her to know that there was no other path for him. What would she demand of him then?

"Like what?" Neon Chow persisted. "I still think I have the best chance. Sooner or later he'll drop something on my pillow or I'll overhear a late-night conversation."

461

Jake appeared lost in thought for a time. "All right," he said at last. "I'm willing to give it another shot. But," he warned, "if you can't bring me results in one week, that will be the end of it."

She seemed unsure. "That's very little time."

"It's all you're going to get." He glanced at his watch. "If I were you I'd make the most of it."

Neon Chow nodded. Went quickly below and, gathering up her things, she went off the junk.

Jake watched her leave. It was easy to pick her out of the crowd. She could stop traffic in a model's convention.

Bliss caught his eye. "Jake—" she began but Jake waved her to silence. Seeing Three Oaths emerging from belowdecks he went over to him.

"It's all done," the old man said. If anything, he seemed in worse humor. "If it means anything, Sawyer's reaction was the same as mine. But he's done as you ordered. The du Long bonds are on the market."

"Good," Jake said, and began to turn away.

"*Zhuan.*"

"Yes, Elder Uncle."

"Bliss told me about what happened at Great Pool of Piddle's and I am concerned."

"We're all concerned, Elder Uncle."

"No. I mean about you."

Jake watched him, silent.

"She told me what you did to White-Eye Kao."

"I don't have to—"

"She admitted her own guilt. The torture—"

"We did what was necessary," Jake said shortly. "Nothing more."

"I understand that there are great stakes involved."

"Greater than we know, I fear."

Three Oaths fought hard to decipher his nephew's words. Yes, he thought, he is greatly changed. His spirit is so far away from all of us. Is this what it means to be *Zhuan*? If so then, truly, I do not wish it for my number one son or any of my sons, for that matter. "Is it true that Chen Ju is alive?" he said finally.

"So it would seem, Elder Uncle."

"And that you and Bliss will seek him out."

"Yes."

Three Oaths gave a great sigh. "It is exceedingly dangerous there. In the Shan."

"I know."

"It is his place, now. Chen Ju's. It is our enemy's seat of power."

Jake looked deeply into the old man's eyes. "Elder Uncle, if I do not do this, there will truly be nothing left for any of us."

"Of course you must go, then, *Zhuan*."

"I will take good care of her, Elder Uncle. She is most precious to me, your *bou-sehk*."

"My precious gem." Tears were glistening in the old man's eyes. "You were right. Times have changed. More, much more than I have realized. Shi Zilin is gone. You are *Zhuan* now. And my *bou-sehk* is no longer a child. It is a difficult realization." Which one did he mean? The first, the last, or all of them?

The madness was growing. Being in her proximity was akin to standing too close to an out-of-control blaze. No wonder, Huaishan Han thought, Colonel Hu was no longer among the living.

Within General Kuo's kingly hut Huaishan Han sat like a misshapen lump of lard. That one shoulder was higher than the other never bothered him more than it did now. It was a constant reminder of the well. Or perhaps she—Qi lin—was that reminder.

Her eyes were like burning coals. Once Huaishan Han had gone tiger hunting in the north, far above Beijing. Siberian tigers, enormous, savage beasts out of a prehistory he could only guess at.

It was the whiteness of the beast that had surprised him the most. He supposed it was because of the snow. There was a lot of snow that far north. He could still see his own breath, a living thing, escaping from his lungs in silver sheets. His hair had been rimed by ice so that he looked prematurely gray. The cold penetrated even through his sheepskin-lined parka.

Huaishan Han and the hunter had spent three days tracking the faint spoor of a massive male. He was like a spirit: they could hear him at times, snuffling, growling low in his throat. Once he was certain he even scented the beast. But they never caught sight of him.

The last night in camp. They had decided to call it quits. The cold was bone-chilling and the quest seemed fruitless.

All they spoke of around the sparking fire was returning to civilization where they could get warmth and real food.

Huaishan Han awoke into utter darkness. The full moon had gone down. A night wind flicked shards of ice and snow through the encampment like the remnants of a defeated army.

Heard a quick, sharp sound and, turning his head, he was aghast to see the massive shoulders of the shadowed beast not a half-a-meter away. He held his breath. Fear was like a living being squirming in his belly. His legs were water and he was certain that he had lost control of his bladder.

The neck muscles displayed so high above him were bunched in tension and, as Huaishan Han stared in helpless fascination, the tiger gave a sharp jerk of its powerful head. He heard a distinct snap, as if a mature tree had been rent by lightning, and the pale face of his companion rolled in his direction.

Huaishan Han started despite himself and the great feline head came up. A rough bestial snuffling and he was staring directly into the face of the creature. For a moment, there was absolute stillness. Then, it snarled a little, black lips curling back to reveal long, blood-streaked fangs.

Those great mirrored eyes, utterly round, yellow and streaked as polished carnelians, gave off their own light, lurid and luminescent. They lay encysted within the encompassing womb of the night, glowing with power, until Huaishan Han was quite certain that only he and the beast existed.

He knew that within the next sixty seconds he would either live or die. Knew as well that he had no say in the matter. He knew if he moved at all the tiger would leap upon him without warning.

It was up to the beast, then. Or Buddha, who dwelt within all living things. *Joss*.

Huaishan Han gave up a tiny sigh of resignation and, looking into the face of death, recognized it as being wholly familiar.

It had not surprised him when the beast turned away from him, all illumination ceased, the extraordinary world that those eyes had revealed to him winked out, the raw power, the indefatigable energy evaporated. And that awesome engine of destruction was again part of the night.

For many years afterward, Huaishan Han was to lie sleepless in his bed trying to decipher the message Buddha had left for him in those eyes. At last, he had decided that it was this: it was not that the tiger killed indiscriminately but, rather, that it did so without the slightest compunction.

Now, humped in the dusty wicker chair General Kuo had provided for him, Huaishan Han stared into Qi lin's coal-black eyes and knew that he was visited again by the terrifying engine of destruction out of his past.

Compulsively he reached out and took her hand in his. Turning it over, he stared down. It seemed so fragile, so pale and beautiful with its extraordinarily long slender fingers. Yet he knew that it must have been this hand that had killed Colonel Hu. He recalled the hypnotic beauty of the beast that had exerted its pull over him. It had made him ache to reach out and caress those velvet eyes. It had made him long to crawl closer to the nexus of that heady power. Did not this female, the granddaughter of his enemy, possess the same disorienting quality?

It was madness to think so, to believe in such power. But madness had been Huaishan Han's constant companion, a piece of the utter blackness of the well dwelling within him long after General Kuo had come to the lip of his world and, reaching down, had pulled him out of that pit of terror.

Huaishan Han closed his eyes and shuddered heavily. Ah, the well! The world of the damned. General Kuo had saved him from that but Huaishan Han knew that he had never truly escaped. His heart was encased in the utter anguish of that endless time. And now, looking into those feline eyes so close to his face, he realized with a start, that though General Kuo might have pulled him from the depths of perdition, he had died down there in the lightless trough of the well.

Realized as well that he had never been so alive as at that moment when he stared into those hot agate eyes in the night. Now he knew just how much he had drawn from that engine of destruction and, with trembling, withered hands he brought Qi lin's exquisite head toward his own. Her cheeks were heated like a mysterious sun burning in the darkness and her skin had the velvet texture he had imagined in his dreams belonged to the white Siberian.

She growled low in her throat as he brought her to her knees in front of him and he was keenly aware of the danger seeping from her, as if a shining blade was at his throat. He swallowed convulsively and bowed his head until his forehead pressed against hers.

The energy flowed into him and he knew that if she reached

up now and broke his neck he would not stop her. But she would not. He was as certain of that as he had been of anything in his life.

No, she would not harm him, this grandchild of his enemy, but she would kill for him. She would kill Jake Maroc Shi.

With an almost religious reverence, Huaishan Han pressed his lips to her forehead and for just an instant the horror of the well faded from his consciousness.

The girandole rose into the black sky, radiating light.

"Someone," Threnody said, "has a sure hand with the fireworks."

They could hear the popping and sparking associated with the display now. Up on the hill, they were quite a ways away from the source.

"When the boy comes," Simbal said, "I'll have to go."

Threnody recognized a threat when he heard one. They were at an outdoor café. It was still so hot he was sweating doing nothing but sitting. He found the climate intolerable and wondered how Simbal could like it here. "I did not come here to tell you about Peter Curran. I could have Telexed that information or have sent Monica."

There was a large Buddha nearby as there almost always was wherever one happened to find oneself in Burma. The figure was seated with his left hand palm upward on his lap, the right resting palm down on his right knee, the fingertips touching the ground.

"Actually," Threnody went on, "I'm glad you're pissed off at me, Tony. It shows you're right on form." He took up his sweating glass of beer and downed some. "I wouldn't want to think I'd misjudged you at this late date."

Threnody seemed very sure of himself and this interested Simbal. This was not his territory and, it seemed to him, Threnody was not a good traveler. He had a weak stomach, a penchant for picking up the local parasite or something. At least that was the story that was commonly batted around at the DEA when Simbal had been there.

"Tell me something, Max," he said. "Did you know that Peter Curran was alive?"

"Now how would I know that?" Threnody said.

"Do you see that Buddha?" Simbal said. "It's many centuries old. Those are diamonds encrusting its base. In many temples, Burmese work full time to restore the gold leaf that is worn away over the years by supplicants touching the image for luck." He poured out a bottle of beer into his glass. "This one is in the Bhumispara *mudra*. He's calling on Vasumdarhi, the earth goddess."

"I didn't know Buddha needed help with anything," Threnody said drily.

"The legend has it," Simbal went on, "that Mara, the god of destruction, sought first to destroy the Buddha's power by unleashing an army of fierce demons against him and then, when that failed, dispatched his three daughters, Desire, Pleasure and Passion, to sway him.

"The Buddha touched the ground, calling upon Vasumdarhi to bear witness that he had found perfect knowledge. With her assent the earth began to heave and shake apart with such violent force that Mara and his daughters were driven away."

Threnody had finished his beer. He pushed the glass away to the center of the table where it stood, a lone barrier between them. "Is that how you see me, Tony, as Mara, the god of destruction come to crush you?"

Simbal remained silent. He was all too aware of Rodger Donovan's warning about Max.

"Today I am a messenger. A bearer of bad tidings, only. Will you listen to what I have to say?"

"All right."

Threnody hunched forward. The fireworks turned his face pink and gold, the colors sliding off the side of his face like greasepaint. "I mean really listen, Tony. To the bitter end. Even if some of it is not what you want to hear. I was your case officer through some pretty hairy situations. I always got you out with your skin whole. I always got my executives out with their skins whole."

"If not their minds," Simbal said. But he knew that Threnody was right. With him his people always came first. He took a great deal of heat from the chair jockeys higher up but he never allowed one iota of that to seep down to his executives. That was unusual. There were plenty of case officers out to make a name for themselves who would take all kinds of savage risks with their field people in order to get a job done. "You forget," Simbal went on, "that I work for Rodger Donovan now."

"Donovan, right. Your own personal contact in the old-boy network."

Simbal eyed him. "Do you think that's why he offered me the job?"

"My God, no. But it does play a factor, Tony. Perhaps a crucial one. I think that when it comes to the crunch Donovan believes that you will remain loyal to him *no matter what*."

"Because we grew up together, went through school together?"

"Don't underestimate the network, Tony. You performed the rites of youth together. That's a bond that is difficult to break."

"Through all of this you haven't said one word about Curran and Bennett," Simbal said.

"I'm grateful to you, Tony. Because of you we've found them. I gave you the motivation, you see. You're such a chivalrous type, I knew what the news of Curran's death would do to you."

"It didn't bother you what it did to Monica?"

"Believe me, Tony, when I tell you Monica's far better off thinking he's dead than knowing the truth about him."

"Is it up to you to play God?"

Threnody ignored that. "I knew once I'd given you sufficient motivation, you'd get your teeth into this mess. You found Bennett. You were always my best bulldog, Tony. I had a hell of a time, now and again, getting you to back off."

"I've done more than find them, Max," Simbal said. "Curran and Bennett are up to something that is larger than the DEA, larger even than the Quarry," Simbal said. "I have some facts but they don't add up to anything concrete. Before he died, Run-Run Yi managed to tell me several things. That the *diqui* is moving arms all around the globe. Not for resale but rather for stockpiling. Yi said that these antipersonnel weapons will have the power to destroy the world. He also called Bennett the jinn who opens the door. Do you know what he meant by that, Max?"

"All I know is what I've given you," Threnody said. "The point is I had the devil's own time getting you okayed for this briefing. There was a lot of—"

"Then this isn't about Curran and Bennett," Simbal cut in. "It never was."

"Oh, yes it was. Bennett and Curran are one issue. Rodger Donovan is quite another."

"Who had to okay me for this briefing?" Simbal said.

"The President."

"The President of what?"

Threnody sighed. "Of the United States. This is straight from the top, Tony."

468

Simbal peered at his former boss. "What do you have to do with the President of the United States except pick up the medals for your executives at closed awards ceremonies now and again?"

"I work for him now. Part time. That's how I'm able to run SNITs like Martine. I'm sort of semiretired from the DEA."

"Since when?" Simbal said skeptically.

"Since about a month after Henry Wunderman was killed. Do you think a thing like that would be let go so easily?"

"And the DEA?"

"As far as any of my people are concerned," Threnody said, "I'm still there full time. They know I'm grooming Boxer as my eventual replacement."

"David Boxer?"

"Yes. You know him, of course."

"What's he been told?"

"That my doctors say I need to take it easy, ease myself out of full-time involvement. He's most solicitous. And very good. I have no worries there."

Simbal watched the colored light dripping from Max Threnody's face. He had always wondered what it would be like to have his world turned upside down. Now that it was happening he knew it was nothing like the fantasy. "What's going on, Max? Why are you here?"

"In a moment, Tony. First, I feel I need explain something to you. The President was not happy when I mentioned your name for this."

"Why?"

"As I said, you and Donovan come from the same club. You're asshole buddies."

"This is about Donovan, then?"

"I told the President that in this case I thought it might work in our favor. I told him I was banking on you, Tony. On your smarts, your honesty, your sense of justice. You're a goddamned paladin, Tony. You like nothing better than to get on your white horse and have at the man in black." He paused significantly. "No matter their identity."

"I see you won out."

"I know you better than the President does," Threnody said. "Besides, this all rests on my shoulders."

Below them lights were on in a square. A bunch of teenagers, naked to the waist, were playing *chinlon*. It was the Burmese national sport and something of a mania among the

469

young. They passed a ball made of woven sugar-cane leaves from one to another using complicated strokes that involved only the feet and the knees.

"Max, what the hell is all this leading up to?"

"I think your boss—Rodger Donovan—is working for the other side."

In the square, the kid with the ball had stepped outside the circle drawn in the dust. It had a diameter of six-and-a-half meters and he lost points for his misstep. Points were also subtracted if the ball hit the ground. One gained points from the degree of difficulty of the strokes one performed while one had the ball.

Simbal, watching the *chinlon* game, felt sorry for the kid. It was a close game and now he was out of contention for the lead. Then he realized that it was really himself for whom he was feeling sorry.

"I noticed," Threnody said evenly, "that you haven't said 'You're out of your mind.'"

"Yet," Simbal said. The kid, rattled by his mistake, let the ball slip off the side of his foot. It bounced in the dirt and a hooting went up. Now he'd have no chance at all. "What makes you suspect Rodger?"

"Quite simply, it begins and ends with a painting," Threnody said. "Except that it's far from simple."

"I don't understand."

"Do you recall the painting Donovan put up in his office when he took over as director of the Quarry?"

"Sure. It's a Seurat," Simbal said, bringing to mind the conversation he'd had with Donovan. "But it's only a copy."

"Says who?"

"Donovan."

"Then he's a liar," Threnody said. "It's the genuine article."

"I hope to God you don't suspect him because it's too expensive for a man on a governmental salary to have," Simbal said. "Donovan comes from money."

Threnody waved a hand in the air. "Of course not. Money has nothing to do with it. The thing is, I've seen that painting before. Years ago I was stationed in Paris. Even then I was hot on the Impressionists. I haunted the galleries, museums. And auctions! My God, I'd've sold my soul to go to just one more.

"That was the only time I cheated on the service. Even in the middle of the business day, I'd sneak off to any art auction

I could get to. That's where I saw this Seurat. It was sold at auction. Sold to a beautiful woman with stormy gray eyes and thick honey-colored hair. I remember her well for a number of reasons. I wanted that Seurat but I am not like your friend, Donovan. I did not come from a monied family, I didn't go to the right schools." He laughed a little but there was a tinge of something dark there, as well, perhaps regret. "I was born on the wrong side of the tracks. I could only look longingly at the daughters of the Boston brahmins and wonder what it was that made them superior to me and my old man. Of course, in a law office on the Hill you never came home with a face black with coal dust and hands so callused by manual labor they looked like rhinoceros horn.

"But by the time I got out of college I knew my painters and, by God, I loved that Seurat. I coveted it even though there was no way I could have afforded it. So instead I concentrated on the buyer."

"The blonde."

"The blonde," Threnody affirmed. "Then I got interested in her for another reason. I recognized the face. I'd been doing some extracurricular research in regard to an operation that was getting somewhat strange. The Russians were apparently involved. More specificially the KGB.

"Which is where," Threnody said, "I'd come across that face. The Seurat had been bought by a KGB lieutenant by the name of Daniella Vorkuta."

Down below the moths were batting themselves to death in the lighted-up square. The kids should have been hoarse by now with all the shouting but the noise, like the energies involved, seemed indefatigable. Looking down there, Simbal saw that the kid who had made the two miscues had rebounded and was in the forefront of the pack again. He wished that he was that young and resilient again.

"That's the sum of what you have on Rodger?" he asked after a time. "That he has a Seurat that you saw purchased by a KGB lieutenant years ago in Paris?"

"At the same time Rodger Donovan was there," Threnody said. "I did some subsequent checking. Lieutenant Daniella Vorkuta was in Paris on recruitment assignment. Her official title then was second cultural attaché, so she moved in some high-powered circles."

"And the Seurat?"

Threnody shrugged. "Recruits like to be romanced. It's part of the game. They all want something tangible the first

471

time out. It's like testing the water, seeing how warm and inviting it is. The Seurat was most likely a gift."

"Some gift!"

"A measure of how important Donovan could be to them." Threnody reached into a pocket, withdrew a sweat-darkened envelope. "And believe me he lived up to his potential, Tony. It's all in there, copies of blown operations, crucial intelligence leaked. It's all very cleverly worked out, of course."

Simbal looked down at the envelope Threnody had placed on the table. "Why hasn't he been caught before this?"

Threnody shrugged. "What would you have me say, Tony? We're stupid. All of us in every service. We stumble blindly on. We all bungle things. As is true in every bureaucracy we fuck up more things than we get right. I admit I stumbled into this. Without the Seurat there'd be no suspicion. At least not in Donovan's direction."

"What do you want me to do?" In the square the game was over. The kid Simbal had been following had pulled it out, his last three strokes blowing away all competition. Good for you, Simbal thought.

"He's killing us, Tony," Threnody said. "He's sucking our blood like a goddamned vampire, bleeding us dry. It can't go on. He must be terminated. Quickly, efficiently, discreetly."

The boy for whom Simbal had been waiting had come. He quickly threaded his way around the tables. He came up to Simbal and grinned. He was from one of the mountain tribes near Mogok, where they mined the gemstones for which Burma was so justly famous. He looked into Simbal's face and grinned. Embedded into his front teeth were a heart-shaped ruby the color of pigeon blood and a diamond-shaped piece of Mogaung Imperial jade.

"They're on the move," Simbal said, rising. The boy had been watching the place where Curran and Bennett were holed up. "I gotta go."

"To the Shan," Threnody said.

"That's where they're headed," Simbal said. "I've no doubt."

Threnody looked up at him. He scooped up the envelope, held it out. "He's a bad one, Tony. The worst."

Simbal, with the kid pulling at his sleeve, took the envelope. "I'll take a look at what you've got."

"There isn't much time."

"What do you mean?"

"Go on, Tony," Threnody said. "The Shan is calling. The land where God dwells."

"Far from where Rodger Donovan is."

"That's part of the briefing. The last part," Threnody said. "My people, who are keeping tabs on Donovan, tell me he'll be here in a matter of hours."

"But why?" Simbal asked.

"That I don't know. In fact, I really don't care. The important thing, Tony, is for you to take immediate action."

"I haven't agreed to anything," Simbal said. "I'm here to track Bennett and Curran down. Do I have to say it again? I don't work for you anymore."

"It's all there." Threnody's forefinger tapped the manila envelope. "Rodger Donovan's a traitor, Tony. A lot of people have died because of him." Threnody's gaze was steady. "You bring Bennett and Curran down. God knows they deserve it." It was a look Simbal had seen before. "But it's Donovan that the President and I are concerned about now. We want him gone." It was the look Threnody got when he had decided to take the leash off his bulldog and give him his head.

The old man had skin like gold leaf. The sun and winds racing along the Shan plateau had burnished him in precisely the same manner he burnished the products of his labor.

He was an artisan of the old school, a Burmese fast disappearing from even this remote sector of the country. He was a master lacquerware maker. He had been born in Pagan where, it was said, his art traveled into Burma sometime during the first century A.D. via Chinese of the Nan-ch'ao Empire, whose great-great-great-grandchildren now inhabited Yunnan.

Nowadays, the pearl-gray liquid, tapped from the *thitsi* tree in similar fashion to the way latex is extracted from the rubber tree, was wrapped around wooden or bamboo frames. This man still did his work the way his grandfather had, using twists of horsehair as his base so that the finished product possessed a marvelously flexible quality.

Jake spent some time squatting beside the old man. He had brought with him two bottles of Johnnie Walker Black and four cartons of American cigarettes, which lay between the old man's legs.

The old man did most of the talking, Jake nodding and occasionally asking a question while he watched the ancient hands deftly molding the lacquer, black when it combined with the atmosphere, around the horsehair.

Above, the sky was the color of cat's-eye, great masses of cloud dimming out all blue. Perhaps it was all the foliage which turned the sky yellow or perhaps the dust along the plateau, great wings hanging like gauze turned by an artist's hand.

After a time, Jake stood up and went a little distance away from the end of the open-air market where traditional plaid silk scarves and opium weights were displayed for sale. In the shade of an overhanging tree Bliss waited. "He knows," Jake said. "He's heard of Chen Ju. Although he's not known by that name here. He's known as the Naga. Very goddamned melodramatic. The great serpent out of Asian myth."

"Jake."

"Uncle Tommy knows where to find the Naga," Jake went on. All Burmese had American names and were known by them. "We're not far. It's just about—"

"Jake." Bliss took his arm, led him around to the other side of the tree, where they were screened from the villagers. "What is it? Since that night on my father's junk you haven't said a word about anything besides Chen Ju. You haven't slept, you've eaten next to nothing. You have a look in your eyes that frightens me."

"It's nothing."

"As nothing as what happened at McKenna's?"

"What about that?"

"You were never so callous. Never so, I don't know, maybe sadistic is the word."

"I didn't enjoy what I did."

"No," she said, "perhaps not. But perhaps you could have considered another alternative."

"There was none. I told you White-Eye Kao was trained by a master."

"If that were truly the case, he would have died rather than reveal anything."

Jake watched her for a time. He was aware of the women in *longyi*, their faces roughly painted with pale yellow pigment. They waited upon the old man as if he were the Buddha himself.

"What are you saying."

"I am *saying* nothing," Bliss said steadfastly. Ever since they had come here she had gotten the impression that Jake was spoiling for a fight. "What I am *asking* you to do is consider the possibility that White-Eye Kao told you just what he was ordered to tell you."

"Chen Ju wants me here."

"Perhaps, yes."

"But, why?" Jake asked. "It makes no sense to lead me to where he is. Far better for him to attempt to take over InterAsia by proxy as he is doing."

"He is afraid of you," she said. "Here, he can destroy you so much more easily than in Hong Kong. And there is no one to make an inquiry."

"It's stupid," Jake insisted. "And Chen Ju is not stupid." He had continued to watch her and now he caught something in her expression that he could not let go. "Unless you know something that I don't."

Bliss turned away. How to tell him about what had happened with his father? How to prepare him for *da-hei*? "I—" And then she shut her mouth. She knew, with a terrible, sinking feeling that there was no way to prepare him for what she had to tell him. But why shouldn't he understand. How many times had she seen him slip into *ba-mahk*? Wasn't *da-hei* similar?

"You've changed," he said.

"As have you. I hope you still remember what it was like when we were together."

Something she said pierced him like an arrow and he let go of her, sliding until he was crouched down, his back against the bole of the tree.

Bliss knelt beside him. "Jake," she said, "what is it?"

"I don't know."

She knew it for a lie and foolishly told him so before she thought about it.

"You know everything now, don't you?" he flared. "You knew when White-Eye Kao was lying and when he was telling the truth. Now you have divined a change in me. What else do you know that you aren't telling me?"

Bliss could have bitten her tongue for saying what she had. "Don't you have it backward?" she said softly. "It is you who can divine the truth. With *ba-mahk* you—"

"No."

"What?"

"I no longer possess the ability to enter into *ba-mahk*." His face was in shadow but she did not need to see his expression to hear the bitterness in his voice.

"Is that what it's all about?"

He turned to her. "Is it so little?"

She put her arm through his. "Now you sound like a small boy who has lost his favorite teddy bear."

"I feel like a man suddenly gone blind."

She said nothing for a time, but took his hand in hers. She made certain that their fingers twined. Together, they watched the restless clouds, piling up like dirty linen until the yellow sky beyond was entirely obscured. In a moment, there was a dull boom of far-off thunder. But it seemed to go on forever.

"Did it ever frighten you, Jake?"

"What?"

"*Ba-mahk.*"

"The power?"

"Not so much that. The insight. The intimations." She put both her hands around his. "The connection to another world."

"I only ever saw it as power," he said.

That's the difference between us, she thought. "Perhaps," she said carefully, "that is why you miss it so."

He turned to her. "What do you mean?"

"*Ba-mahk*, it seems to me, was a great deal more than power."

Jake disentangled himself from her, held out his hands. "Look at this," he said. "They're shaking. It was *ba-mahk* that kept me safe. Through it I could determine strategies, I knew instinctively what was the right step to take and where there was danger."

"And now?"

"Now I have nothing," Jake said. He ran his hands through his thick hair. "There is nothing between me and death."

Bliss was glad that she had not told him what had happened with his father. She had believed, perhaps, so much in Shi Zilin that she had convinced herself that the old man somehow knew of Jake's loss of *ba-mahk*, that his *qi* merging with hers was meant as an aid to his only remaining son.

In this moment of Jake's agony she saw what it was Jake had to do. And she knew that she could not overtly help him. He was like a child who carries his beloved teddy around with him for years and years, even when it begins to wear out, shred and fall apart.

The teddy bear, the child believed, kept him safe from harm, especially when he ventured out into the frightening world away from home. But eventually the bear was gone and the child had to adjust to believing in his own inner power to keep him psychically safe from harm.

This was the point at which Jake now stood poised. Perhaps, she thought, Fo Saan had not done him a favor by teaching him *ba-mahk*. One needed a full understanding of such an extension of *qi* in order to cope with it while it was available and to do the same when it was gone.

"If you cannot trust in yourself, Jake," she said, "how can you expect anyone else to? You are the *Zhuan*. How much truly rests upon your shoulders I think only you know."

A young girl with the face of an angel stopped several meters away. Like her elders, she was painted with powdered *thanaka* bark and her long hair was pinned back from her face with a red clip fashioned into a star-shaped flower.

"I don't think you understand," Jake said slowly. "And I suppose I only have myself to blame for that. I feel as if I have lost something more than just *ba-mahk*, Bliss. I feel as if I have lost a part of myself as well."

"But wasn't *ba-mahk* a part of you?"

The girl was staring openly at them. She put a fingertip in her mouth and sucked on it as if it were a stalk of sugar cane.

"There is a void inside me," he said, "that is more than *ba-mahk*."

"But what?"

She wasn't staring at them, Jake saw now, but at something quite close to them. It was just beyond Bliss's right shoulder, out of his sight. Now the girl began to cry.

"If I knew that," he said, "I'd know everything." But his mind was on the girl and what was making her cry. She took one step backward and on her face Jake could see the desire to flee. But she was caught, somehow, her eyes fascinated.

Fascinated . . .

"Bliss," Jake said softly, "don't move." He could feel the tension come into her body almost immediately.

"What is it?"

"Just do as I tell you," he said in her ear. "All right?"

He could see her face now only at the periphery of his vision.

"Jake, what it is?"

"Don't move, I said!" he hissed. He had to hold her tight because her head had begun that involuntary motion that the body required when it sensed it was in danger.

"Will you do as I tell you?"

"Yes." He could hear the fear edging close to the surface.

"Good. Now listen to me. In a moment I am going to move.

477

When I do I want you to do nothing. Do you understand? Absolutely nothing. You are not to move. Clear?"

"Yes. Jake—?"

"No time," he said shortly. "I'm going."

And leapt over her, kicking out and down hard, his heel smashing the body of the serpent into the hard cracked earth.

It was this that had attracted and frightened the little girl. Nothing else in the countryside would have engendered such a response in a child of the hill tribes.

The adder whipped around and Jake caught it just behind the head. Still holding it with his heel, he reached down and gripped the body with his other hand. It was a *mwe-boai*, Burma's deadliest viper. It was so dangerous not only because of its lethal venom but because it was prone to unprovoked attacks on beast and man alike.

He heard Bliss's gasp and knew that she had turned at last. The *mwe-boai* hissed and Jake tramped heavily on its head. There was the sound of bones breaking as Jake crushed its skull.

The body, perhaps five feet in length, whipped back and forth and Jake let it go. The child, crying in earnest now, was rooted to the spot. Jake left the twitching snake and crouched down beside the girl. He began to talk gently to her and then, as she put her head into the hollow of his shoulder, he picked her up.

Took her over to where the *mwe-boai* lay now quite still. Jake, still talking quietly to her, took her tiny hand in his own. Together they reached out. She gave a little yelp as she saw them nearing the dead serpent but Jake forced her to touch it so that she could feel for herself that its power to hurt was gone forever.

"Bad thing," she said in the accent of the hill tribes, and Jake laughed, saying, "Yes, bad thing."

He took his hand away and the child kept hers on the snake's back. Her small fingers traced the slick, cool scales. But she kept clear of the mashed head that lay half-driven into the compacted ground.

When, at last, he began to stand, she crawled up him, wrapping her arms around his neck. He lifted her and walked back to the shade of the tree where Bliss was waiting for him.

"I hope you understand," she said, "what you possess that keeps you safe from harm."

Jake watched the child as she lay cradled in his lap. Those bright black eyes stared up at him, unblinking, now unafraid.

"You did not become aware of the snake through *ba-mahk*. *Ba-mahk* did not allow you to kill it before it bit me."

"No," he said and she could hear the bitterness welling up from the depths of him. "But my father is dead because—because I lost the ability to see ahead. I was lured away from the junk at just the time when the *dantai* was set to arrive. *Ba-mahk* would have revealed that to me. Instead—" Emotion constricted his throat.

The Burmese girl made a sound in her throat and reached upward. With the tip of her finger she took the tear standing at the corner of Jake's eye, let it roll into her palm. "Bad thing gone," she said. "Bad thing dead."

Bliss wondered at the amount of human compassion in that young mind. Jake felt it, too. He leaned over and kissed the child on her forehead. When he lifted his head, his lips were coated with her *thanaka* bark makeup. She giggled unselfconsciously, and Jake, laughing, too, squeezed her tight.

I wish, Bliss thought with a touch of envy, that I could make him laugh like that. But the child cannot see how wrapped up in guilt he is, so it cannot affect her. The loss inside Jake was not only that the lack of *ba-mahk* had made him, in a very real sense, blind, but that, having been reunited with his father only months ago, he was now alone again.

Jake, his head back against the tree, said, "Maybe you and your father are right. You both think I'm walking into a trap."

"What difference has that made to you?" Bliss asked. It was a loaded question and they both knew it.

Jake sighed. "In Japan, I discovered that the *dantai* sent to assassinate my father was composed of members of the Moro clan."

"Mikio's rivals?"

"No. That was the interesting part. Mikio's battle is with the Kisan clan." Jake pulled his knees up, making a more comfortable cradle for the child. "We penetrated to the core of the Moro clan. Hige Moro told me that my father's death was requested and paid for by a Chinese Communist minister named Huaishan Han."

"That seems improbable," Bliss said. "Since when do the Japanese underworld and the Communist Chinese make their beds together?"

"Never," Jake admitted. "At least not that I've ever heard of."

"Then Hige was lying."

"Perhaps." But his tone suggested that he did not believe it. "And if not?"

"How would it make sense?"

"We're here," Jake said, "in the Shan. We're on the mountain." By the way he spoke she knew that he was working it out as he went along. "I asked Hige the question. He said he had made a mint for his clan by dealing with this particular minister."

"Did your father ever mention his name?"

"No. But Hige mentioned the mountain. I asked him why he was being paid all this money and he said, 'Only the mountain knows.' " Jake's head came down, his hooded copper eyes searching her face. "I wonder if it was the Shan that he meant."

"You mean the tears of the poppy?"

Jake nodded. "Maybe. But the Communist Chinese are set foursquare against its growing, harvesting and distribution. A good part of the yearly disbursement to the army is to cover the Shan through Yunnan province. The poppy generals encounter constant harassment from Chinese Communist army forays into the fields."

"Then it is a false lead."

Jake watched the shadows creeping over her face. The planes, dells and hillocks of her physiognomy were turned by his mind's eye into the topography of a strange and alien place. He knew they were in enemy territory in more ways than one. "Now White-Eye Kao tells us that though he ostensibly works for Sir John Bluestone, he has been trained by Chen Ju. Chen Ju is behind the takeover raid on InterAsia and so is Bluestone, so we know that the two have formed a partnership. Yet Chen Ju has a spy in his partner's employ. Interesting, no? What kind of a partnership could that be?"

"Obviously not one filled with trust."

"No," Jake agreed, "at least not on the part of Chen Ju. But then he would hardly be likely to trust anyone."

"Where does all this lead us?"

"Back to the Shan," Jake said. "That is the interesting part. The Shan is the common denominator in all of this: my father's murder, the run on InterAsia, Chen Ju's scheme of revenge."

"Who is this minister, Huaishan Han?" Bliss asked.

"I wish I knew," Jake said. "That might go a long way toward solving this mystery. I wonder what could bring together Chen Ju, Huaishan Han, Hige Moro, Sir John Bluestone, and Daniella Vorkuta."

"There are a number of natural enemies there," Bliss pointed out.

"That's what makes this so puzzling," Jake said. "And frightening. What is their common goal? It can't be the destruction of the *yuhn-hyun*, as I had originally thought. These sharks would rip each other to shreds going for the spoils. No, it is something else entirely. Something of which we are not yet aware."

The sun, so long obscured by the roiling clouds, was gone beyond the mountains. The shadowless light was gone, too, replaced by an odd illumination that was entirely reflected off the base of the cloud bank. But the heat had not dissipated any and the insects' buzzing was very loud.

"What if it is you?" Bliss said in an ominous tone. "What if that is their goal?"

"From the Shan? I hardly think so."

"This is the one place where your death would go unnoticed," she repeated. "And, perhaps, unavenged."

He watched her carefully. "You'd like me to say, 'Okay, let's get out of here. Let's go back to Hong Kong.' "

"Frankly, yes," Bliss admitted. "But I know that's fruitless. I know you won't turn back now."

"You're right."

"But I wonder why. Something crosses my mind but I hope I'm wrong."

"Which is?"

"That you've got a death wish."

Jake looked down at the Shan girl. Her eyes were half closed. "Mariana used to say that about me. My first wife, as well."

"Does that mean there's something to it?"

Jake heard the tension in her voice. "I don't think so," he said.

"Then why are you out here, in the middle of a red sector? Is it to protect InterAsia, the *yuhn-hyun*, your father's dream?"

"They're one and the same," Jake said. "Yes."

"No!" she said so vehemently she woke the girl. "It's to assuage your guilty conscience. Your mind insists that you are to blame for your father's death. That somehow, if you still possessed *ba-mahk*, you could have deflected the *dantai*'s attack.

"The fact is that with *ba-mahk* or without it the result would

481

have been the same. *Joss*, Jake. Why don't you listen to your Chinese side a little more often. Accept your father's fate. I know he did. *Joss* that he was killed. *Joss* that you were miles away when it happened. Do you think *ba-mahk* would have allowed you to dispatch the tick that was following you any quicker? Do you think you would have ignored her and allowed her to follow you back to the junk where you father was waiting for you?"

Jake said nothing but he knew what the answers were. She was right. *Ba-mahk* would have altered nothing. His father was dead. *Joss*.

He looked down at the small face in his lap. The child was sleeping contentedly. A little fist had grabbed hold of his shirt for security. Staring into that beautiful, painted face, he felt an exquisite pang of longing and grief.

"Funny what you think of at certain times," he said softly. "I miss my daughter now more than I ever did when she was alive and living with that rogue Triad up near the border."

He looked away from the child's sleeping face, to Bliss's. "The most painful memory I have of her is also the truest. It was she who had a death wish, Bliss. Lan, my only child."

In a moment, there were more tears than the Burmese girl could ever hope to wipe away.

"He's on his way!"

Chen Ju was jubilant. He had just taken off the earphones, shut down the powerful transceiver. "Huaishan Han," he said, "I have just heard from White-Eye Kao. Shi Jake is coming, just as you planned."

He stopped at the open doorway to the room. He could see the humped sprawl of the old minister in the dusty rattan chair. At his feet, the girl knelt. They were holding hands. Perhaps they were asleep.

It was an odd symbiotic relationship the old man had with the girl. Did she love him, hate him or fear him? Chen Ju wondered. Perhaps it was a combination of all three. Certainly her brainwashing had turned her into another person. But who knew, really, what she was capable of doing?

Now she was the vehicle of Huaishan Han's revenge. Jake Maroc Shi's daughter.

And what was his own vehicle? No single human being. But rather a *shan*—the implacable mountain, an international organization that had taken decades to build into the most powerful smuggling network in the world. Chen Ju would rather put his faith in the grinding jaws of his *diqui* than in the workings of one psyche.

That his dismissal from Sawyer & Sons had become the single most fortuitous event in his life in no way mitigated his desire for justice to be done. He had turned a devastating blow into something positive. That was his genius. But it did not excuse the wrong that had been done him.

It had, in fact, been Three Oaths Tsun who had given him the idea. Before being brought to Sawyer & Sons for employment by Shi Zilin, Three Oaths Tsun had been the finest runner of the tears of the poppy in the Shanghai area. The money he had made on the periphery of the business was astounding. How much more could be made, Chen Ju had thought, at the very center of the opium trade? All the world would be knocking on his door.

Thus the *diqui* had been born and, with Huaishan Han's aid, had flourished. Yet even this was not enough for Chen Ju. He wanted more. He wanted the world.

And now with the help of the two Americans, Bennett and Curran, he was going to get it.

It was amazing the difference it made, Daniella thought. With the knowledge of Carelin's baby inside her, nothing else seemed quite as important. Certainly not Oleg Maluta's threats against her. It astounded her how much power an unborn creature could possess. The gun, wrapped in its poly bag so as not to smudge her incriminating prints, seemed as distant and unimportant to her as the far side of the sun.

With the future in mind, she picked up the phone and made a date to pick Maluta up after work. A concert and then a late dinner, she proposed. He seemed delighted.

She dismissed both their Chaikas, telling the drivers to take a night off. They were used to such things but were grateful nonetheless. There was nothing so debilitating for a military man as to wait around doing nothing.

At day's end, Daniella signed out for a departmental Volga she had phoned down to reserve early that afternoon. She had one of her people purchase tickets for the Beethoven Quartet. They arrived at the Hall of the Gnesin Music Institute on Vorovsky Street five minutes before the concert was scheduled to begin. If Maluta was surprised at being driven by Daniella in the Volga he made no mention of it. Perhaps he was just as happy that they were alone.

The concert might have been played by four pigs for all

the music that penetrated Daniella's consciousness. She stared at the vaulted, groined ceiling and it was like peering into the convolutions of her own brain. She felt as if she had lost all sense of herself, as if her heart had stopped beating without her knowledge, and now she stood, breathless, staring at the wreckage life had wrought.

She watched synapses spark and snap and, on stage, spotlights were brought to bear upon the musicians and that light, reflecting off their precious instruments, sent jeweled flashes upward onto the faceted ceiling, the massive crystal chandelier that glowed like a star at intermission.

Daniella felt that she was walking through her life like an automaton, the dazed survivor of a ship dashed against hidden shoals. Her homeland, always so dear to her, now seemed nothing more than a cleverly rendered stage set upon which she had been playing out a bizarre and totally inexplicable role. She wondered what it was that she had been doing all her days. And how in the name of God it had ever made her happy.

In fact, she realized dully, she had no real conception of what true happiness was. Or how to do so basic a thing as live. Up until now she had been doing nothing but surviving. Her life had been a day-to-day struggle for power, an endless *agon* from which there could be no surcease. How pitiful that seemed in the face of the kind of love she felt for Mikhail Carelin.

Maluta spoke to her but she had no conception of what he was saying. It was as if she had lost the ability to understand the language, as if she were some cosmic cinder floating in the vastness, the utter blackness of space, cut off from everyone and everything.

"Daniella?"

"Yes." Eyes closed against the bright light. A sun blazing. The chandelier lit up, it must be intermission.

"The concert is over."

"Yes."

"It is time to go."

It is time to go. His words echoed eerily in her mind, as if he had spoken them in a cavern or, perhaps, from the recesses of a church. It was not surprising that she should think of her mother at this time. Religion had played such a strong, though clandestine, part in Daniella's formative years. It was something that never left her. Though she could not, as a member of the *sluzhba*, go near a church, still she could not help but worship in her mind. And hold the precepts of her mother's religion—and in a very real sense, her own—dear.

It is time to go. She rose, bidden by a voice inside her own mind. In the gilt-and-cream lobby, she caught sight of a bleak-faced woman, beautiful but drawn. There was an expression in her clear gray eyes that Daniella had seen many times before in the Lubyanka. Always the "interviews" were completed and the prisoner was being sent down to Level Three, the depths of the prison from which there was no escape.

With a start, Daniella realized that she was looking in a mirror: the woman was herself. With a little shake of her head, she cleared her mind and, pulling on her coat, walked beside Oleg Maluta out into a night spangled with Moscow's streetlights.

The sky was clear and the breeze was freshening, taking with it the choking diesel fumes and the plaster and cement dust. When Daniella suggested a stroll down by the Moskva, Maluta was delighted.

They got into the Volga and she drove to the spot where he had first taken her. She remembered the cautionary tale he had told her about falling through the ice as a child and recognized it now for what it had been: a warning. He had survived that early disaster; he could survive anything now.

In a way, it had about it the aspect of a mystical experience, almost as if there had been a kind of divine intervention on his behalf. *I am among the chosen*, he had been saying, *so be content to do my bidding*. It smacked of the almost supernatural quality he attributed to Oreanda. In a way, he believed that she lived on after her death in the same way he was convinced that his being saved from drowning was fated.

They got out and went down the crusty scree to the glimmering river. This time, Maluta reached back, helping her past the several steep patches where shale was easily sheered off by the weight of a human body.

"Daniella," he said.

But she already had hold of him and, kicking out, dislodged his footing from the mossy rocks along the bank. He fell with a great exhalation of air and she quickly jammed an elbow into his solar plexus.

As his knees rose up in spasmodic response, she shoved him out along the rocks and down until his head and shoulders were beneath the chill water. Her fingers closed around his neck and chin, trapping him there without air.

Moonlight glimmered along the Moskva. She could see

traffic moving as slowly as molten lead across the expanse. The sound of a klaxon littered the air for a time and with great reluctance died away.

He was struggling very hard and she climbed on him to keep his powerful legs from working himself upward into the cool night air. She did not want that, did not want him to get even one small breath. She did not want him to be able to use his superior strength against her.

It was getting very difficult now and she kneed him in the groin. She could imagine the airless dark which he was inhabiting, could imagine his lungs desperate for oxygen, the reflexes wanting to open the mouth, to inhale through the nostrils. Only the brain holding out, desperately seeking some way to be rid of the water.

But there was no way. Daniella made certain of that. And, after a time, there was no movement at all. She found herself wet with sweat. Her vision was blurry so perhaps she had been weeping.

Without taking his head out of the Moskva, she felt with her hands for the chain and the key around his neck. When she found it, she pulled, and it came away in her hands.

Then she set about making quite sure Oleg Maluta's body would never surface. When she was through she pushed him in, wading out until the water lapped at her thighs. It was cold and she shivered heavily.

He sank like a stone, which at this point, was what, mostly, he was made of. For just an instant, the moonlight glistened off his still face. Then he was gone, claimed at last, perhaps, by his Oreanda. And his guilt.

In the shadows of the night, she let herself into the office. She could smell him immediately. His malign presence dominated the suite like the stench in a crematorium. Maluta.

She went immediately behind the desk and sat in his chair. Took the key she had ripped from his neck and, opening the bottom drawer, unlocked the steel case inside.

And there it was. With a trembling hand, she lifted out the poly bag. She recognized the gun inside. The oil had slicked the inside of the plastic. Beneath the gun was the packet of photos of her weeping in the night. She pulled the steel case out of the drawer, set fire to the negatives, using the case to contain the flames.

Putting the gun inside her purse, she was about to leave when she saw the corner of an envelope wedged into the corner of the now empty drawer. She pulled on it but it would not budge.

Looking around the desk, she seized on Maluta's brass letter opener and with some effort wedged it into the seams at the bottom of the drawer. It took her several minutes of intense work but at last she freed the envelope from its hiding place.

She slit it open. There were four sheets of flimsy upon which were typed in single space a detailed breakdown of profits, expenses, percentages and the like as if for some business. But the figures were gargantuan.

When Daniella got to the Mandarin word, *diqui*, she knew she was on to something very big indeed. With every sentence she read she felt her excitement building. No longer were her thoughts filled with home and hearth, with love and an idyllic future that, deep down, she had known could never happen.

Now the old, the true Daniella, perhaps, reasserted itself. She felt the power flowing from the few flimsy sheets of paper into her hands, knew with a certainty that was undeniable what it meant.

It was as if fate had drawn her here, causing her to make this astounding discovery. It was as if fate had handed her back her power—the power she was meant to wield.

So be it.

She knew what she must do.

She breathed in the darkness, the aura of strength in the office that had, at last, delivered up to her its ultimate secret. If there was a God then surely he hardened her heart now. Held within the silence of the night, she braced herself for what was to come.

And found, to her surprise, that it was not that difficult to do.

The storm was at their backs when they plunged back into the triple-canopied jungle. The Shan States. Off the plateau, it was enemy territory, a full red sector. It was the killing ground, from which, Fo Saan had taught Jake, there could be no retreat. Before them lay only victory. Or defeat.

It is determination which wins many battles, Fo Saan had said. *And determination is strictly a matter of force of will. Often the outcome of a contest is not decided by the first strategy or even by the third. Rather, endurance is involved. Force of will is endurance. If you do not lose your sense of self, you will endure and your power will not wane. On the contrary, it will endure even after your body has wasted away.*

Jake and Bliss were following the directions given to them by Uncle Tommy, the master lacquerware maker. But even so it was most difficult. For one thing, the terrain was unknown to them and its density tiring to work through. Without a compass they would have been lost within a few hours. For another, the farther they penetrated up the mountain, the more frequently they were obliged to hide from units of the poppy warlords' independent armies: patrols, heavily armed supply trains and, going in the opposite direction, the mule trains loaded down with the tears of the poppy.

There were the patrols of the Burmese and Chinese armies to be on the lookout for, as well. This is not a country, Jake thought as they moved with almost painful slowness; this is a war zone.

They had set out from the plateau village at first light. By noon, they had covered six hard-won kilometers and were forced to take a break. They ate dried foods and washed the unpalatable stuff down with clear, icy water from a swiftly running stream. Jake, staring into the silvery depths of the river, found himself envying the ease with which the water flowed down the mountainside.

Father, he thought, *I am finally nearing the top of the mountain. I hope I know what to do when I get there.*

Just before one, they broke camp and, reviewing again Uncle Tommy's directions, pushed onward into the forbidding jungle. The towering foliage engulfed them completely. They might have been on the bottom of the sea. The light was entirely green, with an odd kind of luminosity, aqueous and heavy so that they felt weighed down by it.

Above their heads, birds screamed and cried, taking wing, now and again, with a noise that echoed through the jungle. Insects were everywhere, of every description, size and color but as they rose in elevation, their profusion diminished. Uncle Tommy had told them to look out for snakes and leopards.

Twice they had caught sight of monkeys but soon they were too high for many of these primates who seemed to prefer the warmer weather on the plateau.

It was pouring so hard now that even the branches of the lowest trees were turned to a pale green haze. They were soaked through their jackets and Bliss began to shiver. They crossed a crude rope bridge beneath which one of the many magnificent Shan valleys spread out, furry with rain.

Just beyond, they came upon a rough dirt track chopped

into the jungle. The trodden-down ferns on either side attested to the constant use it got. Jake, on the lookout for soldiers, pressed them on. He was seeking some kind of shelter now. This was no weather for a prolonged trek.

Perhaps a half-a-kilometer on, they came upon a bamboo latticework shack. Two crude steps led up to a kind of overhang that could be called a veranda in only the loosest sense.

Jake suspected that there must be more houses in the immediate vicinity but with the heavy weather it was impossible to see more than a meter in any direction.

He took Bliss up the steps. A young boy no more than eleven emerged from the gloom inside the hut. He had a beautiful face with the typically blemish-free Burmese skin. This high up, its golden hue had been burnished copper by sun and scouring winds. His forearms and upper torso were covered with tattoos. He smiled when he saw them, started to chatter in a dialect neither of them understood.

Jake spoke to him in Mandarin and he pointed inside. Jake took Bliss into the hut.

The overpowering, sweet musk of opium pervaded the air and, in the twilight, they could make out an old man. He was turbaned, sitting cross-legged on a mat in one corner. He was smoking and, when he saw them, he lifted a languid hand, beckoning them forward.

He offered them opium, a gesture of friendship and hospitality in this part of the world. He took up a piece of sticky black substance, rolled it between his thumb and forefinger until it formed a ball. Then he popped it into the small bowl of his long-stemmed ivory pipe.

As he passed it around, Jake could see that despite the chill he wore only a loincloth. His thighs and the backs of his hands were tattooed in the same repeating pattern as the boy. It obviously had ancestral significance.

The boy was nowhere in the hut and Jake rose, moving silently to the open door. He looked outside. The world was a teeming mass of gray-green. The rain hissed down, running in muddy rivulets. There was no other sound in the world.

He was turning back inside when a rift appeared at the periphery of his vision. It darkened as it widened and, before he could make another move, more than a dozen Shan tribesmen appeared through the mist and downpour. They were armed with AK-47 machine guns. Soviet weapons. All were pointed in his direction.

Standing in the doorway, totally vulnerable, he made no

move at all. In a moment, the party of Shan moved aside. A tall, lanky figure towered over them to such an extent that Jake knew it was Caucasian even before the face become visible. A pale-eyed man with the ruddy complexion of the true outdoorsman. It was an American face, not a Russian.

"Well," Tony Simbal said, striding up the steps to where Jake stood, "what do we have here?"

"Maroc," he said. "By Christ, Jake Maroc!"

Simbal leaned against the bamboo wall. Outside, rain thundered against the ground like a military drumroll.

"You're the guy who got the mole. Henry Wunderman."

Jake watched him from where he stood near the door. Bliss was still sitting next to the old man, who blithely continued with his smoking as if nothing out of the ordinary were occurring. One good sign: none of the Shan tribesmen had come inside. But the boy was here. Jake assumed that it was he who had gone to fetch Tony Simbal with news of the strangers' arrival.

Secrets stole across the floor, white wraiths, as insubstantial and hallucinatory as the opium smoke the old man was inhaling.

"Rodger tried to recruit you again, didn't he?"

"If you mean Rodger Donovan," Jake said, "the answer is yes."

"Why didn't you accept?"

There it was, Jake thought. The suspicion. "I'm done with that," he said.

"But you're here," Simbal pointed out. "You and I in the same spot on the globe. I hardly think that's coincidence."

"How long are you working for Donovan?" Jake asked.

"Months," Simbal said. "But he and I go way back. We went through high school and college together."

"Stanford boys."

"That's right."

He's going to be no help at all, Jake thought. A company man and worse. Aren't clubs thicker than blood in some circles?

"You worked for Donovan a long time."

"Worked *with* him," Jake corrected. "I worked for Henry Wunderman for a long time."

"The mole," Simbal said. "Daniella Vorkuta's swift sword."

Bliss, listening to the two of them as well as watching, knew what was going on. These were more than two males sparring for dominance of territorial rights. The feint and jab of the questioning held reverberations far beyond the ordinary conversation. Both were trying to probe for certain answers without revealing their own secrets. Perhaps it was she who first realized that what each was concealing was the same.

"So it seemed," Jake said.

"Meaning?"

Jake moved around the room. It was getting damp so near the doorway. It was also disconcerting to see the Shan squatting in the storm, eyes on the hut. He knew the meaning of that display. He knew who was ultimately in control of this situation. There were too many AK-47s for any one man.

"Henry was an old hand. Recruited by Antony Beridien himself, the man who with John Kennedy's blessing created the Quarry."

"Correct me if I'm wrong," Simbal said. "But Beridien recruited Rodger as well."

"At another time," Jake said. "From another place."

"The old guard always resents the presence of the new."

"Yes," Jake admitted. "That's true enough. There was no love lost between Henry and Rodger."

"Did you take sides?"

"I was far away," Jake said, "from it all. Office politics never interested me. I was always a field executive. But—"

"Yes?"

"Henry recruited me. He came to Hong Kong and took me off the streets. I was running for the Triads, doing odd jobs, none of them very savory." Jake looked at Simbal through the smoke. "In a way, Henry Wunderman saved my life."

"Killing him must have been a sad affair."

"It was difficult." Sad, yes, he thought. That was exactly what it was. He paid more attention. Perhaps, he thought, there is more to this man than I had thought.

Which was just what Simbal had on his mind. "Everyone at Central is very grateful to you for what you did. Especially Rodger."

"I imagine so," Jake said carefully. "Especially Donovan."

"You don't like him."

"I don't like what he represents."

Simbal was very still. He could hear the rasping breath of the old man as he sank further and further away from them. "Which is what? The old ways are the best ways?"

"Not precisely," Jake said. "I recall that one of the old man's watchwords was: change. Beridien felt that flexibility in a network such as the Quarry was essential. He was convinced that the KGB's major defect was that it never changed. Invalid thinking, he called it." Jake pronounced it with the emphasis on the first syllable.

"It's more Donovan's attitude that I don't like. The old man thought about his people. He could be ruthless and, I suppose, at times even cruel. But through it all his heart beat for his field executives. He was once with Wild Bill Donovan. He knew what it was like. Rodger Donovan hasn't a clue what it's like out here."

"But he's smart," Simbal said.

"Smarter than any of us thought."

"That could be true," Simbal admitted. Coming to a decision, he pulled out a sheaf of papers. "Take a look at these."

Jake riffled through the flimsies that Max Threnody had given Simbal. "What are they?" Bliss wanted to know.

"Evidence," Jake said. "Proof that someone has been systematically blowing Quarry networks to the KGB."

"Then Apollo's for real," Bliss said.

Jake looked up. "It would appear so."

"Apollo?" Simbal said.

"Henry Wunderman's legacy," Jake told him. "A deep asset inside the Kremlin. My asset now."

Simbal produced a photo. "This was with the evidence." He handed it over.

"It's a surveillance shot of Daniella Vorkuta," Jake said.

"Right." Simbal sighed. "When we were younger Rodger was hung up on a girl in college. Leslie. She and Daniella Vorkuta could easily be sisters."

"That's how Donovan was recruited? Through Daniella Vorkuta?"

"Her and a Seurat in Paris," Simbal said. "It seems so, yes." He gave Jake an odd look. "It occurs to me now that if Apollo really was Wunderman's asset, he'd've known that Wunderman could not have been Chimera."

Jake nodded. "That's true enough."

"Then this evidence can be corroborated by another source."

"It already has," Jake confirmed.

Then Max wasn't lying, Simbal thought. And then, Can I trust this man? He's ex-Quarry. Does he still hold a grudge for his abrupt dismissal? Threnody had called Simbal a paladin, and now he recognized in this man standing before him a kind of kindred spirit.

"But Donovan can't be why you're here now," Jake said.

"No," Simbal admitted. It was easier this way. He was not yet certain what he would do when he met up with Rodger Donovan. "I'm after the end product of two voodoo spooks: Peter Curran and Edward Martin Bennett. They've sold out, joined the *diqui*. Now they're set to meet the Naga."

"We're here to find the Naga," Jake said. "He's set out to destroy me, my work and everything my father built."

Bliss was by his side, staring into his face. "Chen Ju—"

"Who's Chen Ju?" Simbal interrupted.

"The Naga."

"The head of the *diqui*?" He was incredulous. "You know who he is?"

"Yes." Jake's voice was hoarse, as if he had been screaming for hours. "My father, my family knows him." He wiped at his face. "It all boils down to Kam Sang. My father's secret. You see, Kam Sang is a nuclear project in Guangdong province. Ostensibly, work is being done there on a radical way to desalinize water in a cost-effective way for Hong Kong. But there is another, far more secret side to Kam Sang. It is a discovery that my father told me had already changed the world. Until this moment, I did not truly understand how irrevocably it had been changed."

In the ringing silence, the noise of the rain reverberated eerily through the smoke-filled house, repository for dreams of faith and, now, abruptly, of fear.

Daniella Vorkuta hugged the honey-colored rabbit to her breast. Its shining brown eyes stared up at her with an inherently adoring expression.

"He's perfect," Mikhail Carelin said. He was obviously anxious to leave.

Daniella's lips pressed inward in a pout. "How do you know it's a he. I think it's a she."

"Fine," he said. "*She*'s perfect. Buy her."

"I don't know. Martina's particular about her animals."

"Your Uncle Vadim's grandchild is going to be seven, isn't that what you told me? How particular could she be?"

Daniella put the rabbit back among her sisters and they moved on. It was not so easy. They were in Detsky Mir, Children's World, what was renowned throughout the Soviet Union as the largest children's department store in the world. It seemed more crowded than Lenin's Tomb, unarguably the most popular tourist attraction the entire country had to offer.

"It's damned hot in here, Danushka," Carelin said. "I hope

493

we're not going to spend all morning looking." He had more time to spend with her now that his wife had gone to visit her mother in Leningrad.

"When I find Martina's gift, I'll know it immediately," she said.

"Personally, I liked the rabbit."

"Because it was the easy thing," she said lightly, taking his arm.

"No, I quite fancied her face. I could see her whiskers twitch."

She laughed, her eyes scanning the counters on either side of the aisles. "You know," she said, sometime later, after running the daunting gantlet of the store's stock, "you were right." And led him back to the counter full of honey-colored rabbits. She picked up the stuffed creature.

"How do you know your cousin will like it?" Carelin asked.

Daniella stared into the rabbit's face. She could not tell him that this rabbit was for her unborn baby, that she had wanted him here with her this one last time so that, together, they would choose a creature that eventually the baby would come to love, and by which Daniella could someday recall this moment encysted within time, free of anger, rancor or regret.

"Take her," he said. "She's perfect."

Daniella produced her Party card and received immediate service. While the rabbit was being gift wrapped, she opened her purse and took out a square manila envelope. She handed it wordlessly to Carelin.

He glanced at her, then opened it cautiously. "Good God," he said softly. He flipped through the photos, feeling a sinking sensation in the pit of his stomach. It was disorienting, seeing himself and Daniella in intimate embrace. He, too, was drawn to the facial expressions; his embarrassment was acute.

When he came to the last one, he said, "Where are the negatives?"

"I burned them," Daniella said, paying for the rabbit.

"How did you manage that?"

"Don't ask."

"Danushka, I want to know."

Now he sounded like Maluta. "Trust me. You don't."

"How did you get these? Steal them?"

"Hardly," she said, taking possession of the bulky, be-ribboned box. "He gave them to me."

494

"Something serious had to have happened for Maluta to just hand them over to you."

"He thinks I'm cute."

"Daniella!" He went after her as she began to walk away. "He hates your guts."

She said nothing.

He took her elbow, turned her to face him. The crush of shoppers pushed them quite close and Daniella was obliged to switch the package from one arm to another. "I want to know."

"Why?" Abruptly she felt put upon. "Why must you know everything? Do you tell *me* everything?"

"Yes. Of course."

"You're a liar," she said hotly. "How do you expect me to put my trust in a liar."

"I don't understand."

She put her head closer to his. "I know, Mikhail. Do you understand? *I know who you are.*"

"What are you talking about?"

"Stop it," she snapped. "Let's get out of here." Abruptly, the huge store with its surging crowds was making her feel claustrophobic.

She took him to the Hermitage Garden along Karetny Ryad because it was less crowded than Gorky Park at this time of the year. She had had enough of crowds.

They sat on a wood-and-ironwork bench near the open-air puppet theater. It was near dinnertime. Gray squirrels scampered down the boles of oak and beech trees to sit near them, hoping for scraps. Nearby, pigeons waddled, pecking now and again at nothing at all.

The sound of children's laughter was strong on the air and, unconsciously, Daniella touched the firm roundness of her lower belly, imagining the little life growing there. She had almost broken down and cried at Children's World. All the toys, all the children running, pointing, laughing, wanting. She felt a longing deep inside her.

Large, fleecy clouds drifted above their heads and there was only the occasional rumble of the large diesel trucks. "What will you do now that you know?" He did not look at her.

"I want you to understand something, Mikhail," she said deliberately. "Maluta is no longer a factor in anything I do or say."

He looked at her. "Do I have to guess at what that means?"

"I think you already know," she said simply.

"How did you find out about me?"

"Mitre signaled me." He knew that Mitre was her code name for Sir John Bluestone. There was no reason not to tell him now. "You were blown somewhere in Hong Kong."

A little girl came racing by, her arms stretched out to grab the tail of the dog that raced, barking happily, just in front of her. Her cheeks were red, her eyes wide with delight.

"Tell me," Carelin said, envying the girl's innocence. "Do you love me?" His back was ramrod straight. He knew that it would be many years before that girl would have to ask such a question. "Have you ever loved me?"

"I think," she said, "that is a question that we are better off not asking one another."

"Daniella," he said seriously, "I don't believe that I have sinned. It is important—essential, even—that you understand that."

"Do you hate Russia so?"

"I hate what Russia does to its people. To all people it comes in contact with. And Russia is what Russia does. We have not come so far from Stalin as we would like to believe. We Russians are very adept at self-deception."

"No more than any other people, Mikhail."

"In that, I think you are quite wrong. Our capacity for—"

"I will not—*will not*—debate the morality of this with you," she said sharply.

"It was my choice, my decision only, and I do not regret it." He looked away for a moment. "At least, very little of it."

"To answer your question, whatever you are has nothing to do with what I feel inside."

He looked down to see the small-caliber pistol with its silencer pressed against his coat. It was between them. No one could see it but them.

Daniella saw that his expression had grown sad. "Is this how you disposed of Comrade Maluta?"

"This is the answer, Mikhail," Daniella said. "The only answer." In the corners of her eyes, liquid diamonds danced. "There are only lies between us. And that's all there ever could have been. Lies are all that are allowed us in our profession. We knew that when we chose to be who we are. Nothing can change that."

"Are you so certain?" he said.

"I have the power now, Mikhail. What deadly secrets Maluta once possessed—what made him rich, what made him strong—are mine."

"So that's it," he said softly. "You got more than the photos. In the end you got everything." He watched her eyes for signs of life. And when he was certain that she would give him nothing, he offered her all he had left. "You may know who I am," he said, "but you know nothing of my final directive." He looked from the pistol she held at his side to her face. It was such a strong face, he thought. And thought again of Circe, the ancient sorceress out of Greek mythology in whose image he felt she had been molded. How well she had manipulated everything and everyone around her, he marveled. "It was to terminate you, Danushka." He saw the shock forming in her features and pressed home whatever advantage it might have given him. "What else would Jake Maroc want of me?"

In a moment, he rose. "Good-bye, Koshka."

Daniella watched him walk away, wending his way past the running groups of whooping children whose nannies were vainly attempting to gather them up. It was time to go home.

Hours later, she found herself in her office without having any idea of how she had gotten there. She remembered her mother in just such a dazed state after she had been in an auto accident. For a moment Daniella wondered why she had come here instead of to her apartment. Then, as if a veil had lifted from her consciousness, she remembered.

She went to the window and looked out at the night. Stars spangled the heavens. She felt somehow grateful that she was far enough from the center of the city to see those of first magnitude. Below them, the dark mass of the forest, blacker even than the night sky. Part of her wished that she could lose herself in that stygian maze.

She thought of the onion domes gleaming in the spotlights, the crenellated walls within which crouched, like a savage beast, the power to change the world. Now she had within her grasp the means to tame that beast.

She turned and picked up the phone, spoke into it for some time. She thought she knew in which direction Carelin would choose to flee. He was heading for Hong Kong, after all. That much was obvious. But even if he chose another route, her people would intercept him. She had faith in them.

"One more thing, Lieutenant," she said into the phone.

497

"I want the traitor shot on sight. Terminated, do you understand? Terminated."

At that moment, she felt something that she could not possibly feel: a stirring in her belly. She gave a strangled little cry and put down the phone, feeling as if she had come to the very edge of the world.

"You're right," Simbal said into the silence. "Kam Sang is what it has been about from the beginning."

"What do you mean?" Jake asked.

"Kam Sang was the reason Donovan brought me into this. Two of his agents went underground in the *diqui*. They were killed, but just before that they managed to report to Donovan that the *diqui* was interested in the Kam Sang project."

Jake nodded. "That's why. And now you know where Donovan's interest in Kam Sang comes from."

"Daniella Vorkuta?"

"Right," Jake said. "Vorkuta again."

Simbal shifted his position. "But what is it exactly that was discovered at Kam Sang?"

The green bower dripped all around them. The jungle, weeping with moisture, fell away from them in a hard line. It devolved here and there, as it descended in raggle-taggle fashion, into rocky scree upon which great black birds sat, cawing.

They—along with perhaps a score of Shan warriors—had come some fifteen kilometers from the tiny village of the tribe loyal to Simbal. In that time, they had ascended perhaps a further five hundred meters. The air now had about it the tang of ozone that scoured the back of the throat and tended to sear the inside of the nostrils. One had to be in good shape here or the relative scarcity of oxygen would inordinately tax the cardiovascular system.

"We're very near," Jake said. "According to Uncle Tommy."

The storm had not blown over, merely seemed to be taking a breather. But, for now, at least, the air was calmer than it had been for the past twenty-four hours. The two dozen or so Shan soldiers were grouped loosely through the small clearing. Simbal had set guards every fifty meters at a one-hundred-meter perimeter.

"We're into General Kuo's territory now," he said. Wisely, he saw no point in pressing the Kam Sang issue. Deeds not words, he had learned in the Shan, were the only basis of

498

trust. "He's the head man all over these parts," he said. "Very bad dude."

"We're going to have to go right down his throat then." Jake pointed. "Assuming Uncle Tommy was giving me the straight goods."

Through the dense foliage within which they crouched they could just make out patches of a structure.

"Looks like an opium factory," Jake said, sniffing the air.

"Bingo. Maybe the biggest one in the Golden Triangle. Kuo's the only one fanatic enough about security to keep his factory at his base of operations. The other generals like to take it down the mountain before refining it." Simbal shifted his position. "We haven't got the firepower, you know," he said. "Kuo's men will chew us up and spit us out."

"I don't give a shit about General Kuo," Jake said. "I wasn't thinking about taking your Shan soldiers with me."

"You mean just us, don't you?"

Jake looked at him. What did he really know about this man? *At the killing ground*, Fo Saan said, *trust no one*. "That's entirely up to you," Jake said.

Simbal waited a minute. "You're a hard one, aren't you? What do you think you're trying to prove?"

Jake kept his eye on the opium factory. It was important to get a sense of the minute-to-minute movement around the site.

"You've got a bad attitude, you know that?" Simbal tore a bit of fern in two. "That's going to get you killed one of these days." He jerked his head in Bliss's direction. "I hope you've provided for your lady love, 'cause she's going to need some comfort after you're gone."

"Do you always talk so much?"

"Only when I have something on my mind."

"Okay," Jake said, "you've done your duty. Feel better now?"

"That wasn't for me, buddy," Simbal said. "It was for your benefit."

Jake said nothing. In five minutes he had counted no less than forty Shan at the factory. Not a good sign.

"What we've got to do," Jake said, "is find some way in and out of there."

Simbal snorted. "How about a couple of pine boxes. That's the only way we're coming out of that fortress if you insist on doing a duo number. Unless maybe you've got a couple of those miniaturized nuclear warheads we could lob at them."

"You'd better go to a movie for that," Jake said. "We're not likely to get any help here."

At that moment they heard voices raised, quickly stifled. They left their position, went back through the jungle.

They saw a man standing on the periphery of their make-shift camp. He wore a bush jacket over a buffalo plaid flannel shirt, Nike sweat pants and Eddie Bauer hiking boots. On his head was the kind of expedition fedora Harrison Ford made famous in *Raiders of the Lost Ark*.

Bliss, who had been given a spare AK-47 from one of the Shan, had it trained on him. "I found him lurking in the underbrush," she said, when she heard them approach.

"Jesus," Simbal said, "what the hell are you doing here, Rodger?" There was no reason to let him know he had been expected.

Rodger Donovan put his hand out and gingerly pushed the muzzle of the submachine gun aside. "Time for a little vacation from Washington," he said, coming up to them. Turned his head. "Hello, Jake. I haven't see *you* in a while." He redirected his gaze. "The information you gave the Cuban was quite detailed. From that, I gather you never expected me to make it out of my director's chair."

"You're not a field man, Rodger," Simbal pointed out.

Donovan frowned. "Have I dressed wrong?"

Simbal laughed. "If only this were a movie set."

"Never mind that," Donovan said, "I'm here, aren't I? Now I want an update on the *diqui*." He saw the look pass between Jake and Simbal. "I must've missed plenty since you're here, Jake. What's *your* interest in this?"

"What happened, Donovan," Jake said, "things get a little bit too hot for you back home?"

"Meaning what?"

"Meaning this," Simbal said, thrusting the sheaf of incriminating evidence at him.

Donovan took it and slowly went through the documents. "What's this supposed to be?" he said.

"Your epitaph," Jake told him. He handed over the photograph, gave a silent prayer that Simbal would not get carried away and mention Apollo.

Donovan looked down at Daniella Vorkuta's slightly blurred face. "Not a very good likeness," he said.

"And you should know," Simbal said archly. "You know what your mistake was, Rodger? Hanging that damned Seurat in the office. If you'd left it at home, you'd be okay now. But

500

Max saw it and knew it for the real thing right off. He'd seen it before, you see. At an auction in Paris. He was there when it was sold. To a KGB lieutenant named Daniella Vorkuta."

"I see."

" 'I see'? " Simbal cried. "Is that all you have to say?"

"You're Chimera," Jake said. "You're Vorkuta's mole. You always were." He was trembling visibly. "You set me up to kill Henry. My best friend, my mentor. You—"

He leapt at Donovan, who threw up his hands to ward off the attack. Simbal jumped between the two, turning toward Jake, pushing him back. "Stop it!" he shouted. "Jake, that won't solve anything!"

Jake thought of the moment in time when he had first met Henry Wunderman. The man had come to Hong Kong to seek him out. *Tell me*, he had said, *why are you still on this rock, running errands for the Triads? Because I'm half Chinese*, a very young Jake had said. *And if you were fully Chinese?* Wunderman had asked. *I'd find a way to make the Triads work for me.* Wunderman had smiled. *Suppose I can show you a way to do that*, he had said. *Would you be interested?* Jake sure was. And then Wunderman had said to him, *This also might be the way to find out what happened to your father.* Wunderman had known that about him: Jake's secret desire.

"There's Henry's death to be accounted for," Jake said at length.

"And your guilty conscience," Simbal said.

Jake allowed himself to be pushed back. He felt Bliss at his side. "He's right, Jake," she said.

"Sure," Simbal said, a gleam in his eye. "Now that we know about you, Rodger, here's what we're going to do with you. We're going to put you back in place as Director of the Quarry, only now you'll be running for us."

Donovan grunted. "Nice touch," he said, "but someone's already thought of that."

"Yeah?" Simbal said. "Like who?"

Donovan looked at him. "The President of the United States."

"What?"

He turned to Jake. "I wasn't the one who set you and Wunderman against one another. And it wasn't Daniella either, though she thought it was. It was the President."

"I don't believe you," Jake said.

"On the face of it, I don't blame you," Donovan admitted.

"But think about it for a minute. What better way to cement my ties with Daniella?"

"Henry was a sacrifice?" Jake said incredulously. "And I was the stalking horse?"

"That was it, yes," Donovan said. "And who better than you, Jake? Daniella hates and fears you. With you in the picture, she never suspected a thing."

Simbal thought about all this for a moment. "One thing doesn't make sense, Rodger. If you're a triple, working for the President, how is it that Max wants you dead?"

"So it was Threnody who gave you this evidence." Donovan sighed. "I should have known he'd get to you somehow. You were always his fair-haired boy, Tony. How he resented my taking you away from him! I'm still getting interdepartmental memos about agency raiding."

"Come on, Rodger, that's not what this is about," Simbal said skeptically.

"In a way, it is," Donovan said. "You see, Max wants my job. He's got access to the President now himself. Well, I'm sure he told you that. It's been Max's lifelong dream to get that kind of power."

"What are you handing us?" Jake said. "Someone outside the Quarry sphere would never have a chance. It's simply not the way things are done there."

Donovan had a sad look in his eyes. "You've been away a long time, Jake. It wouldn't've been the way in the old days. Beridien never would have permitted it. But he's long gone and times have changed.

"The President needed to appoint someone unconnected with the Quarry to head the inquiry into Antony Beridien's assassination. He needed someone who commanded respect, who had seniority. He chose Max Threnody. Ever since, Max has been working on the President to have me replaced. Once exposed so intimately to the Russians, he maintains, my loyalty remains suspect."

"Does Max know about Leslie?" Simbal asked.

"He seems to know bloody everything about me," Donovan said. "So there it is. I had an affair with a KGB lieutenant in Paris. She looks amazingly like a girl I was hung up on in college. Max put two and two together."

"You make it all sound very innocent," Simbal pointed out. "You can't tell me that you weren't aware of what you were getting into."

"I wanted her," Donovan said in a self-righteous tone. "She knew all the right strings to pull."

"You had no choice," Simbal said, "is that what you want us to believe?"

Donovan stared at them.

"Oh, come on," Jake said.

Donovan watched him, wary for another attack. He almost flinched when he said it. "She's beautiful, sexy and—Tony, you'll understand this—so much like what Leslie was in my mind. I would have to have been inhuman to turn her down."

"When did you start tripling?" Jake asked.

Now Donovan averted his head. The dripping of the water was a doleful sound. "Not for a long time."

"How long?" Jake pressed.

"Jesus," Donovan said.

"Rodger, you'd better tell us," Simbal advised. "I've got orders from Max to terminate you and Jake would just as soon see you dead. It sounds odd, but at this stage we're likely to be the only friends you've got."

Donovan plucked the fedora off his head, flung it into the jungle. "Why the hell am I wearing that, anyway?" One of the Shan sentries retrieved it, stuck it on his head. He didn't look any more ludicrous than Donovan had. "Not until after."

"After what?" Jake said.

"Beridien's assassination."

"Ah, shit," Jake said. "I should kill you right now. You and Vorkuta cooked that up."

Donovan nodded silently.

"Rodger," Simbal said softly, "when Max ordered me to terminate you he said that it was on the President's authority."

"I suppose he knew you were in no position to check," Donovan said.

"Meaning?"

"This is strictly internal. The President wants the matter settled one way or the other."

"Wouldn't the President rather keep you in place as a triple agent?" Simbal asked.

Donovan nodded. "All things being equal. But they're not. Max has seen to that. He's put a doubt in the President's mind as to my loyalty.

"So it's between me and Max," Donovan said. "A fight to the finish. Max wants me out any way he can. He knows it's not going to be easy. But this was a perfect way. I would

503

have done the same thing. Who's going to conduct an official inquiry out here in God's boondocks?" He gave a dry, ironic laugh. "The truth would never come out. Plus you'd be tied to him forever if you managed to kill me. He'd have something on you for the rest of your life." There was a defiant look in his eyes. "Still want to go through with it?"

Simbal turned to Jake. "What do you think? Is he lying or telling the truth?"

"There's one thing that bothers me," Jake said. "You said that Threnody told you Bennett and Curran pickpocketed the DEA computers of names, places, networks."

"Well, there's something I can straighten you out on," Donovan said. "Sometimes half a truth is the best lie there is. What those bastards also took are all the strategic deployment directives for the President's newly formed elite antiterrorist unit."

What am I missing? Jake wondered. Drugs and Kam Sang and the theft of antiterrorist directives. I've got pieces but no whole. Nothing fits.

Outwardly he showed nothing of his confusion.

Simbal, too, had some hard thinking to do. He recalled Run-Run Yi's words, *Bennett is the jinn who opens the door.* With antiterrorist strategic deployment directives? How? *These weapons*, Yi had said, *will have the power to destroy the world.* Blackman T-93 antipersonnel rocket launchers? How? And again he thought, What have I fallen into? He felt like a rat in a darkened maze. "I don't know," he said. "Why would Max lie to me about that?"

"Max probably doesn't know," Donovan said. "He's the consummate bureaucrat, Tony. You know that. Right now he's concentrating on getting me out of his hair any way he can."

"There's too much at stake," Jake said, "to take either of these bastards at their word."

Donovan looked at him. "I see I have more bargaining to do." He nodded. "All right. Do you recall that Henry Wunderman had a deep-cover asset code-named Apollo?"

"Yes," Jake said. He dared not glance at Simbal. He wanted to give Donovan no clue at all.

"Daniella knows he exists and his identity."

"She told you this?" Jake said, damping down on his anxiety.

"She did."

"What's his name?"

"What good would it do you?"

"Tell me," Jake said, "and don't ask questions."

"Mikhail Carelin."

Dear God, Jake thought. Carelin's a dead man. "When did she find out?" he asked.

"We spoke before I left," Donovan said. "She had just gotten the intelligence."

"Jake, what do you think?" Simbal said.

Is Donovan telling the truth about everything? Jake asked himself, or is he taking his own advice and feeding us half truths as lies?

"If you believe me, Tony," Donovan said, "it means aligning yourself against Max Threnody. I don't know whether you're prepared for that."

"I want a chance to get to Daniella Vorkuta," Jake said. "Donovan's the only path." That is, he thought, unless Apollo can get to her before she kills him.

"Is it worth the risk?" Simbal wondered aloud.

"To get to the head of the KGB's First Chief Directorate," Jake said, "I'd mortgage heaven and hell."

Simbal thought of Max Threnody, of what he had done to Monica, to the Cuban, to Simbal himself. That was all part of the game, in Max's book. Was this, too, just another ruse? Who was using him now, Max or Rodger?

"All right," Simbal said at last, making his decision. He called out softly and two of the Shan came and took Donovan. "You'll be in their custody until this is all over, Rodger," he said. "In the meantime, don't do anything stupid and make us sorry we kept you alive."

The rain had come again, the storm backing around from the south and sitting athwart the mountains, banging on them like a gleeful child with a new set of drums.

From where Jake and Tony Simbal crouched in the heavy undergrowth, they could scent the opium cooking. Its stench permeated the heavy air, hanging like pollution over the clearing. Their Shan escort, hidden from view, was entirely silent around them.

"If we can get to General Kuo," Simbal said, "I think we'll have a chance."

"Of what?" Jake asked.

"Of getting out alive." Simbal stretched a cramped muscle in his thigh. "I don't know about you, friend, but I have no death wish."

"Is that what you think I have?"

"If the shoe fits." Simbal shrugged.

"Don't worry," Jake said.

Simbal shifted the AK-47 on his lap. He was checking its mechanism for the third time. It was important to do that: the combination of the atmosphere and the laxity of the Shan in cleaning their weapons could be lethal. "Jesus," he laughed, "what the fuck do I have to be worried about?"

Jake thought about that for a time. "What do you suggest," he said after a time.

"You and I will go in all right," Simbal said. "But not until my Shan have created a diversion at the other end of the compound. That will do two things. First, it will draw General Kuo out in the open where we have a chance of getting to him. Second, it will keep his men busy while we try to find Bennett and Curran."

"And Chen Ju," Jake said.

"And Chen Ju."

For a long time, Jake watched the encampment. At last he said, "I think you deserve to see the whole picture. What the scientists at Kam Sang have come up with is a way to make a mobile nuclear warhead that can be slipped into existing weaponry such as handheld rocket launchers. The project directors felt that what they had come up with was essentially useless since the radiation fallout resulting from the percussion would undoubtedly kill the initiating soldier as well as his target."

"Christ," Simbal breathed. It had all come rushing in on him. "That's why the *diqui* have begun stockpiling Blackman T-93 antipersonnel rocket launchers! With the Kam Sang payloads those T-93s will have the power to destroy the world."

"What!" That was it: the missing piece! "Where did you hear that?" So this wasn't about drugs at all. Chen Ju had a far different objective in mind. Jake's eyes bored into Simbal.

"From a man named Run-Run Yi, the *diqui*'s late New York boss."

"Late? What happened to him?"

"Edward Martin Bennett happened to him," Simbal said. He recounted the incident at the Trilliant.

"That's Chen Ju's strategy," Jake said, so appalled that he felt sick to his stomach. "Members of the *diqui* will be supplied with stockpiled Blackman T-93s loaded with the miniature nuclear ammunition. With the stolen information Bennett and Curran have provided them, a single man could

506

infiltrate any major American city, hold it for ransom, destroy half its population."

"God in heaven," Simbal said. "Knowing the antiterrorist directives, he could make himself virtually invisible. He'd be unfindable."

Jake nodded. His mind was whirling with what they had uncovered. The audacity of the man! "This is what Chen Ju is after." Much more than the destruction of the *yuhn-hyun*, he thought. "He will infiltrate city after city, making his demands. Members of the *diqui* are fanatics; death means nothing to them. Chen Ju wants nothing less than the entire world. It's the ultimate stage of terrorism."

"He's not going to sell this new technology to the highest bidder?" Simbal asked.

"I don't think so," Jake said.

Simbal agreed. "He's changed the objective of the *diqui* from merely transshipping opium to disseminating the ultimate terrorist army. With the technology from Kam Sang, Chen Ju can hold the entire United States for ransom if he wishes."

"And he does, make no mistake," Jake said grimly. "But I think you're wrong on one point. Chen Ju's strategy for his *diqui* did not change at all. I see that clearly now. This is not something one just jumps into. I think his little toy has grown up into this monstrous weapon."

"Jesus," Simbal whispered. "We've got to stop him."

"Let's get started."

Simbal went off to give orders to his Shan warriors. When he returned, he watched Jake's profile for a time. He thought he'd give a great deal to know what was going on inside that mind. "The clock's ticking down," he said eventually. "They're all there. The information's got to be changing hands." He glanced down at his AK-47. His hands had told him. Everything in place.

Jake nodded. The Shan warriors had departed in absolute silence to take up their station.

Simbal glanced at his wristwatch. "Time," he said.

Together they broke cover.

General Kuo first became aware of the attack through the bird call. The sentries were well trained. That was General Kuo's first rule. Sentries were imperative in his line of work. Wars had been lost because of lax sentries. There were no lax sentries in General Kuo's army. At least none who were still among the living.

The bird call—one of his ideas—galvanized him. It had come from the north and he stepped out onto the veranda of his house and shouted orders. They were quick, precise, but unhurried. Precipitous action, General Kuo had been taught, most often led to defeat. He was, further, prepared for all eventualities. He possessed a cool mind in all matters, especially battle, which he loved.

He did not know the identity of the enemy: Burmese, Chinese, Russian, American. Even a ragtag army of one of his competitors. It did not matter. His response was the same. Victory was assured. General Kuo felt no anxieties in these situations but rather an odd kind of elation that was akin to a superbly sharp knife piercing the flesh close to his heart. The thrill took his breath away.

Strapping on his U.S. Army-issue Colt .45, he stepped off the veranda. The northern perimeter of his encampment was where the mule trains departed for their trek down the Shan to market, loaded down with the processed opium. It was most often here that attacks against him were begun. The tears of the poppy were, after all, his life's blood. It was what they all desired, no matter their nationality.

Three of his men went trotting by and he shouted to them, sending them off to the northeast perimeter. No sense in taking chances. He did not want to be enfiladed. In defense, General Kuo believed, it was better to err on the side of conservatism.

He went quickly in the opposite direction, toward the factory. It was where they all were: Huaishan Han, Chen Ju and the two Americans. They liked to talk business surrounded by their wares, General Kuo had discovered. Like the clusters of sapphires and rubies he kept in his pocket, it gave them a physical sense of their own wealth. It was a way of gaining face. It could be no other way.

General Kuo twisted the Imperial jade ring on his finger. It was good luck to have the mystical stone, prized above all others by the gods, against one's flesh. It brought health and prosperity to the wearer.

This was in his mind when he turned the corner and felt the muzzle of a gun bite into the back of his neck. He began to turn his head but was dissuaded by a sharp jab to his kidneys.

"Don't do that," a voice in his ear said.

General Kuo winced and bit his lip so that he should not cry out and thus lose face to his unseen enemy.

He wondered briefly who it was who had the skill to infiltrate his camp so successfully but was distracted as the flap of his leather holster was unsnapped and his prized Colt .45 taken from him.

"I will kill you for this," he said, through lips compressed with pain. "I will have you strung up in the center of the compound and there watch the nocturnal animals tear you to pieces."

"Big talk," Tony Simbal said, keeping the pressure heavy at the back of the Chinese's neck. He risked a glance at the gun Jake had taken from the General. The standard stocks had been replaced by ones made of carved Imperial jade.

"Very impressive," he said to Jake in English. Then, to General Kuo, in dialect, "Send the men guarding the factory back to where the fighting is."

"But— Oof!" Pain lanced through General Kuo's side, making his eyes water. He did as he was told.

When the men had left their position, Simbal said, "Get going."

"Where?" General Kuo asked. He was wondering how he could reverse his current position.

"Into the factory," Jake said.

For emphasis, Simbal jabbed him hard again with the muzzle of the AK-47 and the Chinese stumbled forward. For the first time General Kuo began to worry. These two men were not CIA and not KGB. They had infiltrated his camp. Therefore, they were not fools. When it came to foreign devils, General Kuo was used to dealing with fools and morons. This was a new experience for him and he did not like it. He was a creature of habit, a man who lived by strict rules that he himself had set down. He controlled a vast fiefdom of staggering worth. Any hint of anarchy was anathema to him.

"What do you want?" His tone had changed. It was softer, most reasonable. Perhaps, he thought, I can strike a bargain with these two. "There is a shipment set to depart tomorrow morning. Six hundred kilos of excellent quality Number Four. If this is why you have—"

"Keep going," Simbal said, jabbing him again so that he lurched heavily against the corrugated tin wall of the factory.

General Kuo gritted his teeth and put his left hand against his heavy belt buckle. Felt the comforting configuration of the tiny .22 caliber pistol secreted there. His fingers twitched.

Not yet, he thought. It would do him no good to get one man only to be shot by the second man. He needed an opportunity to shoot both of them at once. "What do you want with the factory?" he said. "This is not where the tears of the poppy is stored."

"It's where they all are," Jake said.

General Kuo felt a little thrill of fear shoot down his back. Buddha, he thought, they are not after the opium at all. His fingers closed over the butt of the .22. Soon, he thought, as he led them around to the front door. Very soon now.

"Here is the entrance," he said. They went up the wooden steps. He quested with his senses, felt both of them close behind him. At the doorway they were crowding forward as he had expected. He could physically feel both of them now, knew where each stood.

He put his right hand on the door handle and pulled outward. As he did so, his left hand jerked the small pistol out of his waistband and he whirled. He was already pulling the trigger. It was point-blank range. There was no question of missing either of them.

Chen Ju was in the process of receiving from the two Americans the intelligence data which he so keenly desired when he heard the gunshots. He whirled, as did they all as the front door to the factory flew open.

Rain spattered inward, the wind howled. Then General Kuo came in and stared at them each in turn with eyes wide with surprise.

Annoyed at being interrupted at such a crucial moment, Chen Ju barked at him. "What is it?"

"What are you doing here," General Kuo said angrily, "when—" And vomited up a river of blood. He took two exaggerated strides into the cavernous room and lurched against one of the zinc-topped trestle tables. His left arm struck outward, sliding across the stained surface. His white, grasping fingers knocked over a Bunsen burner. Then he looked down at the mess he had made of his uniform, said, "Shit." His knees buckled and he slid to the floor. His eyes stared at them accusingly but did not blink; they were already filming over.

Then the doorway was filled, not with rain and wind, but with the bulk of two men.

Jake and Tony Simbal came into the factory. Simbal leveled the AK-47 in the direction of the group of four men.

"Jesus fuckin' Christ," Edward Martin Bennett said.

510

"Long time no see," Simbal said, coming quickly into the room.

Jake, behind him, knelt beside General Kuo, felt for a pulse. "He's dead," he said and Simbal nodded.

Chen Ju, who was standing almost directly behind Peter Curran, kicked viciously at the American.

Curran, taken completely by surprise, stumbled toward Simbal, who immediately opened fire with the submachine gun. The boyish face was caught in midexpression. The body jerked, stood up straight, then under the force of the fusillade, was thrown backward as if by a high wind.

To one side came a crackling. Jake looked around, saw the Bunsen burner General Kuo had upended had been lit. Flames were spreading along the wooden floorboards. In a moment, they leapt upward along the line of freestanding wooden cabinets filled with glass bottles and metal containers.

"Let's get out of here!" Jake yelled at Simbal. "Some of these chemicals are highly flammable!"

"I want these fuckers," Simbal said.

"Now!" Jake went past him, pushed Bennett toward the doorway. The old man with the one shoulder higher than the other looked at Jake with the expression of a sphinx.

"Shi Jake," he said in a reedy voice.

Jake took him up. He did not look like he could go anywhere fast. He had about him already the smell of the grave.

Smoke had engulfed the inside of the factory. It was a virulent gray, acidic, sparking, singeing the eyes, inflaming the back of the throat. There was a heavy roar off to one side and a crash. The chemical cabinets!

Jake rushed Huaishan Han outside, put him down. It was raining heavily and the wind had picked up. The roiling sky looked to be at treetop height. Jake saw Simbal and Bennett, turned, remembering the fourth man, undoubtedly the Naga. Chen Ju. He took two paces toward the factory and with a great, muffled roar, the roof blew off. One wall collapsed entirely and now the flames licked upward, unmindful of the storm.

It was impossible to get near the place. The heat and the thick, acrid smoke penetrated the entire clearing.

Jake turned away, saw the old Chinese, propped against the bole of a tree. Pain made of his face a lopsided mask. He knelt beside him. "You're Huaishan Han," he said in Mandarin.

511

The old man seemed surprised. "Surely your late father never mentioned my name."

"It was given to me at the point of death," Jake said, "by one of your *diqui* network. The *diqui* is yours, is it not?"

"Mine," the old man said, "and Chen Ju's. It gave him power."

"And you?" Jake said. "What did it give you, old man?"

"Me? Why, it gave me back my life." Huaishan Han reached out with a taloned claw and drew Jake toward him. "A life that had been taken from me by your father. He took everything from me: my wife, my child, my career. He ruined me utterly. The *diqui* brought me a reason to live. It brought me back into the good graces of a Communist Chinese regime whose memory had grown dim. I was no longer remembered. The old guard was all gone: purged or died of natural causes. Except your father. He was the only one who would remember. And seek to stop my rise to power again inside China." He cocked his head as if the barking crackle of the gargantuan fire were speaking to him. "He had to die, you see. Only he could have stopped me. And, of course, you."

"You had my father murdered." *Only the mountain knows*, Hige Moro had said. The Shan.

"Revenge," Huaishan Han said, "is its own reward. Your father destroyed me once. He did more than destroy me. He destroyed my future as well. My wife, my dearest Senlin, and my unborn child. In the well at Shuang jing. He threw me down into darkness. Into hell." The old man's eyes were fever bright. The chemical flames were reflected in their glossy depths.

"He had done something to Senlin, you see, your father. Something despicable, something unspeakable. Her mind, her entire personality was twisted beyond recognition. Still, I wanted her; still, I loved her. She was the only one I ever loved!"

It was a wail, a terror-filled, anguished sound unlike any Jake had ever heard before. The rain beat a solid tattoo against Huaishan Han's white face. He breathed as if he were running a race he could never finish.

"In the well," he said. "I lived in that hellish place for almost a week. My back was broken. I could barely move. But when I fell, I took my Senlin with me." His eyes were filled with tears. They made the flames, in reflection, seem chimerical, changing shape in the manner of windblown clouds. "She was above me. My own battered body protected her

512

from serious injury. The same stone outcropping that broke my back now saved us from an endless descent into the depths."

His head drooped on his stalklike neck, his sharp chin brushing his fluttering chest. "Oh," he cried, "she could have saved me. She could have saved us both. But, no, she began to fight me. She was under your father's spell. Some terrible, unimaginable sorcery he had worked on her.

"I could scarcely believe it. I begged her to save us. It was in her power to do so. I could hear your father calling to her from above. How I hated him! I sent my hate upward as if it could entwine itself about him and strangle the life from him.

"But my Senlin was gaining in strength and she began to pummel me. She was a madwoman. I looked in her face and knew that she was no longer sane, no longer mine. No longer Senlin at all.

"She was a stranger," Huaishan Han panted. "A stranger who was trying to kill me." He looked up at Jake. "I did the only thing I could, you see. She had told me that she was pregnant and at that moment I, too, must have gone mad. I remember thinking, It is *his* child, not mine!

"So I killed her and killed it. The baby. The future. In an instant it was all gone. Everything. And for a week afterward they were my sole companions."

Now the old man's head came up and he clutched more firmly at Jake. "So you see, it was not enough to kill your father, Shi Jake." The tears were gone, the eyes were clear and colorless in their passion. Jake imagined that Huaishan Han had gazed upon his Senlin with such a baleful expression in the split instant before he reached out and snuffed out her life and that of the baby growing inside her.

Abruptly nauseated, Jake broke the old man's hold on him. But Huaishan Han's taloned claws sought to hold on. It was like being in a field of nettles.

"It was not enough, Shi Jake," the old man screamed. "Your father took from me not only my love, my life, but my future. Is it not fitting that I destroy his now!"

With a great effort, Jake pushed the demented old man away from him. He was disgusted. Horrified at the depths to which the human soul could sink, he turned away toward the flickering fire. He meant to find Simbal and Bennett but, instead, he saw a figure walking slowly toward him.

The hair was cut short, the fire threw it into stark silhouette against the pelting downpour. Then it turned and he saw it was a woman. The figure came steadily toward him and at last he could see the face, that familiar face that had haunted his dreams from the moment Nichiren had shot her at the Sumchun River four years ago.

Lan, his daughter! Alive!

"Lan," he said, elation filling him. "Lan!"

"Hello, *bah-ba*," she said and, as Colonel Hu had instructed her, pulled out the automatic, aimed it and pulled the trigger.

When Tony Simbal heard the shot, he whirled around, the rain flying off him. He got the briefest glimpse of Jake facing a shadowy figure. Then Bennett took off and Simbal went after him.

The combination of the storm, the explosion and the Shan diversionary raid at the other end of the compound had put the area into chaos. Bennett chose to dart in the direction of the fire. It was the smart move. The factory was on the southern perimeter of General Kuo's encampment. Any other direction would take Bennett into the compound where he ran the risk of being stopped by Kuo's men or, worse, shot by Simbal's Shan warriors.

Simbal had this figured as well so he did not follow Bennett directly but rather made for the place beyond the burning factory he would have gone to were he in Bennett's place.

He was at the edge of the jungle. Already a tangly web of undergrowth was building its way toward the side of the factory, although there was ample evidence that it had been hacked back quite recently.

In the trees, he turned, moving the muzzle of the AK-47 in a slow, steady arc. The rain destroyed perspective and the continuing conflagration just meters away cast bizarre shadows that rose and fell with sickening rapidity.

Bennett was nowhere to be found and Simbal cursed himself. He moved off farther into the jungle, began a sweep that would take him parallel to the shell of the factory.

Saw a darting movement and, crouching down, began to move as quickly as he could toward the spot. In that moment, felt all the breath go out of him. He doubled over as Bennett kicked him a second time in the kidneys. Lost hold of the AK-47 and saw Bennett's bulk diving after it.

Simbal went after Bennett. He grabbed hold of the big man's legs and twisted. Bennett went down but he was already rolling, kicking upward in a vicious thrust.

The toe of his cowboy boot brushed Simbal's cheek and then the heel slammed into his jaw. Simbal reeled backward and Bennett lunged for the AK-47, took it up and aimed it hurriedly.

Simbal leapt at Bennett as the big man pulled the trigger. Felt the heat, the disintegration and he was inside the spray of bullets. Used the edge of his hand under Bennett's chin in a short, sharp chop.

Bennett let go with a "Whoof!" of surprise and pain and Simbal brought him down, jamming an elbow into his sternum. But Bennett used the stock of the submachine gun, smashing it into Simbal's groin.

Simbal saw stars. His breath was steaming in his throat and sickening bile rose upward, threatening to choke him.

Bennett scrambled to his feet, trained the AK-47 downward. "Christ, Tony, but you were always a pain in my ass. What a fucking white knight you are. I really think I'm doing you a favor now by killing you. I'm saving you from a life slaving away in the gray corridors for men with little minds and even littler pocketbooks." He curled his forefinger around the AK-47's trigger. "So long, Tony."

Simbal, his right hand holding his aching lower belly, flicked his arm upward and the thin throwing knife stuck to the hilt in Bennett's chest. He looked utterly astounded and died with that expression imprinted on his face.

Taking three deep breaths, Simbal got to his knees. He took the AK-47 from Bennett's grip and staggered back toward the encampment.

Jake felt the blood running along with the rain. It pumped from him: his life draining away. He slipped to his knees, regained his feet.

"Lan," he called. "Lan! Oh, Buddha."

Saw her leveling the pistol at him and thought, This is a dream, some terrible nightmare from which I will awake at any moment.

But the pain was real and with every beat of his laboring heart he could feel his strength ebbing. How could this be happening? he thought. How?

He struggled toward her. The wind and the rain scoured him. He was beaten again to his knees. Gasping, vision blurred. He tried to assemble his thoughts but the sight of his daughter, and then the knowledge of what she had done to him, unnerved him. He was frozen. Shock and despair gripped him unshakably.

"Lan," he called. "Lan, I love you." Had he ever told her that? When was the last time he had held her, the last time she had come to him for comfort. Had he given it even then? Probably not. He had not wanted a daughter, he realized now, had been disappointed in his first wife that she bore him a female child instead of a male. So he had deliberately set about making her as hard in spirit as a man.

Now he knew that he had squeezed all the joy, all the life out of her. What was left had fled his unhappy household to join the radical Triad, the Steel Tigers at the border of the Mainland.

And now, insanely, she was going to kill him. He looked up through his pain and his grief to see the muzzle of the pistol coming down. It was aimed at a spot between his eyes. There was nothing in his daughter's face: no recognition, no rage, no emotion at all. She was a machine, programmed to perform this hideous task.

Jake made one last attempt to reach her. Got to his feet and took three quick, unsteady steps toward her. Then toppled to the muddy earth at her feet.

He was the only thing of which Qi lin was aware. She heard him calling a name but was hardly aware that it used to be hers. Instead, he seemed to be mouthing some alien tongue, which struck her much like the rain. She was indifferent to its effect.

In her mind, Colonel Hu's hand stretched out along the cradle of the night, caressing her while his mind talked to hers. He told her what to do and she listened. Her finger tightened on the trigger and, for the second time, she began the slow squeezing motion that would ensure a perfectly placed shot.

Then she was lying prone on the ground, gasping in air, staring up at another female face.

Bliss had come at her from the blind side, slamming into her with the full force of her body. She had led with her shoulder, driving her weight up from her planted right foot.

She had no thought other than to save Jake. Breaking away from the diversionary attack at the north end of the encampment, she had been searching through the chaos for Jake. She had been angry that he had placed her away from the main conflict but had seen no reason to argue with him at the time. She knew there were other matters occupying him. She knew she would get her chance.

The explosion at the factory had provided her with that and she had taken it. She had seen Jake shot and had instinctively leveled the AK-47 she carried at his assailant. Then she had heard him cry out and had recognized Lan.

At first, there was no thought of harming the girl, merely subduing her. But as soon as she came in contact with Lan, Bliss knew that something was very wrong. Now that she had been openly attacked, her lips drew back in a rictus, she snarled deep in her throat.

Bliss spoke to her as they wrestled along the ground but the girl either would not or could not respond. She was almost certainly mad. The decision was instantaneous. For the last time Bliss entered *da-hei*. Over the heaving bosom of the moonlit sea she flew toward the strange presence.

And saw the world turning, the world changing, herself changing. Felt the great karmic wheel lurch into motion, begin its swing forward, always forward, carrying her onward toward the edge of the moonlit sea, and the unknown that was beyond. Waiting.

Now she was at close quarters with Lan's qi. And recoiled in horror. Through the twisted tendrils she recognized the endless war that raged like a ravening beast. In and out, like a pristine moon revealed through storm clouds, Bliss could feel glimpses of the true spirit of the girl. But the movement of the beast always cut it short.

The essence of Lan was dying inside a mind that had been tortured beyond all reason. This wanton destruction was so cruel it made Bliss want to weep with pity and rage.

At the same time she knew what she must do, knew now why Shi Zilin had drawn her into da-hei, *and why she felt the qi of the ages roiling through her like a howling wind.*

She set about doing what Shi Zilin had trained her to do. In the back of her mind was the suspicion that he knew that this moment would eventually come. Because now she was no longer Bliss, no longer Jake's beloved, no longer, even, Shi Zilin's godgranddaughter. She was all these things and more. She was the messenger of the celestial guardians of China. The wisdom of the ages resided in her, the ancient magic of an ancient race, the animus of genius that lived on, that must be maintained.

Now she was all spirit. While, quite apart, her body continued its physical struggle with Lan, her qi, spread out across the

517

shining skein of da-hei, *began to infiltrate the tortured spirit of Lan, who had taken the name of Qi lin, the mystical male-female beast of Chinese mythology.*

The beast who possessed Lan's spirit had incalculable strength. But Bliss was not alone. Shi Zilin was with her, and someone else, another female spirit, ancient of ancients.

The two slim forms rolled and battered one another in the mud, while the real struggle was carried on in a secret harbor that no human eye could pierce.

Jake, dragging himself centimeter by painful centimeter to where the two women fought, could only find fear in his heart. In the killing ground there could be only one victor. Death to the defeated.

He loved both of them almost more than he could bear and he had to defuse them before the unthinkable tragedy occurred.

He lurched forward but pulled up short. Startled, he heard the voice that was not a voice, repeating, *Stay away, Jake! I can save her if you stay away!*

"Bliss!"

He went on, stumbled over a root. On his knees, he heard it again. *Jake, please! Stay where you are! You will kill your daughter otherwise!*

His head reverberated with the words and he thought, I must be hallucinating. But knew that was not so. Now the changes that had worked themselves through Bliss leapt up to his consciousness. Ever since his father had died Bliss had been a different person. It was as if some mysterious current was running through her. She could tell lies from truth. What else was she able to do?

"Bliss!" Through the rain, his agony, he called to her as his father had done with Senlin. "I don't want to leave you alone!"

I am not alone, Jake. This must happen if you are to have your daughter back.

"I don't want to have to choose."

Joss, Jake. The wheel has turned.

"Bliss, I love you! Bliss—!"

The sky was a sheet of iron, reverberating with the howls of the beast. A rain of zinc hurtled down upon forms inimical to one another. Clouds of tin and antimony tore at them and a moon of mercury dripped painful illumination.

Bliss or, rather, the essence of Bliss, had made her pact with Buddha. It was time to die. She could feel the comforting presence of Shi Zilin inside her. Lan was the chosen one, the descendant of the line of the guardians of China. It was Bliss's responsibility to cleanse Lan's mind, to rid it of evil just as Fazhan had done with Senlin so many decades ago, to keep the conduit of wisdom and magic alive that would guide China safely into the twenty-first century by transferring all that resided in her into Lan.

Bliss was one with the universe. Totally immersed within da-hei she felt the connection with the generations. She was young and old at once, large and small, male and female. She became the continuum of which life and death were but an infinitesimal fraction, the passive receptacle rather than the fierce avenger. She stole the light from the world, she sought the low ground, became the rivers to the sea.

And the sea became her mantle of power. The wind as well, the rain, the storms. The dragons of the night rose to her beckoning, their fierce breath startling the stalking beast within Lan. It had been made manifest to her that to cleanse the evil that ran rampant within Lan, to transfer the power she now possessed, she must relinquish her hold on her own corpus. That was the only way.

And Bliss found a joy in this, for she was playing a key role in the continuum of China, because she now knew the folly of the concepts of "life" and "death," ideas conjured up by the limits of the human mind.

Now Bliss was much more. She was the energy of the universe, moving and forming in an infinite number of directions. Cradled within the bosom of the eternal elements, she understood how much more there was to existence than mere life.

Bliss was all color, swirling: green-blue of the seas, blue-gray of the sky, gray-black of stone; red-orange of fire, orange-brown-green of the foliage. In her vision now was the hideous noncolor of the evil that gripped Lan's mind. She flew toward it.

Bliss embraced the evil, felt its inimical chill and for an instant sensed her qi begin to shrivel in fear of what it could do to her. Then, thunder rolling through her heart, she understood it all, that fear was another human idea, that it had no meaning in the place within which she dwelled.

Gathering her power like a cloak, she opened her arms. She engulfed it, running through it and, in the end, absorbing it in a burst of light-energy-kineticism that shook her, that roared through streams and fields, oceans and mountains, that thundered in her world for all eternity.

Jake heard something then, like the snapping of a twig. Unmindful of the pain and her warnings, he made it to his feet and stumbled the last paces to where the two of them lay. Bliss was on top and, groaning, Jake went to his knees. He pulled Bliss off his daughter, brought her into his arms.

"Bliss!"

He saw the hole ripped in her chest at the spot where her heart was. Somehow the wound had been instantly cauterized. There was no blood, only, inexplicably, the scent of the sea.

"Oh, no. No!"

The rain beat against him and every drop seemed like a reminder of his sins. "Oh, Bliss," he whispered. It was impossible to believe that she was gone. *I will take care of her, Elder Uncle*, he had said to Three Oaths. *She is most precious to me, your* bou-sehk. Until this moment of utter loss he did not know just how precious.

"Jesus."

Jake turned his head.

"Are you okay, Jake?" Simbal said.

"I don't know."

Simbal knelt at Jake's side, his fingers feeling for the wound. "What happened?"

Jake looked down at Bliss's beautiful face. "I don't know that either."

"Bennett's dead. And the old guy with the broken back's where you left him under that tree. He's laughing his head off. Won't stop for anything. I think he's lost it."

Jake barely heard a word.

Simbal leaned forward. "How's this other girl? Who is she?"

"My daughter," Jake said.

"She's still alive," Simbal said, checking her pulse.

Jake carefully moved Bliss off his lap. He was very tired. With an effort, he bent over his daughter. Her face, so long in his memory, seemed subtly altered somehow. Familiar in an altogether unfamiliar way.

"Lan," he said. "Lan."

Her lids fluttered open. Her eyes were filled with him. "*Bah-ba*," she said softly, disbelievingly. And began to cry.

"Time's gone so slowly," she whispered. "Oh, how I've missed you."

Jake was going to go alone but Lan insisted on accompanying him. The sun was shining with a fierce intensity. The stench of air-drying fish was everywhere. The waves of the South China Sea were chips of beaten brass where the sunlight hit them. In the troughs, deep aquamarine shadows crept, stealing the light.

Jake still did not walk well. The bullet had entered his right side just above the hip. Perhaps it had chipped off a tiny piece of bone or pierced a nerve, it was impossible to say. In any case, the pain stayed with him. Not that he minded that. It was proof that what had occurred up in the Shan had really happened.

Lan, when she awoke, could not remember seeing him moments before, let alone shooting him. In fact, she was a wholly different person. The anger and rage had all been expunged from her. She was his little girl again. Or, perhaps, he had returned to being her father.

Simbal's Shan had taken the head of General Kuo from its corpse and had held it before them as they had advanced into the camp. Without their general, the army could not exist. Those not already dead or wounded were disarmed and beaten and sent scrambling down the rocky scree. The old man with one shoulder higher than the other was flung like a rag doll after them. The Shan had no use for a Chinese.

Jake and Simbal had found him fifty meters down the steep slope, head down, his neck broken by an outcropping of granite. It was an ignominious death for a man who had wielded such awesome power.

Jake, crouching over the frail figure, could only wonder at the furies of the mind which drove human beings to such lifelong quests. His father had been such a man. So had been his enemy, Huaishan Han. That was ironic and at the same time terribly sad. Huaishan Han had been the darkness to Zilin's light. But they were two sides of the same coin and that was a sobering thought, indeed. It made Jake wonder whether the *Zhuan* should retire at this moment. He did not want to look back on a life filled with interminable sorrow as his father and Huaishan Han had.

He recalled the session at McKenna's house with White-Eye Kao and wondered how he ever could have done so much vicious damage to one human being. The cause was just. Or was it? The line was blurring for him and that was a danger sign. It frightened him that he could justify the means through the end. Was that a product of being in the dark and the cold on the mountain? Huaishan Han had been like that. Had his father felt that way as well? Jake thought he knew the answer. Perhaps it was time, then, for him to step aside. Let someone else shoulder the burden of being *tai pan* of all *tai pan*.

He felt Lan's hand warm inside his now, felt the weight of the urn he held against his chest. He breathed deeply, abruptly overcome by sadness.

Simbal and Rodger Donovan had come with Jake to Hong Kong but not for long. There was another battle to be won: the one involving the power struggle at the Quarry.

Alone, Jake and Simbal had shaken hands.

"It's not over yet, is it, Jake?"

"No," Jake had said. "The world won't be safe from Kam Sang until we've managed to dismantle what they've built, dispersed the scientific team that worked on the project."

"The Shan," Simbal said. "The Shan won out this time."

"The killing ground," Jake said. "The place where it all began." *On the mountain it is cold and dark,* Zilin had cautioned him. *That is where you are now.* The Shan.

"I'm going to need your help," Simbal said.

"There's more than friendship between us," Jake had said. "There's trust."

After Simbal and Donovan had left, Jake learned from his hospital bed that Bluestone's combine had at last succeeded in acquiring more than fifty percent of InterAsia stock. But to do that, the *tai pan*'s investors had mortgaged their businesses to the hilt.

He had thrown his head back and laughed for the first time in many weeks, so hard in fact that he had almost popped several stitches.

"Let them have it," he had said to a semihysterical Andrew Sawyer. "They're finished now."

"It is we who are finished," Sawyer said in a lament.

"On the contrary," Jake said, wiping his eyes. He could scarcely believe it. The strategy had worked. His father had said, *Yes, my son, gamble everything. But, Father, if I lose— There is no point,* Zilin had said, *in gambling pennies.* "Bluestone and his combine have paid almost a billion dollars for a company useless for their purposes."

Sawyer was white-faced. "Have you lost your mind, *Zhuan*? The entire fortune of the *yuhn-hyun* is tied up in InterAsia."

"Is it?" Jake said. "This afternoon I want you to go to our lawyer's. Tell him that you require the Redstone file." Jake was studying the other's astounded face. It was running the gamut of emotions. "In it you will find all the applicable papers. You remember the meeting when my father insisted that all the *yuhn-hyun* assets be signed over to me?"

Sawyer nodded. "No one was very happy about that, even your uncle."

"I know," Jake said. "But now you see why it had to be done. Our assets are no longer in InterAsia. Over a period of months after the public offering, they were moved from their various holding companies. Even the Kam Sang holdings are no longer within Pak Han Min. In fact, InterAsia Trading is nothing but a shell. The *yuhn-hyun*'s profits flow *through* it but it owns nothing outright. I hope you don't mind Bluestone taking a one percent cut. That's a helluva good dividend but I think it's a small price to pay for the collapse of Five Star Pacific."

"And Pacific Overland Trading as well," Sawyer cried. "Sir Byron Nolin-Kelly has been a thorn in my side for years. Now we have them all! *Zhuan*, you are a genius!"

You are a genius. Those words echoed in Jake's mind now as he laced his fingers with Lan's. They had a mocking ring to them. A genius. He was nothing of the kind. He was no more than a zombie now. His daughter had returned to him but Bliss was gone.

He clutched the urn tighter to him. It was decorated with calligraphy in blue: "If the seasons did not change/The world would cease to breathe/The universe would give out/And the Buddha would close his eyes."

In the urn were Bliss's ashes. Bliss, who had died in order that his daughter might live. He was grateful for her selflessness but, oh, he missed her with a sharpness that was almost unbearable.

They came to the spot where he and Three Oaths and

T. Y. Chung threw out the remains of Zilin upon the water. Three Oaths and his family were already there. Prayers had been spoken into the wind.

The sea breeze rustled Lan's hair. During the time she had been here, she had allowed it to lengthen. It shone like black gold, drifting off her face in ethereal wisps.

There was no laughter when Jake had confronted Three Oaths. There was little to say. Jake had no explanation for what had happened. He no more knew why Lan had tried to kill him than he did how Bliss had been shot. He had not found the pistol in Lan's hand and no one else had been around to pull the trigger. A gun does not go off by itself.

None of this, of course, allayed his uncle's grief. But in this, at least, they were united.

"She wanted to go," Three Oaths had said. "She wanted only to be with you. I could not forbid her to go." He shrugged. "She did as she wished. As she always has done. It was her way." He turned away, wiping the tears from his cheeks. "I know that you blame yourself, Younger Nephew. In this you are wholly Western. It was her *joss*. I assign no blame. I am proud of what she did."

"Father," Lan said now, "it is time."

Jake nodded. He held the urn in front of him. A solid breeze was at their backs. An orange-sailed junk was leaning into the wind, heading for the typhoon shelter. Further out, tankers were steaming toward Japan. On the beach, children played, building castles out of sand and dreams. With an inward sigh, he inverted the urn, scattering the ashes over the bosom of the ocean.

Reaching out, Lan touched the shining side of the urn. In her mind was a buzzing, a pleasant cacophony that reached down to the soles of her feet. She was warmed by it, calmed. It was almost as if the voice of Buddha spoke directly to her. She heard the calling of the world around her.

She opened her eyes. "Father," she said, "Shi Zilin, Bliss. I feel them. They're all around us."

Jake put his arm across her shoulders. "I know they are, Lan."

But perhaps he would never know what it was she truly meant.

From the beginning of Eric Van Lustbader's novel, *ZERO*, to be published by Random House in May 1988.

He was on one of the top floors, a strict stipulation with him. He was personally comfortable with the vistas thus afforded him and professionally at ease with the view of his immediate environment a high floor provided. He had been taught to be a very careful man.

Beyond the clattering palms and below the tropical profusion of the orchid gardens, the cerulean waters of the Molokai Channel beckoned invitingly. The early wind had died, and with a practiced eye Civet knew that it would be a calm day. A great day for fishing.

He could already see the shining strand arrowing down into the water, could feel the tension on the line, the shuddering, and then the great monster tug as the Onaga, the deep-water snapper he loved to eat, took the bait. Oh, yes, he thought, happier now. The tang of the salt on his face, the challenge in the pull and leap of the big fish. That was the kind of activity that would wash from his emotions the detritus of the aftermath of the extraction.

Extraction was part of the jargon, as odd as the ergot of an African bushman, that men in Civet's profession used to indicate a sanctioned killing.

Below his lanai he saw a couple in their twenties cutting through the grass in their jogging outfits. Disturbed, the mynahs rose, cawing. And as his eyes followed the arc of the birds' flight, Civet saw the figure standing beside the coconut palm.

The figure was partially in shadow, and yet the power that emanated from it reached Civet seven stories above.

Civet forgot the hopping mynahs, the jogging couple; he was oblivious to the soft air, the spectacular view across to the island of Molokai which he loved so well. He was fully concentrated on the figure. Civet, who was as adept at tracking as he was at killing, was used to identifying people at a distance.

Civet was now at the far end of the lanai. Palm fronds waved, partially obscuring the figure. But the angle was better, and at last Civet could get a look at the face.

The glass Civet held crashed to the cement floor, and he

found himself gripping the railing to stop himself from falling to his knees. Vertigo overcame him. His mouth was open and he was gasping for breath. It cannot be, he thought. Not yet. I need to rest; I'm exhausted from all this running. It simply cannot be.

But he knew what it meant: they had already found him.

He turned and rushed back into the room, scraping his knee on the edge of the bed. He staggered into the bathroom where he vomited in great, wracking convulsions. He wasn't emotionally ready. Dear God, he thought, protect me from what I must do. Protect those I love if I don't make it.

His imagination, racing in panic, unraveled what was ahead of him. Stop it! he admonished himself. Getting hold of himself at last, he splashed cold water on his face, into his mouth, across the back of his neck. Then he hurriedly dressed, putting wallet, car keys, passport, and a small eelskin case into various pockets of his tropical-weight jacket. He reread the postcard he had written in the dead of night, and then he went out the door.

He avoided the elevator, taking the stairs two at a time. In the lobby, he hurried past pale-skinned tourists in garish aloha shirts. He deposited the postcard with the concierge, who assured him it would go out with the morning's mail.

In the underground car park, he took a quick scan, allowing his eyes to adjust to the gloom. When he was satisfied with his security, he crossed to his rented Mustang. Gettinig down on his knees, he inspected the underside of the carriage with his customary thoroughness.

He looked along the entire length of the tailpipe as well as in it. Places where the deadly items he had seen in the war's aftermath could easily be secreted. Finishing his check, he began *prana*, the semimystical deep breathing that allowed him to think clearly in difficult situations.

Still on his knees he went over the car trunk lock, looking for the minute scratches that would indicate an intruder's attempts to pop it. There was nothing. He rose and unlocked the trunk.

A couple with a small boy came into the car park, and he was obliged to wait until they got into their car and drove away.

Working quickly, he transferred the contents of the trunk to the front passenger seat. Then he climbed into the driver's seat and put the convertible's top up. In a moment, the Mustang's engine coughed to life and, throwing it in gear, Civet drove out of the car park.

He took the Napili Road because he disliked the new highway that had been built recently further up the ridge slope. This, as well as his driving, was purely instinctual.

The face—the shadowed face! Its features burned into his mind, glowing like coals thrust into his eyes. There was a heat upon him, so unnatural that it made him shiver as if he had the ague. For a moment, his resolve wavered; death cracked its bare knuckles in his face. His fingers, white upon the wheel, hurt with the unconscious power of his grip.

He fled Napili as if chased by a ghost. At the Methodist church he turned right onto Honoapiilani Highway, a three-lane road where he could pick up speed.

He had just begun to accelerate when he saw the black blur of the Ferrari Marcello coming up behind him. It had taken the Kapalua Highway and now shot into the mainstream of traffic not more than a hundred yards behind Civet's Mustang. For an instant, he got a clear look at the driver. His heart began to race once again.

Blinking sweat out of his eyes, Civet wrenched the steering wheel to the right. At the same time, he trod hard on the accelerator. The Mustang gave a shrill squeal and, with a thick cloud of red dirt and torn foliage, he shot off along the wide verge.

Horns blared as startled drivers protested this dangerous maneuver. Glancing in his rearview mirror, Civet could see the black Marcello weaving in and out of traffic as it kept pace with him.

Civet cursed his American car which, in horsepower and maneuverablity, was no match for the Ferrari. Back on the macadam of the highway he took a sweeping curve at eighty-five. On his right, the water of Napili Bay glistened; on his left, the mountains, still mist-shrouded, rose in plateaus. One was open, inviting; the other arcane, mysterious. But both were powerful—much more powerful than I am, Civet thought, a puny human being driving a ton of welded metal.

Past Kahana's ugly new high rises he sped. He used the wide verge to pass when he could. In some spots it was paved, in others it was packed red dirt, the ruts jarring his spine through the Mustang's mushy suspension.

Another glance in the rearview mirror confirmed that the Ferrari was fast overtaking him. It was now barely fifty yards behind.

They were fast approaching Kaanapali, Maui's largest developed resort area. This strip of five hotels and numerous condominiums was the major cause of traffic and pedestrian congestion on this side of Maui. It was to Kaanapali that Civet now decided to head. Within its warren of walks, restaurants, shops, and high rises, he would have the best chance of losing his pursuer.

Civet jammed on the horn, tramped on the brakes as a car began to pull out from the right. Cursing, Civet's foot poked at the accelerator as he heard the squeal of the intruding car's brakes. He had a brief glimpse of a woman's face, white with fear, as he sped by, his horn still sounding.

But the incident had had its consequences. The Marcello, thundering, was only twenty yards behind.

Civet concentrated on the traffic piling up in front of him in anticipation of the first of Kaanapali's three access roads. A road crew was at work here, traffic was being squeezed right. He was going much too fast. One-handed, he was obliged to swerve at a precipitous angle onto the verge to avoid rear-ending a slow-moving Nissan.

Civet was compelled to decelerate drastically, and a glance in his rearview mirror showed the Marcello almost upon him. Unless he could find a break in the traffic, he knew he would be finished.

Already the road ahead of him seemed smeared with grease. Colors fluttered, blue to green, red to orange, and back again. Light dilated as if the sun were running in and out of dense clous with appalling rapidity. He jammed on his brakes, almost on top of the car in front of him. In the next instant, he saw a minute opening as the line of cars siphoning through the work area was halted to allow traffic from the resort onto the highway. What the hell, he thought, tramping on the accelerator.

Taking deep breaths, trying to slow his hammering pulse and, at the same time, ignoring the blare of horns, the shouts, the screech of hastily applied brakes, he shot through the gap.

He was running at eighty again, but now the Marcello was on his tail, and as Civet went through maneuver after maneuver, a growing conviction began to dictate his next moves. When he had exhausted his entire repertoire of evasive measures, he abandoned the idea of ducking into Kaanapali. He had no lead on the Ferrari, and consequently no chance to disappear inside the resort complex.

They were heading toward the major access to Kaanapali.

Here the highway gained a median island, planted with palms and giant ferns, around which the two-way traffic divided.

His mind making rapid calculations, Civet accelerated through the traffic, weaving this way and that. Horns blared, people shouted at him. The median was coming up on his left. Civet slowed, switched to the right-hand lane as if he were about to turn into Kaanapali. The Marcello followed.

At the last instant, Civet accelerated sharply, cut the wheel hard over. He slammed into the rear fender of a Chevy, the right front wheel of his Mustang ran up onto the verge so that for one terrifying moment, he was canted over at an angle. Then with a bone-jarring slam he was down, the Mustang rocking on its springs as Civet faced oncoming traffic.

He swung left onto the far verge, accelerated.

The Marcello, still pacing him, was now at a safe distance, now separated from Civet by a line of intervening traffic and the median island.

Glancing over, Civet grinned. The adrenaline was pumping through him like the ocean shining in sunlight beyond the now impotent Marcello. Civet felt the ocean's power energizing him, looked back to the paved verge ahead of him, and cried out.

Where just an instant before it had been clear, he now was bearing down on a pair of teenage girls clad in their Fila jogging suits. All pink and powder blue, their blonde hair tied in ponytails and flying along behind them. So young, bursting with life. Their browned faces were serene as they ran. They were talking, laughing at something.

Christ, Civet thought wildly, they don't see me! At eighty-five, he was bearing down on them with hellish speed. Even as he applied the brakes, Civet knew that he was going too fast to stop in time. To the left there was a fifteen-foot-high ridge decorated by wild bougainvillea. Bright sprays of pink, orange, purple trailing down the ridge.

He was too close, his speed too great. He was going to hit the girls dead on unless . . .

Civet turned the only way he could: right, into the oncoming traffic. If he could catch a break in the traffic, make the grass-covered median, he would be . . .

Screeching of metal, hot and tortured beyond its breaking point. The Mustang clipped the front end of an oncoming truck, taking out a headlight and part of a fender. It was too much for the Mustang, which lifted upward like a rearing stallion. When it came down he was broken free of the seat-belt.

Instinctively, Civet looked toward where the teenagers stood, backed against the ridge on the far side of the verge, fists in their mouths, horrified. They were safe. Safe.

Then he was tumbling, tumbling. In his mind's eye, he saw that face again. That haunting face! And for the first time today he put a name to it: Zero.

A moment later, the Mustang screamed as if it were a living thing. Flames blew through the passenger compartment, igniting the world.

ABOUT THE AUTHOR

Eric Van Lustbader was born, raised and educated in Greenwich Village. He was graduated from Columbia College in 1969, having majored in sociology. While there, he founded an independent music production company, a move that led to a fifteen-year involvement in the entertainment industry.

Since 1979, Mr. Lustbader has devoted his full time to writing. He is the author of five previous internationally bestselling novels, *The Miko*, *The Ninja*, *Sirens*, *Black Heart*, and *Jian*.

He lives in New York City and Southhampton, N.Y., with his wife, free-lance editor Victoria Schochet Lustbader.

A Master of the erotic and terrifying thriller...

ERIC VAN LUSTBADER